1945. The Nazi forces are in full retreat all over
Europe. Hitler's evil empire is crumbling hour by
hour. Beneath the ruined streets and buildings
of Berlin, the Fuehrer grows ever more demented,
ordering Army divisions that no longer exist into
battle, sending bomber pilots on suicide ramming
missions against the advancing Russians. Soon
the rattle of small-arms fire, the explosions of
mortar shells, the rumble of tank tracks, and the
harsh cough of anti-tank guns can be heard in the
suburbs of the Reich's capital. Harsh, bloody
house-to-house battle has come to Berlin as the
victorious Soviet troops flush out German
soldiers ordered to fight to the last bullet – even
to fight on with their bare hands. But
resistance is futile. Soon Berlin is completely
overrun. A once proud city is submerged in
panic, looting, fire and rape.

Theodor Plievier, although born in Germany,
left his native country in 1933 at the rise of
Hitler. He fought with the Soviet forces in
World War Two. As a result, every word of his
war books carries the unmistakable mark of total
authenticity.

Berlin

Theodor Plievier

Mayflower

Granada Publishing Limited
Published in 1976 by Mayflower Books Ltd
Frogmore, St Albans, Herts AL2 2NF

First published in Great Britain by
Hammond, Hammond & Co Ltd 1956
Translated from the German by Louis Hagen
Made and printed in Great Britain by
C. Nicholls & Company Ltd
The Philips Park Press, Manchester
Set in Monotype Plantin

Berlin

Part One

'Posted to Berlin.'

'I shall probably get there too late.'

'May well be, but we've got to get you moving.'

The telegram from the Army Personnel Office at Zossen posting Colonel Zecke to the Karlshorst Pioneer School in Berlin as instructor in a regimental 'leadership' course had been many weeks on its way before arriving at General Headquarters at Prague where Zecke was stationed. Between despatch and delivery lay nights of heavy bombardment of Berlin, and also the complete destruction of Dresden, which had disrupted communications as well as the postal and telegraph services.

'Probably too late', repeated Zecke. He did not want to leave Prague just when the general collapse was only a question of days, especially in exchange for Berlin which looked like becoming the centre of the maelstrom towards which the whole of Germany was rushing. Marshal Zhukov with his Russians, Siberians and Cossacks was on the Oder, and farther south, on the Neisse, Koniev with tanks and cavalry, Usbeks, Turkomanians – the might of Asia poised to strike in an imminent overwhelming avalanche. In the west the Americans and British had forced the Rhine at Remagen and Oppenheim, and between Rees and Wesel; had encircled the Ruhr and were penetrating further into the Reich. In the south the French were crossing the Vosges and already holding the Black Forest.

Zecke looked out of the window.

The old lime-tree in the courtyard of the General Headquarters was covered with thick buds – they would burst open during the night, and the whole yard, and also the streets, squares and quiet little corners of this city on the Moldava would be gay with the fresh green of Spring.

It was April 1945 – a warm Spring day.

'Nothing can be done about it, Zecke', said the Adjutant-

General. 'Get yourself a bottle of brandy in the canteen for the journey!' He understood Zecke's hesitation and his regrets at having to exchange Prague for the witches' cauldron of Berlin. In this GHQ they assessed the war situation and the probable future of Hitler's Reich realistically.

'You're right, but even the General himself couldn't change this order.'

That was that.

Colonel Zecke took his marching orders. Before daybreak next morning he boarded the train to Berlin. It was one of the new fast army trains, converted cattle trucks with narrow window slits (glass was a rare commodity in bomb-shattered Germany), and wooden benches, chest high wooden planking breaking them up into compartments.

As the wheels started turning, carrying him onward into the awakening day, Zecke thought idly of the peace he was leaving behind him. For more than two years GHQ Prague had been a safe refuge. Since the breakdown at Moscow – his own breakdown – and subsequent sick-leave, he had been sitting in the QM's Section. But his life here, though peaceful, had not been inactive. There had been a whole pattern of journeys, meetings, the diffident sounding-out of opinions, and a network of common understandings. But this net had been shattered by the unsuccessful 20th July bomb attempt, and those on the edge of the net, like Zecke, had been shaken by the blast. Organizing a murder plot was hardly a suitable job for Prussian generals. Especially as their admitted aims – including government consisting of a coalition of parties under conservative leadership and army influence, and an adequate church to counteract the materialistic outlook – were hardly strong enough to assure sufficient support among the population. And there was no proper organization either among the workers, in the army itself, or among the scattered opposition groups.

Fascinating thought – you sit at a desk, seize one of the many telephones and utter a magic formula – and at the other end of the wire, regiments are set marching. But the use of Hitler's own 'Valkyrie-Order', an automatic plan for quelling internal rebellion, proved fatal. It was not the misuse of the available means – in themselves as strange as the circumstances – that proved a failure; the weakness lay in the missing essential basic conditions. Not the least among them was the absence of encouragement from outside. For as things were, it would have been for the enemy powers to legalize the completed revolution. But revolt inside Germany, and a changed government and administration, did not now fit into their concept of the end of the war. Zecke had felt sure of this ever since the conferences of Casablanca, Teheran, and, more recently, Yalta. The enemy had gone a long way from their proclamations of the Four Freedoms to their demand for 'unconditional surrender'.

Colonel Zecke got up and looked through the compartments. Officers of all ranks were sitting on the benches. Officers, and also privates, including wounded and convalescents and a few malingerers who, with their marching orders in their pockets, were travelling up and down the country from one town to another, passing the time left to them, eating pea-soup on stations and dozing fitfully in the carriages. All types were represented in the train, and all regiments and ranks, although the differences between them were in-distinguishable in the general neglect and untidiness. Leathers were no longer polished, nor boots; collars gaped open, caps sat crumpled on the heads of unshaven soldiers, cigarettes stuck in the corners of their mouths, their hands dirty. They scarcely looked at Zecke; no one made a move to salute. Tired after having been defeated on all battlefields of Europe, steeped in a common and general misery, all faces bore the patina of catastrophe.

Zecke sat down again in his window seat. Woods, fields, gentle hills. The countryside of Bohemia – enslaved for the past thousand years. Zecke looked up into the blue sky. The conversation in the adjacent compartment sounded more distant. One of the voices roused a memory in him, a vague picture of falling snow. He could no longer keep awake. The train left the Moldava basin behind, passed through the Elbe sandstone mountains and rolled along the Elbe valley, not even stopping at Tetschen-Bodenbach, the frontier town. Zecke only woke up as the wheels beneath him slowed to a muffled halt.

He glanced through the window slit.

What he saw was Dresden – had been Dresden.

So that was what it looked like – a giant plough had swept

over the earth leaving behind a complete wreckage. Nothing was left of the big hotels – five or six had stood just there. In their place, wave after wave of rubble and masonry frozen into immobility. From the rubble emerged a column here; the arch of a window there; further away the shell of a split tower; a decapitated church; famous Dresden façades motionless in the middle of general collapse, covered by soot and grime, strangely ghostlike. . . .

Who had once spoken of erasing? Who had started it, and who had gone on with it? Good God in Heaven, where is this going to lead, where would it end? Down there in the sea of wreckage the Frauenkirche had stood. Not so long ago he had been sitting in that church listening to the Mozart Requiem, uniforms around him, and the sounds of devout piety, but in their hearts had been the memory of one disgracefully executed – Witzleben. His friends had assembled there and mingled with the official visitors – high dignitaries of the Third Reich.

'Dies irae, Dies illa . . .'

Fieldmarshal von Witzleben on a butcher's hook.

The ordeal of his last journey – actually printed in a macabre filmstrip. Eternal shame . . . and it was not he who was disgraced and defiled, but the Pharisees in their splendid robes. And it was not the Fieldmarshal, with his pathetic clutching hands (his braces had been taken away from him and he had to hold up his trousers during the trial), who was exposed to eternal shame and ridicule – but the roaring President of the Volks Tribunal, the Minister of Propaganda with his flashlight photographs of the place of execution, and those who sat watching the unrolling film-strip. It is they who are in the pillory – and they will never get away from it.

Witzleben, Hassell, Höppner, Moltke. . . . Several hundreds hanged, killed, shot; thousands of others, workmen, students, housewives . . . they are the people whom the Lord has called by their names and who are His, and they will be there when Germany will rise again from the ashes of destruction.

'Dies irae, Dies illa . . .'

The wheels roll slowly over the patched-up Elbe bridge. Two thousand years ago the veil of the Temple was rent. To-day the church itself is torn – the Frauenkirche split open from spire to chancel steps – the organ scattered in the wreckage, the glass paintings and baroque windows fused into ash-encrusted balls.

'Dies irae, Dies illa . . .'

In ruins the buildings of Chiaveri, Canzler, Dunger, Semper . . . the Brühl Terrace, the Zwinger; in ruins the bas-reliefs and frescoes; in ruins pictures by Raphael, Giotto, Holbein, Dürer, Cornelius. Nothing left of Europe's smile but dust.

Did this have to be? Was it essential thus to fulfil Stalin's demand – this wanton bombardment timed to fit the Russian offensive? A shattering destruction that left untouched the one place of military importance: Germany's largest railway terminus!

Since the times of the Saxonian kings Dresden had been known as the city of retired civil servants and officers. Upper middle-class families lived here. Honeymoon couples had unobtrusively strolled through the famous galleries. Names like Dostoevsky, Tschaikovsky, Balzak, George Sand, Byron, were to be found in the visitors' books of small hotels. Dresden was also a railway junction and a transit centre for reinforcements. But what about the unscathed railway station? And the Russian offensive already rolling effortlessly westwards, across the forsaken lines of the exhausted German soldiers?

The untouched station remained a mystery.

And there was another unsolved problem. The final phase of the battle of the Volga two years ago had cost two hundred thousand lives; the whole of Germany had been in mourning, black flags had been out everywhere. The number of lives lost here in two nights was even greater. Here, the casualties were old age pensioners, workmen, women, children and refugees – and there had been no national day of mourning.

'Nobody could ever count those lying buried down there.'

'Even before that, the refugees were already numberless and unnumbered.'

'You, Herr Hauptmann, you were in it, weren't you?'

'Yes, I was there. Got there the same day, on my way to General Headquarters', replied the young captain. He wore a Ritterkreuz, and introduced himself curtly as 'Boehlke'. He was somewhat uncommunicative, but eventually described the night. The increasing heat had driven him and the others out of their bunker; he had been running through blazing streets trying to reach the open spaces. 'In the Grossen Garten I got into a mass of refugees standing there with their carts. Unimaginable. . . . They were rushing from side to side in a blind panic. Every so often machine-gun volleys from low-flying planes combed through the mêlée.

'Terror-bombing!'

The voice came from the adjacent compartment, once more strangely familiar to Colonel Zecke. There sat a young major, his arm in a sling. Zecke suddenly recognized the man. O-17, as they had called him, Lieutenant Hasse from Bomelbürg's staff sat there, or rather Captain Hasse – and as a captain, Regimental Adjutant under him. It had been near Moscow, in a tiny village on the Nara. The hut swaying, the window blown in. He himself thrown to the floor and lying there amidst glass fragments and the smashed oil lamp, snow whirling in through the gaping window panes. The face that bent over him – next to the doctor who gave him a strophanthin injection – was the face of his Adjutant Hasse. A heart attack – with cause enough, admittedly – the hasty retreat amid general confusion, the heavy losses, and, on top of everything, the disappearance that same night of Divisional Commander Bomelbürg, who vanished in the snow and was never seen again.

And now Hasse sat next door.

Major Hasse, a dull somewhat thin voice.

'Terror-bombing!' he repeated.

Down below them the city, turned into a desert in one night, a mass grave-yard beneath the endless undulating mounds of rubble.

Captain Boehlke was still talking. About the heat, the smoke, the despair, the blinding brightness; human beings whirled about like dried leaves in an autumn bonfire. He had been found in the area just outside the storm centre; he had been dipped in water and lifted out.

'Terror-bombing!' repeated Hasse monotonously.

There was something in it, but Zecke, who had been on the verge of getting up to greet his former adjutant, remained motionless. What about Oradour-sur-Glane, Lidice, Treblinka, Auschwitz, the gas cyclon B, the 'Nacht und

Nebel' decree, mounds of human skeletons from the furnaces and gas chambers, and hundreds of thousands more, marked for extermination? Annihilation as a political principle – it hardly befits us to speak of being terrorized. But . . will there ever be an end to it, how is it to finish? God be with us and the others, too!

'If one of them bales out, get after him, and kick his face in! They've asked for it – a hundred times over.' It was Hasse again.

Again Zecke sat motionless.

The train had left the bridges behind and passed through gently mounting hill country. A road followed the railway tracks, on the other side of the Elbe was another road. Streams of refugees were trekking along both roads.

'Where are they heading for? And the others, over there?'

'One stream to Czechoslovakia, the others to the north.'

'They must be completely mad!'

'Who isn't these days?'

Northwards to safety – southwards from the Russians. Both were driven forward by a desperate hope. Behind them – to the north and south – hunger, storm, tears, and the countless dead. Surely somewhere ahead there must be safety – as long as they kept moving forward – to the north – and to the south.

'Are we so different?' asked Zecke, looking at young Captain Boehlke who had already passed through a purgatory of fire and crumbling walls. Now, he sat in this train to Berlin, on his way to start his first post as adjutant. Many others too, those who sat there, had already been in the devil's claws, had escaped and were travelling here and there to continue their service, trying to resume the thread of life which had been snatched from their hands. As if it could go on like this for ever; as if, after the final catastrophe, higher adjutants would be required and new regiments would demand new commanding officers.

And here was Hasse. He was passing the compartment and stopped.

'It is you, Herr Oberst?'

'Hasse, you of all chaps!'

'What a surprise!'

'I thought I heard your voice but wasn't sure. Sit down, Hasse, there is a seat here.'

'Well, Good day, Grüss Gott and Heil Hitler!'

So it was God and Hitler all together, and many other things and questions as to where and whither, and 'do you know?' and 'do you still remember?' . . . and 'On the Nara that day, what happened afterwards?'

They sat next to each other the former Commander and his successor who, in the winter of 1941, had taken charge of the regiment, or what was left of it, and had brought it back to Juchnow through storm and snow.

Hasse, too, had been between the devil's claws, but the devil had dropped him, only to pick him up again and drop him once more; he had rejected him a third time, possibly as an unexciting victim. Not only was Hasse's voice dull, he was a dull character altogether; and all his adventures and gruesome experiences had left him completely unmarked. He had survived the ice and blizzards round Moscow, and a year later had been flown out, with a shot arm, from the Stalingrad basin. At the moment, he had come from Greece, near the Acropolis. The old wound had broken open and he wanted to have it treated in Berlin where he would see his family and convalesce.

The time came when all had been said and Zecke and Hasse had nothing further to impart. Hasse turned to Boehlke whose home division was at the Courland front.

Boehlke was still very young, much too young for a captain, and such a blatant disproportion between rank and age was always suspicious. But he had an open face, and eyes that were apt to disarm suspicion. Zecke was therefore glad to notice, after a little while, that the conversation between the young captain and Hasse had also faded out.

The train crept slowly through the countryside.

The journey seemed endless. Lulled by the monotonous rumbling of the wheels, Zecke slept fitfully. The carriage resounded with loud snoring. The head of one of the men had sunk almost into his lap, another leant against his neighbour, jerking up from sleep and falling back. The dim light of a candle flickered at the far end of the compartment. The night outside was as dark as it had been many hours ago. But although time seemed to creep as slowly as the train, they did keep moving. It was better to sit in a crowded compartment with sweating men than in the middle of a potato field during an air attack.

And this journey did come to an end.

The wheels rattled over points. Clouds of white steam drifted past the windows. The train was shunted on to different tracks. Eventually it rolled into a giant hall and the wheels stood still.

Berlin, Potsdam Station.

The station hall had suffered quite a bit; its thick walls, dating back to 1870, were cracked and blackened by fire. Large pieces of stone lay on the rails. Fragments of glass were under foot. A grey morning peeped through the naked framework of the high cupola.

It was five o'clock.

Zecke, Hasse and the others pushed to the exit and swarmed down the staircase. The Square outside looked like an abandoned civil war. Pieces of masonry, iron bars, removal vans heaped higgledy-piggledy, the pavement torn open for trenches, barricades thrown up, chevaux-de-frise blocked the way. What was there to defend here?

'Not very convincing,' remarked Zecke.

Hasse laughed, but Boehlke remained serious. 'No, not very convincing. From a military point of view completely amateurish!'

A man with steps and a paste-brush was about to stick up a poster. Zecke, Hasse and Boehlke noticed it at the same moment: BERLIN REMAINS GERMAN! May God grant it, but the Minister of Propaganda would have done better to have kept his mouth shut, the matter seemed very much out of his domain, the hour was much too late.

And there again was the wailing of the sirens.

The surrounding ruins re-echoed the rising and falling tone.

It was the signal that a heavy attack was on its way.

'Alarm, get off the streets!'

'Cellar Hotel Atlantic!'

'Cellar Hotel Atlantic!' repeated Hasse and shouted it to those who descended the stairs behind him. You must follow those hurrying before you. Past rubble heaps, empty shells of houses, a tramrail abruptly bent upwards beneath loose high-tension wires; at the end of a narrow path there was suddenly the entrance. No guard in front of it, nor porter or even a waiter. Strange hotel – seen in the dim light of descending electric torches. The Captain in front was immediately swallowed up by darkness. Again steps leading further down. A cave and another cave, hollowed catacombs lying in darkness. Far away the flickering of a candle.

'Can't you watch your step, you fool!'

'That's no way to talk to me!'

'Can't you choose something else to walk on than my belly?'

Hasse turned the light of his torch on a face. A sailor lay on the floor and looked at him menacingly.

'All right, leave it at that, Hasse', said Zecke soothingly.

After all, this was the customary tone in such places, and it was also a sign of the times. You could not be too particular an hour before the mass grave, even if your rank was ignored.

'I hope this place deserves the name "Cellar Hotel" and that there is a cup of coffee or a sandwich somewhere around.'

'Not a crumb. What you don't carry in your pocket don't exist, Colonel.' The seaman talked more politely by now. He had found an empty corner and piloted Zecke and Hasse into it. Candle-stubs stuck into the walls, and Hindenburg lights, were flickering about in the darkness. Their eyes slowly got used to their surroundings. Seamen, airmen, infantry, despatch-riders, pioneers, all lay here next to each other and on top of each other, rifles in their arms, packs under their heads, rucksacks, cases, boxes around them. Other ranks and officers, all covered by the same worn filthy grey uniforms. Outside the ack-ack guns had started.

'Not many of them here, Herr Oberst. Just protecting the stations and government offices – that's all there are.'

The rumbling of the flak; spasmodic detonations of bombs. But the snoring was hardly interrupted. Nor was the grumbling. One half complained of having been disturbed, the other of having been driven into the cellar. There were three heavy attacks on Berlin daily, sometimes four and five, they said; and it would soon be impossible to move about, since everything was disrupted after every attack – the Metropolitan line, the Underground, the trams.

'And how do I get to Karlshorst?'

'We used to make it in an hour, to-day you'll need a whole day, Herr Oberst.'

'And to Potsdam?'

'You'll get there somewhat quicker.'

Boehlke had to report to GHQ at Potsdam. In the circumstances Zecke decided to go with him as far as Wannsee, where he would visit an old acquaintance. After the all-clear they took their leave of Hasse who wanted to go to Hermsdorf to his family before reporting to the Tempelhof reserve hospital. Boehlke bought a newspaper at the Metropolitan Station and on his way looked through the news and even read carefully an article on possible war developments. Zecke sat opposite him and watched him closely. He noticed how carefully he was reading, how he frowned suddenly and that his eyes looked gloomy. When Boehlke folded his paper, their eyes met and he shrugged his shoulders.

'It's one hell of a mess – what can we do now?' he said.

'I think it is too late to do anything,' replied Zecke.

'You are probably right, but I have to report to my artillery commandant.'

'We all have to report somewhere or other.'

Boehlke told Colonel Zecke of his epic wanderings after his General – Potsdam, Bad Kissingen, Prague, Leitmeritz, Dresden, and now Potsdam.

'It almost gives the impression . . .' – the impression that he might be one of those travelling malingerers up and down the country, intent on nothing but to pass the time still left – this is what he meant to say.

'But that is not so, Colonel. It's as if there were a jinx on me – everywhere I'm too late—— Well, you never know. It might be for the best.'

Zecke had judged the young captain correctly – frank and straightforward – he felt an immediate bond between them, but it looked as if it had to remain at that.

He had to get out. A meeting at the roadside – ships in the night.

There was only enough time for a handshake.

After twenty minutes walk Zecke stood in front of one of those tasteless little villas covered with turrets and stucco ornaments from the Kaiser's time. Two families lived in the house; on the first floor a Luftwaffe Colonel, and on the ground floor Zecke's old friend, Dr. Wittstock, the writer.

Once Zecke had been asked: 'What sort of a chap is that Dr. Wittstock?' That was in the days of his previous stay in Berlin, and the question had been asked by someone he had met for the first time, but in whom he had every confidence and to whom he had to give a very precise answer to this particular question.

'What sort of a man is he? . . . a very gifted man, highly-strung – mercurial'. Zecke had started his description on that occasion – it was in the south of Berlin, in a block of flats behind Tempelhof. 'No, he's not an army man, but I used to be stationed in Potsdam as a young officer, and I met him during my off-duty hours. At that time we were all keen on extremist ideas, particularly of the left – after all one did not always lunch at the Adlon – Berlin in the twenties – Reinhardt and Piscator; cafés along the Kurfürstendamm, theatre lounges, cabarets, evening restaurants where you met after the theatre. What a ferment everywhere! We frequented salons where we might meet anyone. That was how I got to know the Wittstocks. As I said before, he had somehow failed to get into the army, but he seemed to have a real craze for uniforms. And though deep inside he was always in opposition to the Party, he couldn't keep away from them. He was never a Party member, they did not even want him, he was much too highly strung for their liking. But he would never stay in opposition for any length of time. Those in power attracted him irresistibly. The press, publicity, cars, march-pasts, the whole pompous pageantry, all that had a strange fascination for him and he had to take part in it. Nevertheless the combination of his nervous excitement and intellectual insight made him capable of abusing Hitler and, for instance, shouting at a party: "You are quite right, it is high time for a murder-plot!" But if nothing happens within three days, he will say: "There you are, those chaps aren't clever enough, and the others are right after all. Those who hold the power also hold the authority for it. They are real men, they have grasped the lessons of history and put them into practice. But you poor intellectuals, you are crippled with your own scruples and moral prejudices." When he has reached that point there is no holding him, and he will run through the whole gamut of modern jargon: a moral outlook is the evaluation of the middle classes of whatever adds comfort to their lives; history does not happen – it is shaped by men of power and determination; and the shaping demands a blood sacrifice of human lives; evil is no longer evil if it is committed on a sufficiently large scale; unless you have the courage to do evil, you cannot take part in the making of history. And, for Wittstock, to make history is a compensation for his lack of religious belief, a kind of tangible intellectual eternity. The rest is all mythology. In certain conditions, and contrary to his outspoken rationalism (but then the whole Wittstock consists of contradictions), he admits the unconscious. The unconscious as a driving force in history is even one of his pet hobby-horses. That is Wittstock, and unfortunately he is not alone in his mental outlook. Many people think thus in these godless times.'

Colonel Zecke was standing at Wittstock's door. The bell did not work. But the siren at the next street corner did – with a continuous rising and falling tone which signalled urgency. The ack-ack guns started rumbling. Zecke thumped with his fist. The door opened and there stood Wittstock, dishevelled, laden with overcoats, including his wife's fur coat, in his hand the shelter luggage.

'What, you, Zecke? Come in quickly – where did you spring from?'

Zecke followed Wittstock into the house and out again by the back door into the garden and a few steps down into a slit trench.

'The second air attack to-day: with one short interval we have been sitting in this trench since 5 a.m.'

'I was here for the first attack as well, down in the Cellar Hotel Atlantic.'

'No mail, no papers, no telephone; very comfortable, don't you think?'

The trench had been dug in zig-zag shape, and covered with planks and earth against the rain. It was very narrow, and people could only stand one behind the other. Zecke greeted the lady of the house. Mrs. Wittstock was a friend of his wife, at least they were on calling terms.

Her first question was therefore: 'How is Lena?'

'As well as can be expected. She is in Friedrichsroda in the

Thuringia Forest, together with Agathe, and writes fairly contentedly.'

'And you come from Prague. That's bad management, dear Herbert! I expect life is still pretty civilized in Prague.'

'Besides you can get such lovely things there, and it's so cheap!' added Mrs. Wittstock.

'That was long ago, my dear lady. And cheapness is relative. All they've done was to push up the exchange rate of the Reichsmark. But that's over now – like so many other advantages which our "far-seeing" policy offered us.'

The bombers were roaring past, right across the trench. But the hits were heard much further away.

'Perhaps it is not meant for us,' said Wittstock. 'When you have seen a bomb go right through a nine-storey house and the twisted corpses dragged from the ruins, you get to appreciate a trench in the open. All that can happen is a direct hit, and then it's over anyway.'

'Yes, it is the same as at the front.'

'You are going to stay with us, Herbert, aren't you? – You will be able to manage?' he asked his wife.

'Gladly. Mr. Zecke is always welcome. He doesn't want to go back to an empty flat; and Potsdam is much too far away.'

'Incidentally, what are your plans?'

'You should ask me what are *their* plans?' Zecke told the Wittstocks about his orders and said that he had to see his army unit first, but would like to accept their kind offer after that.

He made up his mind to report that same day and after the all-clear and breakfast he took leave of them.

The suggestion that it would take him a whole day to reach Karlshorst proved to be very nearly correct. First everything went smoothly, but at Potsdam Square he had to get out and walk to Alexander Square. The Metropolitan line only took him as far as the Silesian Station, where he had to ask his way.

'Walk up that street over there, where you can see a tram running. It won't go to Karlshorst, of course, but you might get as far as East Cross.'

So Colonel Zecke stood there waiting and looking into the mist. At length, the tram arrived and he boarded it thanks to his uniform. Other passengers who could not show a red card were turned off by the conductor – a sixteen-year-old cripple. 'You can walk!' he told them.

'We can take you along for a bit', the conductor told Zecke. 'Yesterday we got as far as the viaduct again, but after the big attack just now I don't know how far we'll get.'

It was not far. Soon Zecke stood again in the street.

'Tell me, how do I get to Karlshorst?'

'If you are lucky, by Metropolitan. They were running a shuttle service yesterday.'

And by the shuttle service Zecke managed to get within walking distance. It was late afternoon when he reached Karlshorst and the barracks.

A row of modern buildings, generously planned. The windows, of course, had all gone, and there were large gaps in the roof. The houses looked abandoned, without life. A sentry in a huge driver's outfit, coat and heavy boots, an old worn pipe in his mouth, the cap lopsided on his head – the type of common soldier Zecke admired – was stamping up and down.

'I am looking for the Pioneer-School, old man.'

The sentry stopped and looked at Zecke. An old Colonel, one of the old guard. He spat out an answer without removing his pipe.

'The Pi-School? This is what's left of it.'

What's left of it . . . that described the scene exactly.

'There was to be a course for regimental "leadership" here?'

'Was; it's all over now.'

'Well, I'm supposed to report.'

'It's a bit late for that, Herr Oberst. Don't you know?'

'I know nothing.'

'Well, then listen. The course was moved west because they were scared of the Russians. But we just heard this morning that the Amis (Americans) caught up with it there and carved it up.'

'Carved it up?'

'Yes, right in the middle of company drill. If you'd been earlier, Herr Oberst, you'd have caught it too.'

Colonel Zecke learned that some other late-comers to the course were billeted in the house and that the Regimental Adjutant had stayed behind.

In the canteen there were some younger men who confirmed the sentry's story and had further news, the whole course had fallen into American hands but had been freed the same day by a German Panzer division. This time they were supposed to be moving to the south of Germany. When Zecke entered the regimental office, he felt he was as well-informed as the Regimental Adjutant himself.

'A very good day to you. I am Colonel Zecke from Prague.'

The Adjutant almost dropped his monocle. He was a Major and in civilian life a teacher at a technical college; but here he represented the regiment and was not accustomed to anything like Zecke's slovenly bearing or jovial tone – even from a colonel.

But Zecke went on in the same vein. 'It's a complete shambles here – why on earth are you still here? I've come much too late. When can I leave?'

Words failed the startled Adjutant. The Senior Paymaster, who sat in the same room, looked up, equally shocked, but quickly bent over his papers again.

At last the Adjutant spoke: 'I am sorry, Herr Oberst, that you have come in vain. But I have received no further orders for the Herr Oberst. In the circumstances I must ask you to stand by.' And he repeated all the details that Zecke knew already.

'But you can telephone to Postings, can't you?'

'The Army Personnel Office has been moved to Thuringia, and at the moment the telephone service with Thuringia has closed down.'

'That means that the Personnel Office has also closed down. In fact, half Thuringia has closed down as far as we are concerned. You can read that in the official army reports. Be a good chap and don't use these silly euphemisms.'

The Adjutant was obviously prepared to fight to the last ditch – even if it meant ignoring the official news bulletins. He was going to out-Goebbels Goebbels in his ignorant perseverance to the end. But just now he had been driven to the defensive, and Zecke seized the opportunity: 'Since we can do nothing but wait for new orders, I shall report here again tomorrow or the day after.'

'But I would like to point out to you, Herr Oberst, that you should really stay in the barracks.'

'Wouldn't dream of it.'

The Adjutant riposted lamely with: 'It would be desirable, Herr Oberst!'

'I have had a look at your sleeping-quarters. Extremely uncomfortable – and the beds too. I wouldn't dream of spending the last two weeks of my life in such conditions.'

The last two weeks . . . How could he dare – what did he mean by it? This time the monocle really dropped from the Adjutant's eye. The Paymaster bent still lower over his desk. Zecke watched them both.

Here they sit, with their useless telephones, in a bombed building, glass splinters on their desks, still determined to win the war at the eleventh hour. But even they should realize the difference between the bombing of a Regimental H.Q. in the front line and the front line itself being in Berlin.

'Gentlemen, I fail to understand your optimism. I have already found a billet in town. I have a number of things to do and want to look round a bit, visit old friends, and so on. And in the present state of chaos I don't imagine it makes any difference if my orders get to me a few hours earlier or later.'

He left it at that.

'So long, gentlemen, see you the day after tomorrow!'

The Adjutant and Senior Paymaster stared at the door as if an apparition had just gone out. The Adjutant shook his head disapprovingly, and the Paymaster agreed with an equally silent nod. Neither of them had ever come across such blatant cynicism. But he must have authority to behave in that way; this Colonel from Prague had been leading a regiment before Moscow and just now was returning from an even more important job. You could never tell these days; there was probably nothing they could do about it.

Zecke reported every second day at Karlshorst, to be told each time that no contact had yet been made with the Army Personnel Office. Apart from that he went to see his 'old friends' and also made new acquaintances. The evenings were mostly spent at the Wittstocks'. Once he went to Potsdam, but returned, sadly conscious of the fact that Potsdam had become past history. The shattering reality of near-total destruction out-did all his imaginings. His empty flat had been bombed and ransacked; he walked through it once without even bending down to pick up any of his belongings strewn on the floor. What do belongings mean when the walls around them are cracked, the wallpaper hanging in shreds, the dust is blowing in through empty window frames? What do belongings mean when they no longer have a relationship to human beings and to normally functioning surroundings; what meaning can there be in a Louis Quinze chair, a Damascus blade, the scattered remnants of a coin collection; when the whole of Potsdam is in ruins, the Garrison Church split in two, the historic crypt broken open, the mortal remains of the Great King removed and bumping somewhere over a German highroad, and when the former members of the Gardejäger Battalion and Life-Guard Hussars and of the Garde du Corps are dispersed over the whole world, never to return?

Never to return! Zecke went back to Berlin with this feeling of irreversibility. Now that Prussianism lay prostrate in the dust, should the Reich metropolis, grafted on that Prussianism, smouldering from hundreds of fires, breaking open over and over again through endless detonations, also be condemned? Should this giant congregation of stone houses with their five million striving inhabitants also be condemned? And should the 'Morgenthau-Plan' come into effect and split up the Reich, would Berlin have to die? How does a city come to life, and how does it perish? Not because a Great Elector has his castle built there and has the road to the town gate planted with lime trees, although this is certainly part of its development just as its location on a river or crossroads. But of equal importance are the travelling merchants, the commercial sense of its inhabitants, the skill of its workmen; the Great Fire, and marauding warriors who were instrumental in creating a fire-brigade and town-guard. A multiple accumulation of inhabitants of all German provinces, of Pomerania and Silesia, settlers from France and the Lake of Geneva – Huguenots, Flemish and Dutch – a huge melting pot. A great deal had to happen, a multiple and multi-farious coupling and generation in citizens' beds and servants' attics or on Mother earth, crouched in the woods behind the Zelten beer-gardens (these are already our grandmothers), or on rambles to the mountains and seaside camps (and these are the fathers and mothers of our cadets to-day). So much had to happen before the Berliner man and woman were created.

Can this entire evolution, can this Berlin 'type' which

finally emerged from the sand and mud of the Spree simply be wiped out by the stroke of a pen? Is it no longer to exist because, due to a special constellation in home politics – and even more in foreign diplomacy – a monster held the reins of government, and at the end of the war the three victorious Great Powers join together and declare that what is must not be?

Impossible! The Spree still flows through Berlin and will still be flowing after the final collapse, even though the bridges crash in a last desperate and futile gesture of defiance.

Berlin is Berlin and will survive.

It will survive because of the Berliners. The ball is still rolling, the word is not yet spoken; no representative of any power – either in a Kaiser's cape, or in a President's frockcoat, least of all in a brown shirt – can speak for Berlin. The Berliners with the cap, the ready-made suit, the blue shirt, the high-collared workman's pullover, the Berlin women in their little home-made frocks – it is they who will determine the city's fate. Hocus-pocus with pens or gunfire is equally futile. It is only Berlin itself who could surrender.

Colonel Zecke strolled across Weidendamm Bridge.

Almost fifty years ago, the same Zecke had been walking here holding his father's hand. Below flowed the slowly moving river, above was the blue Spring sky; and the breeze, of a dreamlike softness as it can only be in Berlin, lifted young Zecke's broad-rimmed hat over the parapet and sat it gently on the ripples. It floated along, vanished under the bridge, reappeared on the other side and drifted away, a tiny bright fairy-boat. 'I say, you down there with the long pole!' shouted his father. And the man with the pole fished out the hat and brought it along, dripping and a little sticky – and was rewarded with a gold piece. That was the Weidendamm Bridge.

Zecke left the bridge behind, passed the bombed-out barracks of the Alexander Grenadiers, and in the Friedrich-strasse suddenly found himself in a kind of rubble ravine, a cañon, between two collapsed rows of houses which had met on both sides, forming bizarre and perilous arcades. Zecke reached the open space beyond. Passing the Opera and Hedwig Church, he came to an area which, with huge squares of stone strewn about, looked more like a marble quarry. The giant palaces of the financiers had stood here – a hurricane had blown them away. Zecke found the house – at least the stump of the house he had been looking for, and went straight there. It was nothing important – all he had to do was to give a greeting to a bank clerk, a man he did not know. Perhaps because of that it was important. The ground floor was still standing, but the three storeys above had collapsed. The street in front was completely blocked, a rubble heap that Zecke had to climb over to reach the entrance that remained strangely untouched; even the revolving-door was functioning. He stood in a big hall. Outside the sun stood high in the sky, but through the rubble in front of the windows it penetrated only dimly. The people here moved about like sightless beings in a deep-sea aquarium.

Zecke went up to one of the counters.

'Could I speak to Herr Schulze? I have a message for him.'

'Schulze? You'd better go to Counter five along there!' The clerk pointed somewhere into the underwater world. Zecke went in that direction and a forlorn candle led him to another counter, where he asked the same question again. Whereupon the clerk went to fetch the head of the department who fittingly appeared in an unpressed suit, a dirty shirt under his pullover. The candle started flickering. Chief and clerk whispered while they looked at the visitor who had asked for Schulze. When the chief finally approached him, Zecke found it necessary to explain: 'All I want to do is to tell Herr Schulze that his brother-in-law in Prague is all right and sends his love.'

'Hm, Schulze . . .'

So it wasn't the usual story after all. Nothing about searching of flats, arrests, Gestapo, and so on.

'Ah yes, Herr Schulze. It's so sad. He had been at the front for the last six months. Left his wife behind, a charming young woman, and two children of four and two years. And then the usual happened: a direct hit right through the house, wife and children buried in the collapsed cellar. Schulze got the usual telegram, you know, bombed out, special leave. That was three weeks ago, Schulze came back on eight days' leave, and for eight days he stood there, from dawn till dusk, while the workmen were digging, staring into the crater. That was his leave. And just imagine how lucky he was: three hours before he was due to go back they found the bodies. . . .'

Zecke groped his way back through the aquarium, knocked against the door that revolved noiselessly, and climbed back over the rubble heaps. He crossed the quarry, saw the Opera, the Arsenal, the University – farther behind in the mist the Abbey and the cracked façade of the Castle. Again he crossed the Weidendamm Bridge where the Spring breeze had once blown away a child's hat.

How lucky he was! This remark stuck in his mind, and it was also there next day when he met Herr Knauer, the General Manager. He was the man on the Mariendorf Estate to whom he had given information about Wittstock. He had had no intention of meeting him and indeed knew no more of Knauer than his name which to him meant the Sirius Works near Stettin. He had meant to visit a young lady whom he had met one day at a sports meeting and whom he had seen a few times afterwards. A typical Berlin girl – realistic, practical, Americanized. She did her own dressmaking and her ironing on Saturdays after the office and took sandwiches along on her rambles. Her realism extended to a sober assessment of her surroundings, but still with a strong strain of romanticism! Once he had rung her while in Berlin, inviting her to coffee and a film. But she could not come, and told him she was going to be married that day, one of those war weddings by proxy: a nuptial by radio-telegram. Her fiancé, a young doctor to whom she had introduced him once, was on the Eastern front. What else could Zecke do but buy a bouquet of white roses and attend the telegraphic wedding. Since then he had not seen her again.

And now, unable to reach her by telephone, he opened the gate and knocked at the front-door. It was opened by a man, Director Knauer, as Zecke found out later. At that moment he was just a man, dressed in an assortment of garments, all of good cut but none of them belonging either to the wearer or to each other.

'I am looking for Frau Halen.'

'Sorry, but she is not in . . . no longer in Berlin.'

'Perhaps you could give me her address.'

'That's not so simple. I am afraid I can't. But do come in.'

They sat opposite each other – Zecke and Knauer, the

Sirius-Knauer, though Zecke did not know that yet.

'Our charming Frau Halen had to leave suddenly for Salzwedel, and after that . . .' He paused, and they looked at each other. Knauer smiled.

'You are looking at my waistcoat, it belonged to my dead brother. The sleeves of my jacket are too short, I know, but it fitted a close friend of mine who was hanged at Plötzensee. I found the trousers here; they belonged to someone who set off for Italy: we don't know whether he got there. We can only hope that the Gestapo won't be looking for him here.'

The man had heavy hands and long, heavy arms. It would not have been easy to find a jacket that fitted him.

He introduced himself: 'Knauer from Stettin'. That meant he was the Sirius-Knauer, one of the richest men up there on the Baltic coast. With these heavy hands and his own strength he had built up the works that used to deliver goods to England, Africa, China and the rest of the world.

'In a single night everything was flattened,' he told Zecke in his low voice, so strangely contrasting with his powerful physique, 'the factories, the stores, the car park and my own flat. The buildings were destroyed; petrol store and coal heap a sea of flames; machinery and tools turned into scrap-metal; even the iron safes blasted and the contents strewn about, charred and blackened. My private safe was, however, salvaged – by the Gestapo. I got away in my pyjamas and slippers, a blanket wrapped round me – and reached Berlin. Here I was introduced to several people and that is how I came to Frau Halen's flat.'

Purple turns the heather . . . now Zecke knew where romanticism could lead a Berlin girl, not only to a wedding by proxy, but to other acts by proxy . . . Frau Halen as well . . . a link in the chain, one of the ring, frequent visitors, among them the prison chaplain from Plötzensee, smuggled letters, refuge for hunted men and women, Jews, officers, and also a director, Knauer. She had to find clothes and food for them: through cunning, forgery, if need be, or even theft, to provide ration cards and personal documents. As could be foreseen in those circumstances, she, too, had to leave one day – for Salzwedel and further – and Director Knauer really did not know her address. Romanticism cannot do without peace, and to preserve peace for the humble hut, big palaces must be fought, the palaces of the usurpers and corrupters of the Reich. Thus romanticism leads back to blood-stained reality.

'Now I have been told that this house is no longer safe and that I should go somewhere else. Dr. Wittstock has been one of those whose names have been mentioned. You know him, don't you? What sort of a man is he?'

'What sort of a man is he . . .?'

That was Zecke's opportunity to describe his friend Wittstock, and his characteristic summing-up was: 'That's the type of man he is. He does not write for posterity, but for to-day. And he claims that the men of to-day are figures of history whatever the outcome. Which means, of course, he is ignoring reality completely, and in lucid moments, he admits it himself. He has even been known to add that not only are they nothing to do with history, but, in fact, they are plain villains. So you see, there is still quite a bit of the old Wittstock left, and it's the best part of him.'

Colonel Zecke had stayed for so long that he was unable to get away before the sirens started. When the wireless announced strong enemy formations heading for South Berlin, he accompanied Knauer into the cellar.

The estate was horseshoe-shaped, its open part showing north towards Tempelhof and Berlin. Residents of neighbouring flats joined them in the shelter. A few women, two old men, one of them a retired university dean, the other a printer, and a youngish couple, Heinrich Putlitzer and his photographer wife. Frau Putlitzer reminded Zecke, in a strange way, of Frau Halen. Not that their faces looked very much alike, but they were like leaves of the same tree, it was the face of Berlin that shone through their individual traits: in their eyes the same expression of foreboding and yet, at the same time, of confidence in their ultimate survival.

The two Putlitzers, the old printer Riebeling, and Knauer, were clearly one group. But the other side had its adherents as well. The retired dean was completely at a loss. His two younger daughters were simple creatures with little imagination; the third one, already ageing, although scarcely forty, was the image of her father, and, like him, confused and bewildered. But there was a special reason for this. All over the neighbourhood it was an open secret that a few days ago the youngest of the family, the nineteen-year-old son, had deserted from the Waffen SS, had arrived home in civilian clothes and was now hidden in a shed. The old man was racking his brain for a solution. To report him would mean that his son, the pride of his life, would almost immediately be found dangling from the nearest lamp-post. But his eldest daughter thought it was their duty to 'the People' to expose him, and she never stopped pestering her father. She was consumed with shame; her long face got thinner and thinner. She hardly dared lift her eyes, nor did she speak to anybody any more, and no longer could she – as she had so freely done in the past – rebuke those who made improper remarks.

This time the attack had not been meant for the south of Berlin but for the centre. They only heard the returning planes, and Zecke and Knauer left the shelter before the all-clear, and went up to the flat.

Here Zecke resumed their interrupted conversation. 'On the whole you need have no fears about the Wittstocks. Even the motley company you'll find there hails from bygone days. For instance, the editor Splüge is always there; in his youth he did not know whether to become a painter, a writer, or a musician, and his most cherished memories are his student days in the cafés on the Kurfürstendamm – no danger there!'

'There seems no other alternative but the Gestapo or the Russians: the former possibly, the latter inevitably. I don't know which is worse, but what more can happen to me? I might just as well stay here.' Those were Knauer's last words, when he saw Zecke off.

In a way he was right, what more could happen to him – his works shattered, his clothes coming from friends, one hanged, another waiting for it, the third on the run, looked after by a charming Berlin girl who travelled continuously from town to town effacing all traces behind her. So, bombed out and burnt out, weighed down by his own burden – he might just as well wait for his fate in the suburbs of Berlin as anywhere else. How lucky the man was!

That same day at Karlshorst the Adjutant had a rather surprising message for Zecke. His orders were to go to Jutland via Hamburg and take charge of the troops there. 'There is a very real threat of an English landing, and all available units are to be formed into a joint command to prevent a British attack from the north.'

'You are speaking of "available units and British attack",' said Zecke. 'Let's pass over that for a moment and just consider the following: in view of the disrupted communications it will take me a week to reach Hamburg, another week to get as far as Jutland, and a further week to gather the available units – if there are units and if they are available. Only then would I be able to start reconnaissance – another week.' Zecke counted on his fingers: 'One, two, three – three to four weeks! Tell me, Herr Major, what do you really think?'

The Adjutant did not seem to understand Zecke; or pretended not to.

'How much time do you think we still have? I have always been used to planning my actions and cannot therefore take on a job which seems completely hopeless from the start. Is this an order from the Army Personnel Office?'

'No; we still have no contact with the Personnel Office.'

'In that case my mind is made up. I am sorry, but I cannot undertake it!'

Again the Adjutant, the Paymaster and a few other gentlemen at the Pi-school were knocked off their feet. They had failed to get rid of that awkward colonel. Instead, they had to listen to a grim assessment, bordering on defeatism, of the overall situation. The Adjutant gave the Paymaster a desperate look, but the presence of his subordinates made it impossible for him to express his thoughts. Must he as a reserve officer and national socialist of long standing really put up with all this from a colonel on active service?

Zecke added to his experience of the Berlin transport system. When dusk came, he was caught in the third air-raid of that day, and found himself in the cellar of a large block of flats. Women in slacks and pullovers, with cases, blankets and eiderdowns, sat down almost without saying a word. The bursting of anti-aircraft shells, the droning of enemy planes, the deafening noise of bombs exploding in the neighbourhood, had become part and parcel of their days and nights. Could they still remember their former life without black-out and air attacks?

'I hardly can,' replied the woman whom Colonel Zecke

asked. 'However, there is an end to everything, isn't there?'

She was a woman of forty, with three children; of her two soldier sons, one was missing in the East, the other a British prisoner of war. She was forty, but actually, if you could forget for a moment the dismal surroundings and her untidy air-raid clothes, she looked much younger. If Zecke looked at her, a smile appeared somewhere at the back of her eyes. The mask of misery was on her face, but her eyes could still smile.

'That one at least is safe,' said the woman, referring to the son who was a prisoner of war in Britain.

'And your husband?' asked Zecke.

'He is no good, never has been. That's why he joined the Party in 1933, but he was no better off for that, Nor was I, but I have never had any illusions. In any case, he left the Party again and that was worse than if he had never been in it.'

Conversation was over. There was a deafening crash outside and all the evil powers were suddenly unleashed on that one house. There were no anti-aircraft guns, no fighters. That one block of flats with its cracked front and unstable gables was helplessly exposed to the frenzy out there. Four storeys of the main building and another four of the side wings had unloaded their human freight into the shelter, an unkempt, unwashed mass of humanity. How could anyone wash or even relieve nature when all the water pipes and drains were broken; what use were combs when, day and night, plaster, soot and dirt rained down? The cellar started rocking, a crack in the masonry widened. Plaster trickled from the ceiling. They felt that the floor might burst open at any moment, or mountain-loads of stone avalanches could sweep down on them – even a single stone would be enough. Man is too small in the midst of such unloosed powers. A woman was praying, but no sound could be heard in all that fury, only her lips could be seen moving, forming the soundless words. Another pressed her forehead into her hands and started crying. A third crept under the bench, and would have liked to creep into the unreceiving earth. A soldier back from the front lost his nerve and turned into a shuddering wretch. An old woman, with an emaciated face, better dressed than the rest, sat motionless, her eyes wide-open, staring. Zecke learned later that she was the owner of the house, a morphia addict.

But the praying, the weeping, the crawling, the staring

woman and the soldier were at first only five faces, and there were more than a hundred sheltering here, women and children and soldiers from the street. Some of them vomited – not because they were so frightened, but from sheer defencelessness. But many, perhaps most of them, did not seem to be affected. Yet in one way or another, they were all affected, and reacted accordingly; by crying, by being sick, by throwing themselves on the floor, or trying hard to convince themselves that they did not mind – but not a single one wanted to die; all wanted to survive.

An interval.

For this, too, had its place between waves of attacking bombers – this, too, was part of the devil's own show, in which the audience was taking part as leading actors, not knowing whether, at the end of the drama, they would be alive or dead, but hoping against hope. And these intervals were filled with typical conversations.

Between the first and second act the woman of forty had told Colonel Zecke about the owner of the house and about the way the people were feeling. She had also introduced him to her lodger: 'This is Franz, who is staying with us.'

Franz had only one hand, the other – the right one – he had lost at Vjasma, and at the same time, he automatically lost his career as an industrial designer.

Zecke and the woman resumed their conversation.

'If your husband is no good, it must be very difficult for you to manage.'

'The little we can get on our rations I can easily earn with sewing at home. I don't want to go into a factory. It doesn't seem right to help to prolong the war, does it?'

'Most certainly not!' was his reply.

The woman did not hide her feelings: why should he? So she does dressmaking, maybe repairing uniforms, and that fellow just idles about.

'Do tell me . . . sorry, it is not my business after all.'

'Never mind: ask as much as you like!'

'I may never see you again. But I am interested – why does a woman marry a good-for-nothing?'

'Very simple, Herr Oberst. Perhaps he was a good-looking fellow, with dark curly hair. It takes only a moment to fall in love – what follows takes much longer.'

'Does he drink, does he go off with other women – excuse me again.'

'No,' was her reply. 'He is just lazy, too lazy to get drunk, too lazy to go with other women.'

The second wave. Again the weeping and trembling and hoping and staring. Man is too small. . . . From outside, people were dragged in unconscious. Flames had spread even to the pavement. Perhaps it was only the house next door. It grew hotter and hotter in the cellar. Zecke had difficulty in breathing and was near to choking. The woman of forty gave him a towel soaked in water and pressed one against her own face. Others had wrapped themselves in wet sheets. A house disintegrated with a terrific crash. It was the house next door.

'Where is Willem?' asked the woman.

'Gone upstairs to rescue his barrel-organ', said Franz.

The conversation stopped. Zecke felt very weak, the towel was taken away from him and he got it back freshly soaked. The landlady was still sitting on the bench staring in front of her. Wounded were brought in. Willem turned up as well, an old war veteran carrying an antiquated barrel-organ on his back. His face was like paper, and he dropped like a heavy sack.

'They've hit the organ', he whispered. But he had been hit as well. On his way across the yard a splinter had penetrated the organ and its case and gone into his back. He sat doubled up.

Bombs were falling one after the other, shrieking and whistling; the earth erupted. The noise rose to a hellish crescendo – evil triumphant!

This was the point of climax; the shelter full of frightened people waiting only for the final catastrophe. And even that moment was marked by apathy and unconcern. After a thousand air attacks the bad air can make one giddy or sick, but one no longer dirties one's pants. Those who once used to, had long since left for the country.

Medical orderlies started carrying the wounded away. They came to Willem, who moaned when they sat him up. He did not want to leave his organ behind. Eventually he called to Franz:

'Look after my organ, take good care of it, Franz! It is an Italian Liratedesca, a Sambuca . . .' It sounded like a bequest.

Suddenly it was over.

The quiet exploded through the open door. Then people started coming in, calling, shouting, arguing about the fire-fighting. In the end they all grabbed pails, shovels, and hoses, and went out into the street to the burning ruins of the house next door.

The woman . . .

She, too, had a pail in her hand. He returned the towel, but what could he do further, how could he say anything nice to her here in this shelter, next to the house in flames? Should he tell her that in such surroundings she did not look her forty years, and that he would have taken her to be thirty? Too silly; and what he wanted to say was even sillier. She noticed his embarrassment and smiled. A smile full of under-standing and consideration, yet touched with sadness; al-though her face was blackened by dust and soot.

What he did say in the end was silly enough, but she had somehow authorized that remark through her smile.

'You have the eyes of a girl of twenty!'

'Only the eyes, Herr Oberst; that's not quite enough.'

Some time later Zecke sat in the Metropolitan train going to Wannsee. He was not aware how late it was and hardly noticed the tired and irritated people around him whose only aim was to get home as quickly as possible, before the next alarm.

Zecke remembered the woman and smiled. That experience was a part of the phosphorous bombs, the collapsing house and the yawning abyss of death, so were the eyes of that woman. A Berlin woman could have such eyes and such a smile even amidst catastrophe.

A romance . . .

A romance behind Alexander Platz. Zecke's smile faded. He found the Wittstocks in their cellar, very different from the one he had been in. It had originally been intended as a bar and was furnished in old German style. Since the be-ginning of the air attacks it had become the family's living-room.

Zecke absent-mindedly welcomed Wittstock's son: 'Home on leave? Is there still such a thing?'

'Oh no, not on leave, on active service with a transport of

badly wounded. Our casualty station is being disbanded; those who could walk have already been dismissed and have had to get away on foot or by train as best they can.'

The hospital in question was in Buckow, a small town in the romantic countryside between Berlin and the Oder, and Frau Wittstock had told Zecke that her son had been posted there as medical assistant.

'Does this mean that you too are moving to Berlin?'

'No, our medical unit is staying out there, and I have to be back tomorrow.'

Zecke was deep in thought. He had not yet been able to shake off the memories of that other shelter – the woman, Franz, Willem with the Sambuca. . . .

'Very good', he said, although it was by no means clear what could have been so good. But Wittstock junior reacted promptly: 'Oh yes, it is certainly good to be with a medical unit, much better than with an anti-aircraft unit or the HJ (Hitler Youth)'; and as Zecke remained silent, he went on: 'All the students in my year have been drafted into the army, some are with a flak unit, some with the "Volkssturm" – not my cup of tea.'

'You are not out for military glory?'

'I am waiting for the end.'

'And the rest of your age-group?'

'They are half-wits.'

On second thoughts it was somewhat half-witted of a sixteen-year-old Wittstock to let a colonel know what he thought about 'military glory'. But then, Zecke was different. Soon afterwards Zecke went upstairs to get rid of all the dirt and soot he had collected on his wanderings through Berlin.

When he returned to the cellar, he was alone with Wittstock, who after a little while remarked: 'So he is waiting for the end.' He was quoting his son who had gone to see a friend presumably not one of the half-wits.

'He is waiting for the end of these saturnalia.'

'Yes,' said Zecke.

'You're very laconic tonight!'

Zecke yawned.

Wittstock went on. He obviously had to talk. Not that he believed in what he was saying, but it was as though he had to argue himself out of his own undigested theories. He spoke of the power of the unconscious, the varying degrees of its existence among different people, the influence of this dark power on politics and the arts. Zecke only started listening again when Wittstock's rambling thoughts stumbled once more on to reality.

Wittstock spoke of painters and the dissolution of line and form. 'When the French rebel against reason they present us with a Matisse, a Braque; the solid outline changes into colour, the picture turns into a boiling pulp – and in literature surrealism, visions and hallucinations are the fashion of the day.'

'And everything becomes questionable, and man is as helpless as a moaning Job,' remarked Zecke, resuming his part in the argument. 'But after all it is only a search for a religious expression. Only those who have been searching for God with brush and colour and in the field of abstract thought, have been labelled degenerate and driven out. I'll go with you so far, but not when you pretend to see anything potent, sub-conscious or otherwise, in the cat-calls and babblings of our present political amateurs and bandits. You call it "saturnine". "Paralysis" seems the right word to me. You call it the "un-conscious", but let me tell you that we Germans are methodical even if paralysed, and when the unconscious gets the better of us, we don't rest until the unicorn, the cerberus, dragons and other fabulous beasts take on human shape, set up in office, and get fat, gnawing human flesh and swilling human blood . . .'

'I really don't know what you always have against the Third Reich!'

This was a new note and put an end to their conversation which had not been more than a skirmish and, as far as Witt-stock was concerned, was an evasion of the real dispute. Splüge, his daily visitor, had come in carrying a brief-case and a parcel under his arm. He put both on the table and started unpacking.

'Spirits and tins,' he announced, and went on enumerating them: 'Corned beef, sheep's tongues, a sausage as long as your arm, Hennessy and Cherry Brandy. We don't need to grumble. Here are cigars and cigarettes, and something special for Madame!'

Frau Wittstock was not with them but, upstairs in their flat.

Splüge was brandishing a box of Russian cigarettes. 'Straight from Moscow – they crossed the Oder and left this behind. Incidentally, I, too, am planning to drive to the Oder one day, just for a day or so, maybe even tomorrow.'

Splüge seemed quite at home and went to fetch glasses. He had already uncorked one of the bottles, and now he filled the glasses, lifted his own and gave them a toast: 'To the Third Reich – or something or other! There was quite a to-do in our department today. A skeleton press conference, hardly a dozen journalists, no foreign ones – they have already taken to their heels. The good Doktor (Goebbels) looked rather pale – but it suits him. I can tell you he let the cat right out of the bag!'

It must have been an overwhelming disclosure by the Minister of Propaganda. Splüge gulped down another glass, filled the glasses of the others and before they could catch up, filled his own a third time.

Lieutenant Splüge was considerably younger than Zecke and Wittstock who were fifty and fifty-two respectively. Splüge had only just celebrated his thirty-fourth birthday. His father was a well-known solicitor and Zecke was on very friendly terms with the whole family. He remembered young Splüge the first day he went to school, with a bag of sweets in his hands, and later on he had had to admire his school reports. He was a gifted boy, and, at the Technical High School, had had many outside interests, painting as well as music and other things. In fact, his bohemian leanings had cost his father a good deal of money and considerable trouble, and finally precluded an academic career. When the landslide came in 1933 he was the conductor of a jazz orchestra. His father being a Party-member, young Splüge slipped one day into a Party job which meant a rapid, indeed, a rocket-like rise for him. By the time the war came, he had reached a key position in the new Reich.

By now Vicco Splüge was grown up, so much so that he could look upon his father's friends with benevolent joviality. Upon Wittstock, whose writings he did not think much of, but whom he admired for his almost encyclopaedic knowledge and also for the gay, if rather mixed, company he found in his house. Upon Colonel Zecke, because as a Staff Officer he had always been an uncertain factor, and after the 20th July, highly suspect. This assessment, however, did not mean that he was not very proud of being allowed to call his school-boy hero by his Christian name, in spite of the rumours which floated around about him. Apart from this, he had his own ideas about Party opinions. He did not by any means put his signature to every bit of nonsense. In particular, he retained his independent judgment in matters of ideas and taste. The Party was his employer – friendships were his own affair.

It was after the fifth or sixth brandy.

Splüge lit a cigar and, contemplating the white ash with a connoisseur's approving eye, expounded: 'As I said, we have no reason to grumble; we, the *élite*, are having a splendid time. In no democracy on earth could I have such freedom as I enjoy in the Third Reich. I can drive through the whole of Europe without having to pay a farthing. Never before could I have earned so much money. And I am still drawing my salary as editor-in-chief into the bargain. I am getting fixed pay as senior lieutenant in the Propaganda Section and on top of it extra fees for all my articles – more money than I could ever dream of spending.'

'You will have to pay for it – and soon!'

'Do you really think very soon, Herbert?'

He grabbed his glass and gulped another brandy.

'In fact, it's all the same, to tell you the truth. Don't think that I can't see where we are heading for. We shall pay by total catastrophe. But then, what is there that you don't have to pay for? If you live a calm middle-class life, you pay in terms of boredom. Or you may, as in the Third Reich, be a European freebooter and for a few years have everything you could possibly wish for, but then you'll be paying for it in terms of a minor European cataclysm.'

The sirens interrupted him. Again belated, so that they heard that alarming rising and falling tone announcing a major attack.

'I've had enough of that to-day!' said Splüge without moving. Nor was Zecke inclined to get up. Only Wittstock had jumped to his feet and got his things ready. Zecke's thoughts went back to the shelter on Alexander Platz and the woman. . . .

'So we'll have to pay for it. . . . Incidentally, the Führer has been distributing poison capsules like a good uncle handing out chocolates.'

The sound of sirens still rose and fell against the droning of heavily laden bombers. A hit – the glasses on the table were clattering. Frau Wittstock ran in excitedly: 'Albert, why don't you come to the shelter?' Wittstock joined in: 'Herbert, Vicco, the sirens!'

Splüge resented the interruption: 'Sirens, my backside – sorry, Frau Wittstock. Run away to your silly little shelter.'

Frau Wittstock ran. Wittstock, laden with his belongings and the shelter luggage, looked round at them: 'As you please, but when you see the blackened corpses being dragged from the cellar . . .'

'Blackened corpses, shrivelled corpses, dried corpses, kidneys shrivelled up, lungs sunk in, hearts like sponges –' Splüge cut in. 'I know it all from anatomy lessons. You can't frighten me! . . . Well, he's gone, and so is Madame. And the bottle is empty, but then we've got another one and we're going to open it, aren't we, Herbert?'

This time Splüge poured the brandy into tumblers. The cellar was a semi-basement with sand bags piled up in front of the window. Again a bomb fell and it looked as if the wall of sacks was going to collapse. The ground shook and something fell on the floor upstairs.

'I say, that was bloody near!'

'Don't take any notice! That's not meant for us. Where were we? Terrible, these constant interruptions. Oh yes, our white-faced Doktor at the press conference this morning. It might well have been his last. He spoke of the German power of resistance, of the well-prepared major offensive in the East, a fight to the last man. . . . You understand, Herbert, don't you?'

'Of course.'

'So that is what we are supposed to write about, and about dissensions in the enemy camp. We are supposed to help him ginger up the people to a last final decisive effort. "But," he said, "don't think I am such a fool as to believe that myself. Germany's defeat is inevitable." And he added: "I have one last ambition . . ." You should have seen him, Herbert, he looked as white and dignified as the dead angel Gabriel – "in five-hundred years time text-books on history shall report that, due to their Minister of Propaganda, Goebbels, the German people did not capitulate but went down fighting!" – You see . . .'

Under their feet, continuous rumbling. That meant pattern bombing farther away in the centre of the city.

'What do I see, Herbert?'

'Your fallen angel and the whole pack from the Wilhelm-strasse and Voss-strasse – these men really seem to think that world history is a Wagner opera. It doesn't even occur to them that gangsters who die like rats, will be eliminated from the writings of history!'

The ground under their feet was shaking incessantly.

'I also got one of those capsules, Herbert, from the Doktor in person. In fact, I got two – the second is for you. Here you are, take it! You never know: the lamp-post, the Russians, anything is possible; it might be just as well to have it.'

Colonel Zecke accepted the small capsule filled with white powder, and put it carefully into his wallet. Vicco was right, you never could tell. A mysterious treasure was now hidden in his pocket, a dark door which he could open but perhaps need not.

He suddenly felt that the cellar was getting too oppressive; he got up and went out into the open. What a strange sky! A cloud glowed red with the light from a huge fire which was reflected back to the ground again casting no shadows. Zecke threw himself to the ground. A tuft of grass touching his nose looked unnaturally large, naked and indented like one of those big cacti in the desert. A storm of red sparks rose over the Avus or by Zehlendorf. Petrol tanks were blazing. Berlin was encircled by huge flames; the centre of the furnace seemed to be near the Castle, the Town Hall or Alexander Platz.

The noise of bombers was fading, the attack was nearly over.

So was the flak – exhausted, out of ammunition, silent. Houses had collapsed across the road, and in the cellars and craters corpses were lying. The moment had come when those who had survived had to say their farewell to the dead.

When Zecke went back, he found Splüge still on the same spot, staring at him.

'You must not think, Herbert, that my heart is not bleeding when I pass through Berlin. What does it look like? the streets, the houses and the people . . .' He was searching for a simile, after all it was his job to find the right expression for horror scenes. But words failed him, he could think of nothing adequate.

'I've got it! Like . . . no, that's no good.'

'Leave it then!'

'Why should I leave it?'

'It would be more appropriate not to use an empty phrase.'

'My life is ruined, Herbert. I have achieved nothing, have never said one significant word, and now I am apparently doomed to be swallowed up in the big cauldron with the white-faced Doktor and the rest. . . . The white face, the frozen heart. So clever, but so cold. So many women and so little love. His Magda is putting up a lioness's fight, wants to leave Berlin with her five children. But he is holding her back. We've lived together – we'll die together! In his country house on the Lanke, while his wife and children were in the shelter, he remained upstairs with another man, my immediate superior in the office, and they looked across to Berlin and followed the air attack in the night sky. He said the time might come when he would not care to live any longer, and without taking his eyes from the incessantly bombed city writhing in the throes of death, he went on to say that he did not know how his children could live in such a world. You must not think, of course, that my boss has ever given me a coherent account of this. Far from it. But here a word, there a word: and I have pieced it all together until I feel as if I had been present myself. Well, after they had been pacing the yard for half the night discussing the question as to whether anybody, even a father, had the right to decide about the life and death of his children, he decided there was a duty to relieve a child under age of a weighty decision beyond its powers.

'Live together – die together! That goes for the children; it also goes for me, Vicco Splüge, poor innocent child. And I did try to grow up and come of age . . . before I have to face the abyss. The demoniac hierarchy dancing on the brim of the abyss; gradually they topple over, yesterday Schliff, Rabenalt, Ristisch . . . I can see it all, Herbert, but if I could stand above it as Goya did; be of age, mature – even a ruined life could be redeemed. Put them all in the pillory; the unicorn, the cerberus, the dragons, as you have enumerated them . . .'

'Listen, you two, I must ask you . . .'

Wittstock was back with his wife and sixteen-year-old son.

'What must you ask us? I am just in the mood to answer all your questions!'

'I must ask you both to lower your voices.'

'What's the matter?'

'Something rather unpleasant has happened. Part of your fatalistic conversation has been overheard. You seem to have completely forgotten that we have a very nice Luftwaffe Colonel with his wife and children living on the top floor. He told me he would not like to report anybody, let alone a comrade of the same rank. But his children were horrified that high officers and Party officials could speak with such defeatism about the future of Germany.'

'Well, I hope you have told him what you think of it.'

'Think of it, Herbert, what are you trying to drag me in for?'

'My dear Wittstock, if you had half your former wits and courage, you would have button-holed him and said: "My dear Colonel, if you are fond of your children, you'd better warn them that in a few days Russian tanks will stop before this house and the best course to follow then will be to hang out a white flag and do what else is necessary when a whole town capitulates." That's how you should have talked. And, by the way, when are you going to wake up? What are you waiting for? Or for whom? For the trembling ghost in the Führer's Bunker, the villain who still hasn't realized that his time is up!'

A heavy knock at the door, someone asking to be let in.

'Now you are for it!'

'For what, you exalted intellectual?'

Frau Wittstock opened the door and let in Oberst Aachern, the Luftwaffe officer about whom they had been talking. He hardly saluted and pretended not to see the chair that Wittstock offered him, nor Wittstock himself, nor Spülge. He went straight up to Zecke and addressed him alone: 'If a senior officer in uniform dares utter words such as I could not help overhearing just now, Germany is doomed. How can one who has taken the oath let down his Supreme Commander in war-time?'

'Well . . .' was all Zecke managed to say. Where did he suddenly find himself? In a world – which he had thought dead – in which the oath of allegiance was still referred to. But he knew only too well what a terrible tie that solemn promise might be and that even with the best of men it often got the better of their reason, their sense of responsibility and their own conscience. However, what might have seemed quite natural with his old friends, still deeply rooted in tradition, seemed almost incredible in a much younger officer, particularly one of the Luftwaffe. After Mölder's suspicious crash, Udet's suicide and the case of the Luftwaffe Inspector Galland, who, faced with the discrepancy between reality and the orders he received, had returned all his decorations to Göring; after the Luftwaffe's having been hopelessly overburdened and coming out of this war just as completely disorganized and demoralized as the Navy in the first world war; after all that, he could not believe that Colonel Aachern was in earnest. He could not possibly be such an immovable rock. The military oath apparently served him as a corset to keep his back straight. But as the subject had been thrown into the conversation, he had to say something.

'I have been wearing uniform for thirty-four years now,' Zecke said in a low voice as if talking to himself. 'Governments have changed and I have had to take the oath three times. The obligations connected with the oath were always the same. The last time, however, contrary to the old Prussian tradition, our promise of loyalty was not addressed to a flag or to a principle, but to a person. Does that mean that we must forget the principle? Because we are tied to a person, who no longer embodies the principle (and in fact never did) – are we really to go on fighting against all reason?'

'To put it mildly, this is another incredible remark, Herr Zecke. What do you mean by "fighting against all reason"?'

'What I mean is simply that everything is smashed and crumbling, that we are finished and have no means to fight the rest of the world.'

Everything smashed – those were words that could not leave Aachern unmoved. He was stationed at Rechlin aerodrome. Out of originally ninety machines he was left with five, perhaps six, which could take off. All the others were laid up in the hangars, either damaged by bombs or with serious engine trouble. Or they were lying smashed right behind the hedge, having been shot down at the moment of take-off.

'You know yourself well enough, Comrade Aachern, that we have neither the material nor the man-power!' Zecke knew this point would go home.

How right he is, thought Aachern. No fuel, and the little he got was potato spirit. The engines were sooted up right from the start. The same with the oil – full of grit, and if it was not changed after ten minutes full throttle, you could throw the engine on the scrap heap. No real fuel, no real oil, the engines hopelessly obsolete. The new Messerschmidt originally devised for a pursuit plane, was refitted as a fighter, and we have still to take off with that old crock, the ME 62.

'True . . .' said Colonel Aachern, 'but I am sorry to hear this kind of talk in this house – under our common roof', he added, turning round to Wittstock.

He was still standing, but after a further invitation sat down, pushing the chair well away from the table.

'By "fighting against all reason", I mean that after the soldiers, we are now sending their wives and even their children to death, and all this in a lost cause, without military or political aim. That's the point we have reached, Herr Aachern, we are burning up the seed-corn!'

That, too, was correct – the children from the glider pilot schools, who after a short course must get into an ME 62 and crash on their first flight: they are the seed-corn.

Aachern sat stiffly in his chair, dismally eyeing the company round the table. What on earth was he doing here, and why had he brought his wife along – he should at least send her out of this poisoned air. But then it did not really matter . . . to be frank, he had occasionally heard her, too, say things which made him go off the deep end.

'What a terrible strain this present situation is!' exclaimed Wittstock. But with an appropriate gesture Zecke wiped away Wittstock's miserable understatement. 'No need to spoon-feed anybody here. We are sitting on a volcano and had better try to be articulate. The lamentable thing is the reason why such talk is necessary. Not only we here, but people every-where in all the Berlin shelters are racking their brains to find a way out of this hopeless situation.'

'Let's have another drink.'

Splüge had the glasses all ready, including one for the colonel of the Luftwaffe. The ladies were offered liqueurs and Russian cigarettes. But for that order in his pocket, received the same morning at General Army Headquarters, Colonel Aachern would certainly have declined – the brandy as well as the company. Never before had he discussed such matters with anybody. 'I have been sitting there behind the stick, doing my job, and that was that.' These problems – and they were certainly weighty ones – were the concern of his superiors, so why should he burden himself with them?

That was his point of view. Had been up to this moment. Perhaps it needed revision. Zecke was right in many ways.

And now that order! He must protect a courier plane due to arrive from the north at half-past midnight by screening the air over Berlin. With what? With all available means, it said in the order. That meant with the five or six machines left over from the squadron. And if arms cannot give sufficient protection, it must be done with ramming. Night chase, 'Wild Boar', against a sky full of Mosquitoes!

'We are still drinking brandy, the others have gone over to cyanide of potassium. Some use veronal or morphia,' said Splüge.

Colonel Aachern looked from one to the other. That grey-haired staff officer, at Verdun as a young captain, later at Moscow, he had been told. The other one a senior lieutenant in a high Party position – but what a way of speaking! Cyanide of potassium, veronal – ramming. . . . Who on earth could think up this crazy order after the ramming squads had proved a complete failure; nor had their copying the Japanese suicide pilots shown any results. The Luftwaffe Marshal must have thought of this when drunk; Galland had told him off properly. No doubt the whole matter was of special importance since the General had warned him that the order had to be carried out under pain of death. We've got to get our backsides into the air as long as they're still warm, and after that . . . poor Lisa. He looked at his wife who innocently believed that he had to go back to Rechlin the next day, the day after, and the night after that to carry out his duties. Poor Lisa . . . and Hans, Joachim and Anneliese.

He hardly heard the conversation going on at the table, and

they in turn respected his aloofness – very likely he had reasons for gloomy thoughts.

But Zecke tried eventually to draw him into the conversation. 'A propos,' he said, 'I have been able to contact Dr. Lemke after all. No, not a question of cyanide of potassium. That's why I want to tell you how I met him and what he went through only a few days ago – this will interest you, Colonel Aachern – he's very much out of step with the general mood of world collapse. Dr. Lemke is an old friend of mine, a highly intelligent man, in charge of a big printing works and also the editor of a scientific journal. I badly wanted to see him, but somehow didn't succeed in contacting him. The telephone was always out of order. Yesterday his sister answered it. Her brother was there, just back from a journey to the West, completely exhausted and lying in a coma-like sleep. I implored her to try to rouse him, to tell him my name and that I was daily expecting to be posted away from Berlin. She returned with the message that her brother wanted to speak to me, that he would have a coffee and after that could spare me an hour. I went to see him. Expecting an imminent final reckoning by the enemy powers, he had taken his family to Lake Constance. Then he had driven to Groningen to fetch his fourteen-year-old son from the famous old college there. While still there, the American advance tanks were within twenty-five kilometres. That was when his adventure started "My dear Colonel," he told me, "I know what I did was completely mad. I could easily have stayed there. The college administration had offered to engage me as an agricultural adviser to hide me from the Americans. I was on the brink of accepting when I suddenly told myself: No, your place is in Berlin, you can't leave your people alone in this catastrophe. At the last minute – the Americans had in the meantime got even closer – I hired a horse-drawn brake for a lot of money and went off eastwards over the fields, right through the collapsing Germany army. I have seen them all: the soldier who simply refuses to advance, and the one who runs for his life. Total disintegration, no more discipline. After five hours – we had just reached a small railway station – low-flying enemy bombers caught up with us. Believe me, Zecke, if in modern warfare a country's airforce has been defeated and the enemy has air supremacy – that's the end, any military operation or opposition is futile. The American dive-bombers are the masters of the highroads and the railroads. As soon as the sun rises, no locomotive can show itself, nor can any vehicle or group of people take to the roads. Down come the planes and throw their shells into everything. I know some of it from experience. I left the brake and took a train. Twenty minutes later: dive-bombers! We had to leave the train on the open track and rush for cover under a viaduct. The planes smashed the train on the bridge. Their projectiles hit right through train and bridge and burst in our midst. I stood right in the mêlée of service men and civilians, old ladies and children. There was considerable panic and I witnessed young officers' nerves failing them. Believe me, soldiers who have gone through this are unfit for battle for quite a while. Everything is finished. This is complete collapse!''

'That was Lemke's story. He speaks of a reckoning and has never made a secret of his antagonism to Hitler whom he considers the main cause of Germany's disaster. But when his people are doomed, he cannot leave them in the lurch – even without the oath!'

'Yes, responsibility for others!' said Aachern. 'But he at least has still got people to be responsible for – I haven't had that, not for months.' When he was posted from fighter planes to jets, he had first disliked the atmosphere and had criticized the pilots' and crews' casual ways and lack of military discipline. But it was much worse now with a heterogeneous collection of pilots from various dissolved units. For though the deportment of the men had not been very military, they had had team spirit. Once, a pilot, his leg in plaster, had climbed into his machine so as not to weaken the formation in the air. The infiltration of this motley crew had put an end to such a spirit. Discipline was thrown overboard. The number of those sentenced by military tribunals on various charges of a personal or political nature was rapidly increasing. Some had simply been too blunt in their complaints about bad material, not to speak of the many officers reduced to the ranks – even colonels with the Ritterkreuz to corporals. There was no getting away from it. This was the end. . . . Some had claimed they were unfit for service, some pretended to be ill, others panicked and took off into the blue, racing their engines to death in the process. It had been a group without fighting morale. But even that motley crew did not exist any more. All he had at his disposal now was a kind of air home guard – instead of a trained crew – and only five or six of them . . . on ground crew at all, and – ramming!

Aachern had to admit that Lemke was right in more than one way: 'Only too true what he said about the importance of complete air mastery. If I come to think of it, Colonel Zecke, what you said about telling my children . . . probably not so wrong either.' He almost felt inclined to have a heart to heart talk with Zecke, without witnesses, of course, but he could not shake off that special order, not for a moment; he would have to cope with it alone. He got up abruptly, kissed Frau Wittstock's hand, and turning to the others said: 'Thank you for your company, and good night.' His wife left with him.

For the last time Colonel Zecke was strolling through the battered city, bleeding from so many wounds, and behind the Spittelmarkt got into an area that was so completely destroyed and abandoned that it gave him the feeling of being among the ruins of an ancient city. Heavy rainfall; grooves and channels had washed deep through the ruins and made them look even bleaker. A tram was clattering over the rails, its bearings ungreased and worn out. He saw the men and women in the street with their luggage on their eternal wanderings to the shelters, housewives, waiting in endless queues for their rations or fetching water in large pails from the next standpipe. He had a few more talks with Wittstock, but, like the preceding ones, they did not get them anywhere. Aachern did not turn up again, and Splüge had left a scribbled message that he was off to the Oder front for a couple of days.

At the Karlshorst Pioneer School, as he passed through the canteen on his way to the office, it struck him that all the faces had changed. So much so that he turned to one man who looked particularly upset and asked him:

'What has happened to all of you?'

'Don't you know?'

'No, what should I know?'

'The Russians have started their attack. About four o'clock this morning, two hours of heavy bombardment. They have crossed the Oder and are said to have reached the Seelow Heights.'

The information they had in the office was based on telephone conversations and rumours, according to which the Russians had reached the Seelow Heights but had been thrown back. There was no doubt that the success of their offensive was due to artillery preparations on an enormous scale and an incredible superiority of material. The Pioneer School had pieced all this together from loose scraps of information, although up to that very day they had expected an offensive on the part of the Germans.

Yet another surprise was waiting for Zecke in the regimental office. His marching orders had eventually arrived from the Army Personnel Office. The commanding officers' course had been moved to Bavaria and he was to report near Regensburg.

'The hour is very late, it will soon strike midnight,' Zecke remarked. He studied his route on an ordnance map. 'A thin neck from the Elbe to the Oder (or, more correctly, now the Seelow Heights). I wonder whether you have noticed, Herr Major, that the part of Germany still in our hands strikingly resembles an hour-glass. A bit of Germany to the north, a bit to the south, and in the middle – just around Berlin – is that narrow waist through which the sand is trickling.'

The adjutant was not in the mood for such fatalistic remarks. But he had to admit that the comparison was all too fitting. In fact, he suddenly felt that many of the colonel's previous remarks which he had at the time found arrogant and cynical, were now assuming an uncanny reality.

'Considering that the route by Leipzig and Nuremberg is now in American hands, it seems I shall have to go via Prague to get to Regensburg,' said Zecke, bending over his map.

Another of those infuriating remarks!

The Senior Paymaster turned round with a jerk as if stung by an insect, but – possibly prompted by the same trend of thought as the adjutant – quickly withdrew behind his papers.

Zecke took his orders from the Adjutant, the Paymaster gave him a slip for the canteen to get his rations for the journey, and, in spite of having so clearly shown his disapproval of Zecke, he added an extra bottle of brandy to the list.

They parted with few words, Zecke was to meet the Paymaster again, but in a completely different world. Among some five thousand prisoners of war, he suddenly stood face to face with a figure in a tattered uniform whom he recognized as the Paymaster of the Pioneer School. 'Fancy seeing you again,' exclaimed the Paymaster, 'you can hardly imagine how glad I am. We used to be absolutely furious about your casual manner and the things you said. You obviously did not take us seriously; but now I realize how right you were; we were behaving like immature children.' But that was some weeks later.

At the moment Zecke was still in Berlin on his way from the Pioneer School to the Karlshorst Metropolitan Station. Behind him he heard isolated explosions of heavy artillery, but so distant that it sounded more like the croaking of frogs than the rumbling of gunfire. As usual, he reached the Alexander Platz and then Wannsee by using various means of transport. His farewell to the Wittstocks was somewhat chilly: outwardly cordial, but what really mattered was left unsaid. The colonel of the Luftwaffe had returned to duty, and Zecke could only leave a message for him. He packed a rucksack and a brief-case with the bare necessities, and set out for Anhalt Station. Like Potsdam Station, Anhalt Station was completely burnt out and the huge shell was filled with shadows. The big carriages rolling in listlessly were shadows with red lights; shadows were soldiers milling backwards and forwards, bent under their heavy loads.

Zecke stopped a railway official. 'I am bound for Dresden and Prague.'

'You'd better go to platform five. They're getting a train together; eight carriages are ready, but the engine is still missing.'

'When is it due to leave?'

'Within the next five hours – if you're lucky.'

Zecke groped his way through the darkness, found the carriages, and was confronted again with rows of silent shadows hunched in their seats and waiting. He lit a match and found a vacant seat.

'Is this seat taken?'

'No, it isn't.'

'Where are you heading for?'

'For the south, comrade.'

These geographical indications were all you could hear mentioned inside or outside the carriages, in fact north and south were the only directions left.

'If we are lucky, we'll still get out, but the next air attack is almost due. . . . Rotten to be right inside the station. . . . We are bound to have a pretty bad night.'

You can't frighten me, thought Zecke. He had bread, sausage, sardines, a hundred cigarettes, and thanks to the Paymaster's generosity, a bottle of brandy – and a second one from Wannsee. I'm certainly not going to let myself be upset by an air attack; nor am I going to drag my rucksack to a shelter and lose the train. Here you are, Zecke, and here you'll stay! The rules about taking shelter when the sirens go are all very well for children. But for me, a bottle of brandy is much more important. He opened his rucksack, uncorked the bottle, took a good swig and ate a roll and a piece of sausage; then he had another drink and another roll, and so on. The bottle was empty – that should do the trick. Let them all come now. Here's to courage, even if it comes out of a bottle.

Zecke sank back, recent memories flooding into his mind. Wittstock and his wife; poor Splüge wanting so badly to be Goya; the man who had been 'so lucky' looked now like Knauer; and the women Putlitzer and Halen and also the unknown woman behind the Alexander Platz had one face; and he remembered Lena – when was that, for heaven's sake? Lena in a full pleated dress, with a straw-hat the size of a cart-wheel – it had happened that week at Kiel, hadn't it? – during the whole of his stay in Berlin he had not given her a thought. He seemed to fall into a deep shaft and was swallowed up by darkness. That lasted until it became very noisy around him, and the shadows near him awoke to their ghost-like lives. They rushed past him with their rucksacks. Then everything was calm again.

'There's another one!'

'Get out, Herr Oberst . . . the sirens!'

Zecke grasped his bottle, drank the last drop and opened the other. It's about time. . . . Here's to you, my children, here's to you, all my loved ones! The wise man travels through the eight barbaric lands, dips into the water of all the four oceans, climbs the five Holy Mountains, returns home after his wanderings, looks at his bare walls and ends his life. A

Prussian colonel needs much less, he starts his journey to a barbaric land with sausage as his Manna and brandy his nectar – and silly sirens can't disturb him. True, these planes here are making a disgusting noise. And bombs are crashing down. How worried I should be if I were sober: I might even think of getting up and running for my life. But no, Zecke, no – here you are, sitting very cheerfully, and couldn't care less whether one squadron or two are buzzing about up there.

One bomb followed the other. Berlin was burning, as it had been burning yesterday and the day before and the day before that. Sparks were drifting into the big hall, flames streaking up into the night. But this time he was not viewing it all from a distance as in Wannsee, nor was he in a shelter under a shaking house; this time he sat plumb in the middle of this primeval uproar and eruption. The red glow of the fire flared into the compartment. The flames flared through the whole gamut of colours, from blinding white to the deep blackness of night. Blazing engines hurtled through the air – souls damned both in heaven and on earth. One man alone stood on the Holy Mountain – one alone. But one should not be alone; should not sit back when the whole world is being shattered. At least one should take cover under the carriage, hopeless though this may be. Zecke took another swig and sat fast.

Quite a character, that Zecke. What was it he had said? You should distinguish between an order and a conversation. If you can only hear orders you are only half a man. And you must also distinguish between a principle and a person. . . .

That was Aachern, Colonel of the Luftwaffe. Yes, he had wronged the fighter pilots of his former set up. What does it matter if a cap is crooked, or if a tunic is a centimetre longer than the regulations allow? It's not the uniform that matters: it's the man inside it.

A belated understanding.

Now all the young ones had gone – shot down – senselessly tossed in the mud. And the most recent ones – two old men and three youths – the Volkssturm of the air.

Now I am in a real mess, and it can't get any worse.

That was Flight-Colonel Aachern, eight thousand metres above Berlin. Five machines behind him, he was flying the sixth. The enemy, according to the last radar message he had received, was flying 'Hanni 25' – at twenty-five thousand feet. Then silence, no more radar, it was destroyed, useless. He was flying at twenty-five thousand feet at a speed of three hundred and fifty miles per hour. Six machines, an armament of thirty-six guns. And without radar he was trying to pin down some of this Mosquito swarm.

A lunatic order! The jovial little bandy-legged general with the red stripes down his trousers and the portwine nose, had no longer been easy-going. 'The courier plane must get through, Aachern, I am holding you responsible with your life!' With guns or by ramming!

But where are they? Radar had announced 'at twenty-five thousand', and was silent after that, interrupted, out – dead.

Down below Aachern saw bombs hitting the ground and squirming up earth and rubble, and above his engine the red streaks of incendiary bombs. So there they are, higher still: 'Bank left and climb up to thirty!' he signalled to his pathetic group, his five men, Crocodile, Elephant, Caruso, Serpent and Polecat. But that wretched box – the ME 109 – could not climb higher than thirty-two thousand, and now their ceiling was thirty only, and the Mosquitoes were perhaps at forty thousand. Again he saw bombs falling on Berlin and the flares dropping through the night, floating down from eighteen thousand feet in white, red, yellow, green and blue streaks; dissolving at ten thousand feet to be replaced by new ones. The flares illuminated a circle from the Brandenburg Gate to Tempelhof Airport, from Neukölln to Schöneberg: the southern sector of Berlin – exactly the area he had to secure for the incoming courier plane. In the bright glare he could recognize the Brandenburg Gate, the Anhalt Station, and, like a pointed needle, the column on Belle-Alliance Square.

They are throwing everything into this marked-out circle. The order cannot possibly be carried out – the sacrifice is in vain. If only he had thought of it before, had got his boys together and had explained to them the hopelessness of the situation. They could then have taken off and flown straight to the west. Too late. Now he was in the middle of it, flying above that devil's cauldron directly in the path of the bombs. Shadows were passing him, ghostly, phantomlike figures. 'Turn 180 degrees, to the left!' Aachern pulled his machine out and banked steeply to the left, the others following him. As he turned he could see flames from the anti-aircraft guns. So they were getting that as well now – fire from their own flak guns. Glowing balloons were drifting up from below, red showers of meteors, bursting right and left, above and below the planes. Whole bunches of splintering shells, searchlights, fires, conflagration. The pale finger of a searchlight caught up with Elephant – yet another searchlight. A radio message from Elephant to Pigeon: 'Hit by flak, hit!' and again a cry of distress: 'Hit again! Elephant calling Pigeon: Must go down, am baling out, baling out!'

Silence. Another one lost. Where are the others? 'Pigeon calling all of you . . . Pigeon calling all of you . . .'

Down on the ground a glowing circle, seething chaos, whole rows of houses wrapped in dark smoke, red flames shooting high, Potsdamerstrasse, Yorkerstrasse, the goods station – a solid island of smoke with red borders.

Where are the Mosquitoes?

Aachern is shouting into the microphone, almost roaring: 'Tuba, Tuba! Cuckoo, Cuckoo! Where is the enemy – what direction, what height, what course?'

No answer.

Fighter control was as dead as the radar.

Where are the other five – or four, or three? An old sweat and two children plunged into that infernal cauldron.

'Pigeon calling all of you! Pigeon calling all of you . . .'

No Viktor, no Ricardo, no 'understood' or 'cannot understand'. No one spoke, no one answered.

Bursting ack-ack guns, one ball of smoke after the other. Dark black flat smoke. Aachern plunged into this jungle of black smoke, still at three hundred and fifty miles per hour, could not see his hand before his eyes, was flying blind, shot through, got into the cauldron again and back into the light – red, green, yellow. Down below, Berlin, in ghostly illumination. Conflagration, mountains of smoke, hissing flashes. If only he could get out of the jaws of hell, the space marked out by Very lights – but he did not succeed, was blinded, could not see any more, unfit to fly by night. . . . You mad red-nosed bastard – your orders are senseless! Zecke, Zecke, where are you? I must talk to you – we must talk over, discuss things.

Too late. Too late!

What is the use of realization now?

He must call off the attack. That's all that's left now. Aachern shot through, got into it again, shuddered again through the shadowless light in the forbidden zone. Then he was outside in a space of drifting phantoms and ghost-like reverberations.

'Cuckoo! Cuckoo!'

The intercom was silent.

'Pigeon calling all of you . . .'

No Crocodile, Polecat, Serpent, Caruso. They were no more. None of them left.

'Pigeon calling all of you: No sense in attacking, we have failed . . . get away, get away, get away!'

No Viktor, no Ricardo.

No one left – I am alone.

Hurrying shadows, a thousand reflections. . . . Glowing streaks from the exhaust shooting past. A machine made of fire. Dropping fire bombs, wreckage, bombs – everything caught in the light and throwing it back, glittering in all colours. Light and dark, day or night, above or below – he no longer realizes any of it, does not distinguish any more between sky and earth. Nothing but shadows, fleeting shadows, lost shadows, damned shadows. Where am I to attack, where is the spot? – I can neither shoot nor ram. . . .

Suddenly he saw . . . he saw a metallic flicker, an illuminated silhouette under his machine. At last! But he could not see, was blinded – could not shoot either. This is it – ramming. He put his machine into a steep dive . . . down, down – no shock, no crash, no end. He had dived far beyond the target but where was the end, where was death?

A piece of tin, of glowing metal, a falling petrol tank – he had rammed or tried to ram a ghost, a will-o'-the-wisp. Aachern pulled his machine up and began to climb. The blood rushed from his head; everything turned dark before his eyes. Everything swam and disappeared in a swirling mist. He was done for; covered in sweat, he trembled and shook; forgot everything around him. Then consciousness returned. He came back to a world of falling shadows. A world in collapse – bursting into a million coloured fragments, all colours of the spectrum. What about the order, was it still in force, was anything in the world still in force? It was past and done – the world of orders drowned in smoke and grime. Why am I still here? Get out – but there is no way out. Out of here – west, south. It's all the same. Bearing south. A last attempt: 'Pigeon to all, to all! Call off the attack. Get out. Bearing south!'

No answer.

No answer.

Bearing south.

Aachern could feel nothing, would not have noticed the pricking of a needle. He was without fear, without thought, was functioning mechanically like a part of his machine roaring through space, like the throttle he held in his hand.

But how am I to get back? Nowhere to land. Never mind, out at all costs, out of this hell – even if another one is waiting down on the ground. Where shall I find myself? Among Russians, Americans, or in no-man's-land?

One thing only remained: to get out.

I am flying – the machine flying with me.

But where to?

Flying, flying – through a thick soup, through snow, through air-pockets . . . over brown desert, the curved earth, a forlorn light among other lights, brother of the stars, so I fly, bedevilled by a red-nosed bastard, straight up the devil's black backside.

A red light – the tank was thirsty. The second red light flashing up. Red lights everywhere, inside the engine, over Berlin, everywhere this is the end.

Aachern woke from his numbness. My time is soon up. I've ten minutes left; five minutes left.

Get out! Get out!

He did not want to die; he must do something, had to do something. Those were his only thoughts. To get out of this machine, to get out! He loosened the straps, pulled up his knees, pressed the red lever and the spring-loaded handle of the cabin roof, and with both feet pressing hard against the controls, he was catapulted out of the top. Mechanically he counted: one, two, three. The parachute opened and he started floating. What sort of a world was he going back to? East, west, no-man's-land? It was night and nothing moved down below. No gun-fire, no bangs, no flames – and no talks in a shelter either. The world seemed asleep. He drifted over a broad light ribbon. It was the Autobahn – but which one? the one to Breslau? or to Leipzig or to Cologne? Hardly the latter. A thin strip of forest was drawing nearer. His feet almost touched the tree-tops. He smelled the fragrance of the firs and the stronger smell of earth, drifted to the left, down a narrow path through the forest and on to a field. Once more a gentle breeze caught the parachute and made him drift a little further. Then Aachern felt ground under his feet.

But only under his feet. The change was too sudden to take it in. Just now he had been sitting in a roaring machine, gliding down through a bank of clouds – and now he was on the ground with soft grass underfoot. For a moment it was a great relief not to have to act, but the sudden inactivity paralysed the willpower that had made him operate the levers of his engine and the strings of his parachute. He almost lost control of himself, a helpless creature, dropped from the sky. Then he pulled himself together and staggered over the field, reached a small lane and followed the ruts of the wheels to the highroad – a signpost!

He struck a match and read: Stadtroda. Where was that? Another post pointed in the direction of Kahla. Neither name had any meaning for him. He went back along the same lane, reached the field, and passed a young forest plantation. A little further on he noticed a house, a lonely farm with a large gate. A dog started barking. Through the chink of an ill-fitting door he saw the yellow glimmer of light. The dog was now barking violently, and someone came to open the door.

'So here you are at last, old man,' he heard a man say. 'You look as if you needed some rest – come straight in and make yourself comfortable!'

Aachern followed the man – he would have followed the devil. They entered a dimly lit hall and from there went into a living-room with peasant furniture.

'We were afraid you couldn't get through. . . . But it isn't him at all! Just look, Luise, it isn't him!'

The man and his wife stared at Aachern, and he noticed that, although it was long after midnight and in a low peasant's room on a lonely farm, they were dressed as if for a solemn occasion.

'That's right, not him at all!'

'But he has had a rough time all the same.'

'Aachern,' the Luftwaffe Colonel introduced himself curtly.

'Rudi Paul is my name, wholesaler in guinea pigs. But gracious me, where do you come from and what do you want?'

'Where from? . . . Well . . .' he vaguely pointed to the wall and the ceiling. 'Yes, from up there – from Berlin.'

'From Berlin? I see. . . . Have you been long on your way?'

Herr Paul noticed that Aachern's eyes were blinking, that his mouth twitched and that he was on the brink of tears. He also realized that the untidy uniform was that of a pilot. In the first world war he himself had been a colonel in the air force.

'You'd better sit down first and rest a little. So you are from Berlin, the centre of the Third Reich, which at this very moment is collapsing. Down in Ulrichswalde in front of the pub, the last four have gone, a lieutenant and four privates. They did not want to, but the lieutenant was determined. The Americans passed along the Autobahn yesterday.'

Aachern sat in a comfortable chair. The furniture was rough but good. . . . The man opposite him reminded him of Zecke and at the same time of 'Portwine nose' – not as the latter had been when they met the last time, but as the little jovial man used to look formerly when his eyes could still twinkle cheerfully. The man here was rather short too, but somewhat broader, with a chest like a barrel, a battered face with observant eyes.

'Where exactly am I?' asked Aachern.

'In Thuringia . . . not far from Gera, at Ulrichswalde, on Dr. Paul's estate. I was a pilot once and a public prosecutor and had my office at Gera. The Third Reich took my licence away. Here on this farm I have weathered the "Thousand Years", breeding guinea-pigs which my wife has been selling to colleges and other institutes. But now that's all over – the guinea-pigs and the millennium. That's how it is.'

'Yes, it's all over; it's the end.'

'No, my boy! Life is beginning again.'

Aachern slowly sipped a cup of tea Frau Paul had put before him. By now he was just about able to tell them, though not very coherently, of the special order he had decided not to carry out, of his lost comrades, and how he had eventually landed.

'Well, and what's going to happen now?'

'There'll be a complete change.'

'The Americans...'

'They are already at Gera and rolling along the Autobahn in the direction of Chemnitz. We can count on seeing them here at dawn.'

'That means I'll be a prisoner of war.'

'Are you married, Herr Aachern?'

'I have a wife and two children in Berlin-Wannsee.'

Dr. Paul looked at Aachern. He had at least seen reason at the last moment and tried to save his comrades. It would not make sense for the poor devil to disappear behind barbed wire. But could he...? After the endless chain of interrogations at the Prinz-Albrecht-Strasse Gestapo Headquarters, the former solicitor Rudolf Paul had been waiting for the collapse of that government of evil and injustice as for the trumpet of Doomsday. Could he, as a man of the law, burden his first step into a new order by aiding and abetting a man in a matter that was not quite correct? But that's nonsense, Rudi, he reassured himself. Haven't you also been a flier, and in distress yourself, and haven't you been helped as well? Undoubtedly, he had to provide him with civilian clothes. Hundreds of thousands were rendering that same service this very hour – how did they justify themselves? By calling it a state of emergency? It was that indeed.

'Do you want to find yourself in a prisoner of war camp?'

Aachern stared at him with wide open eyes.

'Just wait a moment.'

Dr. Paul left the room, and returned with a farmhand's jacket and trousers. Aachern took off his uniform and changed into the earthy peasant's suit. Only then did he realize the full importance of this action.

'I suppose it will be best to burn all that?'

'Yes, burn it, please. . . . Oh, Dr. Paul!' He gripped his hand.

Colonel Zecke emerged from abysmal darkness to the sound of confused voices and shouting around him. Outside, people rushed past the windows. He did not know where he was and tried hard to find his way back to reality. The people outside were shouting:

'The railway tracks...the rails!'

What had he to do with tracks, and what had happened to them anyway?

The rails had been hit, the very track on which the train was supposed to leave the station. Suddenly Zecke realized where he was and that the bomb damage would mean hours of waiting. At least until dawn!

What else could he do but go on drinking? He emptied the second bottle to the last drop to prolong his blissful state – back to the Holy Mountain. He succeeded: once again time and space were suspended around him.

When he opened his eyes it was full daylight, and the train was moving fast. He passed through potato and turnip fields bathed in sunshine – nothing reminded him of Berlin, the metropolis beyond the horizon, awaiting her fate.

There was almost complete calm at Buckow. Situated near a forest and a lake, off the beaten track, the little township had remained remote from the spreading catastrophe. A few staff officers had moved their quarters there, and at night, muffled by the intervening forest, the unending rolling of the rear-guard vehicles could be heard from the highroad beyond. The twenty miles distance between Buckow and the Oder had so far kept Russian fighter-planes away.

Big flies were buzzing in the sunshine outside the Pension 'Waldfrieden', long since turned into a reserve hospital. After darkness had fallen the silence of the night was almost audible and one could clearly hear a lonely sentry pacing up and down.

For almost three months now the Russians had been lying by the Oder. Once they had managed to cross the river, but had been met and thrown back across it. Surely it should be possible to repel further attempts of that kind; surely the expected German offensive would succeed in banishing the Russian phantom to the open spaces of their own vast land.

This at least was the spoken opinion and hope of Staff Medical Officer Dallmann and part of his team in 'Wald-frieden' hospital. Orders came to move the wounded. Those who could walk had to look after themselves and get away as best they could. The badly wounded were hastily flown to Berlin, whether sufficient beds could be found there for them or not. The hospital was to remain a casualty station under Medical Officer Dallmann.

The night of the 15th April was wrapped in peace. It was Spring, a clear night with dawn just around the corner. In the hospital everyone woke up at the same moment. . . . Medical Officer Dallmann, Medical Sergeant Wustmann, the orderlies and the nurses. An alarm-clock had started ringing and did not stop.

A strange noise.

A vibration under one's feet, so gentle that the glass on the bedside table did not even clink. But a strange noise different from anything heard before. Only Sergeant Wustmann, the driver Stroh and some medical men who had taken part in the eastern campaign, were at once wide awake and knew: artillery barrage. It lasted for one and a half hours.

A casualty transport arrived – nothing out of the ordinary. A second one followed soon after. Buckow was not yet in the line of attack, but there was no question of coping with the number of casualties, except to give first-aid. Then an order demanded an immediate move to Werneuchen, where a main casualty station had been established. It was a motorized medical unit with lorries, ambulances and cars; and Werneuchen was only some twenty miles away. But hardly had they arrived there when fresh orders decreed: On to Weissensee. Weissensee – that was actually on the outskirts of Berlin.

Chief Medical Officer Heide, Medical Sergeant Wustmann, the driver Stroh, two lance-corporals and the young orderly Wittstock stayed behind to wind up the affairs of the unit that had been moved so hastily. They would follow later. But they could not help giving first-aid to fresh casualties and arranging for their further transport.

This continued for two days and nights. Buckow and the sector between it and the Oder were still outside the battle, but ambulances and lorryloads of wounded from the neighbouring sectors of the front found their way there. None of the medical men slept any more. Casualties from flak units, from the Volkssturm, the Hitler Youth, the SS-Division Nordland, the rifle brigade. Torn-off limbs, splinters in thighs, buttocks, bellies; burns, scalds, grimy uniforms, blood-soaked rags – the conveyor belt of pallid bodies under their hands did not stop. But most striking was the mental state of these wounded men. Some even suffered from muscular spasms and loss of speech as a result of shock. They all came from the north. A lieutenant with a twitching mouth said: 'Doctor, it's all smashed to bits, wide open, there's no front any more, they are coming. . . .'

Further north the front had in fact been smashed up and pierced. But in the direction of Küstrin and Frankfurt-on-Oder strong, undefeated units were holding their old positions. Three more days. Then the Senior Medical Officer, the sergeant and the three orderlies also mounted the lorry that had been filled with dismantled equipment and apparatus.

They were all exhausted, worn out, longing only for sleep. The driver alone managed to keep his eyes open. He could in any case only move slowly as the bombs had churned up craters in the road. When they reached the main road leading from Freienwalde to Berlin, the movement stopped almost completely. Behind them the rumbling front, right and left shells bursting in the fields. Dive-bombers were sweeping over tree-tops, machine-gun volleys swept the street. The senior medical officer and the orderlies hardly opened their eyes – they were reduced to the state of somnolent cocoons. Sergeant Wustmann jerked up for a moment, blinked into the light and found himself in a mêlée of vehicles, bombed cars, interlocked carriages, horse-drawn carts, hopelessly entangled. 'Dear me', said Wustmann. The driver only nodded. All too familiar. It had looked the same near the Vistula, the same along the Dnieper, and beyond the Don it had not looked much different.

Familiar scenery, familiar road . . . road of retreat.

The sergeant had fallen asleep again. They reached Werneuchen and found the house of the main casualty station. But their unit had moved further on. The driver came back with the order: 'On to Weissensee!' . . . Familiar scenery, familiar road.

Retreating men of the service corps, parts of the support troops in headlong flight, the backwash from the front, soldiers from the rear services first, but behind them the remains of an air division smashed at Freienwalde. Among them civilians, women with prams, pushcarts, wheelbarrows; men on bicycles, some from the adjacent villages, others from far away who had already moved towards Berlin with the big trek of refugees from the east – foreign workers, Frenchmen, Russians, Poles and Dutchmen.

And Splüge was among them – Goya-Splüge. He had driven to the Oder on the eve of the offensive. The village Güstebiese was lying on the farther bank. A horse-ferry used to cross the river in the past. At this spot the Russians had built a bridgehead which they defended tenaciously. Splüge had watched the bridge from an advance post – the death bridge, the devil's bridge, the Berlin bridge, as the Russians had named it. A belt of freshly cut planks, ten yards wide, had grown across the Oder in one night and had for all the following weeks been the target of German artillery and Stuka bombers. By day and night, relentlessly. The grey waters of the Oder on both sides of the bridge were in continuous fermentation, in boiling and foaming uproar, splashing over the roadway and sweeping bomb-destroyed human beings, horses and heavy lorries down into the abyss. Corpses of men and animals were drifting downstream; so were wooden planks and other parts broken away from the bridge. But the bridge still stood, a grey mass of pioneers swarming at both its ends, handling tubes and wires, knocking, hammering away, patching up holes. They were hit by bombs and bursting shells, blown into the waves, some reappeared with hammers, axes, saws – and the banks of the river were constantly changing. The ground was churned up by bombs, pitted by shells, and each crater turned into a workshop of carpenters and blacksmiths. The eastern bank had been an enormous colony of craftsmen from the beginning. The woods were cut down one after the other, and had almost completely disappeared. Now trees had to be brought from further away. Day and night detonations, smoke, spurting water – but when the smoke lifted the bridge reappeared, as it had the day before and many days before that, full of men, horses, service lorries, an endless grey ribbon, slowly moving westward and fanning out from the bridgehead.

Splüge had watched the bridge through the staff artillery telescope of the advance post and had then returned to a lonely farm where the staff officers were quartered. After a bite of food – it was long after midnight – he had driven back in his car as far as Letschin. There, in the middle, between the first and second line, the barrage had caught up with him, shots from distant guns hit the village, all the houses of which were crowded with soldiers. Glaring flashes lit up the fields and mushrooms rose out of smoke and earth. Splüge had come here to look for himself – but what's the good of getting the right impression when your head and the whole of you will be pinned to the next wall by a long distance shell. He would stay in the village, creep into the next shelter, into the deepest hole he could find. But what had the next hour, the end of the attack, the coming day in store for him? 'On to Quappendorf,' he told his driver. But that proved impossible. The advancing rearguard columns pushed them off the road. They returned to Letschin and tried to find a detour via the fortified second line to Berlin. But that, too, was not feasible as the road lay under overwhelmingly heavy fire from medium and heavy artillery.

The battle of the Oder had started. The last big battle in Germany, and Splüge found himself right in the midst of it. He had asked for it, but not quite. He had not meant to be thrown into the frying pan with the rest. He had only meant to look from the edge of it and see for himself. For the next hour, Splüge neither saw nor heard anything. Human eardrums cannot stand such a shattering din. In fact, it took nearly an hour and a half till Splüge could again get out of his cellar and go on – at the very moment when the German soldiers emerged from their dug-outs to try for the last time to stem the onslaught of the grey masses of Russian infantry. But even now he was only just aware of voices, fragments of speech as part of the gigantic fugue around him. The village was no longer a village, nor the road a road. Flames shot out of roofs which rained burning tiles. Horses, carts, among them a flak cannon, its barrels pointing to the sky. A raving sergeant; 'Idiots, dolts, kill them . . . smash them! Break a way through!' His anger got the sergeant nowhere – nor the colonel at his side. It needed a Russian heavy bomber to achieve some sort of disentanglement, turning horses into horsemeat, and sweeping smashed vehicles into a single heap.

But the confusion and panic went on. Pallid faces, quivering eyes, fleeing soldiers on all sides, staggering behind them pathetic figures without weapons, babbling: 'The Russians the Russians . . . !'

That short distance took Splüge and his driver the whole day. They passed through the second line with German soldiers still fighting, soldiers who had abandoned their front positions but were retreating in orderly closed formations, still facing the Oder and putting up a fight.

In one place Splüge was taken across underground gangways to the staff corps office for his papers to be examined. The officer in charge spread them on the table before him. He offered Splüge a cigarette and made a few remarks on the situation. 'It looks as if the Russians have got one gun on top of the other for several square miles', he said. 'We've gone through a lot before, but never in my life have I heard such a barrage. But the attack has more or less been thrown back and the situation is well in hand!'

Staff officers are not in the front line: it is therefore easy for them to keep a cool head! argued Splüge. But after all this man was not one of the Hitler Youth and although only about twenty-one years old, he was an army officer and a staff officer at that. The optimistic tone of the young officer irritated Splüge. He had not been able yet to shake off those hours in the rocking shelter nor his subsequent hopeless progress like a creeping worm, with the mud fountains bursting in the fields left and right. And he could not get rid of the memory of those wretched, disconcerted faces along the roads.

The lieutenant had second thoughts: 'Well, you have seen some of it yourself. Of course, the front is broken in some places. There is hard fighting going on to secure our positions. Unfortunately, casualties seem to be very high, exceedingly high'. The telephone rang. While answering it, the officer had got up from his seat. He gave laconic answers, looked at Splüge, pushed the papers over to him suggesting he should take them back, and seemed on the verge of taking his leave of him with a wave of his hand. But he was stopped short. It all happened too suddenly.

The front line took control for the second time that day. The receiver dropped from his hand, and he and Splüge and another officer who had been in the room, were thrown to the floor. Another barrage; the first time it had lasted an hour and a half; it was precisely 4 p.m. when it started for the second time.

'Four p.m.,' said the commanding officer looking at his watch. This time it was apparent that the attack was not only meant for the front line but also for the fortified positions behind, including staff quarters and support roads.

Again Splüge was caught. But he was taken to a shelter which, though of simpler type without soundproof double doors, had wooden panelling and electric light. At least at the beginning. The current was soon off and Hindenburg lights started flickering.

Soldiers were leaning against the walls....

I have seen it before; I know how it is ... don't want any more of it. He was completely stunned, would have liked to shut his eyes and ears. But he had to see and to hear and was wondering how long he could stand it. The constant thud of falling earth, making him jerk up and sink back again, a grinding movement, fed and kept going by a cataract thundering through the air. A Niagara of iron and fire that did not stop falling, churning, seething. And underneath the roaring of death, yourself not knowing when it will be your turn to be killed, squashed, scorched, buried, flung up into the air and back on the ground; engulfed by the gigantic uproar.

If only one could stop listening and think of something else!

But there is nothing else ... oh yes, there is – quite a lot besides this!

The waving flag, tattered and burnt ... nonsense, complete nonsense. The waving flag ... the beginning of a poem lying on his desk in his makeshift office. And then there was Leonore.

Leonore, who had eight pairs of shoes in her wardrobe but did not think this enough and had to have more. But she did not get any, neither at Leiser's nor Karstadt's nor at Hermann Square or the Spittelmarkt. One of the buyers she knew had told her to come back when the stores restocked. Now she wanted to travel to Cologne, or better still, to Amsterdam, or at least send a courier. What a silly girl – as if one could go to Cologne, let alone Amsterdam, or send a courier anywhere. Incidentally, she did buy that poodle after all. I should have given her a touch of the slipper.

Beate has got one, she says, Beate only has to murmer: I'd like a smart dog, and she'll get him . . . so she has to have one too . . .

Oh, that thundering, roaring, grinding. And that man in the corner over there, one of the rifle brigade! Splüge has been watching his little finger for quite some time – first it was his finger, then his hand, now the whole man. He is trembling all over – and that's catching!

She's already got a canary; now she has the poodle, which I suppose I shall have to take down in the mornings to lift his leg in the Grunewald.

His girl-friend Leonore, his wife Beate, wife only in name . . . poodle, canary, the waving flag, and next to him the staring faces under steel helmets – it made no difference. His finger started trembling, the little one first, then the second and now the third one. How long can one stand it? That grinding uproar, a primeval forest full of shrieking apes, raving elephants; that screaming collapse, that whizzing and bubbling – saturnine bubbling! Wasn't that the word that idiot Wittstock used? How much longer? When does the moment come when you simply jump up and run away – but where to . . . the officer with his steel helmet is also in the shelter and the cheerfulness on his face has frozen into a mask. Now it has caught both his hands and he has entered into trembling competition with that poor rifleman.

'Everything must come to an end!' It was the man at his side sitting on the bench, steel helmet on his head, fieldpack at his feet, breathing calmly. The cigarette in his hand did not tremble in the least. He was smoking as if in defiance of all the howling, hissing and grinding, and the bursting storm outside, and just sat and waited. Like everybody else in this cave he was waiting for the end of the barrage and the arrival of the Russians whose mass formations would be thrust against the second line of defence.

'Everything must come to an end!'

And it did come to an end. The trembling soldier was at the end of his ordeal and jumped to his feet. They all jumped up in order to go on and face other ordeals in different shapes. The barrage had lasted exactly the same time as in the morning, from 4 p.m. to 5.30 p.m. It was still daylight outside.

It looked as if the Russians were expecting to overrun these heights that very evening – en passant as it were. It was time for Splüge to leave. The roof of his car had been squashed in, but the engine was all right; the wheels turned and off they went.

Tiefensee, Werneuchen, Weissensee were lying along the road in front of them. It was not really any distance and there had been times when he had taken Leonore for a drive eastwards, just for a change, to have a cup of coffee on the Seelow Heights. The whole trip including the cup of coffee and the usual row had lasted a little over two hours. But now the road was being used for bringing up reinforcements; bomb damage necessitated detours and everyone was being harassed by Russian dive-bombers.

During the night and the following day troops hastily called from Berlin had priority on that road, but it had already turned into an escape route. Advance and flight side by side, interlocked against each other. On foot – if only he had thought of that at the start! He could have walked it in one night. But that occurred to him much too late, in fact after they had been waiting for a long time for a piece of the road to be repaired, and after having forced their way slowly and painfully through all the mêlée and having lost a lot of time through all the detours. They had been told the Russian bombs were no good and that half were not exploding anyway. But they definitely succeeded in making the fleeing masses panic and Splüge's Volkswagen was flung off the road and landed upside down in a field. Now he had no other choice but to walk, but with all his bones aching that was rather difficult. Even before reaching the tank barrier at Werneuchen, Splüge spent one night in a house on the road. Bombers and the appearance of what could be arrest-parties had driven many from the highroad into the woods, and in all that confusion he also lost his driver – whom he never saw again. When day came he started his trek. Women, children, old men, they were all fleeing along the road, on foot or with horse and cart – in fact every imaginable kind of vehicle flowed in the stream. And from Berlin there came mixed formations and home guard troops, riflemen, Hitler Youth, army, air and sea units, walking or in lorries. Over a stretch of many miles the road was blocked and everything hopelessly jammed and interlocked. One could not move a single step forward or backward. Russian bombers and pursuit planes vied with each other in firing into the mass of helpless humans. Regimental commanders were swearing; officers, sergeants and drivers were doing their best to drive the wandering masses from the road. Those on foot tried to find their way over fields; Splüge with them. The sick had to stay behind and along both sides of the road were abandoned babies, wounded horses, dead horses and smashed vehicles. Everything in disintegration, breathing its last breath. It was evening when Splüge reached Weissensee. I saw it with my own eyes ... and he had had to pay for that with a lame leg; he had got off cheaply. What poor devils he had met! The trembling rifleman in the shelter; the man who did not seem to mind, beside him on the road the old man with his wheelbarrow; the sergeant with a first-aid bandage round his head; the women with rucksacks, babies in their arms and toddlers clinging to their skirts, refugees from far away and others who had only just left their houses – all of them poor devils. The old woman with the push-cart said she came from Gross-Schliewitz in West Prussia and had had an emergency billet up to now. He had wanted to speak to the sergeant with the bandage round his head, but with a weary gesture of his hand the man had indicated that he did not want to talk, had had enough of it all. An increasing number of soldiers from the disintegrating front line mingled with the stream of refugees. Cut-off troops, remnants of battalions, smashed service units, soldiers with badges pinned to their uniforms labelling them as 'wounded', stumps of arms in blood-soaked slings, men limping on sticks, hollow faces, open wounds. The defeated men in the battle of Kunersdorf must have looked very much the same.

'All is lost!' cried the King.

Two horses had been shot dead under him, but when he returned his kingdom was saved. The death of the Czarina and the disunity among the allies saved the Prussians.

> 'The waving flag,
> Tattered and burnt,
> Shines above the Fatherland.
> Onwards,
> onwards ...'

Now Roosevelt had died, just as at that time the Czarina Elisabeth – a great historical parallel. There must be an imminent clash between Americans and Russians – everybody coming over to the Ministry of Propaganda from Voss-strasse says so and it is the last hope in Hitler's Bunker.

The waving flag . . . but this time it was only a wretched dangling rag, a dangling human being without shoes, one that had been hanged from a lamp-post. A piece of cardboard on his breast said: 'My name is Walter Schulz and I am hanging here because I was too cowardly to defend my wife and child.' He had been in the Volkssturm. His feet were now bent downward, the piece of rag wrapped around them had unwound and almost touched the heads of the crowd rushing past.

Splüge also noticed that the throng of people was thinning out, that many made off sideways, some in a northerly direction towards the sewage-land, others in the direction of Hohenschönhausen, all trying to reach the city by side streets.

Windowless façades, bombed blocks of flats soared up from the fields, the first advance posts of the immense, dying city. The main stream of refugees was heading for the suburbs and the defence squads posted there. But for a narrow passage for vehicles the tank barrier was closed. The arrest squads were still functioning and throwing their nets over the newcomers searching for new victims. Suddenly they emerged – faces under steel helmets, tin plates hanging round their necks:

'Your pay-book and papers!'

Senior Lieutenant Splüge was allowed to pass.

He had got this far at least! Now for a tram, an underground or any other vehicle. 'You won't have much luck, old man. There is no Metropolitan, no Underground, and the trams are completely done for. After this afternoon's attack everything is *kaputt*. Nothing before tomorrow morning, and nobody can say what it will be like then.'

Nobody can say, of course not! God alone knows and perhaps the Marshal on the Seelow Heights, for according to all he had seen, heard and suffered, the Russians must have got there. Splüge was dead tired, dragging his lame leg. That somersault on to the field at Tiefensee had left its grim mark. He might try to ring his unit, ring Lenore – that might be an idea, although it would most likely not work either. If he were to hobble into Voss-strasse, it would take him till Doomsday, and Doomsday was anyway somewhere round the corner and might easily catch up with him at Alexander Platz or even near the Friedrichshain. His optimism – and with only occasional intervals he had succeeded in keeping it up until quite recently – was slowly waning. No wonder, since he hadn't even a bicycle and all the rest of Weissensee seemed to be on bicycles at that moment. Besides, he had not seen a single glass of brandy since Tiefensee. What was left in the bottle had vanished with the driver. On top of everything else – Russian planes within Berlin. Are they planning an attack on Weissensee? Well, the eggs they are dropping don't do a lot of harm, besides it can't get that bad here between walls.

But Splüge threw himself on the ground just the same.

Filthy things! Seem to have no speed at all and then to be whizzing all over the place, smashing electric pylons and dangling wires.

Evening at Weissensee.

Poor Vicco in the gully, a burning house throwing a red glare on the pavement. The women at the water stand-pipes pretending not to know what bombs are; either that or they don't take the Russian bombers seriously. But not all Russian bombs are duds. There you are – pails and buckets are rolling across the road, a moment earlier they were in the women's hands. But the women just pick them up, and back they go to the hydrant. Not very cosy, not at all; much better to leave the main road, after all one can get through one of the side streets.

The side street smelt of fire, smoke and dust; and the stench of decay surged up from cellar holes and rubble heaps. Smashed lumber, all the rubbish lying about, old shoes, mattresses, spilled refuse was smouldering and stank. Splüge felt really sick and his back ached. Where on earth could he get a brandy? He fixed his eyes on the shell of a bombed house. A settee was still hanging from one of the iron girders. The house was familiar; so was the street. He had definitely passed through that street before. And more than once; if he continued a few yards, he'd arrive at the Resurrection Cemetery. That's where Haderer lives – not in the cemetery, of course, but in a street behind it; the old chap who makes his shoes to measure. There is no better cobbler than Haderer, and besides there's always a good drink on his sideboard. A good Nordhäuser schnapps reflected in the light of the cobbler's glass bowl, next door the Resurrection Cemetery – how full of associations and how solemn! Splüge found the walls of the old cemetery, and opposite stood Haderer's house, still intact. The old man had his workshop and a bed-sitting kitchen on the ground floor, and he was in. All Splüge had to do was to knock, wait for a moment and then open the door. Here he was – so was the glass bowl reflecting the light of a candle.

Haderer sat on his stool. He was an artist in his profession and a nightworker, or rather a late worker. But he was not alone. Somebody sat opposite him. This was no hour to order boots made to measure! Haderer had every reason to be surprised, but he looked up composedly.

'I happened to pass', said Splüge. 'No more trains, and I haven't a bicycle; I have something wrong with my back.'

'Lumbago?'

'No, the car overturned near Tiefensee. I just want a little rest.' His eyes wandered to the sideboard.

'Perhaps also a schnapps?'

'Not a bad idea!'

He had a glass of schnapps and after that a second one, and was then allowed to sit down in an old armchair which, though no longer upholstered, still had a back. The schnapps was good, and so was the opportunity to lean back comfortably.

'You need not talk, just relax, Herr Splüge!'

Splüge readily fell in with this suggestion. He could have fallen asleep instantly, and it was not long before his eyes closed. Haderer and his visitor were silent, and for some time only the shoemaker's hammer could be heard. Then Haderer said: 'Yes, much has changed since August!'

The hammer again.

'And what about Pauline?' asked the other man.

'You needn't think about her any more.'

'And Riederheim?'

'Destroyed . . . dead – who knows?'

'And Feierfeil?'

'The same – who knows?'

With his eyes shut, Splüge saw the image of the cobbler's

den and the old doubled-up Haderer. He also saw the other person, but only just before sleep claimed him and pulled him down into black depths. He was in the abyss and on the brink sat an unknown figure. An emaciated face, risen from the dead. A thing like that, 'written off', buried – where does it come from, where could it possibly come from – over the bridge of death, or perhaps down the chimney?

An hour might have passed, or perhaps it was only a moment – Splüge woke up with the sensation of supreme danger, opened his eyes and stared into those of August Gnotke*...

August Gnotke had really been buried under earth and mud, had dragged himself through swamps and decay. A certain day two years back – for others no more than a leaf torn from a diary – had meant for him the end of time, the hoarse call of the trumpet of doom, penetrating to the quick; at whose sound the skies were enfolded and the earth became empty, the graves opened and ninety-one thousand selected skeletons started their march to the place of trial. Through wind and snow and over frozen ground; the judgment was: death on the roadside – through hunger and typhoid, red and white dysentery, and slave-labour. Ninety-one thousand, of which three thousand survived – three out of ninety-one. For those who survived the sentence ran again: hunger, slavery and surrender of the living soul. No memory of the past, no thought of a possible future, no compassion for the moaning neighbour, for trampled innocence – their conscience was locked away; neither death nor murder could reach it.

What was left was a being without willpower, without a soul – a human puppet. Left to that puppet was the ability to repeat hammered-in messages and to carry out certain carefully studied movements, among them the ability to creep through no-man's-land to the other side, there either to meet with his death or to return – only to repeat that game with death.

As a prisoner of war at Stalingrad, August Gnotke had witnessed the death of his army. The individual survivor, withered through hunger, lice, propaganda and slave-labour, was, even before his actual physical collapse, pushed back-

*A character from the book *Stalingrad*.

wards and forwards, ordered to work here, watch and drive others there, or he was sent to courses – to learn by heart, repeat like an automation; to confess and to destroy in 'self-criticism' the remnants of his personality. Gnotke had gone through all of it and was then sent with other survivors as 'helper' to the front – first by the Dnieper, then by the Vistula, and even on German soil death had so far rejected him.

Human lives were spent freely.

The other side was continuously supplying reinforcements. Selected from the gigantic columns of prisoners, the probationers were sent back to the front after a short period of 're-education', and hecatombs of them were sacrificed. There was a shortage of proper uniforms, of German arms, of suitable identity papers; they were not allowed to look at a map so that the majority of them actually ended in the minefields before the German lines, wounded or dead; those that got further fell into the hands of military police and were handed over to the SS for execution.

Gnotke was one of those who returned each time he was sent out by the advancing units; was sent out again, and again returned to be brought before the Security Chief. Gnotke had realized that at his sector of the front only bare weapons counted and nobody attached any importance to propaganda. The pronouncements of the German 'National Committee', the proclamations of the German generals in Moscow, their leaflets, newspapers and handbills had to serve other purposes and disappeared in the cesspools of the staff corps.

Arms had the last word, propaganda did not count. The 'front-line helper' in the loudspeaker waggon or with a simple megaphone in his hand who addressed the German trenches and called upon the soldiers to lay down their arms, offering them good food, medical care and a return home, was in fact a deceitful, garrulous and wicked siren. It happened often that deserters were mown down and German prisoners of war were taken behind the front line and shot down. Both German and Russian artillery were firing into the line of refugees.

A savage and licentious soldiery ransacked, murdered and scorched; under their gun-barrels hospitals turned into death-chambers. Gnotke saw quite a lot – both sides of the front lay open to the ghost in no-man's-land. He followed with his eyes a trainload of women with scarves over their grimy hair and faces darkened by soot from the engine. They came from East Prussia and were going to the glassy sea where he had come from. He gazed after them until the last waggon disappeared in the mist, and his eyes remained glassy.

Again he crossed no-man's-land and came to the township of Schneidemühl. Red army soldiers were feasting heavily and reeling through the streets dead drunk. Helpless screaming came through windows, and from cellars. Women threw themselves into the streets from balconies, others ran for their lives and were caught and lost. Gnotke's eyes remained glassy and his ears deaf.

He passed the village of Güstebiese, crossed the Oder over the 'Devil's bridge' and waited at the bridge-head for the new attack. To the accompaniment of bursting shells and carried by the surging waves of Russian infantry, he reached the second German defence line. The Russian battalion withdrew. He remained in a garret of one of the houses. He threw off his Russian greatcoat; underneath was his German uniform. He put a blood-soaked bandage round his head. He had genuine identity papers, pay-book, medical card, even private letters and some money taken from a dead sergeant. Beyond that he only needed darkness, panic and headlong flight. All these came when the Russians moved in and occupied that whole sector of the front. The evil spirits of catastrophe were Gnotke's allies. He drifted towards Berlin as one of the countless faces in the general disintegration, a particle of the dust of the collapsing German front. He passed Tiefensee and Werneuchen and reached Weissensee and the wall of stones, iron bars, overturned vehicles, the tank barrier and control post of the field police manned with units of Volkssturm and tram personnel. Hoarse and tired from watching all those masses pass by, the military police simply bellowed: 'Your paybook!' He was not soft-hearted and did not want to let anyone slip through, but when he saw Sergeant Gnotke's bandaged head, the 'wounded'-card on his coat and his glassy eyes, he waved him away and turned to the next one. He turned round once more as if touched by an icy wind, but the sergeant had been swallowed by the crowd.

In Berlin-Weissensee Gnotke went his own way, for the first time since the sound of the trumpet of doom. There was plenty of time to carry out his orders, to seek out the hiding-places of the 'Werewolf'.* He went to see Haderer, the shoe-maker who came from the same Pomeranian village; Haderer could have been his father and had in fact always looked after him like a father; but he had fallen out with him when Gnotke entered the SA in 1932. He found him in the same street and the same house. Haderer showed hardly any surprise, nor any annoyance about the return of the 'prodigal son'.

'Where do you come from, August?'

He could not very well say 'from the glassy sea'. Nor would that have been true; that was not where he came from: it came with him, and he had not yet noticed that it had melted under his feet and that now his feet trod firm ground again. 'I come from Güstebiese', was Gnotke's reply. 'And what's the news here?'

'What news do you expect?'

'What about Pauline?'

At this juncture the other man had arrived. A senior lieutenant of the staff corps, a small whippet of a man, per-haps the leader of a pack of Werewolves. But he seemed to be under some sort of a cloud. To come in like that, fling himself in a chair and go to sleep – or pretend to sleep.

Riederheim, Feierfeil . . . who knows where they are? Maybe also somewhere behind the lines, behind trains on twisted tracks that make the carriages jump off the line, or behind turn-tables that do not turn, turning the lorries into motionless rocks, in their hands crow-bars that crack and shovels that roll up like paper; bruised skin and scurf all over, ravenously hungry so that their eyes seem to jump out of their sockets, and behind them the Russian taskmaster yelling: 'Don't forget the work target, *daway*, *daway*† . . .' who knows, yes, who knows?

'Who knows?' repeated Haderer.

It looked as if the Werewolf leader had really fallen asleep after all. If only he could penetrate his thoughts and lure out the information about the hideouts of the young 'Wolves'! That was the moment when Splüge opened his eyes and they met Gnotke's.

*Fanatic sections of the Hitler youth sworn to fight to the death. Their vows were actually 'more honoured in the breach'.
†Off you go.

A glassy look ...

Splüge was alarmed, he recognized the sergeant he had met on the road to Weissensee. He now remembered that when he had entered the room the blood-soaked bandage was lying on the table between pieces of leather and the cobbler's wax. The German uniform he is wearing is genuine, but something about the man is wrong. His face could be the devil's own, and there is something uncanny about his apparent good understanding with Haderer. Anyway, how on earth could he have got to this den? It may be a trap, a meeting-place of Seydlitz partisans, dubious, dangerous, not to be trusted.

He must get away, but without giving the impression of flight.

'Well, how are you feeling, Herr Splüge?'

'Thank you, I have slept a little and do feel rested.' And forcing his voice, though not quite successfully, to sound calm, he added: 'I think I'd better leave you now.' Neither of the two seemed to have any objection to his hasty departure.

Ready to go, he turned to Haderer: 'Chin up, old man: stormy times ahead!'

'Very likely', was Haderer's reply.

'And you, Sergeant ...'

'Roeder', Gnotke introduced himself.

'Good luck to you, Herr Roeder.'

Splüge slurred over the usual 'Heil Hitler'. He shut the door behind him and groped his way down the few steps in the dark. When he came out into the starry Spring night, he took a deep breath. Everything was quiet – an unreal quiet. No sound except a continuous murmur in the distance and the flickering in the clouds of the eastern sky. Splüge felt his way along the wall of the cemetery and started running through darkened streets. When he remembered the two men in the cobbler's den, he called himself an idiot. I just don't know, but I'd bet anything that Roeder is not his real name. Somehow I feel it was a meeting of special significance – if only I knew what kind of significance, and who that man was! –

'Oh dear, that's bad!'

'Yes, we've been there before, haven't we?'

Medical Sergeant Wustmann and driver Stroh were exchanging reminiscences. The others were crouching behind them, in the car, sandwiched between crates. As previously at Werneuchen, a message had been left for them at Weissensee to proceed to their new station in the centre of Berlin, in the Reichstag building. They had reached Weissensee goods station where they ran into marching troops and were pushed into a side street.

Tanks, flak guns, artillery, soldiers, rifle butts, vehicles. The procession was moving towards the tank barrier and further on in the direction of Werneuchen – Tiefensee – Semmelberg.

'That's bad.'

'It looked exactly the same at Odessa in 1944. When they reached their positions, the Russians were there before them.'

'At that time we still had brandy.'

'Quite right, at that time there was a lot of drinking and bawling going on.'

Silent columns were driving towards the outskirts of the city. The glare from burning houses flickered over their faces. The stink of unwashed bodies and filthy uniforms mingled with the smell of burning plaster and leather.

'It was not so bad then.'

The Volkssturm was passing them – old men with peaked caps and Belgian army coats. Hitler Youth – even fourteen-, fifteen- and sixteen-year-old boys in uniforms, much too large for them which hung loosely around their thin, un-developed bodies.

Wheels turned slowly and weary feet were shuffling behind. Airmen with infantry rifles, flak units and parts of support regiments, cadets, police with rifles, men of the Berlin fire-brigade and tram drivers. The road was roped off by a chain of military police so that no one could escape to the side. A man passed – a senior lieutenant who stood beside the lorry and asked if he could board it.

'Good day, Herr Splüge', a medical orderly greeted him – young Wittstock.

'Is it you, Günther? Where do you come from?'

'From Buckow – we have cleared out too.'

'Well, you've been lucky! And where to now?'

'To the Reichstag.'

'Excellent, that's where I am heading for. Well, Sergeant?'

'I don't mind, but you better ask our Senior Medical Officer.'

Heide had no objection; so Splüge got into the lorry and was taken along.

The distance to the Reichstag was only eight kilometres, and in normal circumstances this would have meant half an hour's drive. But they had to wait for hours beside the goods station and finally started moving at a very slow pace by detours and side streets. Blocks of rubble lay across the streets. They passed whole rows of houses that were blazing – there was no water to put out the flames, and the fires spread unchecked. They went on step by step. The moon had risen and stars were shining over a world of ruins. Whole blocks were burnt out and abandoned. Dawn came when they crossed the Alexander Platz. Once again they had to wait in a tight bottleneck to let marching troops pass by. It was another two hours before they eventually stood in front of the monumental stone block of the German Reichstag building.

TO THE GERMAN PEOPLE was inscribed in golden lettering over the main entrance. After the foundation of the Reich in 1871, the German States had found a common roof there. Men like Bismarck, Bethmann Hollweg, Prince Max von Baden, had stood at the Speaker's table of the House, but also Liebknecht Senior and Junior, Bebel, Ledebour and Rosa Luxemburg. From a window on the western side, Philipp Scheidemann had proclaimed the Republic on 9 November 1918. There also had been the Reichstag fire and the Reichstag trial. From the smoke of that fire which destroyed the large conference hall and smashed the glass cupola, the Third Reich had sprung forth – and it now looked as if it would find its end in smoke and fire in the same place.

Medical Sergeant Wustmann was old enough to have some memories of the past. He had also been present at a Reichstag session; had gone in when on leave in October 1918. He could not know then that he would witness a decisive session.

A damp and cold day. Berlin was starving. There was no oil left for the lamps; the trams were clattering noisily and car tyres were worn smooth. You couldn't get anything – no soap, no tobacco, very little bread. Everything creaked, rattled, coughed and was on its last legs.

A war was drawing to its close.

The Kaiser's Empire was drawing to its close.

The twenty-year-old medical soldier looked from the visitors gallery into the hall across the rows of Reichstag members – bent and shivering figures, many of them coughing; Berlin was in the grip of influenza. The new Chancellor, who was making his opening speech, was almost inaudible. He, too, had the 'flu and could hardly speak. He was Prince Max von Baden.

One after the other stood at the Speaker's table. Hardly anybody listened. The representatives of the people were reading newspapers. Only once a gust of wind seemed to sweep through their rows. They jumped up from their seats and talked all at the same time, to neighbours and also across the rows. Only much later, from the published Minutes, had Wustmann learned what it was all about. The collapse at the front, the desperate call for help from General Headquarters, and Wilson's Fourteen Points had been on the agenda. The speaker was Haase, an Independent, followed by representatives of the national minorities – Alsatians, Lotharingians, Poles and Danes.

Social Democrats and Independents accused each other of prolonging the war and each took the other to task for having voted in favour of war loans.

'A plebiscite!' suggested a Dane.

'If the dead were to vote as well', remarked a Pole, and demanded: 'Poland for the Poles!'

Retorted the social democrat Noske: 'Logically, America would then belong to the Red Indians!'

Despair reigned supreme over the Government bench.

'The chorus of the jackals!' someone exclaimed.

'Finis Germaniae!' shouted another.

Secretary of State Haussmann quoted Heine: 'Old Germany, we are weaving your shroud and into it the triple curse!'

All that had happened in 1918. Now the same stage had been reached again. No Fourteen Points were on the agenda this time; the slogan was 'Unconditional Surrender'. No debate was required for that. It was no longer a matter of acceptance or rejection. Their fate was sealed.

Finis Germaniae!

Heide, Wustmann, the two lance-corporals and medical orderly Wittstock had been searching the whole Reichstag unsuccessfully. There was no trace of Staff Medical Officer Dallmann and his medical unit. Soldiers were billeted in the entrance hall and the lobbies; the conference hall was one large soldiers' camp under the scaffolding of the high cupola. That part of the building had remained unchanged and unoccupied, just as the fire of 1933 had left it. There had been no time for repairs; they had probably intended to leave it in that state as a memorial for future generations of the beginning of their reign. Rifles were stacked in pyramids; discarded tins, bits of paper, foot rags, parts of uniforms lay scattered about. Soldiers lay sleeping, their heads pillowed on their packs or rucksacks; others were eating or playing cards – it was ten o'clock in the morning.

A medical unit? Nobody seemed to know. Yes, there had been one yesterday or the day before; one man remembered but did not know what had become of it. Suddenly it came to his mind: 'On the first floor, Sergeant; an army medical inspection department or something.'

Wustmann went up to the first floor. All kinds of military units and officials had established their offices in the former rooms of the various political parties. Many of the staff were only just arriving, either they were taking it easy or the traffic was disrupted. There was continuous coming and going. Wustmann stopped a man to inquire about the unit he was looking for. 'Yes, there is such a thing', he was told. 'Right at the back in the very last room.' He asked a few more questions, and realized that it was a central department with a senior medical officer at its head and a number of employees and typists whose task it was to register all sick and wounded of the German army on a card index. He found the door and stood before the Senior Medical Officer who was already seated behind his desk.

'Yes, there was a Staff Medical Officer Dallmann here. Only yesterday. He had thought he could move into our premises. What an idea!'

The speaker was an old man, could have been on active service only in the First World War. But he had held the job in the Reichstag since the beginning of this war. It seemed to Wustmann as if the Senior Medical Officer had a somewhat muddled conception of the sequence of events and considered it as the foremost task of hospitals and field ambulances to furnish material for his card index. But Wustmann gathered from him that Dallmann and his men could not be far away, for they had finally agreed to move into a nearby tunnel originally set aside for the underground.

'What a shame! A few officers up here would have been nice!'

'And what should we do? After all we have to work!'

'Do you really think this is still of any importance? The Russians have crossed the Oder and are on their way to Berlin!'

The senior medical officer made a disapproving gesture. So did employees and typists in the adjoining room, the door of which stood open.

'Across the Oder – well, that does not mean yet on their way to Berlin.'

'I don't think the distance is very great.'

They still seemed to believe in a wonder weapon and a miraculous army. There was no longer any electric current so that they could not listen to the radio; newspapers only reached them spasmodically. All they heard were hundreds of different and contrasting rumours day in, day out. Besides, so many exaggerations and lies had been spread in this war that you could only trust your own ears and eyes.

In any case, the senior medical officer retorted: 'Would you please stop these wild exaggerations!'

'You'll soon see that it is the truth, Herr Oberfeldarzt. Do you really think this is going on for ever?'

'Why do you say that? After all, we have to carry on.'

At that moment he lifted his head. A distant noise, the like of which he had not heard yet in this war but knew all too well from the last one, reached his ears. The others, too, heard the distant rumbling, different from the roaring, hissing and droning of the bomb warfare – another noise but by no means less threatening.

'That's artillery fire', Wustmann told those in the adjoining room. 'From the outskirts, Weissensee probably.'

'That's impossible.'

But the noise went on, a continuous rumbling, a buzzing that had followed Wustmann from Buckow to Tiefensee and caught up with him here. Then something else happened. It sounded as if a clattering train were passing through the clouds at the outskirts, in a giant semi-circle from the east to the south.

'This sounds as if it came from Teltow or the canal beyond', said Wustmann.

'What do you mean by that?'

'That Berlin is also being attacked from the south!'

A moaning tone swept through the air as if from a very great distance, growing louder as it came nearer and turning eventually into a gigantic roaring. Then a detonation. The ground trembled. The first hit inside Berlin from a long-range field gun.

It made the medical officer change his mind: 'In the circumstances it will probably be necessary to close our offices down for a couple of days.'

Senior Lieutenant Splüge had reached Voss-strasse. He passed the Chancellery and stood in front of the Ministry of Propaganda. The building had been badly battered and had partly collapsed; in some places fires were smouldering. To reach his office, that is to say his makeshift office, he had to pass a number of different-sized cellars. High ministerial officers and councillors, other civil servants and secretaries, as well as hundreds of casual visitors. But what was that? Among an enormous heap of uniforms, civil servants in shirts and pants were searching for clothes to fit them. They had ample choice: uniforms of the Party, Luftwaffe, the Navy and infantry. The civil servants shed their civilian clothes and changed into uniform. Splüge went on into another cellar that looked even more like an army camp. The families of the Ministry staff had billeted themselves here, and during air attacks long rows of women with children and soldiers from neighbouring districts came in as well. Many had come to stay with their bedding and luggage. Let the dead bury their dead! Was it Isaiah who said it, or St. Paul? In any case someone who, like him, did not want to take part in it.

Splüge entered his office. His secretary, Leonore Stassen, had arrived before him. She sat there with needle and cotton in her hand, before her a pile of uniforms.

''d day!' said Splüge, putting his cap on the rack. He did not hear an answer, but it might well have been that his eardrums, used to such terrific noises, had not been able to register a faint 'Good day'.

He sat down at his desk.

Miss Stassen got up and went out of the room. She seems furious, possibly she thinks that it was a mermaid that kept me three days at Güstebiese. He was just about to light a cigarette when his secretary came back with a tray, putting a cup of coffee and a brandy before him. Then she resumed her sewing without saying a word.

After a little while he asked her: 'Did anything happen?'

She did not answer immediately but eventually said: 'The Battalion "Wilhelmsplatz II" is being formed.'

'I have seen it – a circus!'

'We belong to the 2nd Company.'

'We? Does that mean women included?'

'Quite right. I got myself a Luftwaffe uniform.'

'Congratulations.'

'Thank you.'

'And what else?'

'Party member Borman promises Junker estates to those who will render faithful and important services in this emergency. He has offered one to someone in the "Kultur" department.'

'Agreed. Let him have two, if he likes! What else?'

'Party member Ley is recruiting a "Death Legion", mainly over there, but he has also done some canvassing in our building.'

'O.K. Let him go on with it!'

'The Führer celebrated his birthday yesterday.'

'Oh yes.'

'A few of his closest entourage left immediately afterwards.'

'Who did?'

'Göring went south, Dönitz and Himmler north. On the whole the great flight has started.'

'And what are you doing here; and what actually are you sewing?'

'We have been asked to sew "Wilhelmsplatz II" badges on army coats.'

'Very useful. Any more changes?'

'Yes. Herr Schmidtke of the Periodical department – poison. And the head of the Legal department, Herr Schmidt-

Leonhardt, took his daughter to one of the upstairs rooms, and they did not come back – shot themselves up there.'

'Do spare me all that, Fräulein Stassen!'

She was offended. It was probably best not to talk at all to this kind of 'gentleman'. I'm always outside. Probably he spent these last nights with his Beate. I expect it is nice and peaceful at Hohenzollerndamm, while I was sitting at Nikolassee chewing half a dozen hankies and being worried to death about my 'darling'. That's how it always was and always will be. Why doesn't he put a stop to it? After all, it is very painful for everybody concerned. He doesn't dream of getting a divorce. Poor me, I am always unlucky – but I'm not going to be a fool much longer!

Splüge dropped the ash from his cigarette into a tray, gulped the rest of the brandy and, half yawning, told Leonore to carry on.

'Well, what else is happening? . . . Oh yes, Dr. Goebbels is having his usual morning conference, but seems to be a bit late.'

'Anything else?'

'Dr. Meissner left for Mecklenburg, and it seems as if all Ministers of the Reich had left.'

Leonore grabbed her army coats and went out. But she was soon back with them. She had sewn the badges on incorrectly, they should have been higher up the sleeves; so she had to do the whole job over again.

'Perhaps you could do it somewhere else', suggested Splüge. He was tired; too many things went through his mind, and in that state he found Leonore's presence rather irritating. She grabbed the coats again and left the room in a temper. He hoped the sewing would keep her busy for some time and that he could gather his thoughts in the meantime.

But there was not to be any peace for him. A Captain Boehlke entered, a Ritterkreuz pinned to his coat.

'Sorry, Herr Ministerialrat, I don't seem to be in the right place, but this is where they told me to go.'

'I am not a councillor. But what can I do for you, Captain?'

'I have been posted to General Meuspath, the general who is to command the artillery defence of Berlin. But I can't find him, although I have been to GHQ, the Bendler Bunker and the Zoo Bunker. I have just come from the Chancellery, where I was told to call here. They thought that communications were functioning so splendidly here that it would be easy to find General Meuspath's whereabouts.'

As he himself said, the young captain was definitely not in the right place. But Splüge would have liked to help him. The building was full of people who were in contact with hundreds of offices. The telephone, too, was still functioning fairly well. He opened the door to an adjoining room and called the lady-registrar.

'We shall see what we can do for you, Captain Boehlke. Mrs. Dannewitz will be kind enough to take you round to a few offices that may be able to help you.'

He gave her the names of some departmental chiefs, and Frau Dannewitz took Boehlke along.

Splüge was on his own again.

He closed his eyes for a moment and tried to relax. A short spell of sleep à la Napoleon was called for; or if he were a Yogi he could achieve a few seconds of complete oblivion. After that his nerves might be rested like a bear after hibernating.

Three nights without sleep.

Haderer, the shoemaker, the buckets of water at Weissensee, Sergeant Roeder whose name wasn't Roeder, departmental chiefs and secretaries in Luftwaffe, SS and navy uniforms. . . . It would be heaven to be able to rest at Nikolassee behind drawn curtains and to sleep, sleep. He did not want to hear any more, see any more, nor to have to make decisions! He took a deep breath, then another one. But now his brain was like a seismograph and registered a distant noise. A rumbling far away, but he knew in advance that it would die over the roofs of Berlin. He opened his eyes and looked round. The cellar was really very well furnished. Red armchairs with engraved swastikas (these chairs were taken from the large conference halls), a divan, book-shelves, china animals, old flower bowls, Japanese lacquer art work all over the place. But two rifles stood in a corner – one for himself, the other for Leonore. Cartridge belts hung down from the walls and the windows were barricaded with sand bags. There would be splinters, and anyway the cellar was no real cellar, as it was on ground level. And that pompous many-storeyed building on top! It had always offered a very poor protection, but what was left of it was just a giant hollow tooth. Live together . . . but they had started deserting.

The distant rumbling went on.

Leonore came back. She did not seem to be aware of that noise, the new tone in Death's hideous chorus.

'It is also in a minor key', said Splüge.

'What are you talking about?'

'That it's a minor, a gentle key!'

'All right. By the way, Miss Hannemann has also cleared out; taking a job with a building society.'

'Good luck to her! And what have you got here?'

'Manuscripts for the "Tank Bear".'

Again the distant rumbling.

'Apart from that I have found out that in Linkstrasse Dr. Weichhardt has got a very fine selection of shoes!'

'Wish I had your worries. . . .' Is it possible that she had no idea of what the rifles and cartridge belts, and her funny masquerading in the Luftwaffe uniform she had donned in the meantime, meant?

'Dr. Weichhardt has also other essential things.'

'The "Tank Bear" – that should have been done long ago!'

'It would be easy for you to put me in touch with Dr. Weichhardt. They say he can also get you wine.'

The incessant rumbling in the air.

'Weichhardt, Weichhardt . . . you should rather have thought of a printer for the "Tank Bear".'

'Of course; what am I but your diary! I'm not allowed to think of myself. You know I wanted to have a rest at Garmisch, but you just cancelled it. I wish I had been born a worm!'

'You are a worm, from very low and dirty surroundings!'

'You seem to take me for Madame Beate, Herr Splüge!'

A crescendo, as the distant rumbling came nearer – then a thunder.

'That wasn't a bomb; what was it, Vicco?'

'That's, that's . . . There goes your room at Garmisch, you worm, you worm, you worm . . . And I, too, am only a worm!'

Part Two

Gods are made, not by goldsmiths but by prayer.
Balthasar Oracian y Morales

A strange old bird, but not unlikeable. A pity to sit together for a whole night without establishing any contact and scarcely speaking a word. But what good would it do? We don't know each other; we don't trust each other. Yet, when the train pulled up at Wannsee Station, suddenly a bond sprang up between us, a bridge which ended abruptly in a void. Pity . . . His name was Colonel Zecke, formerly stationed at Potsdam. I must ask Uncle Raimond about him.

At Potsdam General Headquarters Captain Boehlke was told that General Meuspath, on whose trail he had travelled since Prague and Leitmeritz, had now been entrusted with the artillery defence of Berlin, and that Boehlke was to report to him at Döberitz. When he left GHQ he called at his uncle Raimond's who was still holding out at his post, his wife looking after him. Boehlke's two cousins – Anna and Leonore – however, were no longer at home. Anna studied medicine at Göttingen; a few days ago she had rung up to say that the British had crossed the Mühl Canal and were already in the old part of the town. Leonore seemed to be the worry of the family. 'She has gone into the Civil Service', his aunt said with an undercurrent of anxiety. It turned out that, of all things, Leonore was now a secretary at the Propaganda Ministry. His aunt added: 'Please do not mention her name to your uncle. He gets so upset about it!' Very strange, all this.

Uncle Raimond returned home, as usual his arms full of books and filed newspapers. He was very pleased to see his visitor and regretted deeply that he had to finish some urgent work for the morning. However, he could spare him an hour's talk. They sat together in a corner of his study in deep arm-chairs, on the low table beside them coffee cups and brandy glasses, the books on the walls round the room climbing up to the ceiling and fading into the shadows. Offering his nephew an Uppmann cigar, one of the last in his box, Uncle Raimond said: 'This is all I can spare you, my dear Berthold, the time it takes to smoke this.'

Then he asked for his news.

'Well, Uncle, the removal to Kissingen was a rather hurried affair, and I just could not find time to see you. Pretty eerie, the last days at the course for higher-grade adjutants! In the end we were only a very small group: it was like the "Ten little Niggers": every day we were one less. Every morning, when the Colonel appeared with the transfer orders, we hung breathlessly on his words. One day someone was appointed Second Adjutant to the Action Commander of Graudenz and was flown the same afternoon to the Graudenz basin. Next day another was posted to Breslau, or Königsberg, or to Thorn Fortress, or to another of those foundering Viking strongholds. And once the Reich Leader SS, Himmler, requested the services of a Liaison Officer. He had to have the "Ritterkreuz" (Knight's Cross), and be fair-haired and tall, and had to board a special train the same afternoon at Berlin Zoo Station in which he would find Himmler. You can imagine how the chaps felt when they packed their bags. I myself was told during the course that my home division in Courland wanted me back – so I was left out of the ghastly "nigger" game. I knew, however, all the time, that my destination was a lost hope. And sure enough: even before the course was finished, my division had ceased to exist. I was then appointed Aide to a high-up artillery commander, and this is the man I am trying to find, so far in vain. At GHQ they did not know whether my general was at Döberitz or at Freienwalde-on-Oder.'

Uncle Raimond shook his head firmly, without speaking.

'It's a rotten feeling, Uncle. Away from the front on my own, I feel lost. In the midst of such momentous happenings one solitary person seems like a trapped mouse.'

'True; comradeship . . . the shared daily bread, suffering and privations borne together . . . everything seems easier then.'

'How long can it last?'

'Well, Stalingrad held out for seventy-seven days – but I don't suppose the Berliners will stand too much nonsense. The soldiers, too, are tired of battle.'

'And what are the plans of our "beloved Führer"?'

That question was not a shot in the dark. Uncle Raimond might be in a position to answer it. As head of the vast military library of OKW Army Headquarters, it had been his task since the beginning of the war to read the foreign press and make extracts from it. In the course of this work he had, from time to time, to visit the Führer's headquarters when his superior, Councillor Scherf, was ordered to make his report. He was thus always in a position to gain first-hand knowledge of the atmosphere and changing moods of Hitler's coterie.

Uncle Raimond, though at first taken back by the straightforward question, replied: 'I will tell you honestly, Berthold: up to a short while ago spirits at the Reich Chancellery were extremely low, worse than anybody could imagine. You could hear it said on all sides, even within earshot of the SS guards: These "last convulsions" are unbearable, the sooner the catastrophe overtakes us, the better! That was the general feeling until, suddenly about three weeks ago, the mood changed and everyone felt optimistic again.'

'Why?'

'It appeared that Hitler, in the last stage of his dementia, was suddenly seeing the light.'

'Extraordinary! How do you know?'

'Scherf told me. When he made his report to Hitler, Bormann was called out for a few minutes, and so Scherf was alone with him. Hitler suddenly looked up at him and said: "Let me tell you, Scherf, I think we ought to throw everything we have left against the East and stop everything in the West"!'

'Our Führer, who thinks in terms of a thousand years, is always six months behind the time, my dear Uncle. He could have had that advice last September from every soldier in the army. He should have thought of it before the Ardennes offensive!'

'That Ardennes offensive! – with the last battalions, the beggar's last few remaining pennies. . . . A very high officer in GHQ – I won't tell you his name – said this. Pure hysterics, without any political or military advantage to be gained!'

'We in Courland thought exactly the same. The Colonel was furious: this was not mere gambling, it was an outrageous attempt to dupe the rest of the world; and nobody will fall for it!'

'It was a tragedy for Germany! With that attack he gambled away the last remnants of moral credit – not his own moral credit, but that of the German people. The only result will be that the coming catastrophe will be a thousand times greater. It destroyed the last shred of goodwill, the last shred of inclination to mercy which otherwise might have influenced the decisions of the victors!'

'And now he intends to throw everything against the East?'

'That, too, was only a flash in the pan. You know it yourself: German divisions are still scattered everywhere, in Northern Italy, in Czechoslovakia, Norway, Yugoslavia, Courland. He has not given up a thing; he has only toyed with the idea of concentrating all forces in the east. And every word that is said in the Bunker is repeated outside, snapped up in the passages, commented on upstairs in the big hall. They all saw themselves once more marching against Russia, but this time with the support of the Americans, and their war materials. Anyway, the high spirits only lasted a few days and then again the deepest gloom descended. And so it goes on, up and down – they can only bear it with the help of the bottle.'

'Truly the "final convulsions"!'

'Dementia paralytica – except that the madness in this case does not take the usual two years to reach its climax of raving frenzy, but only two weeks. As for Hitler himself, he is completely spent: sometimes in the middle of a conversation he withdraws into his daydreams – most disconcerting for the person with him. He then completely forgets the present war and prattles about his earlier political life, and his dead eyes suddenly come alive again. He also loves to talk of the magnificent buildings he is going to erect after the war.'

'Magnificent buildings! When everything around him is being smashed! As if the Russians were going to stop at the Oder and ground their arms!'

'I don't quite know whether he is aware of that or not – nobody can really fathom his mind. He is running away from the present, and the little bit of reality that is brought to him has to go through Bormann. That short-legged, fat-bellied, vile intriguer bred in the Nazi gutters, is to-day his only link with the outside. Only one man managed to approach him without Bormann knowing, and that was Hoffmann.'

'Hoffmann?'

'Yes, the photographer, a friend of his from his earliest days at Munich. But that is already an old story.'

'Tell me about it, Uncle.'

'Hoffmann had free access to the Führer, which was always a thorn in Bormann's flesh. When, about six months ago, Hoffmann developed eczema on his nose, Dr. Morell, whom he consulted, made a fæcal examination which revealed typhus germs; a second examination confirmed this. Hoffmann is convinced that, through Himmler's agency, fake specimens were sent to the laboratories for the purpose of keeping him away from Hitler. But Hoffmann had not the least intention of letting himself be isolated from his old friend – certainly not under the usual detention in a villa surrounded by SS-guards. So Hoffmann fled to Vienna and there told his story to an Army Medical Officer whom he knew well. "Don't you see, man, they want to get rid of you!" the doctor told him when he found no symptoms whatever of typhus.

'Of course, Bormann and Himmler soon found out where Hoffmann was. They let him stay there, but put an SS-guard on him and refused him permission to return to Berlin. However, Hoffmann found a way: the Hotel Imperial in Vienna is now full of German agents who have fled from the Balkan countries, and with their help Hoffmann managed to get a plane to Berlin. He called at the Reich Chancellery and asked to see Hitler. With many others he was kept waiting a long time in an ante-room. Then an A.D.C. entered and warned all present to remain seated when presently the Führer would pass through. But Hoffmann jumped up, and when Hitler saw him, he started back with fright and said to him: "How did you get here? You are mortally ill!" Then he quickly passed on. Bormann was furious and cursed Hoffmann: how could he, a carrier of deadly germs, dare to endanger Hitler's life! Baffled, Hoffmann went up to his room on the second floor of the Chancellery and started packing his belongings. Here Fräulein Wolf, one of Hitler's secretaries, found him. He told her what had happened. "You must see him," she answered, "I will arrange it!" After a while she returned and told him: "Hitler will see you tonight at two." At that interview Hitler's first words were: "Don't speak about your illness – I know everything". But their talk only lasted a short while and both felt awkward. In the end Hitler advised him: "You had better leave Berlin." And these were the parting words of an old friend! But had Bormann been present, Hoffmann would not have been allowed to depart, probably would already be a corpse. As it was, he was able to disappear, and nobody knows his present whereabouts.'

'Bormann and Himmler working together will not take long to find out.'

'He will have to race against time to save his life.'

'The Hoffmann affair, too, is part of the dementia paralytica in Hitler's court circle. How disgusting it all is! And in such circumstances I have to join the general directing Berlin's artillery defence.'

'You too, are racing against time. Just as I am. . . . And tonight I have to write out a digest of the American press hinting at a change of American policy since Roosevelt's death and at mounting conflict with the Russians. What else could I do: throw it all up . . . but what comes after?'

'Yes, we are in it up to our necks, in these "final convulsions". Whether we want to or not!'

'I met a nice fellow on the train, a Colonel Zecke from Potsdam; do you know him, Uncle?'

'Oh yes, good old Zecke, always in revolt. What is he doing?'

'Attending a course.'

'You see, they all do something, carry on as best they can. What else can you do – hang yourself on a lamp-post at five minutes to twelve? But now, dear Berthold, the cigar is finished and my digest for Scherf is waiting . . .'

'Thank you for everything, Uncle. I am glad I have seen you before the final debacle.' They did not know then that their parting was to be for ever.

Two days later Captain Boehlke travelled to Freienwalde, but again failed to find General Meuspath. On his return to Berlin he took a room on the Kaiserdamm, and continued his search. This was made specially difficult by the reduced means of transport, and by the continuous air attacks which forced him to spend most of his time in the shelters and cellars of Berlin. He reported to the Deputy General Command on the Hohenzollerndamm – his general was not there. He is probably in the Zoo Bunker or else in the Bendler Bunker, he was told. He found him in neither. Next day at the Brandenburger Tor he heard the roar of artillery from the eastern city boundaries. Soon it would be too late for city walks! Curiosity drove him into Voss-strasse and to the corner of Wilhelmstrasse to see how the massive building of the 'Führer's Chancellery' had fared. Of the old Chancellery only a shattered façade remained, fronted by heaps of masonry. At the Army entrance to the new Chancellery a big Mercedes stopped. Three officers with red stripes on their trouser seams and red facings on their tunics got out; a general, a major and a colonel. One of them was Colonel Boldt, Gerhard Boldt, who had been a captain in the frosty nightmare of Demjansk. He hailed Boehlke:

'Boehlke, old chap, where do you hail from, and where are you off to? Come inside with me!'

'Sorry, old man, I really shouldn't.'

'Oh, come along. Just for a few minutes.' Boldt had to hurry to catch up with the general and the tall, distinguished-looking major. Up a dozen steps flanked by sentries who presented arms, big fellows of the Guards Battalion specially chosen for their height. An immense hall with elaborate chandeliers, liveried footmen. 'Excuse me a moment, my dear Boehlke!' Colonel Boldt went up to one of the counters, said a few words to the man behind the enormous visitors' book, and then turned to Boehlke: 'Could you wait a moment? You have got time, haven't you?' A footman conducted Boehlke down some steps to a table beside a buffet and asked if he could get him anything. 'A whisky and soda, please', said Boehlke. Boldt, following the general and the major, disappeared down a long passage at the end of which stairs went down to the subterranean world of the bunkers, the air-raid shelters. Along the passage lay a brilliantly illuminated red carpet: no trace here of the dust and dirt outside which was slowly advancing on the Chancellery.

The whisky arrived. Boehlke felt extremely uncomfortable so near the entrance to the Führer Bunker. Along the passage there was a continual coming and going of uniforms of the army, the Nazi Party, the SS. He felt relieved when he saw Colonel Boldt return.

'Only a moment to spare', Boldt said. 'But if you have time, we could have a meal together later, here in the main dining-room. I must hear all your news. Are you only just back from Courland?'

'No, actually I left there long ago.'

Boldt seemed disappointed: apparently he had hoped for news from his Home Division. 'Never mind', he said, and continued: 'You can imagine the turmoil we are in here. I am still with the OKH (Army General Staff). When Guderian left, Krebs took me over.'

'That was Krebs then?'

'Yes; and the other is Baron Loringhoven, his Adjutant. But now you must excuse me, I have to go down again – situation report to the Führer.'

Boldt was off again. So the General had been Krebs, the new Chief of the General Staff, who had replaced Guderian.

Situation report by army, airforce and navy. Situation on the front lines. . . . Good God, when Russian guns are already firing across the roofs of Berlin!

One of the many adjutants around the place, an SS officer, in a beautifully tailored uniform, his young face sun-tanned, sat down beside him and tried to entertain him; what a place, what a time to talk of trifles! Boehlke felt as if he were sitting in a theatre watching the entrance and exit of the players along the carpeted passage which led to that other, subterranean world. Among them a navy officer, a Luftwaffe general, a Hitler Youth. The boy looked shabby; his face was pale, but his eyes shone.

'That boy has put a "34" tank out of action with his anti-tank weapon', the adjutant at Boehlke's table explained. 'The Führer has decorated him with the Iron Cross.' Then, with perfect and engaging manners, he begged to be excused. Too polite, too engaging for Boehlke's taste.

Suddenly everyone stood aside, the footmen pressed like statues against the walls; then he appeared, Goebbels; and yet not Goebbels. Sunken cheeks, deep hollows under the white forehead, eyes unnaturally staring. He limped to the exit door, which opened and shut behind him as if controlled by invisible hands. So that was Goebbels – *'The hour before the sun rises'* – *'Berlin remains German'* – *'If Europe and its civilization have not yet gone down into the abyss . . .'*

Europe and its civilization!

The German soldier, the only bulwak against the East, the bulwark that was crumbling and falling under the impact of the great flood! How true, and how false. . . . Had not the same Goebbels once triumphantly promised the German soldier quite different goals: the rich cornfields of the Ukraine, the oil of Maikop, the ore of Krivoirog? Then the war aims had not been the preservation of Western values, but conquered countries and their raw materials as prize for the victor.

A few minutes' drive brought Goebbels's car to his villa near the Brandenburger Tor. He was late. A small group of his closest associates was waiting for him in his private cinema. The windows boarded up, no electric current, the flames of candles flickering in the cold draught.

A dozen tired, drawn faces, eyes dead with despair, were turned towards their master, waiting. He, their strength-giver, would pump fresh blood into their overworked hearts, raise their courage. But he himself was utterly weary and heartsick because he knew that he had come to them with empty hands. His life was finished and he was nothing more than an apparition from the world of shadows. What did they want of him, why did they come here daily? What did they expect of him – a message from Hades? These sorry, wretched associates who could imagine a life without the Swastika! All right, they shall have it, he can once more orate to them, once more let his brain, already turned to utter darkness, sparkle for them. And the dozen faces lit by candlelight became an audience for Goebbels. They all, the old-time generals, the staff officers, the reactionaries in the ministries, the whole German people who wanted to live on and not go down with the burning Viking ship, stood like accused criminals before him . . . too small, too cowardly, too unprepared!

'Treason!' – 'Treason!'

Like the croaking of a black raven his voice hung over the room, the shadowy hall with the boarded windows and the wall tapestries hanging in shreds.

'Treason . . .'

A raven who could not find a perch, who had to perish alone, a fist-full of scorched black feathers, nothing left . . . no resurrection, no trace, no mention in the book of history.

'Treason . . .'

A gruesome echo repeated the word throughout the empty hall. These miserable creatures hope for a continuance of their lives when a Dr. Goebbels will be no more. And now one of the shivering heap even has the audacity to rise and object.

Blazing fury.

Goebbels struck with sarcasm:

'Don't cherish any illusions, I have not forced you to become my associates, just as we did not force the German people. The German people commanded us to lead them. Why did you work with me? Now you'll get your little throats cut!'

Suddenly he was exhausted and staggered to the door; with one foot already outside, he turned round, scanning with hate-filled eyes the frightened white faces, and screamed: 'When we go down, the whole world will shake in its foundations!'

The door closed behind him like a thunderclap.

The young adjutant rejoined Boehlke.

'Did you see Herr Minister Goebbels passing through on his return from his morning visit to the Führer? – I made inquiries on your behalf, but without success. Nobody here knows anything about General Meuspath. But wait . . . I could ask one other man. Will you excuse me a moment, Captain.'

Captain Boehlke had a strong feeling that the polite young man was trying to get him out of there.

When he returned he said: 'It looks as if the situation report will take some time. Extremely important matters are under discussion to-day. I regret to say that the man I questioned on your behalf could not enlighten us either. But surely, the general directing the artillery defence of Berlin must be traceable! Why don't you try the Ministry of Propaganda – the gentlemen there are always in possession of the latest information.'

Boehlke declined another whisky and asked the SS officer kindly to tell Colonel Boldt, with his compliments, that he was unable to wait any longer.

Then he left. . . .

Across Wilhelmstrasse to the Ministry of Propaganda.

Colonel Boldt was not to blame: he had asked one of the many idly waiting orderly officers to look after his friend and to tell him that the discussion on the situation would last longer than he had anticipated. Once he had entered the labyrinth which spread out widely underneath the Chancellery buildings and their gardens – that vast maze of underground passages, garages, barrack rooms, sleeping quarters, store-rooms, and staircases leading deeper and deeper down into the bowels of the earth; once he was in the corridor of the Führer's subterranean maisonette consisting of diet kitchen, guest rooms, servants quarters, lumber-rooms; once he stood in front of the winding staircase leading down to a yet lower and more spacious bunker, the Führer Bunker proper; he could not make the long return trek past the innumerable control posts.

Report to the Führer – it lasted just under one hour.

The three officers – General Krebs, Colonel Boldt, Major von Loringhoven – did not speak during their return drive to Zossen in the big Mercedes. They stared straight ahead, not seeing the burned-out shell of the Vaterland corner house, nor the soot-blackened façades round Potsdamer Platz, nor the long lines of ruins along the streets through which they drove on their way through that vast ocean of destruction which had once been the city of Berlin. They did not look at the mountains of debris flanking the road, and their minds scarcely registered when the driver pulled up sharply to avoid an unexploded shell lying in the middle of the road.

The three staff officers stared straight ahead. . . .

Six days ago the battle on the Oder had begun. The picture presented on the Führer's map bore no relation to reality: a hand had swept over it in a grand gesture from the Oder marshes down to Czechoslovakia, and, lo and behold! it conjured the already doomed Ninth Army into a counter attack against Zhukov's rear. And General Heinrici marched his decimated 'Army Group Vistula' to the south to cut off the Russian flood streaming out of the Bohemian forests.

That had been two days ago, on the fourth day of the Russian offensive, when on the southern approaches to Berlin Koniev's tanks were rapidly advancing, and in the north Zhukov had reached Oranienburg in the Potsdam district.

The same limp hand which had in such an absurd manner swept across the map, was next seen by the three staff officers the same day in broad daylight, where it seemed utterly out of place. That was in the garden of the Reich Chancellery. A number of Hitler Youths, from twelve to sixteen years of age, were presented to the Führer, none of them specially selected, but all of them bold, overbearing show-offs, and, above all, fanatical believers. Insolent, arrogant and fearless in the streets – here they stood with bated breath, overwhelmed by the presence of their Leader slowly pacing along their line. The magnificent, the adored, the wizard who had brought them to life. A sorcerer – and yet he was nothing but a discredited conjurer who could produce no more tricks from his empty pockets.

The magnificent, the adored – a pretentious fool. . . .

This last epithet was conceived in disgust and hatred in at least one mind in the Chancellery garden at noon on that 20th of April.

Many had seen in the pretentious fool a genius; many had revered him as a god; others had been impressed by his extraordinary memory, by his capacity to confound even the experts with his encyclopædic arguments.

The magnificent, the adored, the pretentious fool, now so horribly broken, walked down the line. He halted before each of the youths in turn. Aged, half-deaf, he seemed in his plain coat more like a pensioned bus driver, a retired postman. The large peak of his cap hid the glassy eyes in their deep hollows, hid the unformed features, leaving only the big bulbous nose to protrude. A postman, a retired chauffeur, and yet a monster, product of the dark forests of the Bohemian frontier, product of a soil which has brought forth bigots and fools, cranks and madmen, maniacs and religious and political fanatics. At the foot of this land of dark forests near the border of Czechoslovakia lies the Danube valley, that broad pathway for the migration of Nibelungs and Goths, Huns, Avars, Swabes, Saxons, Croats and Magyars. For a thousand years, the river valley and the forests were the childbed of a mixed conglomeration of the races which had passed through them. Here the Taborites roamed the country with fire, sword and Bible in their hands; here one-eyed Ziska beat his drum made of human skin. This was Hitler's birthplace, this country where every second or third child had visions, mostly to cease with adolescence, but with him to remain until the attempt on his life tore his eardrum, damaged his nervous system and upset his blood circulation. Here, born of one mother, yet at the same time descendant of all the manifold bands of peoples blown and thrown by the centuries through the Danube valley, the forest lands. Campaigners, marauders, proud charioteers were his ancestors, as well as meditators, visionaries, religious and political sectarians. It was not necessary for him to diverge from the rule; he was born outside all rules, and his special gifts, including the store-room memory, sprang from the unfermented wine of a mixture of too many and too diverse races.

And it was in a time of crisis and decay that the drum which he sounded for a quarter of a century, brought streaming to him all those uprooted in their political and religious beliefs, the homeless and the down-and-outs, the dreamers and the fanatics, the brash and the troubled ones, those who had lost their values and those who had lost hope. All the protagonists of decline and decay, the disjointed and the incomplete, felt drawn to him. It was the collected, the complete ones, those true to their moral and inner values, whom he repelled. A dark comet, always turned away from the sun, a creature of the night, he was, even on the triumphal march, in the glare of the flashlights and under the blaze of a thousand arc-lamps, nothing but a ghost, a brilliant apparition. An immense fortune, of many components and saddled with many chance acquisitions, had fallen to him; following the dark commands of his soul, he had risked it and had gambled it away; it was lost, and only the void remained. German youth in arms had laid Europe at his feet, and he had become the storm centre of revolt for the whole world – but this, too, had been of no avail in giving value and stature to the unformed, a soul to the ghost. Himself of no substance, his aims, all his undertakings remained without substance, and in his hands Germany had become a bowl filled to the brim with oppression, corruption, deception, violence and murder. Now he was old and finished. The head shook; the hand would not obey. Sometimes he had to clutch one hand firmly with the other to conceal the trembling. Like a wound-up automaton, he would walk over to the map table, and as a chair was pushed towards him, he would flop into it like a wooden doll. Here, in the garden of his Chancellery, he played the part created for him of the great aged king. He dragged himself along with the slowest of movements – only a crutch was missing to make the picture complete – hesitating, halting, along the line of youths. He lifted his hand in salute.

He lifted his hand . . . and, by God, this one tired searching gesture of the hand was real, was his one genuine expression. No hated generals, no superior diplomats, were here before him, but ordinary children. The hand which he had so often raised in salute or in a clenched fist symbolizing his authority, this hand now lifeless like a wooden ladle, patted a cheek here, there tweaked an ear. By the fourth or fifth time, this gesture, too, had become a routine movement. The ageing uncle, the old postman, the phantom from the forests with the disintegrating features, fondled his boys . . . children of Mother Germany, the remaining few who continued to fight and swagger for him, to bite and to scratch, as the army and even the SS were by now weary of battle. They fought on because they did not know death. The good uncle, the ageing father, the lame and apoplectic old corporal could offer his Hitler Youth nothing but the emergency tank weapon and a dog's death by the roadside:

> 'In the van the drummer boy,
> With gaiety and courage.
> He does not know what love is,
> Knows not the hurt of parting.'

The onlooker's blood ran cold. With horrified awe he watched the phantom groping its way along the line of enraptured children.

In the evening, the onlooker, the young staff officer, saw the same hand sweeping over the map again. The stooping phantom, its head hanging down, its feet dragging, this ghost of whom Joseph Goebbels had just said over the radio – his strength was that of a man in the prime of life; his presence was worth twenty tank divisions; and through him Germany would triumph as Rome never did – he sat at the table and his hand fluttered over the map. . . .

It was after the great reception. The last of the birthday guests had left the Bunker. Göring, who had packed beforehand, was now in Wilhelmstrasse, where a convoy of lorries was waiting for him; he climbed into his big Mercedes-Benz racing car and shot off. He was caught, however, in the thousand-bomber-raid which the Americans staged in honour of the Führer's birthday, and had to shelter for hours in one of Berlin's cellars. The paladins of the Nazi régime filled the last trains leaving Berlin, sat in courier planes, in big cars with armed escorts: to Mecklenburg, Schleswig, Upper Bavaria, Bohemia; the great dispersal, the great exodus, without any hope of return.

The twilight of the gods.

In the Bunker it was Ash Wednesday, the end of the carnival.

The phantom, surrounded by his military experts, was bent over the map. The fluttering hand moved over red and blue markings, ominous lines which signified torn fronts and bloody battlefields. Words, names . . . mute symbols of catastrophe. The British before Hamburg on the western bank of the Elbe; Bremen capitulated; the Americans before Dessau; the Russians marching through the Spree Forest; in the north the German Third Panzer Army cut off from Berlin by the Russians.

The phantom tottered up and down the room like a wounded animal and, exhausted, sank down again into the armchair.

Jumped up and shouted commands:

Offensives, counter attacks, sorties, arrests, executions. His intuition, which had saved him eight times in attempts on his life, was gone. The writing on the Bunker's wall was as baffling as in the days of Stalingrad.

'Berlin will never fall into the hands of the Russians – since 1760 no Russian enemy has entered Berlin!'

A telegram from General Busse, Commander of the Ninth Army on the Oder, requested permission for a withdrawal; encirclement was imminent, he was outnumbered, with insufficient equipment and without air support.

'Out of the question! Busse will counter-attack and fight to the last man. Cable immediately.' That was Hitler's reply.

Then a name was uttered: Steiner.

The head sunk deep between the shoulders, turned sharply from one face to the other. The round eyes goggled. 'Steiner, yes Steiner. . . . All the others, these miserable, despicable, contemptible scoundrels and criminals – shoot them down by the dozen.'

Hitler spoke of his generals.

'They are incapable; if they can't even hold a river, it proves they don't want to make a stand. Anyone can put up a defence on a river. Cowardice, treachery, funk everywhere; now I have caught them out: a man like Steiner appointed for the ridiculous task of defending the flank!'

The old magic began to work again . . . as it had done countless times before, it did not fail to cast its spell over those present in the Bunker, the representatives of the army, the air force, the navy, the orderlies and the aides.

'Steiner, Steiner . . .'

The hand flitted across the map. The twice broken Oder lines rippled in the mist; the fanatic scheme for closing the gap south of Berlin; all other strategic nonsense faded into the background. Steiner, nothing else mattered! Perhaps Wenk too, though even 'Wenk's Relief Army' became a matter of secondary importance now.

'Steiner will effect the relief of Berlin . . . . You will see!'

The staff officers should have known better, perhaps did know better. But under the old spell they succumbed to the inspiration, and stared in fascination at the hand sweeping over the map. The crooked finger went across the road from Freienwalde to Weissensee, the road that in reality was strewn with shelled cars and buses, with dead horses, women in labour, corpses and new-born infants thrown into the ditches. The finger crossed the road between Werneuchen and Weissensee. 'Here Steiner will take up his position. He will advance from the area between Bernau and Eberswalde, cut off Zhukov's vanguard and relieve Berlin.'

It was salvation . . . even the Chief-of-Staff, his aide, and the liaison officers to the army groups, as well as adjutants and orderlies fell for the magic. It was only when Krebs, Boldt and Loringhoven were in their car returning to Zossen, through streets of burning houses, through dense smoke, winding their way amidst columns of tired soldiers marching to the outskirts of the city, that they awoke from the dream. The capital of the Third Reich was nothing but a dismembered body, the centre of a country in ruins with its command towers deserted. Their minds returned to reality, a nightmare come true, in which their troops were no more than a name and a number.

The shining tank corps, the infantry bedecked with campaign medals from all the battlefields of Europe, were burned to cinders. No fresh plan could revive them.

And where was Steiner; who was Steiner?

Krebs, Boldt and Loringhoven did not know. Even the liaison officers in the Bunker had not known. He was the Commander of an SS unit, who was to organize a position on the flank of the Third Panzer Division – that was all they had established. But where was he stationed, where were his staff quarters, and had he already formed a unit?

A bubble, a shadow.

The phantom in the Bunker was capable of creating this bubble, of infusing this shadow, if not with breath, at least with material – with human beings, with weapons, with fuel. At the Führer Bunker everyone was at the ready. The phantom with a new blaze in his eyes, once more grew in stature. Couriers, long-distance calls; motor cycles roared through the Wilhelmstrasse, disappeared into the shell-torn night. At the Bunker switchboard all lines were occupied. Calls to Zossen, to Potsdam, to the Reich Commander SS in Zieten Palace, to the Luftwaffe headquarters at Wildpark-Werder.

Luftwaffe General Koller's day had started at 2 a.m., when he discussed over the telephone with the Chief of the Army General Staff the positions of the enemy and the points where the air force should be deployed. It was 3 a.m. when he heard a car hooting outside and saw Air Marshal Göring (who up to this hour had been delayed by air-raids in Berlin's shelters) at the head of a large convoy of motor vehicles, shoot past his house and out through the main guard gate – without any explanation, without a word of farewell to Koller, now in sole charge of the Luftwaffe in Berlin. Göring seemed to be in a terrific hurry – well, he had to cross the Elbe, and his road could be blocked at any moment. It was not yet daylight. The telephone rang. Adolf Hitler was calling: 'Do you know that Berlin, the city centre, is being shelled?'

'No.'

'Don't you hear the guns?'

'No! I am at Wildpark-Werder.'

'The people are desperately worried about this long-range shelling. It is said to come from a railway battery of the heaviest calibre. The Russians must have thrown a railway bridge across the Oder. The Luftwaffe is to reconnoitre at once and silence that battery!'

'The enemy has no railway bridge across the Oder. They might have captured a heavy German gun and managed to turn it round. But it is more likely that the fire comes from medium-size guns of the Russian army: their shells could reach the centre of the city.'

In ten minutes, Hitler insisted, he was to be told exactly where the battery was situated. In ten minutes! – how did he think it could be done, how could one particular battery be singled out in the midst of the vast battlefield that stretched from Berlin to the Oder, if no details were known, not even the direction whence the fire came.

The telephone in the Luftwaffe Chief's room rang without stopping. Attack Russians here, attack Russians there, attack ... advancing Russians. Our troop movements to be covered by air. Reconnaissance and night fighting operations. Air transport for encircled units. The searchlights from Prague to be taken to Berlin – impossible: before they can be moved, they will be shattered on the ground by enemy fighters.

Again Hitler was on the line.

'Where are the searchlights ...? ... I see ... Well, then we don't need any more searchlights, we don't need any more Luftwaffe. The whole Luftwaffe command should be executed at once!'

At 2 a.m. the working day of Luftwaffe General Koller had started – it was now 21.00 hours – nineteen hours had passed.

Again Hitler rang.

'Listen, the Reich Marshal has a private army at Karinhall. This is to be disbanded at once and every man put into the lines. He does not need a private army.'

'There is no private army at Karinhall, only the "Hermann Göring" division was stationed there. It is already in operation, and only one battalion is left at Karinhall.'

'This battalion is immediately to be put under the command of SS Commander Steiner ...'

Koller was still trying to puzzle out what this meant and who SS Commander Steiner was, when the telephone screamed again and the same incensed, barking voice shouted at him:

'Every available man of the Luftwaffe in the area between

Berlin and the coast from Stettin to Hamburg to be placed under Steiner!'

Steiner, Steiner ...

Koller telephoned in all directions. The Chief of Army Operations thought Steiner was at Oranienburg. An hour later he corrected himself: 'Battle station Steiner is near Lieben-werda.' Major Freigang of the 'Hermann Göring' divisional staff reported that up to now Steiner had arrived with one officer only at Schönwalde.

Where then was Steiner? Where exactly was the attack to take place? Where was the assembly point, and what contingents were to take part?

Koller telephoned the Chief-of-Staff.

'Listen, Krebs, I have no details, neither the exact time for the attack, nor the supply route. I am supposed to brief my men for a fight, but where in Heaven's name will it be?'

Hitler cut into the conversation:

'Have you still doubts about my orders? I think I made myself quite clear. All Luftwaffe forces in the Northern area which can be used in ground fighting, have to go immediately to Steiner. Every commander who does not carry out this order inside five hours is herewith sentenced to death. Tell them this. I hold you responsible on your life that down to the last man everyone is made use of.'

'All to join the attack from Iberswalde southwards,' added Hitler's mouthpiece, Krebs, not having himself any exact information, unaware himself of Steiner's location.

Motor cycles racketed through Wilhelmstrasse. Fast cars sped through Berlin. Planes with couriers took off. The telegraph ticked. Telephone lines hummed.

Steiner is to form a Chief Army Command; every available man for Steiner ... ground staff of the air force, engineers, railway troops, the Berlin fire brigade, police units, the home guard. The Führer leads ... he had always been the top leader of every division, every single battalion; now he is leading shrunken ghost formations that in his imagination still form well-armed contingents of men and horses and guns, complete with reinforcements, commissariats and all equipment.

General Busse on the Oder, and his Ninth Army, are now encircled by the Russians. Again he requests permission to break through.

'No! Busse stays where he is!'

The man who, without rest and without sleep, is groping his way through the long Bunker passage into the conference room and back again, halts, takes hold of a chair back, screams: 'What is he dreaming off! He is where he should be!' Everything was planned, and the decimated shadow of the Ninth Army on the Oder was to play an important role in the coming battle of extermination, the role of a meat chopper. 'Look here, look at the map! Steiner will cut off Zhukov from Berlin. The routed Russian hordes will stream back eastwards in confusion and panic. And here on the Oder, at this very spot, the Ninth Army will smash and chop up the leaderless masses. No Russian who has dared to approach Berlin shall cross the Oder alive!'

By now, everything had been assembled for Steiner, all available ground staff of the Luftwaffe, cadets, relief formations, even units scraped together from convicts and aliens. Everything was ready at hand, and the Department for Motorized Transport had to furnish the cars and lorries. The airfields supplied the fuel. Men and material, sufficient for one to two divisions, were waiting for the word 'Go'. – Go where?

Along roads that were already supply routes for the Russians? Zhukov stood near Oranienburg, his vanguard had rushed forward into the neighbourhood of Glienicke, about to catch up with the First Ukrainian Army under Koniev marching up from the south.

Where were the men and material collected for Steiner to go? Koller still did not know. Luftwaffe General Stumpf did not know. The Chief of Operations Army Group Vistula, General Detlevsen, did not know. The Chief-of-Staff of the Army, Krebs, did not know.

It was the night of the 21st of April.

At Wildpark-Werder the buzzing of the telephone startled Luftwaffe Chief Koller from his short nap. The caller was Hitler:

'Tomorrow morning Steiner attacks. How is the Luftwaffe going to support Steiner?'

Koller explained: 'We have twelve to fifteen thousand men ready. General Stumpf has organized his ground staff into battalions and companies. I must point out, however, that all these troops are not trained for fighting in the line and that they are not properly equipped. They have no heavy weapons at all!'

Hitler disregarded the pessimism in Koller's words and the sombre tone of his voice. He spoke about the situation, and it was apparent that he knew that the Russians had broken through the outposts of Berlin in the north and the northeast, that to the west they were thrusting in a wide sweep round Berlin, and that the two prongs of the pincer movement were about to close. Yet he was full of confidence, even exuberant in his optimistic view of the situation. 'You will see,' he said, 'the Russians will suffer the greatest, the bloodiest defeat in history, outside the gates of Berlin!'

Koller was stupefied, but had no time to reply. In the Führer Bunker the receiver had already been replaced.

'The Russians will suffer the bloodiest defeat in history outside the gates of the city of Berlin!' Hitler said, this time to Bormann. He repeated the words to the Orderly Officer standing by the wall, to the secretary sitting behind her typewriter in his office; he said the same words in exactly the same intonation to the barber who cut his hair.

During that day the Friedrichshain Flak tower counted five hundred shells fired by Russian guns into the centre of Berlin. Fountains of pavement stones, of crumbled asphalt, of mud and dust rose in Berlin's streets. The heavy shells of the long-range guns tore further huge gaps into line after line of Berlin's houses. The people crouched in the cellars with their suitcases and bedding and valued belongings. They would only leave the shelter to fetch water. For water, life had to be risked.

Behind Alexander Platz, in Landsbergstrasse, where once Colonel Zecke had sheltered in a cellar, the same woman who had looked after him then and had offered him a wet towel, was, with others, on her way to the water main. It was about five o'clock in the morning. Dense clouds of smoke and dust hung over the ruins, a green light flickering in them – the reflection of the dying fire that had consumed a timber yard; and green were the faces of the women. Carrying their buckets, they moved along close to the walls of the houses. The frightening wail of the sirens had ceased – no electricity.

'You see, everything has its advantages,' the same Frau Riek told her neighbour. 'At least we are spared that horrible screaming. They say, the alarm will now be sounded by three shots. How ridiculous! as if we could hear them through this infernal noise!' The crash of exploding bombs was now replaced by the roar of the battlefield. Shells whizzed through Landsbergstrasse. Some of them only made a humming noise, other screamed or whistled or rumbled with a hollow sound that seemed to go on and on. The women from the house in Landsbergstrasse had filled their buckets and were on their way back. For a moment Frau Riek put down her heavy load and looked up. From the lamp-post in front of her house a limp figure dangled. During the night a patrol had dragged a sheltering soldier from the cellar and he hung there, with a piece of cardboard round his neck. The other women, too, stopped and stared in horror at the scene.

From the entrance to the house a voice shouted:

'Serves him right! That's the way to deal with cowards!'

The woman shuddered, her face turned deadly pale under its crust of dust and soot. She could not connect the words she had heard with what she was seeing. And she could not and would not recognize the voice, the screeching voice of her pitiful husband.

Franz, too, was there. 'Don't talk such rot!' he said to Riek.

There were still far too many stupid and deluded sheep about. Frau Riek would have liked to give her husband a piece of her mind, but she swallowed the words. She collected herself in time when she saw the leering, expectant expression on the faces of the others. Not yet, not yet. . . . If only the Russians were here already! 'Don't stand about like that. Take the buckets!' she threw at Riek. She put the buckets down and went past him into the entrance passage, past the dead which lay along the wall, carried in from the street: an old couple and their daughter belonging to the house who, an hour ago, had committed suicide. And the old veteran Willem was lying there: during the night he had died from the injury received a few weeks ago from a bomb-splinter. Another of the dead was the landlady who, not being able to obtain morphia, had, without a word of complaint, collapsed and died.

'Why doesn't Herr Splüge come any more?' Frau Wittstock asked her husband. – 'Because he is a sensible understanding fellow', Dr. Wittstock replied, and he meant it. He appreciated the consideration with which his old friend Vicco Splüge had kept away from them since Zecke's departure. 'A nice boy, Splüge, but, don't you understand, this is not the time to receive visits from a Senior Lieutenant of the Propaganda Company.'

Frau Wittstock understood. She had also understood when eleven years ago the faces of their guests had changed; had had to change. Some had remained friends, though pushed into the background. Now Wittstock had to turn to the people in the background again. He had racked his brains to remember whom he could make use of to be re-introduced to the 'people of yesterday' who of necessity would now become the 'people of tomorrow': – Eventually he thought of Dreyer. Yes, Dreyer was the right man! They had never quite lost touch, and he knew for certain that Dreyer belonged to the other side. Wittstock lost no time, things had gone so far that not an hour was to be wasted. The Third Reich was sinking into its grave! Without bothering to change, he went to call on Dreyer at his office in the Potsdamerstrasse – 'Associated Textiles' was the name of Dreyer's department in the Reich Ministry of Trade. Into the office, where generally only Dreyer and a secretary sat, a dozen people were crowded. They did not work, but argued loudly and telephoned. Like all other departments of the Ministry of Trade, 'Associated Textiles' was breaking up. Some departments of the Ministry had already been evacuated, to Munich or Berchtesgaden, to the 'South German Government'; others were being transferred to Schwerin to the 'North German Government'. Two governments: the disintegration of the Reich was clearly demonstrated here on a smaller scale. Wittstock hailed 'his old friend Dreyer' who was busy dealing with minor officials pestering him. What was the matter? What did they want, to go to the Southern or to the Northern Government? No, the excitement concerned one of their superiors, an Under-Secretary of State, who, with a number of motor vehicles loaded with food, drinks and spare petrol, was about to depart for Schwerin. He was taking some of his staff with him; others who felt they had a special claim to this privilege, were being left behind. In their worry and rage they pestered Dr. Dreyer, their departmental chief.

It was impossible to have a quiet talk in all this confusion, and Dr. Dreyer took his friend Wittstock to a near-by café. A small shop, where a short while ago you could still get real coffee and cakes. But there were now more important matters than coffee and cakes – the most urgent a UK certificate (reserved occupation), and also the renewal of the old friendship. Dreyer went back to his office and returned with the Reserved Occupation certificate. Its issue seemed to have been the easiest thing in the world in spite of the dislocation of the department. Dreyer had done even more: had written a letter to Wittstock's home guard unit saying that as a free-lance contributor to the Ministry of Trade, he was to be exempted from all duties. He handed the copy of this letter to Wittstock for possible future use.

When they separated, Wittstock also carried away with him an invitation for the following afternoon. Dr. Dreyer was to introduce him to an 'interesting circle', people who would have some influence in the days to come. Dreyer had been all the more ready to bestow this favour, as Wittstock, on being asked, had at once declared himself willing to hide some of the 'interesting circle's' protégées in his house.

On his return from that first meeting with Dreyer, Wittstock called at the Army Office where he was registered, in order to have his new status as 'exempted' entered in his military pass. 'If it comes to the worst, this won't help you either', the lance-corporal on duty remarked when he stamped the entry. 'It's up to you how you will avoid the home guard.'

The meeting next afternoon took place in a private house – 'Under the Oaks' in the Zehlendorf suburb. It was indeed a remarkable collection of people. The host was legal adviser to the Anhalt Steel and Coal works, among the guests was a member of the Institute of Market Research, several financial and power supply experts, statisticians of the state departments for chemistry and the leather industry.

Outside, the Third Reich was at its last gasp!

In the street below, columns of refugees from the eastern districts of Berlin rushed past, and the unusual traffic attracted Russian fighter planes. Flying low, they combed the road with their machine guns.

On the roads flight, air attacks, extinction.

And in the house the reconstruction of the German economy was discussed at a round table conference; the measures the victorious powers were likely to take were considered, and a précis on the 'Elimination of money surplus after the War' was read out. This recommended steps which, while avoiding inflation and unemployment, would, with purely capitalistic methods, gradually lead to a recovery from the ravages of war.

The debate was a lengthy one.

Wittstock confined himself to listening. He was no expert on the subject. He did not join in the conversation either when other, more general, post-war problems were discussed; when one of the speakers proposed that, in view of the support the Nazis had received from the women's vote, franchise should be confined to men.

A terrific thunder of guns interrupted the meeting. The gentlemen repaired to the cellar, but even here the noise was too great for any talk. The unremitting firing seemed to come from a heavy German battery mounted in the Botanical Gardens. When this never-ending roar was increased by the crash of bombs from Russian planes trying to silence the battery, the house 'Under the Oaks' speedily emptied; they all scuttled out of the dangerous neighbourhood.

Dr. Wittstock returned to Wannsee.

He might have been satisfied with what he had achieved in the last two days, had his friend Dreyer not immediately started holding him to his part of the bargain. Already in the evening after his first visit to 'Associated Textiles', Dreyer had brought to his house two brothers who had escaped from a concentration camp for people of mixed blood. And on returning from 'Under the Oaks', he now found that a third guest had arrived during his absence. A Polish-looking man in military trousers and boots. Wittstock asked him whether he came from Tegel. Whereupon the newcomer related a most improbable story of how, as a student in Poland, he had escaped the Russians. But why was he dressed partly in German uniform? Cornered, the Pole gave a different version of his story: he had been forced to join the German army, had secretly done intelligence work for the Polish government in exile in London. On the discovery of the spy network, he had been arrested and, first in Vienna, then later at Tegel, had been in prison pending trial. Now, after two years imprisonment, he had suddenly been pressed with his fellow prisoners into a unit for the defence of Berlin. When they were marched to Spandau, he had managed to escape.

Already the presence of the two men from the concentration camp was extremely worrying for Dr. Wittstock, but this Pole, Boguslaw Sikowski, simply terrified him. The only consolation was that Sikowski spoke Russian, and this might prove useful when the Russians came. But would Wittstock, with his house full of escapees (Dreyer was going to send him two more, two women from the detention prison of Moabit) still be alive when the 'Day of the Russians' came?

Well, he was now in possession of an 'exemption' certificate; was holder of the red card for priority in transport; Dreyer had promised to secure for him, from a Communist friend, a letter of safe conduct; and with his joining the 'interesting circle', he was nearly raised to the status of a resistance fighter. In spite of all this, the situation in his house preyed on his mind. With the continuous shelling of the city all the windows rattled. Wittstock needed some diversion, he took the special winter windows out of their frames and stored them in the cellar. This occupied him for a while; then he was drawn back into his brooding. What rumours floated through the city! At Schöneberg, someone said, he had seen deserters and saboteurs hanged on lamp-posts with notices stating their crimes – a pleasant thought for a householder who sheltered escaped political prisoners in his cellar. Wittstock wandered restlessly through his house, from basement to attic. For a few minutes he called on Frau Aachern who had given up all hope of hearing from her husband, the Luftwaffe Colonel, and was now in complete despair.

After dusk Dreyer brought the two women from Moabit prison. He himself was in a hurry and did not stay. Wittstock took the two women down to the cellar where his other three guests lived. One of the women had been secretary to a man executed for his part in the 20th July plot; the other's name was Halen: a fragile young woman who walked heavily – there was no doubt that she was far gone with child.

Wittstock resumed his circuit of the house and garden. There he was tempted to hide in the slit trench. He actually went down, but found it damp and smelly. In the end he returned to his room, threw himself down on his bed, and pressed both hands against his temples, as if to shut out the world. The window panes rattled. The telephone rang. His wife talked to a friend of hers from Nollendorf Platz. 'Low-flying bomber attacks and gunfire in the distance,' she reported to her husband, 'otherwise all is well in Nollendorf Platz.'

Wittstock moaned.

'Don't you feel well?'

'I have a headache.'

He took up one of the books which he had selected for reading in preparation for the new order of things. Not quite authors like Karl Marx or Lenin, but Romain Rolland's *Beethoven* and Hermann Hesse's *The Glass Bead Play* and Joseph Conrad's *Typhoon*.

He read Rolland's *Beethoven* until the lines began to swim before his eyes. His wife was on the telephone again, and afterwards said to him: 'Weren't you at Associated Textiles two or three days ago? The SS is occupying the house now and getting it ready as a defence centre. And the main road into Berlin is cut.'

Wittstock let the *Beethoven* drop. He jumped up: 'I must do something, or I shall go mad. I am going to chop wood in the cellar.'

'You are crazy, it's past midnight.'

Another idea occurred to him. He went down to the coal cellar and got the original of a poster for the 'International Aid for Workers' out from its hiding place. The expressionist painter, Wilhelm Seifert, had given it to him in the 'twenties with a personal dedication.

In remembrance of his own youth, his old friends and life in the coffee houses, he had kept it all these years. Now it might come in useful: a view of a factory, with a large yellow moon behind it, in the foreground a worker with heavy fists; the caption: 'Hunger in Germany'. He cleaned the picture and took it upstairs. He would hang it above his desk. But wasn't that a bit premature? The wrong people might discover it. He pushed it behind a bookcase, thought that unsafe too, and was thinking of taking it back to its former hiding place.

But his wife was on the telephone again.

'Stop moving about. Be quiet ... it is Irene from Blanken-felde.'

Wittstock sat down quietly on a chair, his mind full of burning thoughts, his face deathly pale, his hair hanging down over his forehead. He was insufferably frightened.

His wife said to him: 'Do you hear, listen ... the Russians are in Blankenfelde! There was little fighting, and nothing much happened. Irene has only lost her wrist-watch. The District Party Leader has shot himself!'

'If only the Russians were here, too!'

Captain Boehlke had found his General Meuspath after all. At the Propaganda Ministry he had been told that Meuspath's headquarters were at the corner of Louisen-strasse and Dorotheenstrasse. 'You know the big red building there? A university college or a French Lycée. There you will find your general, Captain.'

Captain Boehlke went to the red building in Dorotheen-strasse. Guards, orderlies; furious activity in the corridors; the classrooms converted into army offices, with papers, papers everywhere and people shouting into telephones. It looked like the Bendler Bunker, like the Deputy High Command on the Hohenzollerndamm. Disintegration and confusion, officers running to and fro.

'You are looking for Meuspath, General Meuspath ... Maybe he, too, has already cleared out!'

'I beg your pardon, Lieutenant!'

The first Lieutenant collected himself: 'Meuspath, general artillery commander, you say? Well, that's possible, there is a crowd of service corps people down there.'

Boehlke went into the courtyard: some units of a service corps had been there, but had been moved in the morning. After further questioning he found a First Lieutenant belonging to General Meuspath's staff.

At last – after Prague, Dresden, Potsdam, he had made contact. The General's quarters were at Fürstenwalde, east of Berlin. The First Lieutenant, delayed here by duties, was just trying to find transport to Fürstenwalde. Boehlke joined him. No vehicle was to be had here, but a captain passing by advised them: 'Try your luck in General Papestrasse; from there cars are going in all directions.'

Captain Boehlke and First Lieutenant Hergesell made their way to the General Papestrasse H.Q. Everything there resembled the army office they had just left, but on a larger scale. There, too, utter confusion. Officers shouting, officers telephoning, doors standing open, cans of pork, loaves of bread on the tables. In all corners heaps of equipment, packed rucksacks. Everyone more or less drunk, a major sobbing. A 'gay' last meal before the great scramble or the execution. Before it was Boehlke's and Hergesell's turn, they had to listen to a long harangue given to a captain wanting transport to Southern Germany. The man who spoke stressed the importance of Berlin in the coming decisive battle between Europe and Bolshevism. He ended by saying: 'No good, Major. Nobody's getting out of Berlin. No more vehicles. Berlin will be defeated. Everyone here, even if posted elsewhere on paper, is being enrolled for the Battle of Berlin.'

'You want to go to Fürstenwalde?' Boehlke and Hergesell were asked. 'Oh, you are in luck. A transport is leaving any minute now. You can board it at once.'

The courtyard, flanked by old grey buildings, was crammed with motor vehicles, among them two old double-decker buses of the Berlin Transport Company, nearly full. Boehlke and Hergesell found a seat. A moment later the heavy vehicle lumbered off, through the gate, followed by the second bus.

'We were lucky.'

'So we were. That man reeked of spirits, too,' Boehlke replied.

First Lieutenant Hergesell was Orderly Officer in Meuspath's staff quartered behind the Oderfront at Fürstenwalde. For a week he had been in Berlin. 'By chance I left on the morning when the Russians started shelling. But our lines will stand firm, you can rely on that!'

'Can I?'

'You can be sure, Captain. Up to now the "Courmark" division has fought off every attack. The front line is manned by "Loot Germans": mixed contingents, from Poland, the Baltic, Transylvania, Hungary, and so on. And behind them the SS division "Netherlands". But the "Courmark" is the heart of the front; our boys are all right, all old soldiers from the eastern front.'

Hergesell glanced with disdain at the other passengers who were gazing sullenly at the landscape. They belonged to a relief unit from Spandau. Hergesell exchanged a few words with his neighbour, a metal worker, who up to now had been exempted.

'Are all these exempted workers from Spandau?' asked Hergesell.

'Nearly all,' the man replied. 'But some, mainly in the other bus, come from Tegel or Moabit prison. Two days ago we were put into uniforms at Spandau barracks.'

The man was forty-four years old – every man in the bus was between forty and fifty.

'Much too old,' remarked Hergesell. 'At that age everything gives you aches and pains.' He turned to Boehlke: 'We once had replacements of this kind. No great gain for the front lines, I can tell you!'

'Such men do much better behind a lathe', replied Boehlke. 'But which way are we going? We ought to have passed through Erkner by now!'

The bus went due east, along the road to Küstrin. Hergesell got up and asked the transport leader, who told him, 'We can't go via Fürstenwalde now. But come with us to Heinersdorf; there you can find another connection.'

They passed Rüdersdorf. The road looked like all others around Berlin in these days. Women and children carrying rucksacks, pulling small carts heaped with bedding, trunks, cases. Through the air whizzed 'sewing machines', the small low-flying Russian bi-planes. They did no harm, did not fire, and did not throw 'flowerpots', they flew in loops and circles, watching, reconnoitring. Now and then shots were fired at them from behind bushes. There was some shooting to the north, but it soon stopped. The people in the bus fell silent. The men from Spandau looked more hopeless than ever. They went past fir plantations, once a stretch of water gleamed in the landscape, a small tributary of the river Spree. The placid mirror was covered with the large leaves of water-lilies. In bygone days one or other of the men had probably spent happy hours in a folding canoe on these waters which wound their way through meadows connecting the many lakes. It seemed a long time ago, the time when no danger lurked behind the trees of the forest and the skies did not threaten.

They reached Müncheberg. The two heavy buses drove along the southern outskirts. In the ghost-like streets not a soul was to be seen; in the centre of the town bombs exploded. The hot smell of burning houses reached the bus. When they were past the crossroads and drove on in the direction of Frankfurt-on-Oder, they saw hanging over Müncheberg, a dense cloud of black smoke. Were those only bombs, or had they heard the noise of firing, too? They were given no time to answer this question: bullets whizzed around them, the bus was being fired at by skirmishers hiding in the fir plantation along the road. Windows were shattered, bullets went through the coachwork. On the floor there was not room enough for all. A heap of men lying on top of each other, and the driver raced on as fast as he could. The two large vehicles bounced through a row of burning houses and turned into a side road which was more like a country lane. The shooting stopped, and the fallen heap of human beings separated again into its different parts.

'A few Russians who have filtered through,' Hergesell remarked. 'They will soon be dealt with.'

'You don't really believe that, my dear Hergesell?'

'What else should I believe?'

'Reality, Lieutenant! In any case, we have passed the point where we should have got off, and it doesn't look as though we could get off now!'

No, there was no chance of that. The bus still raced ahead, followed by the second one. Then: stones splashed into the the air, a dust cloud rose. From the upper deck came the screams of wounded. The brakes screeched, the vehicle jerked to a standstill. Flabbergasted, the passengers stumbled out. In the meadows stood mushrooms of smoke and earth. Splinters of bursting shells buzzed through the air. The deserted bus stood in flames. It had driven straight into the battle. The men had no time to think, they tumbled down a slope into a deep hollow. At the bottom a fir thicket promised protection. But they were forced to go on; those who had thrown themselves flat on the ground were ordered to get up; out of the safe-seeming hollow. Fifteen to twenty yards above their heads was a railway embankment, on it German soldiers were crouching in a trench. This was the front, the Oder front, the eastern front, the second line to which the 'Courmark' division had withdrawn.

The line was thin – so thin that there was room enough for the men from Spandau. They scrambled up the slope and were immediately posted into the line, five men from Spandau between two of the 'Courmark'. They had to shoulder their rifles and to fire at such targets as a dust cloud, molehills, shadowy movements in the open fields. It was completely unreal, the change had been too sudden. They had been told they were going to Lietzen for training. Now they were in Lietzen or near Lietzen. But Lietzen and its surroundings was already the front line, and the dust cloud at which they fired was a Russian tank, and behind the gently moving boughs of the trees lurked human beings.

'Urrah . . .'

This was too much. The deep hollow which they had left behind and the dense thicket down there called to them. One of the men broke the ranks. First one, then all. The men from Spandau climbed headlong out of the trench.

Above them shouting: 'Where are you off to? Halt! Get back, all get back!' The men from Spandau did not heed, ran on, threw themselves down in the fir plantation.

'Stand still or we shoot. All back or we shoot!' The men from Spandau hesitated for a moment, but then ran on. Bullets from automatics swished over their heads.

Boehlke and Hergesell stood in front of the battalion battle station.

'Impossible, Captain, it is quite impossible for you to go to Fürstenwalde,' the battalion adjutant told them. 'There is only one road – through Heinersdorf, and it's cut now.'

'Yes, we have noticed that!'

'We cannot understand how you managed to pass through Heinersdorf at all, and moreover through Müncheberg. Our information is that Müncheberg is occupied by the Russians.'

'Quite possibly. It certainly looked like it!'

'Good heavens, and we just drove through it!'

'In any case, the Russians are in part of the town, certainly in the northern part.'

'There are not many of them, and they're spread out over

the fields; with a "Tiger" you would probably get through. That is just our problem here. We could all get through; we could break out at any moment. But whilst we are waiting for the order to retreat, the Russians are getting thicker all the time. The general hangs on the telephone, but the only reply he gets is: The line must be held!'

'Well, we are staying; we make our stand, or rather, we are lying on our embankment: one of our men to five of those accursed Loot-Germans, Volkssturm, Ersatz soldiers, and such like vermin. You have seen for yourselves the kind of heroes they are. All right, we'll stand firm, as long as we have to!'

Yes, they stood . . . it was one of the unshakable divisions of the Oder Front, that 'Courmark' division which, two days ago, on the occasion of the birthday of the Supreme Commander Hitler, had been decorated for special valour.

'That was a damned tricky moment just now, when the new boys shot off during the tank attack. But the old soldiers stood firm, and the tanks had to turn back. We have seen enough of that in the east. We stand firm, but what happens behind our backs? In the north the Russians have broken through and are advancing. And now they have nearly reached Berlin!'

'Break through to Berlin – that is the only thing left to us. But the order does not come.'

'In these circumstances, we, too, can do nothing but wait here for it,' Captain Boehlke said. 'And till then we, too, will have to shoulder our blunderbusses!'

Tumbling houses, cataracts of bricks, fountains of fire and dirt. The dust rising up in glowing clouds. From afar – from Fürstenwalde and Wriezen, from Oranienburg and Hermsdorf, from Wildpark-Werder, and from Maybach I Camp near Zossen it seemed as though the tail of a fallen comet lay over Berlin, slowly burning itself out. An iridescent ball of gas, the Enchanted Mountain in sulphurous light . . . and in the deep cave under the earth the Witches' Sabbath, the apoplectic High Priest officiating at the maleficium – thus the city of Berlin appeared that night to the Commander of Luftwaffe Headquarters at Wildpark-Werder, and thus it appeared to the tankmen of a squadron driving out into the night at Maybach I Camp near Zossen.

The Commander of Luftwaffe Headquarters entered the room of his Chief, General Koller. Koller's eyes were sunk in deep hollows, as if nights of orgies lay behind him. The life without sleep was eating him up; worse were the commands to attend the blasphemous Witches' Sabbath in the Führer Bunker. The constant railing, the snarling, the threats of execution had become unbearable. Now he was again commanded either to spend the day at the bunker, or else to send a deputy; he decided first to send Major-General Christian and later to relieve him. Thus the burden would be borne by two pairs of shoulders.

Another night lay behind him; what a night, what insanity! He felt exhausted; if only he could have one hour's rest. But he had to listen to the report of the Camp Commander. It was the same as always: lack of fuel for the planes. Petrol trains on their way to the airfields had again been stopped by motorized SS and emptied of their contents. Air squadrons without fuel – how was he to deploy them? Well, it had been exactly the same in Russia; so why be surprised? Koller saw his Camp Commander as if through a thick wall of glass. He was half asleep; it was 4.15 in the morning. Suddenly he pulled himself together. What was that, did you say? Havel . . . Potsdam . . . the approach to Wildpark no longer secure?

'What did you say, what was that?'

'Berlin's defence line has been withdrawn to the other side of the Havel, beyond Potsdam,' declared the Commander. 'Our Headquarters are now lying outside the defence ring and are no longer safe.'

'What can we do? We have to organize the defence ourselves.'

'With what, General? The last battalion of the Hermann Göring division has been sent off to aid Steiner's attack.'

'So any moment now the Russians might appear outside our gates?'

'I have placed motorized guards at all bridges and roads leading to Wildpark-Werder. That is the best we can do.'

'All right. At least we will not be taken by surprise when the Russians come!'

'But we ought to evacuate, Herr General!'

'We will not get permission.'

No, we will not get permission. At this hour the 'Fürher' has other things on his mind. The Master in the Mountain cave officiates – has for the last forty-eight hours officiated at the Black Mass. The contents of his sullied tabernacle are smoke and stench, and the monster that is emerging tonight from the cauldron is named Steiner!

The Squadron which, led by a First Lieutenant, had driven out of camp Maybach I near Zossen into the night, was the guard unit of the army headquarters' staff. After reports had shown clearly that Marshal Koniev had invaded the Lausitz and had now passed the Spreewald, it had been decided to send the last fighting reserve of the headquarters' staff to meet the Russians near Luckau. The squadron consisted of two hundred and fifty men with heavy infantry equipment; it was supposed to make a stand against a force of hundreds of tanks and a sky full of planes.

It was 6 a.m. when Colonel Boldt of the cavalry received an urgent telephone call. The caller was the leader of the squadron, First Lieutenant Kränkel: 'Approximately forty Russian tanks have passed us. I shall attack at 7 a.m.'

Two hours later Kränkel reported:

'Attack failed; heavy loses sustained. Our tanks' reconnaissance reports continued advance northwards of enemy tanks.'

There were no further reserves. Neither was there a weapon with which to disperse the Russian fighters circling above the German H.Q. In the ante-chamber of the General Staff where Colonel Boldt was sitting, the hoarse growling of Russian tanks could be heard.

'Russian tanks outside Baruth!'

This announcement was sent to Berlin to the Führer Bunker. There was no answer. There was no order to evacuate H.Q. The 'Führer' was not available – except for reports in connection with the attack Steiner.

'In these circumstances, will there be a staff conference to-day?' asked Boldt.

'As usual at eleven o'clock,' replied the liaison officer.

It was not yet eleven when the three staff officers from Zossen – Krebs, Boldt and Loringhoven – arrived at the

Reich Chancellery. They entered the Bunker and reached the lowest gallery, descended the last spiral staircase, and were taken through the long corridor into the conference room. Hitler sat at the table, staring at the map in front of him, seeing nothing, hearing nothing. Some time passed before he raised his head and gazed at the new arrivals. The air was full of tension; it was like an ammunition factory before an explosion. The spongy face trembled. The look from his flickering eyes begged, implored, demanded, insisted, on news of the Steiner attack. There was no such news. Steiner had not appeared. The attack had not started. When it was to start, nobody knew.

'This morning, early – at least during the morning I had expected the attack to start!' The voice which managed to get these words out was hollow, was like a vacuum which seemed to suck in the listeners. It should have been General Krebs' duty as Chief of the General Staff, to announce that Steiner had not appeared, had not been able to rally his troops in time, and that, although ground crews of the Luftwaffe had arrived, none had come from the army units or the SS; Krebs should have been the one to explain to the Chief of the armed forces, Hitler, that a serious attack by Steiner, or even a part-attack, was out of the question today, tomorrow or any other day. Krebs, the plump gentleman with the Portwine-nose – who had once sent Luftwaffe Colonel Aachern on his last mission – was no longer plump and had lost his gaiety long ago; he too, remained silent, and when he had to speak, took refuge in empty phrases.

An announcement was brought in from Reich Leader SS Himmler:

'Steiner has definitely started; the attack has begun.'

Hitler jumped up.

'The Luftwaffe must at once establish, through air reconnaissance, whether this is true.'

General Christian communicated this order to General Koller at Wildpark-Werder. But Koller was expecting the arrival of Russian tanks at any moment, and his first concern was to find out when he could evacuate Wildpark-Werder. Christian tried to make it clear to him that at this moment the Führer would not consider such a question. This new demand drove Koller almost to despair. Concrete achievements can be established, but how could an aerial reconnaissance work in smoke and mist without information about the area of attack! In any case, it would surely be much quicker to find out on the ground whether Steiner had even given the order for the attack.

General Christian returned to the conference room. Hitler was staring at the map again and it seemed as though his head was about to drop on the table. He appeared to be completely exhausted, and indeed he got up, staggered to the door and turned, indicating with a hardly noticeable movement of his hand the end of the conference.

This was a complete surprise; not only was Krebs left bewildered. Krebs had intended to mention his own predicament concerning the evacuation of H.Q., and wanted to address the Führer but could not very well grab hold of his sleeve. Hitler tottered towards the opposite wall and disappeared into his private apartment. There was nothing for Krebs to do but remonstrate with Bormann about the urgency of his request; but Bormann could take no decisions alone.

Krebs, Boldt and Loringhoven returned from the underworld – without permission to evacuate their headquarters. They got into their cars and roared off towards the outskirts of the town, completely disregarding the obstacles in their way. Their goal was Zossen; considering the circumstances in which they had left it, that could only mean Russian captivity or death. When they arrived at Zossen, the streets were full of refugees, but otherwise nothing could be seen that might have indicated the arrival of the Russians.

Outside camp Maybach I they found a handful of vehicles and twenty soldiers, exhausted and covered with dirt. A figure crossed the road. First-Lieutenant Kränkel – his face barely recognizable under the dried mud – reported. According to him another twenty men and two anti-aircraft guns were actively engaged outside Baruth. And that was all that had remained of the squadron of the headquarters' staff. Baruth had been taken by the Russians. However, halfway towards Baruth, seven miles from the German H.Q., the Russian advance tank force had suddenly stopped without any apparent reason.

How long – for how long will the Russians stop there?

Krebs hurried into his office and Boldt and Loringhoven ran ahead. They pounced on the telephones – four, five instruments were working simultaneously. They appealed to Bormann, Burgdorf, Christian, anyone who might be able to break into Hitler's sinister brooding.

The answers were devastating.

Hitler refused his permission to evacuate H.Q. Thirty minutes passed. Above them Russian planes were circling. The windows vibrated with the detonations of shells from Russian tanks. At last, at thirteen hours, permission to evacuate Zossen arrived. Fall back to Potsdam-Eiche, the order stated; at the same time it was announced that the next staff conference would be at 14.30 o'clock in the Führer bunker.

Hasty departure from Zossen.

Kränkel's vehicles were loaded up. When they drove off, led by Colonel Boldt, they left behind a ghost camp. Doors moved in the wind. The large entrance gates were left wide open. The safe in the office of the Chief of the General Staff also stood open. On the floor papers were lying about. In the conference room the maps still hung on the walls. There had been no time to destroy anything. The automatic news centre – the largest telephone and teleprinter centre in Germany – went on functioning. The first Russian to arrive there had only to lift the receiver to be able to speak to north and south, to Dönitz in Lübeck, to Göring in Berchtesgaden, to Himmler in Schwerin, and even to Hitler in the Reich Chancellery.

The convoy of the Headquarters Staff proceeded in the direction of Berlin, threading its way past swarms of distracted people with horses and carts, wheelbarrows, prams and bicycles. Old and sick, wounded soldiers, whole families with trunks and bedding, some of them only half dressed, tramped through the lanes and sometimes over the open ground towards the west – away from the Russians; their one thought – away from the Russians!

Faster than the refugee hordes travelled the rumours:

The centre of Berlin is under artillery fire. There have been casualties in Dorotheenstrasse. The Russians are already in Alexander Platz. They have by-passed Berlin and have swum the Havel. Glienicke is Russian. Brandenburg has been taken. . . .

The convoy crossed the Autobahn, proceeded along the blocked road via Grossbeeren towards the west. The various cars had lost touch in the general turmoil, and Boldt ordered a stop so that the other cars might make contact again. They arrived at Potsdam as an orderly column. They got as far as the bridge in front of the old castle, and there they had to stop, jammed in between hundreds of vehicles. There was no way out, neither forward nor back. The attempts of Boldt and Kränkel and other officers to unravel the knot of traffic were not very successful. They had to wait until the unexploded bombs from the last attack had been made harmless by the bomb disposal squad. That might take hours.

At the same time as Boldt was stuck at Potsdam with his vehicles, Krebs and Loringhoven were driving quickly along the approach road from Tempelhof towards the city centre. They stopped outside the Reich Chancellery for the second time that day.

It was two o'clock in the afternoon, but of the blue Spring sky there was no sign. Around a periphery of seventy miles Berlin was a heaving jungle of smoke and fiery dust. A fallen, dying meteor . . . the Enchanted Mountain, a sulphuric Walpurgis night, although it was bright day.

The anti-aircraft tower at Friedrichshain had counted five hundred Russian shells the day before and had replied with four hundred. During the last twenty-four hours the world had changed. The ring round Berlin was practically closed. Already thousands of the 20,000 guns which the Russians had dragged across the Oder were turned on the narrow strip between the Müggelsee and the waters of the Havel and were venting fire and destruction on to the multitude of buildings that was Berlin. The air was one unending tumult. Melting asphalt; cascades of tumbling bricks; pavements thrown high.

The small, shrunken, dried up Krebs, the long, elegant Loringhoven, now emaciated like a greyhound, were surrounded by a hail of shrapnel as they jumped from their car outside the Reich Chancellery. The columns of the high entrance hall rose over the ruins. The wooden sentry boxes to right and left of the entrance were empty. Not a soul was to be seen. Ghostly will-o'-the-wisps flickered round the building.

A Witches' Sabbath . . .

Loringhoven stood aside for Krebs and then took the
twelve steps in one leap. Only in the reception hall did one
of the guardians of the Witches' Sabbath appear. A shaking
SS Second Lieutenant allowed the new arrivals to pass
unchecked, and melted again into the dusk of the hall.
Krebs and Loringhoven hurried along the carpeted corridors
and down the stairs; a reinforced door and two SS-guards
with automatics, hand grenades in their belts; a long corridor,
along both walls stood heavily armed SS-soldiers, some leaning against the wall asleep. A crack in the protective concrete
ceiling caused by a direct hit made a detour necessary. Bad
lighting; a smell of new whitewash; the water foot-high
on the floor. The way now led across boards, then through
a scullery and two mess rooms for the troops. Officers of
varying ranks sat there with schnapps in front of them, with
thickly spread sandwiches and real coffee. More stairs, more
double guards; then the last check. Two officers of the bodyguard, giants with cauliflower ears and broken noses, regarded the close-fitting uniforms with well-trained eyes
and examined the attaché cases for arms or explosives. The
Generals Christian and Jodl, Orderly officers, and stenographers, had already arrived. They were waiting for Hitler's
adjutant, Sturmbannführer Günsche, to come and take them
to the lower corridor outside the conference room.

It was still afternoon; twenty minutes had passed since
Krebs and Loringhoven had left the sulphur-laden daylight
behind them. Here, under a layer of reinforced concrete
thirty feet thick, an underground laybrinth which in turn
had a reinforced ceiling twelve feet thick, over fifty feet
below the ground, there was no longer any difference between day and night; this was the domain where the sun never
rose, and humming ventilators sucked out the used foul air.

The hour had come.

It could not be a birth. It was but a question of the death
rattle, agony, rigor mortis, decay.

The mouth of Baal was wide open.

Whom will it crush? – the short-legged Bormann with the
fat belly and the dark intriguer's face, General Burgdorf
whose morale and faith had gone to the dogs in this hole,
General Field-Marshal Keitel with the light blue eyes like

those of a dead codfish, the Chief-yes-man Jodl, the short, bow-legged Krebs, or perhaps the High Priest himself who was now celebrating his blasphemous mass.

The defiled tabernacle was already falling apart. A filthy decoction of lies and delusion and helplessness overflowed. Everything started quite ordinarily in the usual manner of staff conferences. At this table a staff conference was synonymous with glorification of the Führer, and strategy had become a mysterious magic, independent of mathematical exactness and the law of cause and effect. A black magic, which, outside these walls, had to be paid for in real human blood and which hurled men, women and new-born babies into the dust.

Bormann, Burgdorf, Keitel, Jodl and Krebs sat on stools but the chief magician sat majestically at the end of the table in an armchair. As usual it began with the reports of Krebs and General Jodl. Local successes in Saxony, Italy and even by the Ninth Army near the Oder. Apart from that they had no favourable news, but in their mouths it did not even sound unfavourable that the Russians had reached the outskirts of Berlin, that tank spearheads were aiming at the city centre, that the two Russian army detachments operating in the north and south had already occupied eighteen outlying towns. If their smooth words could be believed, it was not even tragic that the First Ukrainian Army had driven a wedge into the German lines of communication and had separated the capital from the southern part of the country. It all depended on how you looked at it. The imminent linking of forces of the Russians and the Americans by the Elbe might, of course, easily lead to a collision which would mark the beginning of the overdue Soviet-American quarrel and reverse the historic turn of events.

Jodl spoke and Krebs. Bormann watched them both with his habitual distrust. Keitel sat so erect on his stool he looked as if he had swallowed a ruler; his features as smooth as his brilliantine-set hair. General Burgdorf, having arrived at the lowest point of his degradation, thought the only thing now was to forget everything. The orderly officers standing along the wall remained passive witnesses, whether of a holy or unholy event they did not know.

Jodl had spoken and Krebs had spoken, and their rhetoric,

their painting of the situation in glowing colours, had been in vain. No, successes in Saxony and Italy and the destruction of two tanks at the Oder front did not interest the Master. The monster remained unmoved, only to hurl into the room with a strength borrowed from a past and more noisy epoch, three significant words demanding a straight answer:

'Has Steiner attacked?'

Silence around the table. A bemedalled Field Marshal and the row of gold braided hangers-on had their hearts in their mouths. None of them answered, but the question remained suspended over the table, hovering beneath the concrete vaults like an explosive gas. The slightest breeze might set if off and the detonation would utterly destroy this construction of lies, this whole world of delusion and pretence, of falsification and deceit and illusion. The silence was ominously penetrating and spread to the other side of the walls. Guards and secretaries, adjutants and favourites held their breath.

The large protruding eyes stared. The expression on the spongy face changed from sheer amazement to fury. Was not one of the miserable poltroons going to answer? The waiting man leant forward, both arms planted on the table, his teeth bared.

Jodl got up. Cowardly evasion was no longer possible. One of them had to draw the avenging flash.

He said, and his voice was hardly more than a whisper:

'Mein Führer, Steiner has not attacked.'

The phantom started with incredulity, then bowed low under the heavy blow. Suddenly his head was too heavy and his eyes were dimmed with tears. His gaze fell on the map spread on the table. He traced the lines on it with his finger around the area which was Berlin. And only now, at this moment, did he realize for the first time the pincers' reality – not for the city and the three and a half million people – but for himself; he felt their razor sharpness, heard them close. And no Steiner to force them open, to break the claws' cruel grip. He looked up – the assembly grew pale, it was the look of a madman. Out of the gaping mouth came a pitiful whimper: 'I have been deceived by the SS! I never expected that from my SS!'

The complaining, whimpering note subsided. The ice

melted. It was Spring and the south wind raged. The sluices of all the damned-up waters opened. It roared, crackled, whipped, bellowed. A storm descended upon the half dozen pitiable figures: 'Deceivers, scoundrels, villains, serpents! I have reared deceitful serpents in my bosom.'

The raving man rose, clutched the back of a chair – his head lifted. The shouting echoed along the concrete vaults and stunned the assembly with its terrible curse.

Treachery and failure as far as one can see. Corruption as far as the hand can reach. And lies, lies, lies. . . . The Luftwaffe has failed miserably. The whole of the Luftwaffe ought to be hanged. The army is not much better. Every general is a traitor and deserves death. All soldiers are cowards. The German people are inadequate. Thus it bellowed from the wide open mouth, was re-echoed from the walls, travelled along the corridors. And suddenly it ceased. But that was only a pause for breath, a short respite from madness.

The hoarse voice bellowed:

'Everyone, with the exception of Bormann, Burgdorf, Keitel, Jodl, Krebs and the two stenographers is to leave the room.'

The Orderly Officers went out, met in the passage the trembling group of favourites, the liaison officers delegated to the various army units and ministries. Luftwaffe General Christian and Himmler's representative, Fegelein, and the Ambassador Hewel stood there next to the dietitian, the chauffeur and the man who took care of the dogs, and also next to Eva Braun who was seen for the first time by the officers who had come from outside the Bunker.

The communicating doors closed again.

The turmoil in the conference room was explosive. A flood raged, turbid with the mud thrown up from the depths. All that had been forgotten came to the top. In the whirlpool the green faces of murdered victims of far-off days went crazily round and round and disappeared again, together with unknown worms and beetles, together with strangled, shot, drowned dignitaries who had met the tyrant once and then once again, and the battered face, full of stitches, with the faithful dog's eyes was amongst them, the face of Ernst Röhm . . . and Schleicher with his wife, and Heines and

131

Strasser; hundreds of only one purge during the early days, and others who had come even before them; Geli Raubal shot though the heart, an unknown communist sewn into a sack; innumerable corpses appeared out of the hitherto undisturbed slime and vanished in the whirl.

All this – for what?

'For what?' hissed the monster.

'For what indeed, if all this is to have been in vain, when there is not to be a Germany any more, when the German people are but a formless mass, nothing but a dead pulp, impossible to mould?

'Don't talk, don't shower me with explanations. Leave those boring SS-leaders out of it, boring, arrogant, dithering ... I don't want to hear any more, any more, any more. ...'

Even the five heads directly in front of him – Bormann, Burgdorf, Jodl, Keitel, Krebs – and the two stenographers were already deformed, over-grown with sea-weed, nibbled by fish and swimming along the Styx. They shall not escape, they are nailed to the same raft. Everything flows, the river flows to the sea. The drifting corpses eaten away by the salts of the sea, become rattling skeletons and sink, sink, turn into calcified bones.

'Calcified bones . . .' it resounded from the ceiling, from the walls. 'And Germany is too small, too limited, too weak. I have wasted my strength on Germany, wasted it senselessly. It cannot be saved now, it is not worthy of me. I shall shed no tears over it. Oh, oh . . .'

He cried, he lamented. The five around the table cowered, shaken to the marrow, unable to hide their faces. The courtiers beyond the walls trembled.

The dying man renewed his raving.

The fallow land broke open. Stony ground that had never seen the light of day came to the top. A cascade of sounds, the growl of the depths, hot lava, word fragments. The stenographers drew web-like lines across their pads that would never be deciphered by any human. And nobody in the room understood the tirade. Nobody was able to follow, long passages were lost, there was no coherence, long-drawn-out gurglings, the wide-open mouth frothed. Foam from it flew into Burgdorf's, into Keitel's face.

The valley of the Danube spoke – the chariots of the vandals creaked, the missiles of the Huns whined. Rome perished once more: *'Terrible derision! What is this Rome? Cursed and doomed be this city! Rot and wither then, Rome! That is the wish of your depraved people!'*

Thus the words of the opera; this was Linz in 1905, a nocturnal hour spent on the Freinberg; a staggering grammar-school boy walking to and fro, his head a-fire, after a Wagner performance. But this was the present. Chariots creaked, missiles whined. Beyond the Bunker walls women were writhing beneath bearded faces, under the leather belts of the Kurds and Tartars. And in the deepest Bunker a man howled: 'Cursed and doomed be this city . . . depraved people, nobody can help you. You shall regret this day . . .'

Three hours the raving had lasted. Three hours of death agony. The phantom from the woods – the schoolboy from the days of the collapsed Hapsburg dynasty.

His father had died at the local inn in Linz. The son, born during confusion and decay, was to die amidst ruins, in the bottom cell of a beehive filled with drunkards and voluptuaries, with braggarts, wasters, and glittering nonentities whose pale fear showed through the made-up skin.

'It is finished, finished . . .'

The Third Reich is no longer. The emblems are broken, the Swastika flags, the SS-banners, the Blood-standard, the Order of Blood, the crosses in silver and gold decorated with swords and diamonds, lie besmirched underfoot.

'Who am I, what am I?'

None of them was able to answer, but the answer came. It came from the exhausted heart. The face fell in, the blood pumped feebly. The skin grew chalk-white and the used-up body began to tremble. A ghost threw its arms in the air and collapsed. Slumped limp in the chair and cried, cried, cried. . . .

The ghost mumbled:

'The war is over, all is lost, sold, betrayed: I shall shoot myself!'

He said it, and . . . nothing . . . no angry teutonic God with the hammer shatters the Bunker. Thunder does not shake the walls nor the resounding ruins of the wicked city. The ground does not open. Heaven has heard and done nothing.

Nothing, nothing, nothing. . . .

Who is he . . . a nondescript coffee house gossip from Munich, a nameless soldier from the trenches of the first world war, a painter of postcards at the Vienna home for down and outs, a pupil from Linz who could be given bad marks? Perhaps a child with measles?

A lame horse?

Or even less. . . .

Once again: 'I did not expect that. This is base; less than I deserve. Mankind is too insignificant to appreciate true greatness.' A race of dwarfs – smash it and from the pulp create a better, abler race. But it is too late for that. The attempt has failed and there is no time to repeat it. The collapsed man was sinking. His face was sticky with sweat, his eyes lacked all lustre. He had been felled, finally.

The door to the corridor was now open. The most intimate of the coterie came in. Outside Fegelein telephoned with Himmler, Hewel with Ribbentrop, Christian with Koller.

'No, I do not need to be relieved,' Christian said to Koller. 'Events of historic significance are taking place in the Bunker.'

The man who was stretched out in the armchair had given up all hope. The doctor could no longer help him. That clumsy oaf Morell could break his syringe. He needed it no longer; neither did he need pills. The quack could go, get out of it, vanish. Everybody could leave now; to wherever he liked.

The war was lost. Now it had been said by the fountain head. The war was lost. But the paladins did not wish to abdicate yet. Soldiers had still to be fed to the guns. The boys of the youth associations had to go on dying. The executioners had to be kept in business. To put a gun to one's head, to swallow a poison pill, was too simple. The power must go on – the hand into which it was to pass was already outstretched. It was the black hairy hand of Bormann.

Bormann talked feverishly to the listless man. How could he leave his people in the lurch who so faithfully and for so long had stood by him? *Faithful, long* . . . the face of the paralytic grew crimson. His arm, shaken by cramp, fell limp.

The incantations went on. Not everything was lost yet. There were still troops stationed in the mountains of Austria and Czechoslovakia. There was still a chance. Wenk's reserve army was approaching. Keitel, Bormann, Burgdorf, one after the other they came up to the armchair which was already a bier. Himmler telephoned, so did Göring.

This was sheer necromancy.

An incantation of the dead.

This went on for days – still time for misty awakenings sudden death sentences, executions, expulsions from the Party, degradations, political disowning, blood-curdling curses, the making of a Will, a wedding. Nights and days went by.

After seven days death came irrevocably.

'Woman, come here,' they said.

'And you, silly goose, take that badge off,' they said.

'Wherever is Wenk's army?' they said.

'We can but stick our neck out and die,' they said.

'You swine, are you going to let us die like cattle!' they said.

'I cannot go on, shoot me', they said.

The brooch with the Swastika and ear of corn, the badge on the sleeve of her RAD (Land army) uniform, and not only the brooch and the uniform, the whole girl had caught Gnotke's eye. This was a Werewolf, a she-wolf. A hunter's instinct told him that, and the official bag at her side and the way she held her hand over it protectively, confirmed his suspicion. The girl was very young, could not be more than eighteen. She came from the direction of Weissensee garden suburb and was making for the city centre. She meant to go on, into the wolves' lair probably. But there were no trams and the underground had closed its gates. Traffic into Berlin had stopped. She was at a loss, tried to stop passing cars. In vain. Gnotke kept close to her. He needed her because up to now he had collected no information, and judging by the increasing artillery fire it could not be long now before his unit would arrive and he could not face his intelligence chief empty-handed after an absence of five days.

A poor thing, the little werewolf. Her uniform was crumpled, bits of earth and straw clung to the grey material. She had spent nights out of doors and her boots, too, told of a long journey. She was tired, the dark-ringed eyes did not fit the young face. When a rocket exploded in the street it made her jump; but she did not take it too seriously. Personally, Gnotke did not wish her any harm. Despite all the obstacles confronting her and despite her fatigue she was firmly set on her purpose. Gnotke could not withhold his admiration. He did not want anything of her except that she should lead him to the lair.

Suddenly it all came to an end.

A siren whined. Once, twice, four times, and did not stop. Not an air-raid warning, that was finished. The whining announced the arrival of the Russians. The sirens screeched. Alarm shots were fired. People ran to their cellars, but even more of them hurried with their belongings, as fast as their feet would carry them, towards an elevated Bunker at the outskirts of the garden suburb, in the belief that behind its solid walls they would better withstand the onslaught of the Russians. Nobody was allowed in the streets. Patrols urged the people to hurry. 'Alarm! Tank warning! Clear the streets! Into the Herzberg Bunker, all of you!'

The concrete lump at the periphery was like a magnet which irresistibly drew the rushing, panic-struck specks towards it. The whole area from the Resurrection Cemetery to Faulen See and far into Hohenschönhausen was almost wholly cleared of people. The RAD-girl, too, had to abandon her plans and hurried along with the others; close on her heels came Gnotke.

It was eight o'clock in the evening; the sky above the allotments was blood-red. In the little gardens the snipers were already in position. But the girl knew when to slip through the Bunker entrance. Gnotke stuck to her. A long passage, stairs and upstairs more passages. Electric lights glowed. On the ground floor, next to the entrance, a first-aid post had been established. Gnotke did not have to worry about his imitation head bandage. The doctor and the medical sergeant-major had more than enough to do. The Bunker was full to overflowing – five, eight, maybe ten thousand human beings were huddled close together. There was a hum as though in a beehive when the Queen bee dies. The ventilators worked at high speed and could not suck out the sticky used air quickly enough. From the latrines, blocked and overflowing, a sour smell pervaded the whole building.

Gnotke had managed to reach one of the staircases. The

cabins which branched off from the passages – small squares with two three-tiered beds, meant for six people – were occupied by many more with trunks and boxes, three, four and five high. Whole families had made their homes here complete with clothes, beds and pots and pans. People, surrounded by their belongings, were even sitting on the stairs.

In one of the cabins a portable radio was turned on.

'I appear, as I have done since 1933, before the German people to talk to them of the Führer . . .' It was Goebbels, his birthday speech broadcast on the eve of the birthday, the birthday itself, and now again.

'. . . The war is drawing to its close. The madness which the enemy has inflicted on mankind has passed its climax. The leader of the enemy's conspiracy has been crushed by fate. . . . Who else is there to show the way out of the world crisis but the Führer? He is the centre of resistance against the disintegration of the world. He is Germany's bravest heart and our people's most glowing wish . . .'

'Isn't there enough noise here – tell them to turn it off!' somebody called.

'We owe him thanks that our nation is still breathing, that there is still a way out of the deadly danger. . . . Defiantly and full of battle we stand behind him, soldier and civilian, man, woman and child. . . .'

'Man, woman and child . . .,' repeated the same person who had interrupted before and looked round him challengingly.

'Nothing is lost yet except for the Russians sitting in the allotments opposite and letting off fireworks!' said another.

'We stand by him as he stands by us, true Germanic vassals who gave their oath . . .' the radio blared.

'Must we listen to that rubbish?'

'Maybe everything is not yet lost. Wenk's relief army is supposed to be on its way.'

'Yes, the relief troops, Wenk's troops!' That was the RAD-girl. It was extraordinary what she had listened to just now. She had not believed such blasphemous words were possible. Her pupils were dilated in astonishment and indignation.

'Nonsense.'

'Madness.'

'It's all humbug.'

'I am fed up,' said a soldier and took off his leather belt with the cartridge pouches and his whole equipment.

'Don't throw it down here; get rid of it.'

'The Russians mustn't find anything here.'

'And you, silly goose, take that badge off.'

The RAD-girl lifted her head defiantly. The soldier took off his uniform tunic and exchanged it for a civilian jacket which somebody held out. Every wave, however high, breaks sometime. Those who had been on top for so long suddenly found themselves at the bottom; those who had been important, now dared not open their mouths; it was the others now who called the tune.

It was No-man's-land.

The Bunker was under fire. The wall facing the allotments was being scarred by shots from rifles and the Russian field artillery; from the west, across the town, missiles from German batteries whined across the Bunker and bounced against the back wall with deafening thuds. This lasted for hours; during the moments of intensified bombardment, the Bunker was like a kettle-drum. Inside the vibrating shell, ten thousand grains were shaken up; the light masts outside snapped off; the water pipes sprang up out of the ground. It was pitch-dark, the emergency lamps, torches meandering through the passages, were but glow-worms in the night. The sound of the 'Stalin organ', muffled by the concrete, grew to a thin whimper, a song of hell, piercing one's very bones.

Ten thousand people – they grew fewer. Many took advantage of the intermittent lulls in the bombardment and wandered off. The Nazis, who had been the bosses for so long, took this opportunity to disappear. A change began to take place in the Bunker. Those who had been silent – for eleven years – tried to prepare for the transition as smoothly as possible. Weapons must disappear. Uniforms must disappear, they said. Casualties were brought in. They told of Russians being stationed among the allotments, less than thirty yards away. If the Russians find weapons on their arrival, they are going to blow the whole Bunker up, it was said. The inhabitants of the Bunker provided civilian clothes for the soldiers; the Volksturm home guard demobilized itself. The men only had to take off their armbands to turn into civilians.

'And what about you, my little one, won't you take that badge off now and the uniform; surely we can find you a dress!' The old cobbler Haderer was also in the Bunker and seemed to be organizing the change-over. The beam of his torch shone on to the badge which caused so many misgivings, and it also shone into the good-looking, defiant face.

'A pretty girl and easily scared; she has put up a brave front. If she wore a dress we could include her in the reception committee,' Haderer said.

'What is your name, my poppet?'

'What does that matter? – Agnes Hasse,' she said in the end.

'Well then, Agnes Hasse, we have four women so far and you would be the fifth. You will receive the Russians, when they come, standing at the entrance with coffee and cigarettes and look as friendly as possible. That will make a good impression and you will see how they melt!'

'Never!' protested Agnes Hasse, 'I'd rather leave.'

'Just as you like, but the badge must come off and the uniform will have to go, that silly despatch case, too. You should carry a little handbag.'

'Never . . .'

'What, never carry a handbag? You poor child, just come to me and I'll make you one. Come on now, off with that badge.'

Others were less patient. Hands were stretched out to tear off her uniform by force. Unexpectedly she found a protector in Gnotke.

'Let her have the badge, let her go if she wants to.'

Haderer was surprised, first at Gnotke's presence and secondly at his unexpected intervention.

'You here? Are you quite right in the head, August?'

'I'm all right.'

He said no more but raised his glassy eyes; an enigma to Haderer. What is the matter with the fellow, what is behind all this? He had come from the other side, he had said, but what did he want here and what was the meaning of his peculiar attitude?

'Anyone can leave who feels like it,' said Haderer.

This was the most opportune moment for doing so. The battering which the concrete mass had endured all night had ceased. Only now and then did a thunder clap serve as a reminder that the war was still lurking. Agnes Hasse pushed her way through the crowd. As she left the Bunker, Gnotke was at her side. Mist rose from the allotments opposite. Under their feet sand spurted into the air from random rifle shots. Gnotke did not even look up, and the girl walked on.

Gnotke asked where she was going.

'To the centre,' the girl replied.

To the centre – that was his destination, too. Not a soul was to be seen. The streets seemed to have been swept clear. The Volkssturm had fled. Even the Hitler Youth with their anti-tank guns had disappeared. At one corner, an assault gun had been left without a crew. A last stand in a burnt-out dairy – the day before Gnotke had watched a group of leading Nazis there – was now deserted. A pale face peeped from the entrance of the house next door.

'What's happened to them?' asked Gnotke, pointing his thumb to the dairy.

'Got on their bikes and beat it.' The man, too, used his thumb to indicate the direction of the city centre.

In the ruins the fires smouldered. Smoke billowed from the gaping windows. The population sat in cellars and shelters. Now and again a face appeared. Nobody took any notice of the fires. The two ill-matched wanderers had reached the area round the toll-house in Landsberger Allee. Now there were more people about. Gnotke and the RAD-girl were stopped by a patrol. A combined patrol: army, navy, air force, SS. The RAD-girl's papers were in order, Gnotke's as well, and the invalid-certificate plus his head bandage completed the documentation. Asked where they had come from, they answered truthfully: 'From the Herzberger Bunker. The Russians are there,' Gnotke added.

They were allowed to continue their journey.

The big bridge near Landsberger Allee Station had been prepared for blowing up. One officer and two men of the demolition detachment squatted in a hole, surrounded by numerous empty bottles. Vermouth, it said on the labels.

The three of them were completely tight – it looked as if the bridge wouldn't be blown up after all.

That made a fair number of details for Gnotke to report to his intelligence chief. Together they would mean that the unit would be able to advance unhindered as far as the Landsberger Allee Bridge. However, to submit this report would mean he would have to turn back and wait for his unit at the outskirts of Weissensee. He did not do that; instead he promenaded this Sunday morning – at the side of a she-wolf with the regular, tragic features of a Roman.

He was a silent companion.

He made the girl feel uneasy. His disfigured face gave her the creeps. Still, he had helped her; had come to her aid when she had fallen unprotected amongst miscreants. She had to go to Potsdam Station where her office was, her head-quarters, she said.

'Ah yes, headquarters,' Gnotke replied understandingly.

'Important news?' he glanced towards the despatch case.

'Yes, that and collect new orders.'

Gnotke nodded significantly.

'Lucky coincidence that I have to go to Potsdam Station too.'

The artillery fire started up again, this time aiming more accurately. Heavy shells roared across the roofs. 'The Friedrichshain Bunker,' Gnotke estimated. But Alexander Platz was under fire as well. Progress grew more difficult. They managed it all the same, dodging here and there along side streets, throwing themselves down, taking refuge in cellars, and after passing frequent controls they crossed the Spree first at Mühlendamm, and then again near Spittel-markt.

She had been on the Vistula, south of Warsaw. Had managed to get out, one of a group. During the day they had hidden in the woods and from dusk until dawn they had marched, up to twenty-eight miles a night, through wind and snow, burdened with their kit. They had fallen asleep walking and had jerked themselves into wakefulness. Death had lurked behind every tree. That much Gnotke learned during the walk from Dönhoff Platz to Potsdam Station.

But about what had happened since her return up to the present he could discover nothing.

She had been in a collecting camp – but where, she did not say. As to what she had done there, she said just a little.

'We had to sew dresses from curtains and tablecloths, each girl two for herself.'

'So that was the trousseau,' Gnotke said – 'the wolf's skin,' he might have said.

'They were clothes,' said the girl and looked at him with innocent eyes.

But apart from that. . . . The training with the anti-tank gun was a matter of course, that could be assumed without her mentioning it. But then: the leap from the darkness, the werewolf bite, not a word was said about it.

The girl was *chitry* – cunning, smooth-tongued, slippery, crafty. Gnotke thought of it in the all-embracing Russian term: *chitry*.

Agnes Hasse was startled at the intensive interest which the otherwise so monosyllabic sergeant showed in her affairs. Should she have told him that she had received a special training at the collecting camp Nauen, that all forms of ruthless extermination had been practised, that she had finished with an 'Excellent' and was now leading a pack herself? If she did that, she might as well open her despatch case and show him the address lists of the Party Member farmers who all had to take in one or two of the girls as liaison for the Werewolf.

No, he will hear soon enough of the Werewolf. But the set faces of those who will be deposited during the nights in streets and quiet squares throughout the land, they, too, will remain silent.

The girl was *chitry*, that was all there was to it.

It was three o'clock in the afternoon when he said good-bye to her in the desolate hall of Potsdam Station. He waited until he saw her disappear behind one of the doors. Then he advanced cautiously, passed the same door and read: Deutscher Reichsarbeitsdienst, Gau Brandenburg (German Labour Service, Brandenburg District).

He knew more:

He was standing before the lair – the headquarters of the Wolves.

At three o'clock in the afternoon the Russians entered the

Herzberg Bunker. They are here, they will cut our heads off! Thus it was passed on throughout the building. Keep calm, it won't be so bad! said others. Thousands of people held their breath.

Five women Haderer had selected, the friendliest and most charming of the younger women. They stood inside the wide open Bunker door, cigarettes and cups of coffee ready in their hands; the coffee had already been kept warm for several hours. Near them stood Haderer and his assistant, the tool-maker Reimann, who had helped him prepare the Bunker for a smooth handing-over. The women tried to look as natural and unaffected as possible in spite of the fact that their hearts were beating in their throats.

Terrible screams, shots, dust. Through the gunpowder smoke a panic surge outwards. The shots went into the ceiling. Plaster fell, the dust settled. A rider in a rawhide coat; flashing white teeth. The horse reared. The naked weapon cut through the air. All those near the entrance flinched, staggered against the wall. On the floor lay the cigarettes, the broken coffee cups. Old Haderer was not able to deliver his intended speech. He saw blinding sparks as he collapsed under a blow from a fist. Those around fared no better. Blows rained on all the bystanders. Toolmaker Reimann jumped forward, stammered a Russian word: 'Sdraswuitje! Welcome!' and added: 'Me Communist!' Diabolical laughter was the answer. A giant got hold of him around the hips, threw him up into the air and sneered: 'A Communist! An Idiot! – Look at him, he a communist and didn't have to be. Nobody's forced him, just look at him, the halfwit!' Reimann was hurled to the ground and there were many who were only too glad to beat him up for his stupidity. The Caucasian rider had slipped off his horse. One of the lovely receptionists, the wife of a butcher with a skin like a peach, was seized by him and thrown down. The other four 'receptionists', too, were writhing on the ground beneath the heavy weight of drunken men. Twenty, forty, half a hundred wild, weather-beaten faces gushed into the Bunker's entrance hall. All were full of Vodka – in order to take a Bunker full of thousands of 'Fascists', they had had to drain many a bottle beforehand. Others pushed their way in, more and more of them. An unending scream of terror marked their progress along the passages. The women in the entrance hall and the first compartments had to endure the worst. Those who had been selected for the reception were no longer able to rise from the floor, as soon as one man released them another rolled across them holding his pistol at the ready all the while.

Body searches, trunks turned upside down, belongings thrown about. Women screamed, screamed . . . children stood. Shots cracked, men collapsed. Whoever could do so, picked up his things and tried to get away.

Herzberg Bunker was a madhouse.

Old Haderer opened his eyes, in his mouth the taste of blood. He caught sight of the butcher's wife selected by him, a prostrate disfigured bundle. Another of the chosen – whimpering in agony. Behind him inside the Bunker sobbing, screaming, crying.

'Watchi, watchi!'

'Woman, come!'

Terrible delusion, terrible idolatry . . . the wailing tower, the cabins full of women crushed under the weight of strange men, accused him. Deceived, dishonoured, besmirched . . . he had lost face, it was more than a mouthful of blood and a tooth he spat out. He felt as Gnotke had done. The trampled innocence cried out and he had to block his ears. The pitch-tanned fist that had wielded the cobbler's hammer through so many years was useless. A drained shadow he slunk along the wall, behind the back of the oppressors who barred the way everywhere. These twisted madmen! Fascists indeed – they were workers from Weissensee and the wives and daughters of workers. He reached the exit, stepped into the searching daylight. A long column of loaded people walked beside him, laden with trunks and belongings; they had but one aim – home. A cloud of approaching riders. Scattering women. Burst trunks, clothes, linen strewn and trampled in the street. Down feathers whirling in the air.

Black Sunday at Weissensee.

Black Sunday. . . . And once upon a time, the people of St. Petersburg led by the priest Gapon demonstrating for the rights of man had been trampled on and butchered by Cossacks. That leaf out of the book of history sprang to Haderer's mind. But why? Are words meaningless? The sons of the people who had risen against oppression at St.

Petersburg now knelt on the pavement ransacking the trunks that their horses' hooves had smashed, looking for articles useful and useless alike, for glittering baubles and knick-knacks.

And this is what happened at the other end of Berlin, the Mariendorf settlement, not far from Reichstrasse 96, in the same cellar where Colonel Zecke had once sat with Director Knauer, the Putlitzer couple and other inhabitants.

'Woman, come! And you, man, *tuda*!' The man was to go, he must not be present. 'Go, Heiner', Anna Putlitzer managed to say with her teeth clenched. What was he waiting for, to be mown down perhaps? And then there was the other thing. One of them held her wrist. Where did he want to take her? – nowhere! With the other arm he lifted her from the floor and threw her down. The cellar was full of shadows, the intruders remained shadows. Only this one she saw clearly and would always know him again. The face roughened by the wind, the eyes glowing white but dark as the night, long oval slits; he smelled of sweat, dirt and most of all of schnapps.

'Go, Heiner . . .' Heinrich Putlitzer staggered before the muzzle of the pistol which urged him on. The sisters Quappendorf wriggled, the little one screamed in a high-pitched voice, the bony teacher wanted to run away but was caught at the door.

'Into yard, all men into yard!'

They left the cellar behind. Putlitzer, Knauer, the old printer Riebeling, the Rector Quappendorf, lurched up the stairs, stumbled into a changed world.

Their eyes had been used only to the dim light of candles. For five days they had not seen the day. Under artillery fire, whining rockets of the 'Stalin Organ', droning fighters, they no longer knew whether the sun shone outside or the moon.

This was no longer their yard – the horseshoe-shaped square, enclosed by walls and flowerbeds, was no longer a yard in Mariendorf, it was a caravanserai. This was Asia, a night in Asia with sleeping shadows and the smell of hay and manure. Carts and unharnessed horses stood there, a female camel nursing a long-legged foal. The front had rolled across them. Beyond the broken walls fires glowed. The horizon was lined with red; above the Teltow Canal smoke billowed.

The Russians fought for the road to Tempelhof.

'You Nazi!' they shouted at Director Knauer.

'You Nazi, too' – that was meant for Putlitzer.

'You too . . . all Nazis, all against the wall!'

Riebeling, Putlitzer, Knauer and even the retired Rector were pushed against the wall. A boy was brought up, with tousled fair hair, a nineteen-year-old SS-man, now in civilian clothes, the son of Rector Quappendorf; he was pushed towards the others.

A terrible mistake . . . the old printer Riebeling had lived for this hour, had waited for the Russians, the liberators. Once, that had been in the main telegraph office in November 1918, he had got a direct line to Moscow, Berlin – Moscow. 'Riebeling here . . .' – 'Here Tchitcherin, Moscow. Comrade Riebeling; get comrade Liebknecht to the telephone.' He must report this, must explain everything. His mouth fell open: Moscow, Moscow, here Riebeling, comrade Riebeling is standing against the wall. A nightmare; speech failed him; no sound came from his lips. Rector Quappendorf thought of his wife at the Stahndorf cemetery – good that she had not lived to see this. And Else, Margot, Lisbeth in the cellar . . . and the boy, the poor boy! He folded his hands, but not the words of the prayer book, a quotation from Goebbels' last proclamation came to his mind: 'The Russian assault will be shattered, shattered, shattered . . .' Knauer was prepared and awaited the end coolly, better the Russians than the Gestapo. Luckily Frau Halen had gone back two days ago to fetch her father.

Riebeling, Knauer, Putlitzer, a seventy-year-old father, a nineteen-year-old son stood against the wall, a flash tore through their eyes and the end of the world had come.

The shots whizzed over their heads and it was not the end. The soldiers put their smoking pistols away. Wild laughter, punches, blows, this time of a friendly nature. It had all been a joke, the whole execution had been a joke. Only now did the five of them receive the death blow; they felt suddenly contemptible. They had to support themselves, one dirtied his trousers, another vomitted, a third cried hysterically.

In this naked misery they experienced a strange phenomenon, each in his own way. The open horseshoe was lifted high complete with carriages, bundles of hay, camel and horses and Tartars, and the countryside right down to Teltow Canal lay before them fully visible in a brilliant illumination. Snapped telegraph poles, dangling wires, a riddled housefront, on an elevated grass verge a ghostly caravan – soldiers marching to the front. The ground shook under a dull blow. The light in the sky died down into rust-red conflagration, and telegraph poles, ruins, soldiers and horses were flung back into darkness.

The yard was once more a yard with a baggage train.

The bridge across the Teltow Canal had been blown up.

Where the Britz-Neukölln roads divide a couple of hundred yards from the settlement, there stood a Russian general. The dark head showed a few grey hairs; the face was strong, the figure as supple as the Russian leather boots on his feet. General Zhukov, next to him Fighter Command Kusnjetzov and Tank-General Voronov; a little way off his first adjutant and chief of the reconnaissance units; further away still some senior colonels.

A few days previously, General Zhukov had passed through the abandoned headquarters of the German General Staff near Zossen. Now he stood at the periphery of a huge sea of ruins. The ragged spikes and irregular outlines of demolished houses, girders bent into fantastic shapes by the fire, towering granite toothpicks lit up momentarily by the flash of the detonation, reminded him of another city. There as here, the façades of houses were only stage props with empty gaping windows, and the streets were valleys of rubble, the inhabitants fled or evacuated to the East or buried under the masonry; only a small portion of the town, the narrow towpath and the banks gently rising towards street level, had survived. And here, dug into gravel and mud, in hole after hole, had sat the regimental and divisional staffs, only a few feet away from the fire-spitting front line. The underground shelter on the sloping banks of the Volga had been the starting point, the turning point, the very spot where the course of events had changed. This had been the limit of the retreats, through Bucovina, Bessarabia, across the Ukraine, the Dnieper, the Don: so far and no further.

So far and no further!

Retreats, blows, dust of the glimmering steppe, snow storms, cold, hunger and marching, marching; entrenchment after entrenchment, each hardly erected before it had to be abandoned before the stampeding horses of the invaders. Each defence line, hardly marked on the ground, had been abandoned and the Russian soldier knew nothing but flight. The cloud of dust thrown up by a troop of advancing tanks had been sufficient to drive Ivan and Nikolai and Kyril and Mathwei from their trenches and scatter whole companies of Ivans and Mathweis.

As far as Stalingrad. . . .

As far as the narrow strip along the embankment and the entrenchment nearby.

'This is the limit, the end of retreats! They shall never cross here, not the Volga!' That was 'Cerberus', as the soldiers and officers and generals of the Volga front had called him. Short, fat, round as a ball, a ballooning beret on his head. When, as usual, he looked displeased, company commanders and old sweats had been known to lose their appetites for two weeks afterwards. Enters the Bunker without saying good day or good-bye, maybe drinks a glass of schnapps or maybe not, and leaves again. He comes and is in a bad mood, is always in a bad mood, but he has a hell of a memory, he recognizes everyone. 'How was that, who was that, Grigorij?' his Chief, everybody's Chief Chosain, would ask him and receive the reply: 'That was the fellow we came across in 1936' (or '38 or '41 at Kharkov or Ama-Ata, in the Kremlin or Livadia Palace), 'that was the scoundrel' (or British intriguer or American fat-head) 'who always knew everything better.' What a memory, particularly for people, which often boded trouble for the future.

That was Stalin's plenipotentiary, member of the Supreme Defence Committee of the USSR. Together with Khrushchev, the member for the Stalingrad front, he had come across the waters of the Volga churned up by German shells, had crept into the underground shelter, in a bad mood of course, had pulled a wry face, looked disparagingly at the Fighter Commander Kusnjetzov and the general in command of the tanks, and had said; 'This is the limit: so far and no further! They shall never cross the Volga!'

And Army General Zhukov had found the right word:

'Only over my dead body will they reach the embankment, Comrade Malenkov.'

'It's the end, the end . . .' he said and crawled out of the shelter hole, this hell-hound from the Kremlin, Comrade Grigorij Malenkov.

And it was the end, the end of the Russian retreat. There came the offensive, a chain reaction of offensives. First to the Mius, then to the Dnieper, the Vistula, the Oder-Neisse line – it followed the march through Lusatia and the Spree Forest. The swastika outside the gates of the German General Staff headquarters near Zossen sank into the dust, crushed by Voronov's tanks.

And here he stood; here they stood, Zhukov, Voronov, Kusnjetzov, a few old colonels. Many others, very many others, had fallen by the wayside. So far they had come – after retreat and advance, after cold, wind and snow, right to their goal. The details of the goal before him, now lit up by the detonation, were fixed in Zhukov's mind without the aid of a map. The pocket of resistance on the other side of the Canal was the factory Bunker of a firm called Lorentz. The tall building in American style was the Ullstein house. Further to the right, behind a small hill and also beyond the Canal, was an old hospital comprising many buildings, the roofs and surrounding walls painted with the Red Cross. We shall have to respect that one – just as well, it will serve as H.Q., we shall just brush it over with *katjushas*.*

Tempelhof, the forecourt of the town – from here a straight road as though drawn with a ruler leads to Hallesche Tor and behind Hallesche Tor begins the city centre. From there it will be no further to Hitler's Bunker than the way from the Tverskoi Boulevard to the Kremlin. And the more 'Fritzes' we mow down on the way through Tempelhof and the airport, the less the distance will be. Much Russian blood has been shed, and Ukrainian, Usbek. Kazak; and no Ivan or Pjotr. no Kyril or Achmed wants to die in these last few yards. Once more, my sons, my obstinate, rebellious ones, one more leap, one leap hardly worth mentioning . . . look at it, the largest Continental city – now only a torso – this great European centre, lies beneath your fist, belongs to you;

*Light field guns.

believe me, it is worth it, worth a last effort.

The bridge was blown up. Masonry had fallen. The blinding flash had gone. There remained only the pale fingers of the searchlight batteries, hundreds placed in the ruins, turning the bombed buildings and battered streets into ghosts.

Zhukov turned to his companion: '*Nu wot . . .* Berlin!'

One more word he said:

'*I na nasche pereulokje budit prasdnik!*' In our alley, too, there will be rejoicing!

'There she goes; pity.'

'Yes, what a pity.'

It was a pity; the Russians had crossed the Don, the Dnieper, the Vistula and the Oder – they would easily manage the Teltow Canal.

'They'll get across this stinking ditch without a bridge. I am sick of it all!'

Sergeant Major Loose was sick of it, too. He did not know the corporal by his side; had been only a short while with this mixed unit. His own troop had perished near Lübben. Already on the way to captivity, he had been able to escape, reach Reichsstrasse 96, and then, caught by another troop, had been forced to take part in the withdrawal to the Teltow Canal and the opposite bank.

The corporal was also new to the company, and had every reason to be sick of it. He belonged to the last fighting reserve of the General H.Q. in Zossen, a squadron of two hundred and fifty cavalry men, who had been sent to meet the Russians near Luckau – with machine guns and rifles; with a sword and naked hands against planes and hundreds of tanks. Twenty of the two hundred and fifty got away and reached Zossen. When the twenty-first, this straggler, arrived at Zossen and the German H.Q., there was no longer a guard outside the vast entrance gates. They stood wide open; not a soul was about, only the fir-trees. The whole place had been abandoned. Moving on, he met a retreating troop who picked him up, and thus he, too, had come to the opposite bank of the Teltow Canal.

'I am fed to the teeth!'

'Me too,' said Loose.

'All I want is to get back to my unit.'

'I'm sure you do,' replied Loose. But to find his twenty men would be hard job in this mess. Nothing left except to get out of it; to watch for the right moment. Above the Ullstein house opposite white flags appeared, chalk-white in the light of the searchlights. Gruesomely beautiful, gruesome... the end of an SS unit, the last step of a long march, through snow, fog, whirring missiles, through howling storms in which human beings were the falling leaves, and none of it would have been necessary. To sit by the fire with Emma in his home, that would have been more worthwhile.

Get away ... but the moment had not yet arrived.

Another two days and two nights the agony lasted around the Teltow Canal. That was the time it took the Russians to advance, and yet there was nothing left. Every sixty yards a man stood by the Canal. Further up the big Gottlieb-Dunkel-Bridge was held by a lieutenant and thirty men. The main pocket of resistance, after the Ullstein house had capitulated, was the factory Bunker of the Lorenz works. Loose had been inside it once when he had taken the place of his wounded superior officer and had been glad to get out again. An ante-room to hell – the stench in there had been hardly bearable, all the lavatories blocked and overflowing. Burst pipes – the drainage and water mains destroyed. Field officers and high ranking staff officers, all screaming at one another. At the entrance one of them shouted into a telephone, deamnded cartridges which fitted foreign rifles, demanded tanks and even planes for support. Did he himself believe in such help? Loose could but shake his head at so much foolishness. He decided that most of them were more or less important Party Members who had been put into officers' uniforms. And all of them were drunk; there was enough drink about, plenty of tobacco too, and food as much as anyone could ask for. The huge store of provisions in the building could not be used up in years. But there was no drinking-water, and in the air-raid Bunker there were about three hundred civilians, most of them women and children, even babies, who could not be given schnapps to quench their thirst. The garrison consisted of sick and convalescent, of soldiers unfit for front-line duty; there were fifty men from the Mariendorf Factory Home Guard and another thirty men of the Tempelhof Volkssturm Guard who had neither uniforms nor papers and had been given no useful weapons. Picked up just anywhere, they had been handed captured foreign rifles for which no ammunition existed. This was the main force which stemmed the Russian advance.

Yet two days went by – the streets were clear of people; nobody was to be seen except a few women who ran to the nearest hydrant with their buckets to fetch drinking-water. The Gottlieb-Dunkel-Bridge went sky-high and Russian tanks with infantry appeared this side of the Canal.

Once again evening fell and night came.

In Berlinerstrasse a heavy anti-aircraft gun fired across the Canal towards Reichsstrasse 96. Between this gun and Stubenrauch Bridge which had been blown up two nights earlier, there lay a lieutenant with a handful of men – one of them Sergeant-Major Loose; another, the survivor from the mounted unit of Zossen. A ditch across the road with walls made of sandbags, a trap from which only death or captivity could result.

'Do you want to be taken prisoner?' Loose asked the corporal.

The hour of the Lorenz Bunker had come. From the opposite bank infantry were firing continuously with countless guns. Searchlights caught the buildings. From the direction of the Gottlieb-Dunkel-Bridge tanks were firing.

'Another candidate,' said Loose.

An officer came out of the Lorenz Bunker, staggered towards the Canal and stood there, erect and chalk-white in the searchlight, then put the gun to his head and fired.

'They are going completely crazy over there, what with the schnapps and all that. So, you don't want to be a prisoner, neither do I', Loose said to the man at his side. 'When the moment comes, jump for it! But in good time, mind you; once the Russian stands before you and shouts *daway*, it is too late.'

Rifle fire, exploding mines, and the twenty-five pounder started up. The Russians were aiming at the Lorenz factory and the whole area around it. The top floor of the factory was ablaze, flames shot out of the windows. Already another suicide stood by the Canal holding a gun to his head.

Further back the end had already come. The heavy anti-aircraft gun was silent. A man who had been sent there returned and reported: 'Lost – all dead except one, and he is out of his mind, doesn't answer.'

This is the moment, the moment . . . Loose thought.

The moment arrived with an exploding shell. Earth, paving stones, splinters covered the ditch, for seconds nobody could breathe. Loose felt something hard hit his shoulder. He clenched his teeth.

'Now or never . . .'

He nudged the corporal, came out from under cover, jumped backwards, darkness enveloped him. He ran a few feet, threw himself down, a few more steps and down again. He felt blood on his hand; it dripped from his sleeve. He touched the arm gingerly. He was able to move it, it could not be very bad. He waited for the corporal. But the man did not come and the Russian machine gun began to rattle again. A twenty-five pounder, too, seemed to aim at the ditch. Sooner than he had thought – it won't be more than fifteen minutes now, maybe less! Pity – he would have liked to take the chap from the mounted unit with him – couldn't be helped. A nagging regret remained – one does not leave others in the lurch at moments like this. There was discord in his heart; he was in a quandary – he was a sergeant-major but he was also something else. He had to overcome his scruples.

Es war einmal ein treuer Husar – once there was a faithful soldier. . . . Now to creep along the wall. . . . But that leads to Tempelhof and on to Belle-Alliance Platz, which means not in the direction of Magdeburg. Yet, the longest way is sometimes the shortest. He groped his way along the wall, but had not gone far before he saw the battered anti-aircraft gun and also the man of whom the reconniassancé chap had spoken. He sat on the gun-carriage, the corpses of the crew strewn around. Fists pressed to his forehead, he hardly looked up as Loose addressed him. Apparently he had not been wounded. 'Get going, the Russians will be here soon.' Unmoving, the man fixed Loose with his stare. Not the light of the moon but the flashes of the twenty-five pounder were reflected in those dead fish-eyes. Mad . . . Loose could not waste time. He made one more attempt, then gave up and leapt back as the searchlight blinded him. The white light had only streaked across the gun, but it shone straight on to the ditch ahead of him. This was it, a white rag fluttered from the wall. Loose saw hands held high and watched them climb out of the ditch, one after another.

Auf Wiedersehen, my friends, au revoir until after the war; beneath the big clock at Potsdam Station; that was still a long way away. He reached Kaiser-Wilhelmstrasse, tried to find his way, had to take shelter again, had only moved past two or three houses. He was standing in the entrance of a house when suddenly he started as though somebody had hit him.

'Where do you come from?'

Illuminated by the flickering lights around and the unearthly reflections, he saw a dim figure. He knew that face; it was the cracked Major with the crippled arm who, waving his pistol under people's noses, was a menace for miles around. What a fool to have forgotten him and the pocket of resistance he had established with men he had picked up.

'Do you come from that trench over there; are they your men?'

'Take that thing away first, Herr Major. It makes me nervous. My own unit was smashed outside Lübben. Over there in the ditch I managed to get away at the last moment.'

'Well done, Sergeant-Major. Better come along with me.'

Loose had no choice. The trench ahead of him had been taken. The anti-aircraft gun was a goner. Lorenz Bunker finished. Now he was made to crawl into a demolished tram car. That was the front line here, and was meant to stop an army. A whole army, so it seemed, and this fanatic Major was intent on personally changing the course of the Battle of Berlin. Oh Emma, the road to Magdeburg grows longer and longer!

Under collapsed lamp standards, under dangling wires, wrapped in barbed wire, surrounded by iron rails, this former conveyance sat like a spider in its web. A barricade of rubble and a removal van loaded with sandbags completed the outfit. The Major at any rate believed that this heap of sand and iron and paving stones was a suitable bulwark of resistance, a sort of advanced fort for the shelter he was occupying, only a small section of which was visible.

On arriving in Berlin, Major Hasse had met his father in Hermsdorf (the rest of the family was scattered all over

Germany), had then gone to the reserve hospital Tempelhof to convalesce and when the front moved towards Berlin from the south, had put himself at the disposal of the nearest unit – a combat group from Reichsstrasse 96.

A 'Stalin organ' hissed, pale lights flickered through the world of ruins. High up, fighters hummed. Windowless house-fronts showed up in the flash of explosions. Hasse had seen all this before. Not during his last assignment in Greece, but two years ago, out East. The same ghostly toothpick-world, and there as here people cowered and died under heaps of ruins. There had been no bread, no medicines, in-sufficient supplies. As a casualty he had been taken off by a transport plane with the same wounded arm that troubled him now. The town in the fighting line two years ago had been Stalingrad; now it was Berlin. And here, if anywhere, was the time and place where the categorical commandment ordered everyone, militia men and all, to join the fellowship and fight to the death.

'Sergeant-Major Loose . . .'

But this was hardly the moment to remind his newly recruited sergeant-major of this old soldiers' maxim, and Loose did not answer. He had to take over the machine gun. His face the colour of mud, his uniform torn; they all looked like that. They needed a fight, they needed the rattling and clanking of the machine gun as a drug-addict his drug. Without this constant stimulus, without the danger, without the ever repeated *Urrah*, they would fade away, curl up like sleepy caterpillars. We are all worn out. We shall have a good sleep when we have won the victory.

Under Loose's hands the machine gun trembled.

In the darkness a fluttering movement – shadowy shapes through the fog covering the nocturnal moors; brown they were and took shape only when a light caught them and they fell on their faces. Hard to believe that they were called Nikita, Kyril, Ivan, Anton; they they had been eating *kasha* and moist bread and smoked *machorka*; that they made a row sometimes and sometimes listened to the accordian playing and sang sad songs. They fell, and from behind scattered lumps of concrete others rose, more and more of them, there was no end of them; impossible to shoot them all.

'We can stand here, stick our neck out and get shot,'

Loose managed to say, 'but at least we ought to know what we are dying for.'

'What was that, Sergeant-Major?'

'At least one ought to know!'

'Here, in Berlin . . .'

The Stalin Organ made its infernal noise, and what good was it to say to oneself that the beastly things were not so bad, that their hellish noise was meant mainly to demoralize. It just won't work, they drive one out of one's mind.

'Surely here, before Berlin, in Berlin, everybody should know what he is fighting for, Sergeant-Major!'

'I don't know it – soon I shall have forgotten my own name, Herr Major.'

The handing-over of the Lorenz Bunker seemed to have been completed. Volkssturm Home Guard, Home garrison soldiers, Works Guards, civilians, all of them walked along, their hands above their heads, and disappeared in the darkness. A searchlight battery probing for new objects, seized the machine gun nest inside the tramcar and did not let go again.

'We can't hold out much longer, Sergeant-Major!'

'We should have given up long ago, sir.'

'No, this is the end, back into the cellar.'

'Yes, straight into the mousetrap.'

Loose covered the retreat. He waited until he thought the handful of men would have reached the shelter. Then he crept after them, together with the crew of the machine gun who were taking it with them. Loose held back, remained lying by the kerb and watched the others disappear into the entrance hole. He had made up his mind. He did not creep up to the cellar but past it. *Es war einmal ein treuer Husar.* . . . This time no madman should stop him from following the straight course. The 'straight course' led to the next street, round the corner, then, with one leap, into one of the ruins, and on till he reached the reserve hospital 122. Past the hospital entrance (he was not going to be involved with the guard), then through a breach in the wall into the garden, through yet another hole and through a wide gap into the interior of the hospital.

He found himself in a long corridor. At the end of it a candle was burning. A lonely candle in a room, underneath it an empty table; nothing else, not a soul around. A second candle led him to stairs leading into a cellar. He went down and found himself in a vault, the ante-room to a labyrinth of underground corridors; doors were being opened, a dim light could be seen and here it smelt of hospital. A nurse with a trolley full of bandages stopped, Loose showed her the blood which had congealed on his hand. It did not look bad. However, he was anxious to get a bandage, the thicker the better, and that with the appropriate casualty certificate would serve him as identity card. The nurse was going to send him on, to another section, she said, where outpatients were treated.

'All I want is a sticking plaster, and then I want to get on', Loose explained. She asked where he came from.

'From the Canal', Loose replied.

'And what is it like there?'

'The Russians are there.'

'Oh well then, let me see – come with me.' These words were spoken by a young doctor who was passing by. The nurse took him into the examination room, made him take off his tunic and push his shirt sleeve up. The doctor examined the wound. A splinter in the flesh – it really wasn't bad. He picked the splinter out and left the nurse to finish the job.

The doctor was still very young. He had a pale face and dark rings under his eyes, and appeared to be as exhausted and tired as the soldiers outside.

Assistant doctor Theysen had watched that very day – near the Teltower Damm in Zehlendorf – a rifle brigade battalion march past. Recruited old men, nearly all of them grey-haired, many without weapons. In loose formation they had walked along. Three men together, five men, then one alone, and many had sat down on the pavement in order to rest before moving on. Where they were heading for, they did not know. All they knew was that they had received their last rations twelve hours ago. 'What is the use of it, Doctor, we are all of us too tired even to run away when it comes to it', one of them had told him.

'When do you think the Russians will be here?' The doctor turned to Loose.

'Any moment now, Doctor. I was afraid they had come already. There is nothing left between the hospital and the Russians.'

'Would you like a brandy?'

The doctor poured one out . . . 'We have plenty. Our Chief reckons the Russians will be here soon and has given orders to distribute all alcohol, insisting that it is drunk.'

In the circumstances Loose drained another and yet another. At the door the doctor turned round and said:

'Take the bottle with you.'

Loose did not have to be told twice. He put the bottle into his pocket.

'A generous physician.'

'Yes, our assistant doctor', replied the nurse. 'He has only just arrived from the front, the Western front. He is the son of the Chief Medical Officer. Actually this is the eve of his wedding; tomorrow he is going to marry one of the nurses here.'

'He has not arranged that very well – the Russians will be his wedding guests. No wonder he looks pale.'

Loose left the place in the same way as he had come. In the garden he followed a number of bearers who were collecting the dead and carrying them to the farthest corner of the grounds to bury them. This was the most suitable hour for it. They, too, had drunk enough brandy that night and it did not worry them whether they carried corpses who had been identified by the administration department and who were laid, two at a time, head to foot, or whether their burdens were those intended for the mass grave left by the bombing as an unrecognizable entanglement of flesh and bits of uniform. One of the wards was ablaze. The rockets from a 'Stalin Organ' fanned the dying fire and provided illumination. Loose left the grave-diggers behind and once again faced a wall. This time he had to climb it. His way led through a park, then through allotments, bombed-out houses – a modern estate where only the chimney stacks and surrounding walls were left.

At the other edge of this nocturnal desert stood the reception hall and the hangars of the airport. Sudden gunfire caused Loose to change his course and try a detour round Tempelhof airport. After a while he could hear only a distant rumbling, and when he looked round he saw the flickering of gunfire reflected in the clouds. He passed through dead streets, through allotments, a cemetery, areas of desolation.

He was by now in the outskirts of the town. Heaps of debris, no streets visible in the blanketing dust; not a soul to be seen. He had to go on; but: where? Towards Magdeburg – was it still possible? What direction, and how was he to get through the tank blockade? Opportunity is there for those who look for it, and luck is with him who dares: 'It's better to be lucky', Emma used to say. Not very far from here, during a meeting on the Hasenheide, was where he had first met her. Too silly that she had to be stuck in Magdeburg just now! Perhaps it was too late to get out of Berlin. In that case he had to get hold of some civilian clothes, had to get hold of trousers, a jacket, a hat. Atze, Willi, Paule – none of them was there any more. They had all flown. And the rest had dug themselves in so deep nobody could get at them. Loose had his story ready. Admittedly, he had been a sergeant-major in Hitler's army, but he had once been a member of the 'Kommune'. Only an ordinary member, without office, that was why he had been able to take cover in another town and had not been molested. Later he had been conscripted, had taken part in half the campaign in the East and in all the retreats from the Don to the Oder and Neisse, until his unit had been defeated. He had his story and also another special reason for avoiding Russian captivity. Well, it should be possible to rake up a shirt and trousers somewhere in this gigantic heap of rubble. In some house or other, from some reasonable person; they must still exist in Berlin, they can't all be block-heads. The thing is not to slip on the cocoon too soon, to wait for the right moment. Until then all that mattered was to avoid the patrols.

Avoid, avoid!

He had seen enough. The court-martial is always round the corner, and even the schoolboys have steel helmets clapped on their heads. Neither T.B., nor a stiff leg, nothing can save you; the small bandage round his arm means nothing at all; he has no exemption certificate to show them. Therefore: avoid, avoid!

Not a sign of life, no flicker of light, however small, in this vast darkness. A dead city, where can they all be? The night sky without a cloud; shells of houses and glistening stars above. Loose stepped up to an iron balustrade and looked down. Below shone black water. It was the Landwehr Canal;

he would stick to it, walk along it up to the Tiergarten. And there, by Bellevue Station, he knew a caretaker's flat. And if the old woman were still alive, he would find help there; a hide-out, even a suit of clothes. Until then – caution.

The stars above the ruins grew paler. The sky looked already like grey cotton wool. He must get across the bridge, then past Hallesche Tor. First he must have a good look round. Day was breaking, more caution needed.

And then it happened:

'Your pay-book; papers!'

It was an army patrol. A sergeant-major and two men.

'And where is your unit?'

'Finished, over there in Tempelhof.'

'All right, come along to the collecting point.'

That was not so good; anything but good; but he had to go, to the collecting point in Lindenstrasse. They left the bridge behind and went around Belle-Alliance Platz. In the middle of the square the tall column of peace, commemorating the battle of Waterloo, rose into the grey day. At its top Victoria, wearing the laurels of victory, looked towards Tempelhof.

In Tempelhof firing started again after a brief spell of rest. For Hasse's unit, for the reserve hospital 122, for the airport, for the whole of Tempelhof, this was the end. The SS-garrison from the Ullstein House, the cannon fodder and the Mariendorf works guard from the Lorenz Bunker, the home guard troops from the Teltow Canal, accompanied by Cossacks on shaggy ponies, were already marched along to Reichsstrasse 96 – a long road which for many of them was to be a road without an end.

Out of Hasse's shelter, amongst sandbags that had been pushed over and put up again, there showed the muzzle of a machine gun. It only fired at lengthy intervals. Hasse was not surrounded by soldiers only, just as in the Lorenz Bunker, there were civilians, women, old men, even children. They sat or lay on the floor, without food, with little water; there was no light and the stock of candles was dwindling. They had to relieve nature where they lay. In front of the cellar door lay the unattended wounded. The air was stale. Blood, excrements, pus; the stench mingled with the reek of gun-powder.

Underneath the layer of dust, sweat and gunpowder Hasse was white – as white as a negro can become through un-speakable fear. He breathed heavily, his chest felt tight; a restless panic drove him through the cellar, again and again he chased his men out of dark corners.

The thought of his father at Hermsdorf had to sustain him. The father, short, grey-haired, undefeated – thus he had left him a few days ago. 'We need you, we all do, and mother most of all', the father had said to him. 'But your decision to volunteer with your arm still in a sling, that shows what stuff you are made of!' The old man's throat had been dry when he spoke the words, and he himself had tried to shorten the farewell. His father had caught up with him at the garden gate.

'Nothing can change it, Wolfgang, victory is ours if we remain steadfast and don't give way!' Those had been the last words with which he had sent him on his journey.

The white flag. . . .

Never!

Outside the bark of an explosion. The sandbags tumbled once again; dust hit the cellar vaults and penetrated into the farthest corners. A hole yawned at ground level and had to be filled in. It had to be done whatever the cost. He managed it; two men helped him. The machine gun again stuck its barrel through the slit and resumed its rat-tat-tat. All were far away, the whole family scattered – only the father re-mained at Hermsdorf, and Agnes was in Berlin, too, sat in this rattling hell, in some hole with the Werewolf. Surrender? Never – he wouldn't be put to shame by Agnes.

'It is hopeless, Herr Major!'

Hasse looked up; a man stood before him, a face with spectacles. A few of his soldiers crowded also round him. What did they want? The bespectacled civilian was the spokesman.

'Major, it is useless.'

'Surrender!' said another.

'Never – to the last shot!'

It was too late – the door flew open. Men, women; women with children in their arms; women and soldiers; a huge wave rushed past him and carried him with it into the street.

Hands held high, in the air white rags.

The Russians.

'Who is *starsche*?' one of them asked.

Who is in charge; who had defended the shelter so doggedly; he demanded to know. He did not have to ask twice. An empty space formed around Hasse. A Red Army soldier raised his fist and felled him. Another, the same who had asked the question, pointed his pistol at the fallen man as he tried to raise himself and shot him in the neck.

'That's for you', he said. And to the women: 'Women go home, children go home!' And to the others, including the civilians amongst the men: '*Nu daway!*'

With the still smoking muzzle he pointed towards the Canal, in the direction of Reichsstrasse 96.

'This is just it – the empty space in the centre provides a first-class firing position and the trees around it are a perfect screen.'

No sooner thought than done.

The battery commander, mounted on his horse, rode through the main entrance of reserve hospital 122. The sergeant-major and the gunners followed with two 15 centimetre field howitzers. Arrived at the clearing in the middle of the hospital grounds they unlimbered. They had not got far with their preparations when the Chief Medical Officer of the hospital, Medical Superintendent Dr. Theysen, approached, accompanied by his sergeant-major and the duty sergeant.

'I think you've made a mistake, Captain.'

'A mistake?'

'What do you think you are doing? Can't you see the Geneva Red Cross on the walls? It's large enough!'

'That is out of date now. You don't understand, sir, what war means nowadays.'

'We have two thousand wounded in this building. We are under the protection of the Red Cross. We cannot permit fighting troops in our grounds.'

'This is where we unlimber and that is all there is to it.'

The sergeant-major intervened. He seemed about ready to let the captain have it. But to begin with he addressed the duty sergeant. 'Those people don't seem to care how many wounded go up in smoke here.'

'Never mind, Sergeant-Major. We shall settle that soon enough.'

The Chief Medical Officer and his companions returned to their quarters. Dr. Theysen grabbed the telephone. It took him more than two hours before he got through to the Commanding Officer of the competent division.

'It cannot be done on any account, Herr General. We are here under the protection of the Red Cross. I have to think of my wounded.'

'Well then, throw the brute out!'

'That is not so easy, the Battery Commander is most aggressive and I can't force him to go.'

'All right then, get him to the phone and I'll let him have a piece of my mind.'

Dr. Theysen sent for the Battery Commander. The medical sergeant who handed the receiver to the captain noticed that the Battery Commander got a very severe castigation from his Divisional Commander. The battery disappeared from the hospital grounds, and the affair was finished.

The danger to reserve hospital 122 was to come from another quarter. Its proximity to the Lorenz Bunker and the three-day defence of this factory proved fatal; the hospital was drawn into the battles which raged around the Lorenz factory.

Bombs, shells, even salvoes from the 'Stalin Organ' apparently meant for the Lorenz factory, showered on to the hospital.

The hospital was overcrowded, it had eight hundred beds, and in addition, it had at the last moment accommodated the evacuated wounded from outlying points, from Mariendorf and Schlageterschule. More than two thousand patients lay in the various wings of the hospital.

And now it was under fire!

Everyone down into the cellars! Temporary beds, between beds, in the corridors, on the floor. Makeshift. Dire need. Everything had to be provisional, even burying.

The wounded, first from the Ullstein House, later from the Lorenz Bunker, from the Teltow Canal, from Berlinerstrasse, from the area Attila Platz to Gottlieb-Dunkel-Bridge, staggered into the hospital turned field dressing station or were carried in on stretchers. The Chief Surgeon, senior medical officers and assistants, men in rubber aprons and with rolled-up shirt sleeves, worked with scissors, knives and saw, bound arteries, sawed through bones. Stench of wounds, stale air, candlelight. They operated in candlelight, and on the outskirts of Berlin was repeated what had happened in all field dressing stations since Stalingrad, Mius, by the Don and the Dnieper, all over the East. Blood dripped from the operating tables, under foot it became mud; it dried no longer. The surgeons became labourers, worked without respite, day and night. Only strong coffee kept them going. Outside, the Lorenz works burned, the light of the flames was reflected in the hospital grounds, flickered on the walls of the buildings. The surgeons went on working; the nurses, too. But others, orderlies, administrative staff, nurses and some lightly wounded, patients from the nose and throat section, left the buildings in their hundreds. Who could stop them, or not understand them – however senseless their panic-stricken flight? But Tempelhof or Alexander Platz, or the Führer Bunker – the same fate awaited them everywhere.

A new day dawned.

In the subterranean vaults and communicating corridors day was as night. Candlelight. Moaning. Dying. A bomb had dropped on to a mass grave and torn it open, scattering the bodies. In the wards they put the dead in the corridors. The rows grew longer. The orderlies and porters no longer dared go into the garden. The dead had to wait.

The following night brought the end. The sergeant approached from the direction of the front gate. 'The Russians are here, sir, they say the officer in command is to come out.'

The Chief Medical Officer, Dr. Theysen, took his scalpel with him. The Head of the Psychiatric Section accompanied him voluntarily. In the garden stood three Russians, one officer and two men with their automatics cocked.

'Hands up!'

Dr. Theysen only managed to lift one hand, the one holding the scalpel; his left arm was stiff, an old wound from the last war. 'I have nothing, no arms', he managed to say.

'You Chief?'

'Yes, Chief Medical Officer.'

The officer, a young lieutenant, came nearer, stretched out his hand to Theysen as a greeting and said: 'Come.'

Come – nothing else. The sergeant-major and the psychiatrist, Dr. Schott, remained behind. They watched the three Russians cross the garden with their Chief; watched them climb through a hole which the tanks had made in the wall and disappear in the night torn by the flashes of gunfire.

Some hours later Dr. Theysen returned, accompanied by the same Russians. At the gate he met the duty sergeant and his adjutant, an elderly major. He sent a message that he had returned to Dr. Schott and his colleagues in the medical quarters and also to his wife and son who worked at their respective stations. 'First of all, Herr Wegemann, all weapons are to be collected and side arms are to be given up.' He himself only wanted to be alone, and this time he did not go to the vault of the disinfection department.

He went to his own flat in the Chief Medical Officer's house.

There he stood in the darkened room, by the open window. It was a night with a star-studded sky. The air was soft, a Spring night as beautiful as a dream. The war, then, had passed him by. The hospital had been left behind like a forgotten island. In the streets right and left the stragglers flowed past. Reichsstrasse 96 and Berliner Chaussee and Berlinerstrasse had become the advance routes. Field howitzers, tanks, men on foot, Panje carts . . . only a stone's throw from his window they rattled and stumped through the flickering glare towards the centre of the town. An unending snake, so full that it bulged and overflowed into the side streets. Cars with engine trouble and punctures; or parked because there was a jam in front and a passage had had to be left in the middle for urgent transport. In the quiet side street too, where the Chief Medical Officer's house stood, and in the park opposite cars were parked. Under the trees showed the glimmer of campfires. Against the park wall shadows moved. The torn walls and the solitary-looking chimney stacks of the burnt-out flats were lit up again by the flashes from distant detonations. Dr. Theysen had noticed earlier the noise of battle from the direction of the airport and had seen flickering gunfire as he returned through the trees. From time to time rattling bursts of fire from the machine guns and the red hot splash from mortars had forced him to the ground; between times, with his companions he ran, threw himself down, then ran again, and in this way had reached the hospital.

He was ready to drop and needed rest in order to be able to face the trials of the coming day, but sleep would not come.

He stood by the window, heard a shot below. A figure collapsed below his window. Another shot, and a second figure, a woman, fell forward hit her forehead on the paving stones and lay still. A match flickered briefly – somebody was lighting a cigarette. The fire beneath the trees had burned down and was now only a faint glimmering. It was not only the night that made the indifferent cigarette-smoker and the shadows huddled beneath the trees seem like lemurs.

Theysen withdrew from the window. Without lighting the candle he had put ready, he lay down on his bed. He had been led into the cellar of one of the blocks of flats which were dotted amongst the deserted allotments. He had been kept waiting and had then been questioned by a major who spoke fluent German. A high-ranking officer was also present, a general dressed simply in a private's tunic, with greying hair and lithe active movements. He remained in the background, hidden by the shadow of the lamp but in a position to watch the face of the man being questioned.

The actual questioning had been short, but this in itself may have been significant. It concerned the preparations for the handing-over of the hospital. The major also asked whether he had been a party member, how long, since when had he been Chief Medical Officer, and had he been East during the war. Regarding the hospital, he wanted to know how many beds there were, how many wounded, how many of those could walk, and how many prominent party members were among the patients and the staff. He showed an interest also in the amount of provisions, the equipment, particularly the surgical outfit. At last he inquired about the villa, as he called the Chief's official residence, the number of rooms and the furnishing. The general in the soldier's tunic got up and went out without a word. The same two

Russians who had fetched him accompanied him back after he had explained that he could not return alone across the Russian-held territory.

Theysen must have slept for a while. He woke suddenly and returned to the still open window. Salvoes of the 'Stalin Organ' flashed across. Over Tempelhof airfield shells burst. Rifle shots cracked. The battle for the airport was in full swing, spread out from the large reception building, and jumped and raged in the endless sea of ruins behind.

On the pavement below his window lay the man and the woman. Whence had they come – risen giddily from terror and fled, straight into the mouths of the lemurs' pistols? They lay there and did not stir. By the wall shadows squatted. In the distance noise of battle. Ghouls stalking the streets. The stars disappeared. The air was black ashes. From the burnt-out powder, from weaving smoke a swaying chimera rose half-way to the sky, assumed shape, bent down to the bleeding hem of the city, armless, handless, swinging the scythe.

With the picture of the sweeping scythe, Theysen awoke the next morning. Before him stood the duty sergeant and outside his deputy, Dr. Kohlhammer, waited. Theysen found himself lying fully clothed on his bed. He had only to put his boots on. The high boots were mudstained and he remembered his last night's journey to the allotments. He called Kohlhammer in; he also looked as though he had not slept.

'Two Commissars are waiting for you in the office', said Kohlhammer. 'They are rather impatient. And some changes are taking place, significant changes.'

Significant changes, very likely. First of all the handing-over of the hospital had to be arranged.

'Changes, Herr Kohlhammer?'

'You will see, Chief. They have been questioning me half the night.'

Kohlhammer too!

With Kohlhammer, Theysen went across to the main building. In the office the two Commissars were waiting, two men in leather jackets.

Changes, that he knew already. And now the questions – or rather orders – hailed down upon him. They were about weapons, provisions, the buildings, the official residence. Stock lists were to be prepared, lists of personnel and material, with the particulars of every individual, and materials divided into sections.

'Beds, chairs, tables, lamps on one paper. Instruments, forceps, scissors, apparatus on another. And where are the weapons? Why not collected? There are far too few. You, Chief Medical Officer, responsible. And you, Kohlhammer, also responsible. With head, you understand.'

'With head – I understand.'

'We shall seek weapons; if we find, you Chief, bang, bang!' He made the gesture of shooting. 'And hospital will set on fire, fire, everything kaput, understand!'

The two Commissars left, taking Dr. Kohlhammer with them. Theysen remained in the office with his adjutant, Major Wegemann, his secretary and the company sergeant-major.

'Now, roll up your sleeves and get going', said Theysen.

It seemed they were going to respect the Geneva flag and it was his job to see that it stayed that way.

'Where are the weapons?'

He was told that the weapons had been collected except those which had been thrown into the reservoir or buried.

'That won't do. All arms must be produced. Herr Wegemann, you'll see to it at once. Sergeant, go and tell the doctors of all divisions and all the assistants I want to see them.'

'That won't be possible, sir.'

'Why not?'

'Because some of the doctors are not in the building.'

Several of the doctors were waiting outside an interrogation room; others were in the street. Doctors, male nurses, walking wounded in institution clothes or in pants and shirt, whatever they stood up in, had been forced to leave the wards and had already stood for hours in the street waiting to be moved away.

'Well then, weapons first; it's got to be done.'

The second item: the lists containing the inventory and names (together with particulars) of everybody in the hospital.

'We badly need some more typists', Theysen said to his secretary, 'get ten or better twenty, Fräulein Kindler.'

A Russian came in carrying a paper with an official stamp. He was to collect half a hundredweight of butter. Another Russian, then a third, all with official papers, all requiring something. No one knew whether their papers were genuine or not, or even what was written on them. However, as they all augmented their requests with cocked pistols, there was nothing anyone could do about it, and they were given what they demanded.

'And what is this, Fräulein Kindler?'

A few folded letters, amongst them a photograph of an elderly man with cropped head and beared, lay on his table.

'Those are the belongings of one of the dead of Berlinerstrasse. The personal data have been passed on for inclusion in the official list of dead. A major who was shot in the neck, he is supposed to have relatives at Hermsdorf.'

More Russians.

Then the paymaster from the supplies section.

'All right, Paymaster. I suppose you have the list of all provisions in stock?'

'No, not yet.'

'It is high time. We need the list urgently.'

'It's going to be out of date very soon.'

'I know; a hundredweight of butter is missing.'

'It is already two hundredweights. You should see for yourself, Chief. The stores are being sacked. They all take what they fancy, and destroy a good deal more in the process.'

Admittedly, the hospital was under the protection of a Divisional Commander. Guards were posted outside, yet many found their way in from the street. Small bent figures, sweating faces, the greyish-brown tunics torn to ribbons. The wards – legs in plaster, beds full of dying, face masks which left only the nose to be seen; they went along into all the rooms and looked around them, unsure of themselves. There could be no question of rape either (one nurse to every two hundred). But they found the kitchen, found the stores. They demanded schnapps.

'You give schnapps.'

'No schnapps here.'

'You lie, hospital always schnapps.'

'What there behind curtain?'

'What in cupboard; what in table drawer?'

'No schnapps.'

Schnapps no longer existed; they had taken care of that. But the gallons of medical alcohol, and the large stocks of surgical spirit had been forgotten.

'Here schnapps, much schnapps!'

For God's sake, what will happen now, half a company of Russian soldiers with severe alcohol poisoning! But the raw spirit agreed with them, even in large quantities; and they drank surgical spirit and eau de Cologne without apparently being any the worse for it. Nor did they have much time. Their officers found them in the corridors of the hospital. They yelled and swore and waved their batons and pistols and chased them off. One more gulp and another; they made off and others came.

'Whatever is all this shooting?'

'Nobody knows, Chief. A little while ago one of the wounded, a lieutenant-colonel, shot himself in his bed, and the chap next to him didn't even notice it with all the noise.'

'Impossible!'

'True, sir', said the duty sergeant. 'The lieutenant-colonel had wrapped the pillow round his head. And half an hour ago four patients wanted to lie down on the terrace. They opened the door and went out and the Russian guard shot them.'

This time the shooting was nearer, outside the gate.

'That is where the wounded are awaiting their movement orders, Chief. Quite a crowd of sightseers are there, too, and when they come too close the guard uses his machine pistol.'

A first lieutenant came in carrying a laundry basket and demanded watches. He waved his pistol about. 'Orders by the Staff – all watchi collect. Deliver in two hours.'

Theysen received the laundry basket and handed it to Major Wegemann. A Russian medical officer with the rank of major came in and greeted his vis-à-vis, the Chief Medical Officer. He looked round the study and noticed a large picture of Hitler on the wall and next to it the portrait of Field-Marshal Hindenburg. 'Oh, not good. Hitler not good.' He took a chair, stepped on it, but did not smash the picture, just turned it round. To Hindenburg he had no objection. Obviously he had never heard of the battle of Tannenberg and the end of two hundred thousand Russians in the Masurian swamps.

'Good man, picture can stay', he said.

Soon after the Major had gone, one of the Commissars entered the room, this time very annoyed and abusive: 'Nothing is being done; nobody does anything. . . . I shall wait five more minutes then everybody will be turned into the street.'

'What is not being done? Who will be turned into the street?'

It turned out that two wings full of seriously wounded were to be vacated. A Russian hospital unit with Russian wounded was to move in. Above ground the buildings were empty but in the upper floors were no beds; also the cellars, full of wounded, were to be vacated.

'I shall see to it myself', said Theysen. However, he got no further than the door when he met the young lieutenant who had taken him to the Russian Staff the previous night.

'Interrogation, at once.'

By the time he got back, it was afternoon.

Outside the gate the walking wounded and some of the nursing personnel were still squatting. For the doctors and nursing staff he had brought an order from the Staff in the allotments to the effect that they were to resume work forthwith. And the hour had not yet struck when the badly wounded would be loaded on stretchers and carried by Russian lorries in an easterly direction, destination unknown. The slightly wounded were allowed to return to their wards.

The machine worked slowly.

Theysen had orders to take care of the evacuation of the cellar wards where the badly wounded lay. He went first to his office. On the way there he met plundering Russians – linen, furniture, books, provisions, everything was looted now without even the pretence of showing official papers. Even medical instruments and equipment he saw in the hands of the drunks. And here he thought he had to intervene. In vain, however; all he could do was to make sure that each piece was catalogued and that, in contrast to the mad looting of everying else, the medical equipment was moved systematically. Just as the collection of the watches appeared to be a systematic measure on orders from the Staff.

The watches had arrived in the meantime. In his office he

found the laundry basket half filled, not only with watches, but also with insignia, medals and badges; even a golden Party badge lay among the gold and silver watches. The statutory two hours had long passed. Theysen had just been informed about what had happened during his absence when the officer in question entered. A captain; surely that morning he had still been a lieutenant?

'Watchi, watchi', he yelled as he came in with his hand on his pistol holder. Theysen indicated the laundry basket, and the captain's mood changed abruptly.

'Oh you goot man!' he pulled a bottle of Vodka out of his pocket and put it on the table. From another pocket he produced a bottle of eau de Cologne. Theysen had to suffer being thoroughly sprayed with it.

'Goot man, verry goot man!'

Theysen doubted that in this case he had earned the praise. But what was he to do? As Chief or 'Kommandant', as they called him now, he had been elevated to the position of confederate of the robbers. He watched the captain disappear with the laundry basket, but was surprised to see a lieutenant, this time undoubtedly the same he had seen in the morning, enter the room.

'The watches.'

'Already collected.'

'Collected, what does that mean?'

This time it was serious. The lieutenant yelled and drew his pistol. Theysen felt the cold steel touch his neck. He was ready to die if necessary, but not for a silly reason like this; that was asking too much. He lost his temper and shouted back.

That did the trick.

The Russian still called Theysen a saboteur and said that he would shoot him later, but first he had to find out where the watches had got to and was ready to listen to Theysen. It was difficult to make him understand – especially as he was drunk. At last he did grasp what had happened. He pulled Theysen with him, and after a short search Theysen recognized the Russian captain in one of the long corridors.

'That's the one, on the bicycle!' The captain was teaching himself to ride a bicycle in the hospital corridor. The lieutenant leapt at him and pulled him off. At the point of his pistol he chased him to the entrance hall, down the stairs and into the yard. The scene that followed stupefied Theysen completely. The captain ran four or five steps, a shot rang out and he fell into the sand, shot dead by the lieutenant A captain – perhaps he had commanded a company, had led them through snow and deprivations and enemy fire and had entered Berlin as victor. Half an hour of high spirits, a laundry basket full of watches and riding a bicycle in a hospital corridor, and now he lay dead in the sand. A summary execution – and by a young drunken lieutenant. . . .

Theysen went on, past his villa. Heavily loaded lorries, private cars, light tanks, vehicles of all kinds had arrived and crowded round the house. The gates were wide open and Russians, both in uniform and in civilian clothing, many in leather jackets, stood around. They had brought boxes, trunks, carpets, even pictures, and carted them into the the house. A troop of women, just arrived and also in uniform, looked entirely different from the robust policewomen Theysen had already seen; they seemed to belong to a different species. Young women (the policewomen had been young, too), but these were well made up, wore high elegant boots, had shoulder bags of leather, some as many as three. One, who wore a Major's insignia, had long red fingernails and smoked a black cigar. The woman's face was powdered, but badly; her skin was dry and grey like that of night workers who never see the sun. She handed her belongings to a soldier and went past Theysen. He wanted to go in, too; after all it was his house and he still had some personal things, and papers there. It was difficult to get through; men in leather jackets stood around everywhere. They were officers, even high-ranking officers, but Theysen noticed that too late: a sinister assembly. He had almost reached his house; in front of him was the woman with the painted nails, standing on the steps she appeared even taller to him. She half turned, pulled at her cigar and looked at him. The scythe. . . .

This time it passed him by. He was but one of the curious, but that alone, he knew, might have been enough. Someone grabbed him and he was pulled into the house. In the hall stood a table and behind it sat an armed official with papers and writing things before him. It resembled the admission room of a prison. He was indeed – as he was soon to learn –

in the Special Branch of the army which was at that moment moving into his house. And the woman outside, the one with eyes like an owl and unhealthy skin, like the other highly painted creatures, was one of the GPU's female interrogators.

At the other end of Berlin, on the road which leads further north part Oranienburg, lies the suburb of Hermsdorf. A colony of villas, next to it straight roads with modest small houses and red tiled roofs, with front gardens and window boxes, amid groups of gnarled fir trees. A few thousand people lived here, workmen who travelled daily into Berlin, retired civil servants, shop assistants, small shopkeepers, teachers at colleges, and amongst them Professor Hasse.

Old Hasse had fallen out not with himself but with the world. It seemed to him there were fewer and fewer now, of the straightforward, honest, clean-living and strong, the people ready to sacrifice themselves for a cause. There were too many shirkers who wavered and fled when the situation became tricky. Even his Berliners, he hardly knew them any more. Unfriendly, nervous, no longer kind and helpful, no one able to say a word or the others would fly at their throats. The bombing war was a test and not everybody passed the test. Admittedly, it was terrible; whole towns had already been wiped out and the refugees from the bombed areas carried the poison of disintegration through the land. So much excitement, bitter feelings, panic – and all this the work of Churchill, the man who by ill-advised propaganda was made to appear ridiculous instead of being taken seriously. This Churchill was indeed the devil in human form, and it was unimaginable madness that a man like him should be free to speak and act and nourish the hope that he might force us to our knees as in 1918. One had to keep one's head.

Never mind – too unpleasant.

Once again it was the 22 April 1945, the day when the ring round Berlin began to close, when the Russians had left Zossen behind in the south and appeared at the Teltow Canal; the night before the Sunday when the Russians lay in allotments outside Herzberg Bunker and pushed forward past Oranienburg in the north.

Professor Hasse sat at the table in his kitchen-cum-living-room, his old cropped head in his hands. The oak top of the table seemed to have become an instrument for receiving and registering distant noises; it trembled continuously. He had already noticed it the previous day but had thought it a hallucination. . . . That was such an obvious explanation; after all, we do live in an era of hallucinations, in small matters as well as great. The official propaganda is always right and deviations of opinion cannot be tolerated. His own deviating opinions of Roosevelt, Churchill, Teheran and Yalta, for instance, were unacceptable. Already prepared lectures – invitations, too, from the Army Command in the North-East and the SS-Junker School in Tölz – had to be put on ice; they were postponed again and again 'in view of the general situation', so he was told, first by four weeks, then by another four weeks, then indefinitely.

Know-alls, shirkers!

Never mind. . . .

The distant noise, the reverberating table top, they were no hallucinations; he could no longer believe that. He rose and went into the garden. There was only a distant rumble, far away behind the horizon. It was difficult to determine the direction unless one was prepared to point in a half-circle from Oranienburg via Bernau to Rüdersdorf and assume a sector of almost one hundred and eighty degrees, and he did not want to do that. Heaven help us, that would be enough to drive anyone mad!

Once again he sat in his kitchen.

All alone in the house, the children scattered all over the world. Walter conscripted, Jürgen Junior Leader in a KLV camp, Almut at Godesberg, Edda in Obersdorf with mother; only Wolfgang, his beloved eldest, was in Berlin and had reported for duty at the front straight from convalescence in the Tempelhof hospital. This is a fact of which I am particularly proud, and about this and the true test of character and the future career of an officer I shall write him a long letter when life has become calmer. Agnes, too, had stayed in Berlin and does her duty as a German maiden with the Werewolf battalion 'Adolf Hitler'. As for mother, he himself has talked her into the journey to the Allgäu. It had been more than necessary after the trials of a year without a maid, after the continuous annoyances with the clumsy Ukrainian home help, after the endless chase after food and the strain of unending packing and sending-off parcels. Lately she had hardly been bearable, with all this talk of hers. He had had to listen to all the whispers circulating in the neighbourhood; so much nonsense, lack of courage, defeatism! In such a poisoned atmosphere even the strongest was in danger of cracking up. He could not expose himself to that danger and, after all, mother's journey was clearly the outcome of what Goebbels had done to him and all good Berliners years ago, in August 1943, when he issued that panic decree. That leaflet urging the part evacuation of Berlin had been grist to the mill of the faint-hearted. Now the poison of disintegration could run through Berlin and was spreading. The panic was almost complete, it had reached the Ministries which were in a state of disintegration. Even the broadcasting authorities had run away then – to Königsberg, Vienna, Luxembourg and Stuttgart, until an order from the Führer had put an end to all that nonsense and called them back. Well then, let mother stay where she was. If the Ministry officials behaved so stupidly, how could a simple woman like his Auguste be expected to be more sensible? She was run down and the bracing mountain air would do her good; by the time she returned the worst would be over and she would have built up her strength sufficiently to cope again.

He was alone. The Ukrainian home help had been given notice because of a particular scheme for the execution of which he needed to be without witnesses. He waited until the clock in the living-room struck twelve, and even then he remained sitting for a while. I believe in victory as strongly as ever, he said to himself, but all the same I must take certain precautions. I shall do it in anger and yet laughing. He pulled on his Wellingtons, put on the old crumpled hat and went out. He had already chosen the scene for his plan. Spade in hand, he now began to dig a pit. He was quite methodical, the measurements were four feet by five feet four inches. A painstaking task, even in the Brandenburg sand and from time to time he had to stop and rest. It was so dark now that the large branch overhanging the pit was no longer visible. The distant rumbling had ceased. The night was more peaceful that it had been for a long time. The Russians had advanced far, but not too far. Surely the high-ups in front of their maps with the red and blue flags knew what was to be done, and if the Ninth Army by the Oder, strengthened by the legions of the SS, manages to free its right arm and grip, a hell of a lot of fun may result – what a catch that will be!

Old Hasse turned the last sod.

The pit was deep enough. He went into the house to fetch the trunk. The trunk had been prepared, first of all the uniforms and civilian belongings of Wolfgang had gone in, and a few things of sentimental value from Wolfgang's childhood. There was still room, and he cleared his desk and added a few manuscripts, amongst them the script of the lecture for the SS-Junker School in Tölz which he had not been able to deliver. Off the wall in his study he took this and that, two cavalry pistols from the Turkish wars and a helmet, not exactly a Carolingian piece but pretty old, a Bavarian Rumford helmet from the eighteenth century. He added all these to the things in the trunk. Then he locked it and lugged it into the garden. Darkness lurked. He could not see his hand in front of his face. 'The darkest hour before the dawn', he quoted and this time he laughed grimly. He was on the verge of collapse, but the trunk now rested in the pit. He wrapped roofing felt around it and put some corrugated iron on top, then boards and earth, and the task was done. Tomorrow, I shall tackle Auguste's trunk. I shan't give in; I shan't weaken. The darkest hour is indeed before the dawn – this time the sharp-witted Goebbels had hit on an expression which appealed not only to reason but also to the heart. Hasse dragged himself rather than walked back to the house. He had got a pain in his side as always after physical exertion. It would pass; he could do with a rest. This time he allowed himself the luxury – no bombers had come over and the night was almost ended – of undressing properly. There he stood in his nightshirt in his almost bare study, bowlegged, his beard untidy, thick white hair on his bare chest, listening to the dawn.

No distant rumbling, but something else.

Gunfire, quite near even!

'Urrah . . .'

What was that?

The shots were so close that the branches of the trees in his garden cracked. The cocks crowed and some geese –

wherever did they come from? – chased through the garden, after them a greyish-brown figure. The figure almost fell when it collided with the fleeing geese. He rose, holding the largest of the fugitives in his arms, and disappeared behind a hedge.

A Russian?

A miracle; a complete mystery.

It was impossible; after all at Oranienburg and by the Ruppiner Canal there were barricades. The Legion Nordland might be occupied further east, but considerable army units and motorized columns as well as the Volkssturm of Hermsdorf, Schönfliess and Birkenwerder were concentrated there.

Nevertheless, it was a Russian, and more were coming. Others appeared from behind the hedge. Troops of them came from the main road, looking at the small white houses with the red brick roofs full of curiosity and acting generally like tourists. And beyond the railway track there rattled and screamed and boomed Wotan's Chase. The dust raised by the motorized columns showered across the roofs into the quiet side streets.

That was no battalion, no regiment; it was a complete army group from the north, the infantry and tanks of General Bersarin who conducted the attack past Oranienburg, Eberswalde and Bernau on the northern boundaries of Berlin. Hermsdorf was nothing but a stop on the way, and the next day it was already the hinterland.

A day and a night, and another day and a night the Russians had been in Hermsdorf, and the third morning dawned. A bright Spring morning, the sun shone. The red flag was hoisted on the town hall. The school had become the quarters of the regimental staff; and the post office, station and other public and private buildings had been occupied by other units.

Horsemen chased along the street and there were countless cycles, lorries, private cars and farmers' wagons parked in the side roads. Hasse's garden had changed, too. The fence was broken, the hedge smashed down: unharnessed horses stood about in the garden, standing amongst them bearded Cossacks with long whips in their hands. From their midst rose a giant of a man with a Cossack's cap, the top of which blazed like a poppy.

In the grounds next door two tanks were parked.

A trumpet signal.

'*Djadja*, little uncle . . .' The one with the poppy-red cap boomed out; a Viking figure that might have come straight out of a picture book. Old Hasse ran eagerly out of the house.

'*Djadja*, you quickly bring schnapps!'

'Have already brought some.'

'More schnapps!'

'No more left.'

'You not lie – you old man soon go to Heaven!' The giant neighed so that the horses even pricked up their ears. What a good joke he had made. But he did not give up.

'You have another bottle, I have seen.'

Old Hasse had to go and fetch the bottle. He had exhausted his meagre supplies, had had to deliver up everything. This one bottle he had put aside, one bottle of old Hennessy, saved for the day of victory, for the day when his eldest son would return. An evil omen indeed to see it flow down the throat of another; he had to watch the giant break off the neck of the bottle on the edge of the wheel, put it carefully to his lips and drain half the contents before handing it on.

It was a farewell drink.

Men ran after the loose ponies, caught, saddled or harnessed them. The engines of the tanks next door started. The regimental signal sounded a second time, and the horsemen and the Panje carts laden with beds, clothes and Hasse's Persian rug, drove across the smashed-down hedge. Outside the house next door the crew climbed into their tanks. And there something unbelievable happened. One of the men carried an unruly burden, a resisting, struggling bundle; it was a woman with flowing hair, wearing next to nothing; he lifted her high and another man on top grabbed her and shoved her through the open hatch into the tank.

Hasse thought he had recognized this woman; he was quite sure of it but could not believe it; how was that possible? The tank rolled away; the second followed. The people on foot, the riders and cars got out of the way. On foot, in cars, on horseback . . . singing, hooting, they all pressed forward. Once again Hasse glimpsed the poppy-red cap, the dark body of the tank in the throng.

Hasse staggered across the forsaken camping ground.

Strewn about in the grass lay empty bottles, debris and torn clothes, a trodden-down military boot. The gentle breeze made the feathers flutter out of slashed eiderdowns.

No longer a miracle, an uncomprehended ghost.

And it is not over; it is coming back.

The first visitor after the Russians' departure and the first news from other parts of Hermsdorf, made that quite clear. The red flag fluttered from the town hall. The station and railway lines were occupied. In front of the town hall they had improvised a smithy where they shod their ponies. Everywhere officers and scattered troops had been left behind. What Hermsdorf had experienced up to now had been a temporary blocking up of troops; the people of Berlin were soon to learn that the worst infliction was not the fighting troops in front but the idle soldiers of the rear. The first visitor who knocked at Professor Hasse's door this morning was old Martha, an eighty-one-year-old refugee from East Prussia. Since her flight she had lived on whatever people had given her. Once a week she came to him to collect her slice of bread. And since there were no longer any newspapers and the wireless would not work for lack of electricity, the old woman was a source of information, at least where Hermsdorf, Frohnau and Waidmannslust were concerned. Her story, how during her flight she had lost her son-in-law (himself sixty years old), and how she had used the corpse to keep interfering Russians from her hide-out; all this was already known to Hasse. This morning she arrived with an overwhelming amount of news, and her old head nodded mysteriously and importantly.

'Well, well,' she said, 'it happened after all.'

'What happened?'

'Well, IT. And the worst is that one is not alone; everyone is watching.'

What did the old hag mean; was she trying to imply that the Russians had raped her? Hasse's expression was one of incredulous amazement.

'What do you know, Professor; not one has escaped, in our road not one. You should have seen the little Steckendorf girl. She had smeared her face all over with jam and stuck breadcrumbs on it, she looked just like a witch. Made no difference, they take witches just the same, tall and small, everything that wears a skirt. And poor Dr. Linth has collapsed; like a dead thing, says the woman who lives below, the wife of the famous actor. You know, the Linths live in their attic. And yet, in the next road nothing happened at all, and a few yards further along, the road where Dr. Linth lives, they were as brutish as in ours.'

'Dr. Linth, what is the matter with him?'

'They have kidnapped his wife.'

That's who it was . . . he had recognized her, the wife of Dr. Linth. He was a doctor both of medicine and philosophy – they had never been very close, not only because of Linth's subject, sinology. Although during the war he seemed to have concentrated more on medicine. Best thing too, it was a full-time occupation. Anyway, they had avoided each other whenever possible except for a nodding acquaintance. He sometimes saw his wife, the last time had been on the way from the station. A young woman still, elegant he might have called her had she shown a little more restraint in her clothes and manner. She had been striking in any event – had been known to visit the Buddhist temple at Frohnau – people turned to look at her. She came from Berlin but might as easily have hailed from Shanghai or Paris.

It was she; the woman this morning.

He certainly was not on friendly terms with the Linths but his duty was clear. He rid himself politely of the old woman and gave her an extra large hunk of bread. Then he was ready: a good deed must not be postponed.

It was a quarter of an hour's walk. He found the house of the old actor-couple. The lady of the house opened the door; she was only a few years younger than old Martha. The husband, too, was seventy but was still able to stand on his hands. This couple did not belong to his circle of friends either, and politically they were as questionable as the Linths upstairs. But on this extraordinary day he could not pass without exchanging a few polite words. The Russians had been in this house, too; several times. Yet, no harm had come to the couple. There was a special reason for this. As an artist, the man had been issued with a so-called letter of protection by the Commandant who was billeted round the corner. The first two Russians had come through the window, a short one and a tall one. The tall one had taken the letter suspiciously and then had read it to the short one; had pointed to a certain passage, and both of them had burst into raucous laughter; after significant glances at the old couple they had disappeared – again through the window. On every visitor this letter had the same effect; throughout two days and nights Dr. Linth's landlord had been able to study all kinds of laughter, from the homeric outburst to tight-lipped grunts; and a whole scale of human feelings, pleasure and sympathy, pity, scepticism and annoyance. The Russians, the landlord said, were all born mimics. The end was invariably the same: all visitors, sometimes several at the same time, left the flat immediately. They did not steal anything and left his wife unmolested. He had only just learned the secret of this wonderful talisman. It was simple enough: 'Just look at her, the spindly old hag,' it said, describing the dignified elderly lady, 'but don't go too close, you son of a dog. This bare broomstick' (and various other adjectives were used as well) 'could once sing like a nightingale and dance like Ulanova and is now under the protection of the Department for Culture. So let her wither and don't you dare touch her! Order from your Commandant: About turn and march. . . . Next door you will find a juicier younger one.'

The talisman had never failed, and only once had one of them not gone on to the next house but had climbed the stairs to Dr. Linth's attic.

'Poor Linth is past talking to anyone', said the old lady. 'He has been sitting for hours in the same spot staring at the wall.'

Hasse went upstairs.

He found a man in an untidy room, everything upside down. The man sat on a chair and seemed unconscious of his surroundings. Even this most unusual visit failed to make an impression on him. Only during Hasse's account of what had happened did a sort of awakening seem to come over Linth. He asked to be told the whole story again. He never doubted for a moment that it had been his wife. And Hasse, too, was quite certain of it. Suddenly Dr. Linth got up and walked to the door. He paused by the opened door as though he were trying to force himself to be calm and move rationally. He thanked Hasse for the news and said that surely there must be a Commandant to whom he could turn for help. He left the house without taking his hat and without looking round.

Yes, there was a Commandant all right, but he was busy with other matters, with the confiscation of provisions and raw materials, with the mobilization of the populace for clearing operations and also with the appointment of a mayor who was to assist him in the execution of these tasks. As a preliminary questioning revealed, this Dr. Linth who had blown into his office had never been a party member. Linth had explained to him what a sinologist was. That made the case still more hopeful; after all, as a Chinese or representative of the Chinese, the man was practically one of the allies, and it seemed that he was the very man to be mayor whether sent by heaven or the devil. 'Ach, wife, not so bad; wife always come back', he tried to calm Linth. 'We will find her or another', he added. Anyway, he had no authority in the matter which was the concern of the Commander who was on his way to Berlin.

Dr. Linth returned to his home.

He had learnt nothing about his wife's whereabouts and had been unable to do anything towards her release; instead he had to decide – and that within two hours – whether to accept the post of mayor of Hermsdorf.

Once again he stared at the wall.

But it was he himself, and not the wall, who had to make the decisions regarding his wife, his own person and his surroundings.

All life is suffering. He had been felled by a blow and left lying unconscious. This was his fate – and also the trials to come. The position of mayor was not to be one of the trials . . . the confusion was too great. The storm does not come without a cause. The buds torn off by it remain torn off.

Dolores . . . a torn off bud?

Linth regarded the wall, lost himself in contemplation of the small Buddha statue on his table. . . . No reply.

Heaven and Earth were silent.

The Berliners had not wished for this, that their houses should turn into burning charcoal kilns, that the tiles of their roofs should drive through the town like a swarm of glowing birds, that tramrails should arch themselves abruptly into the sky, that the gas mains, water pipes and sewers should burst from the belly of the earth, that flaming dust should descend from the sky; they had not wished for this. What city could desire the fate of Pompeii – the living interment under falls of hot ashes? Neither had they desired the ghost in the Bunker in Voss-Strasse, who had but one last messenger to command, the angel with the scourge – destruction and execution.

'Don't you believe that, my boy! At the last almost normal election – you were still in your cradle then – he only got 31.3 per cent votes in Berlin.'

31.3 per cent – medical sergeant Wustmann knew exactly.

'Apart from Cologne and Aachen that was less than anywhere else in Germany. No; Berlin has never wanted him, never given him authority – and to refer to such an authority now is rubbish, I tell you.'

It was a miracle how Sergeant-Major Wustmann found time for such reminiscences. However, in this mad circle he needed some focal point to assure himself that he was still sane. And when the radio was turned on in the Bunker cabin and Goebbels, Fritzsche or Naumann spoke of the task the German people had entrusted to them and that the Party would carry on to the end, Wustmann turned to his young helper Wittstock.

'Don't you believe a word of it, my boy, it is all humbug. And here are a few packets of cigarettes, distribute them. Everybody who carries one of them out of here gets two. Get it?'

Wittstock took the cigarettes and went to look for men who would, for two cigarettes a time, carry a corpse through the long corridor into the street. He only found old people who could hardly stand on their own feet. For several days there had not been any food in the Bunker.

The Anhalter Bunker . . .

Out of the metropolitan line tunnel next to the Reichstag, Heide, Wustmann, Stroh and the helpers had been sent to the aid of the field dressing station in Anhalter Bunker. That had been an immeasurably long time ago, and since then they had existed in utter darkness interrupted only by Hindenburg lights and wax candles.

There was no electricity, but the radio worked.

No current, no light, no drinking water. The ventilation had stopped functioning. The shafting was broken. Nobody could go into the street. Men and women squatted wherever they happened to be – the corridor was one long sewer. No one got up to leave, no one dared face the hail of shrapnel outside. But there was no end to the incoming – a constant stream of lightly wounded and of badly wounded who were carried in from the street. At first one floor had been cleared to serve as a hospital, then another of the five floors, and the people who had inhabited them were squeezed into the remaining floors, whether there was room for them or not.

The radio went on functioning.

Fritzsche or Naumann or whoever it was, had finished his speech and was followed by the Werewolf-transmitter. This time the diction of Propaganda Minister Goebbels was unmistakable. The Minister had resigned, had disappeared with wife and five children into the deepest Bunker of Berlin never to be seen again, but his voice haunted the room: 'under the ruins of our destroyed, devastated towns the last so-called magnificent deeds of the nineteenth-century middle-class have been finally buried. The enemy who endeavoured to lay waste the future of Europe, has only achieved the destruction of the past – that being the end of the old and used. . . . Oh cleansing destruction, there is no end to the revolution . . .'

A voice from nowhere.

Out of a mismanaged life, out of plans that had miscarried, out of the spreading disintegration, out of the destruction of innumerable human lives and treasures of civilization, he now forged a philosophy of nihilism.

Permanent revolution. . . .

War of ashes. . . .

The Werewolf programme was followed by dance music, a somewhat old-fashioned polka helped along by drums and saxophones. The stumbling old men who fought their way through a wall of people for the prize of two cigarettes, almost collapsed under the weight of the carted corpses. In the darkness a baby cried. A dripping wax candle in the hand of a medical orderly threw its yellow light on to the hand of a surgeon and the opened chest of one of the wounded on the board. The concrete vaults resounded with hits of heavy artillery fire. Young Wittstock returned from the entrance and reported: 'The Red Cross has gone from the door and is being scraped from the walls.' Over the radio came a squeaking woman's voice: *'Wir versaufen unsrer Oma ihr klein Häuschen . . .'* – We'll go on drinking, go on drinking, until everything is spent. . . . That was too much! Wustmann had kept his nerve at the battered Vistula front and in dying Odessa – now he lost control; his face contorted, he grabbed something, it was the plaster forceps, staggered across the corridor into the opposite cell and smashed the radio to pieces.

Uproar.

But what was the pathetic protest of the owner compared with the ceaseless drone of missiles which tore large lumps out of the Bunker's shell; how insignificant it was compared with the cries of the wounded who could not be attended to, the death rattle of the dying, the raiding parties who kicked up a row while combing the concrete bulk of half-dead, starved, wounded, sick, lame, aged, and children to find new recruits for the Home Guard.

An ossuary, a mortuary, although the inhabitants were still breathing, crying, even hoping. One ossuary next to the other – next to the Zoo Bunker, the anti-aircraft Bunker at Friedrichshain, the Shell house by Tirpitz embankment, citadels of death rising into the burning blood-red sky of Berlin – and still those buried had hope, could be plunged into worse terrors.

'What did you say?'

'The Red Cross has gone from the Bunker door and is being removed from the Bunker walls.'

Driver Stroh confirmed Wittstock's observation:

'The Commandant has ordered the Red Cross flags to be removed. The Bunker is a strongpoint, he says.'

Wustmann ran to the front, still clutching the forceps. A staff surgeon, another doctor, the sergeant-major of another medical unit, crowded around the Commandant of Anhalt railway station. The Commandant had only one arm and one leg, was only half a man, his dark hair smoothed over the scalp, his deep-set eyes flashing. He banged the iron hook of his artificial arm on the table:

'I am telling you this for the last time. The Bunker is a strongpoint, part of the defence system!'

'Just what do you think you are defending, Herr Oberstleutnant; what are you shooting at? We are right in the centre of the city here, for miles around there is nothing but private houses.'

The Lieutenant-Colonel knew all right what he was defending – one of the approaches to the Reich Chancellery, the Führer Bunker. He no longer took any notice of the protesting crowd around him. He telephoned, shouted into the instrument: 'You must, you must, you must . . .' and did not seem to know himself what it was that must be done. He glanced wildly around him; then he remembered: 'Where are the planes? You must send planes. Russian tanks are nearing the Bunker itself!'

He turned to the staff surgeon and the medical men: 'Get out of here; mind your own business. The whole Bunker is to be evacuated; wounded and civilians must go.'

'Evacuate? How, where to? Into the hail of shrapnel and fire outside?'

'Don't argue, evacuate; I shall obtain the official order for evacuation.'

'That is murder', yelled Wustmann. He was about to throw himself at the Commandant. The others grabbed hold of him, took him back to his station.

'This *is* murder, Herr Doktor.'

Senior surgeon Dr. Heide was incapable of thought. Whilst trimming the edges of wounds, extracting bone splinters, his eyes kept closing.

> '*Wir versaufen unsrer Oma ihr klein Häuschen . . .*
> *ihr klein Häuschen,*
> *ihr klein Häuschen,*
> *für die erste,*
> *für die zweite,*
> *für die dritte Hypothek . . .*'

The Baroness tried at first to keep her partner, a slim SS-officer, at a suitable distance, but he held her close. SS-officers and women, amongst them Hitler's and Bormann's adjutants, officers of the bodyguard, private secretaries, the vegetarian dietitian, Fräulein Manzialy, Gerda

Christian, wife of General of the Luftwaffe Erhard Christian, telephonists, whirled around dancing.

It was hot, the air was blue with cigarette smoke. The ventilators hummed. On the tables against the walls dishes with snacks and sandwiches were displayed. There were cigars, liqueurs, coffee. When a heavy bomb exploded outside, the concrete building shook and the glasses jingled on the tables.

The radio stopped playing. A gramophone was put in its place. Somebody brought English records. 'Hot music', he said.

They played the Tiger Rag.

A naval officer brought a record of a sea-shanty:

> 'I love a girl,
> Why I don't know,
> Tobacco she chews
> And drinks rum too.
> Oh wake her, oh shake her,
> Oh wake that girl with the blue dress on . . .'

It was one of the lateral galleries of the subterranean labyrinth, the Second SS-Bunker. Deep down below the pavement a number of concrete containers lay dotted, each with its oxygen supply and artificial light, each Bunker a world to itself with living quarters, with kitchens, dining-rooms, guard-rooms and sleeping apartments, and each one of these Bunkers – the one belonging to Party Chief Bormann, the one below the Old Reich Chancellery, the one under the Ministry of Propaganda, the First and Second SS-Bunker – they were all linked by passages with the centre of this underworld, the Führer Bunker.

Almost a thousand human beings lived there, mounted guard, patrolled the immediate and farther surroundings, returned, slept, ate, drank, held orgies which grew all the more intense, continuous, shameless and passionate the closer they came to death.

How dreadfully broken 'he' is; hardly recognizable. Whatever have they done to him, Bormann, Burgdorf, Jodl, Keitel, Krebs, and all these . . . flatterers, deceivers, swindlers, nonentities; these vile creatures have reduced him to a shadow.

Smoke them out. . . .

It would only have been a matter of hygiene. It is over though, the plan has been abandoned, dropped. . . .

'No, thank you.'

The man shook his head, the waiter with a black bow carried the plate with salmon and anchovy snacks, with Strasbourg pâté de foie and lobster to the next table. The man refused the delicacies, also the great variety of drinks. He had a cup of black coffee in front of him and when he had emptied it he called for another with brandy.

A few tables away Burgdorf sat and emptied one glass after the other and stared across with glazed eyes.

> 'Oh wake her, oh shake her,
> oh wake that girl with the blue dress on,
> when Blacky comes down to Hilo
> poor old man . . .'

Hot music. The wine flowed. Champagne corks popped. Typists became priestesses of Bacchus. SS-officers in close-fitting uniforms stared unseeingly.

'On patrol to-day', a very young dancer whispered into the ear of Baroness von Varo. He had been on patrol, with a troop of his men behind him. Now he closed his eyes and inhaled greedily the odour of the woman's hot body whilst recalling the day's happenings. ' "I am finished with it; the war is over; there is no sense in it any more", that fellow said. You can imagine, Madam, what I did to him. The only thing one can do with a traitor. I hanged him on the nearest tree.'

Von Varo did not even listen.

'Just for once I escaped to-day, into the Tiergarten, full of Spring . . .' she said.

'And the artillery fire?'

'Didn't worry me. Nobody was in the streets. It was as though Berlin belonged to me alone.'

Smoke them out. . . .

Finished, abandoned; not possible without authority. The miners, the people in the shelters, the German people had taken the authority away from him. The talk overheard in a dark night in a trench on the Western Front – only a few safety lamps had supplied a dim light and nobody had recognized him – this talk between common soldiers had shed a new light on the affair and changed it. It had not been the 12-feet-high tower which the master of the Bunker, full of misgivings, had ordered to be erected around the ventilation shaft (even this additional complication might have been overcome), but the opinion of the man in the street that had led him to abandon his plan. Because many, surprisingly many, soldiers, workers and simple women still believed in him, even in his broken and ruined condition; his halo lived longer than he did. A funeral with a thousand mourners in attendance and the legend would live to haunt them.

The funeral of a Pharaoh . . . that is what it would have meant. And that was by no means his intention. No glorification, no suspicion of greatness was to attach to the affair. The problem had been reduced to a simple equation. A sufficient quantity of some substance producing poison gas introduced into the outer inlet shaft of the ventilator at the time of a staff conference would in no time reach the whole crowd of insincere and disloyal army chiefs; would infiltrate the private apartments, the living-rooms and bedrooms, the baths and cloakrooms, Fräulein Manzialy's diet kitchen and, despite the fortified doors, the corridors and stairs, all the tributary galleries, and in time this substerranean dance hall, and strike the inhabitants dead. The time needed for all this would depend only on the composition of the poison gas and the speed of its penetration.

Finished, over, cancelled. I shall no longer think about it They have to prepare their own funeral.

'No, thank you, thank you . . .'

The waiter with the silver platter passed by once more A direct hit above shook the caverns below. For one moment it seemed as though the lights would fail altogether. The couples held closer together and whirled past him in an old-fashioned waltz. The gramophone stopped: they hummed the tune and went on. Gerda Christian, Frau Junge, the golden-haired Else – he knew them all, he was no stranger in these circles. At Hitler's Berghof above Berchtesgaden, at Rastenburg in East Prussia, the Eagle's Nest near Bad Nauheim, wherever Pharaoh had held court, he had met the same favourites, dignitaries, secretaries male and female, or their predecessors, now delegates to Hades. He knew them all, was one of them, but even as First Favourite he had been one apart, had not joined in the race and intrigues for favour. Favour had come to him without any special effort and solely because his sincerity and dependability in all tasks given to him had never changed, and by a miracle – now after a thousand and one acts of disobedience he still retained it. But he had also fallen out with his Master.

As long as he had been able to build, as long as he had been faced with technical and administrative problems, he had felt firm ground under his feet, had felt that his work was worthy of a human being and that as a creative man he had played his part in the construction of the world. His master in his capacity as builder had seemed adequate to him; he had been able to overlook the shadier parts of his character and circle, and he had closed both eyes to the number of victims. Had not the pyramids been erected only with moans and suffering and the crack of the whip? Every new canal, every railway through a jungle, every mole reaching into the sea, rested on the bones of those who erected it. Only one thing remained without question: the pyramid rising through millennia, the canal connecting oceans, the railway line joining countries, the completed Autobahn bridge. Only the civilizing achievement itself could justify its creator and the host of victims which his creation demanded. But if the order was one of destruction, demanding the blasting of bridges, canals, dams, railways, factories, towns, the rendering infertile of arable ground, the destruction of all provisions, the laying in ashes of all countries between the Pyrenees and Finland ... what justification was there for that, what was left of the mark a man had meant to leave in the world, what of the short span of life itself?

Nothing. . . .

Terrible orders emanated from the Führer's H.Q., and he was supposed to execute them. But he was powerful enough, with his own official channels and a whole army of civil servants, with high-ranking friends in the High Command of the army, the General Commands of Prague, Brussels, Paris, with his liaison officers and watchful agents, to issue effective counter orders. He saved mines and factories in Belgium, and Northern France, canals in Holland, nickel mines in Finland, the ores of the Balkans and the oilfields in Hungary. He had not been able to prevent the blasting of the dykes at Wieringer Sea, so that many square miles of good arable land had been drowned by the rushing salt-water and been made useless for years to come. He was for ever travelling, racing from one end of the shrinking continental empire to the other, and wherever he went he met the raised arm of the destructor ready to strike: a thousand times he had been able to avert it; a thousand times he had failed. Cities were laid waste, bridges fell into rivers. Sluices were blown sky high. Whole networks of roads and essential industrial plants were destroyed. He stood and watched, unable to call a halt to the devastation. He was even more helpless with the increasing apathy, the general fatalistic mood fed from the well of ministerial propaganda. He sat down and wrote an appeal which culminated in – 'The war is lost, militarily and economically. If the whole nation is not to be destroyed too, a material basis must be preserved on which the life of the people can continue.'

The Pharaoh-like philanthropist, the generous master builder, the powerful patron of the arts, the jolly master of the house at Obersalzberg, now appeared to him suddenly changed into a phantom hovering over a bottomless pit. He had ordered him to come to his Headquarters, and there he heard from a foaming mouth: 'If the war is lost, the nation has to go down, too. Its fate is unavoidable. There is no necessity to consider the basis of even the most primitive existence. On the contrary, it is better to destroy it with one's own hands. The nation has shown itself to be weak; the future belongs solely to the stronger Eastern people. What is more, those who will be left after the fight are not worth anything because all the good ones died for the cause.'

Dismissed and relieved of his official positions but still free and in possession of his many connections and powerful friends in industry and the army, he was still able to avert the blows of the destructor. In the midst of the wave of total destruction which now broke over Germany, he decided to strike at its driving power by eliminating the destroyer of Europe and his whole court. But the aura of the 'Führer' (to which part of him succumbed even now) proved the stronger and he abandoned his plan in the conviction that it would deprive the German people of their focal point, would throw it into military and social chaos and increase the impetus towards certain destruction.

Once again Pharaoh demanded his presence, and this time he found him already at death's door. In this fateful hour he submitted once more to the fascination of the dull grey-blue eyes that had made gamblers of able administrators, murderers of medical men, pseudo-scientific quacks of men of science, and turned a whole nation into a conspiring horde of maniacs. And the man who had already freed himself of the uncanny influence, who had remained untouched by the general mental disintegration and who had thought himself able to stop the people from running amok, one again fell under the spell. Their single-mindedness, the fact that they were both possessed by their respective ideas, formed a link between them. Between Pharaoh and his architect a brotherly bond existed. The one a technological magician, and the other . . . what was it that re-established the influence of the already sinking man; what re-lit the fire in his eyes; what gave them plutonic strength?

Albert Speer understood.

It had happened.

He had gazed into the hollow heart of the maelstrom. For that one moment, no longer than it takes to open one's eyes, he met, trembling, the ancient forefather from the jungle, from time immemorial. The ancestor, already discarded in his primitive form, was now burnt out. Even the worm in the crumbling earth, the herring swimming in shoals at night, gives off his own fluorescent light; but here the light on the extinct crater floated on a sea of nothingness. That was what had happened.

Goebbels might compare him to Attila, to Ghengis Khan. Speer had hit on the truth, had espied the ship which had come out of darkness and was now heading compassless for the veiled horizon, and he felt a human compassion and he was forgiven. He was forgiven at a time when every word emanating from the mouth of the Bunker-god spelt revenge and when rivers of blood could not still his desire for more and more victims. In that same hour he sentenced to death by shooting eight officers who had refused to blow up a bridge. Speer's disobedience was a thousand times greater; was

mutiny a thousandfold, and he was forgiven. That was as
unreal as the limp figure stretched out in the armchair:
unreal, too, were the words which the man who had returned
to favour heard himself saying. He explained that he could
not relinquish his post; that it was his duty to remain where
he was and that his Führer could rely on him as much as
ever. The words were unimportant; for the understanding
between the two lay deeper in an unexplored stratum.
After a thousandfold mutiny Speer was reinstated and given
back his powers only to use them, as soon as he returned
to the detonating reality from the twilight of the Bunker,
with all his force against the wave of destruction.

It followed the collapse of the potentate.

In the garden of the Reich Chancellery burned the documents which he personally had selected for destruction.
The paladins in the south and the north prepared themselves
to take over the command. Not Göring, but Himmler
allowed himself to be made party to a conspiracy which
aimed at the murder of the fallen man. Speer ordered large
quantities of explosives to be hidden; made records in
Hamburg entreating the people to oppose all orders for
destruction and to think of the necessity of preserving a basis
for continued existence after Hitler's death; he demanded
immediate capitulation.

After he had made this speech, had it mechanically preserved ready for publication, after he had done all that
could be done in that hour, he resolved to relinquish his
posts and to return to Berlin. The pull from the Bunker was
irresistible. The last visit had left a sore wound and had
drawn him into that twilight of half-truths and hypocrisy
which hitherto he had managed to avoid. He had to go back
to confess his repeated disobedience, he looked forward to
his arrest and was ready to accept death as penalty. A car
took him as far as Rechlin; then progress by road was no
longer possible. He got into a sports plane, reached Gatow,
changed into a 'Fieseler Stork' piloted by a sergeant-major
and after flying through waves of anti-aircraft fire, landed
near Brandenburger Tor.

And there he was, sitting before a cup of black coffee that
had got cold. Eight hours he had waited in the Bunker. He
had not been arrested, was free, could go where he chose,

could step into the hail of bombs and artillery fire. He had sat opposite Hitler, surrounded by Bormann, Goebbels, Ribbentrop, Krebs with his personal adjutants Schaub and Guensche, and had confessed his renewed disobedience. Bormann had sat there, brooding; he and the haggard, ape-like Goebbels seemed to be already hearing the firing of the execution squad. Krebs remained unmoved; he was used to watching sentences of annihilation; blood had flowed as freely in the country where he had played his first puppet part as did the port from the bottle outside in his private cabin. But nothing happened; the master appeared to be in a state of unnatural calm, human – as he had not been for a long time – that was Speer's impression. The act of disobedience no longer interested him. Speer was dismissed the presence.

Eva Braun received him – like a stray ray of sunshine from her Bavarian countryside. This simple, pitiable child, made for the embraces of a busy village teacher, had spent eleven lean years by the side of the phantom. She was now burnt out and nerve-racked. She described the crashing of her idol and the subsequent confusion. Wandering through the subterranean labyrinth he met another remarkable apparition. She came towards him down the stairs. Elegant, slim, girl-like – and yet the mother of six children. Where the stairs turned he had to stop to let her pass. She returned his greeting with a radiant look and smiled at the SS-guard. Five of her children came running after her. Twelve-year-old Helga and the nine-year-old Helmut took two steps at a time, the smaller ones followed. Helga, Helmut, Hölde, Hedda, Heide – in honour of 'Uncle Adolf' whose guests they were and whom they were on their way to see, they all had to be given names beginning with H.

'Uncle Adolf' seemed to have put everything behind him. The ship without a compass was already beyond the barrier, had already invaded the black cloud, drifted slowly over the seabed of monsters and gnawed skeletons and wrecks overgrown with seaweed. He had put everything behind him, and could afford to behave as a 'private person'. He collected a number of children around him and fed them with cakes: at two o'clock in the morning he called Gerda Dardanowski-Christian and Frau Traudl Junge away from the arms of their dancing partners so that they should take part in the tea party. There he sat, nibbling biscuits, chatting about his elevation from poverty to be the ruler of Europe – though his domain had shrunk and was now but a hole in the ground shaken by bombs.

Terrifying to look at; there is nothing left to murder! He had done it himself. His unnatural life, Dr. Morell with his twenty-eight different injections and medicines, his whole damnable, mad, boastful and flattering Court had done it, had left nothing but a used up, rotten vessel. Albert Speer had once spent forty-eight hours in a doomed city, encircled by the enemy, and had observed there how men and women, goaded by the cold breath of the Angel of Death, had tried to compass everything without restraint in a single night, that otherwise would have filled a lifetime. All this he found here, too. The women's skin steamed under their thin silk dresses; their eyes were unnaturally dilated. Wine flowed. Morell and his aphrodisiacs were missing, and whether his successor, Dr. Stumpfenegger, was equally obliging, Speer did not know. But those stimulants were not really necessary. Death at close range was the greatest stimulant of all. Women, SS-officers, guards, chauffeurs, clerks – the Second SS-Bunker with its barbarous gramophone music, with its rows of cells and corridors, resembled nothing so much as a large hutch full of bucking rabbits.

The vacant-looking drunkards were there, too. There was Burgdorf and opposite him sat Bormann. Tied each to the other by their terrible guilt. Had it not been he who had taken the poison to Rommel and left him the choice of suicide or the execution squad? Yes, his friends were right to despise him. 'They are right, I say it myself. It's got to be said. I was naïve, stupid, I allowed you to use me as your lackey. And you . . . you have wasted yourselves in orgies, grabbed riches, stolen estates, plundered Germany.

'Now then, old boy, there is no need to be personal. . . .'

And farthest down there sat the master of the warren with his party and drank lime-flower tea. And when he did not discuss his own marvellous career or the fickleness of intellectuals or the devotion of his Alsatian, he got excited about ineffectual generals, the unfaithful SS, or the stupidity and evil of people in general. That was the moment when he demanded the blood of saboteurs, of hostages and prisoners.

A lunatic asylum throughout, a mine of information for psychiatrists. They drink and carouse and in their staring eyes you can see the Angel reflected with his sharpened sword. They jump and they dance themselves to death; they know it and the next minute they know nothing; they believe that it may all pass them by like a nightmare. Lunatics – but without excuse of extenuating circumstances. Their way has led through blood, and now they drink, they jump, they dance. Leaving a mutilated Europe behind them, they murder Germany in cold blood and even now are strangling Berlin.

Albert Speer rose . . . he was free, he could leave. He had left the 'Fieseler Stork' on a piece of ground behind Brandenburger Tor. The bombardment had died down to intermittent rumblings.

Once more he looked back.

Puppets on a stage as the curtain falls; they know it and yet they don't. There are a few who still believe that the power could be inherited from the weakening hands. Bormann thinks so and the clique around Bormann. Speer had seen a few hours ago how Bormann, using all his cunning, had managed to push his rival aside, the absent Air Marshal Göring (who also still believed in succession), and had obtained the order for his degradation and arrest. Bormann in Berlin, Göring in Berchtesgaden, Himmler in Mecklenburg – each one on his own isolated, splintering lump of ice, stretching their soiled hands out to clutch at an empire which no longer existed.

Speer went upstairs. Steel doors opened for him and closed behind him. He walked along the corridor covered with red carpet and came into the entrance hall. Porphyry and marble; he himself had ordered the building of it. Huge candelabras, but they no longer shed light. There was a smell of picrine from exploded shells and the air was full of dust. It was two o'clock in the morning and in the pale light a visitor was sitting slumped in a chair; he had put his hat over his coffee and brandy to protect it against the plaster which kept falling from the ceiling. Speer was not to know that the waiting man had come here to reclaim his soul. He left the hall and the late visitor and lost himself outside in a street full of broken lamp posts, dangling wires and fresh bomb craters.

The man in the desolate hall was radio commentor Hans Fritzsche. It had been he who, a few days ago in Goebbels' villa behind Brandenburger Tor, had interrupted his master's abusive speech against Germany. Confronted with Goebbels' unrestrained flaring hatred it had taken Fritzsche some moments to collect himself. Then he had rushed after his chief – but he was too late and the door banged in his face. He had to speak to him, had to see his face once more. He had to know whether the outburst had been a temporary nervous breakdown or whether – and it had rather looked like that – the mask had finally come off to reveal the grimace of a cynic who despised tradition, morals and culture from the bottom of his heart. He had to know whether this was the true face of the Master whose example he had followed for so long with devotion, admiration and self-denial.

But the chair of the Minister in the Ministry remained empty. He found only closed doors, mute telephone receivers. He went round and round the house behind Brandenburger Tor. The shutters were up and not a face to be seen. Towards the evening of the second day he saw two small cars emerge from the ministerial villa. Pressing himself against the wall, he recognized in the second car the wife and some of the children of the object of his search. He watched the cars turn into Voss-strasse. In Tiergarten nearby the first shell of a Russian long-range gun exploded deafeningly. The doors of the abandoned villa would not be closed again. The gate and the front door and even the inside doors, the desk drawers, the cupboards – everything was open and cases lay strewn about. He found himself surrounded by telephonists, typists, guards shouting, crying and swearing. This is the end! they lamented; the Minister is gone; he has taken his family to the Führer Bunker and is never coming back!

He went to the Reich Chancellery and sent his name in. Goebbels was not available. He came again and the adjutants offered him the same chair on which Captain Boehlke had once sat. He returned to the Ministry of Propaganda now burning like a torch; he cowered in a corner of the cellar and went over the last eleven years of his life. German foreign policy, the beginning of the war, the conduct of the war and its aims: suddenly it all seemed unreal and distorted. Could it be possible that the widely publicized peaceful intentions of Germany, the vision of a Greater Germany as a power of law and order in the heart of the Continent, had turned out to be nothing but an empty dummy? Why had it never been possible to obtain a clear-cut answer as to the purpose of the war? The Allies had been able to offer the peoples of the struggling countries an Atlantic Charter. German propaganda had at its disposal only the promise of a 'New order in Europe'. A vague slogan – why had it never been filled with a concrete meaning? Why had the French people and all those in the East and the West never been told what was asked of them, and why had the much promised 'Magna Charta Europæensis' never materialized? Was the history of the last twelve years but a repetition of the fable of the 'Fisherman and his wife' who exploited the magic fish and demanded from it first a country house, then a castle and lastly a king's palace, intending to become king, emperor and in the end God Himself, only to be hurled with thunder and lightning into the gutter?

Radio commentator Hans Fritzsche once more returned to the Reich Chancellery. That meant he had to cover the few yards from one side of the road to the other dodging a hail of shrapnel. Owing to the disorganization of the guards he managed to get across the corridor and down the stairs as far as the main Bunker. Only there was he caught and led once more into the desolate dining-hall above. An adjutant kept him company and made some small talk until, tired of waiting, he left again. And he returned, waited all morning, all the afternoon, all the evening until after midnight; he never heard from Goebbels.

'Will never return' – but he had to grasp him, had to see his face once more, had to know whom he had served these twelve years and to whom he had mortgaged his soul.

The fugitive into the underworld was not available.

In his stead Secretary of State Naumann appeared. To the man who was crushed by endless waiting and mental agony the talkative Secretary seemed like an old woman, drivelling about rumours and hot air. According to him political decisions of vast importance had been reached. It was only a question of a few hours; perhaps even of one hour of endurance. Two fighting armies – those of Wenk and Steiner – were approaching and would free Berlin. Moreover, the tank unit of Field-Marshal Schörner was expected within a very few days and would defend the Oder front. The Russians had only broken through a small sector of Berlin. The Oder line would be restored.

Fritzsche saw Naumann disappear again. An ugly old witch riding on her broomstick into the depths of the Magic Mountain. Fritzsche waited, waited . . . from the Master came only one message – and that a lie. After the bombardment was over he would come upstairs in person, the message said. But he did not come. Only as a corpse was he to see Goebbels again.

Albert Speer found the sergeant-major who had flown him over from Gatow still with the plane. The 'Fieseler Stork' rose into the air from Unter den Linden, flew in a circle above Brandenburger Tor. Berlin bled from a thousand fires. Where gaps in the smoke allowed a clear view, neat squares and rows of soot-covered stone skeletons showed. No longer any roofs – nor floors.

From the sea of ruins rose the Anhalter Bunker. They left behind them Siegesallee, the double row of marble statues, the petrified history of Prussia. Broken trees, the goldfish-pond a black garbage can; lonely beside the bank wept the Amazon of Tuaillon. Once again one of Speer's creations pierced the smoke screen; another coffin of concrete and steel: the Zoo Bunker.

Anti-aircraft shells burst around the plane. Explosions shook the air. The wanderers above the ruins had to climb higher, plunged into the black bank of smoke. A blue Spring sky, more explosions, another escape into another jungle of dense smoke. Their way led them from one smoke island to the next. Behind them – Berlin.

Pinned in the small strip between Havel and Lake Müggel, between the sandy heathland of Barnim in the north and the pine forests of Teltow in the south, were three and a half million men, women and children awaiting the great flood.

An order to retreat had never reached the troops near the

Oder. Only when it was too late did the order to break through – more like a cry for help from encircled Berlin – reach the Ninth Army, and part of that army were the divisions 'Courmark' and 'Netherlands', which had been pushed back as far as the old Oder and Seelow Heights.

The road from Falkenhagen to the Scharmützelsee and the area farther on around Märkisch-Buchholz and Halbe was just a walking cemetery for four or five days; after which it was in addition a collecting and departure point for prisoners of war. This was the result of one of the last 'strategic moves' emanating from the Führer Bunker.

'Walking cemetery' was an expression used by Captain Boehlke in one of his letters to his Uncle Raimond. Captain Boehlke had remained with the 'Courmark' division and had taken part in the attempted break-through with this already weakened unit. 'How right you were, dear uncle – dementia paralytica, and we are part of it, must partake of the final convulsions', he wrote. 'And there is no escape. What is more, it is immaterial where any individual may be. You at your table bending over foreign newspapers, the divisional general faced with orders he cannot carry out, the reserved worker transferred from his factory in Spandau, or myself, a misfit from the first day – there is no difference. Neither would it have made much difference had I remained with my old division in Courland or had I found my artillery commander, or if I had met the same fate as another chap from the same course and had been dropped over Graudenz or Königsberg or Breslau; there is ruin everywhere and whoever has been drawn into the whirlpool reacts in the same way, irrespective of where he is, or who he is.

'I have already described our sector of the front to you. The railway line between Lietzen and Falkenhagen, the last stretch of the Eastern front, was one long cliff rising above the waters. There "Courmark" lay, then followed "Netherlands", and further north lay a division under the command of Remer who became notorious on the 20th July. There could hardly be any question of leadership now. The order to break through, when it finally came, only meant a free pass to every little unit to turn back and try to save its own skin. Three divisions, or rather what was left of them, men, horses and the remainder of the guns, cars, tanks, and baggage, all threw themselves into the narrow passage, about twelve miles long, which led to Lake Scharmützel and miraculously opened like the waters of the Red Sea to let through the children of Israel. The red waters surrounding us like a wall gave under the weight of the human avalanche. But the avalanche moved in a disordered rout and not towards the relief of Berlin as had been planned. We were pushed off in a south-westerly direction, towards Lake Scharmützel, and even there the avalanche was not spent. The reduction in weight (and the wrecked cars, abandoned material, dead horses, and people who fell by the wayside, are uncountable) was more than made up by the additions that swelled our numbers when we got to Lake Scharmützel. Once again they were workers transported there in municipal buses, factory guards and firemen, a unit of naval cadets from the college at Jüteborg – but no arms, no reserves, no fuel; each car, each truck only had the fuel in its tank. Moreover, there were the civilians – women, elderly men and children; from the villages they came with horse-and-cart, from the towns on foot, sometimes the whole population of places that had endured Russian occupation for a week, like Bad Saarow, Pieskow, Radlow, Wendisch-Rietz; all joined the passing troops. The avalanche rolled along, in a south-westerly direction as before; in front of them lay Russian-occupied Märkisch-Buchholz and the little town of Halbe, also occupied. It hardly needed any Russians to finish us off. We were so utterly forsaken, without any guidance, a conglomeration of elements, with less instinct than animals in a forest fire, less sense of direction than fleeing game which cross a river and safely reach the other bank. The battle-scarred men of the Eastern front had lost their nerve and steadiness. It only needed a word that there was a Russian position ahead of us – and a single shot, and they all began to bang away. Those who marched in front were shot from behind; fell and never knew why and how. After all, in an avalanche one stone grinds another, one piece of wood smashes the other. The real tragedy did not overtake us until we reached the little town of Halbe.

'At dawn we attacked. Talks had been going on between "Courmark" and "Netherlands". "Netherlands" attacked from a north-easterly direction; we advanced from the south-east. Between us, in a steadily narrowing wedge, stood the

Russians. The general objective was the station. A third of us fell by the roadside during the advance. The whole thing lasted two hours. A fight developed in the haze, on the devastated remains of the almost destroyed town. Only in the hand-to-hand fighting outside the station did we recognize the "Netherlanders" and they recognized us. "Courmark" and "Netherlands" had fought each other with Tiger tanks and heavy infantry weapons, had fought over the road to Berlin, only to be chopped up piecemeal by the Russian artillery.

'Instead of taking the road to Berlin we had to fall back. The next night found us still on the road – only we were no longer "Courmarkers", "Netherlanders", civilians, naval forces and Luftwaffe ground staff. Altogether, the soldiers, tanks and baggage trains and the farmers' carts with their women and children, were just one huge mass of human rubble moving towards Berlin which lay behind the horizon, a yellow flickering glow. At the head of the column were about two thousand men, many officers amongst them; in addition some forty vehicles, two Tiger tanks and several armoured cars, as well as heavy lorries. A general appeared. But unable to bring any order into the milling crowd, and perhaps also realizing the hopelessly inadequate supply of arms, he vanished again. Still, there were lieutenant-colonels and colonels, indeed half the soldiers were officers or NCOs. Not one of them wished to take over command. Everyone wanted to get out of the chaos and every single one knew full well that the way lay through the Russian-occupied Märkisch-Buchholz; but not one of them wanted to be the leader. "I cannot be responsible for the others", one of them said. "I have no orders", said another. "I don't know anything about the situation cut off from my unit", said another. I myself was no different. I thought of the fact that there were no reserves, no supplies, no provisions, no field kitchens, no dressing station, not even the most primitive First-Aid. Those were justified anxieties, but in the circumstances nothing but excuses. I was only trying to fool myself. The truth was that I, just like all the others, was uncertain, undecided, paralysed, inert, incapable of independent action, infected with the rot that spread upon us from the huge burning city on the horizon. In the end a sergeant-major of the military police – he wore the Golden Cross – took over the command. And everyone, even experienced old colonels, majors and captains subordinated themselves willingly. His methods were quite primitive; he walked straight along the road towards Märkisch-Buchholz. A battering ram, the tip hardened by the two Tiger tanks and the armoured cars behind. But he could not prevent unarmed soldiers, women and children pushing their way into the gaps between the tanks which moved about thirty yards apart. The Tigers advanced, fired and stopped suddenly. The tank behind them, then the third and fourth, even the fifth, all ran into one another. Dear Uncle Raimond, I don't want to paint any lurid pictures of the battle for you. All I want is to clear my mind so as to understand myself, and that is why I am writing all this down. Also I want to make you understand and all the others who may perhaps read this letter, that the battering ram made up of women and children and unarmed soldiers, led by the sergeant-major of the military police and directed towards Märkisch-Buchholz, was the essence of the strategy which had been imagined by Messrs. Bormann, Burgdorf, Jodl, Keitel and Krebs in the Führer Bunker. A chain reaction of crashing vehicles. The crowds in the gaps scattered, but five or six were caught each time; perhaps fifty or sixty people run over and squashed to pulp were left lying in the road – but the battering ram moved on, faster, towards Märkisch-Buchholz, until in the ruined grounds of what had been a factory, under fire which suddenly concentrated on it from the night, it flew into fragments, into howling atoms scattering in all directions. I was pinned to the spot, frozen like Lot's wife before Gomorrah and the objects around me whirled past in desperate flight. The bare chimney stacks, the heaps of rubble, burst walls, a dead cow, a snapped telegraph pole, a tree, another tree, trees . . . trees, a wood. I found myself in a wood south of Märkisch-Buchholz. Under the trees I saw a Tiger tank; others saw it, too. About twenty men collected around it. We had a leader once more. A major had taken over command. From the top of a tree we were shot at, five or six dead. The guns of the Tiger dealt with the machine gun nest in the tree. The dead were left behind, the wounded we laid on the tank; we marched on. Straight across the wood until, in the early dawn, we arrived in the rear of a Russian artillery position. Heavy guns; one of the batteries that were bombarding Berlin. No guard; nobody in sight; the crew slept in rough dug-outs. They now lurched outside, looked stupid and were felled by our shots. We rendered the guns useless, but otherwise looked only for something to eat. There were only a few handfuls of barley. It had been the same earlier on when we had shot the snipers down from the tree. "That goes to show why we lost the war", said the Major; "whenever you find a dead Russian he has no bread but ammunition in his knapsack – with us it was always the other way round: no ammunition but plenty of food in all pockets." The one and a half steel-helmets-full of barley were at the moment all the Major could offer his troop of forty men. He decided, therefore, to attack the village ahead of us. The reconnaissance patrol which we sent out returned to say that the place was only lightly occupied. Together with five others I was sent to try an outflanking movement on the right flank, but had little inclination to participate in a game of war that had been worked out with matches beforehand for the sake of a piece of bread. What is more, some of the Major's remarks, amongst them his observation on the reason for the loss of the war, had made me suspicious as to his suitability to be in command. Instead of taking part in the marauding expedition I determined therefore to try and find a piece of bread on my own; two of my five men were similarly inclined and followed me through a ditch and a small valley back to the wood. There we met more soldiers, led by a sergeant-major. We joined forces; there were now twenty of us ."Break-through to the West", "Relief of Berlin", "Rendezvous south of Berlin with Wenk's army"! those were the slogans with which we had started on our journey. Here, no such martial intentions existed any more. On the contrary, "We hide during the day in the undergrowth and march only at night by compass", explained the sergeant-major. "Perhaps we may get as far as the Elbe and then we shall see."

' "I don't think I shall see the Elbe or any other flowing water again!" "Help me, comrade, I cannot go on." And we moved on, past him. "You swine, leaving us alone here, to die." We moved on, and on. What were we to do, we already carried our own wounded; how could one man carry three or four, how could a little troop of twenty-two burden itself with thousands? But they screamed: "Swine, murderers! You only think of yourselves!" They were mad with pain from their wounds; animals don't scream as they screamed. We moved on, across a howling churchyard, and the cries still cling to me; I cannot get away from them. And the shots which in despair they fired after us; they hit me now. The churchyard, Uncle, between Dahme and Spreewald, is immense and I do not know whether only human beings, hundreds of thousands of them, were buried there or whether the idea of humanity itself died there then.

'I cannot go on, Uncle Raimond. Uninjured, I have passed through hell and now I have come to the end. But I had to write this; the report from the German Eastern front. You are to know what happened to it and how it dissolved into nothingness.

'Nothingness . . . nothing . . . I cannot think of anything else any more. God help me!'

This letter, written in a pine thicket between the Berlin Autobahn Ring – Neisse and the village of Dornswalde, was addressed to Chief Librarian Raimond Stassen in Potsdam. Then Captain Boehlke stowed it away in the inside pocket of his uniform. He was wrong though when he thought he had reached the end of his earthly journey. He was to see, for many more nights during his march towards the West, the fiery marks beyond the horizon, the red-hot breath of the dying city as it gradually caved in. It was in the little town of Fienerode, surrounded by marshland and off the main road, that it happened.

The Russians had already taken the town and left it again, only patrolling the area. Boehlke sat in a farmer's house with two others, a staff sergeant and a seventeen-year-old boy from the Volkssturm Home Guard. Boehlke and the sergeant still wore their uniforms but without insignia or brass buttons and on their heads were now civilian caps. It was evening when a Russian *Sanka* stopped outside the house, and two Russians entered.

'You German soldier!'

'Not German soldier, foreign worker, Dutchman', replied the sergeant.

The farmer confirmed it: 'Foreign worker, Dutchman.' The seventeen-year-old boy declared: 'Also foreign worker, Holland.'

Boehlke was silent.

The two Russians went up to the table and one of them un-folded a map. He wanted to get to the next town, a place called Hohenseeden, but he searched for it on the map around Lübeck. He wore a leather jacket and smelled strongly of perfume. But he was not drunk and appeared almost polite. The other, a short fellow with slanting eyes, looked sus-piciously around the room and watched Boehlke who was showing the officer the route on the map.

Suddenly he spoke:

'You German officer.'

Again Boehlke said nothing.

The one in the leather jacket declared: 'Officer or not, is all the same, you come with us to show us way.'

Dr. Linth drifted, allowed himself to be carried along by the same wind that had carried off Dolores. Whilst the tanks were rolling towards Berlin across Oraniendamm and Wit-tenau Station, he drifted through the still unoccupied Tegel, at length crossed Kaiserdamm, passed the entrance to the Avus and found himself in the Western sector of Berlin, which showed that there had been some purpose in his drifting. He was on his way to the Oskar-Helene-Home where he was in charge of an evacuated hospital. He was probably one of the last to make the journey from Hermsdorf to West Berlin without difficulties, although only as far as Grunewald where Russian fighters soared above the roofs. Formation after formation, for this was the hour during which the Russians prepared the Grunewald sector for their attack. A man in uniform pushing a heavily loaded bicycle caught up with Dr. Linth. The doctor was not to know that this man, who dis-appeared a moment later in the smoke and dust of an ex-ploding bomb, was his Heaven-sent guardian angel. Several other faces appeared through the smoke curtain; Home Guard men approaching from the opposite directions, jump-ing from shelter to shelter.

'Get out of it, down into the nearest cellar.'

Linth continued on his way. One of the houses suddenly showed a crack down its front in a flash of lightning, and lumps of concrete were flung over the garden fence into the street. 'Get down, down! Hide your face!' It was the guardian angel with the bicycle, producer and theatrical director Sarfeld, who wore a uniform with the insignia of a sergeant-major and who, until an hour ago, had been announcer with a Luftwaffe fighter control unit.

Air combat was finished; any sort of combat was finished. All that mattered now was to keep one's head above water. Sarfeld's unit had been sent to Mecklenburg and he himself, with his transport and broadcasting equipment, had been ordered to Berlin in order to resume from the Zoo Bunker his air warning service. Absolute nonsense considering the total confusion of all news services. He had no intention of obeying the order and moving into the death trap near the Zoo; instead he went into the cellar on Hohenzollerndamm and telephoned the Flak tower from there. 'What use is another newshound to us?' was their reply. 'If you can find a machine gun, you can come.' This information quite satisfied Sarfeld who continued to walk about the cellar until, most surprisingly, his Commander turned up and shouted: 'What are you doing here, haven't I given you orders to report to the Flak tower? Unless you are there within an hour I'll shoot you. Get into my car at once!'

The Commander's car was waiting outside.

'But that can't be done in a hurry, Major. My things are all over the place and I have to get them together first. You can see how things are. . . .' The Major looked round and saw for himself, how on the tables and under the tables there lay soldiers from units of the Eastern areas; assistants, telephonists and civil servants who could no longer get home.

'All right then, collect your rubbish and report to me at the Flak tower in two hours time', was the new order. Sarfeld watched him depart.

Splendid – now is the time to get out. He collected his 'rubbish', only his personal belongings, though, tied them all securely to his bicycle and made off – in the opposite direction from the Flak tower, towards Monika, towards home, towards Nikolassee; after all he had not fetched Monika with the last train from Prague only to leave her alone in the crash that was coming.

He had managed to get as far as Grunewald; though on the way he had had to duck several times and had even been driven into cellars once or twice. He was again lying close to a garden wall when he saw that strange figure, Dr. Linth, advancing. A suicide case, or at least one showing a peculiar disregard for danger; he did not even bother to throw himself down, or even to flinch. 'I am sorry', Sarfeld said after he had pulled Dr. Linth down on to the pavement. 'I am sorry . . . but those things whizzing past us might easily have hit you.'

'Yes, probably.'

It seemed immaterial to him. Well then, if not exactly a suicide, at least an odd creature; he had surmised correctly.

The two of them, Linth and Sarfeld, continued on their way together.

Once again Home Guard men from the opposite direction came running towards them, out of breath.

'Where are you off to?' they called. 'Get away from here, you cannot get through any longer.'

But Sarfeld intended to get through and so, apparently, did the other man. Sarfeld meant to get to Monika who was staying with his mother, and he also had to get rid of his uniform. Unless he was much mistaken, this was the hour to shed uniforms and to turn into civilians. From the other side of the street came a rumbling as though from a thousand goblins; nothing could be seen but smoke and dust. But they both noticed the old woman, an old hag who not so long ago had been hobbling step by step with the aid of a stick, and who now ran as she might have run years ago as a young girl; a race with the wild smoke of the steppes. She was a witch-like apparition in the shifting smoke – and just as unreal was her sudden collapse beneath a shower of falling tiles. She did not stir; a doll in a pale dress, stretched out under a cover of drifting smoke. Dr. Linth crossed the road which was full of drifting and whirling objects, knelt down by the old woman and only after he had made sure that she was dead did he return.

By Lake Grunewald it was the same story.

Here a Home Guard unit was entrenched, covering the retreat with a machine gun and a few men stuck in separate holes. Yet not one of them was able to raise his head. Wherever an eyebrow showed, a bullet whizzed past. Sharpshooters had occupied the opposite bank; the advance guard of the Russian infantry which had come from Tempelhof via

Friedenau and Steglitz, Breitenbach Platz, Dahlem and the southern suburbs of Berlin, had just arrived at the bank of Lake Grunewald.

It was impossible to get through; least of all with that strange wanderer across the city battlefield. Where did he want to get to? He was searching for something; for his wife. But where? In Grunewald? Yes, there, and everywhere; at any cross-roads she might appear; might be sitting on any Russian tank. He was not actually searching in the true sense of the word; at least not in the world of material appearances. He could find her only in himself. Suddenly she would be there or she would not be there. That was the story as Sarfeld heard it while he was busy making sure that his companion stuck his head deep enough into the grass to avoid the bullets of the Siberian sharp-shooters.

In between he had to fight off a wild lieutenant who was collecting all able-bodied men to lead them to the Flak tower by the Zoo; on the way they had to hide in several cellars and there was some delay near Kleine Stern too, when they met a flying patrol who examined their papers but let them go.

'All the best, and remember me to your wife; and if you should happen to come to Nikolassee and Teutonstrasse, I shall be pleased to see you.' Thus Sarfeld spoke at the restaurant – Onkel Tom's Hütte; then he continued on his way west towards Nikolassee while Linth turned in the opposite direction looking for the Oskar-Helene-Home.

Linth had hardly closed the door of the Home after him and donned his white doctor's overall, when Russian infantry closed in on the hospital from all sides.

Half an hour passed; half an hour full of changes. All doctors and nurses, the staff, and also the less severely wounded had been ordered to leave the hospital; only three sisters remained. Linth stood in Drei-Pfuhl Platz, a narrow bit of parkland near the Oskar-Helene-Home, with a crowd of civilians driven from their cellars and houses, amongst them soldiers wearing hastily obtained civilian clothes.

This odd collection of people was being sorted out. Some were led away to collection points for prisoners, others singled out for clearing work; all had to hand over their gold and silver, pocket knives, watches, fountain pens. The

Russians seemed to be in need of everything, even handkerchiefs were taken off those searched. Then it was Linth's turn.

He wore a white overall, around his arm was the Red Cross band. The temporary commander, a fat officer with a moustache, asked a few questions concerning the foreign workers' barracks which were grouped around the square. One soldier, a short fellow, his finger on the trigger, hopped around him during the questioning: 'You puck, puck', he repeated incessantly. Linth was indifferent to it all, even agreeable to the prospect of being shot, but the drunken buzzing was beginning to irritate him.

The fat officer got fed up as well.

A kick at his backside that knocked the little man clean over, finished the affair. Where education is lacking force has to take its place, Linth reflected; but the impression he received here was totally different from that which he had received at Hermsdorf.

He was told:

'You doctor . . . you go home.'

Home, where was that? The Oskar-Helene-Home was closed to him. Hermsdorf was far away, and anyway he had no business there. His home was everywhere; he abandoned himself to the wind and chance; drifted again, through Zehlendorf, through the Argentinische Allee, again past Onkel Tom's Hütte. There was plenty of work for him in the cellars and the streets. One boy, for whom he could do nothing except close his eyes, carried cartridges in one pocket and sweets in the other. He bandaged the shattered arm of a police sergeant, the last survivor of his unit which had occupied a so-called resistance line off Kleine Stern in the morning; later it had retreated as far as the Avus where it had met massed tanks and total destruction. The police sergeant who was now wearing civilian clothes, had escaped miraculously; and the fact that he had been sorted out and given his freedom by the temporary Commander was another miracle. As Linth continued on his way he was called into the Mayor's house. Mayor Helfenstein had offered to capitulate to the Russians, had handed over the Town Hall and then shot himself. All that was left for Dr. Linth was to confirm his death and write out a death certificate – a formality which was soon to be abandoned. He went on his way again, crossing streets devoid of people. Smoke was everywhere but not a shot could be heard. Suddenly he heard German spoken again, heard an order: 'Disperse!' Soldiers, their lines spread out, filled the width of the road, behind them rolled a tank. The soldiers and the tank disappeared into the fog like ghosts. Another square, Panje carts and unharnessed horses and clusters of rounded-up people, amongst them several who were in need of first-aid. Linth's white overall and the band around his arm acted as a free pass, and his indifference and lack of concern for all danger was an Open Sesame. Another road between the fronts. A dive-bomber hurled bombs and a troop of Russians fled into a shop. Linth, too, sought shelter there. Among the civilians already in the room were two Red Cross nurses who had tried to reach the hospital in Spanische Allee. They asked Linth whether he was perhaps going the same way and whether they might go with him as they were afraid to go alone.

After the dive-bombing attack the Russians left. Dr. Linth accompanied the nurses. Dead horses; dead soldiers; the streets completely empty. A face looking out from a cellar window registered stupefied astonishment. Others from other hide-outs watched the quietly walking pedestrians with the same surprise. Along the main road into which Linth turned with his companions, Russian troops were marching. The two nurses made as if to run away. Linth had to calm them; nothing would happen that was not meant to happen, he said. In any case an orderly marching column was relatively safe. And in fact they were. The marching Russians were equally surprised; then grinned cheerfully.

'You not run away, you not afraid of Ruski?'

'No, not afraid, why should we be afraid?'

Unmolested, the three of them were able to continue their way. Curious, surprised, startled looks followed them from all the houses. Then one of the cave dwellers from one of the houses appeared, another and yet another. More came; they crept from their holes. They waved and the Russians waved back. Encouraged by the shouts of the onlookers one little Russian had his first try on a bicycle, swerving uncertainly by the side of the column. Suddenly flowers appeared from nowhere thrown to the marching soldiers. At last, at last we may come out of our cellars. No more alarms; we shall undress at night; shall be able to rest quietly.

In this street the spell had been broken. Tanks rolled past. Hands were raised and waved, the riding infantry men laughed. A gap, then two Cossacks, their horses rearing abruptly, and the onlookers applauded as in a circus.

At last, at last . . . the end had come, the war had passed them by. Linth took the nurses as far as the entrance to their hospital. Then he continued on his way alone. He did not know where he wanted to go and yet could not remain in any one spot. A bridge had fallen into the water making the road a cul-de-sac. He turned, walked back quietly and found himself once again in a district empty of people. 'Stalin Organs' rained their rockets on the houses. They fell anywhere, into a yard, a garden, a ruined piece of ground. The laburnum was in full bloom; the cherry blossom was over. White petals lay everywhere. It was Spring and above the pall of bursting salvoes the sky glowed pinkly. Linth noticed a fountain and stopped to drink.

It grew dark rapidly. In the park opposite and in the distance, campfires flared up. Loafing Russians and loose ponies moved through the evening. Foreign gutturals floated across.

Linth used his hollow hand as a cup; there was nothing else. 'Are you a doctor? Would you be good enough to come with me?' somebody addressed him. A man of about fifty stood before him. 'My name is Wittstock,' he introduced himself, 'but I am not calling you for myself; it is a woman, a lady to whom I have offered shelter. It happened all of a sudden, during the change-over, so to speak. I was put into the street by the Russians.'

Dr. Wittstock had been thrown out by the Russians. A certain picture, dragged from the cellar, had played an important part in this. Who would have thought it! The picture of a worker and a huge red flag and the caption HUNGER IN GERMANY. Could anyone have thought of a better passport? It was like a membership card of the Communist party buried in the cellar for twelve years, as he had tried to explain to the Russians – a first lieutenant and two privates who had come into the house and searched. When they understood at last, the effect was totally different from what Wittstock had imagined. That picture acted like a red rag on the lieutenant. *Durak*, idiot, halfwit! – that was the reaction to his confession. And not only that; the two soldiers went for the picture with their bayonets and cut it to ribbons; his chest of drawers went the same way. The Pole called to explain only caused a new outburst of rage. And the end of the story was that Wittstock was thrown out, together with his wife and the whole assembly, the Pole Sikorski, the two internees, the two women from Moabit; all of them – even the wife of Colonel Aachern and her children – called 'damned Communists'. The effect of all the excitement on Frau Halen had been that she lay in labour on the floor of her friend's private shelter in near-by Pfeddersheimerstrasse.

His new friend, the architect Poppert of the Dreyer circle, who had offered shelter to the whole crowd, had encouraged him to go to the district hospital for help. The man standing by the fountain in his white overall with the Red Cross band was a friend in need. That meant he would not have to go any further along the Rehwiese amongst the loafing Russians. And the man really was a doctor. It could not have been better.

'As I said, the lady in question is an acquaintance of mine', said Wittstock. 'The baby should be almost due now.'

He did not have to say more. Wittstock led him to Pfeddersheimerstrasse into the private shelter in the garden of the architect Poppert. Women and children, Wittstock with his clique, the family of the landlord, and several neighbours, were all assembled there. Linth found the woman lying beside the wall. A delicate creature, with fair hair and large bright eyes. Her face was almost chalk-white. Her mouth showed the pain she was suffering; yet not a sound escaped her lips and she even managed to give him a grateful and at the same time apologetic smile. Her face smoothed out; the flickering of pain disappeared; the first wave had passed. Wittstock had been right. The baby might be there any moment.

Some drunken Russians entered the shelter. They were led by a German who shrugged his shoulders and turned to Poppert: 'There is nothing I can do; I am sorry. They sit over there with my wife and my daughters. They are drinking and demand another woman.'

Meanwhile the Russians had a look round. They chose

Frau Aachern and her fifteen-year-old daughter Anneliese. The third one they picked out was Frau Halen.

'Impossible, the woman is with child', Linth intervened. 'With child, child . . .', he repeated as the Russian did not seem to understand.

'You say to me: swinja!' yelled the Russian.

'Child', repeated Linth.

'You say swinja!'

The Russian drew his pistol. 'Stop, stop, try to understand!' Sikorski intervened and not a second too soon. The raving man allowed himself to be calmed down and in the end left with his companions and Frau Aachern and the crying Anneliese. The German neighbour, still shrugging his shoulders, trotted after them.

The Russian visit was neither the first nor the last. The same main road which in the afternoon had witnessed the joyful reception of the Russians by the population, had quite changed with the coming of dusk. The marching columns had dispersed and formed into smaller units or marauding crowds. They searched the houses and haunted the cellars. They always appeared in groups; hardly ever singly. Tap, tap . . . up they came, up the dark stairs, soft cat-like steps, a few whispered words demanding admission, and if the door was not opened immediately, a pistol shot would burst open the lock. A face would peer through a basement window – women, schnapps and watches were the most desired articles; women, too, were mere articles; suffering, resisting, dumb and sometimes screaming objects.

A door opened on a woman and her daughter sitting in a room. The mother first, and then the daughter had to satisfy the intruders; at least there were only three of them. A soldier's wife with her small children stared at the man staggering into the room, and it happened while the little ones stood by feebly punching the brute. A father heard the low-spoken foreign words at the door and went away; as he could not save his daughter he thought it would be better to leave her alone with her visitors. 'I am only a child', whimpered a twelve-year-old, only repeating the words which she had heard the adults say; it took a lot of persuasion to make the drunkard leave the child alone and accept a young woman who offered herself instead.

In Argentinische Allee in a first-floor flat sat one in a cocktail frock. Whilst other women did their best to make themselves look ugly by powdering their hair white and smearing their faces all over with soot, she had dressed herself up. She had travelled from Berlin to Moscow and from Moscow back to Berlin seeking adventure, and had been able to choose a different approach to the Russian onslaught. She sat in a soft armchair, the light of a standard lamp reflecting rich carpets and pictures. The window opened and a Russian appeared on the ledge. '*Schto wui jelaetje?*' 'What do you want?' she asked him. The raised pistol was lowered. Hearing the conventional phrase in his own language, he murmured something unintelligible and disappeared as suddenly as he had come. Three times this was repeated. The fourth visitor, though, was not so easily impressed. She screamed so furiously that an officer came running through the door, and the other, quick as lightning, jumped out of the window. '*Kak sche etot moschet büit, wui sche dama!*' – 'But this is impossible, you are a lady!' she heard the officer say, and now it was her turn to stare at him in amazement.

The announcer for the Luftwaffe radio service, producer and director Sarfeld, had reached his home, had put on civilian garb and gone into the cellar together with his mother and Monika, his fiancée. It was a large block of flats, the cellars of six or seven houses were interconnected and a great many people had gathered there. It was hours before the Russians arrived; plenty of time to do mischief with tank guns and other fireworks. Sarfeld watched a few half-grown youths, led by a greengrocer wearing an SA-cap, running to and fro with their firearms from the cellar into the street and back again.

'If you let off one of those things, the Russians will set fire to the whole quarter', Sarfeld said.

The greengrocer just gave him a dirty look.

'The Russians won't get Berlin anyway', one of them said knowingly. 'The Americans have got Teltow and Wenk's army has advanced as far as Wannsee', declared another.

'Are you out of your mind? I myself have seen the Russians in Grunewald.'

Then the greengrocer broke in:

'Comrades, there is someone here in this cellar who is

handing out defeatist propaganda.' At once a whole chorus chanted: 'Out, out!' That was the moment when Sarfeld knew he had to act. He jumped out and without a word of warning grabbed the greengrocer, and before the youth had grasped what was happening, overpowered him. At once several others came to Sarfeld's aid. The greengrocer and half a dozen men and women who took his part, were locked into a neighbouring cellar.

'There they can stay until they are black in the face or until the Russians are here. Now let's put our house in order and make sure the handing over will proceed smoothly.' Sarfeld formed a committee and got in touch with the people across the road. The anti-tank guns disappeared and in their places white flags appeared.

When eventually the Russians did come, the whole went off without any shooting or complications. But at night it was different. 'Woman, come?' 'Watchi, watchi . . .!' One came and got himself a woman; then another. The women returned, some very quiet, others crying. The flats were searched and everything was turned upside down. So that's how it was; quite different from what Sarfeld had imagined. He went to the Russian Commandant who had his headquarters round the corner. An interpreter who spoke fluent German said there was nothing anybody could do and the Germans had not behaved any differently in Russia. That he would not know, Sarfeld said, he had not been to Russia, had been on the stage during that time. The Commandant, a young lieutenant, recognized in Sarfeld the man who had met him at the head of a delegation on his arrival and had handed him a number of anti-tank guns and pistols. A man of the theatre, an artist – that was a further asset. 'You artista. You play on stage?' He turned to Sarfeld. 'Yes, and so is my fiancée; tomorrow she will become my wife.' 'Your wife tomorrow. Wedding. Good. I shall be your guest at wedding. Until then you live next door.' Sarfeld was allowed to move into the flat next door and remain under the protection of the Commandant. He asked whether he might take some friends with him. That, too, was granted and so he took not only his fiancée and his mother but also a number of women neighbours with him when he moved. Almost twenty people thus enjoyed the protection of the Commandant.

Architect Poppert's shelter was visited by different mobs at least every half hour. Sometimes only one man came, sometimes a crowd. Again and again the cases were ransacked, clothes, underwear, women's and children's dresses taken. Each time everybody was forced to stand up to be searched by the light of a torch. But there were hardly any rings or watches left by now; they had all been collected by earlier intruders. Once in a while a few shots were fired so as to create the necessary 'atmosphere'; on other occasions it was more monosyllabic. 'Woman, come!' – a woman was dragged out and returned distraught shortly after. But during the intervening periods, the odd fifteen minutes between raids, they all slept soundly. So dulled were their senses, so indifferent and exhausted were they and so badly in need of rest, that even these short periods of snatched sleep eased their taut nerves.

Two women staggered into the cellar. They were drunk, demoralized and swearing in the filthiest manner. 'Better a Russian on the belly than a bomb; but one, mind you, not twenty, not a whole company.' One of the women wore a fur coat and nothing underneath it. She had run out of her house like that and soon been captured. In her drunken stupor she accused the women in the shelter of being too lazy and leaving all the work to her while they were hiding. The second one, a very young girl, encouraged her. She attacked the men too. They were cowards and frightened rabbits and it would have been better if they had all been killed fighting. But in the middle of her tirade she burst into tears, and the other began to cry, too; both of them were in a state of collapse. In the end Poppert managed to get both into one of the flats above.

Dr. Linth was still busy with Frau Halen. He helped her as much as he could. So far it seemed to be a normal birth.

Half way through, he was called away.

This was the night of suicides and attempted suicides in Zehlendorf, either because of the Russian visitors or the strain of incessant fear. A woman had hanged herself from the post of her rumpled bed. Another woman had thrown herself and her two children out of the window the moment the door to her room opened. There were a great many overdoses of sleeping tablets, and in those cases help was often possible. There was an epidemic of slashed wrists – attempts which succeeded only rarely. Seneca in ancient Rome had known more about anatomy and had cut his arteries lengthwise, thus preventing any possibility of having them closed up again. The suicides of Zehlendorf to whom Linth was called had cut cross-wise and merely damaged the sinews. The worst cases were those where mothers had cut all the tendons and nerves in their children's wrists and had inflicted only minor injuries on themselves.

When Linth returned to the shelter, Poppert took him upstairs to the flat into which he had put the two raving women. He found both of them poisoned. One lay stretched on the bed; the other, still clad in her fur coat, lay in a bath filled with cold water. Death was due to an overdose of sleeping tablets and to drowning. With Poppert's help he lifted her out of the bath, but could only confirm that she was dead. The eighteen-year-old girl, a music student living in the same street, he managed to bring round. Still under the influence of the drug, she tried to pull Poppert down into the bed with her, and when he managed to free himself, she swore at him, using the same expressions she had heard previously from the dead woman.

Linth was then called to Frau Halen. The moment had come and as there was no midwife he himself officiated. A woman received the new-born baby and, after a makeshift bath, wrapped it in a sheet and put it beside the young mother who, now that it was all over, lay limp and happy on her cushions. The relaxed expression on her face remained, although just then the cellar reverberated with the echo of shots.

Three, four, five shots; plaster fell from the ceiling. The candles went out. Darkness and dust and strange faces. Dark ones and fair ones, slanting eyes, big heads and small heads. Roars from the crowd. The leader of the mob shouted loudest of all.

'Where soldier, where German soldier?'

There were no soldiers here.

'Watchi, watchi . . .'

The watches had already been demanded at least fifty times. Air-raid precaution equipment was once more searched all cases turned upside down; all belongings left higgledy-piggledy.

'No good, no good.'

'All men against the wall.'

'You puck-puck now!'

Linth did not care; Poppert did not care; nearly all of them were indifferent by now. None was particularly courageous but it had happened too often and they were tired of it. Disgust was stronger than anything else. Heads pressed against the wall – this night would end at last.

The shots did not ring out.

Voices were heard, surprised exclamations. 'Oh, oh . . . a baby, a baby is crying.'

A new-born child lay on a pillow and cried.

'Just now?' a Russian asked.

'This very hour?'

'Yes, not an hour ago.'

It was the leader of the mob, a huge, wild-looking in-dividual. On a shelf he spied on accordion and squatted down opposite the young mother. He had steel-grey eyes, and looked like a pirate but was suddenly no longer drunk; with a voice like a brass gong, he sang of the wild pear-tree, of the vast steppe behind Lake Baikal and on without stopping:

'*Volga, Volga, math rodnaja . . .*'

He sent his men outside. They were to stop any further marauders coming in. Peace reigned in the shelter. Nobody was to be molested again. The eighteen-year-old girl who had attempted to commit suicide now came downstairs, quite quiet and with large, wondering eyes. All around snoring could be heard. In a low voice the giant sang.

'Is it a boy?'

'It's a girl.'

> 'The apples and pears are in blossom,
> The mists rise over the river,
> And you, Katjusha,
> Where do you climb
> So steeply up the bank . . .'

Rattling and bumping, petrol and oil fumes. A barrel-organ was playing – playing all wrong. The rattling of the passing tank sounded distant; the rank smell hardly affected her.

The tune of the barrel-organ was stronger.

It was she herself, Dolores; it was twice Dolores, once wearing a white children's dress with flowers embroidered on the hem; and the other the same Dolores, grown up and with long plaits. The third . . . but then the barrel-organ had become a rattling monster spitting fire.

'Volga, Volga, our mother . . .'

A film she had seen, a bad film, a sentimental story on the same theme. The fleet of the robber Stenka Rasin is sailing up the Volga. In the captain's cabin lies the kidnapped Persian princess. The crew are watching their love-sick captain scornfully. A mutiny threatens. Determined, the captain walks into the cabin, seizes his love and sacrifices her to the Volga.

It had not saved him.

But it is no longer a film, not even a ballad; it is already a tale from history.

The Czar got him into his power, he was seized and, like a wild animal, without clothes and spat at by the mob, taken in a cage to Moscow and beheaded in the Red Square.

'Volga, Volga . . .'

Reality is so very different.

Rattling and bumping; oil fumes and smoke making the eyes smart. The tank drove through a town and the gun fired, thick smoke came out as the breech was opened and settled on walls, face and skin. And she, miserable and degraded, with only a great-coat to hide her nakedness, driving into nowhere.

Everything is quite different – the cabin is different and the night, too.

A pandemonium of evil spirits. One of them drove; one was shooting, one fed the shells into the gaping metal mouth; a fourth tapped out morse. And the fifth, the 'Kommandirtanka' – with only half of him inside – almost touched her with the tips of his boots while his head stuck out into the smouldering sky and yelled. His body almost filled the hole, blocked out the light and prevented the smoke from getting out. Just enough light to make out the faces of the sweating devils.

She could not lie down, could not stretch her legs, a piece of lumber, a huddled bundle. A moving tomb, a rattling steel coffin; all the others had their slots through which to look out; only she had none. The coffin tilted up in front as it drove up an embankment; everything slid backwards and she rolled about with all the empty shell cases. The driver and radio operator grinned, but the third helped her, pushed some of the cases aside and covered her again with the coat that had been thrown over her. A courtesy, this gesture with the coat; so that, too, existed amongst the evil spirits. Outside, tearing iron, hissing steam; machine gun volleys rang out like giant peas rattling on tin.

The Commander at the hatch shouted:

'Tegel, Tegel . . .'

Tegel was taken and left behind.

The rattling did not stop. The journey continued. The damned inside the tank knew no respite. The radio operator, 'Radist' they called him, was a fair boy with straw-coloured yellow hair. The driver, black as the night, had a mouth like a slit from one ear to the other. The engine roared; the gun reverberated; the ejected cartridges cases jingled. The crew puffed and spat, sweat drew deep furrows across their soot-smeared faces.

Dolores thought of her husband whom she had left lying unconscious. Was he alive, was he dead? His face, pale and distorted, blood running from his dark hair: strangely, this running blood seemed to assure her that he was alive. Everything was very different; that night, too, had been different. In that horrid bed in Hermsdorf, in a house from which the inhabitants had been driven, nothing had happened to her. A methodical young man, full of forethought, her Kommandirtanka. He put her to bed, covered her carefully, and lay down beside her. Before he turned over to go to sleep he called the one with the slanting eyes and explained something, gave an order. Nothing had happened, and only later, hours afterwards, did she understand what he had in mind and what he had told the soldier to do. He wanted to be woken up every two hours. But nothing came of it, because when the soldier came and shook him, he sent him away again, swearing, turned over and immediately fell asleep again. He slept right through the night and she lay beside him and never closed an eye. That was the night: quelle drôle de guerre!

Day broke with a trumpet blast. The strange man jumped up, looked at her frowning. He was furious about the wasted night, but now it was too late. He thought of a fiendish way out, seized her and dragged her with him.

And now, how was it to go on?

The roar, the stench, everything went black before her eyes.

The noise outside was no longer that of bursting missiles. A cacophony of human, animal and mechanical sounds broke over her.

Where to, where?

She staggered to her feet. She could hardly raise her head in her narrow prison of steel. Rattling of chains, hum o running engines, clatter of horses' hooves, voices in the hot air. And always they went on, on. The man in the hatch bent down to her, called out something. The one with the straw-coloured hair helped her into the greatcoat and put a beret on her head. She was allowed to stand up, to put her head out-side and breathe the fresh air.

The fresh air – a changed world. Columns of tanks with lorried infantry, flanked by riders; Cossacks on the one side, Caucasians on the other. Flashing swords, tips of spears, fluttering coloured scarves, stiff coats of oxhide reaching below the horses' tails. The dead straight Müllerstrasse which ran to the centre of the city was negotiated without fighting. On both sides of the road the shutters were taken down from the windows of the blocks of flats. The blackout paper was torn down, white flags appeared.

White flags, as far as the eye could see.

Shouts, waving hands, in the windows ecstatically happy faces. The tanks rolled past. Mounted troops, a mounted band blaring music. The men on foot followed. Pioneers, mine detectors, baggage trains laden with household goods and featherbeds.

Caps were thrown into the air.

'The war is finished. Hitler is finished.'

Rows of people lined the street, their cries mingled and became one mighty roar.

'One of Goebbels' lies again. Such nice people. Just look at that little one on the bicycle.'

The brass band stopped abruptly. The air grew dark. Movement became jerky. Ahead thick smoke. It was at the bottom of Müllerstrasse. Flames soared from Wedding Station. Rockets howled across the sky. The mounted troops rushed forward like brown smoke.

The woman had to return to her steel prison. The Kommandirtanka came down as well and the hatch was closed except for a tiny crack. Dense smoke and heat, they moved forward in jerks. Her head was swimming, her eyes ached. At last the tank stopped. The hatch was opened and she could leave her box. It was night. The empty shell cases were flung out of the car. Petrol was brought in canisters. The straw-coloured one brought some food, a thick millet porridge. She, too, received her portion. The Kommandirtanka cleaned the spoon with sand and a rag before passing it to her. She could not help noticing the gesture. The tank was one of a row, in a huge circle round a church. Straggly bushes divided hers from the next. Should she run away into the night full of strange noises? Where to? How far could she get? She lay down on the bed of horse blankets. The coat she kept on. She had to, as she was wearing nothing underneath. She lay by herself, heard the others talking near her. The Kommandirtanka splashed in a bucket of water. He washed himself, and the others commented on the ceremony with shouts and raucous laughter. The upper part of the church was lit up by distant conflagrations. It was the Thanksgiving Church, the same in which she had been christened, between the pillars of which she had once played hide-and-seek. Many roads met in this square, Müllerstrasse and Reinickendorferstrasse from the north, Fennstrasse from the Canal and Moabit and the west, and Chausseestrasse and Friedrichstrasse which led to the city centre.

She lay alone, surrounded by thousands of men; alone in a night interrupted by sudden fires and detonations. She fell asleep and the shrill scream of a woman woke her again. She was no longer alone. The man next to her said something she understood, would have understood in any language. He tried to calm her, his hand groped through her hair. And what happened afterwards was not rape; she allowed it to happen.

She thought of Peter, of her husband, and fell asleep again.

The following days passed like the first. She sat again in her narrow box, was sometimes allowed to put her head outside. And yet it was not quite the same. Between her and the Kommandirtanka there existed a tacit understanding. There was much driving, here and there, Fennstrasse, Boyenstrasse, along the embankment of the Canal during the first day; and Schulzendorferstrasse, Grenzerstrasse and as far as Ackerstrasse the second day. In the evening the distance covered was insignificant and had almost led back to the starting point. For the two following nights the resting place was the yard of a large brewery. Once, whilst the Kommandirtanka had been called away, she suddenly saw the face with the slanting eyes bending over her. There was a smell of germinating barley, the damp fumes of the brewery; the man's eyes glowed. He tore her coat off, the buttons came off, too. She resisted and to her surprise she got help. Not from the returning Kommandirtanka, but from another of higher rank. He seized the soldier by the scruff of the neck, and flung him into the night. 'You damned slobbering dog', but she could not understand that. 'You used to wipe your bottom with sand in your village; this one is not for you.' In the opinion of the Major who commanded the tank corps she was not for the Kommandirtanka, either. She was put on her feet by the Major and regarded appraisingly, rather like a horse that had been a bargain. She had to spend the night with the Commander, and next morning was locked again in the lieutenant's tank.

The batch of troops moved forward again in jumps of a few hundred feet at a time. Along Chausseestrasse, past the big barracks, they moved jerkily towards the city centre. The tanks rolled on under cover of the artillery. The salvoes almost touched their roofs. The whole street was in flames, from the bridge over the Panke to Löwe's machine factory, and was masked with dense smoke where fire flashed from the guns of German tanks.

The day trickled away in a grey rain of ashes. Chausseestrasse leading towards the centre from the north, ran across Invalidenstrasse. A few hundred yards from where the roads met was the Russian front line, and on the other side, equally close to the crossroads, the people from the defeated factory and the Home Guard, convalescents and reserve troops, all huddled closely together.

Exactly in the middle of the roaring, bubbling No-man's-land, steps led into the shaft of the underground of Stettiner Station. It was four in the afternoon when a face appeared on the top step of the U-station, the centre of this world of collapsing façades, sliding masses of stone, bursting shells. One face at first; others followed and shrank back before the hot breath of battle. It was no use, there was no turning back. The three, the five, the first dozen, the first hundred faces were not the only ones. Thousands, many thousands, a long column of human beings stood behind the first and pushed and drove them into the fire. The earth seemed to burst on that spot and to spit out a fountain of human wrecks, lame, hurt, hungry, drenched. There was no stopping and no return. There was only death through falling stones, shrapnel, whizzing missiles with perhaps a chance of getting through to the main Stettiner Station.

Stettiner Station. There is rest, there is food and drink and bandages, balm for all wounds. Stettiner Station is the goal, the end of all suffering. 'The road is quite clear. Everything is prepared to receive refugees. Food and drink in plenty', so they said, that was what the swine had said, those liars and deceivers. Lies, false information, deception – after ten days without food, without water, without daylight.

The pressure did not diminish.

The fountain hurled mutilated soldiers, disfigured women, emaciated children out of the ground, hundreds and hundreds of them. The fire from the tanks threw them on to the pavement or forced them forward. The road to Stettiner Station was strewn with dead and wounded. The wounded cried but who was to stay with them! Medical sergeant-major Wustmann was not going to stop; driver Stroh would not stop and neither did any of the others. Who would want to expose himself to the lashing shots from German and Russian guns – unless it be a mother who could not leave her dying child and anyway was longing only for death. All the others ran until they fell.

The Bunker at Anhalter Station had been evacuated. All five floors, even the two occupied by casualties, had had to be cleared. The SS had moved in. The Bunker had become a fighting strong point.

Wustmann did not say anything any more; he was past all surprise; had no longer words for the confusion in which he found himself; was incapable of any opinion. Ten thousand or twenty thousand or more people – who could tell – had been disgorged from the Bunker.

Departure had been at 4 a.m. – now it was four o'clock in the afternoon. Along the dark railway tracks, in the direction of Potsdamer Platz, led by soldiers with torches; that was how it began. The soldiers were supposed to search the tunnel for infiltrating Russians. 'Don't talk; keep quiet', was the order given to those behind. The vault resounded with the hits by the Russian artillery. Underfoot water gurgled; in it lay discarded blankets, eiderdowns, trunks. The water on the tracks rose knee-high, then to the waist.

At Unter den Linden the vaulting had been damaged. From a burst pipe water was rushing. The water tasted of chlorine, but after days of thirst in the Bunker those who managed to get near drank greedily from it. On into the darkness. The soldiers with the torches had disappeared. The water rose further, reached to their chests. In the water lay not only trunks and discarded articles. Their feet slipped on soft shapes, on the dead, on those who had fallen and tried to get up again. Women with small babies in their arms or with young children, fell. They screamed and were pushed forward, floated on the whirling waters. Wustmann was a face in the subterranean night, Stroh was another, Dr. Heide a third. Else Krüger, the Frenchman Lucien, the dairyman Dickmann, his wife . . . hundreds and thousands stumbled through the shaft. No longer thinking, no longer human beings; masks moving in an irresistible mass, through a flood of mud, through sunken wreckage, falling concrete, trickling earth following an unknown law. . . .

The dairyman Dickmann was still fairly strong. He had brought a lot of provisions with him into the Bunker and had been careful with them. When soup was distributed, only for young children and perhaps one or two hundred people besides – he would be in the queue and once, when a barrel of butter had been rolled out of the burning Excelsior Hotel, he had been one of the first to kick the barrel open and to pull out the butter with dirty hands. He had got away with a certificate stating he had Angina Pectoris. Now he had to drag his heavy wife through the darkness.

Chief Medical Officer Dr. Heide was only a skeleton; his eyes flickered like a madman's. His white coat was just a rag drenched with blood. He clung to one of the no longer functioning high tension cables; let the stream of whirling masks go past him; tried to get his breath, to feel that he was human and not an insensitive creature on an aimless migration. That was how Stroh had seen him, clinging to the high tension cable; after that he was never seen again.

The water receded; it only lapped around the feet now; in the end it disappeared altogether. Walking across the sleepers was difficult enough. Baggage was still being thrown away, still the feet moved over lifeless bodies. And many who had come so far were no longer able to carry on, were left squatting in recesses and walls of the air inlet shaft. They would still be squatting there when the flood, caused by the blasting of the Landwehr Canal sluices, would fill the tunnel and all its recesses and branches. Underneath Friedrichstrasse Station a diversion was announced. From the City-Railway duct the way led into the underground duct of the North-South line. The sluice gates at Weidendamm Bridge were opened only just far enough for one person to squeeze through. It was only possible to negotiate the adjoining gate by crawling, and after that there were hundreds upon hundreds of barricades to climb. The sluice of Weidendammer Tor, the vertical gate, the horizontal gate, they all claimed victims. The barricades proved too much for many who were exhausted and for mothers who had to carry their children.

The death march continued as far as Stettiner Station where the masses emerged into the light, into a district wrapped in flames. Wustmann no longer said anything, no longer asked after the conveyance of casualties. Dickmann arrived at the top without his wife. At four o'clock in the morning, Else Krüger had climbed onto the City Railway duct with a three-year-old child; she was now on her own. Wustmann, Dickmann, Krüger, and a hundred others ran and threw themselves down. Not all of them rose again.

Wustmann reached the entrance hall of Stettiner Station, a field strewn with dead and wounded. The stairs leading to the tunnel were black with people; refugees caught while fleeing, women and children and old men from the Alexander Platz Bunker. At the platforms were trains with soldiers of the fighting forces.

'Urrah . . .'

Through Zinnowitzerstrasse they went. The breeches hissed. Shot after shot rang out. Swathed in smoke, a sinister colossus of thick walls and arched joists above, surrounded by earth mounds at the base and wound round with barbed wire as far as the windows, that was Stettiner Station.

'Urraahh . . .'

The dismounted infantry men stormed the earth mounds, cut the barbed wire, removed the remnants of the lacerated shutters around the windows and pointed their automatics into the interior.

The tanks turned away. The tank in which Dolores sat returned to Chausseestrasse, passed Invalidenstrasse, rolled on until it was caught by firing from its flank.

A cemetery wall, the cemetery of the Dorotheenstadt and French community; the area reaches as far as Hessische-strasse. The tanks crashed through the wall, rolled across the graves. At Hessischestrasse and before the flat building of the mortuary, firing from German tanks could be seen. The smoke from the shots drifted across the German lines. The spire of the Apostolic Church seemed to float on a cloud of weaving smoke.

'These dogs, these Huns, will they never have enough?'

'Halt, don't proceed.' – 'Halt, fire!'

'Dogs, dogs . . .'

There were Tigers and King Tigers, Panthers also, heavy Panthers. Heavy calibre shells beat against the armour of the T.34.

'What now; we cannot get through.'

'*Job two je* . . . damn them.' A further lot came up, broke through the gap in the wall – reinforcements.

'Fire!'

'Beat the drums . . .'

Right in the middle of the cemetery a 34 tank starts burning. Another, its tracks jammed, turns round and round as though gone mad. Muzzle flashes. Shell smoke. The hard sound of breeches closing. Stickiness, heat, sweat; dirt;

moaning. There is a roaring, cracking, clanging, thundering. The slit mouth screams; not a sound can be heard. The Kommandirtanka yells. The 'Radist' does not hear him. Dolores Linth cowers in the farthest corner, buried under hot shell cases, feels nothing, hears nothing, knows nothing any more.

The ringing, the tearing, the incessant hammering against the tank wall, the sound of crashing steel, dominates everything.

Bursting bombs.

The tanks rolled on, thrust their noses into a blood-red night. Driving, stopping, reloading and driving on. But moving or stopping, firing or under fire, it was all the same now to the woman who lay under the feet of the tank's crew.

Miserable, helpless, stunned.

Sometime a drink was held out to her. 'Moskovski, forty per cent, *charascho* . . .' It was Vodka; it did not make her feel better, but it burnt the smoke out of her throat and she accepted a second.

Suddenly she woke from her half-conscious state. Something outside was different. It was as though the tossed ship had reached the harbour after a rough crossing and the waves were gently lapping against its sides.

She was alone.

All the others had got out. She was alone, but did not remain alone. The wide-mouthed one came into her prison, filling it completely, reeking of sour Vodka. A heavy cloud pressed her down. No way out, no escape, not this time.

'Lieutenant kaputt, Major kaputt, I make you kaputt, puck, puck!' He looked at her with eyes like glass splinters, drew a knife and slit the dress that she had been given by the Kommandirtanka, down from the neck, and rolled over her.

Peter. . . .

She had to endure him. The shell cases clanged underneath her. '*Woina* kaputt, Hitler kaputt. You kaputt. I make you kaputt . . .' Words like rising bubbles, they gurgled in his mouth, he did not finish them. The grip around her neck relaxed. The man did not rise, remained on top of her with all his weight. She lay in a puddle of oil, amidst cold powder smoke, beneath a breathing Vodka mountain; a fallen besmirched rag. The man snored, overcome by his drink. Out,

out of this cave! She managed to free herself, crawled as far as the hatch, and climbed out into the night. But what a night!

She remained sitting beside the gaping hole. All that was below, the past, her own pitiable state, the present time – all was suddenly forgotten. She felt detached from the ground. The tank on which she sat seemed a stool suspended in the air. It smelled of hay, of disembowelled animals and roasting flesh. Peter . . . The tower, the octagonal nine-storeyed tower; howling nomads underneath the nine-storeyed porcelain pagoda.

Heaven and earth had changed. Time was no longer the same. The latitude had shifted. The world was unhinged.

The hands of the global clock showed the end of the world.

Baggage trains, horses, cows, pigs, heads and entrails of animals. Tents like pointed hats, a lane of tents populated with foreign peoples. The structure of a skyscraper lit up by a detonation and the famous porcelain pagoda of Nanking were one and the same. The waters of the Spree and the Yangtse-kiang were the same. The water was black and coloured by fires. The night sky was the same, red and lined with smoke. And the river bank was the same – haystacks, hooting, noise, ruminating animals and carousing barbarians. The emperor's daughters dragged through the camp, dishonoured and mutilated, their heads cut off and kicked into the gutter. But there was no emperor and no daughters of an emperor. There were BDM-girls and air-raid helpers. There was a group of Land army girls whose uniforms had been peeled off and who had been thrown naked on a bloody and freshly flayed horse hide. The head of the RAD-girl clung to her and gave her an address at Hermsdorf. A lightning flash and the girl's head was severed from the bleeding trunk. She was fleeing and she was caught in a thicket of arms. She was speared to a board and was fleeing still. She lay in a hospital bed and the flight did not cease.

'A remarkable case', said the surgeon.

'The great pagoda in pieces . . .'

Pieces indeed, that was easy to see even without a fever.

'And the barrel organ is playing all wrong.'

'It usually does.'

'Berlin is playing all wrong – and not only Berlin.'

'Heaven knows, that is true', said the surgeon. He had

examined her himself. The wound in the arm seemed harmless, the stab wound in the left thigh, probably caused by a knife, had not cut any tendons either; had not touched the bone and was unlikely to lead to complications. The patient's pulse was fast, but she had no temperature and yet talked of strange, irrelevant things.

'And who is she?'

'Can't get it out of her.'

'How did she get here?'

'A soldier brought her, a Russian infantry man, wrapped in a horse blanket. Underneath she wore nothing but a torn dress.

'Apparently she has suffered physical concussion, quite apart from the other injuries and the psychological shock. Let us put her in a quiet place and keep all possible excitement from her.'

Lights like dragon's heads over Berlin, bursting stars, red ones and white ones; and where they fell they cut a bright circle out of the nocturnal sea of ruins.

Anhalter Station and its surroundings glowed like daylight, the Bunker also, the refrigeration plant and the hollow skeleton of the Hotel Excelsior. Flames leapt from the refrigeration plant's many windows and the charred flesh of forty thousand oxen made the air stink. From the cellars of the Hotel Excelsior rose a thousandfold scream: the Russians are here! The Bunker, into which the advance party of Zhukov's infantrymen with raised torches penetrated, turned out to be a stinking rubbish heap; its filthy treasures guarded by silent watchmen – the corpses lining the walls. Mountains of tossed trunks full of underwear and clothes; mountains of heaped bicycles and perambulators. The passage leading to the street and the long duct to the City-Railway were piled feet high. On the two lower floors, in the abandoned first-aid station, only the death rattle of the dying could be heard. In the vaults cowered suicides, under the benches and in the latrines lay the little corpses of children who had starved to death. Hundreds of dead, some by their own hand, others who had died of starvation or exhaustion. The SS had abandoned the Bunker, the station, the burnt-out Excelsior, and had retreated as far as Potsdamer Platz, as far as the ruins of the Gestapo building and the Luftwaffe Head-quarters, and stood, still firing, their backs almost against Voss strasse and Hitler's Bunker.

The cathedral, the castle and the pleasure gardens shone as if in daylight. The castle, its precincts and the pleasure gardens had been abandoned by German troops and the shots from the advance party of Marshal Zhukov's army approaching from Alexander Platz whirred across the bridge, around the statue of Frederic II on his horse, and scattered the whole length of Unter den Linden which was a mass of baggage trains, staff cars, guns, dead horses and dead soldiers.

As bright as day, too, shone Brandenburger Tor at the other end of Unter den Linden. The pillars had burst, the wings burnt out, the quadriga on the pinnacle – which had journeyed to Paris in 1870 and returned in 1918 – vibrated with the rebounding shots. The feet of the horses splintered like glass; their flanks were riddled; the metal heads broken off. The reins held by the winged charioteer dragged in the dirt, and the sceptre with the Prussian eagle dangled downwards.

Like daylight shone the storm centre, Voss-strasse and Wilhelmstrasse, Wilhelm Platz with the smashed buildings that had been the Old and the New Reich Chancellery, the Foreign Office and the Ministry of Propaganda.

The anvil which was Berlin was now reduced to a narrow strip which had to bear the brunt of a collected force that had flattened a continent. Unceasingly, shells flew along the gaunt ruins and hammered relentlessly on the concrete ceilings of the Bunker labyrinth. The upper layers crumbled and gaped open beneath the showers of falling shells from the nearby batteries.

Ghostly lights over Berlin – and through the flickering, the roar and the tumult, a shadow descended from above, searching in ever narrowing circles from a height of thirteen thousand feet. An 'Arado 96', it drifted through clouds of smoke until it managed to plunge through the dense cloud which hung above the streets to land on the East-West axis.

The first plane to land in three days.

Three days before, it had been Ritter von Greim with Hanna Reitsch – the accompanying forty fighters had dropped like flies struck down by a winter frost. Ritter von Greim and his companion had landed on the same East-West axis, the plane without a bottom and von Greim with his foot shot to pieces. The sergeant-major pilot of the 'Arado 96' managed with less pomp, without fighter escort and without loss of life. In the thick smoke he managed to hide his machine amongst the broken trees of the Tiergarten and found his way, partly by getting lifts in passing cars and partly on foot, to the Führer Bunker. He had passed that way only a week before when he had taken the Minister for Armaments, Speer, to Berlin and flown him out again. The approach to Wilhelmstrasse had changed since then.

The quadriga on top of Brandenburger Tor shook like a dustbin in a hailstorm. Pariser Platz was strewn with lumps of concrete. The American Embassy, the Academy of Arts, Hotel Adlon, looked down on him like buildings from an unearthed Pompeii. A narrow canyon of ruins swallowed him up. Death whined from all the torn walls around. Bombs, shells, rockets. And the grenades, the whining machine gun bursts, the single shots of the sharpshooters were Russian as well as German.

Craters; smell of decay; a dead horse; dead civilians. Suddenly it became so light around him that he could have seen a mouse in the rubble. Russian dive-bombers, four, five; it looked as though they were going to plunge down on him. One leap underneath a fallen arch. Bombs crashed and dust flew up, a hot cloud burned his face. From the next rubble heap he could see the blackened walls of the Reich Chancellery. Together with a figure that came running with flying leaps from the Ministry of Propaganda, he entered the deserted entrance hall. Dust blew in through the empty windows; yellow smoke drifted through the room. At the foot of a cracked pillar a few boys were camping, naval cadets and Hitler Youths with rifles and anti-tank guns. The red carpet which led downwards was covered with discarded paper, empty tins and broken bottles. Both of them went downstairs, unchallenged. Only in front of the armour-plated door were they stopped. The Flight Sergeant-Major had to show his papers first and state the purpose of his visit. He had come to report to Ritter von Greim, the new Chief of the air-force who had replaced Göring, and to fly him out of Berlin. The guard stared at him as though he were an apparition from another world. So there was one, after all, who had managed to get through! The news preceded him along the sunken ship cut off from all contact with the living world. When he was shown into the large outer Bunker, the glazed eyes of the hopelessly drunk turned on him. A waiter floated along with sandwiches, a selection of drinks and a box of cigars. He chose a schnapps and a cigar. He did not have time to bite the end off. A high-ranking SS-officer with a fat, vague face offered him a light from the next table; a second one was already too late offering him a match. Damned polite, these high-ups here. 'Passable', said one SS-officer meaning the cigar. And, by God, so it was. So that was where they sat, smoking good cigars, drinking rum and listening to the rumbling concert of death performed above their heads. An uncomfortable waiting-room, even more uncomfortable than the seat in the 'Arado 96' while she was being rocked by explosions. The Russians appeared to have concentrated their fire from heavy and medium guns on this particular spot in Berlin. A thousand iron teeth gnawed the ceiling of steel and concrete and growled around the walls. It was as though they intended to dig this huge concrete cauldron out of the earth. During a short lull the noise of tumbling stones and sliding rubble could be heard.

A collection of smoking, drinking and bemused idolaters; their idol, already worm-eaten, had shown the fatal crack exactly seven days ago and had prophesied the certain end.

At one of the tables, Bormann, Goebbels and Ambassador Hewel were seated. The civil servant from the Ministry of Propaganda, Deputy Press Chief Heinz Lorenz, had reached that table. He handed to his Chief, Goebbels, a sheet of typewritten paper. Goebbels glanced at it and gave it to Bormann, though as carefully as if it had been a new high explosive that could be detonated by the touch of a fly.

A Reuter communiqué – saying no less than that Reich Leader SS, Heinrich Himmler, had asked Count Bernadotte of Sweden to negotiate an armistice. The Reich Leader SS – and nobody else in the Bunker had the slightest notion of it. It was as though neither the Führer HQ nor the Führer himself existed any longer, as though they no longer had the right to give orders or take part in what was going on. Here, where the one explanation for any happening outside, for every

collapse from the Alps to the North Sea, was: 'Treachery!'
But this thing that glared at him from the paper was the
blackest treason of all – and from a quarter where he had
least expected it.

Heinrich, the coach is breaking.

No Sir, it is the iron rings around my heart.

The faithful Heinrich – so that is his true face! A miserable,
mean scoundrel stretching out a besmirched paw towards the
sceptre before the hand still holding it is cold. Neither Bormann nor Goebbels dared appear before their Master with
this news. The valet Linge was called, and was entrusted with
the task.

The three men at the table watched him go. In brooding
silence they stared at the second copy in their hands. This was
indeed highly explosive material, and Bormann and Goebbels
and Hewel knew that it could not be long before it would
dissolve in thunder and smoke.

'When are they going to relieve Berlin?' 'What is Heinrici's
army doing?' 'Where is Wenk?' 'What has happened to
Holste?' 'Where are the searchlights from Prague?' Thus the
telegrams which went into all directions, to Keitel and Jodl at
Fürstenberg, to Dönitz in Flensburg, to the meanwhile
arrested and then released Koller at Berchtesgaden. The
answer was silence . . . deadly silence. Bormann burst out:
'Instead of encouraging the troops who are to free us, the
chiefs don't even open their mouths. There's no loyalty any
more. We remain here. The Reich Chancellery already a heap
of rubble.' Again – silence.

What answer indeed may a tomb expect, even if the
Pharaoh bricked in with his courtiers, is still determined to
continue breathing beyond his time?

The orders from the Führer Bunker were now only the
helpless stammering of a restless corpse. The ordnance map
that had once spanned the area from the North Pole to the
pyramids of Egypt and the Caucasian mountains, was now
reduced to a street plan of Berlin. And even this was dissolving in the sweating hands of a commander who had gambled
away a Continent. And the armies ordered to march and to
break the ring round Berlin were either non-existent or
scattered and broken remnants. Keitel and Jodl had gone –
white ravens flown from the unholy Mount Ararat in search

of relief. Now only Bormann, Goebbels, and the two alco-
holics, Burgdorf and Krebs, continued with the unending
game of situation reports.

News was received from Keitel – excessively encouraging,
with promises that could not be kept. Keitel had visited the
Army Commander Wenk at his HQ, and had tried to persuade
him to hasten the ordered breakthrough into Berlin. Commander Wenk knew the patriotic will to fight was strong in his
seventeen-year-old cadets and matched the high-sounding
names of his divisions – 'Scharnhorst', 'Ulrich von Hutten',
'Clausewitz', 'Theodor Körner', 'Friedrich Ludwig Jahn'.
But he knew, too, that a childish faith and a readiness for
death in battle could not replace the necessary vehicles, communications, tanks and guns. Without these and air support,
any attack was beyond his scope. Wenk would only agree to
form a collecting station south of Berlin for the Ninth Army
retreating from the Oder.

Keitel met the Commander-in-Chief of the 'Vistula'
division somewhere between Neustrelitz and Neubranden-
burg. Heinrici's front had broken and scores of wounded and
unarmed soldiers, with refugees amongst them, swept past.
Columns without guns, without tanks, behind them an enemy
fifteen times superior. Keitel shouted to the Commander:
'If you had done as Rendulic did in Vienna and shot a few
thousand deserters or hung them from the trees, your army
would not be on the run now!'

Keitel did not have Heinrici arrested as the staff officers
standing by had expected. But neither did he intend to
sacrifice to an illusion, the only tank corps left to him, the
Third Armoured Division. Against orders also he withdrew
his right wing from the Oder, and refused to deliver a division
of badly armed seventeen-year-old naval cadets into certain
destruction by making them defend the fortress in Swine-
münde. When Keitel returned to Fürstenberg, he declared
Heinrici dismissed the service and ordered his arrest and
court-martial for disobedience in the face of the enemy.

Hitler also demanded news from Keitel about Wenk, Busse
and the Ninth Army which, with the help of Jodl and Keitel,
he had forced to make a last stand until – like other armies
before – it had bled to death. In fact, the last remnants of
the Ninth Army were being slaughtered at that very

moment, leaving one hundred and ten thousand dead and as many prisoners, between Halbe and Märkisch-Buchholz.

No news of Wenk, Busse, Heinrici, of Holste and Schörner; in the end there was no news from Jodl and Keitel either. The Chief Command with Keitel and Jodl had hurriedly to leave the HQ at Fürstenberg. They were now fleeing north along forest paths. Hitler no longer heard anything. The captive balloon which for so long had been the only means of communication with the world outside, had been shot down. The radio telephone to Fürstenberg, the last link with events outside, was dead. All cables were silent; the ether remained void. Into this state of things came Linge, his dear, faithful Linge, carrying a sheet of paper. Hitler was visiting Ritter von Greim. He was sitting on the edge of his bed and knew at once that Linge was bringing decisive news; the long awaited reply.

'The waggon is breaking. . . .' His face changed colour, grew deep red and bloated, became pulp, a swamp in which the eyes flickered like will-o'-the-wisps.

He uttered a sound.

Treason, disgrace, infamy – it might have meant any of those. He staggered off, into his den, only to appear the next moment violently screaming.

'Poor, poor Adolf', cried Eva Braun, running aimlessly along the corridor. 'He isn't spared anything', moaned Magda Goebbels. Bormann and Goebbels were ordered to a conference behind closed doors, and after a while Krebs and Keitel too were called.

The Flight Sergeant-Major was told to go to Ritter von Greim. He reported there, and that was all that was asked of him. There was nothing to report about the abortive 'Exercise Stork'. Six Storks and thirty fighters had started out from Rechlin in order to escort von Greim and Hanna Reitsch, and neither the Storks nor the twelve Junkers 52 who had followed the next night with SS-crews for Berlin, had managed to get through. And now those enormous efforts and the number of victims that the two enterprises had claimed, seemed no longer important. Neither Ritter von Greim, stretched motionless on his bed, nor Hanna Reitsch, now wanted to fly out. They meant to stay in Berlin; meant to remain in the Bunker, to die with their Führer.

'But how you have changed, my lad!' The Flight Sergeant-Major did not recognize the energetic Commander of Number Six squadron. Now, elevated to the position of Chief Commander of the Luftwaffe and Fieldmarshal, he lay on his bed yellow in the face, listening to what Hanna Reitsch was saying. According to her, they should swallow the poison capsule they had received from the Führer and pull the release of a hand grenade simultaneously so that they would be torn to pieces and not fall into the hands of any Russian No, they no longer intended to fly out. Victory with their Führer, or death with him, that was their motto. However, it was to be different. Their Führer had decreed otherwise.

Nobody knew what had been discussed during the conference. The chairman and the four assessors, facing death themselves, could only plan death for the others, their wives and associates, the five children, and for all those they were still able to contact outside the Bunker. Goebbels, Bormann, Burgdorf and Krebs crept away. Their master remained behind, lying trembling in an armchair. As the retreating steps faded away, so did the lamentations, the abuse and curses, the complaints and assurances which had filled the room until now

'I am innocent, innocent . . . my Führer, I am innocent!' The cries of despair resounded throughout the building, through all the corridors, up the stairs and into the garden of the Reich Chancellery. They were carried into the night torn by artillery salvoes. He who lay prostrate in the lowest Bunker tapped out the beat to the receding sound of the marching platoon. A lieutenant and six men were leading between them Hermann Fegelein, bound, sweat dripping from his forehead. They led him outside into the eternal night. Fegelein, a toad, a cheat, a dirty traitor, in league with the monster Himmler – and he was almost his brother-in-law, was supposed within a few hours to be his legal brother-in-law.

Hermann Fegelein had married Gretel Braun, sister of Eva Braun, and so far had enjoyed the favoured position of 'Crown Prince'. But unlike the others of the Führer's sinister entourage, he had intended to escape the communal death in the Bunker, had left there secretly a few days ago, but had been fetched from his flat in Charlottenburg when a scapegoat was needed for the 'traitor Himmler'. Himmler was out of reach, but Fegelein was his representative accredited to the Führer and had to suffer death as a stand in.

It took a long time, too long, before the trembling man heard that the execution had taken place.

At last: 'Order carried out!'

Fegelein was dead; up there amongst the ruins and unburied dead lay just another corpse. But the end of this one poor fish was not enough; the salvo was meant for Himmler. To get Himmler he had only one weapon at his disposal – Ritter von Greim and Hanna Reitsch.

A shaking ghost with glaring eyes. Artillery fire gnawed at the Bunker walls. How long could the concrete ceiling support the crushing lumps of steel and masonry?

'Eliminate Himmler', said Hitler. 'Eliminate, eliminate!' he repeated. 'A traitor must not become my successor. Start at once; fly to Ploen; arrest him; he must be rendered harmless by any means you choose.'

No use Hanna Reitsch reiterating that she wanted to die with her Führer. It did not save Ritter von Greim that he was unable to move, that his shattered foot had swollen into a shapeless lump and was slowly poisoning him, that fever racked his body. His Führer had two orders for him. First of all he was to arrest Himmler. Secondly, he had to gather all the airpower he could muster to bomb Potsdamer Platz, Anhalt Station, and all the streets in which the Russians prepared for the final attack. Thus another twenty-four hours would be gained, and that had to be sufficient for Wenk to complete his breakthrough to Berlin, Hitler said.

Ritter von Greim, a yellow-skinned wreck hobbling on two crutches, and Hanna Reitsch, were loaded on to an armoured car and transported through the glowing night to the plane hidden in the parkland. The 'Arado 96' rose. The Russian anti-aircraft guns blew furies of black smoke into the sky. The machine, rocked by the detonations like a piece of paper, swayed from one smoke island to the next and gained height. Burning Berlin was left below, then disappeared altogether.

And the Bunker disappeared with its shaking ghost who now decided that the hour had come to prepare his wedding. A wedding with a single registrar; a shot brother-in-law outside the front door; a bridegroom wrapped in sullen silence waiting only for the end and yet unable to face it; his speech to his bride hailing her imminent suicide as a release from all the treachery of this world. During the whole of this time – during the wedding feast, the making of the Will – the silent farewell from his companions – the shells were bursting, bombs were falling, anti-tank fire hit the approaches to the Bunker, the inlet shaft of the ventilation plant circulated powder smoke from above into the deepest corners and blew dust into the filled champagne glasses. In the end the ventilators had to be turned off; the humming ceased and the smell of decay rose from the corners. And all this time the drunken noise from the canteen of the Chancellery never stopped. Jazz, shouting, laughter. He who was occupied with making his Will, had to send a guard up to request some moderation.

The testament was meaningless. The signature, too, formerly indicating perhaps some signs of mental derangement, was now nothing but a bit of fly-dirt. This was no Attila, no Genghis Khan. Was he the murderer of Europe or but the maggot in an already rotten apple? Was the intellectual élite of European capitals already so corrupted that an 'Emperor without clothes' could override them? The map of post-war Europe was already marked out. He who stood entirely in the shadows of his own great past, was no longer concerned in it.

He dictated his Will.

His secret remained untold.

His secret was: non-existence – *niente, njet, nihil.*

But he had achieved one thing: he had mobilized nothingness.

The gate was thrown wide open.

The ball had been set rolling . . . is still rolling. Will the heirs to the destruction; the coalition of the victorious nations, be able to stop it once more and restore the disturbed equilibrium of the world?

On the 30th April, in the fourth hour, deep down in the lowest Bunker of Voss-strasse, behind closed doors, a shot rang out which left all questions unanswered, which did not even stop the fires in Berlin, the blasting of the bridges, the drowning in the sewers. The gramophone record in the Bunker canteen continued to spin. SS-orderlies, for lack of women, danced with one another, hopping frantically around the room. Despairing drunks stared into their glasses as before.

Only in the cordoned-off part of the Bunker, now devoid of guards and orderlies, on the spiral staircase leading downwards, and in the passage, a ghostly crowd assembled: Bormann, Burgdorf, Goebbels, adjutant Guensche, the valet Linge, and last of all, the chauffeur Kempka and youth leader Axmann. Haggard faces; consternation; sudden fear turning just as suddenly to relief at the lifting of a terrible weight: that was all – except for the deed which was still to do.

The 'Chief' was dead.

It only remained to burn his corpse. They entered the room, Goebbels, then Axmann, then the valet Linge. Linge wrapped the body with the smashed head in a blanket, and with the help of one other carried it into the corridor. Bormann picked up the body of Eva Braun without shrouding it. A gloomy procession: Kempka took the dead bodies from the hands of Linge and Bormann, on the stairs Guensche took them, and further up a third SS-officer who carried them as far as the garden. The mourners remained standing in the doorway sheltered from the bursting Russian shells. Guensche threw a burning rag over the petrol-soaked bodies. A flame shot up. For the last time hands were raised in the Hitler salute. Nothing more; not a word of farewell; not one word. 'Stalin Organs' hissed. Bursting shells spread a green light. The mourners disappeared into the Bunker and dispersed.

That was all.

First the flame, and afterwards the trail of smoke, from four in the afternoon until eight in the evening. Watched only by the routine guard on the watchtower. Once somebody came along, kicked the charred bones with his feet and scattered them. Later two SS-men appeared, carried off the remains and threw them into a shell crater, mixed in with the tossed remains of other dead.

No burial mound; no tombstone; never will the nocturnal sky form an arch above this last resting place; never will the stars, the eternal lamps of the dead, keep watch over this grave.

Part Three

*The proposed peace seems to me a frightful sowing of dragons'
teeth.*

Admiral William D. Leahy

A nightmare . . .

And not yet over, still hovering over the injured city, riding
across the desolate countryside, clutching the necks of men
and tearing women with its claws. . . . Boehlke, Loose, Splüge,
Theysen, Sarfeld, Wittstock father and son, Frau Halen and
Frau Riek, the architect Poppert and the dairyman Dickmann, Bauer and Hasse, even Zecke; and the fate of each of
these – Boehlke or Loose or Theysen – multiplied a hundred,
a thousand times.

Colonel Zecke had not escaped the claws of the nightmare
either. The current of defeat had carried him back to the
centre. The train he had taken, the last train to leave Anhalter
Station for Berchtesgaden with two staff coaches coupled to it,
did not reach Dresden. The place they stopped at was called
Elsterwerda. Zecke had watched fields and roads and still-
functioning level-crossings move past like images in a dream,
unreal to him in his fading alcoholic state. When he finally
came round and the wheels had stopped turning, his compartment was almost empty. The passengers were standing in the
corridor. He saw the engine slide past the windows to be
coupled to the end of the train and he heard somebody saying:
'We shan't get to Dresden. We shan't get to Dresden.' Then a
message came from the station commandant that the connection between Elsterwerda and Dresden had been broken by
the Russians and that anyone who cared to do so might continue by road; the train would be re-directed back to Berlin.
Zecke did not want to return, to make unnecessary detours
and double back like a hunted hare – Berlin, Dresden, Prague
– were they not all the same at this time? 'Everywhere is
fairyland . . .' he quoted; and unless he were very lucky, there
would be no help anyway. He decided to continue on foot
with his knapsack on his back. The road ahead of him, and
behind, was littered with similarly laden figures. They did not

get very far; at the first crossroads, a squadron of Russian tanks waited.

After many days' march past Finsterwalde and Luckau, fairyland turned out to be the walking cemetery between Halbe and Märkisch-Buchholz, the grave of the tanks and guns and lorries of the Ninth Army.

The Soviet army report that day said: South-east of Berlin the troops of the Byelo-Russian and the First Ukrainian front completed the liquidation of the encircled German forces. Captured booty included 304 tanks and armoured cars, more than 1500 fieldguns, 2180 machine guns, 17,600 motor vehicles and numerous other weapons and war material. More than 120,000 German soldiers and officers were taken prisoner. Amongst the prisoners are the Deputy Supreme Commander of the Ninth Army, Lieutenant-Colonel Bernhard, the Commander of the Fifth SS-Corps. Lieutenant Colonel Marx, the Commander of the 169th I.D., Lieutenant Colonel Ratschi, the Commander of the fortress at Frankfurt on Oder, Major General Biel, Artillery Commander of the XIth SS Tank Corps, Major General Strammer, and Luftwaffe General Zander.

Generals, colonels, majors in one row, behind them soldiers, dilapidated, dirty, tired, many of them wounded, many limping. One of this grey flood, now trekking with an empty knapsack and without rations amidst rounded-up horses and cows towards the Rüdersdorfer Chalk Hills, was Colonel Zecke.

Another amongst the confused crowd of prisoners of war was Captain Boehlke. The two Russians he was supposed to take with the Sanka from Fienerode to Hohenseeden, had proved his undoing. Their road led past the shattered and abandoned equipment left behind by Wenk's army. This was the area of the reception point for the Ninth Army. Instead, crowds of refugees from the suburbs and south-eastern battlefields of Berlin had streamed into the general confusion. Together with this crowd of belated refugees Captain Boehlke had got as far as Schwielowsee and after further sorting out had been ordered to march in the direction of Kaputh.

The ball had been set rolling . . .

Boehlke was left behind at a camp near Kaputh with a serious attack of dysentery. Colonel Zecke together with ten thousand ghosts, camped in the open, rain or shine, in the grounds of the Rüdersdorfer Chalk pits. Architect Poppert, like Wittstock before him, had been forced to give up his house to an NKWD-regiment and was now with his wife and child on his way, right through the front lines via Wannsee and Potsdam, to Paaren on Wublitz where he hoped to find shelter in a week-end bungalow. Frau Halen, after a rape that nobody had been able to prevent, now lay in another cellar of the Pfeddersheimerstrasse stricken with puerperal fever. Dr. Linth had taken her there after the evacuation of Poppert's house. Walking from cellar to cellar, Linth finally arrived in Teutonenstrasse. The companion of his walk through Grunewald, theatre director Sarfeld, was no longer in his flat. Nothing had happened to him, the neighbours reported; he was well and a big noise with the Russians. The divisional commander from the corner of Teutonenstrasse had taken him along to Schmargendorf police station.

The new Superintendent of Police, Sarfeld, had his hands full. It was his job to prevent the looting of provision stores and empty private houses; his power, though, extended only to the inhabitants of Berlin, not the Russians. The local Kommandatura approached him with various requests which he had to satisfy. He was asked to supply tables, chairs, meat, cucumbers, radishes, lettuce, carrots, parsley, celery, onions, coloured printed paper to be used as tablecloths, and a net so that the Commandant could go fishing. At the moment he was occupied with the printer's proofs of regulations that had been issued by the occupying power, according to which people were not allowed to leave their houses from dusk until dawn, not allowed to use lights without blacking out their windows, and not allowed to light bonfires or use electric light; further, nobody was permitted to receive anyone, not even members of the Red Army, overnight without special permission from the military Commandant.

Director Knauer, together with arrested technicians and engineers, sat in the cellar of the Chief Medical Officer's residence in the grounds of the reserve hospital 122 and was being interrogated for at least the twentieth time, this time by the Chief of the division, the young Major Judanov. He was allowed to sit down, was even offered a cigarette. The interrogating major behaved with perfect politeness. His secretary sat smoking a cigar, flaunting ruby-red finger-nails and taking down every word that was said. The major had the reports of previous questionings in front of him. They were all technical matters, not only about machinery, and covered the textiles industry, paper factories and electrical industries, also industries which had been evacuated from Berlin.

'Your replies are generalizations, Herr Knauer', complained Major Judanov. 'But let us leave it.' He sent his secretary out for some tea and offered Knauer one of his cigarettes.

'Let us leave Ardenne's case then', he said, and with good reason. It was only twenty-four hours since he had received a tip through a British secret agent. 'You are executing a valuable man, the famous atom physicist Baron von Ardenne.' He had called Budin and jumped into a car. They did not arrive a moment too soon at the barrack square where a handful of 'Fascists' had been assembled to be shot, Baron Ardenne amongst them. He had saved him and taken him into the security of the H.Q. Karlshorst.

'Even if you don't know anything about Baron Ardenne', he said turning again to Knauer, 'surely you can tell us where the physicist Hertz is at the moment.'

'I have told you that I know no more than the Berlin directory.'

'He is not in his flat. But he must have a so-called hide-out. Don't you understand, we have only his welfare at heart. We want to protect valuable men in these disturbed times.'

'I am sorry, but I don't know Professor Hertz.'

'We have been told a different story.'

Indeed, Director Knauer had once been introduced to Professor Hertz at a party. Major Judanov used this to insist that Knauer must know the present whereabouts of the famous physicist.

'We know that you have often been to the Kaiser-Wilhelm-Institut.'

'I had permission to go there and have visited it a few times; that is all.'

'You were there often. And now you pretend that you don't know either Professor Hertz nor Professors Thiessen or Döpel. What am I to make of that?'

'I know all those gentlemen by name but have never been in personal contact with them.'

Again a long silence.

Judanov wrote; his secretary blew clouds of smoke into the air. This might go on for ever; there need be no end to it. But this time something happened to put an end to it. A telephone call – obviously something very unusual. Judanov stared at Knauer, then at his secretary. He called his deputy, Budin, a barrel of a man, who appeared immediately. Judanov said one word and seemed to regret it at the same moment: '*Chramoi*!'

The cigar disappeared from the hand of the secretary. Budin stood nailed to the spot. In silence Knauer was led away.

In the cellar he asked someone who spoke Russian: 'What does Chramoi mean?'

'Old Cripple Foot.'

The cellar of the Chief Medical Officer's residence was an improvised prison, the window at ground level. The incarcerated economic experts were therefore able to watch the arrival of an armoured car. Judanov, followed by Budin and several officers, approached the car. Two men got out, one in civilian clothes, the other, a short man with an emaciated face, with the insignia of high rank on his coat; he dragged one foot as he went into the house.

This was the cripple who made the officers of the special division grow pale. . . . The German economists in the cellar could not know what Major Judanov, Captain Budin and the other officers of the division knew: that a visit from 'cripple foot' meant the deportation and liquidation of whole staffs or of the complete management of industrial combines. This man, thin, stooping, pale and short-sighted, had for years left his mark throughout many countries, in Transbaikal, the Ukraine and White Russia, as well as the newly acquired Baltic provinces. His influence was recognizable by sensational suicides in the most elevated circles, by overflowing prisons and overwork for the execution squads. The cripple was Ivan Serov, Chief of the operational divisions, endowed with special powers, and the civilian by his side was Saburov, in charge of the dismantling of the German industrial plants.

In the centre of the city the battle continued; hope still flickered that the fortunes of war might yet turn. A dozen groups stood their crumbling ground, backs towards the Reich Chancellery. The Zoo Bunker still sprayed fire from its 15-centimetre anti-aircraft guns, and in its shelter a considerable number of army units were assembled. And in Spandau, Axmann's Hitler Youth was still holding the bridges across the Havel ready for Wenk's army.

'Where are the Russians?'

'Nonsense!'

Vicco Splüge, too, thought it all nonsense; the crowds in attics and alleys who lashed out senselessly like enraged tigers; the army camp inside the Ministry of Propaganda – councillors and government clerks with steel helmets and pistols; the whole nonsensical war-game; and his own patrol, which had only led him across the street and past the ruins of the Hotel Kaiserhof. Two girls, armed to the teeth and sitting on motor bikes with protective wire cages picked their way through the debris. Two messengers of the mobile women's division 'Mohnke' which was directed to places of emergency. Most of them came from East Prussia, had lost their home and parents, sisters, brothers or children, and could no longer think of anything but revenge. For them nothing was left but this sinister path of sacrifice.

'Two Mohnke girls', said Splüge.

'Nonsense', said the other.

That one word was rather too limited to establish understanding.

'Nonsense, yes, but where are the Russians?' Splüge asked again.

'Everywhere, I tell you, in the street, right on top of you; it is all nonsense.'

A direct hit from the artillery, a ball of fire, flying debris. The two Mohnke girls had disappeared like a vision in the dust. Splüge and the sergeant – the one who had been stopped by the patrol at the Belle-Alliance Platz, Sergeant Loose – lay side by side on the ground, flat as flounders and like them covered up to their eyes – with splinters, bits of brick and the flying earth that had been Wilhelmstrasse. Their eyes squinted into the swaying chaos of plaster dust, smoke and fire.

The sergeant rose and with him two other staggering figures, stumbling across the Wilhelm Platz in zig-zags and disappearing into the ruin of the Reich Chancellery. Splüge remained lying down and beside him and behind him lay the wounded, dying, dead. The muzzle of a machine gun pointed towards the sky. The crew lay around it, some of them torn to pieces, others seemingly unhurt as though asleep. And then suddenly some more of those odd creatures, four of them this time, appeared from nowhere, two of them striped like zebras, accompanied by SS-guards.

'Down!' shouted one of the guards. They threw themselves down beside the dead crew. They too, like the sergeant before them, were on their way to the Reich Chancellery. A large lump of concrete spiralled into the air. The ground shook. Dirt. The moon eclipsed.

Splüge was still lying like a flounder, covered by the dust raining down on him. A Luftwaffe uniform bent over him, a pale, anxiously peering face.

'Are you mad, Leonore?'

'You still alive, Vicco?'

'Are you mad; what are you doing here?'

He pulled her down to him on the rubble. Hit followed hit. All around them the fifteen pounder guns stood like ghosts with burning eyes. Balls of fire fell from the burning front of the Ministry of Propaganda. Burning papers showered sparks over them. Out of the rubble the glassy eyes of a dead man stared at him. But he kissed the girl on the mouth. That was something he had not done during the whole time he had been in the army camp inside the Ministry of Propaganda. He tried to undo her uniform. After ten days of howling death this suddenly seemed real.

'Are you mad, Vicco?' This time it was her turn to ask.

'I think we both are, Leonore.'

Yes, out of their minds, no different from any of the others of the Battalion Wilhelmsplatz. Only yesterday they had dragged Persian rugs and Bokhara carpets out of the Herpich carpet store. Before that they had brought back chess boards, clothes, underwear, teddy-bears from their marauding parties which had taken them as far as the Gendarmenmarkt and Wertheim and Leipzigerstrasse. But now he thought he understood these plunderers, and also the couples in the smashed sewers; he even believed that he had found the key – the key to the mentality of the Russians and their hundred-fold cruelties in this death-swept city.

It has nothing to do with reason, he thought, solely with death, the primeval fear of everything living. No longer to exist, no longer possess anything, not to be able to get a spark from one's body – that must not be, cannot be. And life – living can be proved. I am sitting on a Bokhara carpet and light a cigar with a hundred Mark note; I lie with a woman and all this proves that life is real. But the proof has to be repeated, every hour and many times. More carpets, more hundred mark notes, more women. The dark one stands by inscrutably.

'Oh, Leonore.'

'What is it?'

'We should not have done it.'

'We need not talk about it.'

'No, not talk, but think about it we must. Do you believe we shall die?'

'Yes, if we stay here, soon.'

'Come, on then, away, back into the cellar.'

Hitler was dead and in the Ministry of Propaganda, only just across the road, they had no idea of it. General Weidling who had been appointed Chief Commander of the troops in Berlin with special powers, had been able to suggest capitulation to Hitler, and Hitler had left him without an answer; had instead sent Krebs into the street to look for Wenk's army that – so his intuition told him – was waiting on Potsdamer Platz. When Weidling went to the Bunker the following day, he was told: 'Hitler has committed Hara-kiri.'

Hara-kiri – that was an evasive term for an ignominious desertion from the highest post. And in the streets of Berlin the battle still raged. Streets were lost and taken again. The various fighting groups lacked any form of liaison. No relief nor rest for them, no regular meals, hardly any bread – and drinking water only from the Spree. Nothing could now prevent complete military chaos. Again Weidling demanded capitulation, this time from Goebbels and Bormann, and again his demand was refused. He was forbidden to establish any contact with the Russians. He returned to his place of command and relieved his soldiers and officers of their oaths of allegiance.

Bormann and Goebbels, already doomed to die, were nursing one last ray of hope. They thought they might get official permission from the Russian Marshal Zhukov to pass through the Soviet lines in order to reach the North and – so they explained through Krebs whom they had sent as an intermediary – prepare the capitulation with Dönitz, the new leader of the Government. But when Krebs returned, covered in mud, red-eyed, more dead than alive, and bringing nothing but the categorical demand for unconditional surrender, the hour had come for Goebbels, too. A carpenter had already delivered to the Bunker the coffins for Goebbels' five children. He left it to his wife to poison the children. Nor did he take his own life. He led his wife by the arm upstairs to the garden of the Reich Chancellery, and, together with her, was shot by the guards who had been previously instructed. Hitler was dead; his fire-charred bones were scattered. Outside the garden entrance of the Bunker, not far from the greenhouse, another fire was burning, a smaller one this time, and the flames licked around the dead bodies of a couple named Goebbels.

A typhoon of fire separated the Ministry of Propaganda from the other side of the road and nobody knew of the events that took place there. Secretary of State Naumann had sent word that he would come soon and bring decisive news. The day had passed, evening had fallen, and hundreds of men and women, telephonists, high-ranking officials with their wives and daughters, drivers, casualties, journalists, SS-men, officers, strange women with children, were waiting for Naumann and the promised decisive news.

'Not yet, not yet', the returning Splüge was greeted.

'Naumann has not come yet.'

It was stiflingly hot; the air like an oven. Above the cellar vaults lay the red-hot bricks of the collapsing building. What is happening? Where is Naumann? Where is Wenk's army? What has happened to Steiner? How far has Schörner advanced? Had Naumann not promised relief through Wenk and Steiner and the arrival of a tank army under Schörner's command? Had he not said that it was only a question of a day now, an hour probably? That had been days ago.

What is the position?

During the first few days this stereotyped question had been something of a joke. That was all over now and so were the strategic reflections according to which the Russians would be lured into the city centre so as to perish through the onslaught of an overwhelming force which would ring the city. During the past twenty-four hours, two-hundred thousand shots had been counted which had hit the Ministry of Propaganda, the Reich Chancellery and Göring's Air Ministry. Under this hail of fire neither optimistic nor pessimistic reflections could survive; there was simply no room for thought at all. Naumann was an *idée fixe*, an idle fancy. Naumann, the messenger of the Führer, was bound to bring new orders, deliverance, salvation from the almost unbearable.

And Naumann came.

After having been expected for twenty hours, he emerged on the other bank. During a lull, whilst only stray shots from sharpshooters whipped along Wilhelmstrasse and whilst the 'Stalin Organs' shrieked again behind the ruined façades, he crossed – this time it was a veritable witches' ride – zig-zagging across the ground which was spattered with hand grenades, staggered into the cellar and was immediately surrounded by men and women, by doctors, soldiers and wounded, and opposite him, amongst the crowd of pale and twitching faces, stood Fritzsche.

It was the evening of the 1st of May.

The 1st of May, traditional day of celebration of Soviet youth, the Soviet state, the Red Army; the greatest holiday – with slogans on banners. Was this time also the beginning of victory celebrations, taking place in the not-so-badly furnished cave of the bear. Ivan had got rid of his house – the Fascists had burned it. He had lost his land – the Fascists robbers had taken it from him. In reality the Fascists had never got as far as Archangel. His land had become collective property, and he had lost his house in quite a different way. He had had to exchange it for the joiners' bench in the Krupki forced labour camp until Krupki was blown up and he was enlisted into the Red Army. But the slogans put everything differently and knew everything better, and when they were read out at roll call in the morning, Ivan's face had not moved a muscle. And the faces of Kyrill and Nikita had not changed either. One had to hand it to him, Stalin was a great man. He had invented the steam engine and the combine harvester, and now he had won the war. And it was true that the Fascists owed a large debt and it was time they learnt a few home truths.

Two nights ago, Ivan from Archangel had played the accordion until dawn and sung songs to a young mother. On this day of festivity he raped eight women, seven to be exact because the last one had got away – a leap through the window and she was gone. One teutonic woman less. Chastise the proud teutonic woman, humiliate her, rape her. . . . Kill, kill! In Germany only the unborn children and the dogs are innocent – heard a hundred times, read out from *Pravda* and *Krasnaya Svesda* and elaborated on by a hundred political instructors. Even if now, at the outset of the last great offensive and with Berlin an open window to the world, it could be read in *Pravda*: 'Comrade Ehrenburg exaggerated' – it could not change the rules that had been in existence for so long. Nor could it at once stop the habit of burning, looting and liquidating whole villages. Ivan only left broken pieces behind; if he saw a clock too large to put in his pocket, then it had to be taken apart. The American bombs had left too much undamaged in the Berlin houses and now he had to go through cellars and flats like a bursting shell. He had drunk schnapps like water and in the evening he felt as sober and ready for adventure as he had in the morning when he woke. In the evening when he found himself in an open square, the yard of a removal firm surrounded by ruins, where the guns had been spitting fire since early morning, and when he learnt from the gunners that they were aiming at Hitler's Bunker, he thought he would like to throw a bomb at Hitler, too. The young artillery officer did the six-foot-six giant a favour and allowed him to pull the lanyard.

'*Ogon!*'

Ivan pulled the lanyard. A jet of fire. The barrel recoiled. The shell whined across the roofs and Ivan bawled: 'Hitler kaputt.' He pushed his cap back and disappeared in a dark alley of ruins, just in time to get out of the way of the 'one in the green uniform' who meant to have a look at the 'stray dog'.

Shot after shot rang out.

The batteries were placed in a half circle around the inner city, at Neukölln, Tempelhof, Schöneberg, in the North on the opposite bank of the Spree. They had only three targets now: the Reich Chancellery, the Ministry of Propaganda, the Air Ministry. The burning sky above the city centre was being fed by continual detonations. And between the fires, between fountains of concrete thrown sky-high, between shadowy islands created by the ruins, there moved the pale fingers of innumerable searchlights.

Berlin roared – in hundreds upon hundreds of yards the men stood herded together; in hundreds upon hundreds of cellars women were writhing under the grip of lemurs risen from the night. Berlin, the youngest of the European capitals and yet ground for settlers since the days of the lake dwellers; a market town built on piles; town of the Elector, fortress, barracks, provincial capital; and lastly, metropolis of the German Reich and largest industrial centre of the Continent; almost a thousand years of history hewn in stone – it was being ground, broken, hacked to pieces, mutilated; even the headless torso was being cut and battered. The castle in the heart of the city shrouded itself in waving curtains of smoke. The Erasmus chapel – the foundation stone was laid in 1540 – and next to it the ivy-covered 'Green Hat', a former medieval tower, both collapsed as though a thousand devils were raging in them. The licking flames greedily ate the panellings, the tapestries, the paintings. The chapel of the castle on the western side turned into a glowing furnace. All that remained were the naked walls, the steel structure of the cupola and the roaring lion outside the Eosander Portal. The Nikolaikirche – burnt out during the great fire of 1380 and rebuilt in 1470 – collapsed with a roar like thunder burying the nave and the aisles as it fell. The Klosterkirche, too, became the centre of a field of ruins; like cliffs in a raging sea, the spire and the chancel and one wall pointed upwards.

Conflagration and murder – and the accordion played.

Last convulsions of a war that had stretched from the Pyrenees to the Volga and from the North Cape to the Egyptian pyramids; returning to its starting point. The horsebreaker in the pleasure gardens of the castle, the mounted archer outside the pillared arcade of the Alte Museum, the warrior's mask bursting from the wooden panelling that looked like an air-raid precaution above the window of the Arsenal, looked with stony eyes across the scatter of broken-down vehicles, smashed ambulances laden with wounded. The dead were everywhere, run over by armoured cars and lorries and rolled into the ground.

And the accordion kept playing. . . .

What the Red Army soldiers were kicking along past the police station and across Dircksenstrasse were the heads of Mohnke girls; finally they rolled into the gutter on the Alexander Platz. The retired teacher Quappendorf came up from the cellar in Laubacherstrasse with blood-soaked hands and went up to the first floor to ask for a rope. They got him a washing line from the attic. He had fled from Mariendorf with his three daughters. On the way to Schmargendorf where he had hoped to find shelter, they had been herded into a cellar. 'Shoot me . . .' whimpered the youngest daughter. 'Shoot me', whimpered the others as well. Put an idea into the head of a drunk and he will carry it out. The drunks did shoot but they shot badly. The father was left alone with his shot-down daughters who could not die. He cut their wrists and he cut badly. Death would not come. So he went up to the first floor, came back with the rope, hanged from a gas pipe first Else, then Margot, then the eldest and after he had done that he hanged himself.

And the accordion played. . . .

From the neighbouring cellar, only divided by loosely placed bricks, drunken shouts and a strange squeaking noise could be heard. An old woman, an eighty-year-old widow of an admiral of the Imperial Navy, had been stripped to her grizzled, yellow skin and was then called upon to sing a song whilst the guests sat around. She stood on a table amongst upset glasses and bottles, amongst the tins of American corned beef and pork and beans, which the guests had brought, opened her mouth and uttered those strange, dry squeaking noises. The drunken infantry men from the Don and Kuban clapped their hands, pushed their caps back and left in high delight.

In that same Laubacherstrasse was the office of Günther Sarfeld, the newly appointed police superintendent. Sarfeld had completed his move and, with fiancée, mother, and a dozen protegées, among whom was Frau Halen, taken there by Dr. Linth, he had taken possession of his new flat. That same day he had supervised the painters drawing slogans and quotations from Stalin and also the erection of the painted boards in squares and streets, had mobilized women and men for the task of clearing a road across the ruin-covered Hohenzollern Platz, had formed squads for demolition work, had found red cloth as festive decorations for tanks and lorries, and with all that, he had yet found time to go to the registrar and go through the marriage ceremony with his fiancée Monika.

His area Commandant, a lieutenant from Siberia, had sent for him.

'You marry then?'

'Yes, that's not forbidden, is it?'

'Of course not, marry good, marry on first May twice good. You need something, want something?'

'Yes, some meat, and something to drink, and my wife loves gherkins.'

'Good, good.'

Sarfeld had received a dozen bottles of red wine, and with it meat and gherkins – enough for everybody. The Commandant had announced that he would visit them in the evening and had arrived with much to-do. The requisitioned German army car rocked crazily. Shots were fired into the air so that the people thought the war had started again. They went up the stairs, strictly according to rank, first the Commandant, then another officer, and lastly the orderlies, one of whom, small and with mongolian eyes, looked like an Eskimo. Sarfeld distributed cigars, a precious gift in those days. The Eskimo received one as well and beamed. And the way he smoked that cigar, that was wonderful – one should film that, thought Sarfeld. But there was nothing left to drink. The dozen bottles of red wine had come to an end.

Therefore: '*Pesche, pi . . .*'

That was how the Commandant's instruction sounded to Sarfeld. The Eskimo ran off and soon came back carrying a basketful of bottles.

'And where music?'

'No music, we haven't any.'

Again: '*Pesche pesche, pi . . .*'

An orderly ran off, came back with a gramophone, a very old one with a horn and masses of records, so many in fact that the pile was nearly three feet high. Everything was there, from Schumann's *Träumerei* and the *Pilgerchor* from Tannhäuser to *A Mill in the Forest* and *Ich hab mein Herz in Heidelberg verloren*. And whatever the records played, they danced to it all.

An hour and a half later the Commandant glanced at his watch and his face suddenly grew serious. Again: '*Pesche, pesche, pi . . .*' and everyone got up and, as before, turned to the door according to rank. Sarfeld went downstairs with his guests. Commandant, adjutant, orderlies climbed into the car, drew their pistols, presented their rifles. It sounded like a minor infantry attack.

'Salute for wife.'

The car went shooting off.

Not every storm brewing in the sky breaks; not every flash of lightning spells destruction. There are such things as 'cold hits' and the surprise visit by Ivan Serov at the Medical Officer's quarters in Tempelhof passed off without causing any radical changes. No executions, no deportations. On the contrary, young Major Judanov, thanks to his contact with a British Intelligence Officer and the rescue of the Atomic Physicist von Ardenne, had been promoted to Lieutenant-Colonel and appointed to a more important position. Captain Budin still sat at the same table, but the file containing details of German Atom Physicists and other scientists had been closed; not that the cases were to be dropped, but they were being given to a special group for further research. Budin and his staff in Tempelhof had to turn their attention to a more pressing task. Their desks were piled high with industrial plans. In Berlin eighty per cent, and in the Western sectors one hundred per cent of the enormous industrial centre had to be dismantled. And the demolition squads – Ivan Serov's visit had indicated this – were running short of time. They had only four weeks, or at most six, before the British and Americans were due; in that time industrial Berlin must be wiped out. Yalta had confirmed the decision of the meeting of Foreign Ministers in Moscow approving the plans of the Morgenthau economic experts to turn Germany into a potato-growing and pasture country. The fact that lately other voices had been heard in America suggesting alterations in the American banker's plans, was only another reason for greater speed. The economic expert Saburov had left no doubts as to the urgency of the task and the simultaneous visit of Ivan Serov clearly threatened what would happen to those concerned if it were not completed in time.

The interrogations were discontinued; the engineers who had been called together in the Chief Medical Officer's quarters were sent each to a different place to supervise the demolition work. In lorries they were taken to Siemensstadt, Neukölln, Weissensee, Henningsdorf. Director Knauer, under supervision of a Russian lieutenant, was given orders to dismantle the Lorenz factory for radio components.

Half-the number of workers were provided by the new Mayor. The other half consisted of repatriated Russians and Ukrainians. Up to now they had been prisoners of war or slave workers. On bicycles, motor-bikes, trucks, with cases, with quickly collected or looted possessions, and shouting the slogans 'Long live the Great Stalin!' and 'Long live the Nation of Victors, the great Soviet Union', they had hurried towards the Red Army and had quickly been incorporated into the large reception camps. After delousing – when whatever they possessed or carried on them was flung on to a large heap – they were cleaned, cropped, put into camp uniform, and were now marching out at the other gate as demolition workers.

Here they were then, crowds of them, besides Germans who had been herded together, in the Lorenz factory grounds. None of them had any qualification for the job, neither the Germans nor the Russians nor the Ukrainians! Experts could not be found in a hurry. Spanners and jacks would have been the most essential tools, but where should one suddenly find a complicated set of spanners, and where were the cranes and all the ropes and pulleys to come from? But all hands were kept busy and the work had hardly begun before lorries drove up to receive their loads. There had hardly been time to clear up the corpses of the war casualties and suicides which were lying everywhere in the grounds. Machines, furniture, work benches and cupboards, window and door frames, floors and window sills, water pipes and drains, electricity cables, the 'whole works' as the lieutenant called it, everything had to be dismantled.

After the dapper Captain Budin had come across from the staff building and had chased through all the rooms with a maximum of noise, the work under continuous pressure from the foremen crying '*Daway, daway*' assumed suicidal speed. And hammer and chisel, crowbars and occasionally oxy-acetylene lamps were the tools most often used. When work benches and sanitary fittings were taken down with the help of hammers so that pieces flew in all directions, Knauer kept silent. But when complicated machinery was up-ended and rolled along like lumber, he felt he had to intervene and appeal to his lieutenant. But he only shrugged his shoulders; he had been given a time limit and had to stick to it. Captain Budin was even less approachable; he was already thinking about further targets enumerated on his demolition list – a factory for special tools, a carriage repair works, an installation for the treatment of wood, a large bakery. It looked to Knauer as though the Russians were about to shift the whole of in-dustrial Tempelhof – and not only Tempelhof – to the East within the space of a few days.

Outside, crowds of Red Army soldiers swept past; then a horse-drawn anti-aircraft battery – the spokes of the wheels and the tails and manes of the horses decorated in red with torn-up mattress ticking.

The hammering, cutting, welding, dragging and loading went on. Dismantling here was almost identical with demoli-tion. The time-table and the loaded weights recorded by the checkers were more important than the condition of the goods. Knauer tried to prevent the worst destruction, though at that time he had no inkling that a single damaged machine would have been enough to mark him as a saboteur to be courtmartialled by one of Ivan Serov's summary courts.

Night fell and the work continued. In the beam of search-lights men and women hammered, sawed, worked and moved – like swarms of pale moths.

'*Nu wot* – Berlin!'

The tone was not guttural and the soft B of Berlin was pro-nounced P. Also the speaker added in pure Saxonian dialect: '*Da ham mersch!*'

There we have it; there it lay; the wide sea of ruins, smoking fires everywhere and in the middle a glowing furnace. One sector of the town, the mass of buildings tilted at an angle so that it was possible to see into the burnt-out windows and roofless ruins, turned like a disk beneath the wings of the

Douglas. And the broken-down cars, the battered guns, the lumps of concrete in the streets looked from that height like dotted fly-dirt.

Five hours before, the Douglas had taken off from Tushino airport outside Moscow. After twelve years of waiting, the leap had been accomplished in a matter of hours. Twelve years of methodical desk work, handing on of second- or third-hand orders. The desk in the Komintern building in the suburb of Rostokino which resembled a Lama monastery; the cheerless quarters in the Hotel Lux in Moscow's central street; backwards and forwards from office to quarters by overcrowded tram; murderous self-accusations and whitewashings; fight in the twilight for survival . . . intrigues, denunciations, writs to appear before the Triumvirate who decided over life and death. And many did not make it, very many. Twelve years of waiting and anxiety – and then suddenly the liberating word and the hurried packing of wooden cases and the issue of equipment 'necessary for the capitalistic West' – a pair of shoes, a suit, a felt hat and five hundred or a thousand or, according to rank in that hierarchy, several thousand marks of freshly printed occupation money.

The flight had been bad – stormy weather, air pockets. The machine was lacking in all comfort. The steel walls were bare. On two bare planks without backrest, fixed lengthwise along the centre portion of the plane, the travellers sat facing each other. And if the comrade at one end of the bench should feel sick with all that bumping and vibration, the big galvanized pail had to be handed along the whole row. And the pail did not always arrive in time, and when the slopping contents of the gradually filling receptacle went from hand to hand, even the most hardened looked green.

'*Da ham mersch, Towarishtshi!*'

That was a remarkably long speech from one who had no experience in addressing people privately, who usually confined himself to passing on ready-made slogans.

Well then, that's it; after twelve years, a smoking rubbish heap, a glowing dump as far as the eye can see. That is the end we have prophesied to the destroyer of towns. *Da häm mersch*, and there we have it indeed. All this we have been given by the Red Army 'in good faith', house and land and cattle and wife and child (the men had better remain in the adjustment camps for the time being) to take possession of finally and for ever. And not only Berlin – the zone reaches as far as Dresden; as far as Weimar and Eisenach and Leipzig. So roll up your sleeves and spit in your hands. No ingenious reflections, no clever theorizing necessary; that gets you nowhere. There are examples, ready-made templates – Poland, Lithuania, Latvia, Estonia. We have the map in our knapsack. Land reform – that will wring the cabbage barons' necks and destroy the breeding ground of Prussian militarism. Bank reform – that will take the last reserves from the middle classes. The workers have nothing anyway, and from now on all will have to feed out of the same tin can. School reform – that way we will get hold of the youth and he who has the youth of a country need not fear the future.

Hundreds had perished, in Moscow, Omsk, Tomsk, in Kolyma, Alma-Ata and Ferhana, many of them of a better class, public speakers with thoughts of their own and some even with ideals. The one who led this group was no orator, had never addressed the masses, and the masses had never honoured him. To have thoughts is conceit. To possess ideals borders on metaphysics and political suspicion. Hundreds had perished, and he had not raised a finger. He left without a beard; he returns sprouting a goatee, and that appears to be the sum total he has achieved during emigration. The direct line to the NKWD administration he had already. Caution is the mother of wisdom! Don't pretend to have ideas of your own. Don't ask questions, but when you are asked, answer. And if you receive an order, carry it out. That is the recipe which had allowed him to survive, to make him the No. 1 survivor.

Numbers two, three, four, five . . . eighteen survivors are sitting with him in the Douglas. Some of them have qualities, good ones and bad ones, but nevertheless qualities. The man without qualities will survive them. Yesterday they had been on the shelf – an editor had become a proof reader, and had supervised the dots and dashes, the question marks and brackets of a Stalin translation; a Comintern agent who had been for many years in China, became a radio announcer; a director of a publishing house had been turned into a miner in Kolyma. One had remained the same, a writer of poems – his only change the transition from expressionist pathos to patriotic folk-songs and that not entirely for tactical reasons. That was real, this longing for the lost motherland, the lost middle-class security, this expression of a shattered life, and of personal disaster. The remainder had sat at their office desks at the 'Lama monastery' in the suburb or Rostokino and had chewed their pencils. That had been yesterday. To-morrow they would all be officials, governors of ministers. The men with Survivor No. 1 were not future presidents, but vice-presidents and police commissioners; not the mayor of Berlin, but the first deputy; not the chairmen of the unions and potential political parties but the deputy chairmen and secretaries. That was the principle; the only exception was the poet. This man who would awaken in the morning in a rosy mood and seize his pencil and concoct an endless epic, and in the evening would be fleeing from ghosts who had tempted him more than once to grab his razor and cut his wrists, was the ideal choice as spokesman for the down-trodden German intelligentsia.

> 'And then I knew it; you were but a tomb,
> But still a tomb that strove to rise from death.'

The Douglas circled the perimeter of Berlin, turned back to the east and then landed on the military airport of Schöne-feld, south-west of Johannisthal.

They emerged into the luminous glare of searchlights. Examination of documents. At the roadside sat Red Army soldiers, frying potatoes and bacon over a bonfire of mahogany and rosewood furniture.

The documents were all right: Group Ulbrichta – ordered on special duty by the Red Army. The wooden cases were thrown on to a lorry. The travellers climbed in after them. They drove through Nieder- and Oberschöneweide, past the huge factory grounds of AEG, the great electricity works, where demolition squads worked in the light of searchlights, and on to Lichtenberg. The streets were pitch dark and empty. Dead horses; a smell of fire and decay; from the desolation of the ruins sounded an accordion.

'So this is it!'

'Yes, this is it.'

'A large rat ran across in front of me when I got off the plane.'

'A rat crossed the path of a rat.'

The poet, and president-elect of the planned cultural organization, was fond of cynical remarks.

'And the war goes on.'

A hand pointed to the town centre. There the sky was blood-red. A boiling volcano. Glowing smoke as high as the stars.

Secretary of State Naumann finally ventured the leap across the flaming Wilhelmstrasse. For twenty hours he had hesitated; several times messengers from the other side of the road had hurtled across. Now events within the Führer Bunker were reaching a climax and Naumann, as Commandant of the Battalion Wilhelmplatz and now first chief of the Ministry of Propaganda, could not do otherwise than leap through the fire.

He arrived, choking and fighting for breath. Councillors and ministers, soldiers, women, children, encircled him. He looked around him, wild-eyed; his voice sank to a whisper:

'Adolf Hitler committed suicide yesterday afternoon. Dr. Goebbels is dying.'

Silence. Incredulity.

What about Steiner, Wenk, Schörner; what about the impending relief, the promises from Naumann himself?

Naumann continued in the tone of a press conference:

'The whole fighting unit at present within the Reich Chancellery will make an attempt at escape at twenty-one hours, under the leadership of Bormann. They will be preceded by all available tanks. I recommend everybody, particularly women, to participate. Departure twenty-one hours sharp.'

'Escape? That is madness.'

Naumann stared at Fritzsche, then at the door.

What did he want now – to run away again? Naumann raised a hand dismissing the helpless crowd and remained alone with Fritzsche and a few other intransigents.

'This escape is madness', Fritzsche repeated.

'I don't care.'

Fritzsche, only skin and bones, his clothes singed by the fiery flecks that had fallen on him during his wanderings through burning Berlin, would not let go of Naumann. Goebbels he had not seen again. Was that face emaciated in life, now distorted in death, to be the answer to his question about the meaning behind this bloodiest of all wars? And what about Goebbels' wife, and the children of this father who considered it was his duty to relieve his children of decisions of which they themselves were not capable.

He did not ask Naumann that; he did not have to. The pale, twitching face and the small black button eyes told him everything.

So you don't care?'

Naumann did not reply.

Tell me, Naumann . . .' Fritzsche omitted to address him as 'Mr. Secretary' – 'Naumann', he said and asked him the question that he could no longer ask Goebbels. 'For how long have you, Goebbels and Hitler been leading us knowingly into the abyss? And why, on top of everything else, the Berlin blood bath? Why?'

'I have no time now for discussions.'

He had no time. He was sweating with fear. Fritzsche could smell the man's fright oozing from every pore.

'In that case, listen to me – as a civilian I personally will offer our unconditional surrender. Now, at once – and the soldiers and officers here in the town centre will be with me.'

'Give us time to make good our escape.'

More waiting, more victims? Potsdamer Platz is a field of ruins. At the Pschorrbräu soldiers, women and children are literally stuck to the wall. Wait for summary courts to shoot and hang more victims? To give the fanatics among the Werewolves a chance to wreak their revenge on whole streets?

Fritzsche made one condition:

'I will give you time for escape, only if Bormann in his capacity as chief of the "Werewolves" gives the order to suspend all operations.'

'I agree – for three months.'

'No, for ever – and I require Bormann's confirmation.'

'Come across with me.'

Es war einmal ein treuer Husar,
der leibte sein Mädchen ein ganzes Jahr,
ein ganzes Jahr und noch viel mehr.
Die Liebe nahm kein Ende mehr . . .

But love did end there, had ended already, love and much else.

That much he saw and heard.

'Get up, you bitch, or you'll stay there for ever.' It was no Hussar's bride to whom these words were addressed. A slim woman, her fair hair carefully set, but otherwise the worse for wear, lay in a corner and stammered drunkenly: 'Let go, Fritz, I don't want any more.' And Fritz, an SS-leader, said: 'We are getting out of here and if you don't get up I might as well put a bullet in your head right away.'

Such were the whisperings of love here.

There was a bubbling noise from falling and bursting shells, here underground it was an incessant stamping and gurgling. The SS-Fritz did indeed draw his pistol, changed his mind and leapt upon a round table, firing into the air and yelling: 'Listen everybody! Shut your traps, and let's get on.'

A drunken crowd. To get on, meant drinking, eating, smoking, lounging. They sprawled in soft armchairs. Beneath their feet thick carpets. On the walls mirrors, pictures in heavy gold frames, gigantic old masters – stolen probably from the Louvre in Paris or the Rijksmuseum in Amsterdam. Armchairs, pictures, soft lights. And on the tables wine, brandy, liqueurs, biscuits, white bread, sausage, bacon, ham.

A fools' paradise.

At the side of the armchairs heaps of anti-tank guns. The ceiling cracked ominously. Dust blew in, settled on the SS uniforms, fell into the glasses. That was less like a dream, more like reality; like everywhere else reality triumphed here too. But the gentlemen took little notice. It seemed as though they were used to having light fittings drop into their soup. They did not take much notice either of Loose and his two companions – the two men who had been given into his care in the cellar of the Luftwaffe building. And those two – prisoners from the Prinz Albrechtstrasse – opened their eyes wide and with reason. Paradise with noises off; with the bubbling and grumbling of the surrounding world. That was the last straw, after Luckau, after Tempelhof, after the fracas with the crazy major in the tram car, after the Lindenstrasse collection point and the journey to the Luftwaffe HQ. He had got that far, jumping, creeping, shooting his way through ashes and smoke. There had been constant coming and going from the cellar into the street; they emerged loaded with anti-tank grenades, and hand grenades and returned empty handed back into the cellar. They were throwing 'things' of all sizes, this collection of Hitler Youth, sailors and soldiers. Such a mess, in the end he had not known whether he had handed the grenades to a German or a Russian. He had gone downstairs again to get a little personal breather. He had hardly dropped off when it started again. Suddenly an SS-stormtrooper had stood before him.

'What are you doing here?'

'My unit is gone.'

'I don't care. Do you know what this is?' he said and the 'thing' he shoved under his nose was a pistol.

'Either you come with us to the Reich Chancellery, or it'll bang.'

Such was the friendly invitation and on departing they had handed the two prisoners from the Prinz Albrechtstrasse Gestapo prison over to him. And here he was, obviously having arrived much too soon. And if one of the inhabitants of this fools' paradise should ask him what he was doing there, he would be lost for an answer. But they were all much too busy; they were all absorbed by their efforts to put themselves into a trance or to keep themselves in one. They did that with Danziger Goldwasser, with gin and Cointreau, and when they were soaked through with spirits they stared at their shoe caps or at a point on the ceiling and tried out postures which they probably intended to adopt at a future SS-waxworks. Better to get out of here. But maybe it was not as easy to get out as it had been to get in. The two he had to guard were an additional problem; 'subversive types', how could he possibly act as their warder? As far as he was concerned, they could beat it, but probably they knew no more than he did which way to turn.

Whilst Sergeant-Major Loose was still thinking things out, the SS-stormtrooper arrived from the Luftwaffe HQ with two Gestapo warders and another four prisoners two of them wearing the zebra striped suits of a concentration camp. The stormtrooper approached a brigadier who was almost bursting out of his black trousers, and bellowed: 'Gestapo guard unit and detached prisoners reporting for duty. Transfer successfully carried out without interference or losses; sixteen men ready for action.'

Action, of course, what else? Loose counted the new arrivals – there were only fifteen – sixteen meant he had been counted in.

New supplies, new fighters.

It did not matter that the new ones were recruited from the Gestapo remand prison and the concentration camps. They had suddenly become comrades and were invited to sit at their tables. Cigars, cigarettes, food and drink, they were told to help themselves. The thousand and one nights – the drop into oblivion won't be far off. Meanwhile the brigadier gave orders that the new fighters should be issued with 'iron rations' for three days and were to keep themselves ready for action.

It turned out differently. The time for any kind of action was past. Loose noticed new faces, amongst them that short fellow with the emaciated face and large nose with whom he had lain outside in the mud. Secretary of State Naumann and Councillor Fritzsche, accompanied by several gentlemen from the Ministry of Propaganda, among them Lieutenant Splüge, entered the Bunker restaurant beneath the old Reich Chancellery.

Naumann exchanged a few words with the brigadier. It was something to do with Fritzsche, a request Fritzsche had made to Bormann. Fritzsche was asked to take a seat and wait. Soon after, Naumann returned and conducted Fritzsche and the brigadier towards the garden of the Reich Chancellery. Something was brewing – 'The Propaganda fellow' seemed to value his life no longer. A few figures stirred from their frozen attitudes, and in order not to miss the impending spectacle followed the group into the garden. The garden resembled a lunar landscape; crater upon crater, the ground churned and churned, mushrooms were pushing up between the stones. Nobody noticed a smouldering fire next to the greenhouse. The group with Naumann and Fritzsche felt their way along the wall. They were expected; in a breach in the wall a short-legged jellyfish of a man in SS-uniform was standing – Martin Bormann.

A short talk.

Fritzsche voiced his demand.

And nothing happened; no pistol was raised; no execution squad was called. Bormann waved to all SS-officers within reach, beckoning them to come closer; the civilians from the Propaganda Ministry and Sergeant Loose who had followed them, moved in towards the group.

Bormann raised his voice.

'Listen, everybody. I give orders that all Werewolf actions and executions are to cease. The Werewolf is disbanded.'

Bormann had betrayed his master, had passed over his master's last wish in order to save his own life. Thus he had managed to obtain two hours for his escape attempt.

On the way back the fire near the greenhouse drew Loose as though by magic. He thought he recognized two human bodies – a man and a woman – a gust of wind blew through the funeral pyre and the flames licked around sharp features. Loose was no longer alone. That chap from the street, the lieutenant, stood beside him.

'Are you saying a prayer?'

'No, why should I?'

'He can do with it.'

'Who is it?'

'Don't you recognize that face?'

And Loose did recognize the profile around which the flames were dancing. He had seen it a hundred times, in a hundred newspapers and illustrated magazines. What was happening here was no concern of his, but suddenly he had had enough; he turned and stumbled away. The fire was dying. And nobody came to feed the flames. They were all busy now. No total destruction for them as for that other couple hours earlier – no consuming witches' fire, no trampling underfoot and scattering of bones, no throwing of ashes to the winds.

The Bunker restaurant had changed completely; no longer any lazy figures lounging in the armchairs. The waxworks had come to a ghostly life. They were all packing their knapsacks, and then unpacking them to throw away unnecessary ballast.

'Light luggage and light shoes – we shall have to walk.'

'Through Tiergarten, past the Zoo Bunker, then across Pichelsdorfer Bridge in the direction of Spandau.'

'What nonsense is that? It's not possible.'

No, it was no longer possible. The now classical route, used by Boldt and Loringhoven on their way to Wenk's army, then by couriers with cries for help to the relieving armies, and lastly by messengers with copies of the Führer's will – was no longer passable. Russian machine guns were rattling as near as Brandenburger Tor. From the torn cupola of the Reichstag flew the Red Flag. The Zoo Bunker was no longer within reach. In this direction the road to the Havel and out of Berlin was blocked.

'Attention! We march in three detachments. Through the cellar and tunnels as far as Wilhelms Platz Station, along the lines to Friedrichstrasse Station. There we get up to ground level and near Weidendammer Bridge Mohnke fighting units will join us. After negotiating the bridge we have to fight our way north-westerly as far as Lehrter Station and Moabitstrasse. After that it is every man for himself. Rendezvous point is the German HQ in Plön, Schleswig-Holstein.'

The Gestapo guard came over to Loose and the prisoners who had retired to the farthest corner and would have liked to melt into the wall. A strange fate had led them here after hearing their fellow prisoners being taken out and shot.

There were six of them; the last six from the Prinz Albrechtstrasse.

'Hurry up and get ready. We are off', said the Gestapo guard.

'Not me; this is not my unit', said Loose.

'We haven't any papers', one of the prisoners replied. 'How can we without passes?' said another.

What was going to happen now? Would they be shot down here and now at the last minute? The room was already emptying. The Gestapo guard could hardly stand on his feet. A cloud of alcohol fumes came from his mouth. He looked for the brigadier but he was nowhere to be seen. What was he to do with those six? Wipe them out? But where was the brigadier? Without orders he was not going to do anything.

'Do what you like', he shouted suddenly. 'The Reich Chancellery will be blown up and then you'll go up in smoke anyway.' He consoled himself with that and slunk off.

'The whole thing is nonsense.' A junior stormtrooper took the knapsack off his shoulders again, threw it on the floor and joined three others who had remained, unconcerned by the general exodus, staring motionless into their glasses. They were not the only ones left behind; dead and wounded lay or sat in the armchairs. On a pile of straw lay five Hitler Youths and stretched out on a table was a BDM girl who had been wounded by a grenade splinter; she was whimpering because she would not see Heilbronn again.

New visitors arrived.

A group of soldiers from the street, dirty, their faces blackened by smoke and gunpowder. The sight of all the food and drink that had been left on the tables seemed to deprive them of their remaining sanity. They pounced on the bottles and dishes, made a lot of noise shouting and smashing the mirrors, shooting the light fittings down from the ceiling. And like ghosts at cockcrow they disappeared again. Hardly the right crowd for him to join. But he had to get out of this ghoulish place. The prisoners had already left. Loose followed the last of the soldiers. He watched them crawl from crater to crater through the dust on the huge garbage heap outside the Chancellery, until they finally disappeared.

After the soldiers had left, the Bunker felt as though an invisible hand had stopped all the clocks. The Hitler Youths moaned quietly. The sufferings of the girl from Heilbronn had come to an end. Others lay stiffly in their chairs.

'The time has come', said one of the four lone drinkers.

The time had come. The first got up and pulled his uniform straight; the others did likewise. One moment they stood at their table, stiff as lead soldiers. Left turn – they staggered across the room, through the door and up the stairs. Loose was still hiding behind a pier in the wall, waiting for a suitable moment to cross the devastated street. The four emerged and lined up in a row. The leader caught sight of Loose.

'Come on, line up and join us', he said.

'Join what?' asked Loose.

'The Führer is dead. We vowed to keep the tryst. Finish.'

At the word of command the pistols were raised – four shots rang out as one. They fell over, lay in the street like tailors' dummies. But only three of them fell; the fourth, his smoking pistol raised, stood there unharmed. It was the young stormtrooper who had been the last to join the company. He had fired into the air and now howled: 'No, no, no – I don't want to, I'm not mad; I am nineteen years old.'

'What are you doing here?' he asked Loose.

'Trying to get out.'

'So am I.'

This one was less use to Loose as a travelling companion than the rowdy soldiers.

The little stormtrooper looked around him. Debris. Craters. The main building of the Propaganda Ministry had collapsed. The Palais Leopold was burning. The fire was reflected on his face. 'That was how it looked in Brest – if I had been killed there, or in the Ardennes! But like this, no.'

Brest, the Ardennes, perhaps even Alamein. The world had grown small, shrunk to the size of the Wilhelms Platz.

'It's all the same to me', replied Loose. 'I have no use for you.'

It looked as though the boy would not be easy to get rid of. Loose had no option but to turn back. Back into the desolate rooms of the Reich Chancellery. He, too, had had enough of it – enough of the dead on the stairs, the lonely dying, the ghostly drinkers in high-ranking SS-uniforms. He knew the way to the garden by now. He felt his way there and squashed himself into a recess in the wall. It was a vicious circle; he could not get out. To run into the hail of fire would be suicide, but so would it be if he stuck to the Führer's ruin. . . .

Russian captivity?

He had wanted that once . . . in the morass of Pinsk; that had been the obvious way out for him then, his beliefs still unshaken; it had seemed rather like coming home to the Socialist motherland. Motherland indeed; nine months had passed since then and he could still see the elderberry bush, the country lying under a thin veil of mist; could still hear the cries of the little chap from Hamburg and the student from Leipzig. No, not captivity, as long as he could help it. Terrible dilemma – here the grave, but ahead were terrors still more ghastly than the tomb at his back. Where was he to turn?

Dear God in Heaven . . . Almighty Stalin, why are all

roads blocked, why isn't there a light anywhere to guide us?

'No getting through, quite impossible.'

One of the returned escapists stood before Fritzsche.

Their route had taken them from cellar to cellar, broken brickwork beneath their feet, pots and pans, steel helmets, and dead soldiers lining the walls. Afterwards in the tunnels of the underground they had met impenetrable darkness, beneath them a swamp sometimes waist-high in which floated baggage and corpses. That had been the first lap of their journey, and many had turned back there.

'Later on came the end. In Unter den Linden a naval party was scattered under fire and no officer could be found who was prepared to lead. Everywhere burning vehicles. It was impossible to cross Friedrichstrasse. Not a mouse would have got across alive.'

'They never had a chance of succeeding, at best a chance of dying a soldier's death; that was my opinion all along', said Fritzsche. He had explained all that during his talk with Bormann in the cellar of the Propaganda Ministry and had advised them all to stay where they were. He considered that the ten thousand odd remaining soldiers, police and Home Guard would follow his call to surrender and he sent messages accordingly into the four or five hide-outs around the Hitler Bunker.

Fritzsche's order to surrender also reached a table in the deepest vault of the Hitler Bunker where Hitler's last adjutant, General Burgdorf, sat with Krebs and Stormtroop Leader Schedle, who had not been able to take part in the escape attempt because of a shattered foot.

'He wants to capitulate, the Propaganda-fellow.'

Burgdorf stared at Krebs, but Krebs remained unmoved; he was so far away that nothing could reach him any more. A doll, his cheeks painted red, he sat on the chair without moving. And Schedle poured down another glass; that was his whole contribution. Burgdorf looked around for another helpmate and caught sight of an SD-representative. He rose clumsily, went across to the Security Department officer. 'Come on, up; there is work to do.' Glassy eyes were turned on him. The SD-man was half dead, too, but he got up and automatically followed Burgdorf. Up the stairs they went, into the street and, without throwing themselves down or altering their tempo in the face of the flying shrapnel, they arrived at the other side.

'Where is Herr Fritzsche who wishes to surrender?'

Hans Fritzsche had retired, and was composing a letter to Marshal Zhukov, at his side an interpreter. Burgdorf appeared in the door – a square-set, heavy face – and the eyes stared as once those of the Führer had stared.

'You wish to capitulate?'

'Yes, I am just about to write to Marshal Zhukov.'

'Then I shall have to shoot you. The Führer in his will has forbidden any surrender. We have to fight to the last man.'

'To the last woman as well?'

The pistol in Burgdorf's hand shot upwards. The shot went into the ceiling. A technician had pushed the SD-man aside without effort and had flung Burgdorf's arm high at the right moment. A wave of blood surged into Burgdorf's face and he looked as though he was going to have a stroke. The pistol was taken from his yielding grasp. He allowed himself to be manœuvred like a heavy wardrobe through the cellar and out into the street.

He reeled away – alone now.

It was a disgrace . . . the pistol in his hand had failed him. The man who, as a messenger of death sent by his Führer, had invaded the highest headquarters and offices, and who had once in a suburb of Ulm forced the wounded Field-Marshal Rommel to take the deadly poison capsule, now took his own last steps. He possessed a second weapon; the companions he had left behind at the table, Schedle and Krebs, would not see him again. On his way back to the Bunker he shot himself.

It was the third hour. The blood-red sky grew paler, stained apricot pink.

'What a delicate sky – like the petals of a tea rose.'

'Yes, and Herr Krebs has a face the colour of thick port, and the face of Herr Burgdorf looks as black as horse blood, and that of Herr Fritzsche as yellow as corn on the cob. And you, you . . . You should have other things to think about than the colour of the sky.'

'So I should, Leonore; so I should.'

'And what is more, you should really come to a decision now, Vicco.'

'Many decisions have been made during the night, and I have a feeling they were all wrong.'

'But what are we to do, Vicco? They have all gone; the building over the road is empty, not a mouse is left.'

'Well, then I suppose it is time. But wait, just wait. Don't move; can you see?'

'What, where?'

'There.'

The talk between Vicco Splüge and Leonore Stassen took place at one of the empty windows of the ruined Kaiserhof. It was still dark but not too dark for them to see the shadowy figures stalking like cats round the front of the New Reich Chancellery. They found the entrance blocked by sandbags and prowled on to a gap yawning in the wall. Stepping on the shoulders of one of the men who was leaning against the façade, one after the other climbed in. Splüge counted six of them and the one whose back they had used was the seventh. A second group of seven men, then a third, gained entry by the same means. Suddenly it was deathly quiet, even the whine of the guns had ceased. The stillness within the ruin of the Reich Chancellery was interrupted by a single report from an automatic; after that silence returned.

'It is time to go; those are Russians', said Splüge. He took Leonore by the hand and led her carefully across the debris to the trench which lost itself in the direction of Mauerstrasse.

Another heard the report from the automatic, and at once recalled the elderberry bush in the swamps around Pinsk. It was deadly quiet, but he heard the little man from Hamburg crying and the student from Leipzig. Loose had not found a way out of the vicious circle, was still standing amidst the sandbags and wreckage at the back of the Chancellery, possibly underneath the window of Hitler's former study. With disaster approaching from behind, there was no longer time for reflection, he had to move. He darted outside, into the vastness of the garden; away, only to get away from the cursed ruin. There were craters in plenty and he jumped into one of them. It was full of bones and corpses. He climbed out again, found another hole. This hole, made by a shell, was about two yards across, the walls were concrete and it had no bottom. When he lowered himself down he found himself once again in a seemingly endless subterranean passage, tiled, with a number of shafts branching off it. What was he doing here – this passage could only lead him back to where he had come from. But there was no turning back. The hole torn into the concrete was now so high up that he could not reach it without help.

The first man to balance on the back of the Red Army soldier and to climb through the window into the battered Reich Chancellery, was August Gnotke. He had landed there after leaving the Werewolf girl at Potsdamer Platz and after drifting between the various front lines until he had managed to cross the Spree and reach his own unit. Somewhere near Kottbuser Tor he had hailed a Russian in the street, had been taken to his Commandant and been handed over to an NKWD department. After several questionings, first in Gitschinerstrasse gasworks, and later by a superior authority at Treptow, he had been taken over by an NKWD group. Street plans of Berlin were scarce and anyway the devastated streets could no longer be identified by maps; so the departments took their guides as and where they found them. In those hours the fighting front extended from Hallesches Tor as far as Potsdamer Platz and filtered through various side streets into the city centre. Gnotke's patrol kept away from the fighting, a small unit, consisting of twenty-one men led by a lieutenant-colonel; the presence of this lieutenant-colonel Judanov from the NKWD-HQ at Treptow implied that an important task lay ahead. Their way led them through Saarlandstrasse until progress became impossible because of the number of broken-down vehicles, useless tanks, dead horses and dead soldiers. Below the ruined houses their journey continued from cellar to cellar as far as the Hotel Excelsior, through the reception hall now turned stable and finally through the basement of the Gestapo house in Prinz Albrechtstrasse. A short stretch along an empty street, and they were facing the entrance to the Reich Chancellery blocked by sandbags. On the way Gnotke was always made the first to put his head through the gaps leading from one cellar to the next, and so it came about that he was also the first to climb through the gaping window in between the sandbags.

He found himself in a medium-sized room.

The NKWD soldiers behind him pulled out drawers filled with Ritterkreuz and similar decorations and stuffed their pockets with them. He was pushed forward again and reached a wide corridor. Steel helmets, pots and pans, equipment, abandoned knapsacks, dead bodies, and more dead bodies. A room opened out at right angles and Gnotke found himself facing a machine gun. Behind the machine gun a soldier was cowering, and the soldier was alive, his finger on the trigger; he was staring at Gnotke who still wore German uniform and the bandage around his head. The automatic of an approaching GPU soldier finished the man off.

That was the shot which Splüge and Leonore Stassen had heard and which, at the back of the Chancellery, had made Sergeant Loose jump from his hiding place to flee in panic until he fell rather than climbed into the second crater to find himself in the tiled passage below.

Lieutenant-Colonel Judanov looked around him in bewilderment.

He had seen plenty of dead bodies on his way from Krupki through the forests of White Russia and Poland, but never so many concentrated in so small a space. Here lay and sat suicides who had been alive only a few minutes earlier. And casualties, dragged in here from the street to die, were stacked along the wall like logs. Corpses seemed to be the only legacy in this Hitler cave. But it had not been to gaze at corpses that he has been sent here by Serov ahead of the troops. On! further down! Surely there must be a way? They were in a high-ceilinged room, the walls battered, the tapestry in shreds, lumps of stone on the floor; through the openings that had been windows one could see the mass of rubble which on the map was marked as a garden.

They climbed through the window, searched from outside for an approach into the underworld. Here again dead bodies, some of which had been buried and torn out of the ground again by the bombs. The torch shone on a corpse whose face had been charred by flames; by his side the body of a woman. Then one of the men discovered a place where a bomb had gone through the concrete. By the light of a torch a tiled passage became visible.

A hefty charge was thrown down.

Gnotke was told: '*Daway* – down into the underworld.'

Gnotke supported himself by the cracks in the concrete and then let himself drop. Torches and half a dozen automatics at the ready covered his passage. An uncomfortable cover, especially as the torches isolated him in a circle of light defenceless to the eyes in the darkness, if there were any eyes left in this sinister cave. For a moment it seemed to him that something moved. The automatic of the man following him strewed bullets all along the passage, but nothing could be seen but the blue flash reflected from the tiles and no sound heard but the hundredfold rattling echo.

And yet, there was one in the line of fire.

Paul Loose, driven by panic into the trap, had not found time to get out again. Loose had heard the voice above the hole and his heart had beaten so hard against his ribs that he thought they were bound to hear it. The light of a searching torch chased him still further along. He put about thirty yards between himself and them – that much control over his actions he had retained. An explosion, they are coming down; they shoot – not at him – he understood that. They were only intent on breaking a hole through the air, to free their passage. Yet they remained at his heels. Corridors, this way and that, which one was he to take? A steel door – of course, it had to be steel. That was how things went in a nightmare. And as in a dream, at the last moment an escape hole. The pursuers – but they were not really pursuers because they knew nothing of his existence – made little enough progress, like cats putting paw before paw, yet on they came, unremittingly. And the corridor was narrow, no side tracks any more either, no means of evasion, no escape. A one-way street – at the end of it the glittering steel door and right and left of it, leaning against the wall, two guards. The door gave, turned on its hinges without a noise. The guardians of the door, the head of the one hung down, that of the other had dropped on his shoulders, were no longer interested. They had done with worrying – SS or army,

Hitler Youth, Sergeant Loose or the pursuing Russians, anyone could pass through.

Sergeant Loose passed through, went up the stairs, came through a kitchen; a candle was burning, dirty dishes stood around, plates with remnants of food, half-filled glasses, half-smoked cigars, a dead cook. Loose went along a corridor. Cabins with their doors open, with two or three beds in them, a moaning coming from one bunk.

Idiot, why not have pushed the steel door shut from the inside? The visitors would have been locked out. Now it was too late. They had passed through the door and came down the stairs; they had arrived in the kitchen. That much he could hear; there was the sound of breaking china; plates, bottles, glasses were thrown against the wall. On, on . . . he had to strike a match to know which way to turn. A large room – looking rather like the waxworks he had first entered – but that was a thousand years ago – with those in the zebra-striped uniforms. Where were they now? Dead or alive; was anybody still alive down here? Certainly not in this room, even if they pretend they are, sitting before half-full glasses with plates piled high with sandwiches. That is only pretence; it cannot fool him. The match went out and the whole show disappeared. No more red generals' stripes, no SS-storm-trooper leader, no more rouged cheeks, no face grinning with bared teeth. Paul, old chap, is that all you can think of? It was, but not for long. There came the moment when he was without concern, without fear, without a spark of life and no different from the whitewash on the wall.

The beam of light from a torch now fell straight on to the scene. Figures with flat caps crowded in – five, six, seven. Seven men and an officer. Loose was stuck to the wall, but something within him was still capable of registering events.

Seven men and one officer.

One of them wore gloves, that was the maddest thing of all. The one with the white gloves touched one of the figures. The dangling head fell on one side. The figure fell, hit the floor like a heavy sack and stirred no more.

Dead, all dead, here too – nothing but dead bodies. Lieutenant-Colonel Judanov thought of Serov. He could not bring him a pack of dead dogs. He had come too late, two minutes too late. Only a moment ago a piece had been bitten off the bread which now lay before him. The coffee in the cups was still warm. They did not move; they had breathed their last; their black souls had escaped.

A sound like a death rattle.

Judanov rushed over, shook the man, half lifted him up, looked into a pair of breaking eyes. Too late . . . the dying man was flung to the ground. Judanov's nailed boots smashed in his face. Another dying man was brought from one of the cabins. But nothing could be got out of him; not a single word. He, too, suffered the fate of the nailed boots. Another one; Judanov shook him and only shook the life out of him. He could not bring the dead to life. Fury seized him against these silent creatures. Raving, he staggered from one table to the next slapping faces right and left. Whoever he hit, fell over, a short-legged general, an SS storm troop leader. And if the general's name had once been Krebs, if the stormtroop leader had once been the leader of Hitler's bodyguard and had been called Schedle – the boots of Judanov and the twenty-one pairs of GPU boots which followed him, would be the reason why none of them was recognizable.

In the moving light of the torch Judanov suddenly noticed the ghost of Sergeant Loose stuck to the wall. Ghosts with wide open eyes, with dropping jaws, lying, sitting, standing, holding a gun or a woman – he had seen plenty of them. He turned away, only to turn back again. There was something unnatural about this phantom of a sergeant which he had to investigate. That was the moment when the scene changed once more.

Paul Loose had seen everything.

He was on the spot and at the same time far away. The Bunker and that blood-soaked spot in the swamps of Pinsk were all the same to him. All the fears which had ravaged the Bunker had coagulated within him. When the GPU officer turned to him he had reached the limit. He had no business here, did not belong here, was a casual visitor. He wanted to run; his mouth dropped open and remained open and the lids of his eyes did not move.

From the farthest, blackest spot of the cave a heavy machine gun opened fire. Bottles, glasses, plates were flung from the tables. The leather armchairs and the dead were riddled with holes. Plaster fell from the walls, flaked from the ceiling. Chalk dust spiralled through the room. There were no longer any searching torches. Only the murderous rattling and the thousandfold echo. The GPU crowd disappeared as though swept off the face of the earth. Figures lay on the floor, crowded round the exit, gathered in groups.

It is no use fighting with ghosts, particularly if they possess heavy machine guns. Lieutenant-Colonel Judanov barricaded himself in the kitchen with his little group, sent a second lieutenant: 'Go on, back to the Excelsior, bring reinforcements.'

Loose jerked into movement, jumped through the fire, reeled into the kitchen, fell down before Judanov. The flight had come to an end; the nightmare was ended. The terror remained; reality was still unbearable. A little heap of misery – he wanted to explain: 'Save me. I have nothing to do with it.' He could not get it out. His lips were sealed.

'Where is Hitler? Has he gone? Is he in the Argentine?'

Judanov received no reply. The man before him was unconscious. 'A doctor, a doctor . . .' At last he had a living being. But Loose regained consciousness without medical aid. A sergeant of the army. He did not wear SS uniform. 'Are you a Fascist, do you belong to Hitler?' 'No, no, I have nothing to do with it!' At last Loose found his tongue, explained that he had landed in the Bunker by chance. 'Take your tunic off, let us see the mark below your arm.' He believed him already. The fear of death was showing in his eyes; he could not help but speak the truth. 'Here a map, you Sergeant, you understand? what is that?' It was a lay-out of the Bunker. 'Wonderful, now we need only wait for reinforcements. You can look around meanwhile; bring me somebody alive.'

The reinforcements arrived. Wild, uncouth chaps, their faces bloated from drink. As they did not find anyone to kill, they killed the dead once more, smashed everything they came across. Loose dared not stir an inch away from Judanov and clung to his uniform. Judanov did not stop him.

'Do you remember that priest in Krupki, Budin – the Saint in the labour camp?' (He had taken his old crony Budin with him on this special mission.)

'You are right,' agreed Budin, 'he looked just the same.'

It could only have been the face, still marked by fear of

death, and Paul Loose's bald head, that reminded the two of
the face and tonsure of the Polish priest in the Krupki camp.

The sky was the colour of a tea rose.

In the pale air, only slightly coloured by dying fires,
Weidendammer Bridge stretched across the Spree, the
scene of the last stage of the escape attempt. The tumult,
aroused by several German tanks breaking through the barrier
at the northern end of the bridge, had died down. The tanks
had managed to get a few hundred yards further, as far as the
corner of Ziegelstrasse, where they were blown up by anti-
tank guns.

Hitler's chauffeur, Erich Kempka, had been knocked
unconscious for a few seconds, then rose swaying and blinded
by the light and was now balancing precariously on a steel
girder running parallel with Weidendammer Bridge. He
eventually reached an arch of the underground railway
where he hid all day amongst a crowd of Slav women. Others
managed to get as far as Lehrter Station and on to Alt-
Moabitstrasse, amongst them the last dignitary of the
Propaganda Ministry, Naumann, whose witches' ride took
him across the Elbe into an American POW camp. Another
group drifted past the Stettiner Station as far as Schönhauser
Allee. The Russian infantry men who chased them out of the
cellars underneath a block of flats did not know how big a
catch they had made. They only kept the men – Mohnke,
Bauer, Rattenhuber, the chief of Hitler's bodyguard, and
Hitler's adjutant Guensche. They allowed the women to
go, the secretaries Christian and Junge and Bormann's
secretary. The dietitian, Fräulein Manzialy, was carried off
by an Asiatic giant of a man and was never seen again. All
traces of Bormann, the instigator of the escape, were lost
between Weidendammer Bridge and Stettiner station.

The sky was the colour of a tea rose when radio commentator Hans Fritzsche surfaced at the end of a long subterranean corridor and was driven to Tempelhof, only to
learn that his offer of surrender was no longer of interest
because the last Commandant of Berlin, General Weidling,
had already surrendered in the name of the whole Berlin
garrison.

The sky was the colour of a tea rose when two figures

stepped out of a ruined duct into the open and viewed the narrow shaft, stretching for miles, which was Friedrichstrasse. Vicco Splüge and Leonore Stassen had got that far. Splüge was wearing a hat and carrying a brief-case. Those were his civilian clothes. The girl was still wearing her Luftwaffe uniform, but in the knapsack she carried a summer dress, scarf and shoes. Jumping, creeping, carefully feeling their way and doubling back whenever necessary, they had got through Mauerstrasse and Französischestrasse and had now reached Friedrichstrasse. But they could no longer be called streets – nothing was in place. Where had the gutter gone, the pavements, the road – all was a shambles.

Friedrichstrasse – do you remember?

It had never been very beautiful, never distinguished; cafés, one after the other, restaurants, dance halls, amusement arcades, jewellery shops. And if the stones were not real – the windows sparkled. A thousand shops with colourful finery. Everywhere noise, everywhere neon lights, red, green, blue and an ugly mauve, right down to the pavement. And night porters and chuckers out, and tap-tap, tap. . . . Until five in the morning, little mouse. When the dawn broke over the roof tops, uncles from the provinces were still looking for girls at twenty marks.

'Do you remember how it used to look here?'

'I don't remember anything any more, Vicco.'

'It seems to me, you have never known very much, or perhaps you've read Spengler's *Decline of the Occident ?*'

'I didn't have to – I could always look at you.'

'I suppose you are right.' Spengler and Ernst Jünger and K. Zucker . . . and I've only just come across the jungle doctor Albert Schweitzer. Incredible, unbelievable – he knew everything as far back as 1900; and in 1914, in the African jungle, he wrote down all that can be seen around us now.

Ruins and debris and not a single human being. Only shadows, human fragments – who had said that, surely somebody had written it. But he had not seen the shadows on the walls, the fragments in the dust, the upright shells of what had been human figures in the doorways and shops and snack bars; he had not seen Friedrichstrasse, not like this.

'You really should read more.'

'What should I do?' . . . the girl was looking into a restaurant. That and the structure above it only rested on shaky pillars. But all the shops and snack bars were resting on shaky pillars, too, with the weight of debris on top of them. No doors no windows, no window sills and open to the street. The collapsed ceiling, a canopy of reeds and plaster, a descending arch touched the tables and the people sitting at them. Only the guests had forgotten to get up again. The cashier with the long blonde hair behind the cash desk forgot to turn the cash register. My God, my God. . . . She looked away, only to see in a florist's, in a shop for men's wear half filled with rubble, further scenes from the cabinet of death stretching the length of the street. 'What did you say I should do?' she whispered.

'Read more; Spengler and Schweitzer, perhaps Heidegger, too.'

'Thank you', she said dryly.

She looked at him sideways, looked down at him. He was somewhat shorter than she. They were the only living beings or miles around.

'Perhaps we should first of all think of how to get away from here, where we should go', she suggested.

'Fate, I follow you of my own free will, for if I did not, I should be compelled to do so with tears', he quoted.

'I have had enough of that. With you, I shall really go to the dogs.'

'That's where you are already; that is why you should read so that you can understand it all.' Splüge stopped outside the blocked entrance to a cellar.

'I know that dive.'

'I can well believe it.'

'We should really go down there.'

'Whatever for – still, if you say so.' But it was not possible, they could not get through. Splüge knew, though, that the place had a second entrance in the side street. They turned the corner; here, too, lay stones, rubbish flung there from the road. They had to squeeze under a fallen and bent steel girder that had to support the weight of the whole house. They managed it and arrived in an ante-room with a coat stand where the light from outside penetrated dimly. There was a telephone and a poster showing two naked girls performing acrobatics.

'Now we only have to meet Lola and Yuscha in there, like Frau Krause at the cash desk in the Patzenhofer, and that would be the last straw.'

'Lola, Yuscha, Frau Krause – you seem to have an intimate knowledge of the surroundings.'

'Knowledge is supposed to be part of my job.'

'Your job is finished.'

'How right you are!' And the job was no job, it was service to a lie. And he had done nothing to make up for it. No pictures or symbols of life in his possession. Nothing had come of his good intentions.

'Now let's tidy up . . .' he said.

He opened his briefcase. Papers, cuttings from articles, notepaper with the heading of the Propaganda Ministry, manuscripts: *Fresh reserves on the march. – The Führer's presence means victory. – The longer breath.* It was all flung into the dust.

'Gone for ever – but what now?'

The question was too difficult; he could not answer it.

'Your head is much too small for that sort of thing. You had better think how to get out of your uniform.'

He stared at the coat-stand as though civilian clothes and a summer overcoat were waiting for him; Leonore knew what to do. She took her dress from the knapsack, began to change and gave him the Luftwaffe uniform. It was not all he could have wished for but better than the uniform with the Party insignia. Luftwaffe uniform, a trilby hat, and the briefcase with cigarettes and iron ration, that was his outfit when the two of them emerged from the cellar.

They had not far to go.

The narrow part of Friedrichstrasse was solid with broken-down vehicles; they had to pick their way through them. Untidy heaps flung together and parts sticking out, an arm, a face with its teeth showing. Don't look at it – the squashed dust cart with its horrible load – it will all be entered in the Big Book. 'You'll have to pay' – when had he been so presumptuous, when did he say that? Those in the dust cart have paid. The man belonging to that arm in the dust, he has paid. The women and children with their belongings in the entrance to the station, they must pay.

And he . . .?

The Metropolitan Station was crowded with women and children, a few old men, whole families with bags and cases and cartons tied with string. Splüge and the girl Leonore left the resting place of misery behind them. They climbed down on to the rails, disappeared in the dark shaft, in the direction of Potsdamer Platz. They waded through the sub-soil water and plodded on determinedly. They could already feel firm ground under their feet when machine guns began to rattle somewhere in front of them. The echoes rumbled along the walls. They had to give up, felt their way back through the morass, back to where they had started. Even the short stretch to the underground was impassable. A mob of SS came towards them. They said they couldn't get through and marched on to where the two had just been.

In the end they stayed in Unter den Linden Station. Here, too, the station hall was full of families with beds and parcels. Splüge found near the exit a recess for platelayers and they both squatted down listening to the noises from above.

A heavy machine gun fired along Unter den Linden. The bullets bounced against the metal surrounds of the ventilator shaft, an eerie hammering noise.

Death sat on Brandenburger Tor and beat the drums. It stopped and a grey light filtered into the ventilation shaft; steps could be heard above. Again salvoes rang out and more steps, and voices sounded, but the language spoken was no longer German.

Hours.

The liver sausage from the briefcase did not taste good and was quickly wrapped up again. The cigarette, hardly lighted, went out again. Splüge could not find the right word for that moment. Long, painful waiting.

Hours – and then it happened within a minute. No guard, no Russian came down. The civilians in front passed on the word.

'Civilians outside – Army outside.'

Fate, I follow you, for if I did not . . . it was a quotation no longer; it was bitter realization, a damned necessity which turned thousands of Berliners in this hour into fatalists and let them endure humiliation, shame, rape and murder as though they were natural events.

Woe to those who give up their arms.

But three times woe to those who raise them needlessly, for it is they who summoned the evil forces, who drew this hour of disgrace on to the heads of their women and children.

The hour had come.

It descended heavily upon Berlin, with the last lingering roll of artillery, the last volley from the machine guns. The hour had come and its smell was of corpses, creeping up from the opened shafts, its cry was that of raped women, its sign and message was farewell; farewell to the West, to the decalogue given with thunder and lightning, to the struggles of Faustus . . . and farewell also to the juice of grapes and song of troubadors, to the Pomeranian geese, the cheese from Roquefort and the distillations of the monks and peasants from Nussia, Fécamp, and Cognac; farewell to the books of the church fathers, the French cookery books, the Italian fish soups, cheese and wines, Bohemian glass, homespun, and the sword blades from Toledo. The hour had come, and the end was not visible.

Splüge was herded across the street; shouts in a foreign tongue and pointed pistols indicated the way. Through Wilhelmstrasse they went, through Leipzigerstrasse – and he was not alone; others marched in front of him and behind him, in uniform or part uniform, with a civilian jacket or a hat just like his own; a trickle which was to grow into a stream, a march of hundreds, thousands and then millions. Many Russians came towards them, climbing out of cellars with chairs, with cases, jumping from the windows of ground floor flats with clocks, with standard lamps. Russians, Russian women, cows and pigs; strangely alien behaviour.

And Leonore, what had he omitted to tell her? That suddenly she looked thirteen – a leggy schoolgirl with long plaits? Even with the scarf round her head and her severe and determined look. Not a word of farewell from her; on the top step of the underground staircase she had turned right and he had turned left. The guard there had made the division at the point of the gun. He had looked round for her but she had already disappeared, swallowed up by the other women, the children and the piles of luggage.

The prisoners crossed Potsdamer Platz.

No pavement, no tram line, no asphalt any more. Pulverized, trampled, thrown up like a hilly countryside. A beaten track wound around heaps of debris; amidst the up and down of the rubble a herd of cows, after them a cowherd with a long whip. Burnt out cars, wet ashes, splashed brains from animals, blood, now and then cow-dirt.

'*Tuda*', called the guard, and waved to the caravan to turn down Saarlandstrasse – towards Hallesches Tor, towards Tempelhof.

The hour had come.

Anna Putlitzer wearing long trousers, with a shovel and dust bin from her kitchen, stood before a pile of rubble, filled the pail and handed it on. The pail and the chain of pails went from hand to hand, from woman to woman, from the middle of Berlinerstrasse to the edge where the containers were emptied into cellars and on bomb sites.

From her own house, besides old Riebeling, only old Frau Schulze was there, wife of the magistrates' clerk. The three daughters Quappendorf and their old father had not returned from a walk to Schmargendorf. Making themselves scarce, of course – oh well, if they can get away with it. But the orders are: No ration cards for those who don't clear rubble. No work – no food; fair enough.

Anna Putlitzer straightened herself. Scarf and face covered with chalk dust, she looked along the row of devastation. Huge sections of walls, the rubble in some places swept as high as the first floor, steel joists, abandoned tanks, burnt-out tram cars. Along a stretch already cleared, which led like an unending canal through the broad road, lorries and horse-drawn carts with Russians were moving towards the town. From the town also came vehicles, loaded high with machines and factory equipment, occasionally grey columns of German prisoners of war, in uniform, and men in coats and hats, old ones and very young ones.

'Mine came back yesterday', she said to the woman next to her.

Heiner had been picked up in the street and put into one

of the columns. He had got as far as Lichtenrade, and there had managed to hide in some bushes. His feet sore with walking, he had come back, and Director Knauer had detailed him to one of his demolition squads; there he was safe for the time being.

Riebeling stopped near the women. The old printer had been given the job of supervising the clearance work on that side of the road. Anna Putlitzer pointed to the mass of rubble.

'Enough there, Herr Riebeling. We shan't be out of work for the next hundred years.'

'Yes, it is rather a lot', agreed Riebeling. 'Too much to shift by hand; and shovels and dust bins won't be much good either.'

He limped on. He looked like a crow with a broken wing moving from heap to heap. Since the first world war he had had a bad leg and during a short sojourn in a concentration camp he had had it broken again. Riebeling, who for so long had been handyman at Ullstein's, had this morning gone to see the Commandant and tried to persuade him to release the excavator standing in the tram depot for the clearance work. The commandant had refused. The excavator was classed as salvage and scheduled for removal.

Impossible to see how the job was to be done without mechanization. All the more, as the engineers had estimated the rubble to be removed from Berlin at several million cubic yards.

Garden spades, pails, dust bins, baskets – even crowbars were lacking. Riebeling reached a group of women labouring under a massive lump of stone. He was incapable of heavy physical work but lent a hand all the same.

'Hey-up! hey-up!'

The wreckage around Alexander Platz was still swathed in smoke. A smell of wet ashes and decay filled the air and the 'Trümmerfrauen', the clearance women, were covered with dust, their clothes wet and caked with mud. They gathered iron and wood fragments, collected dead bodies and parts of dead bodies and carted them off.

'You can touch him; he can't feel it.'

'Clearing up is better than pulling down.'

'And to be buried is probably better these days than to go on living.'

'Easier, yes – whether it is better depends; it depends entirely on us.' A middle-aged man, clean shaven and wearing a grey suit, said this to the women. They were all there, Maria Riek and the others from the house in the Landsbergerstrasse, even barrel-organ Franz – he had inherited the Liratedesca, the Sambuco as he called it, from old Willem, but had not had much luck with it so far; a shell splinter stuck in the casing had finally blocked the bellows.

'If it depends only on us, it'll be all right', replied Maria Riek.

'Too good to be true', said Franz.

The gentleman in the grey suit continued to stroll about Alexander Platz. He spoke German, even Berlin dialect; it was amazing. He wore an ordinary suit like others, yet the suit seemed a sort of masquerade. Perhaps it was just the fact that a healthy man of between thirty and forty was walking about freely that was so astounding. How long could that last? Franz looked at the man. He knew nothing of the 'Gruppa Ulbrichta', nothing of the landing of an aircraft in Schönefeld, nothing of a mandate by the Russian army and of the chosen rulers firstly of this wide sea of ruins, then the country as far as the Elbe and finally the whole of Germany.

Chosen – not elected.

The one in the grey suit was on his way to Wallstrasse where the 'ghost government' from Schönefeld was to meet for the first time.

A tall pole was erected, with indicators to the various places. The names of Potsdam, Spandau, Küstrin, Frankfurt on Oder, Karlshorst, were given in Russian script. Outside the entrance to the underground a bearer of the order 'Hero of the Soviet Union' gave a performance of a Caucasian folk dance; others were standing around beating time with their hands. 'How gay, isn't it? only don't go too close.'

'Better not look at all.'

At the beginning of Dircksenstrasse underneath the burnt-out windows of the main police building, a notice board was erected bearing a Stalin text, this time in gothic lettering:

> *'The Red Army is free from all feeling of racial hatred. It is free from such degrading sentiments because it has been raised in the spirit of equality of the races and regard for the rights of other peoples.'* (*Stalin.*)

'Makes you think, Max.'

Max Riek had also been commandeered for the work, his job was to collect scrap; he looked serious.

'Regard for the rights of other peoples – sounds all right.'

'It would sound even better if we had not picked up the heads of the girls with the blonde plaits from this very gutter.'

'The text is all right – nothing to complain about.'

'So?' was all Frau Riek said.

'Riek changes his mind a bit too quickly; only a day or two ago he was still waiting for Wenk's army', said one of the other women.

The hour had come.

In a private flat at the Schulenburgring in Tempelhof the last Commandant of Berlin was signing the official surrender. He was driven to Johannisthal and there he had to record this declaration:

> *'Berlin, May 2 1945. On April 30 the Führer, whom we had vowed to follow, has forsaken us. Because it was an order from the Führer you still believe you have to fight for Berlin although the lack of heavy weapons and munitions, and the whole situation shows this fight to be futile. Every hour of continued fighting only increases the terrible sufferings of the civilian population of Berlin and of our wounded. With the agreement of the Supreme Command of the Soviet Troops I am asking you therefore to cease fighting. Weidling, General of the Artillery and Commandant of the defence zone Berlin.'*

Loudspeaker vans toured the streets of Berlin.

The voice of the General, intensified out of all proportion, sounded through the hollow ruins and down into the cellars and shafts and the holes which shells had torn into underground ducts; it would be heard, too, in the grounds of the Zoo, furrowed as they were by tanks, with the demolished wild animals' enclosures and the lions and bears and buffaloes killed by shrapnel. It sounded through the smashed aquarium and across the stairs leading to the street on which, after a night of farewells, police officers and soldiers and women some in close embrace, lay drunk or dead.

The news whined also around the Zoo Bunker. From the barrels of the 15-centimetre guns on the tower of the anti-aircraft Bunker the last shot was fired. But there was no end yet to the war. Tears and chattering teeth and nervous breakdowns; drunkenness and murder and suicide. . . . The Bunker Commandant, wild-eyed and with one arm in a sling, would not recognize Weidling's declaration. He decided to break out via Spandau towards the west with all those forces still at his disposal and with the civilians who crowded around the Bunker, bombed out, neglected, apathetic.

'We break out towards the west.'

'March to Freedom.'

Behind them they left the Bunker piled high with corpses, with dying and wounded, a medical officer in charge.

The war had not finished yet.

In Charlottenburg, fighting continued from flat to flat, from roof to roof. Below, the population plundered the shops, the bakeries, chemists' and perfumeries. In the street, rows of vehicles, tanks, guns, soldiers with or without weapons, and crowds of civilians, their last belongings on their backs, women, children, old men, trekked via Spandau to the West.

And the bridges across the Havel in Spandau, Schulendorf Bridge and Charlotte Bridge – three times in Russian hands and three times recaptured – were now taken for the fourth time by the crowds from Berlin. Twenty thousand of them crossed . . . in three waves. Behind the railway embankment, on the water towers and the roofs of shattered houses lay the Russians. Below their positions, Brunsbütteler Damm stretched for two miles like a long flat plate. The approaching people fell in rows. Tanks tried to force a way through all the shot human bodies and finally got stuck.

Russian intermediaries.

They warned everyone not to continue their journey and demanded their return to Berlin. The soldiers did not want to go back, and neither did the civilians – they had been through it all and had left Berlin behind them, they feared the Russian 'peace' more than Russian machine guns. The wave was set in motion again. Twenty thousand on their way to nowhere. None of them saw Nauen; none saw Döberitz. The movement dispersed around the suburb of Staaken. All that was left was a track of blood. Blood dripped off Schulenburg Bridge and Charlotte Bridge into the Havel. On the steps lay the dead and in the fields and meadows and in the gardens by Brunsbütteler Damm; in the entrances to houses and in cellars, everywhere lay the dead and dying; the survivors, now only scattered remnants, were taken prisoner.

There was no 'way to freedom'.

The hour had come – no water, no light, no domestic gas supply, no glass in the windows. One had to make do. Water was fetched from the nearest hydrant and if that had been broken the people went to the nearest reservoir. Gas was something one could do without; after all, there was enough broken timber to light fires for cooking. It was possible to manage without light; if none was provided by the sky, one could go to bed. There were no papers either, no trams, no mail; it was not possible to get from one part of the city to another or to send a message.

Riek was working – on demolition work. He had been taken by lorry, together with a whole squad, to another part of the city. He did not return home at night. Frau Riek came home from her clearance job. Franz was sitting in her kitchen. He squatted on the floor, around him innumerable pieces of the barrel-organ which he had taken apart.

'Have you started dismantling, too?'

'No, my dear; I want to make it go.'

'At least somebody who is more concerned with building up than pulling down.'

She was covered with dust, her hands were as rough as bricks and smeared with soot and resin. There was no water; so she took two pails, went to the door and down the stairs. Downstairs two more women joined her. None of them liked crossing the road alone.

Maria Riek was the youngest. She not only pumped water for her own pail, she also began to fill those of the others. Suddenly she found herself alone; only the buckets stood around her. The two women were running towards the entrance of their house. Three Russians who had turned the corner and saw the women run away, shot after them. It was too late for her to follow the others and fear made her grip the pump handle harder and go on pumping as though nothing happened.

One of the Russians came back, a short man.

'Why you not run?'

She stared at him.

'You not afraid?'

What was she to say?

'No, not afraid,' she said.

He touched her, patted her shoulder, repeated: 'You not afraid of Ruski?'

'No, not afraid of Ruski.'

'Oh, you good woman. I water fetch for you.' He took the pump handle from her, filled the buckets, then asked: 'Yours?'

'This one and that one as well.'

'I will carry for you; where you live?'

How was this going to end? Upstairs in the flat Franz was waiting. They arrived upstairs and she knocked. Franz opened and nothing happened. The Russian proffered an explanation: 'You have good wife', he said to Franz. 'She not afraid of Ruski. I fetch water for her.'

The two pails were emptied into the bath. Trying to get rid of him, she picked the pails up again and prepared to go once more. But the Russian stopped her: 'You stay here, I get water.'

He went, came back, went again, filled the whole bath stood about for a while watching Franz at work and then turned to go.

By the door he asked: 'You need much water?'

'Oh, a lot of water. The bombs made everything dirty and it all has to be washed.'

'I come tomorrow and bring water.'

Thus Maria Riek acquired a daily visitor.

When she returned from work at night he would turn up, fetch water and then sit down beside Franz in the kitchen to try and help him with his intricate job. The dismantled barrel-organ interested him more than anything else, more than the woman even. His help caused such confusion that Franz had to work throughout the following day to put things right again. Once the Russian declared that he had leave and wanted to stay the night. There was nothing she could do but make up the couch for him to sleep on. He was content, slept the whole night, drank ersatz coffee in the morning, ate the bread which he himself had brought and left the house with her without anything having happened.

And Riek returned, for one evening, one night only.

They sat by the kitchen table, Riek and a colleague he had brought along, the Russian and Franz. Frau Riek tried to prepare a meal from 'nothing and water'. The Russian had to be back on time and bade them farewell quite early. Riek worked at the Anhalter station signal and telegraph centre, the largest in the whole of Germany.

'At first they broke the lot and set fire to it, all the switches and connections are fused, but that was immediately after the fighting – now they want to carry the whole lot off, but first we are to restore it completely', Riek told them.

'Yes, the Russian is unpredictable', commented the colleague.

'What nonsense – "the Russian", there is no such thing', Franz interrupted.

'I know, I know, there are all sorts of Russians, but at the same time they are all the same.'

He did not budge.

'The Russian is unpredictable. He is capable of raping women and murdering children, but you can twist him round your little finger if you know how to treat him.'

'There are some who know how to do that', said Riek with a sidelong glance at his wife.

'You'd better think how to get some food into the house', the woman broke in. 'With the money you have brought home you can't buy so much as a potato; as a matter of fact, you can't buy anything with money now.'

Franz went to his coat, took out a bottle of schnapps and handed it to her.

'That is different; you can exchange that. I shall get a piece of butter, perhaps even some bacon.'

The hour had come and had already lasted for many days.
The great city, the youngest of Europe's capitals, had been

sacked and was but one large desolate battlefield – without electricity and water, without post or traffic, without food, social services or sanitation. A city without constitution and without administration, split into a hundred diverse villages.

The head of the improvised police station in Schmargendorf, Günther Sarfeld, had gathered his colleagues together; a few solicitors, two judges, an official receiver, an accountant – civilian clothes, a red band around the arm: that was the staff of the new police force.

From his desk he had a view over the Laubacherstrasse. A field kitchen stood right outside the house. Armchairs were standing around it and a couch on which a Red Army soldier lay asleep. Women with sewing machines were making red flags. A horse, its body lacerated by bullets, walked slowly past. Its head was drooping and its hindlegs gave with every step it took.

Sarfeld held a note in his hand, a list with urgent orders from his Commandant. He was to procure one hundred buckets and a number of brooms, find more workers, bricklayers, cabinet makers, electricians and three hairdressers, have another eighty-two red flags sewn and, of course, get the cloth for them. He wrote out the necessary orders and authorities and sent his helpers out to requisition the required goods. He instructed a secretary who wished to know how to arrange the new personnel register. When he looked up again, he saw that the wounded horse had reached the corner. Nobody thought of putting it out of its misery and neither he nor his police officers, had arms. The guard on the couch could have done it but he was still asleep. A number of men were busy cleaning the street, they had no brooms but used torn-off bushes and branches; all they did was stir up the dust. A small group of mourners stopped outside the house, a father pulling a hand-cart, on it a little corpse wrapped in paper; behind him the mother and a few half-grown children. They were asking the women at the sewing machines where to find a burying ground. But they did not know of one.

'Somewhere in a park, in a yard', said one of them.

A car came along the street and stopped. The local Commandant got out and the next moment stood before Sarfeld.

'You come at once, Commandant sitting there.'

Only a few hundred yards further on, sitting on the pavement, was a regimental Commandant with an injured ankle who said.

'I need by . . .' – he glanced at his wrist-watch – 'It is now midday, by six o'clock this evening I need a school building with several hundred camp beds, an enclosure for two hundred horses, garages for fifteen cars, three houses for my officers, and a few more for my subalterns.'

'It is quite impossible to manage all that by six o'clock this evening. Of course, if I had a car — '

Sarfeld got the car, and in addition a major who knew a little German. The school was soon found; but to find women to equip the school, whilst hordes of Russian soldiers were camping outside the building, was much more difficult. However, by six o'clock he had fulfilled the command. He was as tired as if he had done a day's work in a stone quarry. It was easier to direct a Shakespeare play where at the end the main characters lie as corpses under the falling curtain, than to act the policeman amidst a scenery of real ruins and real corpses surrounded by tyrants and pillagers and an apathetic population.

And what sense was there in all his activities; what was the lasting value of this endlessly unfolding drama? In the world of Shakespeare he would arrive at an allegory of life by way of exposition, climax and catastrophe. But here – where was the end here, what was achieved if he commandeered people's buckets, the red ticking of their feather beds, and finally their tables, chairs, beds and whole flats of furniture? He knew no answer to this. True, he was able to avoid unnecessary hardship and murder, but that was too little. Dissatisfied with himself he returned to Laubacherstrasse. In his office he found Dr. Linth, the sight of whom reminded him of the eighteen women he had been able to protect with the help of the Russian Commandant and the activities of Dr. Linth – that was one sensible thing he had achieved.

Too little, far too little – after all, there were three and a half million people living in Berlin and in his district alone were several hundred thousand crowded streets which still froze into silence every night, a silence interrupted only by cries for help which echoed through the darkness.

Annoyed, he threw his brief-case on to the table. Linth looked at him with enormous eyes; his face had lost all its flesh in those few days, the skin stretched tight over the bone structure.

The two were alone in the room.

'I had imagined it would be different. When I took all this over I thought the liberators were coming, and it does not look like that now. The Commandant is not too bad, admittedly. But that changes nothing, nothing.'

'Perhaps it does.'

'How?'

'Human action never fails to produce an effect.'

'What does it matter if a dozen and a half people here are safe!'

'I pulled Frau Halen through. We managed it without penicillin – there is no penicillin. She has got over the puerperal fever.'

'One – and a thousand others?'

A thousand others. . . . Linth came from a cellar of a large block of flats belonging to the AEG, the great electricity concern. There he had seen a sixteen-year-old girl who had been raped many times. She had cried and the Russian with her had said: 'You not cry', and when she did not stop, he had repeated: 'You not cry, you not cry.' The continued whimpering of the girl had irritated him and he had grabbed his knife and stabbed both her eyes. The *arteria orbitalis* deep in the eye sockets had been hit and the girl was bound to bleed to death. She was almost dead when Linth was called to her. He had not been able to help her. A thousand he had not been able to help – one of them he had helped.

'Yes, it is little; human power is limited,' said Linth, 'but human aid, even in one case only, means more than just aid. The idea of humanity is kept alive by it, Herr Sarfeld.'

The hour had come, and they did not know it.

The war had come to an end, and the bells had not tolled, the blackout had not ceased, the herded existence in the cellars continued, and fear was still the guest who sat down at the table and shared the bed. As before, the sky glowed at night – only, now, the dull thud of cannons, the whistling rockets, the rising beams of searchlights were vctory salutes and signs of peace, and there was no longer any hiding or sheltering in cellars or bomb craters. Fear had become personified and had unveiled its face.

In Tempelhof a capitulation had been signed and the news of it had been carried by lorries as far as the cellars and fighting hordes. At Karlshorst, in the grounds of the Pi-school, the last Chief of the Supreme Command of the army lowered his marshal's baton before the representatives of the victorious powers, put his monocle away and with dropped arches trotted to the waiting table and signed, in the name of the whole German army, the document of surrender. A week passed by and another week before rumours of the completed unconditional surrender reached all the inhabitants of the town which still burned and smouldered.

Berlin was given a new Lord Mayor and did not know it.

A sixty-seven-year-old retired city architect, Dr. Werner, whilst watering his flowers in the garden one morning, had been addressed by a gentleman in a grey suit and had been invited to come for a drive with him to meet a former member of the Reichstag. He did not know whether he was being arrested or honoured. In a house in the eastern suburb of Friedrichsfelde he was confronted with the former Reichstag member, a man with a small Lenin-type beard. He was given food and drink and was allowed to lie down on a couch while waiting for the Soviet Commandant of the city, Colonel-General Bersarin. The latter did not arrive until the evening, and then, through his interpreter, informed Dr. Werner that he had been chosen mayor of Berlin.

Twenty-four hours later Dr. Werner entered Parochial-strasse at the head of the newly formed council. Two days later, at a solemn gathering and in the presence of Colonel-General Bersarin and members of his staff, Dr. Werner opened the manuscript of his inaugural speech, which he had composed with the aid of the gentleman in the grey suit, Herr Maron, his First Deputy.

He spoke of Berlin's sufferings under Hitler.

'This tyrant,' he said, 'has outdone even Genghis Khan who, about 1200, raided the towns, burning and pillaging. We breathe a sigh of relief and owe a debt of gratitude to the Red Army, the American and British forces. Hitler has turned Berlin into *a city of destruction. We shall turn Berlin into a city of work and progress. . . .*

Marshal Zhukov, the liberator of Berlin, has already begun to heal the wounds which Hitler has inflicted on the German people. During the short period of occupation the progress made has been considerable. Soviet engineers are helping in Berlin. Their activities are already crowned with great success. The electricity works are beginning to function again. The clearance work is progressing favourably and men and women are working side by side in an admirable manner. We thank our Lord for permitting us to live in these days and to sow the seeds of a new era. A spirit of love and harmony is to prevail once again in Germany. Our united attitude against Fascism has already brought forth the first visible successes; it is the guarantee of a rebirth of the German nation. We close our celebration with the proclamation: Long live Berlin.'

Berlin had a new Lord Mayor and only learnt of the fact days later. Berlin again had a Council and nobody knew the names of the new Councillors.

The former member of the Reichstag, the short-legged gentleman with the Lenin beard, the man without characteristics, who had emerged as Survivor Number One, called a conference of functionaries.

Half the Berlin Council was present – not the Lord Mayor but some of his deputies, the Manager of the Planning Department, the Manager of the Personnel Department, the Managers for Social Services, for Labour Problems, for Church Matters . . . the anti-Fascists working in district offices, at clearance jobs and demolition, women, men and youths, representatives of the foremen, those in charge of houses and blocks of houses, the printer Riebeling and the photographer Putlitzer from Tempelhof, the shoemaker Haderer, the mechanic Reimann from Weissensee.

They all came.

From penitentiaries and prisons and camps came the liberated inmates, those saved from the gallows and those who had been in hiding. How many well-known faces turned up again, missed for a long time, aged by privation and suffering, and some of them crippled, but all familiar. A thousand or more people were gathered together and the hall smelled of destruction and cold smoke. The atmosphere was charged with hope, confidence, and a premonition of something extraordinary. The speaker came from Moscow and was bound to have some explanation for so much that was incomprehensible in the chaos that had broken out. He was bound to offer a revelation to the novices. The old ones, who still remembered him, could expect a comprehensive analysis of world politics after all the time of darkness, of internment, of isolation; moreover, they were of the opinion that he owed them an explanation as to the rather strange attitude of the 'Soviet liberators' which made their work constantly more difficult and hindered their propaganda.

The speaker appeared.

He came slowly, walking softly. A sergeant-major in slippers, an omniscient tom-cat – just the same as during the cell meetings in the old days. He had acquired a beard – an imitation, the original of which was well known.

Solemn commemoration of the victims of Nazi rule. Everybody rose and sat down again, and the Speaker began. Breathless silence, and expectation on all faces. The speech sounded rather like the report of an auditor. He spoke simply; his great example, the original of the beard had spoken simply too, and also, it was said, with just a trace of dialect. The obeisance before the 'Victorious Red Army' was by way of an introduction and unavoidable considering the circumstances. But after a while he could have dropped it. He kept on about the 'gallant Russians' and after all, it was not quite like that. If there was to be a question of being 'gallant', that could be said of others as well, of the few and badly armed factory guards, and the Volkssturm who had been defending the Lorenz Bunker for days; the Berlin police who recaptured the Oberbaum Bridge; the Hitler Youths at the bridges across the Havel, whose number dwindled from five thousand to five hundred – in the end it is only the aim that matters; that was what he should have talked about.

Old Riebeling made mental marginal notes, but he was listening carefully throughout and there was still a tense interest on his face when others had already begun to look about them searching for familiar faces.

Berlin was the robbers' den of the brown hordes – we know all that, comrade speaker! *The capture of the country's capital cut the Hitler gang to the quick*; true enough, but it is over and done with – and now what? *The liberation of our country from Hitler's gang was not accomplished by our own people but only through the armed forces of other nations* – that also is true, horribly true. But that does not establish a purpose either nor build any foundation. Or does it? The speaker at any rate emphasized the fact as if it were a basic truth – as indeed it turned out to be – that much became clear as the speech went on – a barbarous basic truth according to which he calculated the severity of the defeat and, in logical sequence, the denial of all rights on the part of the defeated. No rights – only duties.

The duty to obey and to carry out orders. The duty to work without asking questions, to work and to dismantle, to clear up, without excavator, without cranes, with bucket and broom, and bare hands. The duty to keep silent when human beings are thrown to wild animals.

The speaker consulted a bulky manuscript.

Pay, pay . . .

Destruction in the Ukraine, the Kuban, in Bessarabia, White Russia, Caucasia. The debt grew to gigantic proportions and the man on whose shoulders it was set was crushed, had no longer a human face, no claim to human nourishment, human clothes, was without a house, without trousers . . . a louse. In the end the reparations were calculated to amount to twenty milliard German Marks.

'A hard time lies ahead of our people, a time of trial. Our people must prove that they are capable of transformation. Under the military occupation of their country they will have to make good all damage inflicted upon other nations, particularly upon the great Soviet nation, by Hitler's war and Hitlerite barbarity. Our people will carry out this duty because they recognize it as essential, because only thus can they find their own salvation . . .'

The analysis of the international situation never materialized. The conclusions of the Yalta conference were presented as orders. Not a word about the former colonies which were in turmoil, about the focal points in the post-war happenings in Belgium, in Greece, about conflicting interests, about trends in America, who also had a say in Germany's fate; hardly a hint as to the place which the German people would have to occupy one day.

Proclamation of a working programme, rendered like a financial report. And the proclaimed ethics were not the 'post-Christian and higher' ethics which Socialists all over the world claim for themselves, but pre-Christian and barbaric.

All high hopes had been shattered. A hundred questions were given an ominous answer. The first conference of the officials was revealed as an issue of orders: working discipline, party discipline, submission to the dictum of the victor.

Order: Work according to the set standards and beyond. Work without having a share in the consultations and without any prospect of helping to make decisions.

'Overseer Number One, the prefect appointed by the Emperor, and we are the Emperor's slaves: that is how it was once before, that is how it has always been; nothing new in that.' Thus Riebeling spoke to Putlitzer as they went home. 'But after all, we shall have to work in any case, enough has been destroyed already and there is no new beginning without restitution.'

'Nothing is eaten as hot as it is cooked', Putlitzer commented.

A new beginning was also the theme in a villa in Zehlendorf. There were carpets on the floor, real Bokhara and Persians, antique furniture, comfortable chairs, a library, a view into the conservatory. All the windows had been taken unbroken from the cellar and put back. The Director of the Deutsche Bank, Baron von Stauss, had lived here and had gone. The poet from the Moscow aeroplane, a prominent member of the 'ghost government', had moved into the abandoned house. But a bourgeois house in bourgeois surroundings, without the security of a stable bourgeois milieu, in the middle of the death-throes of the sentenced bourgeois society, is at best a museum and cannot be lived in any more than can a model of a patrician's house from Pompeii. And a Soviet 'Grace and Favour' residence is more fragile than glass and as transparent. Eyes look across your shoulders as you write. Ears hear what you say in your sleep. There are hands to open the doors of your house and your car. You do not trust the chair in which you sit; you do not trust the serving hands; in the end you do not trust yourself. Once upon a time, in this same Zehlendorf, there was a simple bungalow made of plain wood, beautiful as a dream, beautiful was also the retreat in the Sabian valley . . . once so real and now only a line in a poem, written in the early morning while all was still and the piece of paper under his hand was still lighter than the day just beginning to dawn outside the windows.

Gone.

For ever . . .

Real is the unreality, real also is the command: the harnessing of a huge Trojan horse. So far everything had gone according to plan. The leftish sympathies of the Berlin intellectuals of the nineteen-twenties had left their mark. The Berlin intelligentsia displayed open minds. The poet was welcomed; in many places he met old acquaintances, had only to open the door. There were also tired faces and those that turned away – and there were awkward moments – unavoidable in a town where death had already grown tired. He came to a flat and the faces were wet with tears: early that morning the fifteen-year-old son had been taken away as a 'Werewolf'. Yet the boy had never belonged to any organization and Werewolves were not known there. He went to see a well-known architect in Pfeddersheimerstrasse and entered almost at the same moment as the owner returned to it after it had been requisitioned for weeks by the Russians.

'*Kultura*, my dear fellow. Just come and look at this.'

He saw and he heard. He saw the wife crying and heard the children whimpering: 'Papa, we can't stay here.' It was almost impossible to get through. The cellar steps were cluttered with furniture, the remains of a sideboard, bookshelves, chairs, a needlework table, a dressing table, pieces of china and spilt marmalade and preserves and human fæces. It was the same all over; fæces on mattresses, on featherbeds, on carpets and in the corners. In the rooms the cupboards had been thrown over, mattresses lay on their backs. In the garden exposed to the rain stood a wardrobe and armchairs; it was a huge wardrobe, with rich inlay work. The owner opened the door; the wardrobe had been turned into a lavatory. 'We have a W.C. in the house but they found this more convenient.' He bent down, and from a heap of books swept together with a gardenfork he took an old Flemish chronicle. '*Kultura*, my dear fellow – this can't go on; something must be done. I shall be there; thank you for the invitation.'

That was architect Poppert and the visit there had been awkward. In Hermsdorf, where he had called on Dr. Linth, who was also a sinologist of European renown, it was not only awkward but painful. A simply furnished attic, a man much younger than he expected, and in a corner, roughly screened by a curtain, a bed and on it the figure of Snow-white, already covered by an invisible glass coffin. The man with the young face and the ageless eyes had brought her back the day before. She had been taken from him weeks earlier and he had found her again in a clinic in Karlstrasse belonging to a religious order. He, too, Dr. Linth, said he would come to the meeting. The question of culture was sufficiently urgent for all of them. Irrespective of their personal experiences they had all come.

He had gathered an illustrious company around him.

Famous writers, great actors, painters, architects, an orchestra conductor, the sinologist, a theologian, two producers, one of them a youngish man, temporary District Police Chief, who was only waiting for a licence for his theatre. The other had been Director of the Berlin State Opera; he was carried off on his sixty-fourth birthday and had spent a few days herded together with hundreds of others – like a cattle enclosure in the Argentine, he said – thirty miles out of Berlin; he had finally returned to his bombed flat, robbed of everything, his clothes torn, and completely exhausted. He could well have done with a few days rest, and yet he had come to the meeting and had even brought two well-known actors with him.

A new beginning, that was the theme; the whole atmosphere was that of a general *conversazione*. A young woman with a white cap (when the Russians had first come she had been wearing an evening dress) handed round a tray with sandwiches and Vermouth and brandy. Nearly all of them were ravenous, but etiquette was observed and they ate and drank sparingly. The discussion was everybody's real concern. We must begin afresh, we cannot just go on staring at the ruins outside and the empty dishes at home. Start up the theatres; fill the University Chairs; rebuild. One should be grateful and overjoyed to meet so much understanding, to find so many helping hands. This poet from the days of expressionism of blessed memory, with the powerful hand of the Russian conqueror behind him, was he not a gift from heaven? Besides, it was always a pleasure to listen to him; he was clever, very clever, though perhaps a little shallow. A newspaper: *Die Brücke*. A periodical: *Aufbau*. A monthly magazine: *Sinn und Form*. A large publishing house. Half a dozen theatre licences. Permission to form a cultural organization embracing all artists, scientists and others with cultural interests. The only question still open and the only thing the poet had brought with him was – ideology. They might begin to talk about that; after all that had been the purpose of the meeting.

They talked; and for once the talk did not divide but unite. Berlin was occupied by the Russians; that was a fact which they had to accept. It was not necessarily the same as accepting the Russian ideology. Far from it – the Communist Party was by no means ready to accept just anyone. Ideologies cannot be imported and it was essential to build something new. This, said the prominent representative of the Moscow emigration, was what the Russians hoped for – anti-Fascist of course, embodying the idea of freedom and humanism, but in accordance with national traditions. Well, one had had enough of Nazism. The view from the windows across the ruins was eloquent enough. And almost all those here had had nothing in common with Nazism and its ideology. Spreading the truth; regaining objective standards and values; applying democratic methods to the cultural organization which was to be formed, to the Humboldt University which was to open its doors again; to the theatres which were to receive their licences within a matter of days. They were to start where Germany's glorious cultural past had left off, the past which had produced men like Goethe, Hegel, Engels and Marx – that was the only programme, so they were told, and nobody was going to interfere with the professors, the editors, the producers in their pursuance of this aim. On the contrary; they were to receive every assistance from the Occupying Power.

It all sounded good. One had imagined that it would be necessary to tour the villages with carts to keep the theatre going – and now they talked about re-opening the State Theatre and the State Opera. One should not exaggerate the fears about Russian intervention. The theatrical arts in Berlin, as well as other arts, had often found themselves in situations comparable to those in small medieval Republics. The artists and painters had been given commissions by private and civic sponsors, but the artists had worked creatively and independent of any outside influence.

The sixty-four-year-old Opera House Director spoke; after him the theologian, the architect, a painter and a writer addressed the gathering. It was encouraging; there were no controversial disputes, the conversation was valuable and interesting. The host showed himself to be a clever mediator. It's just not true what they say about him: you mustn't offend him; you mustn't make fun of his forty slim volumes of poetry – because he never forgets. You can't depend on him – he never keeps a promise. None of this is true; perhaps it was once, in the old troubled days. He was older now, had returned wiser and more self-assured. Under his leadership the meeting became a working party. The friendly young lady with the white cap appeared at frequent intervals. The name of the cultural organization was decided on: '*Kulturbund zur demokratischen Erneuerung Deutschlands*' – Cultural Organization for the Democratic Renewal of Germany – and it was no longer true, even the Chairman of the meeting almost forgot it that the same name had already been suggested during a discussion in the Hotel Lux in Moscow. The name was born – a preliminary directorate was formed and a date suggested for the solemn inauguration of the Organization.

A very pleasant and productive afternoon. Agreeably impressed, in the best of spirits, and encouraged by the knowledge that a new beginning had been made, the gathering broke up. And six well-known men – leaders of German intellectual life – did not realize that they had been the first to climb into the belly of the Trojan horse.

'There shall not any man be able to stand before thee all the days of thy life: as I was with Moses, so I will be with thee. I will not fail thee nor forsake thee, be strong and of good courage . . .' These words from the Book of Joshua, were spoken beneath the huge guns of the 'Prince of Wales' one summer morning in the year 1941, when the sun fought with the white mist off the coast of Newfoundland – the promise had been fulfilled and it was now up to the people to fulfil the words of the prayer, stammered out at the same place: 'That we may be preserved from hatred, bitterness and the spirit of revenge . . .'

The hour for the redemption of their world-wide debt had come. The representatives of the three victorious powers met in Potsdam for the conference which was to end the war and begin the post-war period.

The Nazi Reich had collapsed – but the trunk which had borne this unruly shoot had fallen as well. Prussia was no more; Germany no more. The country had been divided into four parts and the people had beeen divided into four parts, and powers had been unleashed which meant to uproot the fallen trunk and destroy it completely. Not one of them asked whether a country – even the youngest – whether a nation – even the most military-minded one – could be removed from the heart of Europe without endangering the whole structure. Nobody cared whether a corner stone could be removed from the intricate 2000-year-old structure without exposing the whole building to the danger of collapse.

Did nobody care? The British Prime Minister, in Britain's hour of greatest danger, had urged the pact with the Eastern partner and afterwards had feared his defection above everything else. Ever since the days of the Casablanca Conference he had watched with apprehension the massing of the Russian cohorts on the Eastern horizon of Europe amply equipped with American materials. In Teheran, when the formation of a second front was the centre of discussion, he was already on the defensive – he suggested that the fortress of Europe should be attacked from the 'soft underbelly', that a mass invasion of the Balkans should be started from the eastern side of the Mediterranean in order to carry the attack along the Danube valley into the heart of Europe – and even the already modified plan to turn not to the left (to France) from a certain position in Italy but to turn part of the forces to the East in order to achieve a strategic diversion in South-East Europe, had had to be abandoned, failing the co-operation of the Americans. Defeat in Teheran would have meant defeat in Europe. Churchill's violent opposition was of no avail. Fatigue and fever forced him to a sickbed. After the Conference he had taken to bed – first in Malta, then amidst the ruins of old Carthage, lastly in Marrakesh. And in Yalta it was too late; it was impossible to catch up with developments. All boundaries were fluid, Central Europe was in the melting pot and the Douglas from Moscow airport had already brought the shadow governments for Warsaw, Bukarest, Belgrade, Budapest and Vienna. His suggestion to send an expeditionary force into the Balkans to reinforce the Red Army was but an inadequate shadow of his original plan; and like all inadequate and super-flous ideas it was passed over. Now he stood in Potsdam, found himself on the edge of the maelstrom and looked down into emtpy space – the vacuum that was Europe.

Did nobody care? Did nobody remember the significance of the ground where once the Holy Roman Empire of the German Nation, and still earlier, the Empire of Charlemagne had risen? The President of the United States was the executor of a terrible legacy – and the inheritance resembled a polyp-like monster with a thousand heads, with a thousand gaping mouths . . . the Kurile Islands, Port Arthur, the South Manchurian railways, the Dardanelles, Iran, trusteeships, war criminals, seats in the World Organization, the Polish government, the Oder-Neisse boundary, Morgenthau, reparations: recommendations, open question, concessions and half-concessions, problems half solved, only to be super-seded by changing events. The man who might have pierced the magic circle, who had held in his hands the key that might have opened up the fatal constellation, President Franklin Delano Roosevelt, was no more. The price of greatness is responsibility – and he had shouldered responsibility upon responsibility. Four times the American electorate had given him the mandate to control their armed operations which covered the whole world; he had led the American citizen out of isolationism and had given him a global awareness which he would never lose. The hour of fate struck once for him in Teheran; in Yalta it was almost his hour once again. The constellation of the Powers demanded decisions and he saved them for a future date – for Dumbarton Oaks, for San Francisco, for Potsdam. He reserved for himself 'freedom of action' in an hour which already demanded action itself. And it was not the electorate, not the people, but history itself which took his measure in Teheran and once again at Yalta; his successor in Potsdam could not excape the shadow of his greatness.

One man had observed the lurking vacuum – and saw it as the eagle sees the empty space beneath its wings and was ready to plunge into it with beak and talons. Good 'Uncle Joe', Roosevelt had called him. Good old Joe – the echo rustled through the American forest. 'Let them have it, Frank; don't let those slave drivers repeat the mistakes of Versailles. . . .' Thus spoke the good American electorate – the slave drivers were, of course the former Colonial rulers – old 'John Bull'. Enough to make a bear laugh – the pipe tasted even better with this going on. Gone were the days when 'Uncle Joe' had had to beg for tanks, anti-tank weapons, bombers, anti-aircraft guns, armoured plate; for jeeps, lorries, barbed wire and raw materials; gone was the time when news of Timoshenko's disorderly troops retreating along the Autobahn had come in whilst he paced the room smoking incessantly, and he had sat down once more to appeal to the suppliers of weapons and had sketched wolves, filling in the sky above them red; gone were the times when he had called angrily for a second front. In Teheran the 'rich Uncle from America' had been his only guest, and the scowling 'John Bull' had not seen him face to face, not privately anyway. Some bright ideas 'John Bull' had had – a 'soft underbelly' and things like that, and across the Balkans he had meant to carry the attack into the heart of Europe. What an antiquated idea anyway, as though Europe still existed! A page turned over in the book of history – with the holy knights who were beaten on Lake Peipus, with the Hanseatic ships, with Bonaparte, Frederick the Great, Bismarck. All that is left are political aristocracies rotten to the core, nations who no longer defend their boundaries, artists frozen in formalism, existentialist cafés, mannequins who looked like boys, and boys who looked like mannequins. . . . It is done with, finished, and it only remains to clean the

309

dung out. Europe is an obsolete description, without substance and geographically untenable – a pasture land on the western approaches of Moscow.

Along the southern outskirts of Berlin, via Wannsee, Zehlendorf, Unter den Eichen, and along Schloss-strasse marched a small group of prisoners of war, seventy of them, sick and wounded, picked up between Kladow and Potsdam, a last handful left over from the grey wave which had passed through the streets eight weeks earlier. They stumbled and limped painfully along and time and again had to sit down by the side of the road to get their breath. And the sergeant who, with the help of a few infantrymen, escorted them, did not stop them, allowed the people from the houses around to go near them, even encouraged the women: 'Woman, give bread.' And the women who queued outside the re-opened bakers and greengrocers' shops, shared their poverty with the miserable wanderers, a slice of bread, a carrot. One of those sufferers was Captain Boehlke. He had a fever; cold sweat was running from all his pores and when he looked up he could not see the long row of ruins because of the black spots which danced before his eyes. He still carried on him the report of the defeat of the Ninth Army addressed to his Uncle Raimond. It had been his intention while marching through Potsdam to give the letter to a passer-by, and ask him to forward it. But later he and his little group had themselves passed through the very street; a heap of rubble indicated the spot where the house had stood. And from a women he learnt that all the inhabitants, including Chief Librarian Stassen, Uncle Raimond and his aunt, had met their end underneath this heap of rubble.

'Daway. Go on!'

At the end of Schloss-strausse the little group turned left towards Anhalter Station. They passed through the centre of the city, through Leipzigerstrasse. On Dönhoff Platz a bus suddenly appeared ahead of them, one of the first to pick its way through the ruins of the re-opened route. The sergeant had already lost a lot of time with his exhausted party. He stopped the bus, told the passengers to get out. The prisoners were allowed to sit down. Thus Boehlke was riding once again in a double decker bus of the BVG (the Berlin Transport Corporation), just as he had done a long time ago with the workers from Spandau at the beginning of his Odyssee when he drove along the same route towards the Oder front.

Typhus, dysentery, abortions (now generally permitted by a special regulation), death from exhaustion, venereal disease; those were the cases coming daily into the reserve hospital 122 which had now become a civilian hospital. Drugs were scarce, also cotton wool and bandages, and the patients died of hunger in their beds. The large stocks of medicines, bandages and provisions which the hospital had possessed, had been requisitioned, and the surgical equipment, except for some pitiably small remnants, had been carried off under the dismantling orders.

Those of the wounded who were able to walk had been taken off to prison camps, soon after the Occupation, and the removal of the seriously injured had been going on for several days now. In institution clothes, or wearing just shirt and trousers, they had been loaded into lorries and driven eastwards. Two thousand – and nobody knew where their journey would take them.

The job was done – into the last car climbed Chief Medical Officer Dr. Theysen. By the car stood Frau Theysen to bid him farewell. 'Come woman, you go too', called the guard. In this way Dr. Theysen's wife became a prisoner of war as well. The lorry took them as far as Lichtenberg where they boarded a waiting train. Three days passed – they travelled this way and that. The train was shunted into sidings, halted, and then sent on again. Theysen slept almost the whole time. He was utterly exhausted and could hardly rouse himself to eat, and there was food in plenty. After three days they had only got as far as Frankfurt-on-Oder. Here they were ordered to get out and change into lorries. Theysen had a suit-case with him and was going to lift it into the lorry. An officer was standing by his side: 'You nothing suit-case. You only robots, nothing work.' He consulted his notes again: 'You nothing robots, you leading surgeon. And woman not on list. Woman also doctor, good, can stay.'

Dr. Theysen became surgeon in charge at the hospital for contagious diseases in Frankfurt-on-Oder. A figure in shirt and pants introduced himself as Colonel Zecke – in shirt and pants, that was how they all went about behind the barbed wire.

'This is our uniform here; it's symbolic', said the Colonel. It was the official clothing for everybody – a simple expedient to cut down attempts at escape. Theysen was allowed to continue wearing his uniform, the only one amongst all the patients, nurses and doctors in the camp. Colonel Zecke was busy writing in the office. He explained the situation in the camp to Theysen. Six thousand patients, no beds, all lying on straw. Typhus, spotted typhus, dysentery; TB; seventy to eighty deaths daily. They died and the straw could not be changed; it was simply turned and the next one put on it.

'A summary report', Theysen commented.

'It's a summary existence here – a short hop from childbed to grave', replied Zecke.

To get out, run away! That had been Vicco Splüge's thought from the beginning, and already during the march through the town he had looked round for an opportunity. At one spot, where a house had collapsed right across the road, one of them had tried it. He had hoped to get away behind the heap of ruins, but he was shot down. At the next corner the guard had seized one of the men standing around and thus made up the number. Behind Hallesches Tor, as they marched along the Landwehr Canal, another had a try. He leaped out of the row, jumped the balustrade and meant to reach the other bank by swimming across. Two Russians shot after him with automatics. From their ranks it was not possible to see what happened down in the Canal. But a number of wild duck took to the air and two fell back with broken wings. . . . The same procedure was used, and another man was seized and added to the ranks. Obviously, escape could not be done that way. The right opportunity had to be there and Splüge forced himself to wait for it. Weeks passed behind barbed wire, on the outskirts of Berlin; then the marching began again, but oddly enough the way led back to Treptower Park and then, with a large detour, to the Wuhlheide water works. A large majority were herded farther east. Splüge remained behind together with about fifty or sixty men. The following day they were set to work, clearing the public park and the nearby sports grounds. In the evenings they returned to the camp and next day work began again. Obviously that could not go on for long, and the next deportation to the East must be imminent. The last opportunity for escape seemed to have arrived. And Splüge took the risk, left his place of work, walked slowly to the nearest bush. Nothing happened; none of the guards had noticed his departure. On, to the next bush. But always slowly, never a rash movement resembling flight. Already he had a curtain of bushes and tall grass behind him and at last he reached the road by Wuhlheide, crossed Rummels-burgerstrasse, hid in a ruin in Oberschöneweide until night-fall. Five days passed; it took him all that time to cross Berlin. On the morning of the fifth day he had reached Wannsee. He saw Wittstock's house, only twenty feet separated him from the garden gate. Suddenly he found himself face to face with a Russian who sat underneath a street lamp, busy taking a wireless set apart. He looked at Splüge, drew his pistol and then shot at the street lamp; he seemed pleased with the falling pieces. Splüge went on, quite slowly again. His heart beat wildly. He passed the garden gate, went round the next corner and got into the garden from the back. He was saved; he slipped through the back door and faced his old friend. But Wittstock was even more frightened than Splüge himself had been a minute ago. Frau Wittstock came downstairs too and threw up her hands at the sight of him. They were both very sorry for him. Indeed he looked like something the dog had brought in: he was ravenously hungry and half dead from thirst. They gave him a piece of bread and a cup of ersatz coffee. No, he could not stay the night. Neither could he return during the daytime, friends were going in and out who must not see him. What kind of friends were they that they must not see him? Well, writers, actors, the united front of German intellectuals. 'Your presence here is utterly impossible; surely you understand that', said Wittstock. 'Destruction of Nazi ideology; the fight against the intellectual sponsors of the Nazi crimes. . . .'

'You mean that I am an intellectual sponsor?'

'What I mean is immaterial. What is more, you have been very lucky; if you had arrived two days earlier, you would have found a Russian division in here.' Wittstock had only got his house back two days ago – this through the intervention of the same 'cultural front'. 'No, you cannot stay; if you are found here, we shall both have to pay for it.' Splüge did not understand all this. However, he began to comprehend that Wittstock's world had undergone a 180 degree turn. Wittstock brought him a pail of water from the garden, and he was allowed to wash. He could take off his uniform, too, and change into one of Wittstock's suits which was much too large for him. Splüge's own flat was inaccessible; it had been requisitioned by the Americans, so he was told.

'And Leonore?'

'No idea; I don't know where she lives', replied Wittstock.

But Frau Wittstock was able to help him.

'You will most probably find her around Alexander Platz or Potsdamer Platz.'

'Potsdamer Platz? What is she doing there?'

'She is trading.'

'Trading?'

'All Berlin is trading nowadays.'

In Potsdam the Three-Power Pact lay on the table ready to be signed. The scene was dramatically changed. Of the three Great Ones of the war only one was able to put his signature to the pact. One of the three had died and had a successor. The 'great old man' had once been able to address his nation and say: 'I have nothing to offer but blood, toil, sweat and tears.' And now that the guns were silent, the same nation who had followed him willingly through the dark valley of the war considered him too much of an obligation. The newly assembled Parliament no longer included him as Prime Minister. In the hour when all the problems which had been discussed during the Atlantic Conference were nearing solution and turning into signed and sealed decisions and binding statutes, he had been replaced by another.

'Freedom from need, anxiety and fear', sounded the message from the Atlantic. And the nations, entangled in bloody jungle warfare, benumbed in a torture of snow, fleeing through empty space, moaning under the showers of plaster from collapsing houses, were holding their breath. Only one of the three titans of the war had remained – and with the new men, he brought the peace safely into harbour.

The world had not been created anew; the disturbed equilibrium had not been restored – it has been upset still more. The middle of Europe and also the centre of Asian power-politics had been turned into empty spaces. Between East and West an abyss had opened. The foundations of the previous existence floated above the bottomless pit.

Whole nations had been thrown to a despotic foreign rule, like brushwood on the fire. The rehousing of national minorities – already in full swing – became legalized. Ten million, twenty million, old people, women and chilren were made homeless, bereft of their possessions. The men stayed behind; together with millions of prisoners of war, they peopled the labour camps. Reparation payments in human labour: such was the wording of the harsh law.

'Freedom from need, from anxiety and fear. . . .'

That had been in the Atlantic where the white summer mists had rolled along the Newfoundland waters. And the heavens opened and a host of angels appeared with trumpets:

> 'Glory to God in the highest,
> Peace on earth,
> And goodwill towards men.'

The curtain came down, the curtain rose again, rose above Teheran, above Yalta – after Yalta above Potsdam.

'Freedom from need, from anxiety and from fear . . .' the words had lost their meaning.

At Hermsdorf a man wrapped the fragile figure of a woman in a sheet, carried the still body downstairs, and laid it upon a handcart. He found a cemetery but no grave-digger, dug the grave himself and laid the dead woman into it . . . a torn-off blossom.

At Mariendorf, Frau Halen who had returned with a baby, received her ration card. Valid for a monthly ration of 18 lbs. of bread, 1 lb. of meat, 6 ounces of fat. 'That is what all receive who don't work', said the caretaker, shrugging her shoulders. 'Card V; cemetery card.'

Franz from Landsbergerstrasse also had only the 'cemetery ration card', but he had put his barrel organ together again and was on his feet from morning till night, and when he came back he always brought something home, a few potatoes, sometimes a carrot and always a lot of firewood.

Saburov, the authorized agent for industrial dismantling in Karlshorst, sat bent over the final lists of figures. Ivan Serov should be satisfied with his effort. The time-table had been kept; they were even ahead of schedule. The Germans were good workers and in only six weeks the industrial capacity of Berlin had been reduced to twenty per cent of its former level. Admittedly the damage done by American bombers had been included. But that could be rectified. There was still plenty left around Berlin that could be dismantled.

In the large studio of the newly opened Berlin broadcasting station the invited guests were arriving, drawn from the Berlin intelligentsia. In the stalls, next to the man with the Lenin beard, actors and scientists were sitting, architect Poppert, producer Sarfeld and editor Wittstock. Accompanied by Sebastian Bach's solemn music, the *Kulturbund zur demokratischen Erneuerung Deutschlands* was presented to the public. The poet from the Stauss villa, from the Douglas aircraft from Moscow, opened the programme, taking his text from Gottfried Keller:

'And then I knew it; you were but a tomb, But still a tomb that strove to rise from death.'

Vicco Splüge searched for Leonore.

Potsdamer Platz was lined with ruins and with rows of 'Trümmerfrauen' in their hundreds. The steps to the station the places beneath the sloping stuccoed ceilings of the 'Vaterland' corner house ruin were thick with loafers. It resembled a production of a witches' sabbath on an expressionist stage. Everywhere people in the shadows, shabby clothes, hollow faces. 'No, thank you, thank you. . . .' Splüge had no intention of buying shoes with downtrodden heels. Neither did he want chewing gum; for cigarettes he had no money. All tried to sell something. 'Ami' cigarettes, worn baby clothes, Nescafé, green herrings – from their pockets or palms they offered their wares. Russians were trading, too; sometimes they simply grabbed. A jeep drove up, full of cigarettes, the 'Amis'; the Americans wanted to barter them against watches and cameras. 'Ami' cigarettes were Berlin's new currency; they were reckoned by single cigarettes, packets and whole cartons. Children stood about, stretching out their little hands and begging in English and Russian, 'Give me chocolate. Give me cigarettes. *Dai jleba!* Give bread!' Splüge, searching for Leonore, looked at all the women, the tired, indifferent faces beneath the scarves. She was not amongst them. He would have to look elsewhere and trotted off to the other centre of the black market, Alexander Platz.

What happened at that same moment in Potsdam or what took place in the large studio of the broadcasting house did not affect the Berliners. At the other end of the earth an atom bomb dropped; with two hundred thousand dead, a new era dawned.

It made no impression; they hardly looked up. They had worries of their own. People died of exhaustion; the old and the babies died, and young children; and there were no coffins.

A beaten city; a raped city. Hardly a house had been left untouched, hardly a woman. Stations and tall arched roofs – nothing but rusty iron scaffoldings without glass. Siemensstadt, Daimler-Benz, the AEG, Borsig – Tegel, the large industrial plants, the factories, big ones and medium ones and small ones – stripped to skeletons; the last nail had been taken from the walls; the last wire been pulled from the connections; and even the joiners' benches of the small craftsmen were loaded on to handcarts.

It was August.

Every gust of wind blew clouds of dust into the air. Leipzigerstrasse and Spittelmarkt lost their outlines. The bombed-out houses were only chimerae in the smoke of the Russian steppes.

In Spittelmarkt Splüge saw Leonore.

Without head scarf, her natural blonde hair silky and cared for. A jeep stopped; an American soldier was driving. Leonore allowed him to speak to her. She smiled a somewhat stony smile; but, my God, she smiled and climbed in.

Splüge stopped dead and gazed after the two in the jeep as they disappeared in the rising dust.

You will pay. . . .

A hundred yards further on, at the entrance of a large area of ruins, stood Franz with his barrel organ. The sounds that came from his large wind-filled box boomed across the rubble heaps and through the empty shells of former banking houses. Not a soul lived within miles now, but the world of ruins was peopled by 'treasure hunters'. And they came and laid their offerings, a piece of tin sheet, a few bent nails, some firewood, down by the side of the organ.

Franz played 'Vilia, oh Vilia, thou witch of the wood' and 'That can't shock a sailor'. He played 'We lay off Madagascar' and when after that 'Volga, Volga' rang out, he stopped it suddenly and put another roll in. It was a hit from an old musical; it had been a favourite at the time when candles were still lit in the Berlin windows to celebrate the Kaiser's birthday. This time he sang the words belonging to the music.

It sounded hollow through the world of ruins:

'And through Berlin still flows the river Spree . . .'

Part Four

He who rides a tiger cannot dismount at will.
                                    Indian proverb

Zecke, Zecke, where is Zecke. . . . Once there were conflagrations, mountains of smoke, a spate of falling shadows,
a bewildered cry for understanding, the despairing cry of a
damned soul. . . . That was the past; a world submerged. . . .
There is no Luftwaffe Colonel Aachern staggering through
space; in his place is a chauffeur in the new Thuringian police
uniform, and the chauffeur's name is no longer Aachern,
but Dietershofen, and the chauffeur drives the President
of Thuringia. And chauffeur, President, the President's wife,
a certain civil engineer, and the chief interpreter Irina
Petrovna Semyonova, are all sitting there, with another
seventy or eighty, in a cellar on the outskirts of Erfurt.

Snatched out of the street, arrested.

Two of the women were called Zecke, one of them about
fifty, the other one younger; Helene Zecke and Agatha
Zecke. Dietershofen heard these two names when a list was
read out; a list which also included the names of the President,
Dr. Paul, his wife, Louise Paul, director and civil engineer
Knauer, the interpreter Irina Petrovna Semyonova, and his
own.

Dietershofen spoke to the women. Told them he had
known a Zecke. Not exactly known him, but had met him
once, on a memorable occasion. And they were in fact the wife
of Colonel Zecke and his daughter Agatha. The two women
came from Friedrichroda, where they had lived in a hotel
for nearly a year. Now, with bank accounts and savings frozen,
they were penniless. The Russians had requisitioned the
hotel and had turned them out into the street. They had
wanted to go by train to Berlin, or if there were no trains,
then on foot, or perhaps they might have got a lift by car.
But on the way to the station they were suddenly rounded
up by a Russian patrol and brought here.

What was the meaning of it, what did the Russians really
want? That was the question which troubled all of them.
None knew, and even the President of the province, im-

prisoned with the others could give no information. What will happen to us, Herr President? Where are they going to send us, will we ever be set free again? Will we see our homes again?

'A minor official exceeding his authority', the President replied. 'Soon everything will be cleared up,' he said.

Another man addressed the President: 'You were responsible, President, for the posters with the Russian pledges – freedom for the individual – here is an example of it. This is what it lookes like in practice!'

'And no encroachment on private property', yet another put in. 'When I read that, I thought there'd be some purpose in saving again, and I put my money into savings accounts – and now, Herr President?'

'Yes, what about the bank reform?'

'Now we are all beggars!'

'And the only freedom we have is to starve.'

Yes, it was disgraceful. 'In Thuringia justice and right prevail'; this was the beginning of his first Government proclamation – and it had not been an empty phrase. When taking office, Dr. Paul had left no one in doubt that he came from the other camp, from the liberal side, and the assurance of freedom was the basic condition of his taking office. One of his first actions had been to summon the most capable lawyers of the province, to form a committee to prepare legislation. After twelve years of injustice, justice and law should rule, and security and continuity of social and economic life should be guaranteed. The Potsdam Three-Power Agreement was the foundation for this, and also the orders of the Occupation Authorities which had necessarily to emanate from the same source. Encroachment by subordinate administrators and interference with local authorites had occurred, and it was one of his tasks to use his power, bestowed by the highest authority, to curb and finally to eradicate local acts of violence. And now, for nearly two hours, he had been stuck in that hole. In front of the prison, the deserted official car stood with the standards in national colours and the German and Russian inscription: 'President of the Province'.

It had been an official journey – an order from Marshal Zhukov, that he should personally get production started at the B.M.W. works at Eisenach. He was taking Director Knauer with him to be the new manager of the works. They had passed through Erfurt, desolate and utterly deserted; and then it had happened: they had been stopped by a group of soldiers armed with pistols.

'Where to?'

'To Eisenach.'

'Nix Eisenach, back to the guard house, to the Commander!'

He had sent Dietershofen into the guard house. But the commanding officer, a Major, wanted to speak to him personally.

'What you doing at Eisenach?'

'I am going by an order from Marshal Zhukov.'

'Oh, Zhukov . . . here I Zhukov. You under arrest, nobody must be on street.'

In the town of Erfurt the officer in charge thought he would prohibit all traffic in the district on the pretence of looking for hidden Nazi leaders. Every German, man or woman, on foot, car or bicycle, was arrested and held during the officer's pleasure for an unspecified time.

'Give me the telephone, Major, I want to speak to the Commander-in-Chief, Colonel-General Tshuikov.'

'Here I Commander-in-Chief, here I Tshuikov.'

All proofs of identity were ignored; all protests had been futile.

Indeed they had, like the interference of the Russian interpreter, only aggravated the Major's attitude. Now, two hours had passed, and more and more people had been thrust into the room. By now there was not even room to sit down.

And the interpreter had had enough.

'Leave it, Irina Petrovna; there will be some explanation, here we shall only get the worst of it.'

But Irina Petrovna could not be prevented. She pushed through the crowd, and banged against the door with her fists. No one there could understand her discussion with the sentry, but they understood the two sharp slaps on the face which the sentry received from the young well-dressed Russian girl, and they also understood that this extremely elegant woman could out-swear a Red Army soldier. They were not to know that her vocabulary had originated in Kolyma and other horrible labour camps up in the north, and that it completely bewildered the poor sentry.

Irina Petrovna wanted to see the Major. '*Si tshas . . .* quick, hurry, you half-wit, you dolt! Or I will make you run!'

The sentry was helpless, confronted with this spitting tigress; the pistol on his hip was meaningless. Suddenly the Major appeared, only to be frozen by the stream of 'Wretches' and 'Lunatics' and 'Blockheads'. 'Keep your mouth shut, don't dare touch me. . . . You are a Marshal Zhukov, a Colonel-General, a Commander-in-Chief? You are going to get skinned in small pieces for this, you dim wit. I personally am going to tear off your badge of rank and the order of the "Red Flag" . . .'

The Major's eyes popped in fury, and he was about to hurl himself on the offender when she hissed a word into his face, and the Major was deflated. She had shown him a tiny bit of that power which had made possible the metamorphosis from a condemned Partisan leader in a death camp, into a lady in elegant European dress.

'Come', said the Major, and then corrected himself. 'Please come with me, Comrade!'

The President gazed admiringly at his chief interpreter. A thin face, black hair scraped tightly into a bun. The scar on her cheek served only to emphasize her strange beauty. He had never seen this usually reserved and gentle creature behave in such a way. She was the daughter of a Russian colonel – that was all he knew about her; now he meant to know more.

It did not take long. He was sent for. The Major was no longer alone. A Colonel had arrived; a very polite Colonel.

'Your identification papers, please . . . from the Military administration . . . from the Marshal . . .' His face looked sad. 'They are no longer valid', he said.

'What is valid then, Colonel?'

He did not know; muttered something about a blue ticket on the front of the car. 'Of course, you are free . . . a very regrettable incident.'

'In there, over sixty people are herded together. Why are they shut in?' the President asked. The Colonel did not know.

He also did not know the name of the Major. The Major did not know his own name when he was asked.

'Have none', was the answer.

'That's correct – you no longer have a name!' was Irina Petrovna's final retort.

Only Director Knauer continued the journey to Eisenach in a car which had been ordered by telephone. The President went back to Weimar, leaving the interpreter Irina Petrovna to inform the General of the incident at Erfurt. The President retired to bed. On his desk lay new important instructions, the result of an intensive propaganda campaign – the details of the land reform for Thuringia.

In the Soviet Military Administration Irina Petrovna was standing opposite the Chief and the hastily summoned Colonel-General Tshuikov. And the General and the Colonel-General were both – after they had listened to Irina Petrovna – wild with rage. The land reform, already in effect in Saxony and Brandenburg, should have been effected in Thuringia that day. But without preliminary discussions on the German side and without the signature of the President, nothing could be done. And President Paul had been kept under arrest for many valuable hours and now was ill. Whilst in all other provinces of the zone the land was being divided up, Junker's estates, and large and small holdings split up and parcelled out, Thuringia alone remained unchanged; Thuringia slept.

'Bring Paul here, even if he's half dead; we need him!'

Irina Petrovna was unable to do it. By telephone she was informed by the President's wife that the incident had had a deleterious effect on his heart and that he was not in a suitable condition to undertake the necessary conferences for such a complicated and responsible task.

The two 'blockheads', the General commanding the town of Erfurt and the Major, had been sent for, and were brought in, to be confronted by the Chief of the military administration, and their Commander-in-Chief. The General got off with a few stray gusts of rage, but the Major received the full force of the tempest. It happened as Irina Petrovna had predicted. She herself had to rip off his Major's badge and decorations; this time her finely modelled face remained unmoved. The degraded Major disappeared from Thuringia and in fact descended to the place where she herself had spent some years of her life.

But still nothing was done. The delayed land reform and the illness of the appointed President had to be reported to Berlin to Marshal Zhukov at Karlshorst. The Major's public arrest of the President while on official duty reflected on the entire military administration.

The Adjutant, at the other end of the line, left nobody in doubt that the Marshal was in a raging fury, and that only the speediest settlement of the land reform question would calm him.

It was late at night when Irina Petrovna was once more called to the Chief of Administration and told to go to see Dr. Paul at his flat, with an invitation to Berlin from Marshal Zhukov. If possible, she was to bring back with her the land reform law with his signature.

The windows of Dr. Paul's study still showed light. The President was sitting at his desk, the papers on the land reform and other official documents pushed aside. The writing paper on his table remained blank, the hand holding the pen motionless. The President was thinking; arguing with himself about his first few months of office.

After the bank reform, the land reform was the second measure which vitally affected the life of the people and the administration. He had only briefly studied the project, but it seemed impossible for him to give his consent to the reform in its present form. In Thuringia there were very few really large estates; even large farms were rare. But to limit land-holdings to five hectares would lead to nothing but starvation and beggary. No, he would not take a hand in such measures. The bank reform had already been a heavy blow to the newly revived economy. At the first touch of the whip his office had started humming like an angry bee-hive. From all parts of the country people had arrived complaining of wholesale plunder. The telephone had been choked with cries for help: the Russians have occupied the banks, they have broken open the safes, rifled them and carried off all money and valuables. What shall we do?

What could be done?

The Chief of the Russian administration had told him:

'Mr. President, we are not dicussing isolated incidents in this province, but the carrying through of an order for the whole zone. We want to avoid the mistakes of 1918. The Republic of Weimar went through an inflation because it dragged along the debts of the Imperial Government instead of cutting itself free. One must learn from mistakes. Because of that, all accounts are cancelled. Also, there is a vast amount of paper money with no equivalent quantity of goods. This surplus money must be removed. The order is that all banks must remain closed, except for the National Bank. This will receive from us a credit of over 30 million marks for which we shall have to be compensated by the equivalent in goods.

'Could you not wait, General, until our sick economy has regained its strength and can stand such an interference?' had been his reply, and it had been of no avail. In any case, the Red Army had already introduced the measure as a *fait accompli*. It was unfortunate that thereby the President had started his office with a breach of faith, for, relying on a promise from the Soviets, he had assured the people that all money paid into the banks after the collapse would be untouched. Difficult negotiations – prolonged and unsuccessful.

No, his heart was not so bad. And even if, at the age of fifty, he no longer played football or boxed, and no longer used his punchball, nevertheless he still stood up to the most difficult conferences, and with the aid of coffee and strong cigars, he was able, on occasion, to work as long as twenty hours a day. The incident at Erfurt had not taxed him unduly – much less than these accumulated piles of official documents on his desk which would remain unsettled, like all the others which had passed through his hands. Here too, were breaches of faith – plunderings, arbitrary requisitions, criminal offences, abductions, violence and murder. A long bloody chain, and he could not even name the perpetrators of these crimes as Russians, but had to call them 'Germans in Russian uniform'. They came from Gera, Jena, Eisenach, Nordhausen, from dozens of towns, from hundreds of villages, and all he could do was to pass them on to the Russian general or to the Russian GPU – and that was all. Weeks passed, months passed, and he heard no more.

Again he reached out for the project on land reform.

'But this beats everything! A wretched business, disgraceful, shameful . . .' He had finished with introspection. His thoughts exploded into speech. He was talking to himself so loudly that his wife came in to close the windows and draw the curtains; it was not necessary for the sentry in front of the house to hear him! She stayed for a moment, filled his cup with more coffee, but remained silent.

'I can't believe it! Look at this – written in pig-German. I can see where this comes from!'

The draft of the bill had obviously been composed in the Russian language and had been then translated, almost word for word, without regard to the proper language. 'A miserable concoction – and quite apart from the content, it is completely untenable from the legal point of view. Surely, one passes a law – and separate from the law, publishes regulations for the executives. But this has got the law, the reasons for it, and the penalties, all interlocked one into the other!'

He could not, as a lawyer, sign such a rigmarole.

'No, General, that will not do; the Prussians can't be dealt with in that way, nor the Thuringians. First of all, the law will be handed over to the Legislation Department, where the leading lawyers of the Province will put it into pertinent and legal form. And then. . . . Yes, then we shall see.'

Frau Paul came in again.

'Irina Petrovna, the interpreter, is outside. She has seen the light in your window and won't be sent away. She brings an invitation from Berlin-Karlshorst.'

'Well, then let her in.'

Irina Petrovna brought an invitation from Marshal Zhukov to a conference on the question of Berlin's Central Administrations, a thing which he himself had requested.

'All right, I am prepared, Irina Petrovna.'

'The conference begins at eleven in the morning at Karlshorst. The General will drive there and asks you to join him in his car. Departure from Weimar at five o'clock in the morning.'

'All right, five in the morning – then we shall be in Berlin before 10 a.m.'

Irina Petrovna had something else; the law on land reform. She thought she could bring back the document with his signature this same night.

'No. . . . No, leave it, Irina Petrovna. I am not up to it

to-day. You can tell the General I am going to submit the draft to the Legislation Department, and then everything will be done as quickly as possible.'

Irina Petrovna made no headway. She had hardly left the house when Dr. Paul got hold of the telephone: 'Operator, get me on the special line the gentlemen in charge of the Legislation Board . . .'

'Whom do I want? Are you still asleep? Take it down: Dean of the Legal Faculty, the President of the Court of Justice, also the President of the Chief Administration Court.'

The telephone was buzzing.

The Dean of the Legal Faculty at the University of Jena was on the telephone.

'President here. Sorry about this nocturnal call, but I am being hard pressed about the land reform law. The draft submitted to me is quite impossible. It will be in your department by tomorrow morning. Please construct it as necessary. It is urgent, urgent . . . burning, Professor! Good night.'

He also spoke to the President of the Court of Justice and to the President of the Chief Administration Court. Well, that was done. But communication by telephone is limited, particularly as the wires are tapped. He would be away from Weimar for two or three days, and some details had still to be cleared up. Although it was now two o'clock, he decided to make a telephone call to the Supreme Judge of the Province.

The Judge's wife answered, torn from her sleep, incredulous.

'Please excuse me, Madam, but it concerns a matter which cannot be delayed. I would like your husband to come to see me. I shall send my car immediately.'

Tactfully . . . discreetly, a haycart was standing not far from the President's villa, a haycart in which two NKWD-sentries took turns to watch night and day. The Supreme Judge had not been in Dr. Paul's house ten minutes before the office of the Chief of the Military Administration received a report from the NKWD headquarters informing the General about the nocturnal visitor to the President's villa. The report had hardly been received when the little red lamp glowed on the General's switchboard. This time it was the NKWD department at Lottenstrasse: 'The President has used the special line. He has sent for the President of the Court of Justice and for some Professors to come tomorrow to work on the land reform law. . . .'

Work on, work on. . . . What else is there to be worked on? The Chief of the Military Administration rested his head in his hands. He had a difficult working day behind him; his clumsy peasant's face showed his weariness. Doctors, professors, Presidents of the Court of Justice, the Dean of the Legal Faculty – it was enough to drive one mad! What is it all about? Why must everything be made so complicated? Why should it just be his luck to get a President like Paul? In Saxony, in Brandenburg, in Mecklenburg, it was quite simple: a scrap of paper was laid on the table and came back, signed. But here, he had a Department for Legislation famous professors, nocturnal conferences, a whole syndicate of academicians and legal bookworms. In the end though . . . well, the gentlemen will see what will be left of their sophistry.

The night was advanced, and there was not much time left till the General's departure for Berlin. The Chief stayed in his office, threw himself on the leather couch to try to snatch some sleep.

At the same hour, the Supreme Judge in the President's study folded up the draft of the law and put it in his portfolio. Everything had been discussed. The plan was to be put into legal form, and in addition, using only the existing text, authority would be nicely inclined towards the President with some elimination of the powers of the Communist Vice-President.

Everything was clear, including the details. It was too late now to go to bed. Like the General at the other end of the town, Dr. Paul stretched out on his settee for a nap.

A bare two hours later, he took his place next to his chauffeur Dietershofen, and they drove away to join the General's car on the Autobahn.

Bank reform, land reform, central administration, refugee organizations. . . . It was necessary to make up for lost sleep during the journey in order to arrive fresh in Berlin-Karlshorst, the innermost arena of the battle for Germany. But Dr. Paul could not get rid of his pressing problems, and only managed a fitful doze. When he opened his eyes, he found himself right in the midst of a tormenting and unfinished reality.

Unfinished – or was this already the finale?

The Autobahn looked like a market track. Carts with ponies slowly plodding along; cattle being driven to the east; cows with hollow flanks, horses emaciated to skeletons – all with a long journey behind them, from Saxony, from Thuringia, from the Bavarian frontier, and an even longer way before them. In the middle of the road was a rain-bedraggled armchair, empty boxes and smashed bottles. A marching column; tanned faces; the uniforms poor and torn; the boots worn out.

'How could this wretched crowd defeat the German Wehrmacht?' It was the chauffeur Dietershofen, the former Colonel Aachern, who spoke.

'One must not think of them as individuals, but as tidal waves', the President replied.

'Yes, many dogs are the hare's death!'

A lorry was overtaken, a Russian office on the move. Tables, chairs, cheap straw mattresses, and, to protect this rubbish against the rain, a Persian carpet spread over it.

The President dozed and woke again: refugees, grey crowds, old men, women, children. From Saxony, from the Sudetenland, from Czechoslovakia, from German-speaking Hungary, and the Balkans.

A decree of the Potsdam Conference: Transfer of the German minorities. Such transfer to be carried out in a humane manner. In a humane manner – without inter-allied control and from countries where they had had citizen rights for centuries, had cultivated the soil and created industries. They had been driven away from house and belongings; hunted, beaten to death, robbed of their property, even their clothes and their shirts. In the end they had been thrown across the frontier – fifteen million, twenty million – nobody had ever counted them. And no place was prepared for those starving masses who poured over the country like swarms of locusts, and stripped the unripe fields to the bare earth.

In Saxony, the concentration camps overflowed. In Thuringia, with virtually no catering or sanitary arrangements for such unexpected hordes, it soon became chaos. It needed strong police supervision and tenacious negotiations with Saxony and with the Military Administration in Dresden, to dam and control this flood of misery. And here they were still, drifting along the Autobahn. Now, only the daily contingent agreed on with Saxony was allowed, but nevertheless over one million had been counted in the Heiligenstadt District within a few weeks. Owners of farms, of large estates, of factories, independent artisans, contractors, tradesmen, onwards they moved – and as survivors of murdered families and as starving beggars they reached the West. Transfer according to humane principles – and the pen in Potsdam which wrote it down, has not cried out, and the Christian world ignored completely the fifteen to twenty million people turned into aimless flotsam.

A heritage of Hitler's . . . But not only of Hitler's.

The misery in the streets, the blown up bridges, the workers amongst the debris in their factories, the village population hidden in expectation of the nightly mischief-making – everything echoed another great catastrophe. Germany had survived the Thirty-Years-War, and life had risen again from its hiding place. It would also emerge from this chasm. One must have faith; belief, even if the sky is dark. The eternal stars go on shining. And the stars on the Western sky are: Humanism, Tolerance, Co-operation, and Law. Law – established, binding and coherent.

Dr. Paul continued his thoughts.

The Russians. . . .

A different economic system, different political conceptions, a different Credo, perhaps not a moral one, perhaps only an expedient one. . . . That does not concern him. He has been given promises and has to hold on to them. Even extensive promises, made to him on the day (or rather on the night) of the surprising offer of the Presidency of Thuringia. He had concealed nothing; had made it clear that he was of middle-class origin; that according to his past he belonged to the liberal camp, believed in freedom, also in a liberal economy. He had been told, that was exactly what would be expected of him as future President.

'Our democracy, Herr President, is no export article. We want a Germany built up on democratic principles. It should be founded on the democratic parties. We are here to help the

German people to build up their democracy and economy.'

That was what Colonel-General Tshuikov had replied to him – and had continued: 'You, Herr President, must build up the industries and Chamber of Commerce as they were before 1933. On your journeys through the Province you must emphasize that private property is being protected by us, as well as private initiative and enterprise. The peasant need no longer fear that his cellars and lofts will be rifled. Our fight is directed exclusively against Nazism and Militarism. . . .'

He was in complete agreement. Under Nazism he personally had suffered to the limit. And German militarism had more than once brought disaster to Germany. – Away with it!

And the alternatives – a democratic policy, freedom of the individual, sanctity of private property, were firm foundations on which to rebuild the political, economic, and cultural life; to re-establish the concept of justice; and to join Thuringia once again to Germany and to the family of democratic nations. But this clear vision was distorted and obscured by local commanders – the experience of the day before was an obvious example – and more still by radicals who had penetrated official departments. Transitory symptoms – they would be conquered. He could rely on the pledged word of the Commanding Colonel-General Tshuikov, and beyond it the Potsdam decisions with which the Allies guaranteed binding treaties and uniform economic and political systems for all occupied zones of Germany.

Besides, the strict discipline and orderliness of the officers at that first nocturnal conference – the Army General Tshuikov, the Chief of the Military Administration, and the rest of them, differed pleasantly from the undisciplined hordes in the country. These were independent, intelligent men, amazingly well informed about conditions in Thuringia.

The flow of thoughts could not be turned off, any more than the endless columns of walking figures. Among them, skirts well tucked up, a mother with her daughter.

Dietershofen said:

'Those two were in the cellar at Erfurt, the wife and daughter of a Colonel Zecke; they want to go to Berlin.'

'Stop the car.'

Dietershofen stopped; the two women got in. The drive

went on. They wanted to go to Berlin, or rather Potsdam, where they had a bombed-out flat. They had lived as refugees in Thuringia for nearly two years. Of Colonel Zecke, husband and father, they knew nothing – only that he had been posted to Berlin.

The much needed sleep came after all. The engine was buzzing; Dietershofen avoided any sudden change of gear; the two Zecke women, glad to have left the insecure roads behind, kept still as mice. When the President opened his eyes again, it was on a rough diversion round a blown-up bridge over the Autobahn. Soon the landmark of Berlin, its radio tower, rose before them. At the turning to Zehlendorf, the Zeckes got out and thanked him. The Avus, end of the Autobahn – and the car merged with the picture of the city. – Ruins. . . .

People with grey faces; women in trousers, primitive tools in their hands; a swarming population of ants against gigantic mountains of debris. The Zoo, all trees reduced to stumps, resembled one of the devastated fields at Verdun after the first world war; around the undamaged statue of the Amazon, allotments were spreading. Berliners with spades and hoes cultivated the soil; others dug up tree stumps.

Via triumphalis. . . . Ruins, people in shabby clothes with hungry faces. Unter den Linden was almost deserted; the castle surrounded by ruins. Red flags. Posters: 'Hitlers come and go . . .' Dust of the steppes was driven through the windows into the car. Around Alexander Platz crowds of people trading, offering goods for sale and trying to get food in exchange. The tramway was running, also parts of the Underground and the city railway were again functioning.

The car passed a triumphal arch made of plywood; a few minutes later they were stopped, and after a careful examination of papers, were allowed to proceed. There were the same modern buildings, the former Pioneer barracks with the Pioneer school which Colonel Zecke had visited, now more than six months ago. The blown-out windows had been replaced, the roofs repaired. The desolate and empty barrack squares were now busy with the coming and going of cars and soldiers. In place of the former sentry who, with chewed pipe in mouth, had directed Colonel Zecke to the course for regimental leadership, stood a GPU-sentry, in clean uniform with white gloves. He indicated the building to which Dr. Paul should go.

There was still time, more than half an hour, till the beginning of the conference. The large conference hall was the same in which Marshal Zhukov, the English Air Marshal Tedder, the American General Spaatz, and the French Marshal Delattre de Tassigny had once been assembled, and into which Keitel, Hitler's last Field-marshal, had been led, his baton lowered, to sign the Capitulation document.

Now, there were Soviet Generals and civilians, Russian Chiefs of Administration, and German provincial Presidents and Vice-Presidents, and Chiefs of Berlin's Central Administration. In the corridors and in the hall a multitude of red flags arranged like fans, and wherever there was space, pictures of Stalin, Molotov, Zhukov – many of Marshal Zhukov, ten times life-size. Dr. Paul sat in the first row, next to a benign old man with snow-white hair and blue eyes: Dr. Werner, the governing Chief Mayor of the City of Berlin.

Sixty-eight-year-old Dr. Werner was capable of carrying the burden of his office and the worries of a three and a half million-city, without breaking down. His deputies, Herr Maron and Arthur Pieck (son of Wilhelm Pieck), Jendretzki and others, had taken over a large part of his work and gave him time to keep up with invitations like to-day's reception by Marshal Zhukov.

The Marshal, attended by a circle of Colonel-Generals and adjutants, entered the hall. All present rose. The military men leapt poker-stiff from their chairs. It was not a salute of Generals to their Field-Marshal, but of recruits to their company leader. Provincial Chiefs, in magnificent uniforms, sparkled with orders, like a picture from Tsarist times. The Marshal noticed the white-haired Dr. Werner and stopped in front of him, exchanging a few kind words before going on to open the conference with a welcoming speech.

Paul turned to his neighbour: 'My dear Werner, you'd better reply on our behalf.'

'Yes, but what am I to say?'

Why on earth have they made this doddering white-haired fool Chief Mayor of Berlin, the city with as many inhabitants as the whole of Thuringia?

'As senior it's your right to speak, but if you don't I shall have to.'

'Yes, please do.'

The President of Thuringia replied in courteous words in the same tone as the Marshal; thanked him for the invitation, and then, fixing his eyes upon the assembled Presidents of the Central Administration, and assuming a more severe tone, he went on to the main subject of discussion. After only a few sentences it was clear that he was a forceful and challenging speaker.

The Marshal was an attentive and interested listener. The cards were dealt, and among the ordinary cards from Berlin, Saxony, Mecklenburg and Brandenburg, there was a special card, example of a complex policy operating in Germany. With puppet Mayors, and Presidents who behaved like non-commissioned officers, it was certainly possible to obtain momentary successes. But a long-range instrument was necessary for a war of expansion which would include not only Germany but Europe as a whole. That was the reason for this special card – a President on a loose rein, trained to complete freedom and independence. That was the experiment; would Paul be a complete failure; or would he, on the other hand, grow into an important and valuable figure?

Dr. Paul looked at the Presidents of the Central Administrations. Two or three, perhaps, had brains; but the others . . . unripe, juvenile puppets. What do the Russians want with groups like that? What do they really intend to do with those Central Administrations? And where is the common head of those separate Corporations? This occurred to him quite suddenly as he was speaking. He spoke without heat, with only half his strength; the real discussion was yet to come; it was sufficient to alarm those concerned and convey the information to those on the platform.

The Chief of the Central Administration for Fuel and Power, a Christian Democrat, who came after Paul, elegantly parried a remark of the Marshal about all the members of the Christian-Democrat Union being blockheads.

The next speaker was the President of the Central Administration for Agriculture and Forestry. Dr. Paul listened attentively at first; then shook his head sadly. This man had not the faintest idea – either of agriculture or of forestry;

certainly not of German forests. How could he . . . after a short debut as a country parson in a Swabian village, he had progressed via the Society of Freethinkers and Socialists to the Communist movement. As a communist member of the Landtag he had worked on the subject of the 'Agricultural Labour Question'. Later, during Russian exile, worn out by advanced age, hunger, typhoid, cold, and political hack work, he was employed as an anti-Fascist teacher in a prisoner-of-war camp beyond the Urals.

Not the faintest notion – a bad speaker, a crippled fighter; but who stands behind this broken old man?

Another one took his place.

Just the same . . . cardboard figures, bureaucratic ciphers . . . Paul thought of other matters; only listened with half an ear; had leisure to look round, to observe the rest.

There was the President of Saxony; he knew him, had studied with him in Leipzig. A lawyer, and a capable administrator; at this conference he kept silent; his communist Vice-President and Minister of the Interior apologized for him because of his illness and spoke on his behalf. Paul felt he could expect no help from the Saxonian Minister of the Interior, Fischer, and only empty promises from the Chiefs of Mecklenburg, Brandenburg and Prussian Saxony. Yet, the game must be won – and it was no game.

After an interval, the Russian Administration Chiefs spoke, then Soviet economic experts. The further the day proceeded, the longer the speeches became. The Russians seemed to wake up properly only after dark and in the blaze of electric light.

Suddenly – an interruption. The electric light went out leaving them in complete darkness. On the platform a hurried stamping. When the lights went on again, the platform was deserted – no Marshal Zhukov, no Chief-of-Staff Sokolovski, no Generals, no Colonels; the Marshal with his Staff had disappeared; in their place soldiers with raised pistols were standing both on the platform and below it. The assembly stared into the open barrels.

A short circuit – revealing the automatic security system. The soldiers went out, and the Marshal and his Staff resumed their seats. The conference continued. Nothing was said about the short circuit.

The Soviet expert for finance was speaking and went on for a long time. The Marshal, after a period of rather forced concentration, was obviously becoming impatient. The civilian was as poor a speaker as he was long-winded. He defended the tax on brandy and explained its effect on the Budget. Finally, the Marshal interrupted him and told him to be more concise. But after a quick glance at him, the expert continued as before. Even a further exclamation from the Marshal did not disturb him.

The successful Commander-in-Chief of the Soviet Army – popular hero and soldiers' ideal – jumped up with a red, furious face, and paced up and down the platform like a provoked tiger, while the seedy civilian rambled on. A strange world; of what importance is a Marshal, even of Zhukov's calibre, compared with a politically sponsored official?

At last it pleased the speaker to finish. After a few remaining experts, the Marshal made his final observations. It was more favourable to their provincial administrations than many of them, including the President of Thuringia, had expected. The Marshal showed himself to be a man who could take frank criticism. His knowledge of conditions in the provinces, and his pertinent remarks, made one think he knew of the seven-hundred-year-old saying: 'It is possible to conquer a kingdom from the saddle, but it is not possible to govern it from there.' For the benefit of the Presidents present he announced: 'Nothing must be done on the part of the Central Administrations without the consent of the Presidents of the provinces.'

The President of Thuringia listened with great relief. With the Marshal's assurance that he would intercede in favour of a unified and democratic Germany, the business part of the conference came to an end. A festive conclusion followed – a banquet to which the Soviet Chief Commander cordially invited all members of the meeting.

Aachern-Dietershofen was sent on leave.

He had been allowed to take the service car to his flat at Wannsee. The house there was still the same, but the people who lived in it – Dr. Wittstock and Frau Wittstock, Aachern's wife Lisa and his daughter Anneliese – were not the same any more; they were different physically as well as mentally.

And Hans. . . .

Hans was no longer there. One morning, shortly after four o'clock, he had been fetched by Russian soldiers from the GPU, with Günther, the son of Wittstock, as suspected Werewolves.

'Had he really belonged to something like that?'

'Nonsense, there are no such things as Werewolves, there never were', his wife replied.

'Everybody is laughing about it.'

'There is nothing to laugh at.'

'I don't mean it like that. Only the accusation is so ridiculous. And not only Hans and Günther, nearly all their schoolfellows have disappeared.'

'Where to?'

'Nobody knows. But Sachsenhausen near Oranienburg, the old concentration camp, is again full of people, exactly as it used to be.'

'You used not to know about such things.'

'There were a lot of things I didn't know.'

'And the Russians . . . how did you get on?'

Lisa looked at him, shrugged her shoulders.

'Yes . . .' he muttered.

She told him of their eviction by the Russians – the few days together with the Wittstocks spent in the shelter of an architect named Poppert; their having to leave there too, and their days of wandering backwards and forwards between the fronts before finally they were allowed to go back to their flat.

'You can't imagine what it looked like.'

He believed that he could.

'And this little side table?' he asked.

'I don't know who it belongs to. The owner hasn't turned up yet. We had to gather together all our things, the chairs and beds, and then exchange them for the things we found here. All our shoes here had the right ones missing. And the way they turned the place upside down.'

'Yes, and . . .'

It was the still unanswered question to which he continually turned.

'Oh, Helmuth, what do you think? No one was spared!'

'And Anneliese?'

'She was fetched once.'

'Once . . . that means?'

'Yes, that is what it means. Oh, don't let's talk about it!'

Her face had become very firm, very sober. What had happened in Berlin, he thought, must have been like . . .

He could not keep off the subject.

'Anneliese too?'

'Oh, leave it, leave it. Rather tell me how things went with you in Thuringia.'

Yes, Anneliese too; at that time she had been fifteen, now she was sixteen. . . . He had not yet asked how matters were at the moment. He was still trying to decipher the past, those gloomy days which had swept over Berlin. Those days were past; the gloom had stayed on. Against this dark background, with lowered curtains, the Berliners moved about, compelled to take part in a game which they had not devised. They had to go on living, good or bad, as ordered by four different masters. This he knew, but without any clear conception of what it looked like to the individual or indeed to his family.

He drank coffee, real coffee, no worse than in the President's home in Weimar. Freshly cut bread with tinned butter and liver sausage was put before him; it all came out of American tins. Berlin was hungry and starving. Here, too, the cemetery ticket was valid. The 'normal consumer' was a person who could no longer fit into his former clothes, a shadow of his own self.

And real coffee, freshly cut bread, and sheep's tongue. . . .

He got up, on an inspiration, and went to the little table and opened the lid. Cigarettes, Virginia cigars, all the little drawers filled, and in one lay ten small packets tied together in bundles. He was sitting at the table again when Lisa came back from the kitchen:

'Coffee, bread, butter . . .' he said.

'Yes, Anneliese is working at the PX.'

'PX?'

'Yes, the American PX-shop.'

'Oh yes . . . and all those cigarettes in the little table, who is smoking them?'

'Oh, that is money; it is our currency. You don't get anything for the Occupation mark. But here' . . . (she took out of the drawer one of the packets) 'for one "bar" you can get anything.'

Lisa was changed. There was a matter-of-factness about her, which he had not noticed before. His son Hans had been carried off, was in Sachsenhausen or perhaps in Siberia, nobody knew. His daughter Anneliese was working in a PX-shop and, apparently, provided everything for the family.

He could have learned more about Anneliese, from his wife, from the Wittstocks, or from the grocer at the corner. But so far he had been told as much as he could be expected to take. Lisa kept silent about the rest.

In the evening he saw Anneliese, fair hair and light blue eyes. Her hair was no longer in pigtails, she was no longer a child and could have been taken for eighteen or nineteen. A girl without any illusions, with a philosophy which was foreign to him. One must live and one must pay for it! And all she could spend was herself. After the cellar in Pfedder-sheimerstrasse, after the road from Nikolassee to Paaren on the Wublitz, through the Russian columns, nothing mattered any more. All in all, she was well taken care of, could have been worse off. The driver of the big PX-truck really loved her; was her devoted servant; gave her all he had and everything he could get hold of. And that was no trifle. It meant life, not only for her and her mother, but also for others. And the fact that the PX-driver was a negro was quite accepted by the Wittstocks as well as their neighbours. But now, father had come home, and it was the day on which the PX-truck was due. Sammy could not possibly be allowed to appear in the house. She must try to prevent it.

'Dear Daddy, I'm so sorry; if I'd only known sooner. But I absolutely have to go out again. I'll do my best to come back quickly.'

He had to let her go. He did not ask for reasons. He was a stranger in his own home. An hour later, he and his wife were sitting at the Wittstocks'. With the unexpressed, perhaps inexpressible between him and Lisa, he had welcomed the invitation. It was better to spend the evening with others, than to sit opposite a Lisa he could no longer understand.

Wittstock had other guests. Aachern recognized only one face from former times; that was Lieutenant Splüge, now of course in mufti, and it seemed to Aachern, judging by his look and clothes, that he wasn't doing too badly. Splüge arrived late with his fiancée, a Fräulein Stassen. The rest of the guests were new acquaintances of Dr. Wittstock – one of them was from a newspaper office, another from the 'Kulturbund', one from the 'Seagull', a place frequented by artists in which apparently everybody with special priority tickets could have a meal. Another of them was the architect Poppert, and Aachern was able to express his thanks for the refuge he had offered to his family in those terrible days. He was pulled up sharply by surprised looks around him and felt somehow provincial. A stranger in his own home, and a stranger here also. The oppression of a whole town, murder, homicide, deaths from hunger – nothing was taken seriously here.

'For twelve years we have been impeded in our freedom, in our free development . . . now that we have won back freedom of thought, it is up to us to make this liberty a reality. . . . The Fascist delusions . . . tyrants, enemies of the people, criminal hirelings . . .' Aachern tried to understand, but for him it might have been Chinese. Poppert noticed his embarrassment. Wittstock memorized the catchwords for his next article. 'The point in question is a programme, Herr Aachern.'

'For what?'

'For a moral rebirth of our people!'

'We have still to learn a great deal from the Occupation Powers. They are far superior to us in cultural progress and also in democratic life', Aachern heard.

Perhaps, perhaps not . . . Germany too has something to contribute to the dignity of mankind; even in the much abused Prussian militarism, there was concealed the strength of order. Wittstock abused it for its excess and for 'aims hostile to the people'! Admitted, but 'to empty the bath with the baby' could hardly be an appropriate policy for a national rebirth. Moreover, not so long ago, Wittstock had spoken quite differently. Certainly, time had not stood still in this house. It had been a violent 're-education'. And now, Wittstock and his friends were already 're-educators' themselves. In addition to his professional duties, Wittstock was busily running from conferences to committee meetings and lectures at local branches of the Kulturbund in Zehlendorf, in Schöneberg, in Neukölln. His subjects were 'The annihilation of the Nazi ideology', 'The people as the basic intellectual norm', 'The development of freedom and the humanistic national traditions of our people by the Occupation Powers',

'The purifying effect of the Nuremberg trials', and 'The inclusion of the intellectual achievements of other nations in the cultural reconstruction of Germany.'

'An extensive repertoire!' Aachern thought.

'Yes, Herr Aachern, our Wittstock has something up his sleeve.'

It was the producer Sarfeld who spoke. Then he told Aachern of his own experiences, of the difficulties of a recently opened theatre.

'I soon got a company together. But apart from that, we had nothing, absolutely nothing. Our leading actor went on stage and told the audience: "Listen all of you, we want to make a theatre here. You are going to see a performance now. But tomorrow we must have new scenery. Bring along nails, bring along tools, bring anything you can. We are grateful for everything." We did the same at the second performance, and the third, and now we are established – all done by magic...'

Sarfeld had made the first film after the collapse, a film on the opening of the State Opera. 'That was a long time ago, almost forgotten', he said. 'Yesterday, I had to go to Milasch-strasse about it – I hope for the last time. Very uncomfortable – two hours by bicycle. And when one finally got there, what did one hear but: "Our apologies, Herr Sarfeld, but a few Russian friends from Moscow arrived unexpectedly."'

'Tell us, Sarfeld, tell us the whole story – Splüge and Aachern don't know it.'

'Well, it was right at the very beginning, in Schmargendorf; we arranged popular evenings, piano recitals, exhibitions of books, and so on. At that time, I was summoned to the Town Hall. Then sent on to the Russians, first to Luisenstrasse, later to Milaschstrasse at Pankow. There the Russians had a film department. I saw a Lieutenant Teich, and he took me to his Colonel.

' "You understand, everything come to pieces, kaputt!" he told me,'

'That I did understand; I only needed to look out of the window.

' "Everything come to pieces and violinny nice!" he said. Lieutenant Teich explained: "There has been a war, Berlin has gone to pieces, and now, violins play, music sounds and everything is once more beautiful! In other words, I should film the opening of the State Opera."

'Reconstruction of Berlin – that was the idea of the film.

' "The Liberation of music" would be the title.

'I got three thousand feet of raw stock for a thousand foot film. We soon got a team together. Producer, camera man, cutter, designer; and a programme, too, was found. Of course, most of the people who had participated in the Opera House opening had meantime gone over to the West. "Begin Beethoven, end Beethoven, and in the middle the story!" Lieutenant Teich said. Well, we spoiled most of the three thousand feet of film before we started; everything was damp in the cellar and all the electric installations were faulty. After a bit of a flap we managed to get another four thousand feet of film, and we shot it. Superintendent Legal made his speech, or rather, a part of it. Chief Mayor Werner made his speech. In the boxes Russian Generals were sitting. It was just as at the opening. And as arranged, we had Beethoven at the beginning, Beethoven at the end, and in the middle speeches and a solo violinist playing Tschaikovsky's Violin Concerto. Everyone was very pleased. The film was shown. Legal was satisfied. Chief Mayor Werner was satisfied. At first, Luisenstrasse and Milaschstrasse, too, were satisfied. Until I was asked to go there again.

'And now, Herr Aachern, ladies and gentlemen, comes the point. My Lieutenant asks me very politely: "Herr Sarfeld: the title?" I reply: "But we have agreed that: 'Liberated Music'."

' "Title: 'Liberated Music'!" he repeated.

'He telephoned, he smoked; he asked for cigarettes and tea to be brought in. I sit, smoking, drinking tea; an hour passes. He goes on working in silence, leaves me sitting there, telephones again.

'Then an interpreter arrives.

'Up to now he has always conversed with me without an interpreter.

' "The Lieutenant wants to know the title of the film."

'That really was the limit; I had already heard the same question at least fifteen times, and replied once more: "Liberated Music".

' "Why Liberated Music, Herr Sarfeld?"

' "Well, because previously we were not allowed to play."

' "Herr Sarfeld, liberated music – German music?"

'Slowly I got fed up with it.'

' "Yes, but we have not had it here for a long time."

' "Herr Sarfeld. Question: Liberated Music – German music?"

' "Yeeesss!"

' "And Tschaikovsky?"

'Tschaikovsky, a liberated composer – a political mistake of the first order; deviation, sabotage! My Lieutenant pierced me with his look. And it was he who had thought of that title. Well, all storms come to an end. The title remains. Next week the film will be shown in the cinema at Friedrich-strasse.'

A long story. Aachern thought it was too long. Now he laughed with the others although he was not in the mood. He thought of Anneliese. It had grown late and she had not returned. Splüge and Fräulein Stassen were also waiting for Anneliese. Coffee and butter were at stake – business affairs. They, too, had waited in vain.

Aachern lay awake for a long time. Berlin, ruins, darkness, unsafe streets full of lurking dangers. And a sixteen-year-old girl, with a disillusioned look, does not come home at night. He brooded and tossed in his bed as he listened to the steps in the street. Beside him, in the double-bed which had become strange to him, his wife Lisa lay in a deep, calm sleep.

The banquet at Karlshorst was proceeding.

Speeches, toasts – on the Russian side the toasts were all proposed by the Marshal. To Stalin, to the Soviet Union, to the provinces of Thuringia, Saxony, Mecklenburg and to their Presidents, to the democratic reconstruction of the economy of the Soviet Zone, to a future united Germany.

Once more, Marshal Zhukov got up. At the conference, he said, he had gained the impression that everywhere hard work was being done, and he saluted the people who staked every-thing for the realization of a great idea. The Hitlers come and go, but Germany, the German Nation will remain, that is what Generalissimo Stalin has said, and everybody could be certain of the support of the great Josef Vissarionovitch Stalin for this great project of the future. Now the time has come to realize Stalin's word, and work in one supreme effort for a future united, peace-loving, democratic Germany!

A banquet, as at one time in the white reception room under Kaiser William II. White table cloths made of damask, crystal, Rosenthal porcelain. The bowls, hardly touched, were replaced by new ones. The same happened with the drinks. The glasses were hardly put down on the table when orderlies appeared and filled them again. And so that nobody should be embarrassed by not having a drink when the Marshal should lift his glass, a cluster of bottles was standing in front of every guest. Wine, beer, champagne, brandy. And dishes with roast and other meats, rich foods, game, caviare, meat-pies, twenty kinds of pickled, smoked and highly flavoured fishes.

It was already too much . . . people like a tumult of fishes in a narrow basin, like salmon in the bay of Alaska. Clouds floated through the hall.

There was the Colonel with the head like a polished billiard ball. Intelligent, educated, speaking a refined German with a scholar's vocabulary. Dr. Paul had already met him during the conference. Now, he lifted his glass and drank his health.

And Colonel-General Semyonov drank to him.

Tulpanov, Semyonov . . . the names did not mean anything to him. Standing outside any sort of party, he knew less than the others there. Colonel Tulpanov, however, had been quite an impressive personality at the first meeting. Colonel-General Semyonov, too, with whom he had had a special discussion about the land reform in Thuringia during a long interval at the conference. Colonel-General Semyonov had made his appearance in a black suit, with a black bowler hat, looking somehow odd in this 'western disguise'. But after two minutes talk there seemed nothing odd about him any longer. He was intelligent, educated, with a comprehensive knowledge and culture. And he executed his task – the exposition of economic, political and social reasons for the land reform – with diplomatic skill; moreover, he took his time, the first talk had been mere conversation; a further meeting had been arranged for the next day.

Tulpanov, Semyonov, a third, a fourth . . . Prosit! 'Your health, Herr President! *Da starovje, Gospodin Presidenta!*' The consideration which the Marshal had shown to Dr. Paul during the conference had won friends for him. Lifted glasses, right, left, again and again. It was a lot; already too much. He filled the large spirit glass with beer, let it grow flat until it looked like yellow Vodka. This made the toasts a lot easier to manage.

The Thousand-and-one-Nights – the Marshal got up. With him, all at once, fifty generals were standing at the tables, like tin-soldiers. Marshal Zhukov made a speech to the President of Thuringia.

Fifty generals lifted their glasses.

He, too, lifted his glass – emptied it to the last drop.

'Magnificent; Paul already drinks like a Russian!' remarked Zhukov.

'Your mistake, Marshal. This is not Vodka, but flat beer', replied the keen-eyed Chief-of-Staff Sokolovski.

'Oh, he is even *chitry*; better still, more useful.'

Better still, if one knows about it and can outwit cunning.

'Paul is cheating!' It sounded through the hall, coming from the table of the Marshal. Roars of laughter accompanied the remark, and everybody sat down again. One speech after another – one dish after another. The succession of courses went on uninterrupted and wine and champagne flowed in streams.

Friedrichs passed Paul's table.

Dr. Friedrichs – President of Saxony, a lawyer like Paul – common college days in Leipzig and later in Berlin.

Dr. Friedrichs, on his own this time.

This opportunity must not slip by. 'Well, Friedrichs, how is your Siamese twin, Fischer?' Paul called to him.

Friedrichs sat down at his table.

'It's really not like that with Fischer. Look over there!'

The Saxonian Minister of the Interior Fischer was standing next to Colonel Tulpanov from Karlshorst; they seemed like the closest intimates.

'Tell me, why did you leave me in the lurch to-day, on the question of the Central Administrations?'

'That's why . . . behind my back stands Fischer. He's a really dangerous fellow!'

'And why has Steinhoff shirked the issue?' Dr. Steinhoff was the President of Brandenburg.

'Behind Steinhoff stands Bechler!'

'Who is Bechler?'

'A renegade German Staff-officer, "Free Germany". He is completely in the hands of the Russians.'

'Saxony, Saxony-Anhalt, Brandenburg – anyway, from the very beginning there was no counting on the Mecklenburger.'

'Yes, it is easier for you, Paul! You have Busse as Minister of the Interior. He, too, is a brutal fellow, but you can get the better of him any time.'

Friedrichs drank, emptying one glass after another – he had worries.

'Listen carefully, Paul.'

'Yes, I'm listening.'

'With Fischer; caution. I repeat: caution! This man is a Russian subject, formerly a Russian colonel; and that is not all. He was an agent in France, in China, I don't know where else. He told me all that when he was drunk. Murder, I tell you; murder all over the world – my hair stood on end. And he boasted about it.'

Well, that certainly made things difficult. It was easier with his Minister of the Interior, Busse. Friedrichs was right. Although . . . Busse, too, was a murderer – according to anonymous letters from former concentration camp inmates. Fischer, Busse, Bechler – the Russian system, with its emphasis on the Vice-President, formerly merely guessed at, now became only too clear.

And Tulpanov, what part is Tulpanov playing within this system? Friedrichs, who had come from the SPD, the Socialist Party of the former Germany, knew more on the subject.

'Tulpanov, a Russian Colonel, a Professor of Literature from Leningrad; during the war, Chief of the political department of the army, now Polit-Chief in Karlshorst. He is the one link to every appointed pro-Russian representative . . . a pack of scoundrels, I tell you! Don't drink so much, Friedrichs.'

But again his glass was full. This time he lifted it towards Fischer. A minute later Paul saw both of them walk away arm in arm.

The conference continued the next day. For eight hours the President of Thuringia was sitting opposite Colonel-General Semyonov. After long discussions on the question of land reform, he had managed to get it agreed that the limit for the appropriated estates should be put up to a hundred hectares. The five-hectares limit for the new peasantry had remained unchanged. But he had been able to protect the forests, the backbone of the Thuringian economy, from being cut into pieces. The forests, according to their agreement, should be put under the control of the State. When Dietershofen drove up to the guest house on the morning of the third day, he had to wait several hours before the President appeared.

Back to Weimar.

The President had slept enough, was rested and confident. Not so his driver Dietershofen-Aachern.

'This was once Berlin!' Paul said.

'Shanghai!' was the queer reply of his driver. He had seen Berlin from a different side. Not only at home; he had also looked round in the streets. Life went on – but how? Indifferent to the past, indifferent to the present, weary, morose – that's how he had found many Berliners. As soon as an American threw away a lighted cigarette, someone had bent down for the stump. In the Grunewald, hungry and drenched, they wandered about rooting up stumps of trees. At home, people crouched in the kitchen over the meagre warmth from wood fires. Cardboard instead of glass in the windows. In the whole of Berlin not a single new nail was to be had; old crooked nails could be bought on the black market. But the theatres were open – 'Pagliacci', 'The Bartered Bride', 'The Barber of Seville'; in the Russian sector, 'Eugen Onégin', Ballet and German classics, and the famous old 'Cabaret of Comedians' had posters bearing the slogan fifty times repeated: Life is Wonderful! All the theatres and cinemas were sold out. A flourishing Black Market in tickets for cigarettes. Electric current turned off; darkness in the houses. In the streets people disappeared. At night people could not sleep for hunger. And amidst that gloomy, buried city sprouted oases of light, warmth, jazz music and boogy-woogy. French Foyers, American Houses, British exhibitions – and 'German Fräuleins', that was the new expression. Hunger is painful, and after what had gone before, nothing mattered.

Anneliese . . . ?

He had not seen her again. Lisa had explained that she had to take the place of a colleague who had fallen ill, and as it was not safe for her to return at night, she had stayed there. But at home there was real coffee, butter, everything; and the contents of the little desk represented a fortune . . . and Anneliese was only sixteen.

'Shanghai, Herr President?'

The President looked sidelong at his driver. Dietershofen was driving at his usual speed; looking at the road in front of him with an impassive face. Probably he had not found things at home as he had expected.

Paul was confident. The visit to Headquarters had been very encouraging on the whole. On the question of the Central Administrations the decision had been in favour of the provincial Presidents. The so-called 'Cemetery-ticket!' ration card would be honoured at an earlier date. Ticket VI would be abolished; only five categories of food rationing would remain – still bad enough, but with the shortage of food it could not be otherwise. Also the Marshal had promised his support for the University of Jena. The number of students was to be increased and there would be extra rations for the students and teaching staff. A promising beginning.

Four hours, and they were back at Weimar.

There, work was waiting. Land reform, requisitioning, receptions, cultural contacts with the provinces of the Western Zone. One conference after the other. The discussions went on, day and night. Reconstruction of the province – its economy, its cultural institutions, its judicial system, its administration.

A new day leading to new shores. . . .

'Herr President, the Courts and attorneys must start their activities as soon as possible!' – 'Herr President, teaching should start again as quickly as possible at the University of Jena. It is one of your special jobs to see that all faculties of the University – with the exception of history – should speedily be reconstituted!'

The Russians did not behave like conquerors but like partners in negotiation; in general, they only took refuge in orders as a last resort. They liked to play the part of advisers; they liked to talk, and talk they did.

Their propaganda shrieked from walls in villages and towns:

'*Creation of a united democratic Germany!*'
'*Battle against Militarism and Nazism.*'

'*Furtherance of reconstruction – the German people must live!*'
'*We cannot disclaim intelligence!*'
'*Back to Humanism!*'
'*Protection of private initiative!*'
'*Protection of private property!*'

The Bavarian Motor Works in Eisenach was working again and had reached a monthly production of nearly three hundred cars. The factories of Zeiss and Schott in Jena had re-opened their gates and again manufactured their world-famous optical articles and instruments. The big works at Zeitz reached a daily output of five hundred tons of petrol. In Unterwellenborn the first blast-furnace had been lit. All over the country, knocking and hammering was going on. In the wreckage of heavily bombed Jena University students cleaned up the old bricks, and the stronger ones among them did the heavy work assisting the bricklayers and carpenters. The Friedrich-Schiller University in Jena emerged visibly from the chaos and rubble.

'Herr President, we must show the world how far we have already gone with rebuilding. Arrange for an industrial exhibition on a large scale in which one can see the output of the country since the collapse.'

And so, in Weimar too, knocking and hammering was going on, and lorries and trains came in bringing the goods needed for the exhibition. Almost overnight the required exhibition was standing. The civilian population could admire the achievements to date, and the abundance of goods strengthened their will to rebuild. The Industry Fair, a true reflection of the actual and potential industrial output, was a pæan of praise to the diligence and will of the population and to the country's administrative capability, both technical and political.

The Russians were satisfied. At the opening they showed pleased faces.

'Magnificent, President – congratulations; things are moving!'

The 7th of November – according to the old Russian calendar the 25th of October, most important holiday of the Soviet Union. Anniversary of the October Revolution of 1917. In Weimar in the 'Elephant' filled glasses, full dishes, toasts. The invited German guests were almost entirely from the intelligentsia: University Professors, Directors of Academies, of the Goethe and Schiller Society, high officials. Speeches on the understanding and reconciliation of nations, on democracy and unity. At the High table, Generals, the President of the Province, the Rector of the University, guests from Moscow, from Berlin – Colonel-General Semyonov, a Russian professor, the editor of a West Berlin newspaper, also the poet, the Moscow exile.

This poet, a person with many reservations, at least dared to criticize conditions and official opinions and sanctified taboos. A member of the Central Committee of the Socialist Unity Party, he was, for the rest, a sedate person far from the *Sturm and Drang* of his youth. His father was Public Prosecutor and President of the Court of Appeal in Munich, his wife a Jewess from an educated family. On his own, he was quite frank, but he became stiffer, more careful in his choice of words as soon as his wife was with him. For Paul – President of Thuringia – he used only superlatives. Superlatives spell danger – the President had already realized that.

The toasts went on and on. The German intelligentsia, who had to make do with their scanty ration-cards and did not want to miss the present opportunity, had again and again to put away their knives and forks to listen to the speeches. Colonel-General Tshuikov was dancing a Caucasian *Kasat-shok*, the President of the Province replied with a solo performance of a tango.

At the tables general relaxation. The Russians began to mingle with, and sit among, the Germans. One could hear: 'We have misjudged the Russians. They help to build, they want Democracy! They wish for the unification of all four Occupation zones; they don't keep themselves apart from the German population. We are lucky with the General!'

That was the general impression – it still remained after the festivity.

The representatives of the intelligentsia seemed to be won over and they did their best to understand and approach the Russian partner.

'Don't take it so tragically, Herr President! After all, we know what the German Communists are like. During the time when we were fighting the Hitler gang, they were all working in German factories manufacturing munitions. Go and tell those dirty German Communists that in my view they are riff-raff . . .' That was the Chief-of-Staff, Colonel-General Tshuikov. The Town Councillors, District-Councillors, Mayors, who had been appointed by the Communist Minister of the Interior or by the Party, he only spoke of as *Duraks*.*

No different was the attitude of the Marshal's deputy, Colonel-General Sokolovski: 'How can you get excited over such scoundrels, President!'

Yet, they were in office, holding the highest positions, and it was very difficult, even in the case of proved criminals, to remove a person from office.

Thuringia is a constitutional State. . . .

That was the foundation and the pivot of the agreement under which he had taken office; that must not be touched. But all over the country, peasants from the 'Mutual Peasants Assistance', youth from the 'Free German Youth', were put in lorries and cars and sent to Nordhausen.

There, in prison, was sitting a poor wretch, a Nazi, an informer, whose information had led to a death sentence during the time of the Nazis. Now, he was waiting for judgment. The faculty of law at Jena had been entrusted with this case, but this procedure seemed too cumbersome to the Party. About eight thousand people gathered in front of the prison at Nordhausen, clamouring for the informer, threatening to break into the prison – mob-law. Well, Paul himself, during Hitler's time continually exposed to denouncements and summoned to one Gestapo examination after the other, was far from wanting to protect a Nazi informer, but it was a question of principle. He summoned the police and ordered them to disperse the crowd at the Nordhausen prison by force. In this case, the legal argument finally won. The comment from the Chiefs of the Russian Administration was the same as usual: '*Duraks!*' The question remained, how could eight thousand people get to Nordhausen? Where had the petrol come from? Unless officials of the Occupation Power had been standing benevolently behind the demonstration, or had even themselves been the initiators!

Another alarming sign was the carrying through of the land reform. As suggested by Dr. Paul, the law had been drawn up

*Fools.

by the Commission for Legislation and had been published with the addition of the promises made in Berlin. Then that edition was confiscated and a new edition of the law was hastily released, and he himself had had to put his signature to it. The important alteration was that implementation of this law was no longer the responsibility of the President, but the Vice-President.

And after some months it became clear what the Communist Vice-President, together with the duly empowered Councils, had made of it. There were no longer any estates over one hundred hectares and those above fifty were scheduled for division. The new peasantry had received holdings which were much too small to support them and had been let down over their building programme. The cement from the cement works rolled steadily eastward. The brick-works received insufficient coal. Experimental new building methods were suggested but were of little use. The new peasant looked with envy on the old peasant who owned his house, stables and barns; but the old peasant was angry because he was expected to produce more than the new peasant. The seeds of conflict were sown. The reform resulted not only in a change in the economic structure but in the beginnings of dissolution of social coherence. The 'Mutual Peasants Assistance' movement aggravated the political fight in the villages, gave a political footing to the economically-weak new peasant, and, with their common pool of agricultural machines and priority in deliveries of fertilizers, took the first step towards the collective farm system.

The entire burden of the high output targets was laid on the old peasantry, urged on by threatened, and even actual, imprisonment. Here the formula was an accusation of 'sabotage' which legalized requisition, theft and arbitrary arrest. Long-established peasants and land-owners were beginning to leave the country, and thus there were many women among the arrested, many of them of noble birth, who had stayed behind when their menfolk fled.

The President took up the telephone.

At the other end of the line the Communist President of Police heard: 'I have just learnt from a reliable source that in pursuing the land reform you have been imprisoning innocent people – mostly women. What is your explanation?'

Evasive muttering.

'There is no legal foundation whatever for your arrests. I know you are actually responsible to the Vice-President; but if you think that I will look on, in a Province where I am President, you are mistaken. Those arrested must be released immediately. Do you know what you have let yourself in for? I advise you to read the penal code!'

The laws on land reform, bank reform and requisitioning bore his signature. In the case of the law on requisitioning, on the expropriation of former Nazi property, he had been able to secure the carrying out of the law and he had managed to give back to their owners some factories which had been wrongly expropriated. A solemn act of reparation, authorized by word of the Marshal and carried through under the patronage of the Occupation Power. At a festive gathering, all those fortunate owners who were again in possession of their property, had received documents to that effect – an action which offered material for propaganda for many months.

But what does the word of a Marshal count?

Marshal Zhukov had been relieved and replaced by his Chief-of-Staff Sokolovski. The name Zhukov could no longer be mentioned without provoking an odd look from his Russian *vis-à-vis*. What does a Marshal's word count – or the word of a President? The ultimate authority for the law on requisitioning too was withdrawn from him. The newly appointed Vice-President came to see him. 'I don't know what my predecessor thinks he did. Surely, it is impossible to de-requisition several hundred factories. . . .' Official documents began to disappear. Could Dr. Paul be any longer responsible for what was going on under his Presidency – had the time not come for him to resign?

Decrees, laws . . . level the town population, pauperize the land and you are the devil's law-giver. Take away the horse from the peasant – and you have emasculated him; neither roaring speeches nor mountains of pamphlets can deceive anyone; a creature of God has become a creature of dictatorial despots! Withdraw from the worker the share he is entitled to by virtue of his manual labour and squeeze him till he is below the minimum for existence – and you have uprooted him just as much as the landless peasant. You will have made an intelligent, ingenious and willing worker into a disinterested slave!

Undermine the people's sense of justice, paralyse the individual conscience and sense of responsibility – and the entire social being disappears into twilight, the strongest roots of the community disintegrate and the people, robbed of their traditions and their morale, will soon crumble to pieces!

Is this the future – should this be the purpose of his Presidency? Is it not high time to resign from office?

Get out, get out . . .

This motif was perpetually with him; when he talked to the General; when he was sitting bent over his documents; when he was in his office.

He entered this office, went through the hall, passed a Councillor to the Government who had been posted there, passed Irina Petrovna, Tatiana, Frau Hansen, secretaries and interpreters. He was surrounded by shadows who observed every movement and took in every word he uttered. Recently they had sent him a lady – not from the Baltic (it was the local NKWD-Chief who was surrounded by a circle of Baltic ladies) – of the old Prussian nobility. At the banquet for the intelligentsia – a social event which had not been repeated – he had observed her in conversation with that elegant, German-speaking Colonel from Berlin-Karlshorst, the one with his head shining like a billiard-ball. This young lady was a shade too daring. On her first day in the office she had opened his letters. Coming on top of the army of informers from Government councillor to caretaker, this was really the last straw.

He asked for her ladyship to be sent in.

Not a word about the opened letters.

'Madam, I have good news for you. This subordinate work as secretary in my office is not worthy of you; I am happy to have found you something much more suitable at the Department of Commerce and Maintenance. You will be in charge of receiving all visitors; such as industrialists from West Germany, and people of distinction; you will be personally in charge of negotiations . . .'

Quite a speech.

The lady stiffened, and seemed to find it difficult to find a suitable reply. He did not leave her any time.

'My congratulations on your new post. You can start at once.'

He gazed after her – it was not this unfortunate woman, but that elegant fencer in Berlin-Karlshorst, Colonel Tulpanov, to whom he had thrown down the gauntlet. He had a good mind not to be satisfied with this one case, but once and for all to cleanse these Augean stables. But to what purpose?

Get out, get out . . .

The permanent secretary Hattinger came into his office with some documents, Hattinger would be case Number two this morning. For a long time he had made mischief in the office; he was a daily visitor, first at Schwanseestrasse, where the Party had moved into their 'Palais', after that at Lottenstrasse, the seat of the NKWD. They had let him climb up gradually, till at last Paul himself had come into his field of vision.

Hattinger was sitting opposite him.

Referring to his documents, he unequivocally demanded the immediate dismissal of two officials who had at one time belonged to the Nazi Party. Both had been ordinary members without any special office; and when Paul considered Hattinger's dossier which he had in his desk . . .

'Herr Hattinger,' he began, 'people's lives do not always run on an even keel, they move in waves, up and down. Sometimes they miss the way, get lost, and then find their way back.'

Herr Hattinger did not want to understand, determined to finish off the two accused.

'Listen, Herr Hattinger, if I were to tell you that you were a member of the group of students representing the University of Prague and not just any National Socialist student, but the NSDAP-leader, and then proceeded to dismiss you immediately on that account, what would you think?'

Nothing further was necessary; it was more than Hattinger could stand. His face became waxen, his ears flaming red.

'And suppose I were to go to the General to tell him about you, Herr Hattinger?' Herr Hattinger had disappeared.

He had got rid of an agent from the Chief of the Political Administration in Berlin-Karlshorst, and paralysed one of the chief informers of the NKWD-Department at Weimar. That should have been enough for one morning; it is better to feel one's way slowly. However, it was not enough; within the hour he had to deal with a third case. He had received some visitors and gone through a variety of documents. These were politically exciting days. An election was pending – both for the local and central government. He was interrupted by a telephone call from a chocolate factory in the country, an S.O.S.

The name of a councillor was mentioned, a name which alarmed him. He knew immediately that this would be more than he could take upon himself. Nevertheless, he could not let the matter rest. Councillor Reuter in the Berlin Criminal Department was an acquisition of his Vice-President Busse. And not only that – Busse, himself an obscure and brutal fellow, was afraid of Reuter, had already been afraid of him in Buchenwald concentration camp. Busse was inexperienced in administration matters, knew neither his rights nor his duties, and was therefore comparatively manageable, except for his Marxist Credo which had shrunk to a single, and for that matter unmarxist, formula. The pyramid must be correctly built up from below! His way of doing this was to put former concentration camp inmates into official positions, completely disregarding their abilities; and not only were political victims now holding important posts, but also ordinary criminals like Qualle.

Qualle – the President had already once been compelled to dismiss him from office – that had happened when Qualle tried to arrest the Director of the 'Schwarza-Zellwolle', in order to get the business into his own hands – the most important of its kind in the whole of Germany. At that time, Qualle had been arrested and imprisoned. The Russians had taken an interest and had even kept Qualle longer than his sentence justified. But one day, he emerged again – healthy, well-nourished, sparkling – presented himself at the Presidential office, referred to no less than the NKWD-General Beshanov and declared: 'I am here by order of my friend Beshanov an ı request that you immediately reappoint me as Councillor of the Government!'

'I shall decide that when the occasion arises', had been the reply, and, naturally enough, he had not been reappointed. But after that, the NKWD had, behind Paul's back, got him posted to the Department for Commerce and Maintenance.

And now here he was again. The director of the Berger choco-late factory, the second largest in the country with seven hundred workers, was on the telephone and said: 'A Govern-ment Councillor is here and he is closing down our factory!'

'What is the name of the Councillor?'

'His name is Reuter.' – It was Qualle.

'Bring him to the telephone.'

Qualle came and heard:

'You are immediately dismissed from Government service. If you dare to undertake another official action, I shall have you put under arrest. Anyway, who said you were reappointed to Government service?'

'My friend Beshanov!'

Indeed, it seemed to be more than he could deal with. Never before had he seen the Chief of the Administration – who was in his room at that moment – so excited. Moreover, the General was not alone, a civilian was with him who tried to remain in the background, but Paul knew who he was. He had been introduced to him at a party as Professor Judanov of the Soviet Criminal Jurisdiction. But he had seemed to have very little idea of criminal jurisdiction or of jurisprudence at all; that much had been quite clear at that first short meeting. His importance must lie in another sphere, and in this respect Irina Petrovna's conduct was interesting. Never had the interpreter Irina Petrovna Semyanova translated so sound-lessly, never had she become as much a shadow of herself as during the seemingly accidental presence of that silent Juda-nov. He also heard a few times the General's excited exclama-tion: '*Nje perewod* – no translation!'

What was it all about?

Certainly not about the professional criminal Qualle, but the men behind him who could not get along without such Qualles and without such obscurantists as the Minister of the Interior.

Get out. . . .

The point was not Qualle. There was the Bank reform, the land reform, the sequestrations, there was a great deal more. The money which had been withdrawn on the occasion of the Bank reform had not been destroyed, but had remained in Russian hands and was being widely used; with it everything was being purchased, not only goods, but houses, land, cinemas, business concerns, everything was being paid for with valueless paper. This was just another way of getting hold of German private property. Bank reform, acquisition of private property, the near starvation of the people, the misery of the students! What had become of their pledges – was everything pretence and deceit?

Qualle was merely a symptom – a worm in a rotten apple, there were many like him.

'Herr General, you can choose between the Councillor Reuter, otherwise Qualle, and me. I shall not remain President if a man like that is planted in my office!'

The General looked concerned. Herr Judanov enveloped himself in silence. The wire between the Soviet administration and the head in Berlin-Karlshorst was buzzing. The General left, tea was brought in, and Herr Judanov managed suddenly without an interpreter. He spoke German quite well, speaking only of casual matters.

The General returned.

'To hell with that man, Herr President.'

'All right; but Qualle is only a symptom. The issue at stake is more than one man.'

'You cannot resign now, Herr President. German self-government is imminent. The Germans will be given more freedom. In future, we will only concern ourselves with certain questions – demilitarization, de-nazification, democratization and reparation. For the rest, you will be quite independent. As far as the internal economy is concerned, you can draw up the plan for industry on your own responsibility. Anyhow you have been billed as speaker in the election over the whole country.'

'Herr General, when I speak as President, I am not just any speaker who promises this and that and immediately forgets. What I promise, I must also be able to keep!'

'You are right. You can promise the people that food Category VI will now definitely be abolished. The third hundredweight of potatoes per head will be delivered. The distribution of clothing, shoes and other daily necessities will be substantially raised.' – Again the telephone was buzzing.

'Herr President, important news! We are going to release one million prisoners of war in the course of the next year.'

Get out. . . .

It was not possible. One million prisoners of war – that alone was decisive and sufficient cause to appeal to the people to take part in the election.

'General, the population is greatly worried by the question of the Eastern frontier. Neither in the Yalta Pact, nor in that of Potsdam is there a legal foundation for the Oder-Neisse-Line. I am fully aware of the much discussed remark of the Soviet Minister for Foreign Affairs and must inform you that I am not in a position to accept this frontier as final. May I speak on the Oder-Neisse-Line; may I do that?'

'That's dynamite, don't forget!'

The General shied away from this question; but at last he agreed to discuss it with Karlshorst again. After a long telephone conversation he said: 'You may speak on the Oder-Neisse-Line, Herr President.'

The President remained in office.

He left the administration building accompanied by Irina Petrovna. In the office of the Chief of Administration, Lieutenant-Colonel Judanov – the Weimar professor – stayed behind. The General and the Lieutenant-Colonel reached out for Russian cigarettes, and it was the General who offered a light to the Lieutenant-Colonel.

'The Germans will be surprised', Judanov said. 'As soon as they will have elected their Landtag, they will feel the pinch.'

Lieutenant-Colonel Judanov knew what he was talking about.

As Ivan Serov's representative, he had been living in Weimar for some weeks now. He had to study the economic conditions of Thuringia and had made things easy for himself. Sometimes a good idea is worth more than a staff of assistants – and his idea had been to have the Chief of the Military Administration persuade the President to arrange an industrial exhibition. This industrial exhibition, installed in the old castle of Weimar, had become a living work of reference – cars, chocolate, rayon, cement, raw fibre, potassium, typewriters, electric articles, optical instruments were exhibited, and the firms and the capacities of their works and factories were stated. Thus, all that was left to him was to look up the individual industrial concerns, check their machines, and to confirm that the stated amount of goods were in fact manufactured.

That part of the work was finished.

The lists were ready, had been handed over to the Manager for Dismantling and Reparations on Saburov's staff. The dismantling which Thuringia had been spared so far, would be put into operation at one stroke. First Thuringia must vote, had to appoint an elected government. But after the election, on the Saturday night, the proposed factories would be put under military occupation and Saburov could start. Then everything would be dismantled, factories, shafts, railway lines, everything except certain things which could not be transported. Those, if they were important, like the potash mine at Leuna, would be transformed into Soviet joint-stock companies.

Judanov was living in Weimar.

His staff was always on the move; they set up their office at Nordhausen, at Gera, Eisenach, Heiligenstadt; at present they were at Jena.

Jena: Karl Zeiss and Schott. The world-famous works for optical glass and optical instruments, badly damaged by American bombers, were once again working with about ten thousand men and were making monthly deliveries to the value of several million Reichsmarks as reparations. That was a lot, almost the entire production. Yet, no longer could visitors from West Germany and abroad be shown round the works to demonstrate the German will to rebuild and Soviet support. Those works were intended for Russia, first on the list for dismantling. But it would be of little use to transport only the machines. With the machines must go the workers who understood how to work them – a staff of workers who had a tradition of hundreds of years behind them. To secure and transport those qualified Zeiss workers was the task of Lieutenant-Colonel Judanov's department.

Everything was prepared.

This time his old companion Budin had surpassed himself. The troops needed for the execution of this operation were in readiness. The working-contracts for 'voluntary engagement in the USSR' were prepared. Jena Station was closed. Budin had even procured a sizeable train with goods wagons, carriages and dining cars. After the first shock, it would be a luxurious transportation and the Zeiss workers would arrive at their destination in good working spirits.

'Well, everything ready?'

'You only need to press the button!'

Budin did not say what it was that was ready and why it was only necessary to press a button; nor did Judanov's reply give anything away. The NKWD-Major and the Captain from Lottenstrasse, with whom Judanov and Budin were sitting, did not show any curiosity. The two German visitors, Ministerial Director Hattinger from Dr. Paul's Presidential office, whose usefulness to the Russians was much reduced, and the other one, owner of a commandeered bookshop, could not understand Russian; Ella, Jutta and Liesbeth could understand a little. Ella, Jutta, Liesbeth; at times there were more – a brothel, that's what the Major had made of it. And the old Professor of Medicine who, together with his wife and grown-up daughter, had been pushed up to the top floor of his house, did not know of it – or at any rate, behaved as though he did not know! It was too disturbing, a continual coming and going, daily parties! Judanov would have moved and found other quarters, except that the two rooms which he occupied and had furnished with good taste, particularly pleased him; besides, he did not want to leave the field to the Major from Lottenstrasse. He was sorry for the family. The landlord reminded him of Colonel Revyevkin, one of the old generation who had left on him a strong and lasting impression. It was before the battle for Moscow, and on the Solovyevo ferry they had had to shoot him. A lot of time had passed since, but he had never forgotten his bearing during the interrogation. No, he did not want to leave the field to the Major, not with someone like old Revyevkin and even less to the Revyevkina, his daughter – for had that old staff officer had a daughter, she would have been like this one. Her husband had been killed in the East, and she had returned to her parents. The Major made advances to her – there was hardly any one he did not make advances to; he sent her notes: 'Come to such and such a place tomorrow. I'll wait for you in my car!' He thinks that is extremely refined, this *durak*! Naturally, she did not respond, neither to the notes nor to other allusions, some of them rather crude; she simply did not understand. The Major was again left with his Jutta whom he had brought with him from Silesia, or with anyone picked up in the street – certainly more suitable for him!

This was the day of the elections – an occasion for celebration.

The remains of the dinner were still on the table. The evening was well advanced and Jutta brought in Sauerkraut and herrings. A gramophone played and they danced to it. Budin had disappeared and so had Ella. The Captain, to whom Ella belonged, became worried. This devil Budin . . . Judanov got up; he did not want a quarrel in this house. He found Budin with Ella in the kitchen; the daughter of the landlord was also there. The Captain soon appeared; then the Major, who did not want to be left alone with the Germans over the herrings. The 'unconquered' daughter made coffee but could not be persuaded to come into the drawing-room; therefore the drawing-room had come to her.

The gramophone continued to play in the next room.

'Why don't we go over there?'

'Yes, why not?'

Would the daughter refuse to dance with Judanov? She had done it often enough before. Suddenly and surprisingly she accepted. She danced with him – and only with him. This was a miracle: this reserved woman whom he had courted from the beginning, gave up her reserve for the first time; suddenly she showed a preference for him, approved of him; and he found, as the evening progressed, that she was prepared to go the whole way. When the party came to an end, she herself led the way to her room.

This was an experience. The next night it was repeated; but not the third night.

This was the night of Jena; the night of Karl Zeiss and Schott. Men torn from their beds, shrieking women, howling children. Guns, bayonets . . . and he was thinking of the woman in Weimar.

The blocks of flats were surrounded by Soviet soldiers.

Inside the flats the men had to sign working contracts put before them. There was no choice. They were compelled to sign, and their signature cancelled the outrage, gave the whole enterprise the stamp of legality. They were allowed to take with them wife and children, and a small amount of luggage.

They must leave their houses; they were not allowed to go back to the Zeiss works; Karl Zeiss in Jena no longer existed. At the same moment the dismantling of the machines began.

Judanov was thinking of the woman in Weimar.

The Germans could produce more than first-class spectacle lenses. They have invented the monkey (according to a Russian proverb) – they have built towers and thick walls with city gates, have secured themselves from danger; for a thousand years and more they have been living in stone houses; and then suddenly a woman's form comes towards you. A woman . . . the devil: is that what he is worrying about on a night like this? A thousand and one qualified workers, not one must be missing. Every machine must immediately be manned and ready for production. If only one machine fails, if only one of those devils of workers escapes, the schedule will be interrupted. Not one must be missing.

A mass enterprise.

To be carried out at one stroke . . . there may be mishaps; one has to be everywhere, everywhere at the same time. Budin rushed here and there like a shot rocket. – Mishaps . . .

The entire town of Jena was involved in the riot; the telephones too – between Jena and Weimar, between Weimar and Berlin. Here is the Karl Zeiss management. Here is the Chief Mayor of Jena. Here is the President. Here is the Military Administration.

'Herr President, the Karl Zeiss works are being dismantled, the workers are being deported to Russia – you must help!'

It was a grey morning over the town of Jena.

Trains were still standing in the station. A barrier of Soviet soldiers prevented relations from getting through – friends, relatives, who wanted to take over the hastily left houses. Excitement, despair tears. A car flying the standard of the Province stopped: 'Herr President, there is still time; hurry!' The car went on to the Karl Zeiss management, went back to Weimar, went backwards and forwards between Jena and Weimar, between the works and the Military Administration. The President went through the factory grounds of Zeiss and Schott looking round the spacious buildings. Everywhere hammers lifted, unskilled hands tearing parts asunder, delicate machinery thrown over like dung- carts, heaved and rolled on to the available lorries.

A furious Captain, round as a ball, with a face like a bloated radish, chased swarms of workers from one object to the other. And here the President met a face which passed by like smoke, but which he should impress on his memory as he was going to meet it again. It was a man who spoke Russian with the Captain, German with the workers, and who remained unconcerned and lost amidst the turmoil.

The glassy sea – Gnotke with his frozen eyes.

Back to Weimar. The Chief of Administration was no longer available. The Marshal whose name was now Sokolovski, was also not available, but he had replaced the pledges of his predecessor by new ones. 'The dismantling has come to an end!' The Marshal of the Soviet Army had said this only six weeks ago.

At last, the General! Irina Petrovna had got hold of him. The General did not understand.

'There is no truth in it, they are panicking in Jena. Nobody is being arrested there.'

'I was there, General. They are dismantling the works. The workers arrested by your soldiers are already sitting in trains. The population is extremely worked up by these happenings.'

The General is not the responsible authority; he has no information.

Nobody is responsible, nobody informed; the Chief Commander of Thuringia has no information either. Indeed, who was actually responsible? There was nobody he could reach. The President knew that he was speaking to dumb walls. He had never heard of Ivan Serov, and could not suspect that one hand could break through all authority and was able to thrust through the many-storied Soviet hierarchy as if it were paper. It did not occur to him to think of 'Professor Judanov'; and it would hardly have helped him. Judanov – even if he had wanted to behave differently, would have been at a loss to answer his questions; he was only the shadow on the wall of the violent hand from the Kremlin.

The operation lasted forty-eight hours.

After that, Judanov returned to Weimar. Everything had gone off without trouble, also without bloodshed. An operation in kid gloves, but he had had to be present everywhere, was worn out, dog-tired, and had to have a good night's rest. He did not think of any woman. He woke during the night, and without turning on the light, he tiptoed to the upper floor. He found the door locked.

And the door remained locked.

It was finished; she no longer wanted him. He met her in the kitchen, asked her to account for her behaviour. Was there someone else? No, nobody else; she wanted no one else. She could not imagine anyone better than he, but did not want to continue their relationship. That was all, and he had to be content. He came less often to Weimar, just often enough to keep an eye on the Major in Lottenstrasse. He did not want to withdraw his protecting hand from her house. Most of his time he spent travelling from one town to the other. He had work enough. The dismantling went forward at full speed over the whole country. Apart from complete factories, there was 'superflous machinery' from electricity works, and double-way tracks of railway lines to be removed and sent off. He did not belong to the dismantling staff, but was Serov's representative, and it was his task to control the work of Saburov's groups. And not only Saburov's work, also the activities of the NKWD and the Military Administration.

The surveillance of the President was a special task which needed great tact. So far it had been sheer idiocy – a hay cart in front of his door, the opposite villa empty for more than a year – reserved for a General and constantly occupied by three sentries equipped with telephone and field glasses; also the move into the neighbouring villa by the Soviet attorney-general was pretty transparent; it hardly needed a Dr. Paul to see through such measures. The arrangements whereby he could only move about accompanied by two policemen, one of whom was his driver, and that he must carry the province's standards on his car – all for his own protection – were certainly better. But this arrangement had not been made by the local NKWD; he himself had brought it along from Karlshorst. And this arrangement worked – always. The telephone rings: the President has just now passed through Stadtroda driving in the direction of Ulrichswalde. And whether he drives to Jena or Ulrichswalde, or to Burgk or to the dismantling department at the motor works, to Eisenach or to the Hescho porcelain factory at Hermsdorf – the telephone keeps a track of all his movements.

His personal driver was to be drawn into this system. Lotten-strasse had already tried clumsily to replace his driver with another. But Dr. Paul had resisted – and they had to climb down. Case 'Paul' had to be handled with care. Many mistakes were being made; and not the least amongst the political mistakes was when the NKWD and the Administration consented to the President's being a member of the Socialist Unity Party. The Chief of Administration had actually encouraged him, had explained that this would make it unnecessary to include a delegate from the Socialist Unity Party at their confidential discussions. It would provide a political basis for his so-called 'Government'. What they had failed to realize was that Paul's standing as a political figure-head to impress the West had been depreciated. Nevertheless, for the East-German Federation encouraged by the London conference, the President was still the only possible candidate.

The telephone rang.

'The President has just passed through Stadtroda, driving towards Ulrichswalde.' To Ulrichswalde – he has property there, a small country estate. He is said to be ill – the second time in a short while. The first time he couldn't get over the Karl Zeiss business. The second time he was suffering from the dismantling and the formation of Soviet companies from requisitioned factories. The crisis had been hastened by his being prohibited from making a speech on the 'World Conscience' at Jena University on the occasion of the Moscow Conference of Ministers for Foreign Affairs.

A speech, a desparing cry . . . a drowning man's shout for help. It was the Marshal who had prohibited the speech Paul wanted immediately to fling down everything. He went to the Head of Administration. 'I resign!' His resignation was not accepted. A reply from the Marshal told him to be ill as long as he wished. He would remain President. In the meantime a deputy would be appointed. He recovered, drove from Ulrichswalde to Burgk, from Burgk to Gera, received visitors from the General, guests from Berlin, and all of them had instructions not to mention politics but only to make light conversation. Every five days a bulletin on his state of health was issued. He was allowed to play the sick potentate. Until he was needed – perhaps to dig for gold in

Kolyma, perhaps as President of the East-German Federation.

In the meantime the pages of his dossier increased. Already comprehensive, dating back to 1923 and even 1918 (but some points were still obscure), at any rate there was enough to justify Kolyma ten times over.

Judanov was sitting bent over the document. One day he would have to put it into Ivan Serov's hands. A thick portfolio, prepared, complete, primed for destruction. From the beginning, a fighter and a reactionary. In 1918, Flight Captain; in 1923, he gave orders on his own authority to arrest the leading Communists on the Simsonbrunnen in Gera – even more reactionary than the Weimar Republic. At the same time he released a crowd of Social-Democrats – was that a point in his favour or had he only set them free because somebody else had imprisoned them?

From 1933 to 1945 an opponent of Hitler – sincere opposition or an innnate spirit of rebellion? After the war appointed Mayor of Gera by the Americans.

His history as President contained a unique register of offences!

Bank reform, land reform, requisitioning, dismantling – everything had had to be torn away from him!

Certain character traits completed the picture.

His chauffeur, from whom he would not be separated, was living under a false name, a one-time Luftwaffe colonel, whose family were living in West Berlin. His wife frequented American houses, the daughter was working in a PX-shop. What a chauffeur for the President of a Province in the Soviet zone!

The Chief of Military Administration had presented him with Lenin's collected works, a German edition. The volumes were still untouched in his library. The NKWD-Chief had presented him with a picture of Stalin, not a print but an original oil-painting. The painting disappeared into his shed. He pretended that he had to get a frame good enough for it; the frame never arrived. Stalin in the shed – instead, on the wall of his study, is a print of no other than the old Prussian King Frederick the Great.

However, a President, even though he were ogling the West not merely with one but with both eyes, was needed.

With another bait on the hook, the fish of the West would not even sniff at it.

And now: Munich.

The Bavarian Prime Minister has invited the Presidents of all German Provinces including those from the Soviet-occupied zone, to take part in a conference. His deputy won't do; the barb would be missing from the hook. What was to be done? The sick potentate had to recover.

Judanov reached out for another document – material on encroachments, trespassing, rape, murder, perpetrated by members of the Red Army, which the President had collected through his public prosecutors; the material had been seized and submitted to him as 'secret and confidential' by the Advocate-General.

Excellent, this will be a way to make him recover; Judanov called Budin, explained what he had in mind and told him to visit two or three public prosecutors in various parts of the country at night, with an escort from 'Lottenstrasse', and to interrogate them in their homes. 'The point is to strike terror into them. The interrogations must seem to be leading to the Advocate-General.'

Budin understood.

'It is urgent . . . drive immediately to Lottenstrasse.'

'Immediately, but as I cannot entrust anybody else with the interrogations, I will need two nights for it.'

On the third day the telephone rang.

'The President has left his residence in Burgk and is driving to the Autobahn. The President has just now passed the Hermsdorfer Kreuz in the direction of Weimar. The President has just arrived at the Military Administration.'

Harden your heart against the underling; the people only respect those they hold in terror – a maxim of the Egyptian Pharaohs, more than four thousand years old, and it could have been coined in Moscow!

Nocturnal silence. A dog barks. Creaking steps on the gravel of the garden. There is light behind the windows of the sick potentate.

The bell has stopped ringing. The dog was still barking. The driver Dietershofen-Aachern accompanied the Advocate-General into the house. . . .

'Criminals are hunting the public prosecutors now. Only you can help, Herr President!'

The following day the President went to Weimar. He confronted the Chief of the Administration:

'General, I will resume office.'

Half an hour later, the returned President was sitting opposite the Chief of Administration and the NKWD-Chief.

'I have heard from prosecuting counsel,' the President addressed himself to the NKWD-Chief, 'and must inform you that your suspicions are completely mistaken. I myself ordered the collecting of that information. The Attorney-General acted only on orders. It was I who directed him to have the evidence you were inquiring about collected.'

The President had at least made his position unequivocal. He was not finished yet.

'I have already handed over to you part of the documents', he said. 'I have further material which I shall submit to you, the General or the Marshal in Berlin. This material should establish the truth about offences perpetrated by alleged members of the Red Army.'

The NKWD-Chief knew what the normal result of the President's self-accusation should be – arrest and extermination.

But in this case there were other factors.

The NKWD-Colonel forced his face into a friendly grimace. The General smirked like a sly but friendly peasant The Colonel got up, excused himself, went to the next room and telephoned for further instructions.

He spoke with Lieutenant-Colonel Judanov.

'The main point is his return to office – the Public Prosecutors are unimportant for the moment', Judanov explained. 'Also the material is of no interest, the contents are already known and, moreover, correspond to the facts.'

'What is it you want, Comrade Colonel? The bird is in your hand.'

The President left the Military Administration with congratulations on his resumption of office from the NKWD-Colonel and the Chief of Military Administration.

His office looked exactly as before.

Shadows, shadows . . . he met them on the staircase. They

were sitting in his ante-room, bent over his desk. Exactly as before – only now he could perceive them more clearly. After those months of absence they threw themselves on him like starvelings.

But of the shadow behind the shadows – Professor Judanov – he knew nothing. Nor of one particular scheme. One of Judanov's creatures had placed on his desk a document underlined in red, as well as a newspaper article similarly marked.

He noticed them immediately.

The one was an invitation issued by the Bavarian Head of State, to a conference of all German Prime Ministers, to be held in Munich. The other, the newspaper article, was a clumsily drawn up refusal, written, or at least signed by his deputy. And this constituted an official opinion of the head of the Province of Thuringia.

Impossible . . . blockheads, scoundrels, traitors! The country is groaning under the dismantling operations. Telephone apparatus, electrical equipment, complicated machinery are being loaded with pitchforks. The railway lines run on single tracks. Whole districts, their rail communications dismantled, have become distressed areas. Ration-card VI is abolished – card V instead is now the same 'Cemetery-Card'. He has spoken in favour of the SED – relying on the Marshal's word. A little old woman stopped him in the street: 'Herr President, I have voted as you asked us to – where is the third hundredweight of potatoes? The promised clothing concessions were ludicrously meagre.

Concessions. . . .

Scoundrels!

'We are a German Party!' comes from all loudspeakers. But on the occasion of the dismantling of the Zeiss works, the man with the Lenin beard in Berlin declared to about eighty members of the Tribunal of the Executive Committee: 'The Zeiss works are in better hands behind the Urals than here with us.'

A German party?

Scoundrels, riff-raff, rats . . . the foundations have been gnawed away; the building is tottering. The economic structure of the country is on the verge of collapse, the population on the verge of starvation! One hope has remained: the

Potsdam Agreement, the solemn pledges given by all three Powers for the restoration of Germany's geographic economic and political unity. And here a hand reaches out, the Bavarian Prime Minister calls a joint meeting, and the hand is refused.

Scoundrels . . . enough to drive one insane.

Generals, agents, traitors – and fools; he himself with a lifelong lawyer's experience, up to every trick, and yet has fallen into the trap like a simpleton! – Why?

Because he has believed in the law, in the meaning of history, in humanism, in a world-conscience.

Law, humanism, world-conscience under Russian management? No, no . . . he has ceased to believe in it. He has caught sight of the partner's concealed face. But the Three-Power-Agreement, the only remaining foundation for a united Germany: he must hold on to that.

The battle for 'Munich' starts!

'We have a President again, you can see it!' – 'He is giving the Comrades from Schwanseestrasse a run for their money.' – 'It is good to have such a pike in the carp-pond!'

The Chief of the Administration, the Chief of NKWD and Lieutenant-Colonel Judanov were sitting cosily together. It was in the General's house. On the table were herrings, bread and Vodka.

'Yes, in the end we shall probably fall into the traps of these *Duraks* ourselves!'

'He is *chitry* . . . and comes out with some surprising things – like the bridal procession of Anna Pavlovna.'

Colonel-General Tshuikov had discovered a safe fixed in a wall in the villa he was living in, and had had it broken open. The President had been told that it contained jewellery and valuables from the wedding trousseau of Princess Anna Pavlovna, who had been married at Weimar in the eighteenth century. The same explanation had already been given to him at the carrying-off of art treasures and gold, silver and precious stones from Weimar, Rudolstadt and other towns. This time he had replied: 'The wedding procession of Anna Pavlovna must have reached from Petersburg to Weimar!'

Roars of laughter. The General, Colonel and Lieutenant-Colonel took another vodka and went on eating their herrings. They were satisfied with their President – an animal which does not keep still while being slaughtered but accompanies the slaughtering-feast with suitable roaring.

'*Karasho* . . .'

'But now "Munich", a very intricate business!'

And it had looked quite simple. One simply refused and was rid of the matter. But it was not so simple after all. The newspaper article had released a wave of fury among the population. At a conference of the SED-executive committee in a big hotel in the Harz, one voice was raised openly against participation in the Munich conference. And Colonel Tulpanov from Karlshorst, who attended the conference, listened without saying a word.

'A hot potato! Nobody wants to touch it.'

'Except Paul?'

'And Tulpanov?'

'Quite clear; he wants to torpedo the conference, but he can't do it openly.'

Now 'Munich' was playing the same game. In their reply to Saxony any possible failure of the conference was blamed upon the East Zone Presidents.

'This is unbearable – for years we talk about unity and now we are caught in our own propaganda.'

'How can we get out of it?'

Colonel Tulpanov already knew. At a new conference he made the SED-Central Secretary's Office decide to order the Eastern Presidents to propose at the beginning of the conference as first point on the agenda:

'The Formation of a German Central Administration by the German Democratic Parties and Trade Unions for the creation of a Unified German State.'

And if this were refused, the Presidents were immediately to leave the conference!

That should be safe enough. It only depended on the reliability of the delegation. And Paul was to be leader of that delegation. His position had to be weakened in such a way that he could not jump out of line. There was nothing to be feared from Mecklenburg; but already Brandenburg even if wavering, had supported Paul. The two Presidents from Saxony-Anhalt and from Saxony, who also came from the middle-class camp, were the danger. In league with them,

Paul would be capable of going beyond his instructions.

'And what is Paul doing now?'

'He is conspiring', was the reply of the NKWD-Chief.

'That's what he is always doing.'

'He rushed through the country like a thunderbolt, from Weimar to Dresden, from Dresden to Halle. Just now he is bringing President Friedrichs from Halle to Dresden.'

One language, one people, one country; that was the content of the prohibited Jena speech. Two of the Western Occupation Powers had meanwhile gone one step further. Between the British and American occupied zones, frontier barriers no longer existed. The French-occupied zone was still lagging behind. But for the Soviet-occupied zone, unification meant rescue from a paralysed isolation, liberation from a political and economic yoke.

Dr. Paul was sitting in the car beside his former fellow-student, the Saxonian President, Dr. Friedrichs. Fighting days lay behind them. It was now certain that the Eastern zone would be represented at the Munich conference.

Friedrichs was looking fixedly at the road. He looked tired; the skin of his face drawn tightly over his cheek bones.

The car was driving through the Klosterlausnitzer Forest.

'At least, we are going to Munich', Paul said.

Friedrichs put his hand on his arm: 'Will you please stop the car. I must speak to you alone', he said.

They both got out and walked together under the tall trees into the Klosterlausnitzer Forest. Friedrichs looked back at the car some twenty or thirty yards away. He was breathing heavily and the expression in his eyes was such that Paul would never forget.

'I am being murdered', he blurted out. 'I am not the first, there have been others before me. Those villains are poisoning me. I don't eat or drink outside my house any more, but it doesn't help.'

'Murdered . . .'

Friedrichs looked terribly ill.

'Listen . . . you don't know Fischer, not as I know him. At the banquet, during Zhukov's time, I told you about his amorous affairs with policewomen. One young thing – I am sure you have seen her at his house, with brown hair and doe-like eyes – became pregnant by him and then disappeared.

Another one took her place – the same thing happened to her. Now he has got a third one. Then there's the business of Goethe's letters to Count Brühl. He confiscated them and gave them to you for the Thuringian archives in exchange for motor tyres. But he kept some back. I have seen them myself. And that's not all – a whole series of crimes, and I kept a record of everything. Finally, I couldn't stand it any longer, I went to Berlin to the Party Secretary's office and put all my material on the table. He listened quite unmoved, just looking at me with his blue eyes. He sent cold shivers down my spine. Then he shook his head as if he had been hearing about the misdemeanours of a naughty child.'

'What happened then?'

'There was a conference in Berlin; Fischer was asked to attend. But he came back. They didn't drop him, not him. Do you understand? . . . No, you don't understand; you think I am ill. I am not ill, I had to tell you, you are going to Munich, but you must know what is happening. Someone must know. . . .'

They drove on to Dresden. Friedrichs disappeared into his house in Meisenweg. Paul watched him; then he looked along the quiet street, once a residential street for retired middle-class people; now it was the home of the Heads of the Party and Government, blocked at both ends by barriers guarded by police.

Here lived Friedrichs, and opposite him, so that he could see into the windows, lived the Minister of the Interior for Saxony, Fischer.

The barrier went up.

Dr. Paul left Meisenweg and Dresden behind him, and drove on to Weimar that same night.

The next drive along the Autobahn brought him back to Hermsdorfer Kreuz, to the lonely spot in the Klosterlausnitzer Forest where the East-West Autobahn crosses the North-South one. He went on for a few kilometres. The car stopped. Near here the Eastern Zone Presidents were to meet before continuing the journey to Munich. None of the others had arrived. At the edge of the forest there were red and yellow valerian and foxglove. A car came from the north and stopped.

Inside sat the Mecklenburg President. He had voted against Munich, and nothing else could have been expected from him, sitting there in Mecklenburg like the Administrator of a Russian colony.

Dr. Paul looked towards the north.

He was waiting for Friedrichs and for the Brandenburg President who, though hesitantly, had voted for 'Munich' with him.

A car approached, but it was one of the BMW-limousines which were only driven by representatives of the Occupation Powers. Next to the driver could be seen the silhouette of a Russian officer. Another car came, with the standards of Saxony on the wings. But it was not Friedrichs who got out; in his stead appeared his Minister of the Interior, Fischer.

What had happened?

'The President is fatally ill. His condition is hopeless.'

Tall firs, above them the blue sky. But an Asiatic air blew through the Klosterlausnitzer Forest.

'We cannot wait any longer. We must start. I must remind you of the instructions from the Central Office – we must leave the conference immediately if our proposal is not accepted!'

That was Fischer again.

A secret agent in China; during the war Commissioner in a mobile column of the Red Army, dismissed after the breakdown before Moscow, and then announcer on the 'Free Germany' Radio. And now suddenly the 'Good Life' in the capital of Saxony – valuable paintings on the walls, luxurious carpets, a huge polar-bear skin as bedside rug, a gourmet's table, and a wine cellar, a liqueur cabinet full of exquisite brandy. This new life had changed his appearance and had given him a mask of middle-class respectability and solidity – a bloated mask, and in his thick neck the blood pulsed angrily. And yet he could become sentimental when, after a lapse of thirty years, he suddenly visited his old parents in a working class district in Leipzig. From the best motives, he had taken a woman into his house from among a crowd of human wrecks who were being chased across the border, and had adopted her daughter; and yet in his luxurious lair he could keep young policewomen, spoiling them with luxuries and Pekinese lap-dogs.

The Minister of the Interior for Saxony and the Minister

from Mecklenburg, both declared opponents of the Munich meeting, and the liberal but weak President of Saxony-Anhalt, were Paul's companions on the way to Munich. The Brandenburg President would have restored the balance, but he had not come. It transpired later that he had been deliberately delayed.

Dinner in Munich – for the first time since the collapse, the Presidents of all the German provinces were sitting at one table. The atmosphere was relaxed, and a spirit of conciliation seemed to be in the air.

Drive to the Chancellery.

A warm summer evening, bright lights under a green foliage roof, people at the café tables, 'Normal Consumers' living on ration cards, just as in the East, but here they were sitting together, relaxed and happy; in the streets young people were strolling along arm in arm, laughing and chatting.

An unusual picture for a man from the Zone of Silence, in which, two years after the end of the war, there were still no lights in the towns, and where at nightfall everybody hurried back to the safety of their homes.

The first surprise in the conference hall of the Bavarian State Chancellery was the agenda already planned. The list of speakers comprised only Presidents of the Western Zone; no representative of the Eastern Zone would have an opportunity of speaking. The atmosphere in the conference hall was in sharp contrast to the generally relaxed attitude at the dinner.

Dr. Paul looked around him, looked from one face to another – was there really nobody who could reconcile these opposite camps? Have they forgotten that Eastern Germany did not invite the Russians to occupy them? In this already tense atmosphere the Prime Minister of Mecklenburg's proposals conforming to SED orders sounded like a Prussian drill sergeant's commands.

It was not necessary for the Western Presidents to pass a formal resolution; they were unified in their refusal. The course of the rest of the conference was now decided.

According to Party orders, Paul, as leader of the delegation, should now get up and leave the conference. He did not get up – and knew what this meant. He was searching for a compromise, for a chance to be able to remain at the conference table. His proposal that after the Bavarian Prime Minister's welcome address one President of each Zone should speak for up to fifteen minutes, met with little encouragement – even with discourtesy.

The majority vote was: No.

A second rebuff – yet, he again remained seated, broke the Party order for the second time. Fischer's face grew red with anger; only with an effort did he contain himself. No encouragement could be expected from Mecklenburg, but Saxony-Anhalt failed him too. No assistance from any side; no help.

He made a new proposition.

At least one representative of the Eastern Zone – perhaps he himself – should be allowed to speak after the Bavarian Prime Minister.

A hurried to and fro.

What do they really know – in their streets there is light, their railways run smoothly, their economy, though damaged by the war, still rests on its old foundations. How can they imagine what is going on behind the Iron Curtain! What do they know of the paralysis of people who no longer grumble, who no longer speak, who hardly notice whether it is raining or whether the sun is shining. Should eighteen million Germans still be condemned to silence, even here?

But he spoke.

Desperation, indignation, impotent fury, uncontrolled words. The misery of a whole Zone was trying to find expression. Burdened by the weight of his feelings, words failed him. His fist crashed on the table.

Dr. Paul left the conference hall; with him Brandenburg, Saxony-Anhalt and Dresden.

The eyes of the Saxonian Minister of the Interior, Fischer, gleamed benevolently. The conference had gone exactly as desired. He could go back with an easy mind, and did so that same night, accompanied by Mecklenburg. The Thuringian President and with him the Prime Minister of Saxony-Anhalt and the Prime Minister of Brandenburg waited at their Munich hotel in case of a possible communication. In vain. After ten hours, they, too, returned to the Eastern Zone.

Public mourning in Saxony.

A Prime Minister was being carried to his grave. A State funeral on a grand scale. Flowers wherever one looked.

Everybody was assembled in the big hall for the funeral service – the Prime Ministers and Ministers, representatives of the Military Administration, Presidents of the Diets, and representatives of the Provinces, the complete Saxonian Government, the Heads of the Party, and delegations from the factories. There was also a delegation from the police . . . policewomen, too, including the third protegée of the Minister of the Interior for Saxony. The head of the Party in his Sunday suit, Lenin beard and blue eyes . . . 'Cold shivers down my spine!' was what the dead man had said. Professor Judanov was there too; a queer professor, he was now wearing the uniform of a Lieutenant-Colonel, and it seemed to Paul that his silhouette was the same as the one he had seen pass by in the BMW-limousine in Klosterlausnitzer Forest, going in the direction of Munich.

One man amongst the mourners, in black suit and hat, was standing on his own. No one around him, nobody came near him, nobody spoke to him. And yet he had many acquaintances among the assembled Government representatives, old Party friends, whom he had not met for more than a decade. The shunned one was Ernst Reuter, the Chief Mayor of the city of Berlin, elected after Dr. Werner had retired through age and Luise Schröder through illness; he had not been acknowledged by the Russians.

Lowered flags.

'Immortal victims . . .'

'Immortal victims, you departed . . .' the policewomen sang, the Minister of the Interior, Fischer, sang; the Head of the Party and the Senior Chief of the firm sang. Both the senior and junior chiefs had at one time been wood workers, and with plane and saw they could create useful things, could give form and permanence to solid wood. And now . . . they were like restlessly drilling worms, and the tree fast disintegrating into dust.

The political activities did not even stop during the obsequies. 'Immediately after the State funeral a meeting of all Prime Ministers. Everybody must come!' somebody whispered into Paul's ear.

Two large eyes were looking at him.

A woman who would not be denied; she had to speak to him.

Trap? Agent-provocateur?

'You are being abused, Herr President. In your name the people are being misled. How long are you going on with this?'

The woman was only telling him what he knew himself; asking what he had often asked himself. He arrived home, got out of his car and met the glassy face which had first passed him in one of the empty workshops of Karl Zeiss and Schott. August Gnotke, with hose, sponge and rags for polishing, started to work on the car; he smoothed the cushions and inspected all the side-pockets of the car....

His chauffeur wanted to speak to him. Everybody wanted to speak to him. That lady in the office, another one in the forest, Councillors, his chauffeur Dietershofen – and to all of them it is as urgent as if their lives depended on it.

But his life does depend on it! Dietershofen was clutching his cap in his hands: 'Herr President, it is difficult for me, but I must ask you to dismiss me.'

'What is the matter? Is it Gnotke?'

'I have nothing against him; I even feel sorry for him. But I ask you to dismiss me before it is too late. I don't want to be disloyal to you.'

Well, Dietershofen too. It had to come. They had got hold of them one after the other. Only the day before he had had to say to one: 'You must leave here, I can no longer protect you.' He was being isolated; nothing from the outside world – no hint of reality would be allowed to reach him.

And now Dietershofen.

'No, Herr Aachern', he said – for the first time he addressed him as Aachern – 'don't worry and don't put yourself in danger. Anyway, there is nothing they could get from you that they couldn't get from other people. Put up with it a bit longer; I have to.'

But the reports sometimes travelled in the opposite direction. 'We approve of the fact that the President clearly expresses his German point of view.' This sentence uttered by a high official was intended for the President's ears, and was quickly reported. 'If the President continues in this manner he will get a stone in the back of his head.' This was not intended for his ears, but yet it, too, was reported to him.

A stone at his head – it would be a matter of little importance amidst the political, economic and moral landslide of which he was an unwilling part. Every decree carried his mark – the signature of a patriot, of a protector of tradition, a guardian of the law.

A Constitutional State. . . .

'Hell and damnation!' the President screamed, flinging open doors, running through all the rooms. A Constitutional State with professional criminals in charge of rural districts, with rogues as trustees and pickpockets as Prison Governors; with a President surrounded by Generals, informers and traitors; where the Vice-President could be a mass-murderer of political prisoners, and who, as a privileged prisoner, had himself selected the victims in Buchenwald and 'splashed them off', as it was termed, with his own hands. A conspiracy of silence had protected those guilty of mass-murder – until it had leaked out that Russian prisoners of war had been among the ones 'splashed off'. The Vice-President was no longer acceptable and another took his place, a clumsy oaf whose memory was so bad that he had to make notes of the President's conversation even before he had left the room.

Dullness and stupidity connected with loyalty to the Soviets – and he was the second man in the country. Generals, informers, traitors . . . and a population of physically and spiritually starving people.

'Helots and slaves – and the President the chief slave!'

A vase, a valuable piece from the Hermsdorf porcelain factory, flew against the wall and smashed to pieces.

His wife came in.

'Have you gone mad?'

'Yes, mad . . . Don Quixote in a desert.'

'That beautiful vase!' But she did not regret it. At last, the bomb had exploded.

'Hell and damnation.'

'For goodness' sake!'

Only a few days separated the throwing of the Hermsdorf vase from the throwing of another object. But this second article, a bronze ashtray, hurled through the shattered window by Irina Petrovna, was a night alarm, a cry for help in the direction of the neighbouring house in which lived the Soviet Advocate-General.

Again official business, receptions, signatures, conferences with Councillors, discussions with the General. Days of horrible soberness – at the same time filled with the effort to hide his new awareness.

It was finished . . . but it was no longer possible to report ill or resign office. He who rides a tiger cannot dismount at will!

As usual, he went to the Chief of the Military Administration.

He had always been on good personal terms with the General, a thick-set, bluff individual, with a sense of humour and a great deal of peasant cunning. Paul had been his mentor on questions of West-European economy and also West-European thought. He had taught the General's wife to dance expertly on the smooth parquet of social life. It had started with simple things, with the etiquette of the table; once he had been sitting next to her and had held her arm unnoticed when she wanted to stand up at the introduction of a Western dignitary. She had been a grateful and an assiduous pupil, and had quickly transformed herself from a Russian village woman into a lady. The General understood and was grateful for what Paul had done.

The General was not alone. The first President of the FDGB, the 'Free German Trades Union', was in his office. This authority had come from Berlin to enforce the closing down of the allegedly Nazi-infested one-man businesses and independent craftsmen. The President was quick to point out the scarcity of workers in the country, and the impossibility of replacing chimney-sweeps, tilers, tin-smiths, cobblers and blacksmiths by untrained women.

The General took no part in the discussion.

It was clear that the Trade Union leader was concerned both with destroying the middle-classes and at the same time with getting new recruits for the uranium mines in Saxony. But why the effort? It was yet another battle against windmills. And tomorrow, or the day after tomorrow, he would no longer be there to fight. They would get what they wanted.

The discussion had been broken off without any conclusion.

The next visitor, a guest from the Soviet Union who should not be kept waiting, had arrived.

A legal authority from Moscow.

It was going to be a tough fight; that was obvious after the over-complimentary tone of the first introductory remarks.

'Herr President,' the General started, 'last summer, according to an order of the Control-Council, a number of concerns were handed over to Soviet limited companies.'

Ordered and grabbed – after the Marshal's solemn promise. 'The Soviet Union claims none of the requisitioned companies!' And then, a number of them had been handed over to the Soviet Military Administration as part of reparations, other concerns had been bought up with money stolen at the time of the Bank reform.

The lawyer from Moscow was pointing out that the transfer of property had not been entered into the register of landed property, and was asking the President to instruct the magistrates to repair this omission.

So that's what it is; after a year they have noticed it in Moscow, and now they want to get the stolen property formally transferred.

'I very much regret,' the President replied, 'that I am not in a position to comply with your request. Legally I have no right to give instructions, either to the Minister of Justice or to the Courts.'

'But it is only a question of putting the change of ownership in a legal form.'

'You are a lawyer and must know that the ownership of property can only be transferred on the basis of agreement and transfer. Both bases – an agreement on the purchase money, and the resulting transfer, are missing. You are in actual possession of the works; but that is all. According to the Constitution, questions on property of the country can only be decided by a two-thirds majority of the Diet'.

This was not what the legal expert wanted. Publicity was not desirable.

'Suppose we leave the bulk of the cases to be dealt with later, and restrict ourselves to the potash mines of Thuringia.'

Restrict? Those potash mines, the most important in Europe, of priceless value! As these mines could not be transported like dismantled machinery, they had been made into Soviet companies, like hundreds of others.

And the President forgot that the day after tomorrow, or tomorrow, he would be gone. Once more he started with a run, this time against the biggest windmill.

'Herr General, if you take the potash mines from us, I will have to ask the Soviet Union to pay back to the country approximately thirty billion in gold standard.'

Thirty billion in gold – the reparation claim of the Soviet Union had been marked as ten billion dollars in gold by the Minister for Foreign Affairs, Molotov. The General and the lawyer from Moscow leaned back in their chairs interestedly.

Dr. Paul continued:

'The available potash is estimated at five billion tons: potash can be extracted for a thousand years.'

'We shall only pay for the equipment', declared the General.

'Herr General, if you will allow me a comparison: I am in possession of a vein of gold, five yards under the surface, which can be mined by hand. Instead of the value of the gold, you only want to pay for the wooden ladder leading to it?'

A shrug was the reply.

Paul went on: 'The potash mines are encumbered with an English mortgage of nine million pounds sterling.'

'The mines have to be transferred to us without debt!'

'One can only transfer an object as one has it oneself. That is a legal maxim many thousand years old.' Then he turned to the General: 'General, I have an apple in my hand, the apple is worm-eaten. You order me to hand over this apple. I can only hand over the apple as it is, together with the worm-hole.'

'We will eat round the worm and throw the rest away!'

It was hopeless; like running in circles. The Russian lawyer suggested continuing negotiations the following day.

Next day and the day after, the President kept exactly to his time-table. He had done everything he had to do; had been as tough as ever in negotiations with the Military Administration; in the Government conference he had led a long debate, and at the end of it called his First Secretary: 'Tomorrow is the reception for the Ministers of Hesse, in the Oberhof, a golf hotel. After the State reception I shall spend a day with the guests, and then I shall drive from Oberhof to the Leipzig fair. The next conference should be called in three days time.'

He had gone home, and looked at documents and sorted out a lot of them for burning. Then, to keep everything as normal as possible, he had gone to a birthday celebration and had spent the evening there in a pleasant and relaxed company of about forty prominent people from the Party and the Government. He had done everything to conceal his intention – except for a few small mishaps, due to over-strained nerves. Perhaps he had been a little too brusque during the negotiations in the Military Administration; the instructions he had given to the office chief on the programme for the next three days had perhaps been spoken a shade too loudly; and it was a pity that Irina Petrovna should have noticed the disordered documents on his desk. But the real mishap was only to happen later – again with Irina Petrovna.

Irina Petrovna Semyonova was the most inconspicuous, most attentive, most skilful and at the same time the most uncanny of all the interpreters and secretaries; to call her restrained would be an understatement. Her face was like porcelain; there was, however, the pale scar which, when that occasional explosive violence burst through the assumed passivity, could become red as burning stigmata. In contrast with the rest of the women agents who made full use of their charm, or as in the case of the second interpreter, of their coarse voluptuousness, and who accepted debauchery as compensation for their miserable existence, Irina Petrovna lived like a nun. What was happening behind that pale forehead? Was he confronted with the one true believer? She seemed to be beyond physical fear, and yet she knew fear. Once she had come to him in terror, had screamed like an animal. She was to have been replaced.

At that time he had gone to the General, had explained that he could not have his staff continually changed, and she had stayed on.

And now the real mishap: at the birthday party everything was in full swing – drinking, dancing, and the privileged behaving like human beings still capable of spontaneous joy. Irina Petrovna was there with her impassive porcelain face and the black, tightly fitting hair. The festivities went on through the night; at two o'clock Paul left and drove home. In the meantime his wife had packed, and as it had grown late, she had left the house to fetch him. Thus, they passed each other – he in the car without noticing her, she on foot.

He arrived home.

His wife was not there; there was no note or letter from her; the still open suitcases were standing in the room, clothes lying on the floor and chairs.

He telephoned his host of the evening:

'Is my wife at your house?'

'No.'

'For God's sake . . .'

The telephone was taken from the hand of the man he talked to and he heard the deep voice of Irina Petrovna:

'I've just heard . . .'

'It is all right, Irina Petrovna, there must be an explanation; it is quite all right!'

Stupidity . . . how could he show his excitement! And Irina Petrovna had to be there ready to jump at the opportunity!

But where is she; what has happened?

And here she was at last. He was relieved, but now his strained nerves snapped. He shouted at his wife – how could she go off like that in the midst of their departure preparations? Didn't she realize what it meant to him always to have to hide his feelings, whether in his office or in social life? How could she terrify him like that?

That was the point he had reached. . . .

Irina Petrovna had left her car, had asked the sentry in front of the house to open the door for her, and had come noiselessly up the carpeted stairs. She had been standing in the open door listening to every word and had noticed the packed suitcases. Her face was no longer porcelain; the mask had fallen; the scar on her cheek blazed. On the table stood the heavy bronze ashtray. . . . The first thing Paul and his wife knew of her presence was the ashtray flying through the shattered window in the direction of the villa opposite.

In that villa was the Soviet Advocate-General; in front of the house paced the sentry; in the front garden Gnotke, the chauffeur Dietershofen and the other driver; and in the room full in the light stood Irina Petrovna. . . . She screamed, and it was no longer alarm, but the scream of a creature in deadly danger. Suddenly Paul realized that. He drew the heavy curtains to cover the windows.

Irina Petrovna fell into the arms of his wife.

'Calm down, Irina Petrovna!'

Her screaming merged into a wild sobbing. A tigress, who had torn hundreds of men both Germans and Russians to pieces in the forests of Byelo-Russia – she was now suddenly the spoilt and terrified daughter of a father who had disappeared behind the power-smoke of an execution squad. And Paul understood.

The agent's existence is limited. It was of no consequence whether she exposed him or not. After the part she had played here – witness of many hundreds of State discussions – her life as an agent was near its end.

'Do try to calm down!'

Frau Paul's quiet voice, the comfort of the closed thick, green curtains, and the stillness of the night outside, helped her to recover.

'So you are going away . . .' she stammered – 'go! go – but you must take me with you!' This was a sudden inspiration, a way out; in the land of the dead, suddenly a bright light and a shining gate. Once more she broke out sobbing. Outside in the street the car with the Russian driver was still standing. Paul went down, looked for Dietershofen: 'Send the car away and say . . . yes, but what? . . . Tell him whatever you want, only he should drive off, he need not wait for Irina Petrovna.'

When he came back, Irina Petrovna was sitting on a couch, completely broken down. His wife gave her a sedative to drink and soon she fell asleep.

The programme for the escape was now timed to the minute; there must be no further mishaps. Before the reception in the Oberhof Golf Hotel, he had to receive the Bishop of Saxony-Anhalt in his office. At the same time he must keep an eye on Irina Petrovna, both in Weimar and in Oberhof. His wife could not help in this; at dawn she had to leave for Berlin to effect the necessary preparations for their flight to the West.

In his office the bishop was sitting opposite him.

In the East it is difficult to be the Head of the Church. Some time ago, the President had helped the Catholic church in the question of Corpus Christi Day, and the Bishop of Fulda had already personally expressed his thanks for it. Now it was the Protestant Bishop of Saxony-Anhalt who had come to tell him of his worries. They were interminable. There must be no more mishaps. . . .

He had to stick it out; then he had to dictate the necessary letters arising out of the points discussed. He dictated, and was thinking of Irina Petrovna, now lying in his house. She had woken once and wanted to run off, but his wife had managed to give her another dose of *Luminal*. If only she would not wake, not regain consciousness before he got back!

He dictated and was thinking of his wife who was at this moment on the Autobahn, driving towards Berlin. Why did she have to take along so many suitcases?

Lot's wife. . . .

Don't turn round; let everything go or you will lose your face, your soul, your life. He could almost have addressed to this ecclesiastical dignitary a sermon on Moses 19 – the evil of clinging to earthly goods.

The bishop put forward a further request; one word followed the next; the minutes moved on slowly.

Irina? Ise?

His eyes were fixed on the big golden crucifix on the chest of the bishop and he broke into a cold sweat. The roles were changed. If he could only go down on his knees, implore him: Help, mercy, leave off, go quickly!

His lips remained shut. The bishop went on talking.

At last he got up; but his leave-taking was also a leisurely ceremony - two high Mandarins exchanging compliments. At last the moment came; it was over; he had got through it. A few last pressing matters; signatures, then back home.

He found Irina Petrovna half conscious, pale with bewilderment, visualizing the end. He managed to calm her down. But she had missed a conference with the General, had to telephone him.

The General heard the confused and rambling voice – still drunk from the birthday party! She explained that she was ill – in Dr. Paul's house. So at last this stubborn virgin had found her man! A matrimonial quarrel in Paul's house –

and in the morning the wife had left with her suitcases going towards Leipzig. Lottenstrasse had already informed him about that.

To Oberhof? The President wanted her to accompany him. All right, granted – the General could not refrain from telling her to enjoy herself. Young love – in Russian villages shutters are closed for eight days. Semyonova and Paul – that might work out all right – the affair of the potash mines would soon be safely nailed down. However, an open scandal with the wife would have to be prevented.

Dr. Paul went to Oberhof.

In the car Irina Petrovna was sitting next to him. She was pale – as usual. No one could guess that she was driving through a thick fog incapable of recognizing anything outside the car.

In the Golf Hotel rooms were reserved for the President. During the visit of the Western guests, the hotel resembled the NKWD-Central Office. The NKWD-Chief from Weimar had arrived. An attorney-general, also from the capital, who had been sponsored by the NKWD in spite of his former Nazi party membership and activities as public prosecutor at the Berlin special court, was purposefully spending his week-end at the same hotel. Among the porters, waiters and chambermaids, hardly one did not serve as an 'ear' for the NKWD.

State reception.

Dinner, official speeches – then the more festive part – dancing and entertainment. And Ise was not yet back from her journey to Berlin, and upstairs lay the woman to whom he was suddenly and perilously chained. Irina Petrovna, her mind still disordered from the *Luminal*, was capable of chatting with the chambermaid, or might even appear at the reception in her disarranged clothes and with her large gloomy owl-like eyes. Either possibility would be the beginning of the end and would lead to the NKWD-Chief, whose curiosity was already aroused, even if in a different direction.

Dr. Paul was leading a lady from Hesse to the dance-floor, and as in the morning with the Bishop of Halle, he broke into a cold sweat. He was laughing with some Russians, and perhaps he laughed a little too loudly.

Two representatives of the British Occupation Power were there. One, a Scottish colonel, provoked with his short skirt the naïve and continuous delight of the Russians. The Scotsman had other attractions and was closely attended by two Baltic ladies, one a Baroness, and the other the President's second interpreter. The ladies' activities redoubled after the Scotsman and his English colleague had mentioned their intention of driving to Chemnitz. The NKWD-Chief had planted his 'ladies' just to prevent any expedition in the neighbourhood of the mines. A lively contest developed between the ladies. As Paul passed through the hall to go upstairs, he observed two of them slapping each other's faces.

He found Irina Petrovna as he had expected – completely unstable, in a violently changeable mood, and capable of cancelling their arrangements. A Don Quixote who had lost all illusions and an NKWD-agent at the end of her career – two rabbits in a snake-pit. The NKWD-colonel downstairs had reason to look mockingly at him as he left the ballroom.

'No, Irina Petrovna, that is impossible!'

'Why impossible?'

It was the time at which she had to report to her Chief, wherever she was. Failure to comply with this regulation could arouse suspicion and immediate investigation. So she telephoned, asked the NKWD-exchange in the house to connect her with Karlshorst, and then asked to speak to her Chief under the pseudonym 'Kostya'. All this she did still wrapped in a cloud and with *Luminal*-dulled reactions. Paul stood next to her listening, although he could not understand Russian; he wanted to watch her porcelain face during the conversation. He felt as though he were wandering across very thin ice and could almost hear it cracking. One thing he did learn, and for the moment it came as a relief to him. The man downstairs in the banqueting hall, the NKWD-colonel, had no power over her. She was answerable not to the local NKWD, but to a higher department in Berlin-Karlshorst or even Moscow itself. This woman was not just any agent, but the chief spy.

At the other end of the line, Lieutenant-Colonel Judanov listened.

Can a wire communicate disorder, trouble, fate, a soul's

distress, the perilous entwining of two people's destinies, the atmosphere of a hotel room charged with mortal terror? It could. Irina Petrovna had nothing of importance to report. It was just one of her routine reports. The fact that she telephoned from Oberhof and had accompanied the President there was nothing unusual. It was her duty not to lose sight of the President. But there was something out of the ordinary. What was the matter with Semyonova? At times she hesitated, seemed to want to say something, yet said nothing. It was almost as though somebody was standing behind her. Inconceivable, that would have been an outrageous transgression. Judanov broke off the conversation. He stared at the wall. He had no proof, nothing palpable, but the bloodhound too has nothing but the smell in his nostrils and yet it knows the game to be there. He was alarmed.

Go to Weimar? But that was not possible till the next day, and perhaps not even then. Judanov had come back to Berlin a few days ago. Together with the Chief-Commander from T⁺ uringia, Tshuikov, Ivan Serov and the dismantling chief, Sa urov, he had driven to the Dalgow-Döberitz airport.

A very important matter.

A guard of honour of the flight division Wassili Stalin, Stalin's son, was standing at the airport in full dress. The representatives of the German Party too, Pieck, Grotewohl, Ulbricht, had been commanded to be there and fell in with solemn-looking faces.

A plane from Moscow was about to land.

A man looking like a ball, in a simple blouse, on his head a cap, got out of the plane, looked over the civilians and military, ran past the guard of honour as if it had been a wooden fence. He shook hands with Marshal Sokolovski without saying a word. Tshuikov and his confidant Ivan Serov were greeted almost with cordiality. He glanced at the Germans and shook hands with each one.

Grigorij Malenkov – Stalin's ambassador. If it were true that Stalin was only intermittently capable of working, then he was not only the hell-hound from the Kremlin but the infernal fire itself.

Karlshorst was in a state of alarm. Headquarters was in a state of panic. The telephone and wireless stations were humming like angry bee-hives.

The guard was doubled in front of the villa of Marshal Sokolovski where Grigorij Malenkov was staying. One secret conference followed another.

About twenty people, military and civilians, were sitting at the round table with Malenkov, Ivan Serov, General Tshuikov, Marshal Sokolovski.

The dismantling expert was addressing them.

He spoke for nearly an hour.

Malenkov smoked one cigarette after another, then he leaned his head against the cushion of his chair and listened with half-closed eyes. When he interrupted Saburov his voice was like restrained growling.

'Yes, yes, all that is correct. I also believe you have done your best, Comrade Saburov; but you have not concerned yourself enough with the cement, I mean the cement-works; we don't only need the cement; even more important are the machines. We need equipment for twenty-four new cement-works in the Soviet Union. Where should we take it from? There is plenty of it here in Germany!'

Saburov was again allowed to speak.

Malenkov's fat hands turned over the leaves of his scribbling-pad on the table in front of him. He restricted himself to interpolated remarks, sometimes in agreement, sometimes with an almost threatening undertone.

'I must say, Comrade Saburov, the work of the Soviet Bismuth Company in the uranium mines is inadequate; it is proceeding too slowly . . .

'And how are the quotas of the timber deliveries, Saburov?'

Saburov mentioned the figures, and added that sixty thousand cubic yards of oak had been sold to Scandinavia on behalf of the Russians.

'We must try to get still more out of Germany – everything that can be got out. Comrade Saburov! What has happened about the removal of the seven bread factories, the four margarine factories, the shoe factories and the glass works in Thuringia?'

'The factory plants are dismantled and ready to be transported, but the trains are missing, Comrade Malenkov.'

'Saburov, don't pretend to be so helpless. Don't they build rolling stock in Leipzig and Erfurt?'

Saburov spoke softly. The figures he had mentioned

necessitated borrowing from current production. 'One has to add, Comrade Malenkov, that a preliminary condition for borrowing from current production is reconstruction in the Soviet Zone. And the progress of this reconstruction is rather slow, Comrade. The shortage of cement is a large factor.'

'Oh, do stop with your cement. What do we care about German reconstruction! Haven't we also dismantled a dozen cement factories in Poland? We got them – and the Poles had to manage; why shouldn't the Germans also manage without cement factories!

'And now tell me, what about the transformer we have ordered from the Saxony Works in Dresden; can we get three million volts?'

'The work is progressing, Comrade Malenkov; the transformer will be ready for transport in a short time.'

'Aren't they the same works which also manufacture the Micro-motors for the V-weapons, and which in spite of their promises have fallen so far behind in their deliveries, Saburov?'

'Unforseen difficulties which can easily arise in the production of these delicate mechanisms, Comrade Malenkov!'

'What does that mean? What are you? – are you a specialist, or are you not? Why do you tell me of difficulties? Isn't it your job to overcome difficulties?'

Malenkov was about to break off the conference. Apparently he had been out to terrorize the dismantling specialist Saburov and had succeeded.

'Is there anything else, Comrade Saburov?'

'Yes, Comrade Malenkov, the question of the machines of the Meissner porcelain factories.' He had had to swallow so much, at least he might unload one complaint. 'The German Minister Dickermann on our instructions had the famous Meissner porcelain factories dismantled and sent to Leningrad to the Limonossov works. They are now standing there unused and are getting rusty. We have no one to work them or even to look after them.'

'Some trees cannot stand being transplanted. Instead of the white porcelain of Meissen, there are now black saucers in Leningrad.' A joke – the necessary grins were forthcoming.

The conference had taken place on the very first evening. That evening a meeting had been arranged with Ivan

Serov, at which Judanov would have to be present, either in the ante-room or at the meeting itself.

What was the matter with Irina Petrovna?

Judanov's feeling was that it was a matter of urgency. He ought to go immediately and surprise her in the Golf Hotel! But this was not possible, he would have to telephone Ivan Sergevitch in Weimar; but no, nobody else should have a hand in this game!

It was time. . . . He had to put on full dress uniform for the conference. Half an hour later he drove up to Marshal Sokolovski's villa.

Irina Petrovna?

If not the NKWD-Chief Ivan Sergevitch, he could have called the General – or Budin. Why had he not thought of Budin?

Now it was too late.

The conference had already begun.

Malenkov and Serov were alone together; later General Tshuikov and the Marshal were drawn in. When some of Serov's staff and Judanov himself were ordered into the conference room, the air was blue with cigarette smoke. Marshal Sokolovski was sitting with an icy face. The questions discussed concerned a sphere in which he was, after Marshal Zhukov, Governor-General. But against these two political favourites – Tshuikov and Serov – he was in a difficult position, and could hardly do more than answer questions which might have been put to any expert. Malenkov was reclining comfortably as at the first conference. 'Don't tell me so much about the German character; I know all about it', he said and exchanged a glance with General Tshuikov. 'I know them, the German Communists and the rest, Serov; I think as little of the one as I do of the other.'

Ivan Serov emphasized the results of his re-education work and thought it necessary to draw attention to the positive aspects of the German character. But he had to admit that the bulk of the population in the Eastern Zone had assumed a negative attitude towards the Soviet Union.

Malenkov became angry.

'I should have thought it is your task, Serov, to dispose of bad feeling against us. Those who remain intransigent will meet the same fate as the people in the Soviet Union who resisted re-education!'

But what was the cause behind the discontent of the German population – he wanted an explanation from Serov, from Tshuikov and from Sokolovski.

The presence of the Soviet Army in Germany was suggested as one factor.

Marshal Sokolovski spoke forcibly.

A total of six hundred thousand Soviet soldiers had to be fed from the territory of the Soviet occupation zone – the 3rd Counter-Attack division, the 2nd and 3rd armoured divisions, the 16th air-fleet, the 4th artillery corps, as well as the 4th Baltic Fleet with a hundred and twenty thousand men who had their permanent quarters outside the Soviet Zone, at Königsberg. These units were using up daily eight hundred and forty thousand pounds of bread, twelve thousand pounds of wheat flour, thirty thousand pounds of fat, thirty thousand pounds of sugar, three hundred and sixty thousand pounds of meat and fish, and over a million pounds of potatoes.

'The six hundred thousand members of the Red Army are consuming as much meat as three million six hundred thousand normal consumers of the Eastern Zone population', said Marshal Sokolovski.

Grigorij Malenkov spoke with suppressed anger:

'Comrades, there is an old Russian proverb: The fish is stinking from the head!'

This was an undisguised threat directed towards those at the top. Malenkov looked round the table. 'It seems to me that many are lacking both in necessary severity and in necessary talent. It also seems to me, Comrades, that some of you have neglected your duties. According to reports, staff-officers as well as soldiers occupy themselves mainly with making up parcels for their families at home.'

Again he turned to the Marshal:

'How do you explain, Comrade Marshal, the farms of which I have received remarkable details?'

Sokolovski admitted that several military staffs kept farms in order to improve their rations.

'Improve?' Malenkov asked.

His eyes flashed angrily, and he dropped his hand heavily

on the papers in front of him. Remarkable documents, which disclosed that every NKWD-department had a farm which supplied them with as much food against their normal rations. The 283rd Regiment of the Guards at Wismar alone had requisitioned three large cattle-breeding farms. A unit near Chemnitz, consisting of thirty officers, had one large farm of forty cows and twenty-five pigs. The Command at Oschatz, Saxony, held a farm with several hundred cows and pigs for the enrichment of their menu. The taverns 'Moskva' and 'Neva', both situated at the Stettiner Station in Berlin, had their own farms, as had nearly every Russian restaurant.

'Comrades . . .'

The hand which had been resting on the papers clenched into a fist. 'It is to be regretted that high Soviet officials do not know better than to surround themselves with a circle of female and male coquettes. The war with Germany has come to an end, but not the battle for Socialism. This battle will never be won by a body of Generals whose pleasure consists in meaningless debauchery.'

He came abruptly to an end:

'I must ask you to leave me now. Comrade Serov . . .'

Ivan Serov alone remained behind with the mighty one. Colonel General Tshuikov and the Marshal withdrew. The Adjutants and Judanov were waiting in the ante-room. There was no allusion to the discussion behind the padded doors. It was not necessary. Comrade Serov . . . it was the call of the gallows for the rope.

Another purge!

Lieutenant-Colonel Judanov received new orders on the following day. It was not necessary for him to attend the conference which Malenkov was holding with German Government representatives, with Pieck, Ulbricht and Grotewohl.

'Whatever is necessary has to be done!' was Ivan Serov's advice to Judanov. Necessary were arrests of City Governors like the Governor of Gera, whose wife had just ordered a series of forty dresses – evening gowns in red and green and white, skiing outfits in blue and white, lace negligées, pink night-gowns, and another forty cocktail dresses; it was necessary to purge the Thuringian Government of American influence; arrests were necessary, exterminations, and deportations to the East. The storm had to be prepared to break over the heads of the victims at one blow.

Immediately Judanov had taken his orders he hurried to his car.

Irina Petrovna?

This was the first thing he had to clear up. His suspicions had grown. Budin had been unable to contact Irina Petrovna either in Oberhof or Burgk, or in Gera or in her flat in Weimar. It had something to do with President Paul and, Paul was said to be attending the Leipzig Fair. Judanov turned towards Leipzig.

Whilst Stalin's Ambassador, Grigorij Malenkov, was speaking to the German representatives on the friendship of the people of the Soviet Union towards the German people, promising Moscow's help to the East Zone Government shortly to be appointed, and indicating that the Oder-Neisse-Line must remain the final Eastern frontier of Germany – Judanov's car drove along through the streets of Berlin, reached the Autobahn and turned in the direction of Leipzig.

At the same time, Dr. Paul was driving from Leipzig on the other side of the Autobahn and caught sight of Berlin's radio tower – one more Russian barrier to be passed.

The night before – when the velvet darkness of the Thuringian Forest was fading into grey, and the stars were already pale, as the last couples moved in a ghost-like dance in the hall of the Golf Hotel – high-born women agents and guests from Hesse and England, NKWD-officers at the tables still conversing with visitors from other Zones – Paul had gone in search of his driver Aachern and had told him: 'Will you please have the car ready in front of the hotel in two hours' time. I want to arrive a day earlier in Leipzig; but please tell no one.'

They had left with both cars.

On the open road he got out of the big official car, with the pennants of national colours, and got into his small Mercedes. His wife and Irina Petrovna got into the official car. They would go through Weimar to let the car stand in front of the house for two hours, before continuing the journey. He himself was driving in the small rather antiquated Mercedes towards Leipzig. Military controls passed the car. An NKWD-troop were erecting a mobile transmitter at the Hermsdorfer Kreuz. He wondered why. The Autobahn was quite deserted. Sometimes the Soviets stopped all approaches to the Autobahn. Had they also done so to-day? The driver wanted to turn off to Leipzig. 'No, drive on to Berlin. I have something I want to attend to; it will be soon enough if I get to the Leipzig Fair by tomorrow or the day after.'

The four hundred miles seemed interminable.

'Faster!' Aachern looked at him askance; for a long time he had been driving at too high a speed for the car. Then a car came towards them and later another. Paul was relieved – the Autobahn was not closed.

At last the radio-tower of Berlin rose up before them.

In front of him was the demolished and dishonoured city, enveloped in a veil of dust from the thousands of ruins a circle of satellite towns surrounding an extinguished crater – the Americans in Zehlendorf, the English in Charlottenburg, the French in Frohnau, the Russians in Karlshorst. A babel of confusion, an arena for secret service cohorts from all over the world, but a city which still strove to read the signs of the time, and which, with every day, raised its voice more urgently in support of the threatened values of the West – in big headlines, in discussions, in radio comments – a salvation and an asylum to the fugitive at her gate, a towering cliff amidst the sea of lost freedoms which had spread from Vladivostok to the Elbe.

The barrier.

It opened; closed again behind him. They passed the first houses of Berlin.

'Drive to the right and stop. . . . Now, let me take over the steering wheel and you get out!'

A pair of questioning eyes.

'Herr President . . .'

'That is over; I am President no longer, Herr Aachern. Wait over there at the petrol station for the official car with my wife and Irina Petrovna.'

A handshake.

'We shall meet again.'

Part Five

'*And he that was dead came forth, bound hand and
foot with grave clothes: and his face was bound
about with a napkin.*'

John 11.44

Posted to Berlin!

This time it was spoken with a Russian accent and was
meant for the sons of Social Democrats and of politicians; the
fathers were needed for government posts in the Eastern zone
– their sons were the bribes. It was also meant for political
enthusiasts who had gone through prisoner-of-war schools,
and prisoner-of-war Communists who were intended to fill
up the Party cadre; and also for Colonel Zecke, who was intended for Ivan Serov's proposed sham anti-Soviet organization.

'Berlin! *Domoy!* Home!'

The officer on duty had suddenly appeared.

'Zecke, *daway*, with all your things! Quickly – you have
only half an hour!' It all happened in such a rush that Zecke
had no idea whether he had drawn a lucky or an unlucky lottery ticket. He was the only one to go from the Ivanovo
Camp.

Ivanovo, four hundred miles north-east of Moscow – that's
where Zecke had go to. Years had passed since he had been
taken prisoner-of-war at Elsterwerda. The march to the
Rüdersdorfer chalk mountains, a few months in the military
isolation hospital at Frankfurt-on-Oder, then transported to
Moscow, where as a general staff officer and former Seeckt
officer he had gone through many months of interrogations,
then he had been sent off to the generals' camp at Ivanovo
– those were the stages of his captivity.

The generals' camp . . .

The fragments of the former 'National Committee of Free
Germany' were interned here – Field Marshal Paulus, Generals Seydlitz, von Daniels, Schlömer, Korfes, and others. . . .
Whatever their names had once been; in the world outside
they no longer had names. Generals of the army which had
decreased from three hundred and thirty thousand to ninety

thousand, and later, in the POW camp, to three thousand survivors. It was not the military bankruptcy, but the crashing
of their political card-houses which was the cause of the inter-
necine and pathological hatred, of the threats and even the
occasional undignified scuffling of these two hundred generals
living together in the same camp. Once – during the first
phase of the 'National Committee', the honeymoon with the
Soviet power – they had considered themselves almost as
equal partners, and, as the future German government, had
already started to quarrel over departments. They recognized
only too late that they represented nothing but a Soviet propaganda move, no longer of use as soon as the German
Wehrmacht was beaten and the war had come to an end.
The compulsory dissolution of the committee had been a
kind of suicide. Now, humiliated and rejected, inside the
barbed-wire fence of Ivanovo, they received the bread of
charity for 'past services' – cabbage soup and millet gruel.
From time to time one of them was required for unknown
reasons – perhaps for the gallows, perhaps for a high position
in Germany. The officer on duty called a name and the man
was sent off within the hour.

The lottery ticket . . . this time it had fallen to an outsider,
Colonel Zecke. Zecke packed his things, shouldered his rucksack, and hurried along though the camp with the officer on
duty.

Hopeless, desperate, terrified looks followed him: eyes full
of hate turned as he passed.

A gabbling voice:

'*Otshen, otshen, otshen – otshen karasho!*'

Prisrak Stalingrada . . .

'*Prisrak Stalingrada* (the ghost of Stalingrad) enters the
court and gives evidence against the Nazi criminals', the
Russian reporter had written in *Isvestia* on the occasion of
Field-Marshal Paulus's testimony at the Nuremberg tribunal.
But if Paulus were the ghost, Artillery General Walter von
Seydlitz, with his long cavalry legs, was the skeleton. '*Otshen,
otshen,*' he cried and then more loudly still: '*Otshen, otshen,
otshen, karasho* – very, very, very well!' That had been his
reply to the Russian Commander after the dissolution of the
National Committee, over which he had presided, and their
transport by lorry to Ivanovo. Ever since, these babbled

words had been the stereotyped expression of his despair.

He is going to pieces; he can't go on much longer; was Zecke's thought. They are all going to pieces. During the war they had lent their names to the biggest Russian propaganda trick. Used, abused, cast away, and confined. They played bridge, football, staggered through the camp; days, weeks, months passed, till the morning arrived when they finally lay stretched out on their bed with scrubby beard, parched skin and glaring eyes. A pistol would have been kinder!

The camp gate closed behind Zecke.

He was sitting in the train to Moscow next to the officer who escorted him. Used, cast away, abandoned – the system treats human beings as if it were God, or at least as if it were the Church of the dark ages; but there is no thought of mercy . . . there is no such thing as mercy; from Vladivostok to Magdeburg on the Elbe, mercy has been wiped off the earth.

An endless country, devoid of trees or bushes; the seemingly limitless earth was rolling away below them.

'Could you give me a light, please?' It was the major sitting opposite him.

'Who are you, oh, a German, so *domoy*?'

'Yes, *domoy*, home!' Zecke replied; it was the reply which was expected of him. But 'home' no longer had any meaning for him.

'I back from leave; am also in Germany,' the major told him, 'there in Dismantling Department, always very busy. Yes, the Germans are all good workers, one command is enough. You tell them more – they get angry. Don't like if you drunk.'

At his request Zecke lent the major his workbox with needle and thread. The major took off his uniform tunic, and sitting in a glaring red-striped shirt, sewed a white stripe on the tunic. '*Nje, Kultur*, if you travel with a dirty collar', he remarked.

A small station.

A peasant woman forced her way into the compartment. 'Scoundrels, robbers, cannibals . . .' she insulted the railway militia who had not wanted to allow her into the train. 'It's true – a dog's life and for what? And who does the train run for, if the *Kolchosniki* can't get into it? You just come to our village and have a look. After the harvest we used to have plenty of corn, but the mill didn't work. Now the mill works, but we have no corn. We have delivered up everything, we all decided that, and it's right, that's why we are there – to stick our hands up at the village meeting, and what else . . .'

'Don't listen; *prostiyi lyudiy* – simple folk!' the officer escorting Zecke remarked as the peasant woman started anew in violent terms.

'It is not really so bad.'

'Yes,' the major agreed. 'Russians always grumble, but they don't mean it.'

'You tell me then, sonny – no corn, no bread. What is going to happen, what do the high-ups really think?' asked the peasant woman.

The day dwindled away as they travelled over sticky grey plough-land.

A dim miserable lamp illuminated the compartment. Indistinct faces, puffed-up lips, feet in trodden-down army boots, a warm vapour – from the many people, from sour cabbage soup, from stale tobacco. The wheels were rolling, stopped at a siding, rolled on, stopped again, rolled on again.

Berlin, *domoy*, home. . . . If one could only believe it!

The sergeant-major who had got in at one of the stations escorted by a sergeant, really believed in it, and for him 'Berlin' and 'Home' were synonymous. Zecke went like a sea captain with sealed orders – what was awaiting him in Berlin, he did not know.

In the corner someone coughed interminably, like a death rattle. The peasant woman woke again: 'Oh, dear God: "Happy life" and "Meat combine" . . .'

'Leave it, *Babka*, you don't understand anything about it.'

'Before that, we had pigs and in the autumn we slaughtered them. Good old times.'

'Forget it, be quiet . . .'

At last, Zecke fell asleep. When he awoke it was day. The sergeant-major had managed to get hot water and offered him some of it for his tea. He was a medical sergeant-major who had been taken prisoner during the last battle for Berlin in 1945. Sergeant-Major Wustmann, asked for in a special list – not as a son, but as a brother – to bribe a Social-Democrat politician, who was needed in the Eastern Zone Government.

They arrived in Moscow, had to go to the White Russian station, there to take a train to the West. After another day and night, the town of Brest-Litovsk lay at the end of the long railway line, under a grey sky.

But Brest was not an open door into the world, nor was it one of the usual frontier crossings with perhaps some lengthy procedure of passport and luggage control. No, Brest was a prison camp surrounded by barbed wire; a watch tower, small wooden huts, a headquarters, a Camp Commandant, a wall news sheet; a camp with food distribution, with a quarantine room, with a lock-up, a parade for morning and evening roll-calls, and with work distribution. Again there seemed to be no end to such an existence.

Zecke realised this, after he had gone through the usual procedure – filling in questionnaires, bathing and delousing – and was assigned to one of the groups of repatriates and led, together with Sergeant-Major Wustmann, into one of the small wooden huts.

Zecke took off his rucksack and looked around. A rather dark hole, the floor unswept, the table dirty, through the newspaper-covered window a gloomy light filtering in.

The door to the neighbouring room was open; Wustmann had been taken in there.

'Where do you come from?' Wustmann was asked.

'From the station.'

'Fool! We didn't think you'd walked from the Crimea.'

'In any case, here I am up to my neck in it again, and I thought . . .'

'Yes, we thought too!'

There were two men in the next room. One was sitting at the table, the other lying on his plank-bed. These two were unwell, the others were out at work. Here, it was not a question of common crop-headed prisoners, but specially selected individuals with long hair – anti-Fascists and old Communists, thrown together from camps in the Caucasus and Murmansk, from Bessarabia, the Ukraine, Siberia. So far there were ninety-eight in the camp, and the transport would not leave until they had a hundred and fifty.

'And you, both of you, where do you come from?' Wustmann inquired.

'I am from Wolsk, and Paul too is from Wolsk.'

Emil Nolte and Paul Loose – Sergeant-Major Loose; like Wustmann, he had been taken prisoner during the final battle in 1945.

'And what is the matter with you, why are you on the sick-list?'

'Still a little weak from the journey.'

'But why from the journey?'

'Well, it's quite a thing, to travel on the buffers for days on end; not everyone can stand it – especially, if you haven't "been" for a week; Paul felt so miserable that we had to tie him to the buffer.'

'But why did you have to travel on buffers?'

'Well, listen to him! – Did you travel by sleeping-car? Of course, the transport leader had pocketed the fare money – for five of us – quite a nice little extra for him.'

Once more Zecke was called into an office, and after again giving his particulars he was told by the Major of the 4th Division that he would have to wait till the next transport was complete. Of course, he would not be assigned to a working party, and he need not attend re-education training.

In addition to the politicals and old Communists ordered back to Germany, there was a regular contingent who paraded in columns in the morning to go to work and came back in the evenings. For the rest, things went on as in any other camp. The cooks stole the best food. The bath orderlies stole the soap from the new arrivals and sorted out the best underclothing for themselves. The members of the ambulance corps sold the medicines to civilians. The Camp staff strutted about in impeccable uniforms with boots and shirts made to measure.

It was like any other camp.

One evening, Zecke was sitting with a man from the neighbouring room – a fellow called Koppmann, a transport-worker. He had worked in the dockyards of Königsberg as a concentration-camp prisoner, and at the first opportunity had snatched a private's uniform and gone over to the Red Army. 'Of course, I thought I'd arrive as an honoured prisoner amongst comrades . . .' Honoured prisoner – that was a cause for general amusement; there was hardly one amongst them who had not at one time thought the same.

'You needn't go on; we already know the rest!' – Koppmann continued nevertheless.

It was a report on his first camp and the 'disgusting corruption' of the German staff – a story which Zecke too knew a hundred times over. 'For *Plennij** Koppmann,' he told them, 'there was never an easy job; I never got a crust at the bread distribution, only the soft middle. Of course, I complained, and so I was hardly ever out of detention. They obviously wanted "to get me down", but when a Committee from Moscow arrived, I told myself: Now, come on – it's win or bust! In my detention cell I roared as loudly as I could and drew the attention of the Committee. When I was called out, I introduced myself – illegal work, Party membership, etc. And I talked fast – for I had known what a Party-book looked like since 1922, and what the inside of Buchenwald looked like. Well, to cut it short: the staff was dismissed, and I was put in charge.'

'The question is, whether the new staff didn't also become corrupt?'

'Of course – but not immediately, only gradually!'

'Yes – circumstances determine people's behaviour!'

'But why should circumstances let some starve and others survive, and provide them with felt-boots, lined trousers and a second, third, and even fourth portion of millet porridge?'

'I have gone through a German concentration camp, and these scars are not from the war but from the class-war. That should give me the right to have a pair of proper trousers and boots, and occasionally a piece of soap!'

'No, that's not right. What you have been in the past cannot give you any right to-day.'

'You think so? You are wearing damned well fitting trousers yourself, August!'

'That's right. And my boots are made to measure; and so that you should know everything, I too had my second portion of porridge. I suppose as senior *Plennij* I couldn't help it, but perhaps . . .'

The speaker got up, he was as lean as a whip-stick.

Everyone waited for him to continue.

'Well, August?'

*Russian for 'prisoner'.

August Meerkatz first lighted a cigarette. He knew it was heresy, but he felt that he had to speak: 'Perhaps it would have been more correct to arrive here in tattered trousers and old boots,' he said and with that remark evoked nothing but laughter from his companions who were all as smartly dressed as he.

'Yes, you are quite right, and you could not have done better in prison camp than to read the *Communist Manifesto* and Lenin's *Imperialism* and the *History of the KPdSU(B)*', Sergeant-Major Loose said to Wustmann, after everybody had gone to work and they were on their own. 'You couldn't have done better, because you've got to toe the party line. The historically right position, that's what they too believe . . .' He glanced at Zecke's door. 'They also believed that they had taken up the right position. "A dignified treatment of prisoners-of-war is guaranteed" – that's what you could read on the pamphlets from the Moscow Generals. "With us there is progress and peace", that, too, you could read. Well, if everything were as written down on paper. . . . Sometimes I really don't know which is Right and which is Left! Yet, at one time, before 1933, everything was simple – on one side the exploited and on the other side the exploiter. "Two large hostile camps, two classes directly opposed to each other", that's what Marx said, and it was as clear as glass. And if you went to sea and had nothing but your kitbag, or if you worked on a crane and your money was not enough, then you knew exactly where you belonged. Become a member of the IWW or the Communist Party, attend the cell-evenings, engage in agitation, do "red" trade-union work, and everything will be all right. Everything was simple, it only became complicated if you should touch on anything pertaining to "higher politics" and if you actually went to the country where the exploited had already been victorious. Why do I tell you all this? I have had a restless night and you are the type one can talk to. After all, each one of us has a stomach-ache sometimes, but it soon passes. What do you think about whilst riding on the buffers from the Volga to Brest, your life depending on one string – and that no more than a twisted paper tape? A lot passes through your mind. You curse your father and mother and the day you were born, and you curse the day you entered the Party.

But that is only at the beginning and is not to be taken seriously. Later you get sea-sick and you curse no longer and also stop thinking. There is nothing but flat earth when you lift your head, and the thick dust rises and gums up your eyes and closes up your nostrils. In addition there is a heart spasm which you did not get from smoking, but which you got in Wolsk, whilst heaving stones. And then there is no longer earth or dust; there is nothing, and you don't get any air, and you are afraid. Then, when the brakes shriek and the train stands still, and the pressure goes and you can again somehow breathe, you suddenly remember that your name is Paul Loose, that your name is on a special list, that you are a long-haired one, an anti-Fascist, that you are a lucky chap and belong to the privileged class and all the others, a hundred thousand others, envy you and would without any hesitation betray their Lord if they could be in your place. And then, you laugh; there is nothing else you can do; you laugh so much that you nearly choke yourself. And Emil, who is next to you, is tapping you on the head and talking to you gently. Well, then you are laughing again, but this time quite differently. And Emma, that is really something, that is the thought you are holding on to, and you can safely do it, because Emma . . . well, that does not belong here. And the wheels begin to roll once more. Emil is right really, you can't let go so near to Magdeburg! I was actually nearly home and on my way to Emma once, but something went wrong. That was after the defeat at Lübben, but they caught me again near Zossen, and I had to go through the whole smash-up of Berlin. But that is a different story. Yes, you are capable of doing anything on such a journey, and the things that go through your mind . . . finally you must also think dialectically on the buffer, and you cannot make the great Soviet country responsible if there is a sergeant who cheats his country of the fare money and lets five *Plennij* travel without a ticket. And if the sergeant has not wasted the money on drinks, but has perhaps bought a kitchen-pot for his farm, you can at least tell yourself that you too have served the holy cause and supported Soviet reconstruction, and thus there are two sides to everything!' – Loose was interrupted.

Colonel Zecke came in, with some newspapers he had borrowed. East Berlin newspapers. When Loose took them and put them away, Zecke noticed an edition of the *Telegraph* and one of the *Tagesspiegel*.

'Oh, I would like to read those', Zecke said.

'Some of the fellows must have brought them along by mistake from the station.'

Zecke took the West Berlin newspapers, but was asked to read them on the spot; so he, too, sat down at the table.

Paul Loose got out a small carved box and a penknife, sat down with the other two, and began to carve busily.

He was silent for a while, then again took up the thread of his talk.

'Karelian birch-wood,' he began, 'well, I didn't fetch the wood from Karelia myself. I was on the lower Volga and there is no wood there, hasn't been any for the last thirty years. They can't even get four planks for the coffin which everyone needs at some time. And I am not talking of our *Wojenij Plennij*, but of the Volga peasant who has to do without the four planks and go to his hole without a coffin and without a parson and without a prayer. A *Kolchosnik* who stood in front of his wretched house watching as they unceremoniously carried away his neighbour, said to me: "Without anything, just like a dumb beast; why not tie a rope round one leg and have a horse drag him off!" A *Kolchosnik*, but as you can see from his words, one with *Kulak* sentiments, a thoroughly reactionary type. The churchbells which faded away some thirty years ago are still ringing in his head, and he wants to hear a Memorial Service at the grave and perhaps still thinks that man has an immortal soul. A man of about fifty, a generation with exaggerated imagination, but they are going to die off gradually – My apologies, Herr Colonel, you too are around fifty, I suppose?'

'Yes, even a bit more – but it is quite correct, my generation is still cultivating conceptions which are gradually being depreciated nowadays.'

'In any case, what does it mean, "what everybody needs"? Four planks – to start with that – and before that, soap and toothbrush, a panama straw hat, perhaps chewing gum in his jaw and a platinum denture, and porridge in the morning, lamb cutlets for lunch, and oxtail in the evening, and clean underwear weekly, warm stockings in winter, and even in the summer, shoes without holes. Does one "need" all that – sheer romantic nonsense, as we all know nowadays . . .'

Wustmann knew it.

Colonel Zecke also knew it.

'But about this little box and the birch-wood of which it is made. Well, there is no wood on the lower Volga. And the fences have been broken up long since, and the *Kulak* houses have all been used up as firewood. But the System is not responsible for that. Only subordinate local posts, who cannot come to terms with the fact of the absence of wood and who are still in the grip of that romantic nonsense we were just talking about, and who, every winter, think that they must have warm stoves and, as there is nothing else to burn, use up the *Kulaks*' houses and fences. The System is not prepared to accept nature's conditions and will eventually grow woods – they are planned and already planted in some parts on quite a big scale by mobilized NKWD-columns; but then there were no fences; an idiotic Planning Commission had not made the necessary arrangements – for that they were shot or liquidated somehow – in this case therefore one may speak of idiots. Nevertheless, in the winter the hares came and nibbled at the newly planted trees. So there was nothing else for it but to float down the wood on the Volga. And in this direction the System is doing what it can; but in spite of the fact that with vigilance and gunpowder large crowds of "parasites" and "enemies of the people" have been exterminated, an administrative inefficiency prevents the wood from reaching the woodless south. Well, now you understand and can judge for yourself what sort of wood this is – Karelian birch – grainy, as brittle as our native alder – and, without any interference from Administrations, unguided, and in an almost anarchistic freedom, it floated down the Volga one day straight into my lap, and I have made this little box out of it, have made it for Emma.'

Both Wustmann and Zecke, who had stopped reading the newspaper a long while ago, understood everything – all about the Russian wood and a great deal more. Zecke also understood quite well that Sergeant-Major Loose liked fanciful exaggerations. If an ordinary *Plennij* had been sitting on the banks of the Volga – but an ordinary *Plennij* would not be sitting there; he would be crawling about in the mountains

on all fours breaking stones for the cement production. But it
was different for Sergeant-Major Loose. He sat there near the
water, looking across at the other bank where, since Katharina
the Second, approximately eight hundred thousand Germans
had been living until yesterday, Germans who had all
disappeared overnight through administrative methods, and
had been forcibly transported to the northern forests to fell
trees. There they would leave behind them deforested
swamps and would be buried, man, wife and child, on the
bleak edges of the clearings. There Loose was sitting, looking across the empty water and the empty land and musing
on the coming and going of nations, on war and revolutions
and administrative measures, and the waters of the great river
which carry the earth and mud and flotsam from the far
north, brought him a gift in the form of a Karelian birch-tree
or rather the stump of a Karelian birch-tree. And if an ordinary fellow travels on a buffer, after a while his hold will slack-
en and he will fall off, smash his head, and that is the end of it.
But Loose's hold slackened and yet he still held on, hanging
on to a cord of twisted paper for eight days. And at last,
here he was in Brest-Litovsk telling the whole story and
carving the story in strange designs on the outside of his
birch box.

It was one of those evenings; Meerkatz, Koppmann and a
third by the name of Schwender, were sitting under the oil
lamp: opposite them Sergeant-Major Loose. The others
were lying on their beds, smoking, dozing or sleeping. Meerkatz, Koppmann and Schwender – three men had got together for a conference, if one could call it that – and Loose
and his small box, or more precisely an event which was
marked down on the box, was the object of the conference or
investigation. The preliminaries had been dealt with. Paul
Loose, seaman, dockyard worker, Party member since
twenty-eight; called up, had been through half the Eastern
campaign and the whole succession of retreats, from Donetz
to the Dnieper, and to the Oder; and had been taken prisoner
during the last days of the collapse.

Max Schwender wanted to establish all these facts and was
trying to give to the matter the appearance of Party procedure.
'As this matter has come up, it must be clarified.'

Schwender took the birch-wood box into both his hands

and with an angry look at Wustmann, who was also sitting at the table, put it down again.

Meerkatz did not much like this imitation of Party procedure. The result of such an investigation might well have harmful consequences, and they were all too deep in the muck, too precariously hanging each on his thin thread.

'Well, all right, but I should like to look upon it as a comradely discussion.'

Schwender turned the little box round in his hands and looked at the surface divided into separate panels, all except one covered with carvings. This blank one Loose had left for his home-coming, for Magdeburg, for the apotheosis of his wanderings. When he looked at the surface still untouched by the knife, he could already see what had to be done . . . a face, and not just any face – a definitive, devoted, expectant, living face. 'The sails spread, suspended across unknown depths', all must be expressed here. 'It is time, be ready!' – all that and more, all that with one stroke, with a single sign. But now this cowhead, this drayman (but a drayman, too, is a transport-worker) is holding the little box in his hand, and Party discipline demands, and rightly so, that one reveals with the utmost honesty one's innermost secret. There is no such thing as 'hands off, this is private'.

Schwender had inspected the blank panel, showed it to Meerkatz and handed it over to Koppmann who also inspected it, then gave it back.

'Well, are you two of the same opinion?' Schwender asked.

Yes, those two were of the same opinion, and Schwender announced: 'There is nothing on it!'

'You're wrong!' Loose shouted. 'On the contrary there is a great deal, but so far only planned.'

'What then?'

'Oh a great deal . . . home, a chair, a table, a bed . . . cooking, hissing, the dampness of the earth, the light of heaven . . .'

'That's a great deal all right!'

'All compressed into one word: "Ahoy!"'

Schwender passed his hand over his scrubby head, looked at the box, looked at Loose, looked at the two others and again at the box.

Meerkatz shrugged his shoulders.

Koppmann said: 'So you want to carve the word "Ahoy".'

'Yes.'

'What do you think of it?' Schwender asked.

'Well, for a seaman and organized transport worker, that smells a bit fishy,' was Koppmann's considered judgment.

'An organized transport worker wouldn't perhaps do anything of that sort, but a seaman, well, that is a different matter,' said Meerkatz.

'Well, if you think so, August, then it is all right. Now to number two: I can't make head or tail of it', and again Schwender passed on the little box. Koppmann shook his head.

Meerkatz said: 'Yes, obviously a seaman; on which lines have you sailed, Paul?'

'Levante Line, Bremer Hansa, banana ships, from Valparaiso to Adelaide, then Malay Archipelago, the Cocos Islands . . . but at that time I still had all my hair on my head.'

'Malay Archipelago!' Koppmann groaned. 'That can really be amusing. Anyway, who started all this nonsense?' And he too threw an angry look at Wustmann.

'Leave Wustmann alone,' Loose said. 'When it comes to Party matters, he hasn't been weaned yet; he is being repatriated as brother of an SPD-party boss, he has heard of Marx and Engels, but more of Charlemagne and Widukind I believe, and in camp he has studied the Prussian vagaries from "Old Fritz" up to our Adolf; all that is a little confusing to him, so I have helped him to get it clear.'

'Well, that's nothing to do with it!'

'But it is!'

'Besides, he is no longer called "Old Fritz", that's too familiar, he is only referred to as "Frederick II". You as an Activist should know that!"

'You seem to be deviating to the left – patriotic and National, that is the line now. Wustmann, and even the Colonel next door can tell you that.'

'Don't joke!'

'It is not a joke; this is quite serious – you may think "International", but your arguments have to be "National".'

'Stop this nonsense.'

'This is dead serious and it's something you still have to learn,' Meerkatz, too, asserted. 'But now let's go on with this damned birch-wood box. A peculiar notebook. Is it art?'

'Art or no art, that question doesn't concern us here.'

'You have started from the end, with number six which is blank, that is "Ahoy!", you understand that!"

'Yes, we understand.'

'Number five is "Fire-horse" – that was the journey to this place.'

'Yes, we understand.'

'Number four is "Hundred and twenty-six per cent" – that was the cement camp. Look here, this stroke is the living standard, let's say, of a normal unemployed with all comforts, with W.C., toilet paper, etc., and down there, these thick lumps, this is us, as hundred and twenty-six per cent below the line.'

'Yes, that, too, we understand.'

'Number three is "Gone to pieces" – that was the first transit camp.'

'Yes, one can even recognize it; look here, Max'; Koppmann turned to Schwender: 'The long stroke that is one, and these two strokes, that are two, and these two are carrying away the one, holding his head and feet. We know; we have seen it happen.'

'Yes, that was the transit camp, our first, after we had arrived here.'

'Well, let's go on, what is number two?'

'Number two is "perambulator tipped over". That was at Lübben, on the road from Lübben to the West, it was in the month of May, asparagus time, and I thought...'

'You think too much altogether, and that's all I have to say about your bloody birch-wood box. Asparagus time and prams, what has all that got to do with it?'

'I told you, we should not have started this nonsense. But let him tell us now.'

'All right then, but to the point and self-critically.'

'Self-critically, I must say that I did not want to be taken prisoner. Yes, at one time I did, that was still in the Pinsk marshes; at that time I wanted to run over to the "Socialist Fatherland". But afterwards, after the happenings at the elder-bush, I no longer wanted to; ten horses could not have dragged me across. And at Lübben it was exactly the same – lose a leg, lose half your behind, but get across the Elbe. And even if you should arrive on the other side without your head, at least you're away from the Russians. That's what I have self-critically to admit. There I was as crazy as all the others. Even Magdeburg, a stone's throw away, had completely gone from my mind. Well, there we were, and the order was: Break-through to the West. And you should have seen them – people from West Prussia, from Schwerin, from Pomerania, families with wheelbarrows, with bicycles, with packed prams. A woman, on the trek from West Prussia, was lying there giving birth to a child. Prancing horses, behind us the bustle of armoured cars, and then a pram tips over – pots and pans, beds, preserves, everything scattered about the field. The woman from West Prussia moans: "Help me!" But nobody has time, everybody is running past her. And there we are, lying shooting behind a collapsed horse, behind a pram, behind burst-open suitcases, and the women always with us. We jump up again, are fired on from all sides and throw ourselves down again in the mud. But the women don't think of throwing themselves down. Always in front with open, streaming hair, and they turn round to us, and one of them shouts: "Are you cowards?" So up we jumped again, but it was useless. We were shot down and beaten up and driven together with spades, with spikes, even with clubs, and there we stood until the evening. . . .'

There we stood until the evening. . . .

So far the description was correct, corresponded with the events which had taken place at Lübben. But later, he had got away, had been snatched up again on Reichsstrasse 96, had seen the blowing-up of the Stubenrauch Bridge on the Teltow Canal, later he had manned a machine-gun in a BVG-vehicle under Major Hasse, had run away, again being snatched up, and then had met horror in the deepest Bunker of Berlin. This had left ineradicable marks on his mind; it still made him turn white and stammer.

He could not speak about that; he passed over it.

He wiped his forehead and looked at his hand, wet with perspiration.

'There we stood until the evening. And at night, marched off towards Königswusterhausen', he said; and only concealed the fact that it had been three weeks later, after the events in the Bunker and after his escape by leaping into a column of prisoners being driven through Wilhelmstrasse.

'The camp was in the Rüdersdorf chalk mountains. . . . The whole Wehrmacht was there and not only the Wehrmacht, but women and Hitler Youths and NSV-sisters, schoolmasters and retired Admirals; the whole of Germany was sitting there, hungry, thirsty, waiting. Everyone thought it couldn't get worse.

'A day came – a goods train, one hundred and twenty axles long, and all of us got into it. But what these hundred and twenty axles had to carry – I believe even old Karl Marx himself would have said: "God forgive them, being of course elements unaware of the class war". All I can say is that the waggon doors were locked at Königswusterhausen and were opened again a fortnight later, deep in Russia. And whoever had enough strength left, crawled out into the light. But how many remained lying in there – and how we had the strength to unload them – I am not going to say. The Camp Commandant came, saw our small party and saw the corpses piled up on the platform, a heap of them next to each carriage. And what did he do? – put the transport leader under arrest on the spot. To us he apologized in German for the bad transport conditions. It was neither hunger nor thirst, nor the fact that we had been lying on bare planks in our own filth, nor that the vicious transport leader had been arrested; it was the Commandant apologizing to us stinking beings with tears in his eyes, either from anger or from shame, that turned me upside down; I had to howl. This Commandant really did everything to get us on our feet again. From morning till night he was running about the barracks taking care of each one of us and literally spoon-fed us into well-being. After that we worked in a steel works without asbestos protection, with wooden slats burning up under our feet; two shifts a day and night without a break, a mad drudgery, and even if you were a bull of a fellow, in a fortnight's time you were ready for the mass grave. Well, that is already another chapter, that was reparation work. . . .'

'I think we haven't got so far that we are blaming the Russians for our dead!' This remark came suddenly from a grey-haired former Trade-Union Secretary who sat up importantly on his bunk.

'Nobody is blaming them, but Paul can't say that they got into a char-a-banc for a happy excursion into Siberia. We all know that prisoner-of-war camps are no child-welfare centres.'

'We should know things that concern us – wars of aggression, concentration camps, shooting of Jews, a long list, there is enough to talk about.'

'You are quite right, but what Paul is saying . . .'

'He should not talk about it.'

August Meerkatz turned towards the grey-haired man: 'Listen, Atze, haven't you spoken about your camp in Siberia? You told us that the East Prussian women there died like flies. Soon we are going to Germany . . .'

'I hope we are – but with talk like that things could easily go wrong.'

'So that's why you're so excited.'

'I am an old SPD-man – on a special list, because I am for the unification of both parties, Socialists and Communists, and I don't want my way blocked by talk like that.'

'It is even more necessary then that you differentiate between principle and accident. We are going to Germany and if we are asked about sons and brothers and fathers . . . what are we going to reply – we don't know, we haven't seen anything? Are we going to plug up our ears? The questions will be there, despite plugged-up ears and hardened hearts, and if we are not going to answer them, we can't answer anything at all in Germany. We know what we have seen; we know there has been inhumanity . . .'

'There cannot be inhumanity in a country where exploitation has been ended.'

'If you tell that to the soldiers' wives in Berlin and the Ruhr, you will only harm your cause. What has been done cannot be undone by denying it. Someone said, "the East Prussian women died like flies", and that is literally true. And in the asbestos factory and the coal-pits and the forests, our people are breaking down in hordes. But one must believe in the will to progress even if the reality looks otherwise. Orders from above are sometimes misunderstood by those below, and sometimes interpreted disloyally. Everywhere there are loyal and disloyal followers. There was Sister Schura who stole cotton wool; but there were also Sisters Tanya and Sonya who carried out in one night from the hospital for contagious diseases twenty-two corpses (I counted them myself) and one hundred and eighty buckets with typhoid excrements; and as there were no rags available, they washed those buckets with their own hands. There was the cruel Transport Leader, but also the Commandant who so assiduously looked after the prisoners. And another example: on the way to be de-loused one of us fell into his own filth because of weakness, and not only because of weakness, he was not only starving, he was ill from utter loneliness and degradation – and the Russian *Matkas** – if I didn't have to think as a Marxist I should say there was light in their souls – they saw this staggering misery and consoled him: "*Nitshevo . . .*" they said, "never mind, never mind, sonny", they repeated and helped him up again.'

Meerkatz broke off. The door opened. The senior prisoner entered, and another camp informer was with him. 'I saw your lights still on; so I just came in.'

His eyes looked round. The bunks were all occupied except four, and their occupants were sitting at the table. He stared at the little box on the table. 'Peculiar box; and you are sitting round it as if it were a monstrance, that's the correct name, isn't it? But what is this thing?'

'A snuff-box, you can see that, can't you!'

'Rather big . . . I only thought there must be something the matter because the light is on so late.'

He went again, looking once more at the box and at Loose.

'Well, there'll be an end of that too,' someone was saying.

'It's all the same how one arrives at agreement with oneself,' Meerkatz said, 'and if you do it with a penknife and a piece of birch-wood and achieve clarity over "fire-horse" and "126%", "Gone to pieces" and "Perambulator", that's all right. As we have gone through the whole lot to number two, we can now listen to number one.'

'Yes, number one is still missing.'

'After all, that was the reason why we sat down here. We might have just been amusing ourselves.'

'There is no need for Paul to amuse us.'

'Is everyone going on nattering?' Schwender turned over his shoulder towards Nolte who was crouched on his bunk. What had started as a matter of serious Party vigilance,

*Women—here nurses.

seemed more and more to slip off into general entertainment. 'We could just as well have arranged for a poker evening,' he grumbled.

'Yes, much better.'

'Well, come on, Paul, number one now!'

'Yes, that was before, as I have already said, in the Pinsk swamps, in the neighbourhood of Olevsk and Slavetshno, that's where I got my horror of the Russians. Number one, that is the "Crack".'

'There is hardly anything on the wood here; anyway, that's where you got your class-hostile crack from!'

'I said: horror!'

'No prejudices', Meerkatz warned.

'Something cracked inside me at that time.'

'Well, tell us about it.'

'The swamps of Pinsk during the retreat. The middle of the front had already been smashed, but as soon as we had got to a standstill, our old boy had plans again – back to the East. Well, he comes up to us, that was in Olevsk, and I only hear: "Volunteers for a scouting patrol!" So I said to myself: "Here is your big chance, this is the moment!" and I volunteered. The next morning, while everything was still grey, we set off towards Slavetshno. As N.C.O., I was in charge. Well, the direction was all the same to me; as far as I was concerned it could have been Gomel or Vitebsk or even Moscow. Anyway, I was going to find Ivan, and then after the first awkward ceremonial it would be over, I would be demobilized, at home welcomed. So we were trotting through the haze, and I was looking for a tree or a large bush in which to hide till evening. But there was no tree; far and wide nothing to be seen. We all rested a little and then we tramped on. As we got up, I said, "Damnation, now we're for it, I have sprained my foot!" The others had to believe me. "No, don't worry about me," I said, "I can manage." And so I limped along about twenty yards behind them. The sun was rising, a glowing red, and there was still nothing. No woods, no trees, not even a bush. And then, right under my nose, suddenly there was a bush, stretching out its branches to the sky. There, I thought, that's my elder-bush. Well, the others went on and I was going to sit down for a little while. And there I was sitting, and had just decided the position couldn't be better, when Ivan appeared. In front of the others, about six or eight men sprang up from the ground. And, God help them, our boys were quite confused. One shot was fired and that was all. The Russians, their machine pistols pressed closely to their bellies, clubs and spades lifted, were already on top of them. There was nothing else they could do but raise their hands. They did – and that wasn't all. The little Hamburger, a smart fellow, spoke a little Russin, he lifted his hands high above his head and roared *"Stalin sdrasdvuitye!"** and he roared *"Voshd sdrasdvuitye!"* Another shouted: "Hail Moscow". But there he got *"sdrasdvuitye"* with a club on his head. And the other one got "Hail Moscow" with a spade through both his eyes. A hand grenade exploded, and the Russians didn't get it all their own way at first; but they were far too many. For a long while the Hamburger was lying on his back, next to him the student from Leipzig. And I saw everything, *bolshoi Stalin*; I saw them finishing them off, the spades on the throats of the fallen. And I still behind the bush . . . as a class-conscious element I had wanted to go over to their side. Yes, you think – but what you do is a different story. They were already bending down, thinking: "Let's take off their wrist-watches and perhaps their boots." But then my machine pistol was spurting out of the elder-bush, and I didn't know any more. I leapt up and threw hand grenades, and if I could have done it, I would have exploded myself. One was falling over, and another one, and another was crawling about, another running away. And I was roaring like ten naked savages. And I heard a chirping behind me and right and left of me; they were shooting at me, but I got through and finally I joined my troop again. And I had actually wanted to go over to their side, had wanted to get to the great Homeland. And only then, as I thought of it, something cracked within me. . . .'

'It cracked.'

'Yes . . .' Koppmann said.

'Hm . . .' Schwender grunted.

Meerkatz looked at Schwender and Koppmann, and there was a gleam of understanding in his eye. Those two were themselves much too involved, too near the filth and sweat

*Good-day, Stalin.

and groans, to be able to give an answer to the dilemma between class-consciousness and the urge for self-preservation. Meerkatz knew the only possible answer which theory would have in such a case. It was easy for him to imagine a different three-man-board. A real *Troika*, as it had been in Moscow only a short while ago, and was functioning now in Berlin. He had a vivid and detailed picture of their forms and faces; he knew them, and quicker than the blinking of an eye, in the case in question the verdict would have been. 'Of course, you should have come out from behind the bush and raised your hands!' And to Loose's obvious objection: 'Nothing else could possibly have been considered!' Meerkatz heard the verdict, could even hear it in Saxonian dialect, as clearly as if it had been spoken in the room.

'Well, Schwender; well, Koppmann?' he turned to his two colleagues, as neither of them said anything.

'Tell us, Koppmann, what do you think of all that?' Schwender was saying.

'Yes, difficult . . . Let us leave the matter alone. It is up to Loose to come to terms with it', Meerkatz said. He was quite content that the affair had turned out that way.

'Sometimes things just do crack,' he added, and with that the matter was apparently settled. To complete the story they learned that Loose, after returning to his troop, had been promoted to the rank of Sergeant-Major and had received the Iron Cross First Class. He had never thought of going over to the other side again.

'It's very late, and tomorrow morning we have to be at the station'.

'Yes, we'd better turn in.'

Germans, Hungarians, Croats, Austrians, Italians . . . thousands of them paraded every morning to be marched off in long columns to their various places of work. There were building sites, gravelpits, mechanized brick-works and primitive hand brick-works. Everywhere – in the gravel-pits and clay-pits, at the furnaces, at the concrete and cement machines, on the lorries and in the long caravans of the *Panje* carts, close-cropped *Plennijs* were working. Many of them from the repatriation camp worked in the enormous yards of the railway junction where the Russian wide gauge ended and the western railway tracks began. Brest-Litovsk Station, with its interlocked wide and narrow tracks, achieved for the first time under the German-Soviet Pact special importance as a junction for corn, sugar, naphtha, butter and other supplies that Russia was sending to Germany. But now for years the transports had been rolling across the Oder and through Poland, to stop with shrieking brakes after their five hundred mile journey at one of the hundred tracks of Brest Station. Goods trains fully loaded (sometimes twenty a day) by whole brigades of German prisoners-of-war as well as Russian workers.

'Hey-up! Hey-up!'

'Soviet transport is the most progressive in the world. The reparation transports require redoubled efforts to bring the transport battle to a victorious end!'

August Meerkatz's look was fixed on one of the banners hanging everywhere; the words on it formed no image in his mind. It was nothing . . . in his eyes no more than a glance into the empty sky or across the wide countryside or over the heaped-up rubbish of this station.

'Hey-up! Hey-up!'

With crowbars and ropes and with 'Let go; careful!' and 'Ready!' the party had managed to get a turret-lathe on to the board and let it slide slowly downwards. There it stood now, canted a little forward. 'Well, off we go, you hang on to the back and press on its tail, and we'll lift up the front, Careful, it'll tip . . . *Nitshevo*, it'll go: it must go! Hey-up! Hey-up!' And the machine, half a ton in weight, moved over as planned, A few parts got bent, a couple of levers broke off. '*Nitshevo*; could have been much worse! Let's get on to the next. Remember our quota.'

The next was a boring machine, after that a steam hammer.

'Co-operative property' – it is all written down. Cars with bent axles, a lathe with broken-off levers, a press with missing parts, and power looms, milling machines and electrical apparatus, standing in rain or sun, in dust and wind.

Meerkatz was absent-minded.

'You are working for yourself . . .' The words which were carried into the room through monster loudspeakers were nothing but a meaningless roar. August Meerkatz thought of

Loose's story about the birch-wood box, also about the epilogue smouldering underneath, these thoughts adding to the long argument which was going on inside him.

'A higher standard of work! Accomplish the quota and surpass it . . .' Yes, accomplish and surpass – we have already surpassed ourselves for a long time, in the will to make reparation, in self-imposed tasks, in submission. We have surpassed ourselves so much that we have shrivelled up, have become skin and bone, not only we, the Committee Members, the Camp Leader, but everyone.

And over there about twenty carriages loaded with human cargo from the interior of Russia are standing next to dismantled machinery, next to goods from current production and piles of scrap metal, squeezed in between empty trains from the East. A part of the million repatriated German prisoners promised by Molotov. Nameless, worn-out wrecks, lying huddled like dead flies. Some, hollow-cheeked, in tattered blouses, hobbled along the railway tracks, with saucepans, to fetch drinking-water. A human cargo of tuberculosis, jaundice and malaria – the only cargo now to travel back to the West in the waggons which had brought railway bridges, steam-generators, radio stations, laboratories, firebrigade ladders, radiators, wash-basins, carpets, church-windows, old paintings and manuscripts, rainpipes, typewriters, and tools.

But it was not those consumptives lying in the carriages – others lay on Meerkatz's conscience. The sudden emergence of a face from former times – the unfortunate Auschug, once a close friend from his Berlin cell; a face from a submerged and almost forgotten time, lying in the isolation ward of the camp. And one cannot simply ignore his arguments, one has to disprove them.

'Slavery, caste-system, stupidity,' Auschug said.

Reminded of the ultimate aim he gave a hollow laugh. Well, he was embittered – he had gone through the whole process of democratic 'construction', until one evening it had tipped him out at Brest Station, a dying man. The transport had come from Berlin, to be exact from Oranienburg, from the concentration camp which used to be there, and, in fact, still is.

And yet, despite all, one must go on!

'*Tovaritsh* Meerkatz . . .' Meerkatz was called to the dispatch room for new instructions. More carriages for unloading were assigned to him. When he came back he had to get his team together.

Some of these he found beside the carriage with the 'hardly worth looking at' emaciated wrecks, as one said.

'All of them saboteurs!' another one exclaimed.

'They don't want to do reparation work and have made themselves ill. They have starved themselves and then stewed up cigarette ends and drunk it, so that they can get home before their proper time!'

'Swigging cigarette water?'

'And refusing to eat!'

'Trains full of saboteurs – and they are being rewarded and sent home!'

'Now you've talked enough rubbish,' Meerkatz said. 'Don't stand about any longer – we have our quota; back to work; *daway!*'

Perhaps thirty goods trains were standing one next the other in what seemed to be a hopeless block. This station had daily to cope with as much as a medium-sized seaport, but without any modern loading equipment, not even ramps. All they had were crowbars, hemp – and wire-ropes, planks, and for the rest – brute human strength.

'*Daway* . . .'

'You are working for yourself; the harder you work, the richer the Soviet will get,' he shouted through the loud-speaker.

Daway . . . Hey-up! Hey-up!'

Whilst Meerkatz with his party was unloading rails from the lorry at Brest Station, Colonel Zecke was standing opposite the Soviet Major with the pinched face in the office of Department No. 4. A thick portfolio was lying on the Major's desk – Zecke's file! He hardly looked up:

'*Ssaditje!* Take a seat!'

The typist sharpened pencils.

The interrogation started with the same questions he had answered a hundred times before and which had a hundred times before been written down. Social origin, education, cadet corps, service in the first world war, joining the Reichswehr, Rapallo and the secret German-Russian treaty, co-operation of the Reichswehr with the Red Army.

The interrogation came to a stop at Rapallo.

Rapallo and Tauroggen – the association of the Rapallo treaty in 1925 with the Tauroggen truce between General Yorck von Wartenburg and the Russian General von Diebitsch on 30 December 1812, was important to the Major, and he needed Zecke's acknowledgment of the parallel.

'Historical situations are nearly always unique; it is difficult to draw parallels,' Zecke said.

'But you do recognize similarities between these two treaties, Herr Zecke?'

'One can admit a similarity between two situations', Zecke replied.

'Good,' the Major said – it sounded like a reproof.

'General Yorck von Wartenburg, who in Prusso-German history is a hero and liberator, was a model for Bismarck as well as for the German politicians who signed the Rapallo treaty. The spirit of Tauroggen lived on at Rapallo; that same spirit was still alive at the time of the Hitler-Stalin Pact, but later Hitler turned away from it.'

'That seems to be taking a great deal for granted, Herr Major.'

The Major looked angry.

'Listen: without Yorck von Wartenburg and the treaty with the Russian General Diebitsch, no rebirth of Prussia . . .'

He had only got that far when the door opened and a Soviet Colonel entered. The Major and the typist stood up, Zecke too. The Colonel stopped in front of Zecke, sketched the indications of a bow, and said: 'Yegorov.'

Zecke did not immediately understand; then he realized that the Colonel had introduced himself: most unusual.

He, too, bowed: 'Zecke.'

They all sat down.

The interrogation continued.

'Without Tauroggen no Prusso-German Reich, no Bismarck and no German Empire', the Major said and continued: 'Without a new Tauroggen, without honest and close co-operation between Germany and the Soviet Union a rebirth of Germany is impossible.'

Colonel Yegorov broke in.

He had icy grey eyes, blond hair, an intelligent face and spoke German with a slight Slavonic accent.

'At that time, Napoleon had crushed Prussia. Are you not of the opinion, Herr Colonel Zecke, that the discussions of the Russian General Diebitsch and the Prussian Yorck von Wartenburg proved the turning-point for Prussia after the Napoleonic war? Are you not further of the opinion that the state of Prussia, humiliated and torn as she was after the truce of Tilsit, is desperately like the state of Germany after 1945, and is it not obvious that German-Soviet co-operation would also bring advantages in Germany's present case?'

'Are you speaking to a prisoner-of-war, Colonel Yegorov?'

'I am speaking exclusively to you, Colonel Zecke! I am speaking as one soldier to another, as one officer to the other, as one human being to another, and I should like to hear your personal opinion.'

'As Colonel Zecke, soldier, officer and human being, I must reply: the Russian General von Diebitsch negotiated with the Prussian General Yorck von Wartenburg from power to power. Yorck's army could have turned the balance in the struggle between the Russian and the Napoleonic armies at a historical moment. The situation for Prussia at that time was fundamentally different from Germany's to-day.'

'What, Colonel Zecke, does that fundamental difference consist of?'

'If you are speaking to me, Colonel Yegorov, as a soldier and a human being, and not as conqueror to the conquered, it is hardly necessary for me to describe the situation of my country occupied by the Soviet army; nor to point out the sad role which would be expected of a General Yorck to-day. I am far from putting Napoleon and Stalin on the same political and ethical level, nor would I put Napoleon and Hitler on the same level, My respect for Napoleon is too high. But there seems to be a parallel. Napoleon's position after the Tilsit truce is at least comparable with Stalin's – except that Napoleon did not evacuate the populations of large territories under cover of night. Considering the Oder-Neisse-Line it is difficult to speak of a new Tauroggen and of German-Soviet co-operation. You, Colonel Yegorov, are a soldier of a great power which has presumed on its military victory to annex a third of my Fatherland and to dispossess and throw out the populations of the annexed territories. What would you think in my place, Colonel Yegorov, of a soldier who could even think of a new "Tauroggen"?'

The Major did not conceal his fury.

But Colonel Yegorov did not seem to notice. He remained calm and replied courteously: 'Other German officers, your comrades, not only think of a new Tauroggen but have moved towards it. Would you deny Marshal Paulus's patriotism and responsibility to his people?'

'Field-Marshal Paulus will have to come to terms with his own conscience. To my mind, only a fool or a scoundrel would apply the conditions of the truce between Yorck and Diebitsch to the present situation of Germany.'

'In which category do you count Herr Paulus or Herr Pieck?'

'I will leave that answer to you, Colonel Yegorov.'

The Major could hardly contain himself. He fretted like a chained-up bulldog.

'I admit,' Colonel Yegorov continued in the same calm voice, 'that certain conditions do not exactly seem to speak for Soviet-German co-operation, although one must take into consideration the world's political framework. Only one third of Germany is Russian, two thirds are occupied by the Western powers. A number of conditions favour German-Soviet co-operation. From the German point of view, which circumstances seem to be unacceptable?'

'Germany must obviously make reparation for the damage which under Hitler she has done to your country. On the other hand, I would suggest – a suspension of the Oder-Neisse-frontier; restitution of the annexed provinces and assistance with the return of the evacuated population. . . .'

The Major had come to the end of his tether. He struck with his fist on the table and shouted: '*Idi k tshortju*, go to hell, *jub tvoi* . . .' This unexpected outburst brought the conference to an end.

Colonel Yegorov got up, bowed.

'I thank you, Colonel Zecke. By the way, the London conference will take place shortly. I will see to it that you obtain the newspapers reporting it.'

Zecke was dismissed; was again outside, not knowing what

to make of it all. *K tshortju* . . . that was honest; but what did everything else mean? He did not know what to make of the over-polite Yegorov.

Days passed. Zecke was summoned to no further interrogations. He saw a German lieutenant march into the camp in front of forty men. Rows of four, equal step, uniforms from captured stocks of the former labour corps. They even had a flag, and they were singing: 'Higher and higher . . . despite hatred and scorn . . . each propeller sings as it whirrs . . . we protect the Soviet Union. . . .'

With those forty men, trained in the Soviet Union for the people's police, the repatriation list was complete. Zecke had not yet been struck off. His name was still on the list and he was still with the crowd of repatriates when they were marched off to Brest Station. He had been given all the newspapers reporting on the London Conference which had been broken off without result – not only the East German newspapers but also those from West Germany with commentaries from France and England.

They were standing on the station. All of them. . . . Zecke, Koppmann, Meerkatz, Sergeant-Major Wustmann, also Sergeant-Major Loose, over whom the mounting storm about his birch-wood box had passed. They waited. The empty goods waggons which had arrived from the East with their human wreckage, had already been switched on to the departure track. Two passenger carriages were being attached to the back of the train for political Activists from the repatriation camp. At last they were allowed to get in. From his seat Zecke saw the miserable figures getting out of the wide-tracked train and taking their seats in a carriage of the German width track. Some of them could only move with assistance. Some could stand on their feet, but could not walk without being supported; others had to be carried. All of them were ill, some dangerously, some on the point of dying. It was only the thought of being buried in their native land and not in Brest, which gave them the strength to hold on. The train stood for a long time. The change-over had been of no use to those poor wretches. They had to get out again and stand between the tracks. To be left behind, here at the last Russian station, as 'unfit for transport' was the worst that could possibly happen, and so even those who could hardly lift themselves upright climbed out of the carriages and took their place in the file; but they had been mistaken, it was not a question of a last inspection. Brest did not have enough workmen to replace those who were dying. Among these recruits, dismissed from the camps in the East as unfit for work, might be some who had recuperated after one or two weeks' rest. There they stood, their knees straightened, their chests thrust out, trying to make a good impression. The Camp doctor had already discussed the matter with the Transport Leader over a glass of Vodka, and both of them now walked along the lines. It was not necessary for the men to strip off their tattered rags as they did for the periodical examinations in the camp. There was no question here of the usual qualifications – fit for work I, II, III, or unfit I, II, III. If a pair of eyes were not yet completely sunk in their sockets, or a head not so emaciated that the coronal sutures could be seen under the skin, the doctor would expose the chest and pinch the skin over the breastbone; if there was so much as a trace of underlying fat tissue, a worker replacement had been found. A few days in hospital and some extra portions of *Kasha** and the patient would be ready for one of the working parties. After a number had thus been picked out, the rest were allowed to get into the train again.

Finally this too was over – the chosen stood miserably between the tracks watched by the political Activists in their carriages. The man with the red cap: the departure signal. The wheels were rolling, the train was gliding out of Brest Station, rolling on a track of German width, driving to the West.

Incredible . . . neither the consumptives stretched out on the bare planks of the goods waggons, nor the Activists in the passenger carriages could quite take it in, least of all Zecke. There are Potemkin villages – perhaps there are also Potemkin journeys on tracks of Western width? But the river spanned by an improvised bridge which they crossed the same night, was said to be the Vistula, and the gaunt city of ruins which slid behind them in the darkness was undoubtedly Warsaw. The journey took them through barren country, past depopulated towns, stations still with the names in

*Millet porridge.

427

German. And nothing happened; no order overtook them; nothing made them turn back.

A grey morning; wet streets drowning in mud.

The wheels rolled slowly. Alongside the train women were running, German women, and they called,: 'Have you got bread?' Surely they must see – forty carriages with repatriated prisoners of war, starved, emaciated, ready for their graves. They saw and knew it and yet they still begged, and threw themselves down and wrestled with a pack of rickety children for a piece of dry bread which a *Plennij* had thrown out. That was unexpected; and to those who watched – Zecke and Meerkatz and Wustmann and the *Plennijs* through the open doors of the cattle trucks – it seemed worse than anything they had experienced in captivity.

They got out of the train at Frankfurt-on-Oder. Zecke wandered with the others across the wooden bridge to Gronenfelde. The Square was decorated for the new arrivals, flags were waving, and there was an enthusiastic speech of welcome from an SED-man from Berlin: 'You are now again on German soil. Not everything is as you might have imagined it. There is still a great deal to be done. The German people have incurred a great debt and we must work it off. That's why we are proud of you, because you have already begun the work of reparation and you also know what a systematized economy is . . .'

Zecke received his discharge papers, stood at the station beside the others, who for the first time were allowed to buy their own tickets and go off on their own, without escort. The train for Berlin was running into the station and everyone was climbing into it when a hand was put on his shoulder and a soft voice said: 'You must come along once more to the *Budka*,* Colonel Zecke.'

You must come along, Colonel Zecke. . . . A door was shut, a door in a boarded-up carriage on the German track; and then later on the Russian track, the door of the 'Black Raven' which had brought him from the White-Russian station in Moscow to the Lubyanka prison, the door to the solitary cell in which the light was turned on day and night.

No difference between day and night, between days and

*Guardroom.

weeks. Periodically the march through subways to interrogations – still the same – cadet corps, first world war, second world war, Reichswehr, Rapallo, Hitler, the 20th of July. Back through the subways, and the guard stops, offers you a cigarette and a light (he has orders to do this), and you don't know whether this is the moment when time will snap and you too will be extinguished.

Again days, weeks, months.

No human sound, no human face. . . . If a door opens, the passage behind it is empty. Passages, steps, underground communication doors, and silence is your companion. This time the points are shifted differently. You arrive in a yard. There the 'Black Raven' is waiting, carries you to the station. You can hear the puffing of the engine; you get into a carriage, a boarded-up box. The train is roaring along below a steel-grey sky. You can see the sky and distinguish between day and night; light trickles through the shutters. Days and nights, outside howling snowstorms, then silence and the journey continues over frozen earth.

A camp, an officers' camp. . . .

Ghostlike figures muffled up in rags stagger through knee-high powdery snow, are standing at the end of the camp fence, staring towards the West over twisted barbed wire posts; always towards the West. There is still a glimmering spark within them; they still have hope; and you too are staring again, standing next to the others, a scarecrow with fluttering coat-tails; you are staring through the falling white flakes and are thinking of Germany.

Is there still such a thing?

'*Daway*, Zecke, transport!'

Once more the boarded-up box; outside the snow is melting into water; the train journey takes many days. At Yaroslavski Station in Moscow the 'Black Raven' is waiting. At the end of the journey through Moscow's streets the Lubyanka is waiting.

The Lubyanka, house of silence; at one time a large business house, now a prison amidst Moscow's sea of houses. A prison full of peculiarities and contrasts, a caricature of life outside, of life and death. There is the solitary block with single cells; there are whole buildings with interrogation rooms tightly screened with green curtains. There are blocks with mass-cells, also with mass-tortures – at one time the *Valutshikis*, hoarders of currency and hidden gold, were put in those same cells and slowly suffocated by piped-in fumes until they revealed their hiding places. The *Valutshikis* were succeeded by political prisoners who, watched by doctors through thick glass panes, were driven to confessions and self-accusations. There are suits of offices with concealed lighting. Studios with skylights and drawing-tables and diligently working designers. Ramsin, condemned to death and then pardoned, had at one time worked with a staff of engineers in such a department and had designed plans for the industrialization of the country. There are also apartments with GPU-attendants who are dressed like valets and behave as such. There are cabinets with heavy oak doors which suddenly open after weeks and reveal to the starving inmate a gaily decorated table laden with delicious food. There are always surprises, each time different.

Zecke went back to the Lubyanka.

This time not into the solitary cells but into an apartment – a study with a sleeping alcove, his own bath next door. Bookshelves: Meyer's Encyclopædia, an old edition, Clausewitz's *On War*, Delbrück's *History of the Art of War*, Rüstow's *History of the Infantry*, military journals and military annuals from the USA, from England and France, Fichte's *Speeches to the German Nation*, many books on German and Prussian history, some recent books: Clemenceau and Churchill, reports of the Casablanca Conference, Teheran and Yalta – but no belles-lettres. Every morning he received the latest newspapers, German, French and English. When he drew the thick green curtain back, there was no window – only a white-washed wall. His fate seemed finally sealed. It no longer meant anything to him when the guard said: 'There's no longer any need for that' when he began to straighten his uniform. And again it meant nothing when, walking through the subway, he was suddenly told to stand still, and instead of the expected detonation a door sprang open and he was confronted with a woman dentist in a white overall who silently examined his teeth. Apparently even the dead had to be prophylactically treated against tooth-ache.

He read newspapers, occasionally referred to one of the available books. He developed an almost professional interest in military and political events in the world outside.

Why should he be interested at all? Why did he still play the game? He had been told too much: it was impossible to think of a return. His life had to end there in the marked-out circle.

But his life did not end. Death had left his scythe outside and let him go on alone. Why continue? Why didn't he himself bang the door shut? Religious reasons? Perhaps; once he had wished that he could look down from a star after his death. Here it was; his wish had been fulfilled.

Once more he was called out for an interrogation. The walk through many corridors, many doors, staircases, a labyrinth of empty passages. The examining room and the usual GPU-official; next to him an Army officer from the fourth division of the Red Army. He recognized him immediately, Colonel Yegorov. Yegorov had been promoted, he was now Major-General. Yegorov got up, with a stiff bow; Zecke too bowed. It was as though it had been yesterday that they had stood opposite each other in Brest-Litovsk Camp.

'Take a seat, Colonel Zecke.'

Zecke and Yegorov sat down at a round table. The GPU-official remained behind his desk, half hidden behind the dimmed desk lamp. The thick 'Zecke' file remained unopened in front of him.

It was the first interrogation for a long time – the first of a series which were to take place nightly – and they were hardly interrogations, rather dicussions concerning Germany and the Berlin of this period.

What was Zecke, and what did he mean to the polite Yegorov, what was his function in Yegorov's researches? He was a specimen, a nearly extinct specimen, but politically he could again become a determining factor. He was the chemical in the retort, the object under the concave glass of the microscope, he was the sample that indicated possible reactions from parts of the German population, a key to the limits of their endurance, to the amount of pressure which could be exerted on a population without explosion. Zecke was all that – a human sample always accessible for observation. He reacted without reflection, without hope and without trepidation. He was an inhabitant in the abode of departed souls from which no return was possible. Thus he spoke at each of the nightly conferences as though it were his last hour, replied to questions as if answering a divine judge. He did not weigh his words, nor did he soften any criticism of the Soviet system, and that made him even more valuable.

Major-General Yegorov had reasons to congratulate himself. Personally he had no ill feelings towards Zecke, and at Brest-Litovsk he had not wanted to harm him. He had only written an objective report on the interrogation which indicated that Colonel Zecke at liberty could be a potential opponent, and that he seemed capable of giving important information. He was surprised when a year later – just at the beginning of the political battle for Berlin – he found the 'Zecke' file on his desk and learned that Zecke was still in captivity in one of the camps behind the Urals. It was he who had given orders for him to be transported to Moscow and given special treatment.

All Zecke said was permeated with his education, his experiences, his whole background and he spoke from the bottom of his heart. The theme was Berlin, the fate of the city and the possible consequences in the arena of world politics. And Zecke was well informed – no less well than the Kremlin, Downing Street or the Quai d'Orsay. And he was more concentrated. For him there was no diversion. His look came from the yonder side, untroubled by vanity or personal wishes, unencumbered by hope. His telescope was adjusted towards one single object; but whatever concerned this object was open to him – secret reports, newspapers, illustrated magazines, confiscated documents from the Berlin magistrates, even piles of stopped letters from Berlin to the West (already inspected and filed according to special subjects).

His telescope was directed towards the city of Berlin – towards the battered metropolis buried under dust and ashes, beneath whose crust of rubble there was still a beating heart.

Three cities had gone to utter destruction during the course of Western civilization. And had not monotheism arisen out of Jerusalem's ashes like the Phoenix? Was not the passion for philosophy, for truth and beauty the legacy of Athens? And had not the idea of a binding and fixed world law arisen out of annihilated Rome?

What sort of red bird would arise from Berlin's ashes?

What ideal would be born from shattered Berlin?

But Berlin was condemned, dead and buried, cold in its shroud, wrapped in winding sheets . . . Yegorov, a legion of Yegorovs, rolled the sepulchral stone, would imprison her for eternity. . . .

Condemned . . . and the condemned did not accept the judgment, the deceased did not acknowledge his death; that was the problem; that was how Yegorov saw it.

Berlin was the theme of the first series of discussions between Yegorov and Zecke. Berlin ground between East and West; the focus of the cold war, in darkness and hunger and cold. The comedy of the dancing puppets had ended. The gigantic Trojan horse in the middle of Berlin had burst. The crew had climbed out, and their faces had been seen by lantern light.

What was the result?

A friendly, amiable Mayor, old, hopeless and helpless. A Police-President appointed by the Russian Secret Police. A Personnel Chief of the Berlin magistrates who had his Russian captain's uniform still hanging in his wardrobe. And for the rest, spite-motivated ex-prisoners in charge of social welfare and labour, and providing local mayors and town-councillors. A President of the Kulturbund vapouring end-lessly on German tradition, German character, German classics and German humanism . . . a resounding brass, a hollow cold tintinnabulation; and the lantern light which had fallen on his face showed a leaden despair.

What had come out of the belly of the Trojan horse? Lying poets, chained politicians, lost souls – they could not get the Berliner's vote.

One of Yegorov's predecessors in the succession of inter-rogation officers had asserted, in reply to Zecke's different opinion, that the pressure of the Soviet Occupation Power would result in a resounding election victory for the Com-munist party.

Berlin voted – the Communists remained in a hopeless minority.

Berlin – plundered, robbed, raped, and dishonoured – was no longer moved by verbal exhortations. The only means left was open violence – a bad means. Grigorij Malenkov had warned:

'We are sitting in the heart of Europe and the convulsions of this heart will be felt far afield.' However he had added: 'Which does not mean that we should not therefore . . .'

The machine was put into motion.

The cohorts stormed the newspaper kiosks. West Berlin newspapers and books were confiscated and publicly burned. Picked crowds stormed the Berlin magistrates, chased away the Town-Council to Schöneberg in the West sector.

Berlin was split – into East and West. That was the beginning.

'Blood is thicker than water: Rixdorf against Schöneberg, that is impossible; it won't work', was Zecke's comment. He could produce a vivid picture from a newspaper report. Two hundred thousand Berliners on Platz der Republik. A grey September sky; rain falling, a sea of opened umbrellas surrounded by the amphitheatre of ruins. The faces under the umbrellas, under turned-up capes, under hats and caps. 'Think about those faces, General Yegorov. Spectacled student, railway worker, labourer, housewife, disabled former officer, ex-actress, milliner. Think about those faces, General . . . they are all grey, sunk in with hunger. "It won't do" – that's what all of them are saying, Herr General. Study those faces; you can rape them (and indeed have), but they stand up again and believe in themselves. Those two hundred thousand people standing there in streaming rain represent the whole of Berlin, east as well as west. They have learnt about Communism. Not the violence and pillage – the Berliners would have got over that – but the continued systematic plunderings, the sequestration of businesses, the organized buying up of daily necessities with valueless Occupation money, the rigid control in all spheres of life, the return of husbands and sons from captivity as emaciated ghosts; all that amounts to an unforgettable lesson. Many had once interpreted Communism as a spiritual union of the community with the highest source of life – with God, the all-comprehensive idea. You yourself know, Herr General, how favourable the Berliners used to be; how many "drawing-room Bolsheviks" there were amongst artists, theatre people, even bankers, not to mention the workers. Not without reason was it referred to as "red Berlin". But to-day they see it as a union with an insatiable monster devouring values and souls, a blasphemous alliance

434

with the devil's representative. That's how they see it to-day, and you can read it again and again in their letters, General Yegorov. The Berliners say, "No, thanks", and you won't hear anything different from them.'

The GPU examining magistrate was sitting behind his dimmed lamp – distant, nebulous, non-existent. Unmoved, however thick the blasphemies flew. The prisoner had been given permission to speak, and the General from the Fourth Division of the Red Army must know how far he could allow him to go.

Major-General Yegorov took a cigarette, offered one to Zecke and gave him a light. 'General Hunger and General Cold will have to say something too; you will find them irresistible, and both of them are old Russian allies', he said.

'Hunger and cold are irresistible forces in the immensity of Russia – not in Berlin. But is it an irresistible force when the Autobahn bridge across the Elbe is suddenly smashed; the sluices necessary for water transport left unrepaired? Rail transport is being stopped; whole trains disappear in the Soviet-occupied zone. At Helmstedt Station long columns of goods trains are blocked. Provisions inside the waggons are rotting. This is not a play of irresistible forces but merely an interminable game of cat and mouse.

'And now: blockade.

'And the electric current from the Eastern Zone and the Eastern sector of Berlin is cut off. Blockade . . . hunger, cold, darkness. No hope for the old; no food for infants. Two million Berlin hostages for political power. Whatever happens, happens under the searchlight of world publicity. Berlin is the balance in which a system is being weighed, in which the truth and the falsehood of Communism will be measured.'

'I am interested in other aspects of the difficulties which have arisen in Berlin, Colonel Zecke. A. – the capacity of the airlift. B. – the possibility of a widening of the conflict. C. – what will the attitude of the population of West Germany and of France be in case of war with America? Can the Red Army count on actual assistance such as sabotage, blowing up of railway bridges, and so on? Will you kindly give me your opinion on those aspects, Colonel Zecke?'

'Out of two million West Berliners hardly twenty thousand

have put down their names for the food tickets offered by the Soviet – and that at a time when cold and hunger are already a solid reality, when the old and weak are dying and children are failing: that is your reply. The attitude of the greater part of the Western population can already be deduced. The blockade has reduced Berlin's opinion of the Soviet Union to its lowest point.'

'The airlift, Colonel Zecke, is at the least a rather uncertain undertaking. To supply two million people even with only the absolute necessities is an unprecedented task.'

'Yes, Herr General, a gigantic, unprecedented task, and without preparation. The achievement so far is the more to be admired. Think of it, Herr General, all the American General in Berlin had at his disposal were some twenty freight planes. He exercised his initiative. The British and the French followed. And the Berliners – indeed all the Germans – suddenly became allies, allies in the battle against hunger and cold and against a system which would try to make use of those horrible scourges. Americans, British, French and Germans are working hand in hand.

'Freight planes from the distant Caribbean in Berlin's sky, from South Africa and New Zealand. A great technical performance; yes, a miracle. And now . . . bursting Flak shells within the air corridor, parachutists leaping down from the huge transport planes. Over Berlin a Yak-plane has rammed a British passenger plane. Both planes down in flames. A sacrificed Soviet pilot, and on the other side thirty-four victims. A second, or a third case, and the "Cold war" would be transformed into a "Hot war" – that is my opinion, which you do not want to hear. The moral responsibility for the outbreak of World War Three would be firmly on the shoulders of the Soviet Union, General Yegorov.'

'But if it does come to it; if the Americans attack – how do you assess the military position, Colonel Zecke?'

'If the Americans attack; it is you who are the attacker: that's what I'm trying to say. The military position of the Americans on the Continent is weak because at the end of the war they were thinking only of peace, and therefore they have demobilized their Army and their Air Force. At this moment, they would be unable to equip and man a fighting front. But their moral credit would enable them quickly to mobilize their own country and half the world as well.'

'I should have liked a more concrete reply to my question, Colonel Zecke.'

'To speak more concretely, General Yegorov, I should like to point out to you that the Americans had only mobilized a fraction of their potential during the last war, and of that only a fraction had been sent to Europe. Consider, General Yegorov, what your country must expect from a fully mobilized America fighting a life-and-death battle. There is, of course, a comparatively unstable political situation, and the American working class could become a risky factor in a long-term war. But in this direction the Soviet Union is doing everything to show itself hostile to the workers and to the people. After the period of Soviet "Vetos" in the World Security Organization, after the colonization of the Balkans, after the inclusion of Poland, Czechoslovakia, and East Germany into the Soviet satellite system, and after the Berlin blockade, any sympathy towards your country will have been destroyed.'

The rest of what Zecke added was complete sacrilege:

'If you will permit me, at the same time, General Yegorov, to remind you of the limits of Soviet potential – the repeated crises in the Red Army during the German-Russian war which were only surmounted with the help of American Lend-Lease deliveries. We can well imagine what would have happened without American assistance.'

That was enough, even for General Yegorov. He left abruptly.

The miracle of one night had lasted for nearly a year. About a thousand planes landed daily in the Tempelhof, Gatow and Tegel airfields bringing the necessities of life for Berlin.

The Soviet whispering campaign according to which chaotic conditions prevailed in the Western sectors and hundreds of dead were lying on the streets, had been a pitiful failure. The West Berliners were eating potato crisps, their children had dried milk. Tables and floors in the dark flats of Berlin were spotted with candle wax from American candles.

'The worst is behind us; it can only get better!' – 'Better to be blockaded by the Soviet and fed by the Americans than the other way round!' That's how the Berliners consoled themselves. They tightened their belts and proceeded with the new election of their Municipal Council in spite of ceaseless Eastern propaganda. The elected Chief Mayor exclaimed: 'Submit? It is better to be threatened by hunger and cold than to go into certain slavery!'

The man in the death-house in the Lubyanka was praying for the continuance of the miraculous air-lift; was praying for a permanent result from this spirit of rational co-operation.

Was the misery not great enough? Were the hearts of whole nations not ready for a great enterprise? Did Europe, changed by two world wars, not require a final liberating deed? Three million Europeans without political frontiers, fed by a common spirit of charity! Should not the nations burn their boats behind them and consolidate their new fraternity? Their hearts were ready for it – but not their heads! Zecke kept a cool head in the sulphur fumes of the Lubyanka. He devoured all the newspapers at his disposal and he saw: they do not burn their boats; they are clinging to the decayed and riddled planks. Opposition between England and the USA, opposition between France and Germany . . . Persian oil, the Saar question, mining-shares, French need for security: All these prevented Germany's integration.

Whither Europe?

Zecke studied the actual events feverishly. He relaxed only to write a monograph on besieged towns, starting with the siege of Troy by the Greeks, the siege of Carthage by the Romans, the siege of Vienna by the Turks and Paris by the Prussians: he ended with the blockade of Berlin.

The door opened – in place of the attendant a GPU-sentry entered:

'Zecke, *daway*, transport. Leave everything here, no longer need anything!'

Don't need anything . . . Lena in besieged Berlin; Lena, Agathe, champagne, vice, morbid drinking-bouts, that is the fate of women in the American sector, Yegorov had said. . . . No longer need anything; whither Zecke?

He went through the large hall, and the 'Black Raven' was waiting for him in the yard. The Yaroslavski Station was again the starting-point for his week-long journey.

This time Zecke was not sent to one of the camps. He was

already considered too unsound to be with condemned prisoners of war; he knew too much. This time a village took him in, a silent village in the far East. Here were only Russians, released convicts who avoided any sort of contact with him, and a GPU-post. An abandoned hut was his shelter. He had no blanket. His rucksack had stayed behind in the Lubyanka with everything else, also his spectacles. That was perhaps the worst; he was helpless without his glasses. He was lying stretched out on the bare planks. Outside a storm was howling Rats were sqeaking in the decayed timber. No longer did the thick walls of the Lubyanka prison separate him from the bustle of the world.

He left the village behind him and wandered outside. Nobody stopped him. Steppes without tree or bush. Wind, wind, storm; very bad for his chest – now a bony cage from his long imprisonment. He walked on, but the scenery did not change. From the next hill deserted grey steppes swept to the horizon. He had thought the end of his life would be different . . . but what was he thinking of, had it not come to an end a long time ago, had not the door shut behind him long, long ago? He had to make it clear to himself – a shadow arguing with his own shadow. During his last banishment he had already been a ghost among ghosts, but with the others he had walked to the camp fence and looked towards the West. Sometimes even human words had occurred to him which he could exchange with one or the other. Mostly with the bird-faced Vilshofen, Manfred Vilshofen, a man of his own age, with the same background, with similar interests – even ghosts still have interests. Until: 'Vilshofen, *daway*, transport!' and he saw him disappear for ever in a snowstorm. A voice, the last in his life it seemed, had faded away for ever. Vilshofen had come to an understanding with a propaganda brochure he had found in the camp.

'Whither Europe?' – It was Vilshofen who had spoken these words and had then disappeared in the snow for ever.

'Zecke, transport!' he heard once more.

Train journey, Lubyanka. The old cell with books, even his spectacles were lying on the table. Books and newspapers. The Berlin airlift had come to an end .The blockade had been smashed. Atom-bomb tests over Eniwetok. A 'Liberty-bell' with Lincoln's words cast in bronze 'That this world under

God shall have a new birth of freedom', was hanging in Berlin. But the cold war continued, and it was a 'hot war' in Korea.

Again discussions with General Yegorov, Again the sudden stop.

Again transport!

And again a banishment to a village of silence. The faces in the village were Mongolian. The language Chinese or Burjat or a dialect between these two languages. It was quite meaningless. The language of his neighbours meant nothing. Winter or summer did not mean much either. Lubyanka – village of silence – Lubyanka – a nomadic cycle: that was his rhythm.

Last time his cell had been full of American and French material on the war in Korea. What could he say to all that; of what value could his opinion still be to Yegorov? The weakness of the Americans in Korea; the serious military blows – that was obvious anyway. The American weakness was the weakness of the West – a multiplicity of opinions and a desire to evade conflict . . . but to draw conclusions from the military weakness of the Americans in Korea about their real strength would be as misleading as it had been to draw conclusions from the Russian debacle in the Russo-Finnish war about the weakness of the Red Army, that's what he had replied to Yegorov.

Burjats – thin women, and cows with legs like greyhounds. The Burjats took down their tents and departed, taking with them their thin women and their thin cows. All that was left behind was a trampled encampment and a grazed patch in the interminable steppes.

Was this now final?

At one time in Novgorod Cathedral he had stood in front of a glass coffin in which the remains of a Swedish princess transplanted to Novgorod were preserved, and he was strangely touched by that forgotten gloomy fate. The castles of Peterhof and Moscow are full of paintings, many by Italian masters, whose earthly existence is long gone and forgotten. How many destinies – painters, merchants, soldiers, workers, scientists – are scattered on lost roads! Russia spreads out inexorably; the far eastern Steppes are a graveyard for lost souls. There will be space enough for the bones of a Prussian Colonel. In sand and wind, on grazed Mongolian Steppes, unseen by human beings, he would disappear without trace.

But it was not the end.

A cloud of dust rolled nearer. A fellow in tattered GPU-uniform on a thin hack pulled up: 'Zecke, *daway*, transport!'

The routine was as before – till the Moscow Yaroslavski Station. There the points were set differently. The 'Black Raven' did not drive to the Lubyanka but stopped at a wide arterial road after a journey through Moscow's sea of houses. A few yards from the pavement was a narrow passage between high houses; some thirty to forty yards further it gave on to a square of single-storeyed apartments separated by flower-beds. Zecke was led into one of them – kitchen, living room, another room behind a locked door. A little old Russian woman busied herself in the kitchen. Without a word she put on the table some tea, bread and butter and disappeared again.

Zecke's sleep was restless.

Prisrak Stalingrada at Ivanovo; Vilshofen behind the Urals; Zecke in Moscow; whither?

He woke and found himself behind unbarred windows. The *Matka* appeared again and brought warm water for shaving, also a safety-razor, soap, and a towel. He had just finished with his shaving when there was a knock on the door. General Yegorov came in from the second room of the apartment, wearing plain clothes.

'Good morning, Colonel Zecke; would you be good enough to join me for breakfast?'

'Thank you, General Yegorov.'

The conversation during breakfast and also later during several short visits was limited to polite small talk. Yegorov asked no questions and seemed to have nothing definite to say. He did not mention Zecke's changed situation, and Zecke did not ask about it. Yegorov came and went, and between whiles Zecke was left to his own devices.

Where was he?

The only window still overlooking the square had been bricked up. There were pavilions; a long barrack hut, divided into apartments, each with its own entrance, apparently inhabited by families, and not only Russians. All his neighbours seemed to have something similar in physiogomy and movements, a common military bearing. They hardly spoke to each other and Zecke spoke to no one. He surmised that the inhabitants of the huts were high officers who had acted as agents and were being sent to Moscow after many years abroad. There was a continual coming and going. His next-door neighbour was a man of about forty with a black beard and spectacles, probably an officer in mufti: in the morning he was no longer there; a foreigner and a Russian woman had moved in. The old *Matka* remained silent – she was doing the cooking both for him and for the family next door. A silent tailor appeared; a silent shoemaker – they took his measurements and after a few days brought a suit and a pair of shoes.

Two weeks passed. Zecke was wearing a new suit, new shoes, a white shirt and a tie. As on the morning after his arrival there was a knock on his door and General Yegorov entered, again in plain clothes. He handed Zecke a railway ticket: Moscow-Berlin.

Nothing else; identification papers were not necessary. Zecke would stay with him as his companion on a journey of inspection, Yegorov informed him.

They left the apartment in broad daylight. A limousine took them to the White Russian station. The blue express to Berlin was standing there, ready. They got into a reserved compartment. Two sleeping bunks, a table near the window.

The train rolled slowly along.

Fili – here Napoleon had his headquarters in 1812, and from here he had looked towards burning Moscow. Fili was left behind and the train moved more quickly. Lubyanka – village of silence – Lubyanka – village of silence: the merry-go-round! Not this time. This time the train is running to the West. The clock has moved on from 1945 to 1953 - the 15th of June, 1953. The dead has risen, is walking about, eating and drinking.

Yegorov ordered meals to be brought into the compartment. He looked exhausted and hardly touched his dinner. Only later, with the approach of darkness, did he seem to wake up. He looked thoughtfully at Zecke. He called for the waiter, ordered the table to be laid once more. Cold buffet – wheaten bread, butter, cold poultry, smoked *Sudak* from the Caspian Sea, beer and Vodka.

'*Da sdarovye* – *Gospodin* Zecke! – Your health, Herr Zecke!'
Yegorov filled the glasses once more. He drank quickly,

one glass after the other, was mildly drunk. Had he not been Zecke's fate? Was it not he who had thrown him into darkness after their first meeting in Brest! Always correct, always polite, never without a feeling of sympathy towards him. And Zecke himself had always been sincere, had held nothing against him, had always spoken frankly.

That had been in the Lubyanka and in the East. Now it was different. The train was rolling along to the West – and in the West it was different.

Zecke kept to himself.

The dead has risen . . . but it is not quite like that. In Berlin, too, he will arrive as a dead man, as companion and mentor of a Major-General of the fourth division of the Red Army.

What would he actually do there?

What did Yegorov expect of him? Information on former officers of the German Wehrmacht who are now Inspectors and Generals of the People's Police or in charge of high Government posts? He had never given this information. Yegorov could hardly expect him to now.

Yegorov spoke; Zecke remained silent. At this table they had exchanged roles. Yegorov spoke and filled the glasses again and again.

'I know you, Zecke, as nobody knows you, not even you yourself. I know all about you, even things you have long forgotten. From your childhood to your grave, till the Lubyanka; what you have done and thought, I know it all. But you don't know me, Colonel Zecke. All you know is a mask. You can only see the machine which has taken note of each movement of your heart and has reported it. Who is this Yegorov; is there still anything in him that is alive? Once there was Volodya, a child Volodya; was this little Volodya already a machine? Was he born dead? What do you think? Speak, Zecke . . .'

Zecke was silent.

'You don't answer, Colonel Zecke; you want to be *chitry*; that doesn't suit you. You can't really do it. Well, all right, you remain silent; block up your ears. Go on believing that Major-General Yegorov, thirty-five years in the Red Army, came into this world as part of a machine, as an agent of the fourth division. Haha . . .'

The bottle was empty.

Yegorov got up and called along the passage:

'*Offiziante!*'

The servant came and brought another bottle.

'Ah, Zecke, were not K. Zucker and J. Plenge and von Scheltema once on your list of wishes for books, and didn't I let you have them though they had nothing to do with the actual subject of our discussions? As a boy I read many books about the Red Indians and felt a strong pity for the last Mohican; later on I felt quite melancholy when I read the story of the last knight, Don Quixote. And that time I could not refuse a request to the last monk of the West, I fulfilled it; you got your books. But believe me, the West as you think of it, can only be dreamed of in the cell of a Lubyanka. In reality . . . there are too many Wests; the OEEZ, the EZU, the EVG, the Council in Strasbourg, the Union in Luxembourg; a lot of it is only paper, and a lot of it is a bureaucrat's game. And the gentlemen behave as though they had a thousand years before them. Meanwhile we extinguish one light after another. Whilst you, Colonel Zecke, were dreaming of Europe in your cell I was travelling – I was in Prague, in Warsaw, in Budapest, Vienna – these we have cast into darkness. Around Berlin the grip is tightening. Around Europe the grip is tightening.'

He pushed the door open.

'*Offiziante*, another bottle!'

'I always return from my journeys in a melancholy mood. I was also in Paris . . . there the people are sitting at the café tables drinking some green concoction. Women and young men, and men with beards, and they talk and talk; they no longer believe in anything; in no painter, no politician, no God; in no Emperor, no Government; they are completely free. . . . And the walls, the old houses, the grey stones are all hot from the embraces of so many people from so much freedom. And light, light . . . do you think that the chandeliers in Rome under Aurelius spread as much light before the barbarian invasion? I am sad for those cities plunged into darkness and for those which are blazing with light. That is how lost I am. Who am I; who was I? Do you know who Vladimir Nikolayevitch Yegorov was once? A person who had faith, and that's something which the gentlemen with their big attaché-cases who travel from conference to conference don't have. Do you believe that Volodya was once a youth and even once a baby – but not with round cheeks like the little Zecke. No, no round cheeks. We are of the same age, Colonel Zecke, 1901. You in Berlin, I in Moscow. The axis Berlin – Moscow: but that, too, is over. There is now only Moscow – Moscow – Moscow: the axis of the world. What should I tell you about Volodya? There is nothing, no old officers' family, no tradition. There is Moscow, not so far from the Obsheshitye, from your lodgings of the last two weeks, there was only suburb, dilapidated log-houses, paraffin-lamps, no drainage, no water. Mother had to fetch it from the well. By the way, it looks exactly the same to-day. The white walls of Gorki Street are a façade, but behind it . . . Nowhere does one dream as ardently of freedom as behind prison walls. Nowhere could one wish as fervently for drainage and water and electric light for all people as there in the Butyrki suburb. Do you know Maxim Gorki's *Night Asylum*? But how can I ask such a question? Of course, you know Gorki's *Night Asylum* from the grammar-school – was it not in the upper second form? – and you saw it on the stage – a Reinhardt production. In such a house as Gorki's *Night Asylum* Volodya grew up. The father was a peasant and remained a peasant even as a worker. I hardly knew him, only knew that he could get angry; that he could drink and that then he was even more torn in two than at other times. Father went to the war and was dead before 1915. *Golod y Cholod* – hunger and cold! War, then revolution. Volodya went on to the barricades. Something like that would never have entered the mind of the young Zecke – after all, he had everything, drainage and light and libraries. To the young Yegorov it was something quite natural. War, civil war, Red Army. Thirty-five years have passed almost to the day. In June 1918 I read Trotski's proclamation and Tukhatshevski's appeal: "Enlist into the Red Army!"

'Trotski, Tukhatshevski . . . softly, you must think softly, Volodya! Have we already passed Brest? But it doesn't matter, the frontier is no longer a frontier. The Kremlin is omnipresent; its ear is everywhere. Therefore, even more softly . . . what am I talking about, who do I talk to? To the grave, that is permissible, isn't it! I can trust the grave, and you,

Zecke. At least once one must speak, and with you, Colonel Zecke, my words will be safe. I know it; didn't I want to get information from you about Paulus, about Seydlitz – *Prisrak Stalingrada* (this expression you used once under narcosis); we thought the ghost could be still of use as director of a stud farm in Germany, then we gave even that idea up – I wanted information about Paulus, Seydlitz, Lenski, Vincent Müller, but you did not reply; you remained silent. "I'll leave that answer to you", you said once. It concerned the Minister of the Interior of an Eastern Zone province, a former Hitler Major and a Prussian-born soldier. And that was all, it was all the information I could get from you about your comrades. I know . . . you can talk to Zecke, you are safe with him. As safe, Volodya, as though you were already eight feet below the ground. "Enlist in the Red Army! Rescue the proletarian Fatherland from the White Guards and from Interventionists!" that's how it was written in the Tukhatshevski appeal. Interventionists . . . now we are the Interventionists, and our white guards are Ulbrichts, Piecks and Grotewohls, and the Müllers and Lattmanns with the Vopos and the Zaissers, with the SSD! A world turned topsy-turvy, what do you say, Zecke?' – Zecke remained silent.

He kept silent and thought: is this, too, an interrogation like that time in Brest-Litovsk, and where is it going to lead? But Yegorov in his drunkenness seemed to be able to read thoughts. 'No, my dear Zecke,' he said, 'of what use could it be? The "Zecke" file is finished, the lid closed; Zecke is not going to be taken over by somebody else, I shan't allow it. The name is blotted out and all I have to do is to make the final report. A diversion, where did we stop? Volodya in the Red Army. Training, forced marches, the battle. The battle of Busuluk, the first great victory against a regular army. *Da sdrastvuet Raboteni Krestnyanski Krasnaya Armiya!* Greetings from the Red Workers and Peasants' Army! *Da sdrastvuet* Lenin! *Da sdrastvuet* Trotski! *Da sdrastvuet* Tukhatshevski. . . . Did you know Tukhatshevski? Ah, Volodya, *durak*. . . . Shall I tell you where and how often you have met Tukhatshevski, and what you talked about? Yegorov knows. Tukhatshevski . . . what has happened to him? Tukhatshevski, Trotski, who has killed them – the White Generals?

'Speak up, Zecke, tell me! Oh well, don't speak. It is now my turn to speak – Vladimir Nikolayevitsh – Major-General Yegorov we will leave out of the game for tonight. There is time enough tomorrow; tomorrow he will be here again! Where was it we had stopped? Busuluk on the Volga, Stenka Rasin in tattered Red Army clothes. Red flag, hammer and sickle, people's liberation. Ah, my dear Zecke, *nasch, nasch*.* You are one of us, you understand our misfortune. What has happened to all those ideas? Where have they done to us....?'

Yegorov had reached a maudlin despair; as was to be expected. And the train stopped – stopped at the frontier station Brest-Litovsk. Movement outside in the passage. Inspections from one compartment to the next.

Yegorov pulled himself together and recited from the civil war:

> 'And the steppe-grasses whisper
> How we in bright night,
> How we in rainy days,
> How we hunger,
> How we endure the cold ...'

The door opened for the inspection; a Captain and a Sergeant appeared in the doorway. Their eyes were fixed on the table, on the emptied plates and bottles.

Yegorov continued with his recitation:

> 'Lead us, Budyenny,
> Into battle still more boldly!
> The thunder may rumble,
> A sea of flames surround us –
> Our life is a battle,
> Our whole life battle ...'

The Captain looked at the document handed to him, returned it and saluted. His face remained stony. He closed the door behind him.

'Our life is battle . . . battle – for what? To put out the lights in Prague and Vienna? Oh, my dear Zecke, who is to be pitied: I or you? You on the merry-go-round Lubyanka – Siberia – Kasakstan – or I who work the merry-go-round?

*Ours.

447

You, who are still of some use tomorrow and then of use no longer – or I, who must use you to the last bit . . . and then, after that, I, too, am of use no longer? Already I have seen too much, spoken too much, with you and with others! Who is to be pitied more: you Colonel Zecke, already dead, whose heart can be moved by a conception of human society – or the working-class lad from Moscow, the bare-footed Army fellow who was leading a battalion at the age of eighteen, who was sent to the Kremlin Officer School at the age of twenty, who had risen higher and higher under Radek, under Primakov, under Bersin, who became a wheel in the destroying machine of the Fourth Division and who once had striven for the happiness of all humanity and who now has no longer any ideal at all? Who, Zecke, who? Say something; do speak! Do you know Radek? Oh, what a blockhead I am, of course you know Radek. Where is Radek now? Where is our Red Cavalry General, the Chief of our Officer School Primakov now? Who was shooting so well – the monopolist-capitalistic Imperialists? Radek – bang! Primakov – bang! Tukhatshevski – bang. Marshal Blücher – and the one whose name was Yegorov like mine, my chief in the Fourth Division, then Yakir, Ulorovitsh, Rykov, Bucharin – bang, bang, bang, bang. . . .

'That was my career. I learnt German and English. In 1923 I went to Germany as an expert on revolution, to the Ruhr district where Wilhelm Zaisser was in command. Tomorrow we will have to report to Zaisser; tomorrow in Berlin. Ah, Zaisser, a very old friend from China. And my Chief in China, Colonel-General Bersin; in 1938 he was ordered to Moscow. Lubyanka, a door opens, a woman dentist, you know all about it (but you don't know that Volodya's hand has protected you). Bersin in the dentist's chair – bang! Bersin, Tukhatshevski, Blücher, Yakir, but Vladimir Yegorov – no bang! Why not; was Vladimir Nikolayevitsh worse than the others? Must have been worse. But he just happened to be in China, far away from the mark, and too subordinate to be ordered to Moscow; that's how he stayed alive. Did he stay alive – or is the man running about in a Major-General's uniform, sitting in the blue express to Berlin, no longer the old Volodya . . . ?

'Zecke, Herr Zecke, Colonel Zecke! Comrade Zecke, tell me, what is right and what is left? Yesterday Tukhatshevski, yesterday still Clara Zetkin . . . and to-day? Dammed be the lips who call Herr Ulbricht *Tovaritch*! Look at my hand, my right one! It is not defiled by the hand-shakes of Wrangel, of Denikin; and it is defiled now by the hand-shakes of Pieck and Ulbricht and the white Vopo-officers. Look at the defiled hand! And now wipe away the whole disgrace. Take it, that's it . . . *Tovaritch* Zecke! That's it, and now to Berlin!

'When you wake up tomorrow we will be there!'

The train arrived in Berlin at Friedrichstrasse Station at about ten o' clock on the 16th of June 1953.

'I must ask you, Colonel Zecke, to remain at my side during the time of your stay. If I should be compelled to keep you occasionally for a few hours or more behind closed doors, I ask you not to regard it as an arrest but as an inevitable necessity.'

How we in bright night, how we in rainy days. . . . Everything seemed to be forgotten, the long speech, the handshake, the maudlin despair which had taken hold of him. But it was not forgotten; he had only put it aside; there was a shade of difference in his relationship with Zecke and in the way he addressed him. He said 'we'. 'First we have to meet the SSD-Minister Zaisser and after the discussion with Zaisser I shall be able, Colonel Zecke, to tell you more precisely about our mission in Berlin.'

A rainy grey sky spread over Berlin. It was Tuesday, a day like any other day. A train was pulling in from Moscow. Officers and civilians were getting out. On the platform, order-lies were waiting, and porters. Friedrichstrasse Station was still untouched by the erupting events which were swelling up to a bursting climax and which would disrupt all arangements for this day – in Karlshorst, in the Soviet Embassy, in the Ministries, in the SED glass palace – Major-General Yegorov's arrangements too.

A Lieutenant-Colonel waited for Yegorov, an officer who did not belong to the Fourth Division but to a different machine. He was appointed to accompany him for the time of his stay.

'Lieutenant-Colonel Judanov', he introduced himself. He led the General and his companion to a car.

The dead is arisen. . . . Here lay Weidendammer Bridge, seagulls floating in the spring wind, as once when the wide-rimmed straw hat of a boy swam away under the arch of the bridge and appeared again at the other side like a bright fairy-tale boat. The car did not drive across the bridge but stayed this side of the river, over Weidendamm and along Kupfergraben. In front lay Lustgarten, the dome, the castle. Lustgarten . . . Marx-Engels-Platz. The dome is decapitated. The castle . . . he knows already, has seen photographs of the falling walls, the wreckage sinking down in the smoke of the dynamiting. The castle has disappeared together with a hundred other stony witnesses of Prussia's past. Lustgarten, Schlossfreiheit, up to Bruderstrasse a wide, desolate field, a parade ground. He knows about it, has read the reports, seen the pictures, but it is only now that the castle is really destroyed as he drives by the side of a Russian major-general in mufti and a Russian lieutenant-colonel over the advanced battlefield of the Russian conquerors.

A battlefield for all time – that's how it appears. From the other side, from Königstrasse – and it is no longer called Königstrasse but simply Rathausstrasse – gesticulating crowds with flags and raised hands are approaching.

Students on bicycles, women with umbrellas, men in working clothes, in white mason's overalls, in wooden clogs. Men, labourers, women, an ever-increasing throng. The car in which Zecke, Yegorov, Judanov were sitting could only move forward slowly and after a while got completely stuck.

What was it?

Building workers from Stalinallee. . . . An hour ago, as he came from Karlshorst on his way to the station, Judanov had seen the workers coming down from the scaffoldings along Berlin's magnificent new road and grouping together for a demonstration.

'What is it; what is the meaning of it, Comrade Lieutenant-Colonel?'

'A demonstration, Comrade General.' A demonstration, obviously ordered by the Occupying Powers – anything else was unthinkable. The People's Police were quite convinced of that. Nothing else would even enter their heads. They made room for the demonstrators, stopped cars, re-directed the traffic into side-streets.

The car with Judanov, Yegorov and Zecke stood still as people whirled past them. Flags, posters. A big wooden board dragged by two men: FREE ELECTIONS! And why not? One slogan is as good as another; any stick will do to beat a donkey. So why not the uplifting words: FREE ELECTIONS?

'FREE ELECTIONS!' – 'DOWN WITH THE QUOTA!' – 'WE DON'T WANT A PEOPLE'S ARMY, WE WANT BUTTER!' – But rather strong; going a little far; playing with fire, in fact.

'DOWN WITH PIECK!'

Down with Pieck, with Ulbricht – not quite foreign to Yegorov's ears. Something like this, a change of course, a loosening of the Eastern Zone Government had been arranged after all; (his mission and his meeting with Zaisser had to do with it). But these arrangements had been behind closed doors, far away in Moscow. This is Berlin, in the open street.

'Herr General, we must have lost our way, we must be in the American sector!' Zecke was as if drunk, his mind as confused as Yegorov's had been last night. The grey sky hung low over their heads. The air was thick – but it was the air of Berlin. And there were Berlin faces, as he knew them; familiar Berlin sounds, not heard for a long time, splashing round him like warm water. Lubyanka, Buryat village, American sector . . . where was he?

'No, we have not lost our way, Herr General.' These battered houses – it was undoubtedly Alexander Platz. In that street, a woman had once lived; he had never known her name; bombs had been falling. The woman . . . she was here, hundreds of them were here, milling around a newspaper kiosk. He smiled. This was quite unexpected. The newspaper kiosk went up in flames. Sheets of newspaper were flying about in the air. The woman . . . or another one, picked up a page and read the headline; it sounded like a fanfare: 'Growing confidence in the Government!' Demoniac laughter was the reply.

Burning sparks flew over the car. Zecke smiled. Yegorov asked:

'Have those people gone mad?'

'No, Herr General.'

'Comrade Lieutenant-Colonel, what does it mean?'

Yegorov turned to the people who were whirling past them.

'What is the matter?'

'To the Government!'

A chorus of voices:

'Colleagues, take your places in the line; we want to be free!'

Monstrous, inconceivable. Great things were happening. Had November 1918 come back? The car with Yegorov, Judanov and Zecke was able to get through to Dircksenstrasse, then the road to Karlshorst was clear. It was not November 1918 – it was the 16th June 1953. A different world . . . a world of workers and peasants. Demonstrations, revolts, risings? Impossible; there was no place for that! Those one or two thousand hotheads would soon be sitting behind bars!

'Why exactly did you grin, Zecke?'

'I don't know myself – I suppose it is the air of Berlin, Herr General!'

'Well, here is Karlshorst; remember what I said; you need not regard yourself as under arrest, Colonel Zecke; it is merely a formality!' Yegorov locked the door behind Zecke and took the key. He was in a three-room suite.

Berlin demonstrated.

The telephone was buzzing at the Fourth Division of the Red Army. Suddenly the situation was reversed; instead of receiving information they had to ask for it; it was disgraceful. Under the eyes of Major-General Yegorov, just arrived from Moscow, the Chief of the Department tried with difficulty to obtain a picture of the situation. – 'What is the matter; what is happening?'

The SED glass palace knew nothing. The Ministries' building did not know either. 'A demonstration, it is supposed to come from the FDGB. We don't know anything about it!'

And the FDGB?

The FDGB didn't know either. . . . 'A delegation is on its way to the Ministry. The building workers want to negotiate about the ten per cent increase in the quota.'

A nice delegation . . . members of the People's Police being beaten up, newspaper kiosks going up in flames, Stalin's portraits being thrown down – Yegorov had seen it with his own eyes.

'Who are those responsible? What are their names? Ulbricht, Grotewohl, Pieck?'

The telephone was buzzing. It was a long time before the answer came.

According to this, Ulbricht was in Karlshorst, discussing

with the Chief of the Political Department of the Soviet High Commission the 'New course' of the 'German Democratic Republic'. Otto Grotewohl, the Prime Minister, had gone to Radio Berlin in Grünau in order to make a recording of his speech. Wilhelm Pieck was on sick leave and had gone to recuperate at Ak-Mechet in the Crimea. And the Minister of Security, Zaisser, was on an inspection tour in Halle. Yegorov reached him by telephone and arranged a meeting for the following day.

Zaisser did not seem surprised about the events in Berlin. It was not the first strike, he declared. In Eberswalde, in Zwickau, in Leuna, he mentioned another half dozen places, there had been demonstrations, and after Ulbricht's increase in the work quota nothing else could have been expected.

General Yegorov returned to his lodgings, drank tea with Zecke, told him of the newest developments and asked his opinion of the situation.

'You have had access to all the existing material on Germany – what are the causes of this movement, and will it be possible to stop it by peaceful means?'

'The causes are obvious, Herr General Yegorov. The Social-Democrat Scheidemann once said that a crowd which had forced its way into a conference of the workers and soldiers Council in 1919 had painted their faces grey. The people we saw to-day did not need to do that. All the faces were grey, emaciated. The two who were carrying the poster "Free Elections" were like skeletons from the Chinese famine areas. Cause enough for a revolt. I don't think you can stop it. The pitch of human misery has risen too high. You can't stop a bursting dam with your hands, perhaps not even with armoured cars!'

With armoured cars . . . that had to be prevented at all costs.

'We are not in Alma-Ata or Ferghana – the "peace-loving Soviet Union" shooting at workers: we can't have that said.'

'The lie and truth of Communism – the question has been asked; here it must be answered!'

'What you mean by the lie of Communism I know already; but what do you mean by the truth of Communism?'

'Its antagonistic attitude, its polemics against the really dangerous abuses of capitalism. It means the unmasking of

Christian sins and a reminder of the shortcomings of the Christian way of life. That's what the Russian Nikolai Berdyaev, who was once on your side, said, General Yegorov.'

'Yes, Berdyaev, he is on our list of prohibited authors. But don't you see anything creative in Communism—'

'No, General – I can't find it in the industrialization of your country. The industrial revolution is something you have taken over from capitalism, and they still do it much better. All I have seen – especially after the war – has been dismantling, breaking up, destruction. To the subjugated nations Bolshevism is the biggest destructive force of all times.'

'And what is it all about now in Berlin?'

'It is about getting their daily bread, and also about eating it in freedom! I have already pointed out, General Yegorov, that the division of this city is an artificial one; East and West Berlin and the divided parts of Germany are all of the same blood. Four years ago the inhabitants of West Berlin refused to accept Soviet slavery as the price for Soviet bread. They got through hunger and cold and blockade and have preserved a comparative independence. The demand for independence is the least you must expect from the East Berliners, if not to-day, then certainly tomorrow.'

Lieutenant-Colonel Judanov brought further news. He also brought an eye-witness who had accompanied the demonstrators to the Ministries' building. Yegorov asked him to come in – a German who spoke Russian soldiers' slang. It was August Gnotke; he had gone with the demonstrators through Leipzigerstrasse and had been up in front at the Ministries' building. 'So many people,' he said, 'the street was black with them and all shaking their fists. The notice "President of the Republic" *daway* under foot! "Pieck! Ulbricht!" – A woman came out; they did not want her. "Ulbricht with the pointed beard, the Siberian goat . . ." they all shouted.

'Another one came, a Minister, his name is Selbmann. He climbed up on a table: "Colleagues . . ."

' "We are not your colleagues!"

' "I too am a worker . . ."

' "But you have forgotten it!"

' "You are not a worker; you are a traitor to the workers!"

' "Workers, look at my hands", Selbmann said.

' "Well, your hands are quite fat!"

'And we whistled and shouted, "Go away! Get out! Ulbricht, Grotewohl – the whole Government: get out!" Then another one came. a professor – Dr. Wittstock, but he spoke "Party-Chinese", laughable!'

So it was 'Party-Chinese' and laughable.

Judanov gave Gnotke a strange look.

He scarcely recognized him. Gnotke did not report with his usual frozen matter-of-fact tone. He spoke as if he were a participant – a new aspect for him.

'And tomorrow it will really start; tomorrow is a general strike!' Gnotke finished his report.

That same evening Yegorov with Zecke and Judanov visited a special Party meeting where Grotewohl and Ulbricht were announced as speakers.

It took place in the 'Theatre of the Five Thousand' on Schiffbauerdamm, the former great playhouse of Max Reinhardt, once the Schumann Circus and later the scene of many mass meetings and of revolutionary matinées.

Just before 1933, Zecke had seen 'Battleship Potemkin' there, also Gerhart Hauptmann's 'The Weavers', 'Florian Geyer', and Büchner's 'The Death of Danton'. He recalled a Sunday moring: Isadora Duncan had danced the *Internationale* and had put the audience into a frenzy. He had been there with Lena. At that time they sometimes did that – visited a matinée and went afterwards to the restaurant 'Schwarze Ferkel' ('Black Sow') or the Hotel Adlon in Unter den Linden to have a meal. Lena . . . it seemed incredible that she should be only a few underground stations away! Lena and Agathe; he knew nothing about them; they never had exchanged any letters.

Zecke, Yegorov, Judanov and Captain Budin, all in plain clothes, were sitting in a box. They looked down on to the stalls. Semi-circular rows of faces, a pale crater of heads rising up to the galleries. A murmuring like the rumbling of an ocean. Four thousand – the most faithful of the faithful were sitting there. Wounded, damaged, burnt fighters who time and again had seen their hopes rising only to be blown away again like smoke. Isadora Duncan had danced the *Internationale*, and they – the same people who were sitting here now – had been stirred to frenzy. 'A ghost is moving around in Europe . . .' and they, whose century-old manifesto begins like that and who had been feeding the ghost with their blood until it had grown into a colossus, could not understand that the ghost would not assume the warmth of flesh and blood. Meerkatz, Loose, Schwender . . . August, Emil, Paul, who had been waiting in the Brest-Litovsk camp for their departure to Berlin. Would they by any chance be sitting amongst the audience? For a moment Zecke thought he saw the long whip-lean August Meerkatz.

It was he, August Meerkatz, and Paul Loose was there too.

Meerkatz pushed along the row and took his seat next to Loose. Meerkatz and Loose had kept together after their arrival in Berlin, after having received their settlement in Wilhelmstrasse (three pieces of cheese and some white bread), and after having been assigned political work in Lothringerstrasse, After their first sporadic employment, Loose had obtained a position as caretaker in the Ministries' building (his wife Emma was employed there too, in the canteen), and Meerkatz had become Distribution Manager of the Soviet-edited *Tägliche Rundschau*. Those two greeted each other with a look . . . no words were necessary. A look of secret understanding, a look as of one prisoner to another, was the greeting of many in that place. The air was loaded with explosive. This evening the man with the pointed beard had to speak, must give an account, must say whether the 'New course' was genuine or whether it was again a mere tactical manœuvre. He would certainly give an analysis of the events of the day with a concrete suggestion as to how to deal with it.

Beneath the spotlights the dozen expected speakers went on the platform, among them Ulbricht, Grotewohl, Jendretzki, also Ackermann and Zaisser.

So they hadn't yet skipped off, as had been said.

'Comrades . . .'

But what is Jendretzki talking about? Has nothing happened in Berlin? Have the building workers not marched from Stalinallee to the Ministries' building, adding to their number at every street? Were the portraits of the figures now sitting on the platform not trampled underfoot? And was it a lie that a general strike had been called for the following day?

'In Berlin everything seems to be all right!'

'A speech written the day before yesterday', Lieutenant-Colonel Judanov remarked.

'We must wait for Grotewohl!'

Grotewohl, too, was a disappointment. Well, after all, Grotewohl was only a be-spectacled SPD-intellectual unsanctified by Moscow. It was up to Ulbricht; he would show that there was more to him than the beard – 'as good as Lenin's!'

Ulbricht spoke. . . .

Yegorov lit a cigarette.

'Would Himmler have been as lost at a time like this?'

Lieutenant-Colonel Judanov shrugged his shoulders.

'Perhaps Herr Zecke will be able to give you information on that point!'

'They say he's cold. But he hasn't even got enough blood for that. He's a little man without orders. A puppet without strings.'

' . . . undoubtedly the Party and the Government can record important successes through the efficiency of the people. After the removal of the wreckage of Hitler's war a great new construction programme has been started and the standard of living of the population has been considerably raised. Economic plans have not only been fulfilled, but have been more than fulfilled in a number of important spheres. Of course, in agriculture. . . .'

That's how it went on; that's how it rattled on for a full half hour. The audience became restless. People started to talk to each other. A murmur was running through each row. Above the murmur impatient exclamations.

Yegorov was at the limit of his patience.

Would a general strike be called? Would a strike of Berlin's workers spread to the whole zone? And then . . . Would the Red Army have to crush the rebels? And then . . . what about the Western powers? Were they on the threshold of world war number three? Would the next event be an atom-bomb descending on Berlin? He was in the wrong place, wasting valuable time. Yegorov asked Judanov and Budin to remain and observe, got up and left, together with Zecke. They drove through the night, across rainy Berlin squares, through Frankfurter Allee flanked by chains of People's Police, which appeared to him, with its white façades, like a desperate and provincial imitation of Moscow's Gorki Street.

Zecke was sitting next to him.

Zecke . . . an experiment which he had recommended and had persuaded his Chief to approve. Zecke, a blank page, had remained untouched by the intrigues, the clique battles, also by the flickering ambitions and secret hopes of the former Hitler officers now in leading positions. He must be exposed on the spot to a flood of impressions – as just now, confronted by the inevitable structural changes within the eastern German Democratic Republic. Zecke . . . an absorbing seismograph – he would then disappear, must disappear – the recorded diagram would remain, a witches, pentagram, a formula against Prussianism, against German unification, against all kinds of 'Western' magic.

He asked Zecke's impression of the public meeting in Friedrichstadtpalast and received only general comments.

'Humanity without destiny, without ethics. The helplessness of the people as a final condition: that seems to be the aim in the DDR; unfortunately not only in the DDR!'

Zecke was holding to his opinions.

'Ulbricht a homunculus. The whole Politbureau a group of specimens in a bottle. And take away the bottle, take away the protecting cover; they will disappear like smoke, as if they had never existed.'

It was late at night when Yegorov learned in Karlshorst about the latest attitude of Ulbricht.

An analysis which analysed nothing.

It seemed that Ulbricht had arranged preventative measures, but was convinced that it would not come to a revolution. The manual workers in the workshops of the DDR were standing fully behind the Government. What had happened to-day in Stalinallee was the result of a few agitators. The disturbance was over. A general strike would certainly not take place!

What should one say? The first man in the country tried to make a trifle of the most critical situation since 1945 – clearly, he could not remain the first man in the country. 'Besides, he's already changed his mind several times, shuttling from panic to bombast. Even now, at two o'clock in the morning – he is actually giving orders to evacuate the glass palace. So he must expect some sort of attack. Well, we wouldn't think of relying on the People's Police. General Gretshko has mobilized the 12th and 24th tank divisions, about six hundred tanks and fifteen thousand men. In one hour, at three o'clock, the tanks will be in full readiness.'

Karlshorst continuously passed on reports to Moscow. Yegorov, too, telephoned the Chief of his Department. He was told: 'The Zaisser question must for the time being be postponed, When the recent events in Berlin have been clarified, we shall know more about the other men in Berlin . . .' Yegorov already suspected that they were incapable of handling the situation.

'Stay at your observation post, Yegorov. It is most important to avoid serious clashes and bloodshed. Not a single shot must be fired without the permission of War Minister Bulganin!'

Yegorov smoked another cigarette with Zecke in his quarters. He pushed the window open. Rain, summer lightning, and the rumbling of thunder.

'That is the lightning . . . tomorrow in its light we shall see what is the matter with the German Democratic Republic and who will be for purgatory! A quotation from Lenin, Colonel Zecke. That was the lightning which illuminated reality far better than anything else, that's how Lenin commented on the Kronstadt revolt.'

On the following morning it was again impossible to drive to the centre of the city. Yegorov was informed that he could join a patrol of six tanks and be put down at the Ministries' building. He got into the tank of the Company Leader, together with Zecke. The Leader, a major, had strict orders from the Garrison Commander to abstain from any hostile action. No shot must be fired! And every tank should withdraw without delay in case of armed resistance. Yegorov looked out from the open hatch, Zecke from the observation slit. White façades, sky scrapers with small windows and encrusted balconies, the former Franfurter – and the present Stalinallee, where in the early morning, in spite of the People's Police barricades, the building workers had assembled again, and again moved forward in a long procession towards the centre of the city. The day before, it was building workers – to-day, rain or no rain, the whole of Berlin had been drawn in.

The tanks turned in towards Jannowitz Bridge, and drove past the Trade-Union House in Wallstrasse. Giant portraits of Stalin, of Pieck, of Grotewohl were lying about in the streets, torn and trampled. The Spittelmarkt resembled a big pumping heart, absorbing from three or four approaches the whirling masses of people and pressing them on, accelerating and shouting more loudly, into Leipzigerstrasse. Yegorov and Zecke looked down at the streaming crowd, looked at single groups, at individual faces, wet from the pouring rain. The demonstrators were running in front of the tanks, were running beside them; only reluctantly did they let them pass and immediately the column joined together behind, filling up the whole width of the street. Some were standing on heaps of rubble and shouting encouragement. The tanks could only drive along in low gear. The clanking of the tracks could hardly be heard against the shouting and howling and whistling. 'Pieck, Ulbricht . . . down with them, down! We don't want to be slaves!' They were as foolhardy as they were incomprehensible; no one was afraid.

'It might get a bit warm for you; you'd better go home!' the Major of the tank division called to the demonstrators.

'Ivan go home!' was the reply.

The radio operator reported: 'Demonstrators are pulling down the sector barriers! The red flag has been taken down from Brandenburger Tor. Workers from the northern suburbs are marching through the French sector!'

Zecke saw fiercely arguing groups, a car turned over in a hand-to-hand fight; an HO-shop was burning like a torch; red flags dragged down from the walls. Members of the People's Police were pointing a fire brigade hose at the crowd – screams, howls, raised fists. A burning flag was flying through the window of a Government building.

Stones were already flying, some of them towards the tanks.

Karlshorst was asking for report by radio.

'The demonstrators are aggressive, are throwing stones and attacking with iron bars', the Commander reported.

'Remain passive. Interference with weapons is prohibited.'

The tanks stopped. A battalion of the People's Police in olive-green uniforms guarded the entrance. Yegorov and Zecke jumped out, from another tank Lieutenant-Colonel

Judanov and Captain Budin climbed down. Yegorov began to reflect upon these two officers from a unit not his, so strangely attached to him.

In the hall of the Government building Zecke encountered General Vincent Müller – like himself, he had been Reichswehr officer and member of Seeckt's staff. In Russian captivity he had become a member of the National Committee, and like Zecke was attached to a high Soviet officer. Müller in the shining new uniform of a General of the People's Police appeared with the Chief Commander of Karlshorst – Zecke was in mufti and still bore the sulphurous halo of the Lubyanka. The other did not recognize him and Zecke left it at that. He saw the Permanent Secretary to the Ministry, Professor Dr. Wittstock – and Wittstock did not recognize him either. Not surprising after eight years on the merry-go-round of the dead. The merry-go-round was still turning. He had not yet got off; would never get off. He had just been swung this time to the West instead of the East. Here, too, were masks, evil spirits, dead souls. And yet nothing was really changed; Wittstock as over-excited as ever, panicky, almost in tears, rushing from room to room, snatching at the latest news, and leaving confusion behind him. And Zecke saw Vicco Splüge; who, startled, turned and waved to him, but whose expression remained that of a stranger; he, too, had not really recognized him, had mistaken him for someone else. So Splüge was here too – just as he used to be, gesticulating and talking vehemently to a group of newspaper men.

He caught sight of Loose – and that was a meeting.

'Herr Colonel . . .' A handshake. 'Things are moving, Comrade Colonel, all sorts of things. Well, we shall see. Come here, Emma.'

Zecke shook hand with Loose's wife. They were in the canteen. Officials, secretaries were sitting at the tables. The woman was standing behind the buffet in her white overall., 'I have made it for Emma' (the little box of Karelian birch) 'well, that's neither here nor there . . .' so that was Emma. A lively, friendly face, comfortably contrasting with the painted dolls' heads and frozen secretarial faces of the others.

'A good friend from Brest-Litovsk, you know', Loose said. He put on his raincoat, had to go out in the street.

'Into battle . . .' he said. Information had come from Pankow indicating that the middle and lower official channels of the Party and the Trade-Unions had failed. Accordingly, contact with the people had to be re-established as quickly as possible. All Party leaders, responsible members of the Government and Trade-Union secretaries had to go out into the streets and into the idle workshops to talk to the diverging comrades. 'Now you can show what you can do, what the Party has taught you!' As the Party leaders and members of the Government and the Trade-Union secretaries had more urgent tasks on hand, instructors and organizers were quickly sent out instead, among them Loose.

'Well, adieu Emma!'

A mob of people, mostly women and civilians, swarmed through the big entrance hall under the Ministries; women were pushing their way through to the telephone booths, speaking of their husbands of whom they were without news. There was a babel of German and Russian. With staring eyes they listened to the news. Eye-witness accounts from the streets. One said; 'Comrades, it is not the people who are rising, but American boys with Texas shirts from West Berlin. I have seen it myself, Americans in uniform stirring up the passers-by; I've seen it with my own eyes!'

'Listen, the Americans are very silly, but you can't really believe that they're as stupid as all that!'

Soviet officers, privates, members of the People's Police were moving from group to group. It was as confusing as a disturbed ant-hill. The air was blue with cigarette smoke.

'What a helpless crew!' was Yegorov's opinion. 'How did you put it, Herr Zecke; The people's helplessness as a final condition.'

'The demonstration outside is a vote – if this is the last word then the Government has been sacked.'

They moved through the crowd to the stairs. On the staircase women were crouching; they seemed utterly exhausted. Judanov, Budin, and the tank Major followed.

The Major was looking for General Dibrova, to report. In the large assembly-hall he was immediately besieged by the people standing around; 'Comrade Major, what have you seen? What is going on?' 'A great deal and nothing', was his evasive reply. It was not easy for him to get away. Everyone wanted information. They themselves knew nothing; since the beginning of the revolt on the previous day they had not left the building.

Upstairs, too, the air was blue with cigarette smoke. The ashtrays overflowed. Yegorov and Zecke sat down together. The rest were standing about helplessly. Here, too, the telephones were constantly besieged. A Government conference was to take place. A few members of the Government and expecially General Dibrova, who was in charge of the garrison troops, were still to come.

That was the lightning . . .

By its light Paul Loose was running through the streets silenced by scornful laughter, contempt, pitying looks, and more than anything else, by his own insecurity and doubt. The dished-out propaganda stuck in his throat. Youths, vagabonds, hirelings, Texas boys. . . . They are crazy, they should go out and tell such stories to the Berlin workers themselves! Paul, what are you doing here? 'Down with Grotewohl! Down with the Siberian goat!' Loose shouted. 'HO makes us k.o.! Free elections! The pointed beard must go! We are not monkeys!' the other shouted. The crowd moved along towards the police chain. Wooden clubs and rubber truncheons, the Vopo were beating up the demonstrators. But in front the seamstresses from the Fortschritt-works were beating back with their umbrellas. Reinforcements came – the olive-green People's Police, also FDJ-boys, ten and fourteen years old. Just like under 'Adolf'. – 'Sonny, throw that away! Go home!' – 'Traitors to the people, what do you want? Shame on you, we are workers! Come with us!' The Vopos none of them more than seventeen or eighteen years, stood rooted to the ground. The crowd opened like a theatre-curtain, and workers with thick planks, heavy timbers, and battering rams rushed forward. The policemen scattered to escape. The cordon was broken. the demonstrators swept through. Among them was Paul Loose. He had forgotten that he was one of the caretakers of the Government building and that he had been sent out to 'enlighten' the demonstrators.

He bent down, picked up a paving-stone.

'Loose, are you mad!'

Max Schwender stood in front of him.

'It is you, you donkey, you traitor; have you forgotten how they have kicked us down!'

That was the lightning . . .

August Meerkatz had been struck right in the heart. The long argument within himself had come to an end. Ordered about, pushed this way and that, a puppet, obeying the gentlest pull of the string – to-day he moved about of his own free will. When the Berlin Municipal Council had been still undivided, he had taken his orders, represented the 'wrath of the people', had helped to split the Municipal Council, to split Berlin; during the railway strike he had worked as a strike-breaker and had done it from discipline, not conviction. But had he not once stood against a whole world against outlawry and persecution for his convictions? Where had all that gone to? What had become of his rebellious spirit! Ideals have degenerated into empty clap-trap; dogma has taken the place of thought. Now he was on the right side. Hey-up! Hey-up! . . . he had been there, as a big-wig, who wanted to gape, who had been thrown into the Spree; and he had felt as if a bit of the mammoth bureaucracy was sinking in the water. Hey-up! Hey-up! . . . A concrete idol had been thrown down, lay there on the pavement beheaded, with broken arms. 'You shall have no other Gods' . . . your own conscience is sufficient; despair, resignation and weariness left him. He was there at the Chausseestrasse sector when the border notices and barriers were torn out of the ground. No more frontiers, not in Berlin, not in Germany, and none to reason and justice. Hail brother! Hand-in-hand, arm-in-arm, he was marching with the Henningsdorf steel workers through Chausseestrasse, across Oranienburger Tor, passing the Soviet Embassy in Unter den Linden, paying no attention to the ostentatious marble façade. State proletarians, State helots, controlled, trained, regimented, directed. . . . Here we come: 'Away with the work quotas! United German elections! Unified Germany!' A system of hunger and deprivation; indifference and inefficiency: 'Down with them! Down!'

That was the lightning . . .

Propaganda boards flaring; sector barriers falling; Columbia House aflame; police uniforms and files flying out of the windows. Window panes bursting at the back of the Government palace. The people forcing their way into the yard, being

pushed back again by the Vopo. The Soviet flag on Brandenburger Tor flutters down into the howling crowd and is torn,
to pieces. People in long army columns, here twenty thousand
there forty, there sixty thousand, the whole of Berlin . . .
Loose, Meerkatz, Halen, the old cobbler Haderer, all of them.
. . . And August Gnotke . . . the glassy sea has thawed, the ice
is breaking. 'I am guilty', Gnotke howled. 'Everyone is guilty!
Everyone could be accused! Everyone is condemmed to a
living death!'

That was the lightning . . .

General Dibrova entered the large Government conference
hall. No one spoke. The roar of the rioting people could be
heard through the just open windows.

The tank Major presented himself.

The General turned over some pages, crumpled a few –
decisions of the SED, reports of the Vopo, no longer seemed
important, were already out of date, time had marched on. He
had already had a discussion with Karlshorst on the necessity
of proclaiming a state of emergency.

One of the Secretaries of State dared to speak:

'Comrade Garrison Commander, will you please tell us
what has actually happened! What is going to happen? What
have you seen on your tour of inspection?'

The General smiled.

'There is no need to be excited. Comrades Ulbricht and
Zaisser are still to come; I shall report when they are here.'
He turned to the tank Major.

'Comrade Major, will you make inquiries by radio whether
these two Comrades have yet left Karlshorst.'

The Major took one of the telephones, asked for the operator. He had to cover one ear; the assembly was again buzzing
like an angry beehive. They were leaning against the long
table, standing around in groups, smoking one cigarette after
the other.

Grotewohl, the Prime Minister, entered the hall, was immediately surrounded by a group. He could give no information,
shrugged his shoulders, brushed back his hair which kept
falling over his forehead; when he managed to get away from
one group, another stopped him.

'Comrade General, the two expected Comrades have left
Karlshorst in a T.34 and should be here any moment.'

The General was drumming restlessly on the table with his fingers. Grotewohl, now next to him, talked urgently. He hardly seemed to listen.

'After my report on the situation you must go at once on another patrol', were his orders to the Major.

Outside armoured tracks clanked – a tank convoy was driving up.

Ulbricht and Zaisser got out and hurried to the conference hall.

General Dibrova lost no time with introductions.

'After my third inspection drive this morning,' he said, 'I am under the impression that the situation can only be saved if one can get the people off the streets. That, however, can only be brought about by ordering an immediate state of emergency.

'I have already asked Colonel-General Gretchko to empower me to do that. Of course, the situation demands the most carefully considered decisions. But a state of emergency is unavoidable.'

Ulbricht nodded in agreement.

Grotewohl again brushed his hand over his hair. He thought force at such a time was a very dubious line.

Zaisser grinned broadly.

The howling of the crowd was again swelling up through the window.

'Comrade Major, you will immediately drive off with your tanks', the General ordered.

Ulbricht explained that one must not be afraid to use force. He, too, had already demanded a state of emergency, and felt certain that both the High Commissioner, Comrade Semyonov, and Comrade Judin, would decide in favour of it.

'One must make an example; and not trouble too much about facts', was Zaisser's opinion.

'Shoot a few civilians; report it over the radio. Choose metaphorical language; no logic. You understand, Comrade?'

The radio man nodded his head.

Grotewohl cleaned his already shining spectacles.

'In any case, one had to avoid the appearance of force. The position of the Government is already extremely difficult.' Minister Selbmann, who had been pushed down from the table by the building workers on the previous day, agreed with him.

'You don't understand this, gentlemen; only practical men who have already had to deal with things like this, can understand.'

The 'practical man' Ulbricht smiled at the General. . . .

Zecke was sitting in the canteen. For company, and probably not only for company, he had the small, round Budin. Budin was not too definite about his orders. But a German on a special mission in Berlin, who spoke Russian as well as Zecke should be closely watched, just as Judanov watched General Yegorov. Yegorov's and Zecke's paths had been divided and Judanov's and Budin's watching had followed suit. Again and again Budin jumped up and rushed through the building – through the hall with its discussion groups, upstairs through the Government chamber where the SED big-wigs were staggering about with pale faces, up to the door of the small conference room where Garrison Commander General Dibrova had settled down with his staff, and then back to the canteen to Zecke.

After all you don't have a revolution every day, nor a state of emergency. And it had come to that; the Minister of War, Bulganin, had given his consent. All tank squadrons were standing by to receive orders. 'Bloodshed is to be avoided; only shots in the air are to be fired. Order to shoot will only be given after special permission from the Garrison Command', Dibrova informed all units. 'It will be all right,' he asserted confidently, 'we should have started sooner.'

Western instigators – of course that was nonsense! A strike, discontented workers, oppression, and they are simply defending themselves! Nobody knew it better than Budin. The farm is taken away from the peasant, the ration card from the middle-class – all that is left for both of them is to starve. The old type of society is just being trampled down. And the workers get higher quotas and lower wages. More work and less food. Budin knew it all – many of the tank personnel knew it, too.

Budin met a tank Captain he knew; had a drink with him in the canteen.

'Well, have you seen any American tanks in the Eastern sector?'

'No tanks, only workers! Many mistakes have been made, too many. They are defending themselves. Have they the right to or not?'

Budin shrugged his shoulders, looked around. He noticed that a civilian sat down at Zecke's table.

'We are six hundred thousand soldiers', the other continued. 'We want to eat, smoke, drink and the rest of it. It's too much. The Germans don't want us and in fact cannot pay for us.'

'Do you think this is a genuine rising in Berlin – workers and not provocateurs!'

'Don't you?'

'Of course', Budin said.

'And for that we should shoot them?'

Budin left this question unanswered. 'I have to attead to something', he said and went over to Zecke's table.

'An old friend, Comrade Splüge from the ADN, from the news service', Zecke introduced his companion. Budin had another drink and looked with interest at the people sitting at the neighbouring tables. High officials. lady companions, secretaries. They were sitting eating, drinking, bawling . . . the end of the world.

One piece of news exploded like a bomb.

'Comrades, the Deputy Prime Minister Nuschke has been arrested in the American sector.'

'Are you sure, Comrade?'

'It is very likely. That pig is capable of anything. He would know how to manage it.'

Cursing. Despair. A woman howling.

Budin marched off again. Zecke and Splüge were left alone. Wittstock – Zecke had already renewed his contact with him – came back to the table.

'Have you heard the news about Nuschke? Half a man, he was also only half ours.

'Ours?' Zecke asked.

'You mean . . .'

Zecke could not say what he meant, he could explain nothing to these two – Splüge and Wittstock. There was also no opportunity in the uproar. They took Zecke to be one of the inhabitants of one of the thousand offices of the Government building. Wittstock was always an unsteady figure;

Zecke had never realized how unsteady. Splüge was only drunk. Wittstock was drowned, bleached, deformed.

'Luckily, I have kept my flat in the American sector', he whispered, and was off.

The first machine-gun salvo.

Its echo in the canteen caused new confusion, shaking, desperation. And Wittstock was back again, suddenly paralysed, crouching over the table, staring in front of him.

The second salvo.

'Herbert, this is the end; but I have seen it coming, I told you so!'

'When did you?'

'We don't have to pretend, Herbert.'

One salvo followed the other.

The picture in the streets had changed. People's Police advanced in tight formation. Lorries with Soviet soldiers drove through the streets. From time to time the T.34 fired live MG salvoes.

Loudspeaker vans bellowed: 'A state of emergency has been proclaimed. . . . Gatherings of more than three people are prohibited! Violation will be punished by martial law.'

But the demonstrations had not come to an end.

Twenty thousand people stormed the SSD building in Friedrichstrasse. Piles of documents and furniture flew out of the window of Columbia House. The officials escaped to the upper storeys of the building, barricaded themselves in.

'What do you want of us, why do you chase us along the streets? It is our city, and we are worker; we are demonstrating for our rights!' Meerkatz turned to a man on the tank, a Lieutenant.

'We have a *Prikas*,* we don't know what is the matter. We have heard about agitators.'

'Agitators? These are discontented workers!'

'Are you being oppressed?'

'And how . . . "twenty-five years", if one is speaking one's mind!'

Another officer came: 'We don't know anything; we have orders.'

Meerkatz went on. . . . The Petersburg Cossacks, 1917 on

*Order.

the Nevsky Prospect, in full career with swinging swords, fraternized with the people, and now your tanks, if they would take our side, the world would be shaken not in ten days but in one day! What use was it raising one's fists against tanks, fighting with the Vopos, trampling down propaganda posters – one has to get into the vital works, to get busy at the waterworks, the power stations, the metropolitan railway! But the workers are without organization, without leadership or a plan – the revolt has broken out like a steppes fire and is flickering away unco-ordinated, in all directions at once

The old cobbler Haderer from Weissensee was carrying a flag from the year 1848, and from 1918. In front of a column of workers he had carried it from Weissensee through Landsbergerstrasse, across Alexander Platz up to Brandenburger Tor on which the same black-red-gold banner was fluttering. He was still holding it firmly when the column behind him was forced open and separated by tanks, leaving only a small body of men marching behind him. He was still struggling forward when bullets rebounded from his flagstaff. That's how Gnotke caught sight of him. It was in Unter den Linden, in the wide area which had already been swept clear but across which the demonstrators were once more advancing. Olive-green police, covered by Soviet tanks, came forward in wide chains, separated the crowds and turned them into the side streets. Haderer marched on. Vopos tried to snatch away the flag, but he held on firmly. It all happened within a few seconds – a hand-to-hand fight, the flag was lying on the ground. Haderer, seized by two Vopos, was thrown into the lorry like a sack of coals, joining a heap of others, both arrested, and wounded. The Vopos did not discriminate between the two. Gnotke had rushed forward to help Haderer; determined not to be overpowered, he was swearing in both German and Russian and flailing about with fists and feet; he was left behind, a smashed and battered little heap. The People's Police went forward. Demonstrators spread the black-red-gold flag over Gnotke's dead body.

There were dead and wounded . . .

They were routine casualties of the state of emergency.

The order to fire in the air was still in force for the Soviet tanks and infantry. The Russian Garrison Commander had already considered withdrawing the German People's Police from the firing line; reports had come in that the People's Police had lost their nerve and had been firing into the crowd.

In Unter den Linden, near the Arsenal, the unrecognizable remains of a man were lying covered with the black-red-gold flag under a hastily contrived wooden cross. Soviet tanks were driving along Brandenburger Tor as in the battle days of 1945. And here, close to the sector border, another victim fell at the same time. Well, Adieu, Emma . . . The sixth field on the little birch box remained for ever blank, nothing of a voyage across the lake, no waves, no stars, no heavens, not even the little word 'Ahoy'; nothing. Paul Loose, who had completely lost his head and no longer knew whether he was in Zörrgiebels' 'Bloody May' or Hitler's night of the long knives, who could only think of one thing, 'to smash the face of the class-enemy', tried to lock the tracks of a tank with a beam of wood. His flying raincoat was caught and he was dragged under the monster and crushed.

'Unfortunate', General Dibrova said.

The General reported to the depressed and troubled members of the Government: ' . . . at Brandenburger Tor a demonstrator was caught by the tracks of a T.34 and run over. A serious accident. Very unfortunate!'

'Comrade Major, let the message be given over the radio! All bloodshed is to be avoided. The same directive applies to the German police.'

Looking at one of the reports concerning an arrest, General Dibrova turned towards Zaisser: 'Here is your victim; as far as I am concerned you can have a few more. But make quite sure that the incident gets known.'

Once more Grotewohl drew attention to the critical situation of the Government and advised that it should be publicly announced that the Occupation Power had sentenced the agitator; at the same time it should be announced that the Government had sent a petition for a reprieve to the High Commissioner.

Zaisser laughed loudly.

Grotewohl was behaving according to form; as though there were no real decisions for him to make. The Russians had given advice to the Germans regarding methods. In Germany those methods had not stood the test. But as a German, Grotewohl should have known which would be the best methods.

'You too don't know your own people; that is quite clear now!'

A message was handed to the General: it again concerned the Vopo. He reddened with anger – the German Vopo were either running over to the demonstrators or hiding in lofts or firing on the crowd without orders.

'The German People's Police must be withdrawn from the firing-line!' the General ordered.

The Government members present became even more nervous. This instrument, too, was falling to pieces – first it had been taken out of their hands and now it was being discarded altogether! Pale faces, vacant looks, jerky movements. One of them was opening and shutting the lid of his watch. Another could not conceal the shaking of his hand. A miserable, wretched, unfortunate company. Were they already condemned, doomed to extinction?

'It is time you understood what is happening!'

The General stood in front of a large be-flagged map of Germany hanging on the wall. Halle, Wolfen, Merseburg, Bitterfeld, Magdeburg, Jena, Gera, Chemnitz . . . there was no end to it. The whole zone was seized by revolt. Strikes, demonstrations, freeing of prisoners. Already suppressed by the tanks, the fire was flaring up again in the towns of Rostok, Eisleben, Sangerhausen, Nordhausen, Apolda, Calbe and Wernigerode. In Schwerin, Stern and Buchheim the entire People's Police came out in open mutiny. In Leuna the workshops were burning. The conflagration grew and spread.

The roar of approaching tanks.

The 'infamous' and 'condemned' went to the window.

They saw Colonel Kotzuba, Semyonov's Chief of Staff, get out of a tank. A minute later Kotzuba brought them an invitation from the High Commissioner. High Commissioner Semyonov wanted to discuss with them 'necessary steps and decisions'. They would be informed later about time and place. An invitation to a discussion. . . . So they still existed, were still a factor to be considered. They were still allowed to breathe.

The lightning had revealed it – no one had come through!

The SED was a heap of fragments; a dust-heap to be swept aside or not, as one willed, For Germany, for all its social layers and for the German workers, the SED régime was an irrelevancy. All that had to be done was to make sure that World War Three should not accidentally arise out of that heap of fragments, torn flags, smouldering propaganda boards; out of that human mass of limitation, defectiveness and insufficiency.

The 'German Democratic Republic' no longer existed, the Government had fallen to the ground like a withered leaf. 'Specimens – let them out of the bottle and they will disappear like smoke!' that's what Zecke had said. Yes, Zecke, too, was in a glass-bottle, the Western monk in the Lubyanka cell. Now, he no longer had a meaning; it is superfluous to look at the seismograph when the earthquake is already here. A diagram was no longer necessary. The whole of Germany from the Elbe to the Oder-Neisse was now the witches' pentagram. The 'Zecke' file was to be closed, finally and decisively. That still remained to be done.

Major-General Yegorov had a busy day behind him.

Conferences, frenzied attacks, break-downs, death sentences, all surrounded by the flickering panorama of the rebellious city. And everywhere he was the observer, in the Soviet Embassy, at Colonel-General Gretchko's headquarters, at the Ministry of Security in Normannenstrasse, at Garrison-Commander Dibrova's office. And everywhere Lieutenant-Colonel Judanov stuck to him, determined to keep him company at mealtimes and even when he was washing his hands. Beyond it he could see the outstretched hand whose shadow Judanov was.

No, he was not yet ready for that.

Volodya was still not as 'ripe' as the others who had been strangled by this hand. The 'direct wire' to the Kremlin which was at his disposal was still intact – amidst the burning Babel, he found time for a special conversation – and the shadow disappeared. Lieutenant-Colonel Judanov gave notice and withdrew from his 'command'.

Zecke, though, still remained.

Yegorov was sitting in a canteen, greeting an old comrade, one who had not been at Busuluk but was old enough to have seen the worker and peasant soldiers still bare-footed, and who had served under Tukhatchevski and Primakov. Yegorov got up; he was suddenly tired. Outside in the fresh air, in the open hatch of a tank, whilst he was driving through the city hearing shots in the distance, he wakened again.

Liberation of the people. . . .

And the steppe-grasses are whispering. . . .

The 'Zecke' file had to be closed. But truth, justice, conscience, morals, honour, conscious will – is it only magic, only an unruly chaos, only a nightmare? Was Christ not born for Russia too?

And the world Zecke had dreamed of. . . . Had Yegorov himself not pitched his tents there too? Could he destroy his own dream too? But a Zecke in freedom would be a token of hope – and he, Yegorov, would have a part in it.

He found Colonel Zecke in the canteen under the Ministries' building.

It was the devil's 'at home' day. The accused accused themselves and each other. They had run ahead too hastily, too carelessly, had lost all contact with the people . . . now the catastrophe was here! Staggering figures. One of them screamed: 'Yes, I have made many mistakes, but all with good intentions!' Zecke in the midst of it all. A blonde woman, a waitress in a white coat, her face wet with tears, nearly fell into his arms: 'You knew him. you are an old friend of his, tell us it isn't true . . . Paul, Paul, it can't be true!' From the other side and old goat drivelled at him.

The 'old goat' was Wittstock.

'We have not yet really spoken to each other, Herbert, the way we used to, heart to heart, Herbert.' He looked around fearfully and whispered: 'You seem to be quite at sea here. I know a way. Come with me, we'll get out the back way and we'll soon be in the American sector.'

'Will you please come with me, Herr Zecke', Yegorov was saying at the same time.

Zecke got up. He left the canteen at Yegorov's side without looking round.

'That's right,' Yegorov said, 'don't turn round. All that belongs to the dust heap. Someone will shovel it away.'

He found another room and a table. They sat down.

What should he say?

The matter between them was beyond words. We must

close the 'Zecke' file – no, that wouldn't do. That was not a beginning.

'I have just come from the canteen,' he said, 'from the canteen in Karlshorst. I was asked: "What do you want, Comrade General?" "Nothing, I have no appetite", I replied. The waiter looked at me. He understood. I looked around. At every table somebody was sitting who had lost his appetite. And I too understood. What can I tell you: we, too, have to pay for your miscarried revolt. In Magdeburg, in Chemnitz, in Berlin, in Rostock, they have already shot a dozen of our people. I listened to a discussion. "What are you going to do?" someone asked. "Perhaps I will become a Berliner!" the other replied. That was not a joke; I know. I was the one who asked the first question; I cannot become a Berliner. I cannot escape my own past. But you can, Zecke!'

Yegorov pointed towards the flashing neon signs on the other side of Potsdamer Platz beyond the sector border. 'There is your past and your future. Let's go!'

And the dead one emerged. . . .

Zecke was being driven in a tank. The streets were empty. At the crossroads Soviet soldiers were camping. A few shots sounded in the distance. The tank stopped in front of desolate ruins. They got out. Twenty steps. 'Doesn't mean anything', Yegorov said as he drew his pistol. He shot into the rubble. Then he took Zecke into his arms and kissed him.

'Run, Zecke . . .'

When Zecke had crossed the street and was on the other side, swallowed up in the world of ruins, he could hear the clanking of the tank's tracks as it began to move again and turn back towards the East.

Yegorov went to Karlshorst, to the High Commissioner's conference. He arrived late: he was not Chief of the Political Department in Berlin, but an Ambassador from Moscow; so his unpunctuality was of no importance. The conference was in full swing. The German representatives of the 'German Democratic Republic' were sitting in the white indirect light of the numerous heavy chandeliers. Crumpled penitents, they had already apologized, acknowledged their mistakes, accused themselves of insufficient vigilance and the application of wrong methods.

The High Commissioner raised his pale thin hand, taking the draft of a letter from one of his staff. He turned to Major-General Dibrova, saying in a soft voice: The Commanders of the British and American sectors won't stop their protests until they are given a suitable reply. Tomorrow I shall submit to you, Comrade Major-General, a letter of protest for signature.

'In it we shall complain that our efforts to ease the situation in Berlin have been answered by the dispatch of agents with orders to engage in agitation, arson and looting. Those accusations we shall support by evidence.

'Beyond that' – he continued – 'I don't think I am mistaken in supposing that Comrade Zaisser will devote himself indefatigably to the task of ascertaining the "real" culprits. The Government of the German Democratic Republic must never again remove themselves so far from the ear of the workers. Self-congratulations for fulfilled quotas are not enough.'

With this admonition the German Comrades, crushed and yet thankful to have escaped so lightly, were dismissed.

Only the higher Soviet officers remained behind.

The High Commissioner looked tired and worn out, almost ill. But now he straightened; the conciliatory attitude which he had assumed towards the Germans disappeared. He covered Dibrova with reproaches. The higher officers were to be blamed because the army had shown so little energy in the interests of the Soviet people.

'I have seen dozens of tank officers in Berlin. Instead of crushing the rebels they have been taking photographs!'

He gave Colonel-General Gretchko permission to speak.

And what Gretchko had to say was also a bitter reproach:

'Soviet officers have been guilty of betrayal and mutiny. Whole units have disobeyed orders not to shoot at the demonstrators. Units of the Second Tank Army deliberately fired on different targets from those ordered.'

Semyonov spoke once more.

'It is well known that the troops of the Red Army in Germany are living far too well. They think of nothing but enjoyment. Therefore I can tell you, Comrades, that there will most probably be courts of inquiry for many units. Only an energetic political sweep will prevent such a disgraceful spectacle happening in the future.'

The High Commissioner left the conference room without a greeting.

The officers stayed behind in consternation.

It was past midnight.

And the dead one came forth . . . and only now was he tied hands and feet in shrouds and his face wrapped in a winding sheet. Only now. . . . Brought past the camp-fires of the Red Army by a Soviet tank, sent on his way with a kiss from a Major-General of the Fourth Division of the Red Army, how would he be able to get through the questions and interrogations?

He was wandering through streets of ruins. Later he found himself in a miserable Broadway, flat white shop-halls, neon lights – behind it, still the dismal world of ruins. Figures out of Kafka – like Wittstock, like Splüge, like the howling poet in the Government canteen – were crossing his path; or was he mistaken and was he a mirror in which only wanderers into nothingness and darkness could be reflected? Didn't he know, had he not learned in the Lubyanka nights, that consciousness was glowing and awake here in these ruins! Berlin . . . he could only think of it as a whole. Unimaginable that a black curtain was hanging down the middle.

A face glimmered like a lantern and drifted along. He looked searchingly through the heavy make-up; a worn-out soldiers' drab, and God help him, at that moment he had to think of Frau Putlitzer, Frau Halen, also of Agathe and Lena. Where were they? In front of him and in the side streets there were still more of those painted lanterns floating past.

The streetwalkers of Berlin.

The great Gospel; and the guiltless guilty; cast out, outlawed, persecuted. Sinners and sinned against. Witches and witch hunters. Medieval shadows on the brink of the atomic age.

And Berlin is torn open, a wild crater; and Berlin has spoken:

'Hephata!'

The bleeding crater cannot bring forth more:

'Hephata . . . Be open! Hear me!'

'If the salt has lost its savour . . .'

The putrid water is eating up the living water. The monster is living on betrayed virtues. I have brought a secret from the yawning abyss of the monster. It has no morals; it has only teeth. It swallows up all; and thus all needs are solved. It has no dreams and has no need for truth and certainty because it swallows up all, the great and the small, the mature and the immature, the minor and the major races as well; and man and woman and child are no more than a few scattered bites.

World without mercy.

Man is matter: that's how all problems are solved.

Zecke entered a beer house, took a seat. A few men were standing at the counter playing a game of dice with the publican.

'A pint and a schnapps', Zecke said.

A formula not used for a long time, and it worked. The publican's wife, a friendly woman like Emma Loose, brought along a glass of beer and a schnapps and put them in front of him.

Hephata . . .

Only when the moral world and the technical world are one, can the new era begin. Justice, wisdom, courage, truth, honour, charity – the new Reich cannot begin without virtues; and a new beginning can only spring from justice and truth.

There are even soused herrings; everything as it used to be.

'So what!' exclaimed one of the dice-players who had lost three rounds.

'Who cares!' another said, and that was their comment on the events of the day; and that was the attitude of the West towards the events of the day.

But the time has been spent, and this night thy soul will be demanded of thee!

Open your hearts! Listen!

Reach out for understanding! In seven days the earth was created. You have less time. Listen! And open your hearts!

Mayflower War Books for your enjoyment

Fiction

WOMEN'S BATTALION	W. A. Ballinger	35p	☐
FROM THE CITY, FROM THE PLOUGH			
	Alexander Baron	35p	☐
BRANDENBURG DIVISION	Will Berthold	30p	☐
CASTLE KEEP	William Eastlake	50p	☐
THE WAITING GAME	Alexander Fullerton	35p	☐
A WREN CALLED SMITH	Alexander Fullerton	40p	☐
SURFACE!	Alexander Fullerton	35p	☐
THE LIEUTENANT MUST BE MAD	H. H. Kirst	40p	☐
PATROL	Fred Majdalany	30p	☐
'H.M.S. MARLBOROUGH WILL ENTER HARBOUR'			
	Nicholas Monsarrat	60p	☐
THREE CORVETTES	Nicholas Monsarrat	40p	☐
THE HILL	Ray Rigby	35p	☐
VERDUN	Jules Romains	60p	☐
THE CAMP ON BLOOD ISLAND			
	J. M. White & Val Guest	30p	☐

Non-Fiction

SEVEN MEN AT DAYBREAK	Alan Burgess	35p	☐
RICHTHOFEN (Illustrated)	William E. Burrows	40p	☐
PATTON: ORDEAL AND TRIUMPH			
	Ladislas Farago	50p	☐
HUNTING THE BISMARCK	C. S. Forester	35p	☐
HOUSE OF DOLLS	Ka-Tzetnik	50p	☐
FIVE CHIMNEYS	Olga Lengyel	35p	☐
LONELY WARRIOR	Jean Offenberg	40p	☐

All these books are available at your local bookshop or newsagent, or can be ordered direct from the publisher. Just tick the titles you want and fill in the form below.

Name ....

Address ....

....

Write to Mayflower Cash Sales, PO Box 11, Falmouth, Cornwall TR10 9EN. Please enclose remittance to the value of the cover price plus: UK: 18p for the first book plus 8p per copy for each additional book ordered to a maximum charge of 66p. BFPO and EIRE: 18p for the first book plus 8p per copy for the next 6 books, thereafter 3p per book. OVERSEAS: 20p for the first book and 10p for each additional book. *Granada Publishing reserve the right to show new retail prices on covers, which may differ from those previously advertised in the text or elsewhere.*